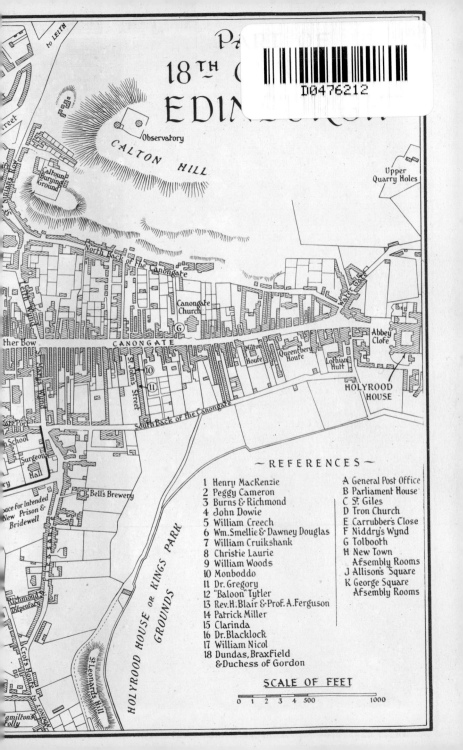

THE WONDER OF ALL THE GAY WORLD

THE WONDER OF ALL THE GAY WORLD

*A Novel of
the Life and Loves
of
Robert Burns*

by

JAMES BARKE

COLLINS ST. JAMES'S PLACE LONDON

FIRST IMPRESSION   AUGUST, 1949
SECOND IMPRESSION   SEPTEMBER, 1949
THIRD IMPRESSION   JANUARY, 1953

PRINTED IN GREAT BRITAIN
COLLINS CLEAR-TYPE PRESS: LONDON AND GLASGOW

THE WIND THAT SHAKES THE BARLEY

THE SONG IN THE GREEN THORN TREE

THE WONDER OF ALL THE GAY WORLD

THE CREST OF THE BROKEN WAVE

In preparation

THE WELL OF THE SILENT HARP

*These novels when completed will
form a work to be entitled*

IMMORTAL MEMORY

NOTE

BURNS'S EDINBURGH days (November, 1786—March, 1788) were the most crucial days of his life. Perhaps for this reason the biographers have accorded them scant attention. Or perhaps they shirked the labour involved in uncovering the facts of this period. But, whatever the reason, the reader 'hot for certainties' concerning Burns's life in Edinburgh gets a decidedly 'dusty answer' from every biographer.

But, though the novelist can get much closer to life (and hence truth) than the biographer, the best he can do is to reflect life in its odd moments. He can however select his odd moments from the flux of time. I have made my selections with such care and honesty as I possess; and the reader may be assured that no vital fact has been suppressed deliberately.

If there is no account, for example, of the meeting between Burns and the young Walter Scott, the reason is that there is no proof that the meeting ever took place. Indeed such proof as does exist (and it is considerable) decisively explodes the legend.

If I have identified Christina Laurie as the recipient of the "My dear countrywoman" letter and not Margaret Chalmers (as the historians have hitherto done) it is because the available evidence is slightly in Christie's favour. But I am conscious of the fact that in giving her the benefit of the doubt I have here, willy-nilly, removed it.

And so with Jenny Clow. There is insufficient evidence to assert without fear of future contradiction that she was Clarinda's maid. But that she was a poor Edinburgh lass who stood in some such relation to Clarinda is vouched for both by Burns and Clarinda. Since this is the only conclusion that makes sense I have adopted it without undue misgiving.

With these indications of where I may have parted from

the strict tenets of historical accuracy I leave the remaining facts to speak for themselves.

For facilitating my fact-finding labours I gladly acknowledge debts to the following: Mr. Robert Butchart and Miss Balfour, Edinburgh Public Libraries; Mr. W. J. Murison of Duns Public Library for taking up the history of Cimon Gray with rare enthusiasm and intriguing results; Mr. and Mrs. R. Rae Hogarth of Stodrig House, Kelso, for doing me the honours of the house once occupied by Burns's Border host, Gilbert Ker; and to Mr. "Topaz" Hogg of Fochabers in his role of incomparable guide, and piquant philosopher, around bonnie Castle Gordon. I am also under a special debt of gratitude to Mr. James Campbell of The Mitchell Library, Glasgow.

To the erudite contributors to the publications of the Old Edinburgh Club it is difficult adequately to express thanks; I have drawn heavily on their brilliant research work.

Lastly: the dedication of this book to Professor Ferguson is but a token acknowledgment of my indebtedness to him, not only for sharing with me his unequalled knowledge of Burns but for his advice and guidance. This does not necessarily imply that Professor Ferguson is in any way committed to my portrait of Burns and his contemporaries. Nor does his published work on Burns need any suggestion of endorsement by me. But I welcome the opportunity of expressing gratitude for his indispensable public labours and his many private kindnesses.

J. B.,
Daljarrock House, Ayrshire.
November 3rd, 1948.

CONTENTS

Part One

THE CUP OF FAME

9

Part Two

THE LONG WAY HOME

Part Three

JEANIE'S BOSOM

Part Four

OSSIAN'S COUNTRY

Part Five

DIALECTICS OF DESIRE

Part Six

OF A' THE AIRTS

CHARACTERS

in their order of appearance

(Fictional characters are printed in *Italics*)

ROBERT BURNS.

ARCHIBALD PRENTICE, farmer, near Biggar.

JAMES STODART, farmer, near Biggar.

MRS. STODART, wife to James Stodart.

JOHN BOYD, street caddie, Edinburgh.

JOHN SAMSON, brother of Tam Samson, Kilmarnock.

JAMES DALRYMPLE, squire of Orangefield, Ayrshire.

MRS. CARFRAE, landlady, Baxters' Close, Edinburgh.

JOHN RICHMOND, writer, Baxters' Close, Edinburgh.

JOHN DOWIE, vinter, Libberton's Wynd, Edinburgh.

JAMES CUNNINGHAM, Earl of Glencairn, Coates House, Edinburgh.

ELIZABETH MacGUIRE, Dowager Countess of Glencairn.

LADY ELIZABETH CUNNINGHAM, sister of Earl of Glencairn.

WILLIAM CREECH, bookseller, Craig's Close, Edinburgh.

WILLIAM SMELLIE, printer, Anchor Close, Edinburgh.

MR. and MRS. DAWNEY DOUGLAS, tavern-keepers, Anchor Close, Edinburgh.

HENRY MacKENZIE, author and lawyer, Cowgatehead, Edinburgh.

JAMES BURNETT, Lord Monboddo, 13, Saint John Street, Edinburgh.

DUGALD STEWART, Professor of Moral Philosophy, Edinburgh University.

REVEREND DOCTOR HUGH BLAIR, Argyle Square, Edinburgh.

REVEREND WILLIAM GREENFIELD, Bristo Port, Edinburgh.

PETER HILL, clerk to Creech, 160, Nicolson Street, Edinburgh.

ELIZABETH LINDSAY, wife to Peter Hill.

MR. (and MRS.) JOHN WOOD, solicitor and surveyor of windows, Libberton's Wynd, Edinburgh.

JANE MAXWELL, Duchess of Gordon, George Square, Edinburgh.

HON. HENRY ERSKINE, Dean of the Faculty of Advocates, 27, Princes Street, Edinburgh.

14

COL. WILLIAM DUNBAR, Writer to the Signet, 18, Princes Street, Edinburgh.

SIR JAMES HUNTER BLAIR, Lord Provost, George Street, Edinburgh.

JANE ELLIOT, Brown Square, Edinburgh.

CAPTAIN MATTHEW HENDERSON, Saint James's Square, Edinburgh.

REVEREND ALEXANDER (JUPITER) CARLYLE, Inveresk.

ALEXANDER, Duke of Gordon, George Square, Edinburgh.

MRS. PRINGLE, tavern-keeper, Buccleuch Pend, Edinburgh.

ELIZABETH BURNETT, daughter of Lord Monboddo, 13, Saint John Street, Edinburgh.

BISHOP JOHN GEDDES, Saint John Street, Edinburgh.

PROFESSOR JAMES GREGORY, 15, Saint John Street, Edinburgh.

PATRICK MILLER, 18, Nicolson Square, Edinburgh.

MARGARET (PEGGY) CAMERON, serving-girl, Cowgate, Edinburgh.

CHRISTINA LAURIE, Shakespeare Square, Edinburgh.

ARCHIBALD LAURIE, divinity student, Shakespeare Square, Edinburgh.

JAMES SIBBALD, bookseller and librarian, Parliament Close, Edinburgh.

MRS. ALISON COCKBURN, Crighton Street, Edinburgh.

ANDREW DALZEL, Professor of Greek, Edinburgh University.

JAMES (BALLOON) TYTLER, Hastie's Close, Edinburgh.

ALEXANDER NASMYTH, portrait painter, Wardrop's Close, Edinburgh.

JOHN BEUGO, engraver, Princes Street, Edinburgh.

HENRY DUNDAS, George Square, Edinburgh.

ROBERT MacQUEEN, Lord Braxfield, George Square, Edinburgh.

PROFESSOR ADAM FERGUSON, Argyle Square, Edinburgh.

JANET BERVIE RUTHERFORD, wife to Reverend William Greenfield.

REVEREND DOCTOR THOMAS BLACKLOCK, West Nicolson Street, Edinburgh.

MARGARET (PEGGY) CHALMERS, cousin of Gavin Hamilton, Edinburgh and Harviestoun.

REVEREND WILLIAM ROBB of Tongland and Balnacross.

WILLIAM WOODS, actor, 4 Shakespeare Square, Edinburgh.

WILLIAM NICOL, teacher, Buccleuch Pend, Edinburgh.

ALEXANDER YOUNG, lawyer, Hanover Street, Edinburgh.

CHARLES HAY, lawyer, George Street, Edinburgh.

ALEXANDER CUNNINGHAM, lawyer, Blackfriars' Wynd, Edinburgh.

ROBERT AINSLIE, law student, Carrubber's Close and Saint James's Square, Edinburgh.

ROBERT CLEGHORN, farmer of Saughton Mills, Corstorphine.

ROBERT BURN, mason and architect, Edinburgh.

BARBARA ALLAN, wife to Robert Cleghorn, Corstorphine.

JAMES JOHNSON, engraver, Bell's Wynd, Edinburgh.

WILLIAM TYTLER, Laird of Woodhouselee, Glencorse.

STEPHEN CLARKE, teacher of music, Gosford's Close, Edinburgh.

PACK-MAN at Fasney Burn.

LANDLORD, change-house at Fasney Burn.

DOUGLAS AINSLIE, brother of Robert Ainslie, Berrywell.

RACHEL AINSLIE, sister of Robert Ainslie, Berrywell.

ROBERT AINSLIE, land factor, Berrywell.

CATHERINE WHITELAW, wife to Robert Ainslie, Berrywell.

WILLIAM DUDGEON, farmer, East Lothian.

REVEREND DOCTOR ROBERT BOWMAKER, minister of Dunse.

CIMON GRAY, retired London bookseller, Dunse.

PATRICK BRYDONE, traveller, Lennel House, Coldstream.

MARY ROBERTSON, wife to Patrick Brydone, Lennel House, Coldstream.

MR. and MRS. FAIR, Jedburgh.

MISS LOOKUP, sister of Mrs. Fair.

MR. POTTS, lawyer, Jedburgh.

REVEREND THOMAS SOMERVILLE, minister of Jedburgh.

MISS HOPE, Jedburgh.

ISABELLA LINDSAY, sister of Doctor Lindsay, Jedburgh.

PEGGY LINDSAY, sister of Doctor Lindsay, Jedburgh.

DOCTOR ELLIOT, Bedrule.

WALTER SCOT, farmer, Wauchope House.

ELIZABETH RUTHERFORD, wife to Walter Scot, Wauchope House.

ESTHER EASTON, Jedburgh.

GILBERT KER, farmer of Stodrig, Kelso.

SIR ALEXANDER DON of Newton-Don, Kelso.

LADY HENRIETTA CUNNINGHAM, wife to Sir Alexander Don.

DOCTOR CLARKSON, Selkirk.

REVEREND JAMES SMITH, minister of Mordington, Merse.

ANDREW MEIKLE, farmer and inventor, East Lothian.

THOMAS HOOD, farmer, Merse.

ROBERT and WILLIAM GRIEVE, merchants, Eyemouth.

BETSY GRIEVE, Eyemouth.

MR. SHERRIFF, farmer of Dunglass Mains, Dunglass.

NANCY SHERRIFF, sister of Sherriff, Dunglass.

JOHN LEE, landlord of Skateraw Inn.

JAMES MITCHELL, merchant, Carlisle.

REVEREND WILLIAM BURNSIDE, minister of New Church, Dumfries.

ANNE HUTTON, wife to Reverend William Burnside.

PROVOST WILLIAM CLARK, Dumfries.

MR. and MRS. JOHN DOW, The Whitefoord Arms, Machlin.

JEAN ARMOUR, eldest daughter of James Armour, Machlin.

GILBERT BURNS, brother of Robert, Mossgiel.

WILLIE BURNS, brother of Robert, Mossgiel.

ISABELLA BURNS, sister of Robert, Mossgiel.

ANNABELLA BURNS, sister of Robert, Mossgiel.

AGNES BURNS, sister of Robert, Mossgiel.

MRS. AGNES BURNS, mother of Robert, Mossgiel.

JAMES ARMOUR, mason and wright, Machlin.

MARY SMITH, wife to James Armour, Machlin.

ADAM ARMOUR, brother of Jean Armour, Machlin.

JOHN RANKINE, farmer of Adamhill.

GAVIN HAMILTON, writer, Machlin.

HELEN KENNEDY, wife to Gavin Hamilton, Machlin.

MARGARET (PEGGY) KENNEDY, sister of Mrs. Hamilton, Daljarrock House.

DOCTOR JOHN MacKENZIE, physician, Machlin.

ROBERT AIKEN, lawyer and collector of taxes, Ayr.

WILLIAM FISHER, farmer of Montgarswood and Machlin Kirk elder.

REVEREND WILLIAM AULD, Machlin Parish minister.

ELIZA MILLER, Machlin belle.

MRS. CAMPBELL, mother of Mary Campbell, Greenock.

DOCTOR GEORGE GRIERSON, Glasgow.

LANDLORD of Inn at Inveraray.

MR. MacLAUCHLAN of Bannachra, Loch Lomondside.

DUNCAN MacLAUCHLAN, son of Mr. MacLauchlan.

MARY MacLAUCHLAN, daughter of Mr. MacLauchlan.

A HIGHLANDER, Arden, Loch Lomondside.

JOHN MacAULAY, Town-clerk, Levengrove House, Dumbarton.

JAMES COLQUHOUN, Provost of Dumbarton.

REVEREND JAMES OLIPHANT, minister of Dumbarton.

CAPTAIN GABRIEL FORRESTER, officer in charge, Stirling Castle.

CHARLOTTE HAMILTON, half-sister of Gavin Hamilton, Harviestoun.

MR. JOHN TAIT of Harviestoun, and Park Place, Edinburgh.

REVEREND DOCTOR DAVID DOIG, Rector of Stirling Grammar School, Stirling.

CHRISTOPHER BELL, Stirling.

LANDLADY, Dunblane.

NIEL GOW, Dunkeld.

JOSIAH WALKER, tutor, Blair Castle, Blair Atholl.

SIR JAMES and LADY GRANT, Castle Grant, Speyside.

JOHNNY FLECK, coachman, Pleasance, Edinburgh.

MRS. ROSE, cousin of Henry MacKenzie, Kilravock.

MRS. ROSE, mother of Mrs. Rose of Kilravock.

REVEREND ALEXANDER GRANT, minister of Cawdor.

WILLIAM INGLIS, Baillie of Inverness.

MRS. INGLIS, wife to William Inglis.

MISS ROSS, Kilravock.

JAMES BRODIE OF BRODIE, Nairn.

JAMES HOY, librarian to Duke of Gordon, Castle Gordon.

JAMES CHALMERS, printer, Aberdeen.

PROFESSOR THOMAS GORDON, King's College, Aberdeen.

BISHOP JOHN SKINNER, Aberdeen.

JAMES BURNESS, lawyer, Montrose.

DOCTOR JAMES MacKITTRICK ADAIR, Edinburgh.

MRS. CATHERINE BRUCE, Clackmannan Tower, Clackmannan.

WILLIAM CRUIKSHANK, teacher, 2, Saint James's Square, Edinburgh.

MRS. CRUIKSHANK, wife to William Cruikshank.

JENNY CRUIKSHANK, daughter of William and Mrs. Cruikshank.

WILLIAM NIMMO, Supervisor of Excise, Alison Square, Edinburgh.

MISS ERSKINE NIMMO, sister of William Nimmo, Alison Square, Edinburgh.

MRS. AGNES MacLEHOSE, General's Entry, Potterrow, Edinburgh.

JENNY CLOW, maid to Mrs. MacLehose, Potterrow, Edinburgh.

ALEXANDER (LANG SANDY) WOOD, surgeon, Edinburgh.

ALLAN MASTERTON, writing master, Stevenlaw's Close, Edinburgh.

JOHANN GEORG CHRISTOFF SCHETKY, musician, Foulis's Close, Edinburgh.

MRS. STEWART, Alison Square, Edinburgh.

SAUNDERS TAIT, Tarbolton tailor and rhymster.

WILLIAM MUIR, The Mill, Tarbolton.

BALDY MUCKLE, tailor, Backcauseway, Machlin.

MATTHEW MORISON, cabinet-maker, Machlin.
JEAN SMITH, sister of James (Wee) Smith, Machlin.
JOHN TENNANT, factor-farmer, Glenconner.
NANCE TINNOCK, ale-wife, Backcauseway, Machlin.
MRS. MARKLAND, merchant's wife, Machlin.
JAMES FINDLAY, Excise Officer, Tarbolton.
DAVID CULLIE, farmer, Ellisland.
NANCE CULLIE, wife to David Cullie.
FIDDLING SANDY, itinerant fiddler.

' Every pulse along my veins
Tells the ardent lover.'

From: "Thine Am I, My Faithful Fair."
By: Robert Burns.

Part One

THE CUP OF FAME

GREY DAYLIGHT

IT WAS a cloudy lowering day and visibility was something less than an honest Scots mile. A dowie day, when the trees stood listless, dripping and clammy with dampness, in a slouched halt by the roadside. The saffron-grey grass seemed to have decayed so long in death that it would take all the miracle of spring to resurrect in it the green sap of life. A few white-breasted sea-mews, freshly daubed on a withered lea-rig, appeared curiously disinterested in the new-turned furrows. Above them, some tattered crows flapped disconsolately—occasionally venting an inconsequential caw.

The November day was wearing late: it was at its dowiest. And Robert Burns, as he jogged in the saddle and allowed the pony to pick his own way, felt leaden-dull. Lack of sleep, hard riding and an unaccustomed overdose of alcohol (pressed on him by ardent admirers) had lowered his spirits and vitiated his immediate appetite for life.

When he had made his halt in the early evening of the previous day, when he had ridden into the snod steading of Covington Mains, on the Biggar road, his host, farmer Prentice, had at once hoisted a white sheet on a pitchfork and had planted it in his highest grain-stack.

It had been a pre-arranged signal: the neighbours knew its meaning. Big Jamie Stodart had seen it flutter in the evening breeze and had gone into his wife saying: "That's the Ayrshire Bard arrived—I'll awa' ower and grasp his hand afore they hae it shook aff him." And then, as he had busied himself with a rough toilet: "Guid kens when we'll be back —but see and keep a hot stane in the bed for him."

They had made merry at Prentice's till early in the morning. When at length he had expressed the wish that he might be bedded, Big Jamie had linked him across to his biggin where, as she had been instructed, Mrs. Stodart had the bed warmed.

But it seemed he had hardly slept when the house began to fill up for breakfast. Those who had not managed to see him the previous night began to clatter into the courtyard.

At breakfast, as at supper, the whisky and the home-brewed ale had flowed with a friendly freeness. It was only with the greatest difficulty he had escaped from their exuberant hospitality.

There was not so much to wonder at here: the folks about Biggar were kind-hearted honest country folk such as he had always known. Aye: kind-hearted free-spirited folks—but foolish company when so much of his journey lay before him. . .

He eased himself in the saddle and pressed his hand across his stomach. The excess of alcohol had outraged his innards and he twisted his face in a grue of nausea. He had never drunk much at any time and only to excess in moments of great emotional crisis. But now, in addition to the alcoholic reaction, there was the nervous agitation of anticipation. He had taken a big step in severing his Ayrshire roots and staking his immediate future on the gamble of an Edinburgh edition for his poems. The nearer he approached the Capital, the more violent did the nervous spasms become. His star had ever been a malign one. Was there any reason to suppose that his fortune would change with a change of country?

And yet, as always, his profound sense of the inevitability of events saved him from despair. For good or for evil, he must go forward and press his fortune in Edinburgh. What would come to pass would come to pass. For his own part, he would strive with all his strength for success. But, if success was not to be, he would weep no tears of useless regret. At best, fortune was but a bitch: cold crafty and senselessly cruel. When she smiled, the other side of her face was never very far away.

His arches were sore pressing on the stirrup irons. Maybe it would be easier if he dismounted and walked for a mile; but then, if he did, there would be the effort of remounting!

Surely by now he must be nearing the Capital? But he was past the Toll and jogging down the Twopenny Custom

Road when he raised his head and there before him, and above him, the Rock and the Castle that crouched on it seemed to hang in the damp grey mist.

The pony placed a hind foot in an awkward rut and sprachled clumsily to regain a surer footing. The movement, coming at so abstracted a moment, almost unseated him.

He patted the beast reassuringly on the neck. "Steady, boy, steady—if you throw me now I'll never rise."

Having recovered his balance, he found his jaded nerves responding to the sight. Auld Reekie at long last! God, but he was pleased to see it, even if it was shrouded in a cold damp of misty twilight.

But this was not how he had pictured the scene. He had always imagined the Castle and the Rock responding to strong sunlight, grave yet gallant, head upwards-thrown in proud and gay defiance. And there was little in the towering masonry of the town that suggested the canty hole Robert Fergusson had sung about.

Glad as he was to be within sight of his journey's end, he could not wholly warm to this sight of Scotland's capital. It was too grim and grey, too cold and blurred in its outlines to cast forth anything of its essential inner warmth. But perhaps there was greyness within him as well as around him; and the tired tail-end of a dowie day was not the best time to witness the realisation, in stone and lime, of a long-cherished vision.

The pleasant familiarity of Machlin and Mossgiel lay sixty miles behind him; and many a wet moss and weary hag lay between. From the ridge of Mossgiel, Edinburgh, lying beyond the far blue hills, had beckoned in his imagination like a city celestial.

Now he was about to enter the gates of the city and meet the challenge of a new world. Never before had he felt less like meeting any challenge. Maybe he had been overbold, over-venturesome. To stride and dominate the centuries-hardened ridge of Scotland's capital was a vastly different business from striding and dominating the ridge of Mossgiel.

But he must go forward and face it. Maybe once he was

settled in with his old Machlin friend, John Richmond, and had enjoyed a night of quiet rest, things would take on a different aspect.

He shook the reins; and the pony, with a tired pent-up snort and a shake of the head, hastened his forward step.

He wheeled sharply to his right, came in the Portsburgh road where tired bedraggled and dilapidated houses flanked either side, and entered the Town by the West Port. Here, even as his Ayr friend, Robert Aiken, had predicted, a caddie came forward and offered his services as messenger or as guide. He asked to be directed to the White Hart Inn in the Grass-market, that he might stable his horse and make arrangements for him to be taken back to Ayrshire by carrier Patterson.

John Boyd, the caddie, tried to take him in with a swift penetrating glance. "You're in the Grassmarket noo, sir! That's the Inn ower there on your left. Will I tak' the beast?"

He dismounted; and the caddie led the pony forward.

He looked around him. The Grassmarket was a vast rectangle, and though the fading light was deceptive, he reckoned it was close on two-hundred-and-fifty yards long and maybe forty full yards in breadth.

Above it, on his left, with vague sinister menace, towered the south cliff of the Castle Rock. Beyond the quaint irregular buildings on his right loomed the turret towers of Heriot's Hospital, while farther up towards the Cowgate corner and the slit of the Candlemaker Row he could discern the ghostly bulk of the Greyfriars Kirk.

These landmarks, though he could not as yet identify them, he noted in a sweeping glance. Then the Market itself fascinated him. He had never seen so many well-made carts, carriages and hand-barrows. And here and there about the causeway, placed with no seeming order, stood little wooden booths about which groups of idling gossiping folks were loosely knotted. And occasionally above the rattle of wheels on the paving stones he could hear the harsh but indistinct call of a vendor or the curse of a carter.

A great pile of hay was stacked in front of the inn door. And above the door, on a painted board, he saw the sign with the name of the proprietor, Francis MacKay, inscribed in bold, if irregular, letters. It seemed that he could not have entered the Town by a more convenient route.

No sooner had he made his business known to the groom than he brought out Tam Samson's brother John to greet him.

"By God, Rab, you're a sicht for sair een. Man, but I'm glad to see ye. I heard ye were on your way: so I've been waiting. I want to borrow your pownie so that I can ride back to Kilmarnock at my pleasure—and do a bit business on the road."

"Well . . . it's no' mine to give, John. It belongs to George Reid o' Barquharrie; and I promised him I would return it by Patterson. . ."

"It'll be safer wi' me; and Geordie Reid and me are good friends: he'll raise no objections. . ."

While they were discussing the matter, out came James Dalrymple of Orangefield. He too gave him a hearty welcome. The Bard shook his head in perplexity. He had never expected to meet two Ayrshire men the moment he entered the Town. He explained his difficulty about the pony to Dalrymple. Dalrymple was decisive. He knew John Samson. He would vouch for him. The Bard decided that Samson must carry back with him a letter of explanation to George Reid. This was agreed upon and they entered the inn to have a drink while the Bard penned his brief note.

"Yes," said the Squire of Orangefield in his large and elegant manner, "I stable my own mount with MacKay here—and my carriage beasts, of course. Good fellow, MacKay—and he keeps damn good grooms—ken how to treat a good animal—especially after a hard day's riding. Noo see here, Burns: you give me a note of your lodgings in the Town and I'll keep in touch wi' you. Maybe the morn—or maybe the next day—I'll tak' you out to Coates House to see my cousin Glencairn. I ken he's delighted wi' your book and will gladly give you his patronage. No reason why you shouldna hae a happy time in the Town, Burns: no reason at all. And you deserve it. But—you're not drinking?"

"If you'll excuse me, sir . . . I never had much of a stomach for drinking, and the savage hospitality I have had thrust upon me on my journey here has ruined what little stomach I had."

"Ha! we'll soon put that right for you here. Your stomach hasn't been properly tanned: that's what's wrong with you. In no time you'll turn the bottoms of five bottles with the best. But I see you're tired, Mr. Burns. Get up to your lodgings and have a good night's rest and you'll be as fit as a fiddle in the morning: it's damned hard riding to make Edinburgh in twa days. The caddie will carry your saddle-bags up the hill for you. And don't worry: Samson will look after the pony . . . You ken, Burns, the Town's waiting on you. Your fame's here afore you. Indeed . . . eh . . . there's been a lot o' talk about you. One of the prints here has been carrying some of your Kilmarnock verses."

"What print would that be, sir?"

"Eh . . . the Edinburgh Magazine."

"Edited and wrote mostly by a Mr. James Sibbald, I understand."

"In the Parliament Close—that's the fellow! Well . . . I suppose a man canna have friends without he has enemies as well. I'm glad you had the good sense to visit the Town. I'm sure your appearance, in person, will have the effect of laying much rumour i' the dust."

Beneath his tan the blood ran hot. "What rumours, sir? Have the goodness not to spare my feelings in a matter that so closely affects my honour."

"It's difficult, Burns. But we're friends. . . The fact is that some nasty rumours have got abroad affecting your moral character. I was about to rise to your defence the other night when Sir John Whitefoord immediately manned the breach and defended you so stoutly that your enemies were completely routed."

"Sir John Whitefoord rose in my defence?"

"That he did, Burns, and did nobly. Of course I backed him up—though as things turned out there was little need for my artillery: a musketry ball or two cleared the field. No: don't thank me, Burns—— What I mean is that rumours have a way of spreading in the Town—and your friends canna be

everywhere to defend you. But—you will be your own best
defence. And that's why I'm glad you have made your
appearance. Think no more of it, I pray you—I merely put
you on your guard and, at the same time, let you know that
your friends are with you."

"But I must thank——"

"No, sir: I will hear of no thanks. And once my worthy
kinsman Glencairn takes you under his protection no one will
dare to utter a word against you."

For some moments the Bard remained in gloomy silence.
So the Holy Willies were here in Edinburgh as well as in
Machlin! Well, he would make his stay short. The *Roselle*
was due to leave Leith for Jamaica at the end of December—
he could always work his passage there—and be damned to all
the Holy Willies and evil-tongued gossip-mongers of Scotland.
But there were men like Sir John Whitefoord—and Dalrymple here! He took his hand slowly from his head.

"Forgive my manners, sir. I have a miserable aching head
—and I confess your news has depressed me."

"Ah, you mauna be depressed, Burns. If you would have
fame you must learn to reckon with envy. Why! people say
of me that I am a foolish man squandering my estate and
riding to the devil. Am I depressed? Do I give a damn for
what they say? But just let any damned cad say ocht to my
face and I'll whip the lights out of him. . . Now a poet——"

"A mere rustic bard, sir, who was foolish to abandon the
plough——"

"Stuff, sir! You are under the weather for the moment.
Toss back your drink and have the caddie take your bags up
to the Landmarket. You have more friends in the Town than
you think. Come—finish your drink and think no more of it.
Here's John Samson back from having seen to Reid's pony. . ."

When he ventured out into the wide gloomy square of the
Grassmarket, the weather seemed to have changed. A keen
wind sliced at his face and hands. But the thinly-clad caddie
grasped his bags and did not seem to mind it.

Inside the mellow warm inn Dalrymple and Samson had

seemed big hearty fellows, their personalities roundly and warmly defined. Now they seemed small and insignificant specks of humanity in this mass of beings weaving about the causeway. Even his own identity seemed to ooze away from him among the press of individuals as unknown to him as they seemed to be unknown and indifferent to each other.

Unlike his caddie, many of them crouched in their walk against the bitter winds that knifed through the narrow streets, the narrower wynds and the yet narrower closes: winds that cut and slashed from all angles like sword blades in desperate and closely-joined battle.

As he approached the head of the Grassmarket, walking east into the biting east wind, the great gloomy lands of tenements seemed to rise to fantastic heights. Noticing a long pillared roof that stood on the causeway at the foot of the tenement crags, he asked the caddie what it was.

"That's the Corn Market, sir."

"Ah! The Corn Market, is it? And where exactly did they murder James Renwick?"

"Murder? I heard nocht about that, sir."

"James Renwick, the last martyr of the Covenant. Murdered on the gallows-tree somewhere hereabouts."

"Oh, the gibbet, sir? Ye see that meikle stane wi' the hole in't. That's whaur the gibbet was fixed. Aye, sir; mony a guid man met a sair death here—in the auld days. Aye, but mony a weel-deservit hanging too. The last man that was hangit there—let me see noo—aye, jist twa year ago come Feebrywar—aye, he robbit a man in the Hope Park... They string them up now fornenst the auld Tolbooth—no' a dizzen o' guid steps frae whaur ye're for biding at Baxters' Close... Aye, an' Half-Hangit Maggie Dickson was hangit there, sir. It's a wee whilie back—but my faither saw it. Aye, the surgeons' laddies were for takin' her awa' for cutting up at the Surgeons' Ha'; but her frien's wheecht her awa' in a cairt. Syne, the dirlin her banes got on the causeway, sir, set her heart beating again. Aye . . . and she had bairns efter that, sir, and sold salt aboot the streets o' the Toon for mony a day."

But the Bard was listening with only half an ear. His mind

was turning back the pages of history and he was seeing again the ordeal of the Martyrs. . . And as he stood there, his head bowed, he knew that every generation had its martyrs and that the fight for liberty had to be endlessly waged. He sighed deeply and turned to the caddie who was beginning to show signs of impatience. They moved up into the steep chasm, the dog's hind leg, of the West Bow that led up and on to the high ridge of the Town.

As they moved up into the ever-narrowing street and the buildings began to overhang him, he felt that now he was entering into the city of which Robert Fergusson had sung so bravely and Tobias Smollett had written so graphically.

The caddie, seeing that his fare was interested in the Town and its history, and thinking also that he might win from him an extra bawbee, voiced a running commentary as they proceeded.

"This is ca'ed the Bowfoot, sir. When there was a hanging taking place the crowd got a grand view frae the brae here: packed like herring in a barrel they were. Aye: if thae auld stanes could talk they would tell a queer story. . .

"See that arched pend there? Aye: well, it was through there that Major Weir bided wi' his sister. Him that sellt himself to the Devil. Damn the doubt about that, sir. His ain confession. Na: he didna recant even when they put the rope round his neck and lit the meikle bonfire ablow him. That was a wheen years ago noo; but the house is still empty. God help onybody that tries to bide in it! For the Major pays it a visit back and forwards. It's no' the yae body aboot the Bow that's seen him. Hunders, sir. Aye, and hunders mair hae heard the ongauns when Auld Nick drives up wi' a carriage-an'-fower to convey him back to Hell. God's truth, sir! If I were you I wadna think o' venturing aboot the Bow after twelve on a dark nicht. . .

"That's the auld Assembly Rooms, sir, whaur the Quality had their dances: my auld faither used to tell me how he'd seen the Bow fair chokit on an Assembly nicht wi' sedan chairs: lords, dukes, earls and their leddies, sir: a grand sicht: aye, and the attendants wi' their lanthorns on a bit pole and the chairmen cursing and swearing in Erse through each other, and the bits o' laddies egging them on and laughing at them. Ah, but ye'll get a better view o' the place in full daylicht. That was Provost Stewart's hoose. He entertained the Prince when he was here in the Forty-five. The hoose is fu' o' secret chaumers and stairs and passages. Mony a murder would be done there in the auld days that naebody ever heard aboot: aye, and could be yet...

"Ah well: here we are, sir, coming up onto the Landmarket: the Bowhead, sir, fornenst the Weigh-house. Aye, it's a stiff brae and a damn rough causeway: if ye ever think o' takin' a beast up or doon it, ye'd be weel advised to lead it. Break your neck gin ye were coupit on thae causeys: aye, bluidy quick. Here ye are then, sir: this is you in the Landmarket."

Against the clip and drawl of the caddie's accent the Bard had swivelled his head from right to left, fascinated by the amazing diversity of architecture displayed by the façades of the Bow houses. Not only were there no two houses alike: almost every stone seemed to have been laid without artistic reference to its neighbours. And yet the seemingly haphazard craziness of the architecture gave the place a fantastic charm that could not be denied. But there was a grim, almost diabolic, element in the fantasy that repelled. From such dark and foul-smelling entries any imaginable evil might well emerge under the cover of darkness. He was glad to stand for a moment and take his breath in the airier Landmarket.

Many of the Machlin streets were narrow enough in all conscience. But the buildings that flanked them were small and seldom climbed beyond a modest attic. But here, every-where around him, the lands climbed to the appalling height of six and eight storeys. And the gaunt lands of dirty grey stone and soot-black ashlar were separated by the narrowest of slits of closes and wynds into which only the greyest and dirtiest of daylight ever managed to filter. The builders had grudged these slits of openings. From the second floors the building lines projected over the base, so that the upper tenants could grip hands and hold intimate converse with their neighbours across the gap...

Coming after twenty-seven years of farm life in the uplands of Ayrshire, all this had a stunning effect. He could well remember the narrow vennels and the high buildings of Irvine; and he could recall the stenches and stinks of that seaport town. But the stinks of Irvine were scents compared to the vile stenches that had assailed his nostrils since he entered the Town.

And now he was standing on the south side of the Landmarket, part of the uninterrupted mile that ran upwards from the Palace of Holyrood through the Canongate and the High Street to the Castle. It was a moment he had long imagined, and indeed many a time in his imagination he had traversed this far-famed mile of history.

The caddie saw he was lost in a dwam and sought, tactfully, to rouse him from it.

"Aye: it's a great Toon, sir. Ye could look aboot you a' day an' never light on Mr. Richmond. Aye, and ye could just as easy lose yoursel'. On your left, sir: that's Castle Hill straight up to the Walk and the Castle. To your right here, the Landmarket: that's the Toll and the Luckenbooths ye see doon there i' the middle o' the causeway fornenst Saint Giles's . . . And further doon's the North Brig that tak's ye to the New Toon. Oh aye: they're comin' on weel wi' the New Toon. Will ye be biding lang, sir?"

The Bard roused himself.

"Biding? I don't rightly know. But as like as not I'll be here for some time—a week or two anyway."

"Ye'll hae business in the Toon, sir? It wouldna be a law plea? If it's the Court o' Session, ye may hae lang enough to wait: the Lords'll no' gee themsel's much unless ye can mak' it worth their while."

"That, my lad, I know only too well. No: what my business is in Edinburgh will be known to you soon enough—if it prospers. And if it doesn't, then it'll be of no interest to you —or to anyone."

"It was just that folk micht be spiering for you."

"Give them my best compliments and tell them where they can find me."

The caddie was an excellent judge of human nature. But he found it difficult to place Robert Burns. The West country was in his intonation but it was not in his speech. He spoke much too correctly to be a country farmer or a small country squire, though his dress indicated that such might be his station in life. He might be a teacher of languages or a tutor to one of the sons of the nobility. But here again the coarseness of his hands and the rhythm of his gait—to say nothing of his weather-tanned and exposed complexion—belied anything but an outdoor life. Close and observant, it was clear that he had all his wits about him. A kindly man; but a tough customer if he were crossed. . .

"I suppose you could direct me to my Lord Glencairn, or the Honourable Andrew Erskine, or Sir John Whitefoord, or Doctor Blacklock, the blind poet. . . .? Do all these good gentlemen have their residences about here?"

For a split second the caddie was nonplussed. "The nobility of Scotland live in thae lands, sir. Some now bide in the New Toon; but the maist o' them prefer here—or the South side o' the Toon: the other side o' the Cowgate. The New Toon's on the North side, sir. The Earl of Glencairn bides just outside the Toon here at Coates House. There's nothing aboot the New Toon but a wheen braw buildings and a lot o' cauld winds. I've heard mony a gentleman lamentin' aboot the cauld since he flitted across: it's far too open: ower much o' the cauld nicht air's no' good for a body—unless, of course, they're brocht up to it in the country. . ."

"Well: it's getting too dark to see much now. Lead on, my lad: I am grateful for your intelligence."

"Follow me, sir: we're almost there: across the street and to your right. Excuse me, sir: Mr. Robert Burns is no' an uncommon name i' the Toon: how would I ken you were the gentleman I micht be askit for?"

"Robert Burns: the Ayrshire ploughman."

"You wouldna joke wi' a puir caddie, sir?"

"A poor ploughman, my lad, has little authority to joke with a poor caddie—or with anyone."

A bluidy queer ploughman, thought the caddie as he led

him diagonally across the street and entered Baxters' Close. He took him along the narrow passage and up the narrow flight of rough worn steps. He indicated a narrow door.

"That's Mistress Carfrae's, sir. Gin you're looking for anither caddie, there's aey a wheen o' us aboot the Luckenbooths."

The Bard thanked him warmly and handed him a small piece of silver. The caddie was delighted: he expressed his satisfaction and quickly disappeared down the dark stair.

The middle-aged widow, Mrs. Carfrae, had been apprised of the Bard's visit. After making a few cautious but shrewd enquiries she conducted him along a dark passage to Richmond's room.

"Weel now, Mr. Burns: I hope ye'll be contentit here. It's a respectable hoose I keep: which is mair nor can be said aboot some folks; and I wad like it keepit that way. It's a sinfu' warld, Mr. Burns; and the Toon's gettin' wickeder and wickeder every day. . . Aye; but nae doubt ye'll be tired after your lang journey. Mr. Richmond's siccan a nice quiet gentleman. He doesna drink and he doesna gandie wi' the bawds. I just canna abide my gentlemen rinnin' after the bawds, Mr. Burns. . . Ye'll ken that I dinna serve ony meals: excepting a bowl o' guid parritch in the morning? I aey say that whan ye hae a bowl o' guid parritch lining your stammick i' the morning, ye dinna need to fash yoursel' for the rest o' the day. Mr. Richmond'll no' be lang now."

There was a sudden interruption of high-pitched laughter from above, revealing that there was little or no deafening behind the internal lath and plaster walls and ceilings. Mrs. Carfrae screwed her face in disgust.

"That's thae bawds abune, Mr. Burns. Wicked shameless hizzies. Ah, but the pit o' hell's lowin' for them: that's a punishment they'll no' escape. Weel may they hae their fling now, for they'll hae a' eternity to squeal and skirl. . .

"But it's a terrible affliction for a decent Christian widow to lie in her bed i' nichts and be keepit aff her Christian sleep by the gandie ongauns o' brazen bawds and their filthy fellows.

Aye: and the Sabbath nicht worse nor a'. Sae dinna you be
tempted up the stair, Mr. Burns, or you and me'll fa' out
completely. . . Ah, but I see you're a decent respectable man
and think mair o' yoursel' and your Maker than degrade
yoursel' in the company o' abandoned women: you wadna
be a friend o' Mr. Richmond if you werena. . . And here's The
Courant if you want to pass the time—juist in."

When at last the garrulous landlady had retired, the Bard
sat on the bed and surveyed his room. It was furnished barely;
but it wasn't a bad room. There was a double bed that at one
time had been an elegant-enough four-poster; but the trap-
pings had long disappeared. The walls, above the half-panelling,
were roughly plastered and were in a dirty and dilapidated
condition. The floor was sanded with coarse yellow sand which
helped to fill in the gaping seams of the floor-boards. A once-
scrubbed table, with a missing leaf, stood against the wall.
The small window that looked out on Lady Stair's Close had a
bunker-locker beneath it. There was a deep press with a door to
serve as a wardrobe. On the table sat a basin and a water jug.
At the foot of the bed, covered by a rough wooden lid, was a
large slop-can suitable for all domestic needs. . . There was a
polished stone fire-place with a corner of the mantelpiece
broken off.

It would be possible to sit into the table and write in
reasonable comfort—if the bawds did not prove too distracting.
He was intrigued at the thought of living immediately below
them. With the thin roof it was possible to hear all that was
going on there. It would be interesting to see them, to speak
to them and to find out what they were like and how they
reacted to life. . . It was obvious that the landlady protested
too much. She envied the bawds: that was plain. He knew
well enough that a bawd was not to be envied; but he knew
also that a bawd was a source of interest. It was strange that
Richmond, in his letters, had never referred to them. But then
Jock had always been a canny cautious chiel. . .

The noise from the adjoining close filtered into the room.
It was a drowsy noise: the murmur of voices and the scliff of
many feet on the paving. Now and again there was the sound

of a voice raised in a high pitched call as if it might be hawking some ware or other. . .

He lay back on the bed and closed his eyes. He was dog-tired; but it was a great relief to be within the four walls of a room and resting quietly. And he would rest quietly for a day or two. At least he wouldn't stir much until James Dalrymple sent word to him. Had he been serious when he had spoken of the possibility of Glencairn's patronage? Ah, that was too much to hope for. An earl didn't bestow patronage on a ploughman merely because he had written a book of verses. Yet Sir John Whitefoord, who had once been the laird of Ballochmyle and who had once been the patron of his Tarbolton Masons' lodge, had stood up among the gentry and defended him! He would have to write a letter of thanks to Sir John.

He sprang up from the bed at this thought and looked underneath it. Thank heaven his sea-chest had arrived safely before him! Maybe his white buckskin breeches and his tailed blue coat would serve him well enough for dress. If he could add to this a pair of polished knee-boots and a new waistcoat he would be elegant enough to call upon any of the gentry.

Darkness had come down on the Town. He lit the candle, waited till the flame reached its full brightness and then spread the *Edinburgh Evening Courant* before him on the table.

But apart from learning that William Wallace, Sheriff-depute of Ayrshire and Professor of Scots Law at the University, had died that morning it contained little news to interest him. It was Wallace who had ratified Hamilton of Sundrum's findings regarding the dispute between his father and MacLure; and James Armour's writ against him had issued from the same office.

His eye travelled over the small print listlessly. Just as he finished reading that the pupils of Mr. Nicol's class at the High School were to dine at Mr. Cameron's Tavern, and before he had time to speculate about Mr. Nicol, there was a sound from the front door.

As he folded the paper he heard the stair door shutting and the sound of steps in the passage. Before he could rise to his feet John Richmond, in his great-coat and cravat, hat in hand, was in the room.

"Well: you managed at last, Rab! Damned, but I'm real glad to see you. I got away as early as I could. You'll have had a word with Mrs. Carfrae? Good! Now I daresay you'll be feeling like a bite of meat?"

"Aye; and your bowl o' parritch will be far down gin now, Jock?"

"It's the cheapest way to live. I can feed well in the howffs here for sixpence a day: sometimes fourpence: aye, and many a day I've put in for twopence. I've got to practise an extreme economy. I hope to save up enough to go back to Machlin one day and set up there for myself. How was Jenny Surgeoner when you left her? Dammit, Rab: I canna marry her the now. But one of these days I'll do the right thing and go back and marry her. You say the bairn's like me?"

"Well: who else would she be like, Jock? Only you might write and tell her that: it would ease her mind."

"It's a bad thing to write to a woman. What you say by word of mouth is one thing: what you put down on paper is another. Never put pen to paper, Rab, unless you're dead certain; and seldom then. I've seen more lives wrecked through folks putting down their silly notions on paper than by ony other cause. But come on: we'll find a quiet place where we can talk. Oh: I was forgetting to congratulate you on the success of your turning author in print. There's some talk in the Town about your verses as it is. . . Sibbald's Edinburgh Magazine has been cracking you up and publishing some of your verses. The Town's talking about them. I listen and say nothing. I wad hae sent you copies o' the papers—only I knew you'd be here ony day. Come on out and have a bite and let me hear a' the Machlin news. Mind you, Rab, there's times I miss Machlin—and John Dow's. . . Damned, and I was forgetting to congratulate you on being the father o' twins! So Jean Armour did pay you double! But maybe I should be careful o' the word father, seeing you managed that bachelor's certifi-

cate out o' Daddy Auld. . . . But come on: get into your coat
and we'll go out and celebrate wi' a bite and a sup o' ale. I ken
a good place, down Libberton's Wynd across the street. God,
Robert, but I'm glad to see you. . ."

And for the moment, in the emotion of seeing his old friend
and hearing his voice, the Bard's tiredness left him and he
was eager to fall in with his plans.

They went out onto the Landmarket in the darkness relieved
only by the feeble lights from the windows. An odd public
lamp on an odd corner provided more stink and fumes than
illumination.

Though the business of the day was over there were still
folks about and not a few skirling urchins.

The wynds and closes that led off the main thoroughfare on
the crest of the ridge descended either to the drained basin of
the Nor' Loch or to the sunken Cowgate.

They crossed the Landmarket and descended Libberton's
Wynd that ran down to the Cowgate.

Richmond explained something of the geography of the
Town as they went along. . .

At a gushet in the narrow rough-cobbled wynd they
entered a tavern whose host, John Dowie, was one of the most
popular in Auld Reekie.

Dowie was in many ways an older and more mellowed
edition of Johnny Dow in Machlin.

At the moment Dowie was not too busy; but in an hour or
so his apartments would be packed, almost literally, to suffocation—as the Bard was soon to know.

Dowie, like a good landlord, never forgot a face. Richmond
was not one of his regular customers. But a customer was
always a customer. Two customers at the quiet time of night
were more welcome than one.

"A cauld raw nicht, Mr. Richmond. Aye . . . and are you
for a bite, maybe? Something tasty to warm you up?"

Richmond introduced the Bard. "Aha now. The Ayrshire
bard! And verra welcome, sir, to my bit place here. Aye:
the Toon's talking about ye, Mr. Burns. . . The skirl o' the

pan, Mr. Richmond, certainly. I'll send a lass ben wi' a platter
for ye... No: there's naebody in the coffin the noo—aye, aye:
just the thing if ye're wantin' a quiet jaw thegither."

The main room in which they now stood was used mostly
for casual drinking. Beyond that was another room where
folk who liked to spend a while over their meal might do so
in better comfort. Beyond that was a tiny room that held a
small table and two wall seats.

The place held two folks in modest comfort and complete
seclusion. It was incapable of holding three.

And so it was that Richmond and the Bard sat and talked
in the coffin, as the room had been named.

They had much to talk about. Richmond asked many
questions about Machlin: the Bard asked many questions
about Edinburgh. But they had many personal things to
discuss...

"So you got a bachelor's certificate frae Daddy Auld?"

"I did. And Jean has no legal claim on me."

"Don't you be daft enough to admit of ony other claim.
What's your plans?"

"Plans, Jock? I wish I had some kind of a plan. I came
here on impulse—and maybe because I couldna bide Machlin
ony longer. First I hope to get my poems brought out in a
second edition here. I don't suppose that'll be easy; and even
if I succeed I don't suppose I'll win more money than I did out
of Kilmarnock Johnny. But if I can make fifty pounds maybe
I'll sail for the Indies yet. I see the Roselle sails frae Leith at the
end o' December——"

"You'll no' get your poems printed before then."

"No . . . I don't suppose I will. But as a second line I'm
thinking o' exploring the ins and outs concerning the Excise.
A gauger's job is nae catch: I ken that fine enough. But there's
a measure o' security attached to it that I could fine be doing
wi'."

"We're a' looking for security."

"Well, I'm coming twenty-eight, Jock—and I'm about ready
for turning beggar ony day. That's a fine look-out after all the
years I've slaved on rented ground."

"You canna live in Edinburgh on nothing, Robin. But surely you had some plan about publishing your verses?"

"Well, Bob Aiken spoke about a William Creech—I understood he was writing him."

"Creech? A most important man in the Town. But don't build your hopes too high, Rab."

"Why?. Do you think my verses are too poor for the great Mr. Creech?"

"No, no! But Creech publishes only the most elegant writers. I don't know that he would look too kindly on the Scotch dialect. . . He holds court every morning. Creech's Levees they're called. The first wits and scholars i' the Town gather there. Nothing can hold a candle to them for wit and learning."

"I'm hoping that my Lord Glencairn will maybe do something for me by way o' patronage."

"Glencairn! You're moving in exalted circles now! Creech used to be some kind of a companion and tutor to the Earl o' Glencairn: travelled abroad wi' him, I believe. If my lord takes notice of you, you're made. Creech'll fall on your neck."

"I would like to have my poems published without anyone's assistance. But I'm told that's no' the way to go about things."

"That's true: without influence you'll get nowhere. Everything's influence here. . . You'll be tired after your long ride?"

"Tired enough. I'd a night o' dissipation on the road here: I don't want to see drink for another year. . . Jock: how long did it take you to get used to the smell o' this place? No: I mean the whole Town. The one place seems to smell worse than the other. . ."

"You soon get used to the smells: except on a right hot day; and then when they start throwing the slops over the windows it can be wicked. You've got to keep to the main streets after dark or you might get yourself into a hell o' a mess."

"You mean that they just open the window and throw everything out?"

"What else would they do? They've got to throw it somewhere: they canna keep it in the house—unless them that hae gardens. Of course they get fined if they're caught throwing muck out the windows—but everybody takes the risk. You'll get used to it. You see, there's not a hole or corner in the Town but has got somebody living in it. Plenty down in cellars below the street level, without windows or a damned thing. Aye; and you'll find pig-styes right in the highest attics: so that when the beasts get ready for the knife they've got to lower them down to the ground wi' ropes. It cost me a bit o' influence to get in wi' Mrs. Carfrae. She's an auld bitch like a' landladies; but she could be a lot worse. For God's sake dinna go near the bawds up the stair or she'll fling the pair o' us out. Besides: there are better places; and you're better to go as far away from where you bide as possible: that's only sense——"

"The only sense about brothels, Jock, is to give them a wide berth. I've never been wi' a bawd yet; and I never hope to be."

"Don't be too sure: there's some fine lassies i' the Town; and when you've paid for their favours they have no come-back on you; and that's a big factor—as you should ken. I had my lesson wi' Jenny Surgeoner: I don't need another."

"Whatever you say, Jock: we won't quarrel about that: or anything else. You're free to go your way and I'm free to go mine. I don't know that I'm going to like this place: I'm going to miss the caller air for one thing."

"Don't worry, Rab: once you've had a night's sleep and a look round the Town in daylight, you'll think differently. I was hame-sick when I cam' here at first. By God I was hame-sick! And that's when you're damned glad to go to a bawd. At least *she'll* speak kindly to you; and you can speak to her; and you can forget that you're paying her. A human being needs company in a place like this more than in Machlin; and sometimes that's the only way you can get company. Aye; and you could get a damned sight worse. Besides, everybody does it here. They have different values on such things than they have back hame. Folk are sensible here: civilised. Damnit, I hardly ken a man that doesna pay a regular visit to his own particular house."

"Are there as many houses as that?"

"There's thousands o' bawds in Edinburgh: thousands! That's no exaggeration. I could take you to a dozen houses in the Landmarket alone. Some are damned particular: it's no' everybody they'll let in. A lot o' them you've got to be introduced into; and vouched for. Some o' them are harder to get into than a Masons' lodge. You don't judge by Machlin standards here, Rab. Aye; and some of the ministers are as bad as onybody else: you want to be here when the General Assembly's meeting. . . And then the hypocrites go back to their parishes and rate poor devils for a simple houghmagandie ploy."

"I've heard tell o' the wickedness o' Edinburgh. I never thought it was as bad as you suggest."

"You'll see for yourself."

"So we're just a lot o' puir gulls in the country?"

"You're no gull, Rab. You'll soon find your feet; and when you do you'll no' want to go back to the plough: you'd be a fool if you did."

"You don't paint a pretty picture, Jock."

"You'll need to forget a' about pretty pictures, Rab: sentiment doesna count here. Life's a grim struggle for lads like you and me; and we've got to fight with every weapon we can lay our hands on. If you go down there's nobody weeps for you: or cares. And why should they? There's no money in it."

"And money's the talisman?"

"You see how far you can go without it. I ken I've got to make every bawbee I earn a prisoner. If you have to take to your bed wi' an illness, unless you have money, they'll let you lie till you die: if they don't throw you out into the gutter to die there!"

"So it's not surprising that they let puir Fergusson die?"

"Don't say ocht about Fergusson wi' the literati here. They hate the very mention o' his name."

"Oh, they do?"

"Fergusson was only a poor scrivener; and he made the

mistake of insulting Henry MacKenzie: see that you don't make a like one."

"I mean to pay my respects to Henry MacKenzie; but first I'll pay my respects to Robert Fergusson: or to where his last remains were cast into the earth. I don't suppose they were laid there with any pious reverence. But never heed me, Jock: we'll have some good nights together in this same stinking Auld Reekie. I'll maybe have to go back to the plough some day; but before I do I mean to enjoy myself. I must confess that when I rode into Embro this afternoon . . . and the great bustle o' folks and not one of them paying the slightest attention to me, I thought that my poetry would hardly affect them either."

"I'm glad it's you that's saying that, Robert, and no' me; for the truth is that there's nobody gives a damn about poetry here unless it's the poets themselves . . . and the critics. Since poetry neither fills bellies nor purses, why should they?"

"What's come over you since you left Machlin? Something's hurt you, Jock. You've become hard in your judgments. Are things no' prospering wi' you? You don't need to tell me if you'd rather no'."

"Maybe I'm a bit bitter nowadays. You're a success: our old friend Jamie Smith's gotten a good partnership in Linlithgow. I'm just a lawyer's clerk working my fingers to the bone for a miserable pittance. No: don't think that I grudge you or Smith your success: I'm more nor pleased about it: especially you, Robert. You're a genius; and you've more right to success, to fame and fortune, than ony other man I know. Only I don't see you getting justice. I came to Edinburgh wi' high hopes; and I see you've come the same way. But I ken what goes on; and you dinna. But go forward your own way and maybe things will turn out for the best: I don't suppose they could be worse than Mossgiel."

"We'll see, Jock, we'll see. I've kent misfortune a' my days. I don't think I'll start shedding tears now."

"You'll be all right. I wish I had half your chance. Well . . . I've to get up in the morning and get along to Willie Wilson's desk. Come on: we'll get away up to bed."

Night had settled down on the capital of Scotland, the Athens of the North. . . A cold biting darkness it was. This side of the Ural mountains the wind sprang up and swept across the snow-deep steppes of Russia and the frost-iron plains of Europe; from its sweep across the North Sea it gathered a keenness and a new vitality to attack the great stone-scaled dragon that crouched on the ridge of the rock that was Edinburgh. It clawed at the serrated stone scales with a cold ferocity: it lashed and tore at the beings who huddled there.

The Town Guard, muffled to the ears, came down from the Castle: the wind whipped the drum-beats from the glinting skin and scattered them through the wynds and closes.

It was the official signal that the day had ended. From the howffs and the taverns folks muffled themselves up and bent their heads to the homeward journey.

Before another hour had passed the great dragon crouched on the ridge was asleep. The blade-keen winds howled and moaned and shrieked and clawed at the rattling pantiles. Only in some of the clubs and taverns did parties sit drinking and eating. The bulk of folks, their work before them in the morning, were snug abed.

Stretched on the chaff bed beside John Richmond, the Bard lay listening to the howling winds, though sometimes a busy bawd, entertaining a more than usually boisterous customer upstairs, distracted him with the fear that the ceiling might come down on top of him. His own thoughts were distracting enough. It seemed like a century since he had said good-bye to Jean Armour in the Cowgate of Machlin and taken the long hilly road to Muirkirk; and it seemed that nothing short of a century must elapse before he became familiar with the strange new life the city offered.

But before he slept he remembered Jean Armour and thought of her lying in the Cowgate with a twin in either arm. His heart softened towards her: softened and melted. He was far from her now; and it might be a long time before he saw her and the twins again. He had no regret that he was legally free of her. But he knew he would miss her: that no matter what happened in this life he would never again be able to shut her out of his mind. She would always be there to haunt him. Haunt him with her body and the music of her voice: with the memory of those nights they had spent together beneath the green thorn tree by the banks of the river Ayr... Nor would all the melody in Scotland ever drown the haunting measure of that slow strathspey she had lilted to him. No: whatever happened to him there would always be Jean Armour ... and the twins. Robert and Jean: she had paid him double as he might have known she would. Jean Armour and he had not given their love by halves. Doubly they had loved: doubly their love had borne fruit.

And yet the love and the fruit of it belonged to the past. There was nothing but the memory of it for the future. Nothing but a memory that carried with it an agony in the core of its longing.

But there was agony at the core of life as he knew only too bitterly. Why had death come the way it had to Mary Campbell? His blood ran cold at the thought of her, at the senseless pitiless cruelty of her dying. What had she thought of him before she died? The agony of her longing must have been terrible. But he would never know. Here lay the burning hell of his torment. He would never know what poor Mary had suffered in her bitter brutal death. If only he could have spoken to her once before she died. If only he could have assured her that the thought to betray or desert her had never once found a lodgment in his brain. . .

He groaned involuntarily and turned on his side. . . The wind howled and shrieked through the grey town and bawds plied their trade for the hunger of men for their bodies never ceased. Always man craved to be free of the agony that was at the core of life; and only with woman could he share the agony of creation, however corruptly and unequally divided the sharing might be. . .

If only men and women would cease to bind life with their petty laws. If only men would free themselves from the menace of morality and realise that the laws of life were more profound than the depths of man's mind. Life was but an endless dance of endless patterns. No one had yet been able to solve the riddle of the patterns. But the measure of the dance was knowable: this was the deepest knowledge to which man could attain. When a man and a woman danced against the measure there was confusion and unhappiness. When they danced to the measure the harmony of life was restored and there was deep fulfilment. Yet to find the measure of life's dance, man had to be free; and the evil was that everywhere he was in shackles and in thrall. And while one human being remained in thrall, mankind could never be wholly free. . .

The truths of life were simple profound and clear. Only the lies of life were strange and shallow and confused. Herein lay the terrible evil of morality: it sought to give the sanction of law to the lies of life. . .

Once more in the circle of his thoughts he had encompassed the riddle of the universe. To-morrow when he awoke he would find the circle broken. But in daylight or in darkness he must cling steadfastly to his simplicity and clarity; and profundity might be added unto him.

Slowly the wheel of his thoughts ceased to turn. . .

PATRON

James Dalrymple, the Ayrshire Squire of Orangefield, was a man of his word. He took the Bard out to Coates House (it was but a short walk) and introduced him to his kinsman James Cunningham, Earl of Glencairn.

The Earl was good-hearted, good-looking and he wasn't over-clever. He liked the Bard. He insisted that he stay for a meal, meet his mother the Dowager-Duchess and his sister Lady Elizabeth.

The Dowager had a hard unemotional face and a hard unemotional voice. She was somewhat given to religion. But she spoke sparingly.

"Tak' your meat, Mr. Burns: it'll stick to your ribs when words winna."

Lady Betty, on the other hand, was soft and coy. She was young and life had treated her gently.

" I thocht your verses on the Mountain Daisy so filled with sensibility, Mr. Burns. . ."

The Dowager clattered her spoon unceremoniously on the table and rifted with loud but evident satisfaction.

When the Bard took his leave, the Earl said: "I'll tak' you to Willie Creech's myself. I'll send word to you. We'll fix you up somehow, Burns. We canna let the Bard o' Ayrshire down. Na, na. . ."

Robert took an immediate instinctive liking to James Cunningham. It was difficult for him to believe that a man of such rank and wealth could be so unaffectedly modest and warm-heartedly interested in his welfare. After all, he had nothing to give him; and the Earl had nothing to gain by taking him by the hand.

PUBLISHER

From early morning the Landmarket clattered with life— hummed, jostled, throbbed and hog-shouldered.

The wynds and closes emptied their life onto it in the morning even as they emptied their excrement onto it in the night.

In his shut-away narrow segment of Edinburgh the Bard was conscious of its jundying and hog-shouldering . . . and the interminable scliff-scliffing of feet in Lady Stair's Close. . .

He emerged rather late in the morning from Baxters' Close, almost colliding with a bleary-eyed bawd at the close-head. He grued; for he was not feeling well. The unaccustomed alcohol still played havoc with his stomach.

The Landmarket was cold and grey and bitterly windswept for it lay high on the ridge of the Rock. The booths and stalls that were put up close to the side-walk were bare and hungry and Decemberish enough for this time of the year. But they had potatoes and kail and a few turnips and plenty of leeks and some roots fresh dug that morning from the Portobello sandpits. . .

Had he been an unlettered rustic he would have stood and

stared in wonder and awe. But he was a much-lettered rustic and his wonder and awe were of a higher order.

He had read much about Edinburgh—and even about London and Paris. Many things did not surprise him. But he thrilled to the active physical contact of Edinburgh; its cobbled causeways; its high tenement lands piled stone on stone to dizzy heights; its noises and stinks and smells. And above all: its humanity.

The citizenry of Auld Reekie were an amazingly diverse yet homogeneous lot. All classes intermingled and jostled and yet did not quite mix. There was every variety of dress and clothes imaginable. Many clung to the styles (and perhaps to the actual garments) of half a century ago. Some were in the latest fashion. And so many of the very poor were clad in the patched cast-offs of the wealthier class. . .

Such Landmarket (and Gosford's Close) personalities as James Brodie, the surgeon, John Caw, the grocer, and John Anderson, the wig-maker, could and did exchange pleasantries whenever and wherever they met. Even James Home Rigg, Esquire, of Morton, having a chat with General John Houston, would bow to Mrs. MacPherson who, though a landlady, described herself as a setter of elegant-rooms and who was considered a distinct cut above Mrs. MacLeod who let rooms in the same close. Nor was it thought amiss that Robert Middle-mist, the dancing master, stood laughing and joking with Mrs. Robertson who kept "the best ales." They were more than citizens: they were all inhabitants of the vertical street that was called Gosford's Close, emptying on to the Landmarket. Stephen Clarke, the organist of the Episcopal Church, might not care very much for James Leishman, the bookbinder; but both were very civil to Mrs. Harvey, the writer's wife.

The Bard, as he slowly sauntered down the Landmarket, could not tell General John Houston from organist Stephen Clarke, nor had he any means of knowing that they both lived in the same dark smelly turnpike-staired vertical street, with slum-dwellers on the ground and slum-dwellers in the attics and with various grades of gentry in between.

But he was aware of a close familiarity between many of

the folks who jostled about the narrow side-walks or who exchanged greetings or conversed on the causeway: conscious of the fact that pools of human friendship or neighbour-liness gathered on the edge of the general stream of human indifference.

He sauntered slowly down to the Luckenbooths—that long rectangular block of narrow buildings (the locked booths of the merchants) that almost blocked the street in front of the four kirks that huddled beneath the crown spire of Saint Giles's. . .

In front of the Luckenbooths (and attached to them) stood the Tolbooth—the grim prison where so many famous and infamous Scots had dreed their weirds, and where, even as the Bard passed it, languished many debtors and felons in incredible dirt darkness and pestilential foulness. Yet such was the thickness of its walls that nothing of the human misery and suffering seeped through to the passers-by. In the stillness of the night weird and pitiful shrieks and groans sometimes emerged half-strangled from the narrow slits of windows. . .

But the Bard was conscious of outlines and façades in a generalised way: the scene was too variegated and diversified for him to note (and relate) the details.

He went down through the Buthraw between the booths and the close-mouths on the left side of the High Street. He now emerged onto the broadened High Street at its greatest breadth. Here faced the east gable-end (and entrance) to Creech's Land and, in the Saint Giles's corner, the main entrance to the Parliament Close. Though Creech's Land dated back to the year 1600 the wretched Luckenbooths to which it was attached dated back to the year 1400.

A couple of hundred yards from Creech's Land and a little to the right side stood the Mercat Cross, the centre of Edinburgh and hence, in a very true sense, the centre of Scotland.

Already, for the morning was wearing on, there was a great crowd of people, apart from the ebb and flow of traffic, gathered round the Cross. It was an extraordinary crowd of people; but then it was rather extraordinary that here (unless the weather were too inclement) the business and gossip of the Edinburgh morning was done. Almost anybody of even the least consequence could be found about the Cross between eleven and twelve o'clock on every working day. At twelve o'clock there was a general break-up and men moved off to their respective howffs to enjoy their meridians!

As the Bard emerged from the narrow Buthraw the morning session of gabble and gossip was at its height.

Some chatted gaily and some discoursed gravely and many listened with an anxious and attentive ear cocked over two or three twists of knitted cravat. It was a raw morning and hats were well pulled down where wigs allowed. And what a variety of hats there were: cocked hats, three-cornered hats, beaver hats, hats trimmed with lace, slouch hats, hats with brims that drooped and hats with brims that curled—and some blue-bonnets. All, except the blue-bonnets, sitting or perched on as wide a variety of wigs.

Since the day was raw everybody was wrapped to the chin and clad in great-coats with frilled and embroidered skirts, sporting shoulder capes plain or scalloped. Some huddled in capes with arm-hole slits. . . Many men wore mittens and some went to the extravagance of gloves. . .

An occasional sedan-chair, carried fore and aft by Highland porters, steered an uneven course through the crowd carrying a fair damsel to an appointment for tea, or with the hairdresser —or maybe to get fitted with the latest outsize in artificial bums from London.

And on the fringe of the crowd passed up and down the tradesfolk of the Town—working women in their shuffling wooden pattens and striped petticoats and servant-lassies in bare legs and shawls. And occasionally came a fisher-wife or lass from Newhaven, bent forwards, creel on back, making for the closes and wynds of their choice with the early morning's catch from the Forth.

This heterogenous press of humanity almost bewildered the Bard. For a brief moment he wanted to turn and seek an escape from it. But the moment passed. He had come to Edinburgh in order to win a measure of success for himself. And if the

Earl of Glencairn could interest himself in his affairs why should he fear a crowd that neither knew him nor cared for him?

He smacked his riding-crop sharply on his booted leg and turned on his heel.

Creech's shop faced him in the gable-end with his name painted in distinct lettering above his entrance door.

He approached the building slowly. It was difficult to believe that his fate might be contained between those two windows and behind that narrow doorway. And what was the knot of folks doing round the door? What were they talking about and what were their interests? But he must not allow his fears to overcome his resolve. There could surely be no harm in a rustic bard taking an interest in a bookshop or making enquiries about Allan Ramsay's library.

He plucked up courage and mounted the three semi-circular steps to the doorway. Inside there were groups of people talking and laughing. He was conscious that they eyed him with some curiosity. He looked around him; but there was little evidence of books. He had imagined that the shop would be full of them. Instead there were some small tables with a number of volumes laid out on them—much as if they were samples not to be handled.

While he looked about him with a growing sense of confusion, a small dapper fellow in shiny black silk breeches detached himself from a group and approached him with a somewhat supercilious air.

"You wish to make a purchase: a Bible perhaps?"

"Not at the moment, sir. I wished to know if I stood on the floor of Allan Ramsay's celebrated library?"

"My dear fellow, Allan Ramsay is dead this long time. His library was above this: premises now occupied by me."

William Creech was long used to summing up his customers at a glance. He prided himself that he could anticipate their wants almost before they had given expression to them. He had assumed that the Bard belonged to that nondescript class whose sole interest in entering his bookshop was to make the common purchase of a Bible. He was somewhat discomfited to find that he was mistaken. But the look in the stranger's eyes and the quality of his voice also discomfited him. Both were remarkable. This stranger to the Town was no less a stranger to his wonted method of classification. Mr. Creech was puzzled; and he did not like to be puzzled.

"Perhaps there is some other volume you would care to purchase?"

"Had I money, sir, there is scarce a volume I would *not* care to purchase."

"Well, well, now! You may look around you: something may strike your fancy." And with that Mr. Creech returned to his companions and the Bard walked out of his shop.

When he returned a few days later in the company of the Earl of Glencairn, his reception was vastly different.

Creech had spied them from his inner office, and came tripping down the wooden stairs to meet them. He made a low bow to Glencairn, who then extended his hand.

"Willie: I hae come to introduce to you a countryman of mine—the justly-celebrated ploughman-poet: Robert Burns. Burns: mak' the acquaintance of my good friend William Creech."

A shifty look crept into the corner of Creech's cunning eye. He had just finished reading the proof of Henry MacKenzie's review of the Kilmarnock *Poems* for *The Lounger* which he published. The meeting could not have been more opportune.

"You do me a great honour, my Lord. But indeed, if I am not mistaken, Mr. Burns and I have already met. Did you not ask me a question the other day about Allan Ramsay's library? But do me the honour, my Lord, to step with me into my inner sanctum where we will enjoy some privacy."

When they were seated, James Cunningham came to the point.

"Willie: I want you to bring out an edition of Burns's poetry. The Kilmarnock edition is sold out and yet everybody is clamouring for a copy; and richtly so. Burns, I believe, has some excellent pieces by him that have not yet appeared. Mak' it an elegant edition, Willie. I'm arranging for the Caledonian

Hunt to subscribe in a body at half a guinea. That'll more than ensure the success o' the volume."

"A new edition? My Lord can be assured that I'll give the matter my earnest consideration."

"Damn your consideration, Willie. You'll bring out the edition wi' all the speed you can command; and that's an end to it. I want a parcel o' subscription bills within the week."

"My Lord kens that I will treat his merest request as it were a royal command. But my Lord well understands there are business matters that'll require some consideration."

"I'll leave such to Burns and you. And I want Burns treated with every consideration. He's a worthy and excellent fellow. See that he meets all the literati here—introduce him into the best circles. Let me know if at any time I can be of use in furthering his interests. When you hae settled all the details, bring him out wi' you to Coates House and we'll hae a party. My kinsman Orangefield, Sir John Whitefoord and Harry Erskine have all taken him by the hand: so you needna think I'm imposing some upstart on you."

"Indeed, my Lord, the thought never crossed my mind. Mr. Burns's fame has already reached me. I had a letter about him from Mr. Aiken in Ayr. The next copy of The Lounger will contain a most enthusiastic review of the Kilmarnock volume from the distinguished pen of Henry MacKenzie."

"And why shouldna he be enthusiastic? I'd like to see him write half as well as our young friend here."

"Still, my Lord, Henry MacKenzie's seal of approval means a great deal in the literary world. Indeed, I would not be exaggerating to say that he settles the question for all time."

"These are literary matters, Willie; and I don't give a hoot for them. I can settle my own judgments without any assistance from Henry MacKenzie. Now, I'll leave you twa to settle matters atween you to your mutual satisfaction. But remember that Burns is my verra special concern. Don't allow Willie Creech to overawe you, Burns. He is a canny business man; but for all that he's a sterling good fellow and will do his best for you. . ."

When Glencairn had gone, Creech thought for a few

moments. What worried him was how Burns had managed to secure Glencairn's patronage. But the Bard had nothing to hide.

"I first made the acquaintanceship of Mr. Dalrymple of Orangefield through one of my Ayr patrons—Robert Aiken."

"Ah, worthy Robert Aiken! He is, of course, sib to the Dalrymple family through marriage. And Orangefield introduced you to my Lord Glencairn?"

"Yes; but the Earl's factor at Finlayson, Mr. Alexander Dalziel, also introduced my Kilmarnock volume to him; and then a worthy friend of my father, and of mine, Mr. Tennant in Glenconner brought the volume to the notice of the Earl's mother, the Dowager; and my Lord tells me that he had brought a copy here with a view to making its merits known among the first people of the Town."

"Indeed, indeed! Most interesting, Mr. Burns! You are fortunate in having so liberal and distinguished a patron. The Earl and myself once travelled together a great deal on the Continent. I am much attached to the Glencairn interests."

"That I can well understand, Mr. Creech. I cannot imagine a more worthy man or a more noble Lord. His taking me by the hand in the manner he has done: the fact that he has shared with me the honour of his table at Coates House, has more than endeared him to me. I shall ever be in his debt and shall ever remember him with the deepest gratitude and affection."

"Yes, indeed, Mr. Burns: yes, indeed. . .! I gather, Mr. Burns, that you are an unlettered ploughman? You will not misunderstand me when I say that you dinna speak like one. It is patent, sir, that you've been more than ordinarily educated."

"My education is nothing. I owe a great debt to an early childhood dominie: I owe more to my worthy parent who was a man of very singular parts. The rest I owe to my ability, such as it is, to read books and profit from them."

"And you've read widely and well, Mr. Burns. D'you intend to embark upon literature as a career?"

"I hadn't aimed so high, Mr. Creech. I'm not at all confirmed in myself that my abilities would in any way be equal to the support of such an ambition."

"Very commendable, Mr. Burns. In a pecuniary sense there is little profit in poetry. Indeed, I know of no other branch of literary commerce so attended with disappointment. That, I am afraid, is what my Lord Glencairn does not so readily understand. I will, of course, assist you with all my powers. But I'm afraid I couldna bind myself to the loss that such a project might well entail. Still: I should be more than delighted to act as your agent in this matter. I could, for example, undertake to arrange the printing, binding and sale of the volume: provided that you paid for these expenses out of the proceeds of the sale of the volume! The profit—less a small percentage to cover my own expenses of the sale—would accrue to yourself."

"I'm afraid, Mr. Creech, I've no funds at my disposal to finance any such venture."

"I understand that, Mr. Burns. Suppose we get Mr. Smellie to print and Mr. Scott to bind? I think they might, like myself, be prepared to stand out their money until the returns from the sales come in. Of course, we would require to put out a prospectus to gauge the pulse of the public. If the subscription was well taken up, I fancy that would be enough guarantee with Smellie and Scott. Would you care to step across with me to the Anchor Close where we could have a word with Mr. Smellie? 'Tis but a step. Smellie is a very shrewd man: it would be well to have his observations and advice. . . "

PRINTER

William Smellie was a very different man from William Creech. Where Creech was finicky elegant supercilious and formally polite, Smellie was rough direct and brutally unceremonious. His great flabby jowl was unshaven and his grizzled grey hair was unkempt. But the moment Creech made the introduction his face broke into a great wreath of soft smiles and he extended a ready hand.

"Shake, Mr. Burns, shake! I've been reading the extracts o' your verses that Jamie Sibbald has been publishing in the Edinburgh Magazine. I'm beggared if I can lay hands on a copy o' them. . . By God, sir, and you look the part too! A plough-man-poet, eh? And I'll warrant you can drive a bonnie furrow! But welcome, Mr. Burns; and what can I do for you?"

Somewhat embarrassed, Creech outlined his plans. Smellie rasped his forefinger and thumb along the stubble on his chin.

"So that's the airt the wind's in, is it? Weel, we'll no' see you stuck, Mr. Burns, however the thing works out. We'll get you out a volume some way or other. Dinna believe a word Willie Creech tells you, for he would lie his best friend into the Tolbooth if he could make a bawbee o' profit out o' the transaction. But I'll tell ye what, Willie: send me down a rough o' your prospectus and I'll see about running off a wheen o' quires. If I decide to print, Willie Scott'll bind: I can speak for him. Mind you: we couldna dae ony less than twa thousand to mak' it pay."

"Yes indeed, William: two thousand was the edition I had in mind."

"Weel, Mr. Burns: it rests wi' the prospectus. . . Creech and me hae a prospectus running the now for my Natural History. . . Aye, we ken a' aboot that side o' the business. But if the Caledonian Hunt start the ball rolling I dinna think you hae much to fear. I'll mak' a good job o' the printing; and you can rest assured that Willie Creech'll mak' a good job o' pushing the sales. You certainly couldna get a better man to look after that side o' the business. Now: what about a drink? Will ye tak' a step up to the close-head to see Dawney Douglas?"

"You have a drink with Mr. Burns, William: I have much work to attend to at my office. I'll tell you what: come and have breakfast with me to-morrow morning: Craig's Close, first on your left: Henry MacKenzie and one or two others will be there. We'll all be very glad to welcome you, Mr. Burns."

Coming out of Smellie's office the daylight was good since there was an open yard immediately opposite; but as they walked up the close it became darker and gloomier as the tall lands rose on either hand. Indeed when they turned into Dawney's entrance, Smellie had to lead him for it was unbelievably dank and dark.

"Tak' it easy. Watch the scale stair noo. Man, I could find my road here in my sleep. Aye: count the steps—there's only seven o' them. Here we are."

Smellie opened the door on the landing. At once they found themselves in the kitchen. The hot air smote them as they entered. The landlady, an enormously fat woman, sat into a table working on a heap of oysters. The great folds of her buttocks overlapped the stool. Her arms, thick as a maiden's thighs and red as a lobster's claw, were bare to above the elbow. The expression on her heavy face was passive. But the moment she heard Smellie's voice she turned and nodded to him with odd, almost comical gravity.

The Bard took her in in a fascinated glance. He knew her type. He wouldn't have been surprised to find that she sweated goose-fat: a typical landlady even if an out-sized one. As long as she was about there would be plenty of good food.

Her husband came forward from the blazing fire wiping his hands on his once-white apron. He was a thin stooping fellow with a straggling apologetic moustache and a weak and watery eye.

"Weel, Dawney: my friend and I will just step ben for a minute. Bring us your best whisky and some cappie ale . . . aye, and bring us a platter o' herrin', trotters—or ony damned thing you've ready to taste our gabs. Through here, Mr. Burns. . . We hae the place to oursel's. Weel noo: this is where ye throw care aside and talk your mind. As I've said already: I'm damned pleased to see you. How long hae you been in the Toon? Since Tuesday night! You don't let the grass grow under your feet. . . I see, I see: weel: you've done the right thing. You'll need to keep an eye on Creech of coorse: there's nae sentiment about him; but the best man for you if you manage to handle him the right way. . . Aye; and you'll be twenty-eight in January! I would hae taken you for a lot more than that. The world's afore you. . . But a word o' advice: don't pay too much heed to what the gentry say to you. Don't be disappointed if they turn and leave you high and dry and pass you on the causeway and never see you. As for the literati: there's no' one of them I couldna write aff the face o' the bluidy earth. I was editor o' the Scots Magazine for five or six years and I was the first editor of the Encyclopædia Britannica. *I* don't give myself airs. There's Creech: he writes a fiddling wee thing for The Courant and thinks he's an expert in the department o' belles-lettres. By the way: Creech is a partner of my printing house here: he passes me a lot o' work. But I've nae illusions about him. But it wad gie ye the dry-boaks to see the airs the literati gie themselves. But ability—real sterling ability—it's just no' there. . . No, Mr. Burns: look about you and say as little as you can. And then once you hae gotten your book published, tell them to go to hell. For you hae genius; and what is genius but ability carried as far as it can be carried . . .?

"But if you've been ahint the plough a' thae years, it's time you enjoyed yoursel'. We've a grand club meets here every week. Some o' the best fellows i' the Toon. I'll introduce you some night. Bawdy songs: that's one of our specialities: I'll warrant ye ken some toppers! We're organised on a military basis: The Crochallan Fencibles: Crochallan is Dawney the landlord's favourite Gaelic song: that's how we picked on the title. . . I'd hae thought you were a good singer. But that's no' a great drawback as lang as you can join in a chorus: I'm no' much o' a singer mysel' come to that. . . And don't miss Creech's levee in the morning. You've got to get that subscription o' yours going; and the only way to do that is to meet as mony folk as you can: you canna meet ower mony. . . It's been a rare pleasure meeting wi' you, Mr. Burns: I can see we're going to hae mony a merry nicht thegither. . ."

"I think we'll get on, Mr. Smellie."

"Aye: what's to hinder us? D'ye ken ony other folk i' the Toon besides Glencairn?"

"I met Professor Stewart in Ayrshire——"

"Dugald! I ken Dugald Stewart fine. A bit staid. No' very

bright—a kind o' plodding philosopher. Oh, but Dugald's a' richt. He'll no' dae ye ony harm. Onybody else?"

"James Dalrymple of Orangefield."

"No. . . I dinna ken him. Heard tell o' him of coorse. One o' the Caledonian Hunt. You're a' richt there. And noo that Glencairn's sold his Kilmaurs seat and is settling up wi' his creditors, Creech'll be ready to sing his praises again—and do his bidding."

"I reckon Glencairn a noble man."

"There's worse than Glencairn, I'll grant you that. Keep him on your side as long as you can."

"It seems you can't have too many patrons here."

"Or onywhere! By themselves, honest worth and sterling ability get nae place. I should hae been professor o' Natural History at the College here. What was against me? I hadna the richt influence. Hadna the richt friends in the richt places. So they gave the post to a bluidy eediot that kens a damned sicht less about natural history than you do—aye, a damned sicht less.

"Ye see: I ken a' their weaknesses. There's damned few o' them can write. When their manuscripts come to me I set them in order. Aye: I've been daft enough to rewrite some o' them. Of coorse that's a' richt as lang as I'm Willie Smellie the printer. But they wouldna tak' that sae nice frae Professor Smellie."

"That's sense enough. You must know all the literati here then."

"Every one o' them. Aye: and the law lords. They're the boys! Wait till ye meet wi' some o' them. Monboddo, Kames, Gardenstone, Hailes. Oddities ye ken. Brilliant—but oddities. They'd just be village eediots in your part o' the country. Oh, but there's some great characters aboot the Toon. Man, you'll meet wi' mair wit worth and learning in the Crown Room through the wa' there when the Crochallan Corps is in session than you'll meet wi' onywhere else. I'll get you doon some nicht soon and put ye through your paces—and then you'll be able to say you've met wi' folk in Edinburgh that were worth meeting. . . But here's Dawney wi' a platter o' something that smells guid.... Dawney! This is Scotland's poet, Robert Burns! Tak' a guid look o' him, Dawney, and ony time he comes in here—which I hope'll be often—see that he's well served wi' the best that's gaun."

"Indeed yes; that is so, Mr. Smellie. Och, but Mr. Burns will be finding nothing but the best here at any time."

"And never pay more than saxpence for what you eat. Leave the drink to Dawney: he'll charge you honestly for that."

"You are indeed a kind gentleman, Mr. Smellie. You are a stranger to the Town, Mr. Burns, sir? Ach well, now: I am a stranger myself."

"Stranger be damned! You're here twenty year to my knowledge. And yet maybe you're richt, Dawney. I doubt if you've been the length o' the Castle Hill?"

"Indeed now and I havena. I have enough to do here. Well now, gentlemen, if I can leave you—for it's a busy time."

"On you go, Dawney. Dinna keep the customers waiting."

Dawney thanked them, nodded sadly and withdrew himself apologetically.

"Delve into the hash and grab a pig's clit!" said Smellie. "Damnit but Dawney's dishes are aey tasty." His loose lips smacked round a trotter as his yellow stumps of teeth fastened into the gristle.

The Bard could not help contrasting the man who was to be his publisher with the man who was to be his printer.

Creech was prim pert elegantly supercilious mannered politely haughty, correct in everything from his carefully-powdered hair to the silver buckles on the shoes that protected his silken-hosed feet.

Willie Smellie was somewhat like an intelligent boar: bristly dirty slouchy clumsy inelegant: but with a rare light shining in his eye and a glorious directness burring on his broad warm tongue.

It was difficult to think that this was the man who had edited the *Scots Magazine*, written and edited the *Encyclopædia Britannica* and was about to put a great and learned work

The Philosophy of Natural History before the world. But that he had extraordinary and unusual ability he did not doubt for a moment.

In a sense everything about Creech might be doubted—the man was so manifestly artificial. Everything about Smellie was so obviously genuine that it was inevitable that he should be taken on trust.

And a man like Smellie who knew everybody in the Town, and especially the literati, would be a great help to him.

THIN ICE

Being a bachelor, Creech had more room in his Craig's Close apartments than he would have had he been married and had anything like the family Henry MacKenzie was able to boast. The Man of Feeling had caused his wife to throw him some thirteen children in some eighteen years; and he had no intention (such was the quality of his sensibility) of stopping at the limit of the baker's dozen. The result was that few people had ever been inside MacKenzie's old house—where his father's three wives had died—at the corner of the Cowgate and the Grassmarket.

Nevertheless the Man of Feeling envied Creech his comparative spaciousness and was thinking of moving soon to the new square that builder Brown had erected close to Argyle Square (south of Hume's Close and the Cowgate) in the still-fashionable south-side of the Town. He would have liked to be able to move to the New Town; but the expense of a large family and the fact that he would be expected to entertain there instead of in the tavern had to be thought of.

He was discussing this projected move to Brown's Square with Creech and Lord Monboddo of the Court of Session when the Bard and Professor Dugald Stewart (whom he had met outside) were shown in.

To the Bard, the meeting with Henry MacKenzie was not without a quality of emotion. He recalled how, some five years ago in Irvine, he had first read *The Man of Feeling*. This best-selling novel of sensibility had had a very deep and profound effect on him. He was not to know that he had given more to the book than the book had given to him, and that he had come to place in its hero's hand a sword of a sharper social sensibility than the author had intended, or could have been capable of intending. And now the author's elegant equine countenance (for it was something more than a common face) smiled to him; and well-modulated periods began to fall with a proper elegance from his carefully-manipulated lips.

"Mr. Burns: my verra dear sir! How glad I am that I should so soon have the pleasure of greeting you in person—having so lately laid aside your volume, not without a sigh, for the noble proof it contained that the heavenly light of poetical inspiration rests not where we list, but rather—eh—where the inscrutable will of the Almighty directs: yes. . . There have been few occasions when I can say I have met a man who was also a poet of nature . . . indeed you are the first poet of nature I have met; and I trust you will find your stay in Edinburgh maist pleasant and . . . instructive."

"Mr. MacKenzie, sir: you pay my rustic bardship an honour dear to my heart. Since I was a young man I have read the Man of Feeling with much pleasure and more edifying instruction. . . Since I arrived in the Town I have looked forward to meeting you in the flesh more than I can say."

"So you liked my Man of Feeling?"

"'Tis a glorious book, sir, and one that had a great influence on me in forming my opinions on the society of men and of manners. It proved to me that the injustices of this world were recognised and appreciated far more widely than I had had reason to suppose. Indeed, sir, it would not be too much to say that Harley gave my knowledge of the inequalities of this world a political and philosophical direction that they might not otherwise have taken so soon: I mean that Harley proved to me that I was by no means alone in seeing how this world operates against sensibility: especially when that sensibility is translated, as Harley translated it, from the personal field of experience to the moral and political field."

MacKenzie's horse-face assumed an involuntary expression of vacuous alarm.

"God bless me! Did Harley do all this to you, Mr. Burns?"

"That and much more, sir. When Harley put his finger on the evil of the nabobs, he put his finger on the social evil of our times."

"Did he indeed! Do you mean that Harley conveyed to you a political message? I had not intended that: in your sense, Mr. Burns."

At this point Dugald Stewart, who had listened to this conversation with some amusement, said:

"I warned you, Henry, that Mr. Burns has a political philosophy he holds to with the utmost tenacity."

"But Harley was innocent of politics! Perhaps you are thinking of the passage about India? But I didna intend that that passage should be read as a political message but merely as an illustration of Harley's feelings under circumstances of peculiar import . . . of a moral nature."

"But can morality and politics be separated? Or do you regard politics as a party game?"

"I regard politics as being outside the field of literature. A novel ought not to be regarded in the same light as a political treatise: far from it, indeed. I should be very distressed, Mr. Burns, if you saw in Harley a political lesson that had a direct bearing on the politics of the day."

"And why not, sir? There are political lessons in the Old Testament that have a direct bearing on the politics of the day."

Lord Monboddo smacked his lips in a curious fashion. "Mmmyes. . . Verra weel put, Mr. Burns: verra weel observed. There's nothing like the study of ancient history to show up the shortcomings of the present day. Have you Greek?"

"I have some English and some Scotch: did I live to the age of Methuselah I doubt if I would be able to master either."

"Ah! but without the classics, sir, you canna go far. The Ancients, my dear Burns, knew everything that was worth knowing."

"But would you say, sir, that knowing their languages was the same thing as having their knowledge?"

"What's that? Having their knowledge? Pray, how else can we have access to their thoughts did we not know their language?"

"But surely every generation must *think out* its thoughts afresh? Else how came it that Greek and Latin are now dead languages?"

"Dead languages! Greek and Latin will never die: they are eternal! Nae man can think properly except wi' their aid."

"But I'm a rustic who has followed the plough. Am I not to think because I've no Greek? What you say, sir, is no doubt true for scholars; but the bulk of mankind must go about the tasks of mankind without the assistance of scholarship. And because of this they must be allowed to think in their own way: and give expression to their thoughts in their own language—whatever that language may be."

"I think, gentlemen," said Creech, "we had better be seated. We seem to be in the mood for talk this morning and we might as well be comfortable."

Creech had a fine room. It was oak-panelled, carpeted, and there were pictures on the walls. The chairs were of polished oak and high-backed. A good coal fire burned in the grate which was framed in highly-polished marble. . . A man-servant waited on the table; and there was a variety of cold meats and chickens, kippered salmon, bakers' bread and both oaten and wheaten cakes, to say nothing of smaller delicacies. There were coffee and tea and small ales. . .

The Bard was becoming used to the well-stocked tables of the Edinburgh gentry. Glencairn's table at Coates House had been a shock to him. Now he realised that the rich did not live by bread alone and that a well-stocked sideboard was one of the infallible signs of a well-lined purse. But as his stomach had been conditioned to scarcity and to a severe limitation of variety, he surprised his hosts by the smallness of the food he ate. . . But the literati were not so limited. One witty hostess had named them the eaterati. Henry MacKenzie had a voracious appetite and could stuff himself at any time of the day with whatever was going. Dugald Stewart was not far behind him in this respect. As for James Burnett, he slobbered like a

W.G.W.   C

toothless dog that hadn't seen food for days; and always he kept smacking and clacking his toothless gums in his curiously-detached fashion. Creech, with characteristic finickiness, was more dainty with his food and though he ate little he ate with a show of discrimination.

Creech's breakfast table was inexpensive, however; and he more than made up the expense of it through the business it brought him. He was not in the habit of selling any of his numerous hens on a rainy day.

Soon the gathering consisted of MacKenzie, Burnett of Monboddo, Professor Stewart, Doctor Hugh Blair and his assistant-to-be the Reverend William Greenfield. . . Dugald Stewart, who had already sampled the Bard's forensic powers in Ayrshire, was anxious to see how he would conduct himself in the company of the first brains in the Town. With some skill he led the conversation into channels he thought would produce the best results. But the Bard needed little encouragement from Dugald Stewart; and the company was only too anxious to hear the quality of his conversation. They had never before been in the company of a ploughman, far less a ploughman who wrote poetry.

The Reverend Doctor Hugh Blair was a vain and pompous cleric who had gained the reputation of being the most elegant sermoniser of his day. So elegant was he thought in this respect that the King had granted him a pension of two hundred pounds a year; and the Senate of the University, with pressure from the Town Council, had created the Chair of Rhetoric for him to grace. In an even more official capacity then Henry MacKenzie, he was reckoned the arbiter of literary taste and fashion. He advised the Bard to abandon the use of the Scotch dialect.

"It is a dying dialect, Mr. Burns. You are restricting your audience to the ever-decreasing number of those who understand its meaning. Besides, your dialect will never be understood in London; and it's to London that Scottish writers must increasingly look for the suffrage of intelligent readers."

But the Bard was not dismayed. "I've no great ambition to

woo the suffrage of London, sir. I'll be happy to be understood by my compeers in Scotland."

"Then you must realise that we are of small numbers."

"When I refer to my compeers, sir, I refer to the common people: I make no pretence to write verses for the polite and the learned. I fear that my homespun muse would look ridiculous in the elegant robes of classical learning."

"That, sir, I can well appreciate. Nevertheless I dinna think you are wise to aim so low. There's no reason why a man of your ability should not take steps to remedy the defects o' an imperfect schooling."

"Ah, yes, Doctor," said MacKenzie, "but what I take Mr. Burns to mean is that he is a bard of nature's making and that as such he would prefer to remain; and there, I think you'll admit, lies his present strength."

"Sir: I do not admit that nature has the advance on art. Nature can always admit of improvement and refinement: this I take to be the object of all learning. . ."

Lord Monboddo clacked furiously with his tongue. "Nature, my dear Blair, leads us back to the origin of all custom. It is from nature that we must draw the lesson that all things hae a beginning as well as leading us to an understanding of *how* they began."

Blair spoke in his haughtiest tones. "We need look no further than the Creation for any explanations. The duty of scholarship is to expound fundamental truth and not to confound with a multiplicity of non-scriptural . . . er . . . ah . . . explanation."

Monboddo waved this aside impatiently and turned eagerly to the Bard. "Mr. Burns: ye are a man much endowed wi' sound native sense. Has it ever occurred to ye that there's a striking resemblance between ourselves and the monkey tribe? Have you ever had the good fortune to clap eyes on a new-born infant? I mean in all its nakedness as delivered from its mother's womb? It is my convinced opinion, sir, that many babes are born with tails, and that it is the practice of midwives to bite off the offending appendage in its rudimentary state. . . If monkeys could be prevailed upon to sit about on chairs instead of swinging about on their ancestral branches, they would very soon wear away their tails as we have done."

"It is a barbarous notion, sir, and not to be thought of."

"There, Blair, you speak as a Doctor of Divinity. Mr. Burns: I await *your* opinion."

The Bard realised that Monboddo was perfectly serious. He determined to give him a serious answer. "If you mean, sir, that all living things have a common origin then I can only say that, there, I am with you. On the other hand, it may be a factor in your favour that the Devil had not the services of a Scotch midwife at his delivery."

The company roared with laughter. But the learned Lord of the Session was not the man to be put off with a joke.

"There, sir, you hae hit on a link in the chain of evidence that the Ancients had not thought of: you must come round to my house, number thirteen Saint John Street, and sup with me."

And with that Lord Monboddo clacked his tongue, waved an impatient hand in Creech's direction and shuffled from the room.

When he had gone Creech said: "You must not mind his Lordship: there are some points on which he is thought to be a trifle peculiar."

"Does he carry his peculiarities to the benches of the Court of Session?"

The Reverend William Greenfield, a man of thoughtful and refined countenance, said: "There are many men of peculiar ideas gracing the benches of the Session, Mr. Burns; but in matters of law they remain singularly free from absurdity."

"I must confess, sir, that to one of my humble situation in life, much of the law seems an absurdity—though often very cruel in its absurdity. Hence it may well be that absurdity breeds absurdity."

"There, indeed, Mr. Burns, you speak literal truth. But then, if there were no absurd laws there would be no need for absurd lawyers."

Blair turned to Greenfield with a severe look. "I need hardly remind you, Mr. Greenfield, that the law is a very ancient

institution and that without its guidance we would find ourselves in a sorry state of barbarism. Moreover, secular law
exists to reinforce divine authority."

Greenfield bowed to his superior. "I was merely discussing
the aspects of the matter, sir, on the secular plane; and I
would humbly suggest that as our laws are man-made they
carry with them, inherently, all the imperfections that are in
man."

But Doctor Hugh Blair was not the man to brook contradiction in any shape or form. He rose and bade the company
a very good morning. But he had not gone further than the
door when he returned.

"I understand, Mr. Burns, that you have some compositions that you intend to publish. I should be glad to be
of assistance to you where improvements might be made and
. . . ahem . . . indelicacies removed."

"There," interrupted Creech, "I think I may speak for Mr.
Burns in thanking you for your great liberality, Doctor. We
shall be only too glad to submit to your judgment any compositions of which we are in the slightest way doubtful. If,
in addition to your generous offer, sir, Mr. MacKenzie and
Professor Stewart were to join with you in helping us with
your advice, then our proposed volume would be free from all
those little complaints that were detected in the Kilmarnock
one."

As MacKenzie and Stewart readily agreed, the Bard felt
that he must thank them. "There are a number of compositions
I would like to see added to my second edition; and nothing
would give me greater pleasure than to know that they had
your approval. I shall immediately take steps to see that they
are available for your strictures."

Henry MacKenzie said: "Not strictures I hope, Mr. Burns.
A suggestion perhaps here and there, and, as Doctor Blair
suggests, the avoidance of indelicacies . . . so that the most
sensitive of female susceptibilities may have nae need to fear
offence. But strictures! Heaven forbid!"

When the Bard and his publisher were alone, Creech said:

"Whatever else happens, we must have the approval of the literati. If it got around that any of them were against the volume, it would fall stillborn from the press; and of course, Mr. Burns, it would be idle for me to point out that the loss would be yours: my reputation would survive since it is not founded on any one author."

"Which means in plain language, Mr. Creech, that what is not approved by the literati of the Town will not be published in my book?"

"We understand each other perfectly, sir: there can be no question as to the respectability of any book that I handle . . . irrespective of terms. And I think you will find that my Lord Glencairn and the gentlemen of the Caledonian Hunt will be very much of the same mind. And now that we have the literati on our side . . ."

"But do you think they are on my side?"

"My dear fellow: do you think that any money or other inducement could prevail upon Doctor Blair or Mr. MacKenzie or Professor Stewart to read your verses—far less criticise them —unless we had got them on our side! I confess that they would do anything for me. But my good sir: Lord Monboddo has invited you to sup with him and Doctor Blair has asked you to bring him your compositions. . . Why, the highest in the land could not command more—to say nothing of a ploughman just arrived in Town. Believe me, these gentlemen do not give idly of their favours; and they are very busy and important men: none more so in the realm."

Creech smiled importantly and patted the Bard on the shoulder. "Now you realise why it is so important that we give them no cause for offence. You must feel very proud, my dear Robert, that you have so captured their attention. And they tell me that your verses have captured the fancy of Her Grace the Duchess of Gordon! But a word, my dear Robert! The Duchess has her little peculiarities: you will not misunderstand her? But I know you will be discreet. There are many things about the Town that will no doubt surprise you; for aught I know they may even shock you. I may say—but only in your private ear—that there are many things that shock me; but it is most essential to keep a discreet silence. Mixing as you now are with the highest society in the land, you will understand that the gentlemen and their ladies have learned—as an essential part of good breeding—to be most discreet. And no verses, my dear Robert, no verses, epigrams or satires: on no account and no matter how you may be tempted—or even provoked! I must charge you on this. Not even the smallest line on paper—lest anything come to light. It would never be forgiven you and you would be ruined immediately and beyond any possibility of ever getting into their good graces. The ice upon which you skate, Robert, may seem very polished—as it undoubtedly is. But it is also very thin. . ."

SCOTIA'S DARLING SEAT

One of the principal streets (soon to become the main thoroughfare) in the South Town was Nicolson Street. It was modern and eminently respectable. Its good sound tenement blocks housed such worthy and reverend divines as James Bain, Adam Gibb, James MacNight; such gentlemen of quality as Captain John Inglis of Redhall, William Fullerton, James Stewart Monteith, Dr. Alexander Monro the Professor of Anatomy, Colonel Thomson, Captain Robert Irvine and Sir James Wemyss. True, there were also sundry merchants and lawyers including an odd Writer to the Signet. And Angelo Tremamande, the riding master and celebrated equestrian expert, graced the street with his flamboyant personality.

At No. 160 lived Peter Hill and his high-born wife, Elizabeth Lindsay. Lizzie had married beneath her for she was the daughter of a Perthshire baronet. But even a baronet's brat, like other folk's bairns, must either marry or burn. So Lizzie married Peter Hill, the son of the comparatively humble collector of shore dues at Dysart on the Fifean coast.

Six years married, Lizzie was still burning and had already gone a third of the way towards bringing fifteen children into the world.

And if her ardour was not yet cooled neither had her social snobbery abated. To be married to a bookseller's clerk, even though that bookseller was the great Mr. Creech himself, was humiliating.

"And where do you think you're gaun?" she challenged when Peter came back from the kirk with his eldest son and did not immediately take off his sober Sunday braws of good black broadcloth.

"I told you, Lizzie, that Mr. Creech asked me to show Mr. Burns the Town."

"*Maister* Burns, indeed! The Ploughman-poet! And my man's to be seen trailing an ignorant lout o' a ploughman round the Toon on a Sunday!"

"How can he be an ignorant lout when he's a poet? Mr. Creech is for publishing him."

"You and your Mr. Creech! I suppose you canna let doon your breeks withouten you ask Maister Creech? I've the weans to haud i' the hoose the whole day and you go gallivanting and stravaiging wi' a ploughman! If you canna think on your ain position, you could at least try to think on mine. . ."

Peter at last escaped from No. 160 with red ears and jangling nerves and cursing under his breath. He was in his thirty-third year and was six years married. But he wasn't yet broken in to the matrimonial state. He would show Lizzie Lindsay yet that there was more to him than she thought. . . .

He trudged up Nicolson Street, turned down to his left round the back of the College, through the Port of the Potter-row, down the Horse Wynd, across the Cowgate and up the steep Fishmarket Close to the High Street at the Cross.

Here Robert Burns was waiting for him.

The Bard had been kicking his heels about the Cross for a good half-hour; but he had not minded waiting.

It was a fine clear December morning. There had been frost in the night; but now the midday sun had thawed it away and left the air clear and sparkling. A snell but bracing east wind from the North Sea had lifted the smoke-pall from the Town. Even the stinks were somewhat in abeyance.

The Cross of Edinburgh was a fine place to stand on a clear

Sabbath morning. The canyon of the High Street fell away with the falling canyon of the Canongate. From this vantage point could be seen to the east, the grey-blue waters of the Firth of Forth. . .

But the Bard's great smouldering eyes saw far beyond the Firth; saw across the Tay and up through the Howe of the Mearns to Clochnahill; saw the road his father had travelled south till he too had reached the Fife shore and had stood staring in hungry anticipation at the smoke-pall above Auld Reekie lying like a cloud by day. . .

Douce citizens turned to stare at this strange man so strangely clad who stood with his back to the Mercat Cross and gazed into the distance with such abstracted wonder.

"Wha the deil can that fellow be?" asked John Wood, solicitor at law and surveyor of windows for the county. He addressed the question to his wife as they emerged from Borthwick's Close where they had been visiting George Cruickshanks, the writer. But all his wife could say after staring hard was: "A stranger, whaever he is."

"Aye," said the window surveyor, "and a gey queer stranger."

The Bard had bought himself a new hat with a wide curl to the brim: he had bought himself a new waistcoat bold in its horizontal stripes of buff and blue (the party colours of Charles James Fox). As a final touch he had invested in a pair of sound and extremely good-looking top-boots of highly-polished black leather with a broad band of white doeskin round the top.

His handsome rig-out was completed by his blue tailed coat with large brass buttons and his white buckskin breeches. A strong sturdy independent figure he looked as he stood there staring into the distance or when, with a sudden crack to his booted leg with his riding-crop, he took a turn and a swing about the High Street.

Peter Hill certainly thought him a commanding figure. He apologised for his lateness. But the Bard would have no apologies.

". . . I've been enjoying the scene, Mr. Hill; and it certainly is a scene to be enjoyed. When I was here the other day I had to elbow my way through the multitude o' folks pressing round the Cross. This morning I've the breadth o' the street to myself. And mind you: I never thought that, some day, I'd be able to stand at the Cross o' Edinburgh. And yet I should have minded! Many a time I've heard my father tell how he came to the shore and stood staring across at the great cloud o' smoke that hung about Auld Reekie——"

"Oh aye: on a clear day you get a grand view frae the Cross and just as guid frae Creech's front steps. Well now, Mr. Burns: what part o' the Toon would you like to explore first?"

"For that I'm no' particular, Mr. Hill. For the moment I'm puzzled wi' the lie o' the place. Looking down the High Street here I'm looking east . . . to where?"

"Follow your nose and you follow the Canongate richt doon to the Abbey and Holyrood. Now the lie o' the Toon, Mr. Burns, is simple enough. The Auld Toon lies on either side o' this ridge we're standing on. East is Holyrood: west, the Castle. On your left hand, to the north, the New Toon: to your right, the South Toon. Three Toons, Mr. Burns, divided frae each other by a valley as it were. The Nor' Loch divides us frae the New Toon: the Cowgate—that some say is juist a dried-up loch—divides us frae the South Toon."

"Aye . . . that's simple enough, Mr. Hill—as simple as the four points o' the mariner's compass. . . And what connects the Auld Toon with the New?"

"Doon the High Street there to your left—the North Bridge. Opposite it they're working hard on the South Bridge over the Cowgate to connect up wi' Nicolson Street. And a great convenience it'll be when it's finished—it'll save folk the traik awa' doon to the Cowgate juist to climb up again."

The Bard wasn't really listening. It was difficult to listen to Peter Hill on such a morning. What did it matter how Edinburgh lay in the sun or whether the Cowgate ran east, west, north or south, up or down, sideways or zig-zag? The Cowgate! That word had another connotation for him. The

Cowgate signified Jean Armour and all that Jean Armour signified.

On the sudden he was restless. Peter Hill had a plain white pock-pitted face and eyes like a dog that had got a boot brutally planted in his rump when he was hungry and a whine had escaped from his twisted entrails. A good honest man, Peter Hill, notwithstanding. . .

"Let's walk over your North Bridge then, Mr. Hill."

Away they went swinging down the High Street of Auld Reekie, capital of Scotland, the Northern Athens. On a bright Sunday in December; about midday on the Tron steeple; about the time men in their sober Sabbath braws, having stewed themselves in Auld Reekie's high-flown Presbyterianism, under the shadow of John Knox (made elegant by the Reverend Doctor Hugh Blair, minister of the High Kirk of Saint Giles, sometime Professor of Rhetoric and pensioner of Royal Geordie . . .) about the time they were repairing, without any indecent haste, to their favourite Sabbath howffs, gin cellars and drinking dens; that they might wash out of their mouths and drive out of their consciousness the sour baby-pap of the reverend and right reverend divines—for never, since John Knox came thundering out of Geneva, had the Scots, as a race, been able to imbibe their Presbyterian theology without the aid of strong drink. . .

Anyway they went swinging down the High Street and Peter Hill had to shuffle his step repeatedly before he fell in with the Bard's rhythm.

On the North Bridge they stood to survey the incredible scene. Below them to the west ran the great gully where but lately the North Loch had stretched its dirty dishclout waters.

Now the loch had been drained and in the middle, almost opposite the foot of Baxters' Close, they had commenced to unload the carts of soil dug from the building excavations from the New Town with the object of building, by this great mound of earth and stones, a road across from the middle of Princes Street up onto the Landmarket. . .

Peter Hill explained the project:

"And how will they ever get access to the Landmarket?"

"Oh, they're getting ready to demolish Upper and Lower Baxters' Closes to mak' way for the new road. But you get a grand view o' the New Toon frae here, Mr. Burns. That's Princes Street running along the top o' the gully. . ."

The Bard glanced at the New Town which was well advanced in its building. The houses were certainly big and spacious looking. Big but not high. But there was a rawness and uniformity about them that did not attract; the great jagged lands of the Auld Town were far more imposing, far richer in character. . .

And then the Bard was conscious of the most damnable stink in his nostrils—a dead foul decaying putrefying stench. He turned away in disgust and nausea.

"That's frae the shambles just doon below the Brig. There's nae activity seeing it's the Sabbath. . . And on a hot summer's day the stench can be fair overpowering."

"I shouldn't like the stench here on a hot summer's day, Mr. Hill. . . What's on the other side o' the Brig?"

Now the Bard had his eyes to the hills. On his immediate left rose the great steep bluff of the Calton Hill, on his right the great mass of the Salisbury Crags beetling bare and bleak and precipitous: the great ridge crowned by the peak of Arthur's Seat. In the valley between ran the Canongate down to the Palace of Holyrood. Here the cluster of high tenement lands huddled and smoked in the hollow.

The Bard could have drunk in the scene for hours. He listened with but half an ear to Peter Hill's running commentary. He would get the details later: meantime it was more than enough to gather the impression of this extraordinary town where every step and every turn of the head brought fresh angles and new vistas. . .

Below them lay the Physic Gardens, College Church and Lady Glenorchy's Chapel. . . It was too much to take in: the names fell dead on his ears. . .

"Don't tell me any more names, Mr. Hill: I canna take them in. Auld Reekie, I can see, will have to be wooed gently and over a long period o' time. . ."

Where the North Bridge joined the ridge of the New Town,

in the right-hand corner, stood the Theatre Royal dominating Shakespeare Square. . .

"You attend the theatre, Mr. Hill?"

"Weel . . . no. No' since I got married. A wife and weans, you ken, Mr. Burns. . . Oh, but there's mony grand performances given i' the Theatre Royal so I hear. There's a bill on the door there, you can see what's on."

"Aye . . . we'll see what's on as you put it. I've never been inside a theatre but I've aey had a hankering after it."

They examined the Theatre Royal's bill of fare. The Bard found it well worth examination. The entertainment offered seemed amazingly diversified. He ran his eye over the items:

THEATRE ROYAL

Last Night but Two of the Company's Engagement
On WEDNESDAY Evening, December 6, will be exhibited,
A Variety of Performances
by a
Select Company from Sadler's Wells,
As performed not only there, but at the Theatres
Royal of Paris, Dublin, Liverpool,
Manchester, etc., etc., etc.

TIGHT ROPE DANCING
By
THE LITTLE DEVIL
THE LITTLE PEIRE
MADAM ROMAIN,
AND LA BELLE ESPAGNIOLA
CLOWN, BY PIETRO BOLOGNA

The Little Devil will dance on the Rope with Baskets—Madam Romain will dance on the Rope with Swords to her feet—and La Belle Espagniola will dance on the Rope with Fetters on her Legs, and Likewise dance the Fandango with Castinets.

A Favourite Song by MISS S. VERNELL

TUMBLING
By the Inimitable
LITTLE DEVIL
MR. LAURENCE
MR. FAIRBROTHER
MR. BALMAT
and SIGNOR PIETRO BOLOGNA

Who will exhibit, this evening, a variety of New Performances;
particularly, Mr. Balmat will throw a most surprising Somerset
from off three tables and a chair; and the Little Devil will, in a
most surprising manner, fly over twelve men's heads.

SIGNOR PIETRO BOLOGNA
will exhibit some new comic and entertaining performances

ON THE SLACK WIRE
He will balance a Straw, a Peacock's Feather, display two Flags,
and beat two Drums, in a manner never attempted by any but himself.

A Comic Song by MR. HERMAN

To which will be added a Pantomime, never performed Here, called

THE LOVERS OF COLUMBINE
Or a Trick of the Devil

Harlequin	*by the* LITTLE DEVIL
Pantaloon	MR. FAIRBROTHER
French Servant	MR. BALMAT
Magician	MR. HERMAN
Clown	SIGNOR PIETRO BOLOGNA
Lover	MADAM ROMAIN
and Columbine	LA BELLE ESPAGNIOLA

In the Course of the Pantomime will be introduced the much-admired
Dance, called

LA FRICASSEE

After which SIGNOR SCALIONI *will exhibit with the*
Original Surprising
DANCING DOGS
Particularly
GENERAL JACKOO
and
THE LITTLE DESERTER
will be tried by a Court Martial; condemned and shot by a party
of his regiment.

The whole to conclude with the
Wonderful EXERTION of an English Bull Dog
Who will ascend in a PARACHUTE, surrounded by
FIRE WORKS

Tickets may be had and places for the boxes taken at the Office of
the Theatre.

PIT AND BOXES 3s.—FIRST GALLERY 2s.—SECOND GALLERY 1s.

"This is something I must see, Mr. Hill. If this La Belle
Espagniola is as good as she sounds, she'll be worth the price
o' the ticket herself."

"Oh, I hear they give good value."

"I should think so! And this Little Devil! Aye: a most
amazing programme, Mr. Hill . . . and not a Scot amang the
bluidy lot. . . ."

"I wadna be ower sure o' that, Mr. Burns. For a' ye ken
La Belle Espagniola may hae been nae further abroad nor the
foot o' the Canongate and the Little Devil may have come oot
o' the Baijen Hole. . ."

Opposite the Theatre stood the almost finished Register
House, a grand and imposing building—but the Bard was no
longer interested in buildings.

His eyes were now on the citizens who lived in the New
Town and on the folks that passed between the Old and the
New by way of the North Bridge. Interest and activity was

added to this corner by virtue of the fact that the road to Leith sloped away from the corner of the Register House.

It didn't take the Bard long to notice how sharply, in so far as dress was concerned, the classes in Edinburgh were divided. The female gentry were gorgeously clad in the most extravagant of styles. Their dresses consumed yards and yards of expensive materials; and between canes, hoops, cages and enormous artificial bums they sailed about the foot-walks with the bulk of haycocks. The hats they supported were equally bulky and hideous and of the most grotesque designs.

Such were the ladies of fashion who blocked the side-walks of the New Town—the wives and daughters of the rich merchants, the landed aristocracy, the wealthy law agents. . .

The women of the middle classes were more soberly and less extravagantly attired. Their clothes were designed to last more than the season's fashions and for them a bonnet had to last for several years. Here were the wives and daughters of the small tradesmen and shopkeepers, the impecunious gentry and the middling lawyers.

Then came the douce women-folk of the artisan class. The wives were drably put on though they were invariably clean and respectable. The daughters were more daring. They liked brightly coloured silk shawls and coloured worsted stockings —when they sported the luxury of stockings; but they were outside the pale of the hoop and cage stockade. Their dresses did not sweep the causeway—indeed some of them were surprisingly high kilted and did not hesitate to display a shapely leg.

Then there were the poor; and the poor predominated. Auld Reekie's poor were indeed very poor. Dirt, poverty, ill-health, undernourishment, beggary and destitution were stamped on them. They were bundled in hideous evil-smelling rags. And yet the New Town gentry did not hesitate to recruit from them their lowest menials. For cleanliness and elementary hygiene, except in odd individuals, was something unknown in the Athens of the North, even as it was unknown in London or Paris . . . or Saint Petersburg.

The Bard had seen poverty in Ayrshire: he had even seen

beggary and destitution. But he had never seen such a mass of suppurating poverty as he witnessed in Edinburgh.

And on this bright December Sunday, at the point where life flowed betwixt the Old and the New Towns, it was seen in the most glaring contrasts.

He commented upon this to his companion. But Peter did not seem to be affected by it.

"There's rich and poor no matter where you go, Mr. Burns. The Book says that the poor shall always be with us. But, now that you mention it, I think I see what you mean. Still, apart frae that, Mr. Burns—what d'you think o' Edinburgh?"

"Oh, I'm impressed, Mr. Hill: impressed more than I can say—now! You get a wonderful view of the Auld Toon from Princes Street here. You can almost hear poor Fergusson's glorious lines singing in the air. . . ."

Viewed from Princes Street, across the drained but still marshy bed of the North Loch, the old tenement lands rose fantastically out of the rock like great ragged-edged blocks. It was difficult to believe that they looked up to what were the principal dwellings of Edinburgh, those precipices of stone and lime and narrow slits of windows that until a few years ago had sheltered the entire population of the Capital.

And then the whole jagged fantastic panorama was crowned by the Castle—the Rock terminating abruptly and falling sheer into the morass below. Grey rock and grey stone. Grim austere hard and enduring—but massively, impressively so.

Peter Hill saw that the Bard was impressed.

"It gars you think, Mr. Burns."

"Aye . . . and gars you dream too. That's the Capital of Scotland without doubt; and a fitting monument to our race. What a tragedy it was that robbed us of our parliament and our independence. I doubt if there's another country in the world could boast such an inspiring capital!"

"Ah well: them that's been in London says it's just a flat overcrowded midden o' a place. And them that's been in Paris say it stinks worse than either o' them. I've heard Mr. Creech tell about his travels abroad wi' the Earl o' Glencairn. . ."

"Yes: I've read about those places—and seen prints of them.

But no: I can imagine nothing finer than Edinburgh. It lifts up the mind and the heart even as it lifts up its palaces and towers."

"Maybe you'll write a poem on it, Mr. Burns?"

"Aye: did my Muse feel adequate to my inspiration I might do that. Well . . . much as I like the clean tidiness of your New Town, I doubt if I would care to live out my life in it. I am a countryman and I'll gladly return to my rural shades when I've completed my business with your master—but, had I on compulsion to choose a city to dwell in, I would choose Auld Chuckie Reekie. What a pity you didn't know Fergusson! If you only knew how I loved that poor lad's gift for rhyme. Listen: ' Auld Reekie! thou'rt the canty hole, a bield for mony a cauldrife soul, wha snugly at their ingle loll, baith warm and couth; while round they gar the bicker roll to weet their mouth. . . Auld Reekie! wale o' ilka Toon that Scotland kens beneath the moon; where couthy chiels at e'ening meet their bizzing craigs and mou's to weet; and blythly gar auld Care gae by wi' blinkit and wi' bleering eye. . . Now morn, with bonnie purpie-smiles, kisses the air-cock o' Saint Giles. . . On Sunday here, an altered scene o' men and manners meets our een. In afternoon, a' brawly buskit, the joes and lassies lo'e to frisk it. Some take a great delight to place a modest bon-grace o'er the face. Though you may see, if so inclined, the turning o' the leg behind. Now Comeley Garden and the Park refresh them after forenoon's walk . . . while dandering cits delight to stray to Castlehill, or public way, let me to Arthur's Seat pursue, whare bonnie pastures meet the view; and mony a wild-lorn scene accrues befitting Willie Shakespeare's muse '—

"Befitting Willie Shakespeare's muse . . . aye: puir Fergusson—his words and rhymes drip like honey from the tongue. And I suppose from Fergusson and Allan Ramsay I've had Edinburgh bright and clear in my mind's eye. And yet, Mr. Hill, Edinburgh in all the majesty o' its naked stone is finer than ony description o' it could be—no' excluding Willie Shakespeare's muse."

"Well, sir, I've never heard poetry spoken with such meaning before—and I've heard poetry spoken about Mr. Creech's shop mony a time. You must have had a great admiration for Fergusson—as weel as a great memory—to say his lines like that. You ken: the literati hereabouts never mention him."

"There's not one of them—or a dozen of them together—could write poetry like Fergusson. He was my first real master —and he may well be my last. Believe me, Mr. Hill, and I say this in all truth and modesty—my verses are poor stuff compared to the glorious lines of Auld Reekie's Bard... Could you take me to his grave?"

"No . . . that I couldna, Mr. Burns—and sorry I am to say that. He might be buried in the Canongate Kirkyard. You see, I wasna in Edinburgh when he died and, well, I never thocht he was important—never heard onybody about the shop talking about him. Though I did hear, elsewhere, that Henry Mac-Kenzie doesna like him."

"I can understand that—though Fergusson's satire on his Man of Feeling was harmless. MacKenzie should have been big enough to look over it. But if you can't direct me to his grave I'll need to make enquiries elsewhere. Smellie should be able to tell me."

"Oh aye: Mr. Smellie kens a' aboot the Toon and a'bodies in it. He's a verra clever man is Mr. Smellie. Indeed, between ourselves, Mr. Burns, I doubt if there's a cleverer man i' the Toon for learning o' a' kinds. Of course, there's some clever law lords. Lord Monboddo is a great scholar though plenty think he's clean gyte——"

"What's your own opinion, Mr. Hill?"

"Weel, Lord Monboddo's nae doubt clever—but I think he's a bit gyte too. I've watched him coming up the street to the Parliament House—that's where the Law Courts are held—behind Saint Giles's. As I say, I've seen him coming up from Saint John Street and the rain coming on; and he would hire a chair and place his meikle wig in it and walk beside the chair-men—and ne'er fash about getting drookit himsel'. You see: he doesna believe that folk should tak' advantage o' modern conveniences—because the Ancients—the auld Greeks—hadna onything like them. And he'll travel on nothing but horseback. I heard him mysel' telling Mr. Creech, when he was for London one time, that it was degrading for a man to be dragged at a horse's tail instead o' sitting manfully on its back as master. And he's no' a young man—he'll be over sixty. Makes his dochter ride wi' him to London and up Aberdeen way to his estate—in a' weathers; and I wadna say she's a strong lass though she's a good-looking one."

"So that's Lord Monboddo—and his daughter!"

"Aye, but they're a' a bit touched. You'll need to visit the Court o' Session and see and hear them. The like o' some o' the arguments baith in defence and prosecution you wadna believe till you heard them wi' your own ears. Of course, Mr. Burns, this is a' verra confidential atween you and me. Mr. Creech wadna like to think I was saying ocht aboot the Law Lords—they a' come aboot the shop even them he doesna publish.

"And it's the same wi' the professors doon at the College. Some o' them are right enough—some o' the younger men. But among the older generation there's some queer characters. The like o' Doctor Adam Ferguson. He resigned the Chair o' Moral Philosophy that Professor Dugald Stewart took up last year. He used to be Professor o' Mathematics—John Playfair tak's that now."

"But are they able to change from one Chair to another as if they were chairs at a table?"

"Change? No' so much now, of course. But tak' Adam Ferguson. I understand he was an army chaplain at one time. When he left the army he was made librarian of the Advocates' Library—that's just about the most important collection in Scotland. Then he was appointed to the first Chair in the College that fell vacant—and that happened to be the Chair o' Natural Philosophy. Of course he knew nothing about that. But he took it over and they tell me he made no' a bad job o' it. And then he took over Moral Philosophy; and about ten or twelve years ago he published his Institutes of Moral Philosophy —and made a name for himsel'. Then for a while he was away travelling abroad wi' Lord Chesterfield—met Voltaire and a' the literati abroad. That wasna the finish o' him. About '78 he went on the Commission to America to see what could be settled wi' the rebels—and came back empty-handed. But the purse would be well filled! Then he manipulated the Chair o' Mathematics. But he did better than that: he gave the Chair to Mr. Playfair and kept the salary—draws it still."

"And what does Mr. Playfair live on?"

"Oh, Playfair gets the students' fees—and they come to a bit if you're onyway good at tutoring—and Mr. Playfair's good they tell me."

"And how much is the salary?"

"Over a hundred pounds."

"And is this a proper proceeding?"

"You wadna think so. But then it's managed wi' the consent o' the magistrates. There's wheels within wheels a' the time, Mr. Burns. But I meant to tell you about the way he goes about —summer or winter. Lord kens how many clothes he wears. But at least he wears twa great-coats—one o' them fur-lined— a fur hat and a great meikle pair o' fur-lined boots. You'd think he was biding at the North Pole. Just a piece o' nonsense if you ask me. I saw a lot o' him when he published his History of the Roman Republic two years ago. And I thocht he was about the oddest man ever I saw. Aye: shivering wi' his way o' it—and the sweat running down the sides o' his wizened cheeks on a hot summer's day. And as crabbit as Auld Nick. Flare up in a temper about the least thing that didna please him. I'm telling you, Mr. Burns—and I don't mean this to flatter you in ony way or to insult you either—you're the first sensible-speaking, sensible-looking man that's been connected in ony way wi' the literati."

"I'm a ploughman who writes poetry for his own amusement."

"That's your modesty, sir. And it becomes you. But your poetry amuses—and instructs—everybody that can read. And you're not just a poet—you're Scotland's poet now, sir. I think your book will do well in Scotland——"

"We'll see what we'll see, Mr. Hill."

"And you'll make money too—though I don't know exactly what Mr. Creech and you have arranged on the financial side. But you should clear a good three hundred pounds."

"A fortune, eh? I'll be pleased if I clear my expenses. Don't forget that I'll have to pay Smellie for the printing and Willie Scott for the binding—apart altogether from what Mr. Creech will need for his share in the business."

"Ah weel . . . Mr. Creech will be looking for something."

"And I'll not grudge him it. I don't expect him to be a philanthropist in this matter: he has his living to make even as you and I have to make ours. And without Creech to publish —or act as my agent in the matter—I'd go abegging."

"That's your modesty again, Mr. Burns. . . Weel: will we hae a bit look at the South Toon?"

"If you have no objection, Mr. Hill, I'd rather for the moment look at a pint o' ale. There's plenty o' questions I want to ask you—the kind o' questions that are better discussed round a tavern table. Is there such a place convenient to us?"

"That's one thing aboot Edinburgh, Mr. Burns: a dozen steps in ony direction'll land you at a howff o' some kind. So we'll just turn into Shakespeare Square here behind the Theatre. Bayle's is as good a tavern as you'll find in the Toon. Mind you: it's a superior place to Dawney Douglas's or John Dowie's though there's plenty wouldna like to hear me say so. But there's mair room aboot Bayle's. . ."

"Lead on then to Bayle's, Mr. Hill. For I have plenty to ask you concerning Mr. Creech and the literati."

THE TENTH WORTHY

Richmond and the Bard had much to talk about in the evenings before they snuffed the candle and turned into the chaff bed.

He had been nine days in the Town. What he had accomplished in those nine days astounded Richmond more than the Bard. Apart from his leisurely stroll round the Town with Peter Hill the previous Sunday, he had spent his time meeting one person after another and being introduced on all hands as the celebrated Ayrshire Bard. He had already made firm friends with Willie Smellie, Peter Hill and Willie Scott. . .

And to-day he had attended a sale in the Exchange Coffee House (by order of the Lords of the Session) of the lands that had but recently belonged to David MacLure of Shawood and his partners Campbell and MacCree.

It had been a historic occasion for the Bard and it had evoked many bitter and ironic memories. But Richmond was the only friend in Edinburgh who understood something of its import.

"Little did I think, Jock, as I posted between my father's death-bed and Bob Aiken in Ayr that I would ever see the day when I would stand in Edinburgh and watch MacLure's land come under the hammer."

"Aye—if only your father had lived to see this day."

"It was MacLure—as much as any physical illness—that killed him. . . . But I suppose I'd better write to Gavin Hamilton before it's ony later: I promised to send him details of the sale."

"There's no hurry: the mail doesna go till Thursday. But how are you feeling?"

"No' a damned bit better, Jock. I'd some greasy titbits in Dawney Douglas's in the Anchor Close with Willie Smellie the printer. My stomach's been in rebellion ever since. The fact is, Jock, I've never fully recovered from that night's debauch in Biggar on my journey here. Either that or the whisky must have been rank bad. Sometimes it's my stomach, sometimes my head—sometimes both."

"Maybe it's the change o' air and food and water. I don't think the water's ony too good in Edinburgh. Or maybe you're missing the open air and the exercise."

"Aye . . . and too much excitement. I've only been a week here and I've eaten more strange meals with strange folk than I've done in the whole of my life."

"By God, you havena been idle since you arrived. Are you sure Creech is for printing your book?"

"I'm as sure as I can be: the subscription bills may come out to-morrow."

"Has he given you onything in writing?"

"No . . . but does that matter?"

"It would matter wi' me. I wouldna trust ony o' them— Mr. Creech least of all."

"The strange thing, Jock, is that nobody seems to like Creech though everybody thinks highly of his ability."

"Creech is about as clever a man as you could find in the High Street—too clever to be trusted."

"Well, I find him honest enough for my wants. I've a lot to be grateful for. . . Where's Saint John Street: I've to sup wi' Lord Monboddo to-morrow night?"

"Lord Monboddo? Who next? It's aboot half-way down the Canongate on your right going down. Let me see. Aboot a dozen closes past Saint Mary's Wynd: you canna miss it."

"Do you know Lord Monboddo?"

"I ken who he is fine. He's one o' thae auld humbugs o' law lords that would be better retired out o' the road to make room for some o' the younger and more up-to-date men. You'll need to come round to the Court o' Session some day. You'll see and hear some of the greatest oddities on the face o' the earth—and Monboddo's as odd as any o' them."

"I met him at Craig's Close. He's odd without a doubt—but he's no fool for all that."

"No . . . no fool for himself—like the rest o' them. Oh, they ken what side o' their bannock's best toasted."

"There doesna seem to be any fools in Edinburgh?"

"Plenty—but you're meeting only the privileged ones that are fooling the public—and robbing them at the same time."

The Bard laughed. "By heavens, Jock, but you've become sour: there'll soon be no living wi' you."

"There'll soon be no living wi' you, you mean! The next thing is you'll be taking up rooms wi' some lord, duke, earl or countess. I can see you marrying into the nobility a' richt—and going hame to Machlin wi' a crest on your carriage."

"Aye—and the beggar's benison written underneath it for a'bodies to see half a mile away."

He drew his chair into the table and wrote to Gavin Hamilton in Machlin:

7th December 1786

Honoured Sir,

I have paid every attention to your command, but can only

say that Adamhill and Shawood were bought for Oswald's folks. . .

For my own affairs, I am in a fair way of becoming as eminent as Thomas a Kempis or John Bunyan; and you may expect henceforth to see my birthday inserted among the wonderful events, in the Poor Robin's and Aberdeen Almanacks, along with Black Monday and the Battle of Bothwell Bridge. My Lord Glencairn & the Dean of Faculty, Mr. H. Erskine, have taken me under their wing; and by all probability I shall soon be the tenth Worthy, and the eighth Wise Man, of the world. Through my Lord's influence it is inserted in the records of the Caledonian Hunt, that they universally, one & all, subscribe for the 2nd Edition. My subscription bills come out to-morrow, and you shall have some of them next Post. I have met in Mr. Dalrymple of Orangefield what Solomon emphatically calls "a friend that sticketh closer than a Brother." The warmth with which he interests himself in my affairs is of the same enthustiastic kind which you, Mr. Aiken, and the few Patrons that took notice of my earlier poetic days, showed for the poor unlucky devil of a Poet.

I always remember Mrs. Hamilton & Miss Kennedy in my poetic prayers, but *you* both in prose & verse.

> May Cauld ne'er catch you but a hap,
> Nor Hunger but in Plenty's lap!
>
> Amen!

He read the letter over. Aye: that would make Gavin open his eyes a bit wider. The tenth worthy, no less. But true enough if he was a fit and proper judge of all the signs and omens.

Maybe—maybe his luck was about to take a turn for the better. Maybe he was on the high road to success.

But deep within him there was doubt. Maybe he should write to his brother Gilbert—or to Robert Muir in Kilmarnock. To Gilbert he could express some of his fondest hopes.

But no: he would wait until he had his subscription bills in his hand. No doubt Gavin Hamilton would be so taken with his letter that he would show it to Gilbert.

And no doubt, if he knew Gavin, he would add his own comments—and Gibby would have a double message to take home to Mossgiel. . .

THE EDINBURGH GENTRY

Jane Maxwell remembered the days of her girlhood spent in Hyndford's Close near the Netherbow at the foot of the High Street. They had been the happiest days of her life when, with her sister Eglantine, she was free to ride the backs of innkeeper Peter Ramsay's pigs. She had never known such freedom since she had left the close as the second daughter of the late Sir William Maxwell of Monreath in order to become the wife of the fourth Duke of Gordon.

Jane was reckoned one of the most handsome women of her day: she herself was quite certain she had no rival. And even if she had not been born with good looks and an elegant figure she knew that her intense and magnetic sexuality would have won for her an unrivalled position with men. Holding such an infallible power over them, what consideration did she need to give to women?

From riding the back of an innkeeper's pigs, it was an easy step to ride the back of Scottish convention. She broke all the laws of social etiquette and social decorum and, as a consequence, found herself the more toasted by the bucks and the beaux.

She had early discovered that men have one set of manners in the company of women and another set when they are by themselves. She did not relish the tame conversation meant only for ladies' ears. She relished masculine bawdry and the jocose incongruities of sexual anecdote. But indeed her mind had a strong masculine bent: just as her sexual passion was ever aggressive. Women secretly hated and feared her; and though there were many men who feared her, only a John Knox could have routed her on the plane of morality. Many men in her circle thought her scandalously indecent; but this did not prevent them thinking her the more attractive for her daring charm. . . . The Duke, in self-preservation, patronised the brothels. . .

Hearing that the Ayrshire ploughman's poems were in places rather daring and given to 'qualities of libertinism,' she immediately borrowed a copy of them from Henry Mac-Kenzie and read them through at a sitting. . . They were very much to her palate: and very much beyond her palate. She relished their uncompromising realism and thrilled to the touches of bawdry though here she found them rather tame. What she found she did not respond to was their social senti-ment. There was a quality in *The Twa Dogs* and *The Address to the King on the Occasion of his Birthday* that caused her to wonder. This author, she was sure, was hiding more than one light under the bushel of his genius. . .

Jane did not for a moment doubt the high quality of his genius; and she needed no assistance from Henry MacKenzie here. She was not without a streak of genius herself.

She must get to know this man. She made enquiries. She spoke to the Earl of Glencairn. "James," she said, "I believe you have taken the Ayrshire ploughman under your patronage? Is he presentable? Can I meet him? Or should I send him a couple of guineas and subscribe for his new edition?"

"You should meet him, Jane: he will surprise you much. He makes no pretence to being other than a ploughman. But he kens how to conduct himself before his superiors."

"You make him sound very dull, Jamie."

"I find him a trifle dull myself. But I fancy you micht be able to draw out his parts."

"You, at least, Jamie, never flatter me. But I find authors disappointing—and damnably unlike their works."

"I havena much interest in them myself, Jane. Maybe you'll find Burns like enough his works."

"I've heard that he has quite a small regiment of bastard bairns in your part of the country. . . Oh, I'm not censuring him: it becomes both his talent and his station in life."

"It's an untruth though. I've had the maist carefu' enquiries made as to his conduct; and I find that his regiment of bastards amounts to no more than two very young recruits; and even they might have been lawfully born but for some disagreement with their mother's parents."

"Like patron, like poet! You're a gey canny man yourself, Jamie. But I've seen the day you micht hae tried to seduce me! Now dinna blush: you're too handsome as it is without that. Tell Andrew Erskine I would like to meet your poet at the Buccleuch Street Assembly—before the ball. I shall be at my best then. . ."

The Duchess was always something of a trial to James Cunningham. He found it difficult to keep up his end with her. To cover his embarrassment he produced his silver snuff box. The Duchess held out her hand: she took a liberal dose, paused for a moment and then returned the box. Her parting shot left him speechless.

"Your poet, Jamie, had better have more kick in him than your snuff."

There were two main assembly rooms in the Town. The New Assembly Rooms in George Street, soon to be opened, were as grand and spacious as the New Town. But in Buccleuch Street, in the South Town, the Assembly Rooms, if smaller and less pretentious, had a charm of their own. The Duchess of Gordon, whose Town house was in George's Square, liked to think of them as her own: she looked rather sharply down her sharp nose at the New Assembly Rooms.

In this she was not wholly snobbish. There was much that was raw in the New Town. But George's Square was still the residential gem of Edinburgh. It was a self-contained socially-powerful community lying in the eye of the sun and on the flank of the Meadows, the pride of its owners and a credit to its builder, James Brown.

The Assembly Rooms adjacent to the elegant and tasteful square might be fighting a losing battle with the New Town; but the battle was not yet lost; and as long as the Duchess of Gordon led fashion within its precincts there could be no thought of defeat.

Indeed the Duchess would not allow herself to be on the

losing side. She was beginning to formulate a plan of campaign for the conquest of London. Meantime, if this was to be her last winter in Edinburgh, she would continue to dominate it on her own terms.

"Ah! Mr. Burns! Welcome to Edinburgh. . . No, no, no, no! Please don't let us have any ceremony: there's no one at the moment who can overhear us: unless you shout. You are not my humble servant at all: only formally. And I would much rather have my poets informal."

"And it please your Grace, then, you have me as God made me."

"I shall remember in my prayers to-night to thank Him for His handiwork. But don't let's bandy pretty compliments, Mr. Burns. May I congratulate you on the excellence of your poetry? It would be wrong of me to say I found it charming; but I did find it wonderfully fascinating."

"Then in the reader my volume has met its compeer! But perhaps I should first ask you to excuse the rusticity of my manners. Perhaps I am over-bold in telling a duchess that she is fascinating?"

"Of course you are over-bold, Mr. Burns: I should think that is part of *your* fascinating charm. . . But I should be very annoyed with you if you *didn't* tell me I was fascinating: I am well aware of the fact: just as you are aware of your boldness. . . Am I not right?"

"I am aware that your Grace has a sense of character above that possessed by some of the more discerning of the literati; but boldness in a poet of humble station in life is not an advantage. . ."

"When you make the mistake of being born into the wrong family, Mr. Burns, you must try to remedy the defect by suitable marriage."

"But one of the disadvantages of being a poet is that a poet marries for love."

"Then poets are bigger fools than I tak' them to be. They should marry for money—and love for pleasure."

"Then I perceive your Grace has not yet been loved by a poet."

"Now, Mr. Burns! You are in danger of taking me out of my depth."

"Nay, madam; but I may be in some danger of taking you *into* your depth—did not the mountain barrier of our respective social positions prove insurmountable."

"I'm afraid it isn't the barrier that is insurmountable but rather your inordinate consciousness of your class. I guessed that too from your poems. It is perhaps their one defect. You canna forget that I am a duchess and you are a ploughman; and that is a gey pity. . ."

"In the harvest field, I make so bold to suggest, you would find the barrier even more insurmountable."

"I should do very well in the harvest field; and when the hairst was hame I should have earned my nicht's frolic at your kirn dance."

"And I'd be poet enough, and dancer enough, to give you frolic."

"I fancy you would be no gentle shepherd, Mr. Burns!"

Internally Jane Gordon began to quiver. She rocked for a split second and took a half-step backwards. This man overwhelmed her. It was not what he said: it was not even how he said it, though she had never heard from any man a timbre of voice so powerfully and yet so exquisitely moulded. It was not the unnatural purity of his English though it was, as English, purer than she had ever heard. What was it then? His eyes? She could not look for long into them without fear that she might betray, in weakness, the weakness of her sex. What was it then? The total impact of all his qualities, his personality? She could not put words on it; but she was overwhelmingly conscious of the waves that vibrated from him—and vibrated through her. Ah yes—she had it now! Behind those great burning pools of his eyes was a sharp penetrating intelligence. Not cleverness, though it was obvious that he had cleverness enough. Not cleverness, not mere intelligence, not wit, not cunning. . . Insight: that was it! Nothing was hidden from this man—and yet he had the devilish cunning to hide what he knew—to seem not to see all that he saw. . .

This flashed through Jane Gordon's keen receptive analytical mind. She felt uncomfortable. She wanted to escape. She had used the wrong tactics with this man who was no more a ploughman than she was a scullery maid. She could not change her tactics without lowering herself in his eyes. But next time they met she would be prepared. She had not expected at her age, and with her experience, to be caught on the wrong foot by any man.

Hitherto she had always been the one who had done the catching—and triumphed in the catching.

She plied her fan with quite uncharacteristic agitation and looked round her. Then she saw the elegant figure of the Honourable Henry Erskine, Dean of the Faculty of Advocates, advancing towards her.

Her breath came in a quick gasp as the tension eased within her and she turned her eyes to those of the poet. And then she knew his had never left hers.

"No—no gentle shepherd, Mr. Burns. No... Ah! but here's Harry Erskine to shepherd you away. . . Harry: I have just been telling Mr. Burns that you must bring him round some afternoon for tea."

"Delighted, my dear Jane; shall we settle on a day now?"

"If Mr. Burns has a fancy for some of our Edinburgh belles, let me know, Harry, and I'll extend them—or her—an invitation . . . if I approve!"

"I would rather I left the choice to your Grace. I could survive the disapproval of the literati for my verses; but I could not survive your Grace's disapproval of a belle fille."

Again the quivering agitation shot down from her diaphragm. The man was like a charge of gunpowder, like the twang of a bow string—and the barbed arrow that sped from it to flash in the target's heart.

There was no reply she could make. She must divert the attention from herself. Again, beneath her heavily brocaded dress, her foot slipped backwards and she raised her fan.

"Harry: I see that the agitated bosoms of many of the young ladies threaten to burst their stays apart. Introduce Mr. Burns to them and put an end to their misery. Enjoy yourself,

Mr. Burns! You may be sure I shall sing your praises—with genuine enthusiasm."

Instinctively the Bard bowed; and, to the astonishment of the eager onlookers, the Duchess returned him a very pretty curtsey.

"Aye, aye, Mr. Burns! I begin to see why you're the famous Bard of Ayrshire!" said Henry Erskine. "Well, for my part, I'd rather hae a full belly than a belle fille—partial as I am to the belles! Aye. . . But now that you hae won the approval o' the Gay Duchess—and she used to be fully gayer—you need hae nae fear o' Edinburgh society."

"Does it mean as much as that, Mr. Erskine?"

"Certes, there's no' a hostess i' the Toon but apes her—in so far as she can; but ye ken what monkeys the women can be. Invitations'll pour into you now. Your difficulty'll no' be knowing which to accept but which to refuse."

"In that event, sir, I'll be glad to have your good advice and guidance."

"And by the look o' things you'll be the better o' a chaperon too. You're in a fair way to capturing the Toon, Mr. Burns. My guid-brither Glencairn and his sister were singing your praises. It's a pity you hadna a supply o' your verses wi' you. Everybody's raving mad to lay hands on a copy; and such copies that are i' the Toon hae been read to tatters—or so I hear. But there's one thing does surprise me—I meant to speak about it afore—and that's whaur you got your English tongue. I canna see you learned *that* ahint the plough in your native Ayrshire."

"It seems to surprise most folks—but it's a long story, sir. And dinna think that guid braid Lallans doesna lie warmer till my tongue and my heart nor the English. Only I see nae reason why a man shouldna hae the twa tongues. Nae doubt if I hadna had the English hammered into me as a scule-laddie I wad hae thocht different. But there you are—and I see nae need to apologise for mysel'. I will say, however, that I had thought to hear more polished English in the Capital than ever I heard in my rural shades."

"Oh, there's some hae polished themselves up till you wadna ken what they were saying. It's the fact that you've nae Anglified accent to your English that surprises me. But I'm neglecting my duty to you. I see there's plenty here waiting to meet you."

Erskine was a pleasant fellow. The Bard could appreciate his intelligence and the wit that twinkled in his eye. If his tongue was not Anglified his dress was. And he carried his sartorial finery with a very gallant and becoming air. He was some dozen years older than the Bard; but a life of comparative ease, and the skilful use of silks and powders, enabled him to carry his years with a touch of lightness that was deceptively youthful. The women adored him for his great personal charm; and as the younger brother of the Earl of Buchan and a relation by marriage to the Earl of Glencairn, he was a man to whom much social deference was naturally due. So sound indeed was his social position that the extreme liberal views he held concerning the affairs of state were not counted seriously against him even in reactionary circles dominated by uncompromising Whigs. For all his reforming zeal Erskine's fundamental Whiggery was not in any doubt even by his bitterest enemies who were closest to Henry Dundas. And as things were going nicely for Premier Pitt's Scottish henchman he had no wish to exercise the more brutal side of his dictatorship merely for dictation's sake. He knew his powers and how best in his own interest to exercise them.

As the elegant people gathered in the large rectangular hall and chatted in little groups or sat into the small tables by the red plush-lined wall-seats, the Bard experienced a moment of fear. This gathering was much bigger and much grander than he had been led to expect. He consulted Henry Erskine.

"Oh, this is nothing—just a preliminary to the grand Hunt Ball which will be held in the New Assembly Rooms in George Street. Just a gathering o' folk that matter are here. I canna introduce you to them a'—nor wad you enjoy that. But here's a man you should get to ken—a grand fellow: Willie Dunbar."

Colonel William Dunbar was a different specimen of

manhood from Henry Erskine. Willie was a bluff bachelor
and a successful Writer to the Signet with chambers in Princes
Street. He had once served as an officer in the Earl of Home's
regiment and he liked to think of himself as a military man
who dabbled in the law more as a hobby than as a means of
earning an excellent living. But his bluffness was not assumed:
there were many things for which the Colonel did not give a
damn; and the scraping and bowing of the foppish rising
generation was one of them: his approach to life was fairly
honest and direct.

He grasped the Bard firmly by the hand and looked him
keenly in the eye.

"There's nae good in me saying that I've read your poems,
sir: I dinna read much beyond the necessity o' legal documents.
But I promise I'll give your book a ca'-through when it comes
out: I canna do fairer than that, can I, Harry?"

"If you have ony skill wi' a bawdy ballad, Mr. Burns,
Willie's your man: maybe you'll meet him at the Crochallan
Fencibles' Club one night and you'll hear him bawling like a
Gilmerton coal-vendor. But I'll tell you, Willie: I was thinking
of introducing Mr. Burns to the Lodge. What d'you think?
He is depute-master of his own Lodge in Ayrshire. . ."

"Aye; and I'll warrant ye can pass and raise in your
country wi' a bit o' honest ceremony: they're a damned genteel
lot o' beggars gotten in the Capital. But up in my hame
country, by certes, we used to gie them something they didna
forget in a hurry. . . Certainly, Harry: bring Mr. Burns alang
to the Lodge. . . How are you enjoying your stay in the
Town, sir?"

"I've hardly had time to know whether I'm enjoying myself
or not. Everybody seems to be set to show me the heights of
hospitality and kindness. To be taken by the hand by so many
of the nobility makes it difficult for me to find my way among
them."

"We're a' nobility hereabouts. To hell: what's a title
amang friends?"

"Ah! but you'll find that our friend is a stickler for the
niceties concerning such matters. Still he's done no' bad: he's

gotten the Gay Duchess on a string after two minutes o' conversation."

"Hae a look out, sir. By God, Harry, gin she took a notion o' me I would post out o' the Town by the crack o' dawn. . . I was hearing about you from Willie Smellie, Mr. Burns. I don't give a damn for the Duchess o' Gordon; but when Auld Smellie tak's a notion o' onybody that's enough for me. And I think by the look in your eye, Mr. Burns, we could hae a grand session at the Club. Smellie'll fix you up. . . I think, Harry, we'll better arrange to assume Mr. Burns into the Lodge. . ."

Erskine took him by the arm and whispered in his ear: "Here's a worthy gentleman that you maun meet: Sir James Hunter Blair, Baronet . . . almost brand new . . . Provost of the Town and a partner in Coutts' Bank."

They moved towards the burly provost.

"Sir James: may I present Mr. Robert Burns, the Ayrshire Bard?"

The banker's stern-cast features relaxed into a broad smile of welcome. He extended a ready hand. "Man, man, Mr. Burns: this is a verra welcome meeting. Ayrshire's Bard? That's the Wast country for you again, Harry. I'm an Ayr man mysel', Mr. Burns, and real proud o' the fac'; and real proud that ye've done such honour to our native land. I've no great interest in books; but if I can be of ony assistance to ye, Mr. Burns, ye hae only to seek me out and say the word. Now dinna hesitate, Mr. Burns, for I'll count it a verra great privilege to serve your interests ony way I can; baith for yoursel', sir, and for the honour ye hae done for the Wast. Noo, Harry: I tak' you for witness here. See that Mr. Burns is no' keepit standing oot in the cauld where I can be of assistance. . ."

When they had passed on, Erskine said: "That was an honest welcome you got from Sir James: actually he's a bit of a terror and brooks interference from naebody. But an administrative genius, to give him the fair. He has carried through far-reaching plans—like the brig over the Cowgate— that have been for the Town's good; and he'll do more good yet—despite the opposition. That's why I'm glad he took to you for he'll probably be the biggest man in Scotland before he's done: that's why so many fear him. But that's how it is, Mr. Burns: to be successful you've got to drive over all opposition and do good by force where you canna do it by stealth. It wouldn't suit my temperament; but then it takes all kinds to make a world just as it takes all kinds of writers to make a literature. . . Now we maun return to the ladies so that they may not burst their stays, as the Duchess had it. And there I'll leave you for a time. A man gets on better with the ladies when he has them to himsel'. . . But you see that one there wi' the haughty air and a meikle mouth you'd think had been made wi' a trowel? That's her. Well . . . avoid her as you would the plague. She'd deave you wi' her Anglified accent. That's Jane Elliot: wrote a version of The Flowers o' the Forest but doesna like onybody to ken aboot it. And come back when you've tired o' the ladies: I see Captain Matthew Henderson's come in and I'd like you to meet him."

But the Bard found the ladies a great trial. He had never imagined that he could possibly be asked so many foolish questions about the writing of poetry: questions not so naïve as downright silly. But he did not lose his patience and answered their queries with such a mock gravity that they never suspected for a moment his tongue was in his cheek and were convinced that not even Henry MacKenzie had created a character so full of sensibility as this heaven-taught ploughman.

Who the young ladies were into whose hands he had fallen he had not the slightest idea. Though he had been introduced to them with the usual formalities he could not distinguish one from the other and rested content by addressing them in the most general terms.

But he could not help reflecting that if they were the products of the fine boarding-schools for young ladies of title, of which the Town was so proud, he would rather have any one of the Machlin belles for wit, looks or intelligent conversation. They simpered and blushed and lowered their eyes so affectedly (and shamelessly) over the edges of their fans that

there were moments when he thought they must be creatures
from a different planet.

Their dress also amused him. They were so tightly laced
that they could hardly breathe. Their breasts were forced
upwards to their chins and their bare shoulders were draped
with the flimsiest of scarf-shawls. Some of their dresses were
hooped with canes; and they stuck out behind like lop-sided
haycocks. Others had such great padded artificial bums resting
on their natural hurdies that they were totally unable to sit
down and, in dancing, must have sweated like brood mares
heavily yoked. . .

Yet he stood there with his arms folded across his chest,
his head held erect, his weight resting on one leg while the
other, placed slightly forward and bent at the knee, gave to
his posture an independence and an elegance that drew
admiring glances and comments from the older folks.

The Duchess of Gordon, stopping for a moment to talk to
the Dowager-Countess of Glencairn and indicating the Bard
with a slight movement of her fan, said: "You must be proud,
my Lady, of James's protégé. He behaves very well for a
ploughman: you see how he has captivated the young ladies."

But beneath her title, the Dowager-Countess could never
forget that she was Lizzie MacGuire, the Ayr joiner's hard-
bitten daughter. "Tach! a wheen silly gawkin' bitches couldna
wash through a luggie o' clarty hippens. That's a decent
ploughman-laddie that didna ken when he was weel at himsel'
in his ain but and ben."

The Duchess laughed heartily: she always appreciated the
Dowager's sallies. "But he's a gey guid poet as weel."

"I dinna need you to tell me that, Jane; but we'll see how
mony bawbees that'll put in his pouch."

Some of the younger fops thought to ridicule his dress—
the same dress he had donned that Sunday he had gone round
the Town with Peter Hill. His tied hair was innocent of any
powder or grease. But his dress, though it was so individual
as to be almost eccentric, suited his character so well that it
could not have been bettered; and since he was well aware of
this, he suffered no embarrassment on its account. He might

be dressed outside the character of a tenant-farmer or a plough-man; but he knew he was dressed within the character of a ploughman who was also a poet, and a poet who was essentially a peasant. He never sought to contradict anyone who described him as a ploughman, and of himself never hinted that he was also a tenant-farmer in his own right. Ploughman he had been all his life; and if they sought to add that he was heaven-taught, he had no objection to that either. It saved a lot of tiresome explanations and was the perfect disguise to enable him to pursue his hobby of catching manners living as they rose. Only to those who proved themselves worthy of his confidence would he bestow his confidence; and there was plenty of time to think about that.

John Richmond listened to his recital of the evening's proceedings.

"I don't know, Jock. Here I have invitations to dine or sup, aye, or even breakfast with half the nobility of Scotland and every family of note in the Town. There's something wrong somewhere. Some of them have read some of my poems—those printed by Sibbald. Most have read none. A few, a very few, have read the Kilmarnock volume. But it seems to make no difference. They are all equally enthusiastic, tumbling over themselves to do me some honour or kindness. Oh, I'm a ploughman—a prodigy, a wonder, a seven days' wonder——"

"You're not complaining, are you?"

"No . . . I'm not complaining, Jock. The tide o' good fortune's running high just now. Higher than it should by all natural laws. It'll ebb, Jock."

"Wait till it ebbs—though why should it? It winna turn in twenty-four hours."

"They don't know me, Jock. I very much doubt if they want to know me. I'm a curiosity—much like that performing pig in the Grassmarket. I doubt if they know the difference between a good poem and a bad pig."

"If you sell your book and make some money what does it matter? And get after them for a job while they're thinking so highly o' you."

"The Duchess o' Gordon has a glimmering o' the truth. By God, Jock, that's a woman for you. They tell me she's had six o' a family: you wouldna think she'd had one."

"Aye . . . and she couldna tell you the father o' any o' the children—so they tell me."

"I could believe that. The martial chuck I met in Poosie Nancie's in Machlin and her hae much in common. A crab-louse is but a crab-louse still. . . She may have a woman's body; but she's gotten a man's brains: the best quality at that.

"And I've to be introduced to Lodge Canongate-Kilwinning by Henry Erskine and William Dunbar—and it seems everybody will be there."

"I only wish Daddy Auld and the Kirk Session o' Machlin could see you now, Rab. Aye: or the Armours. Huh! And you werena good enough to marry Jean! I wonder what they'll say when they get to know?"

"They won't believe it. Nobody but Daddy Auld will believe it. Auld was well acquaint wi' the Town in his day: so I've been hearing. It seems he used to be a great friend o' James Boswell o' Auchinleck the time Boswell stayed in Saint James's Court up the Landmarket there. Aye: Auld will understand—and Doctor MacKenzie . . . and maybe Gavin Hamilton. . .

"Howsomenever, Jock, you've to go to work in the morning and I've to have breakfast wi' Mr. Creech at Craig's Close.

"It's a gay world all right. Gay and mad. Starved, dirty and stinking like a cesspool. Painted and powdered and hanging in rags. And a ploughman, because he's a poet, made the toast o' the Town. . ."

But while the Bard was talking to John Richmond (indeed long after they were stretched together on their chaff-packed mattress) many of the assembly gentry were drinking and wenching.

The Earl of Glencairn, Dalrymple of Orangefield, Harry Erskine, Henry MacKenzie, Sir James Hunter Blair, and others had been carried in sedan-chairs to Fortune's to finish the night's celebration.

The tavern had been warned in advance of their coming and was ready for them with platters of tasty food and plenty of drink—and bawds to hand.

The long low-roofed dining-room was given over to them. . .

A couple of hours later, too drunk to rise from his chair, Glencairn said: "Where's my poetic ploughman till I get him to sing for us?"

"Burns is awa' hame to his lodgings, Jamie," Dalrymple informed him.

"Awa' hame! That's—that's—— Send for him! Send for him—— You! MacKenzie! MacKenzie! Stop fiddling wi' that lass and go and fetch Burns. See here, cousin James, I maun hae Burns. Damnit, I'm his patron, amn't I? Ah weel . . . if I canna hae my ploughman-poet I maun hae my wench. Wha's got my wench?"

Beads of spirit were beginning to condense on the low roof. The stench was appalling. The Provost was lying sick in the corner; and a wench was trying to clean his waistcoat with a large napkin. At the same time she was feeling in his pockets for any loose change. . .

Only two candles had been left burning on the table. The light was so dim that it was hardly possible to distinguish who was in the room. . .

There was a dull thud on the floor and Henry MacKenzie slid off his chair taking his lass with him. Seeing that he was insensibly drunk and that she had already been through his pockets, she staggered to her feet and, clutching the table, made her unsteady way towards Glencairn. . . She put her arms round his neck.

"Tak' me to bed," he mumbled. "Tak' me . . . to . . . bed." He buried his face between her naked breasts. "My plough-man-poet," he moaned in a thick drunken slobber: "my ploughman-poet's awa' and left me. . ."

Harry Erskine came staggering into the room oxtering

the Duke of Gordon. Both were very drunk. "Where is she?" demanded the Duke. Erskine, swaying on his feet, bleered round the room.

"There she's—wi' Jamie Cunningham. The best wench in the High Street. Come on—Jamie's ower drunk to bother wi' her. . . . Where did you leave Jane? Can you mind?"

"Ah . . . she'll be lying in some corner wi' the ploughman-poet."

"The ploughman-poet's in his bed sleeping. He left early. Damn you, Sandy, d'you want this wench or do ye no'?"

"No. . . I want nane o' Glencairn's. . . Come on, Harry— oot o' here. We'll tak' a chair to Baxters' Close. . . I ken a lass there . . . and we can lie till mornin'. . ."

"Is she young?"

"Fresh's a daisy—there's a dizzen o' them. Fresh's daisies and cheap."

The wench freed herself from Glencairn. He toppled sideways from his chair and sprawled on the floor.

She lurched towards the Duke of Gordon, tearing apart the remnants of her torn clothes.

The Duke staggered back and then, coming forward with a lurch that nearly upset Erskine, gave her a shove that sent her reeling backwards, screaming.

"Come on, Harry! Come ye to Baxters' Close and I'll show you wenches. . ."

The Bard got little sleep till the late hours of the morning. He had never heard such a noise from the bawds above him.

The Duchess of Gordon came to earth in a corner of Lucky Pringle's howff in the Buccleuch Street pend above which Mr. Nicol of the High School was sound asleep. Drunk though she was, Jane had all her wits about her—as had her companion, Captain Matthew Henderson.

"I wish I'd been twenty years younger, Matthew."

"You're as young as you feel, Jane."

"No . . . I'm forty, Matthew. And you're?"

"Fifty."

"A nice age for a man. . ."

"No' so nice an age as Burns is at—in the prime o' his life."

"God! but he's a handsome coarse beggar, Matthew."

"Coarse?"

"Aye, coarse as a bull or a stallion—but handsome, Matthew, in the same way. I ken he's a poet—— What do *you* ken aboot him?"

"I like the man, Jane—damnit, I thocht he stood head and shoulders above every other man at the Assembly."

"'Coorse he did—and he kent it."

"Think sae?"

"Yes, Matthew: he kens his worth—baith as man and poet. . . If he hadna been a ploughman and I had been ten years younger. . . Get mair gin, Matthew. . . I'm upset the nicht . . . you ken me."

"No. . . I admire you, Jane; and aey have. But I canna say that I ken you. . . Come on, Lucky, I ken we're keeping you oot o' bed. Fetch ben a bottle o' gin and ane o' whisky— and ye can gae till your bed."

"Aye . . . awa' to your bed, Mistress Pringle. Matthew and me winna steal ocht—or set the place on fire."

"Thank ye, your Leddyship—gie a rap ben when ye gan awa'."

"You've read his poetry?"

"Aye . . . wonderfu' stuff."

"A genius, Matthew—a genius that only a woman can understand. But a silly headstrong independent beggar for a' that. Pride and poverty'll mak' his bed gey sair to lie on."

"D'you think so, Jane? I think he's modest enough—and sensible too."

"He despises us, Matthew—he thinks we're gay and stupid."

"No, no: ye canna think that."

"Oh yes, I can. Robert Burns, the heaven-taught plough-man! No: he's prouder than Lucifer. Aye; but whoever marries him will be a lucky woman."

"Damnit, he seems to hae impressed you, Jane."

"You're a good man, Matthew—and very gallant to me. I can tell you what I wouldna tell anither living soul. Of all the men I've ever known that ploughman-poet . . . Well: as a poet he's a genius. As a man he's got something of the quality Adam had when he walked in the Garden of Eden. Oh! I'm getting poetical myself, Matthew——"

"You havena fallen in love wi' him, have you?"

"Puif! I'm a duchess and he's a ploughman! I micht overlook the fact that I am Duchess Gordon. But would he ever forget that he's a ploughman! You winna breathe a word of this, Matthew!"

"Jane: for a' the time I've kent you, you've never even given me a kiss."

"Oh, Matthew! I never suspected you had feelings that way."

"D'ye ken what I'm for doing when I've finished this bottle?"

"You're going under the table."

"Aye, and you wi' me, Jane. I'll tak' the taste o' Robert Burns oot o' your mouth."

"You'll do nothing o' the kind—you'll go out and fetch me a chair!"

"There's nae chairs at this time o' the morning—and you ken that."

"When I was the toast o' the Toon, Matthew, there were chairs whenever I lifted my pinkie. The Toon's changed. . . To think this is probably my last winter in Auld Reekie—and I have to meet Poet Burns . . . and walk hame on my ain feet. . . You could at least offer to carry me on your back, Matthew. . . Why didn't Burns stay . . .? I could talk to him now. I'd mak' his lugs burn and put him fidgin' fain even if I am forty. I've done it wi' younger men than him. . . Maybe if I'd been a milkmaid . . . He said he'd give me a dance—at a barn dance. Give *me* a dance, Matthew! Did you ever see the man I couldn't dance to his knees?"

"I never did, Jane."

"No. . . But maybe Burns could dance me to my knees. I . . . I believe he could, Matthew."

"Damnit, Jane, what's come over you? This is maist unlike you."

"You dinna ken me either, Matthew. You're the only man

in Edinburgh I'd trust. . . I believe I could tell you my life story, Matthew. And what I told you would never pass your lips."

"Weel . . . I hae some few points o' honour, Jane. I canna say I ever betrayed a confidence in my life."

"Aye . . . I ken that. There's no' a woman in the Toon but adores you, Matthew."

"Maybe they do, Jane. But if they do they bestow nane o' their favours on me."

"That's why they adore you, Matthew."

"Weel, to speak the truth, Jane, womanising's never had much appeal to me."

"I ken, Matthew. . . You were jilted?"

"Weel . . . I suppose I was—you've heard the story?"

"I've heard. . . I made a mistake too, Matthew. There was a fine lad I loved: the only lad I ever loved. I heard how he'd got killed abroad. Heart-broken, I married the Fourth Duke. . . That was a mistake, Matthew. He wasna killed, he cam' hame again. . . I'll tell you a great secret, Matthew——"

"You had twa bairns to him?"

"God in heaven, Matthew! Does everybody ken that?"

"Only me, Jane. You told me that one night. . . Ye mind we were in the Coffin at John Dowie's?"

"What else did I tell you, Matthew?"

"You told me that o' your six bairns not one o' them was to the Duke."

"Did I tell you that?"

"That and a lot mair I forget noo."

"I blether a lot when I get melancholy fu'."

"Ye shouldna drink gin."

"It's easy on the water-works, Matthew. And sometimes I like a good greet."

"Oh, you women . . . I'm afear'd I never kent the sex, Jane."

"That's how you got jilted. A man that kens the ways o' women never gets jilted—neither does a woman that kens the ways o' men."

"D'you think the ploughman-poet kens the ways o' the women?"

"Nane better that ever trod the planestanes o' Auld Reekie."

"I wadna hae thocht that, Jane. How d'ye arrive at a' this after five minutes on the Assembly floor wi' him?"

"I learned more about Robert Burns in that talk than I would gin I'd spent a nicht in bed wi' him. . . I learned a lot about mysel' too. . . But what was it he wrote, in one o' his poems? ' Aey keep something to yoursel' you scarce wad tell to ony?' I'm getting tired, Matthew—tired o' the men aboot the Toon. There's no' the gallants there were. . ."

And Jane, Duchess of Gordon, sighed a deep nostalgic gin-sodden sigh and rested her head on Captain Matthew Henderson's broad and gallant shoulder.

THE BARD AND THE BISHOP

Lord Monboddo's house at number thirteen Saint John Street, leading off the Canongate, was a good solid house furnished in good solid style. Here on most Friday evenings when Monboddo was in Town he gave a supper. This supper was something of an event. Not only was it given in what the host thought to be the manner of the Ancients—plain fare, good wine, old silver and flowers, herbs or leafy twigs scattered about the table—but he always managed to invite to his board some remarkable characters.

James Burnett was an eccentric; but he was an erudite one. And for all that he was a law lord and had an extensive estate in the North-east country, he was no snob. Provided a man had intelligence and could talk well and wittily (and listen quietly) he did not care what his social standing was. He even liked to entertain men who held political and religious views in opposition to his own—for the dialect of argument was as the breath of life to him, as he was assured it had been to the Ancients.

From the moment he had heard Robert Burns in argument with Henry MacKenzie and Hugh Blair he had taken to him. He was intrigued at the fact that this vigorous-minded outspoken young man was a poet and a ploughman. He dismissed as sentimental nonsense the thesis of MacKenzie that Burns was heaven-taught. What intrigued Burnett was that he had brilliant ideas of his own; and he was curious to know how he had come by these ideas.

He had ploughmen in his own employment on Monboddo estate. Many a time he had conversed with them (or rather had lectured to them) on a variety of topics. But he had to confess that the Aberdeenshire ploughmen in no way resembled this specimen from Ayrshire. Maybe there was something peculiar about Ayrshire. . .

But Monboddo got more than a surprise when he found out that Robert Burns was the son of William Burnes of the North-east—and that he had worked on his estate in days gone by.

"So . . . Mr. Burns, you are not pure Ayrshire after all! Your mother, yes. But a man takes his blood from his father. You are of good Aberdeenshire stock, my lad—and the North country men have good clear heads like the good clear air they breathe. I must tell my daughter. . ."

Elizabeth Burnett listened with patient attention to her aged parent. Occasionally she smiled to the Bard—her smile emphasising some point of special agreement.

He was highly susceptible to the smiles of a fair maid. And Miss Burnett not only smiled to him: she was solicitous of his comfort in every way.

"Do you find your chair to your comfort, Mr. Burns? Shall I fill up your glass . . ?"

"Madam!" he said at one moment when she was enquiring about his comfort: "believe me, madam, a whinstone by the roadside would be comfort itself in your presence."

"What's that?" cried Monboddo. "A stone seat, Burns? There again I'm persuaded that the Ancients preferred stone seats to the corroding comfort of the stuffed abominations so much in favour among this soft-spined generation. Stone seats—you have given me an idea. Eliza! remind me to have a word about this with old Smellie the next time he sups here. Smellie's father was a stonemason, Burns, and Smellie who kens something about maist things will like as no' ken something about stone seats. Noo I won'er . . ."

"Wouldn't they be heavy to move around, sir—apart from the obvious disadvantages?"

"Disadvantages! My dear Burns: all this generation can think about is disadvantages. It'll soon be a disadvantage for them to use their legs: syne it'll be a disadvantage for them to use their arms: syne the tongue: syne the brain. All our faculties are the better o' proper exercise; but folks noo-a-days seek for excuses to avoid these right an' proper exercises. But you, my lad, that's been born to the plough, you ken different. Aye; for when you were exercising yourself between the stilts you were exercising your mind too. The Ancients kent how a healthy mind and a healthy body went thegither. And this is where you hae the pass on thae puir bits o' toon scribblers that spend their days bent ower a desk or a tavern table."

"After a day at the plough, sir, I'd been gey glad the opportunity of either; and many a cold wet day I wad fain have changed the plough for the desk."

"Cold and wet? What are they, sir, but nature's whips for our lazy hides? Rain never did a man ony ill—barrin' he didna keep his bluid moving. And when folks had nae fires to sit roastin' themsel's at they had to move about damned smairt to keep themsel's warm. Aye, certes, they had that. . . What's that, Eliza? Oh aye. Aye . . . that's so. I hae a maist important visitor the nicht, Burns. A man that's anxious to meet ye. Aye; and you'll be glad to meet him. Bishop Geddes: a verra fine gentleman and the son o' a Banffshire crofter. Aye. A Roman Catholic—o' sorts. One time Bishop of Dunkeld. Of course a titular honour. Aye; and sometime rector o' the Scots College at Valladolid—in Spain. A most intelligent cleric. Maybe ower meikle brains for his Kirk. Oh, but Geddes'll be a great power in his Kirk yet. Rome'll no' see a man o' his abilities gan to waste. I trust, Burns, you're no' bigoted about the Romish persuasion?"

"I trust, sir, I am bigoted about no man's beliefs. And I have long ceased to judge a man by what beliefs he professes. I prefer to judge him on his own worth. And if he is a good honest man and does well by his fellows I care not what label he hangs round his neck. Aye: even though the label be atheist. It is the hypocrite, sir, I scorn—the man who acts against the creed he professes to believe in. I'll be delighted indeed to meet your friend the bishop as I have had little opportunity to observe the Romish mind in action."

"Well spoken, my lad—that's how I like to hear a man talk. We have mony narrow-minded bigots in our Presbyterian Kirk, Burns. Mony narrow bigots."

"I have suffered from them, sir—I know their kind only too well."

"Aye, weel—though mind, gin the Catholics had the upper hand I've nae doubt but ye'd find some gey fanatical bigots amang them. We hae the lesson o' the Inquisition as testimony to that. No' that we can preen oursel' ower meikle on that score. An' the way thae auld wives were burned at the stake for witches—shamefu', downright shamefu'. It's a terrible thing, Burns, when humans in a' their weakness and ignorance think that God's wisdom rests only in *their* Ark. . . Ah, but ye'll find my friend Geddes is nae bigot. . ."

And indeed the Bard had not been in conversation with Geddes for more than a few minutes before he recognised the soundness of Monboddo's estimate.

Geddes had a mild and benign exterior. He spoke softly; and there was a gentle caressing cadence in his voice. Yet for all this he spoke not humbly but with a firm authority that came from a deep inward conviction of his essential rectitude.

He eyed the Bard keenly.

"Forgive me, Mr. Burns, if I seem to scrutinise you too closely. I have read your poems. To say they have given me great pleasure is to say what is obvious. A man would need to be a dull clod not to enjoy them. But the fact is that I never met with an author who was more like his work than you are. As I sit here I realise you could have written not otherwise than you have done."

"Is that so strange, sir?"

"It shouldn't be. I have met with not a few of the great

writers gathered in London. But never yet have I fallen in with an author who resembled the picture I had drawn of him from a reading of his work. I had a picture of you—not so much in the physical sense as in the spiritual sense."

"I am not a very spiritual man, Father."

"What nonsense is this, my boy? Of course you are a spiritual man. You have a very fine spirit. What you mean perhaps is that you find yourself in rebellion against certain of the outward tenets of your faith—as reflected by your pastors. This much at least I have gathered from your book."

"I'm afraid I am."

"Ah well: let me confess, Mr. Burns, that I have some sympathy with you there. But come: we must not spend our time on theology——"

"But we could spend our time on a less profitable subject— and I have not hitherto had the pleasure of conversing with one of your faith. You mentioned orthodoxy: do you think orthodoxy in itself is to be admired?"

"In itself, yes. In the ideal state we would all be orthodox because we would all believe the same truths and all truth would be divine. But we are very far from living in an ideal state—not even our worthy host's Ancients experienced that pre-Christian uniformity of belief. There were orthodox and unorthodox among them. And so it must ever be—this is the burden of our earthly heritage. But orthodoxy *for* itself: that is a very different matter. Man loses the spirit and clings to the letter. He turns aside from revelation and clings to ritual. You, Mr. Burns, cling to revelation and care little for ritual—and I am much of your mind. And yet the poet and the preacher should have this in common: theirs is not so much to discover truth as to propound it, lead men to it, explain it to men. And in this the poet may be more successful than the preacher. He should be more skilled in the harmony of words—so that his words—and his truths—fall on the ears of mankind as a sweet music."

"All this I can appreciate, Father. But surely the poet— and the preacher—must have faith and be able to draw strength and inspiration from his faith. A preacher may echo the truths of his Church—a poet must echo—nay must give direct utterance to—the truths he finds within himself."

"Yes: the truths he *finds* within himself. But whence come such truths? From God—or from the echo of other men's thoughts in his own mind?"

"From nature's God come all truths—if a man can win himself free from the corruption of orthodoxy. All this, Father, I'm afraid must sound like heresy to you. But I must be honest with myself if I'm to be honest with you. It's difficult for me to accept as truth that which I have not experienced as truth in myself."

"And this is what has brought all heretics to the rack, the wheel and the stake! Yes: we have here one of the fundamental problems besetting mankind. The strength of orthodoxy—or conformity—is that it is—or should be—a collective strength: its wisdom should not be the wisdom of the individual but the wisdom of mankind—the sum total as it were of the universal revelation of God. Yes: that is indeed its strength and my Church places great reliance on that strength. But the danger of conformity is that it can too easily harden into dogma and empty ritual. The rebel on the other hand, especially the individual rebel of high spiritual quality, may be capable of revealing afresh to men the divine purpose. My Church recognises this in the recognition it gives to gifted sons by canonisation into the sainthood. You, my dear Burns, are a true poet and therefore a true rebel. And it is because I feel your rebellion is essentially on the side of the angels that I find your verses so appealing. But you are also a lay poet. So you must not be surprised if secular society seeks to excommunicate you."

"You are certainly the first cleric I have ever known who could argue with such elegant common sense, Father; but I am in no danger of excommunication from society since I have never and can never be a member of the gentry. My society is that of the common people of Scotland. They may excommunicate me: they may reject me: only they have that power. But as long as I speak their language and give voice to their sentiments I think I can be sure of my ground."

"Ah, the voice of the people! Beware, my dear Burns, of danger here. You are not the voice of the people: you are the voice of your own conscience, your own will, your own inward necessity. The common people can be very cruel in their blindness."

"I know my people, Father. My thoughts may not be their thoughts; but their thoughts are mine. It could not be otherwise. I eat as they eat, live as they live, toil as they toil: when they hunger I hunger; when they are cold I am cold. I am of them, bone of their bone, flesh of their flesh. And even as I share their virtues I share their vices, their loves and their hates. In so far as I am a poet, in so far as I have gifts that they have not, then in so far am I privileged—but privileged to give expression to their hopes and fears and aspirations. It cannot be otherwise since I have no ambition to be other than of them to the end of my days. As I said to Lord Monboddo the other day when we were discussing the Greek and Latin tongues: I have at my disposal but the tongue of my fathers, the language of the common people of Scotland. And this is the only tongue in which I can speak."

"No. . . Even now you don't speak the language of the people—you speak the language of scholarship—the language that pays no attention to social boundaries. I myself am the son of a peasant and was brought up in the peasant's shed. But I neither think nor speak as a peasant though I understand—and appreciate—their thoughts and speech. And I think our worthy host will support me in this."

Monboddo clacked furiously with his tongue. "A more interesting and edifying conversation I havena listened to this while back. I'm loth to interrupt it. About poets I ken little and for the subtleties o' theology I care less. But then we hae here a maist extraornar poet and a maist extraornar theologian. And I flatter mysel' that mine's the only table in Edinburgh whaur a conversation like this could tak' place. You said Doctor Gregory's coming later, Geddes? It's a pity he wasna forward. This talk wad dae him a lot o' guid. But . . . ahem . . . if I'm to give learned counsel's opinion I maun state that I canna accept the premises either o' ye hae advanced wi' sic skill—and—eh—eloquence. For, ye see, a' things hae a history: they hae a beginning; and hence they hae a development. A' history begins in ancient times. And the first important development in man's history begins wi' his learning to speak. Aye; but what garred him learn to speak? The need to communicate his thoughts! Simple thoughts at first to answer simple needs. And syne the needs became mair complex and sae the thought became mair complex. . . .

". . . now what Burns here, as poet, seeks to convey is the thought in his brain—and he wants that thought understood by the folk he understands. Had he been brought up familiar wi' the Latin tongue he wad hae socht to express his thoughts in that tongue since the best o' mankind has been doing that since the Ancients perfected that language. That's the reason why Burns writes in the Scotch dialect."

"And why doesn't he speak it?"

"Oh, he can speak it fine. The fact that he learned guid English is but an accident though it proves his great mental ability. Noo you, Geddes, are a scholar first and a theologian afterwards. A' the sources o' learning are open to you. Noo, for the scholar, learning is the goal o' a' activity. A simple priest may be like a simple ploughman—the one may hae nae mair learning nor the tither. Ah, but you're a bishop, Geddes. An' a' bishops are learned men and scholars—whatever their piety or otherwise. It's no' essentially a bishop's job to be pious—he's there to see that piety is guided on the right lines —as his learning has taught him. Shake your head as ye like, Geddes—what I'm saying's the historical truth."

"The only historical truth is God's truth."

"Sophistry, Geddes. The Almighty works through history —the Almighty, in a way, *is* history. Eh . . . did you want to say something, Burns?"

"Only this. I think scholars and clergymen are too apt to be on familiar terms wi' the deity—and a long-faced familiarity at that."

Geddes laughed; but Monboddo thought the interjection irrelevant.

"No, no, James—Burns has the right of it. We *are* too

solemn; and we *are* too familiar with the mysteries of creation. Laughter restores sanity—and a sense of humility."

Monboddo performed some high-speed clacking. "Mysteries of creation, ha! Investigate, investigate—and the mysteries disappear. Aye; but mystery is half the craft of the clergy. . . ."

Robert Burns was intensely interested. This was conversation after his own heart. It was glorious to be in the company of men whose minds were vigorous and adventuresome. He could go on all night listening and arguing. He had been told that Monboddo was an eccentric. Maybe he was; but the man possessed a lot of shrewd sense for all that. He was unfortunate in that he lacked any sense of humour.

John Geddes was a very different type of man. Geddes had the lively intelligence that is founded on humour, and the deep elemental seriousness that is the base of all humour that is not cruel and senseless mockery. If he was truly a Popish divine then he put all the Presbyterian representatives he had met completely out of countenance. His cast of mind was utterly at variance with that of Father Auld. Auld was never in doubt, never uncertain of his doctrine. Geddes might not have doubts of any fundamental kind; but at least he was prepared to admit that doubt was possible—and that those who doubted were not necessarily heading straight for hell. Or at least he was prepared to give an opponent the benefit of his unbelief.

Tolerance and kindliness were hall-marked on the man. Erudition sat easily on his shoulders. His speech was soft and sought not to offend by an intolerant righteousness.

What the Bard did not realise was that John Geddes had long held a position of authority in Valladolid in a stronghold of his faith where no challenge had to be encountered from without. In this atmosphere Geddes had acquired grace and poise and assurance. There was nothing of the martyr about John Geddes. As a shepherd he was prepared to lead and guide a flock: he was not prepared to identify himself with them. This measure of detachment—as Monboddo correctly assessed —was the detachment of the scholar-divine rather than the divine scholar.

The Bard was disappointed when Professor Gregory was shown in and Elizabeth Burnett announced that the supper was served.

James Gregory, who was professor of the Institutes of Medicine at the University although he was still in his sunny thirties, was a very different type of man from any of the Edinburgh literati he had met.

Gregory was an Aberdeen man (here he had affinities with Monboddo and Geddes); and the quality of intellectual conceit was marked on his features. He carried his head slightly back so that his straight if rather prominent nose seemed tip-tilted. His voice was inclined to harshness for he was in the habit of rasping out his lectures without much ceremony—indeed he was but biding his time till old Doctor Cullen retired and he assumed the chair on the Practice of Physic.

But James Gregory did not think that his intellectual range should be confined to medicine. He was not afraid to pronounce judgment on any topic that came before his attention. To give him his due Gregory was no fool: he possessed great intellectual faculties and his judgments were often based on sound native common sense. But he was young in experience and arrogant in his tone to those he thought beneath him. He had heard of the ploughman-poet; but any real knowledge of his poetry he had obtained by second-hand means—and in conversation with his friend Geddes.

He had not come earlier because he had thought the evening would be dull—and he had no intention of showing deference to a ploughman merely because he had written a few verses.

The first thing that surprised him about the ploughman-poet was his appearance. The Bard rose and shook hands with him on introduction; and in that moment of introduction Gregory realised that he was meeting a man who would at least hold his own in any company.

"Let me say, Mr. Burns, right at the outset, that I havena read your poems—I canna tell whether they merit the praise they've gotten or no'."

"And do you think, sir, you would be in a position to tell if you had read them? I am not, you see, in the position to tell whether your judgment of poetry would merit *my* attention."

"Oh, nae offence, Mr. Burns."

"And none taken, Doctor Gregory. Believe me, we might as well understand each other in this matter. There is no compulsion on any man to read my verses and I would not have it any other way."

Geddes took the Bard by the arm and led him to the table.

"Gregory is a professor, my dear Burns—a professor of everything under the sun. And, except on medicine, he dispenses his advice gratis. But he's a good man for all that when you get used to his conceits."

"Ah, damn it—I didna think a ploughman wad be sae sensitive."

"Now, now, James," urged Geddes: "Robert here has put you nicely in your place—so you might as well put a good face on it."

Across the table Elizabeth Burnett smiled at him. He relaxed immediately.

"The fault is mine. Of course a ploughman has no feelings and precious little brains. I sit at your feet, Professor."

James Gregory drew down his brows while at the same time managing to tilt his nose a portion nearer the ceiling.

But most of this was lost on Monboddo who was eyeing the table to see that everything was in order. He was anxious that both the Bishop and the Bard should be suitably impressed with the way he observed the practices of his beloved Ancients.

But the Bard was not impressed: he was merely curious. But he accepted a boiled egg from Elizabeth Burnett as if it had been a rarity he had never seen.

"Now, sir," said Monboddo, "tak' a boiled egg! There's a dish for you supplied by nature—complete in itself—and packed with honest nourishment. Where's your French chef and fiddle-faddle who could concoct a dish to equal it?"

"Ah, yes, Monboddo—but the French cooks we see over here are poor examples of their nation's cooking. The honest French and Spanish cooks are masters of many fine dishes."

"If folks wad eat mair honest food there wad be less need for me to prescribe my purging mixture."

Elizabeth screwed up her face; but Gregory, undeterred, launched out on a panegyric on the merits of purging in general and the merits of his purge in particular.

But the worthy Monboddo was not to be bested: he too had his sure and certain specifics and was able to relate them to the Ancients.

The Bard made no contribution to the subject. His anger at Gregory had vanished and his interest in purging was negligible. But he was interested in Elizabeth and he watched her closely. He would much rather they had conversed on a topic upon which she could have entered. Instead he had to content himself with odd snatches of commonplace remark.

And then, with a suddenness that startled him, Gregory lost all interest in his purging powder and said: "And now, Mr. Burns, what think you o' Edinburgh?"

"As a town, Doctor Gregory, I am unable to think of anything finer. But then I have not travelled."

"But you like it?"

"I do."

"And what about the folk you have met?"

"I have met with marked kindness and attention—far beyond my merit, I'm afraid."

"Ah, dinna be ower modest, sir: dinna be ower modest. Folk tak' you at your own valuation. And what about the ladies? A' poets are admirers o' the fair sex, are they no'?"

"Well, sir, there are many opinions on that score—and we need not enter upon them here. But I welcome the opportunity of stating my opinion that Miss Elizabeth here outshines the ladies of Edinburgh for every female virtue I can think of. . ."

Monboddo's face softened and his daughter blushed; and before either Geddes or Gregory could say a word Monboddo rose to the occasion.

"Noo that was verra nice o' you to say that, Burns—for I ken you mean it. Aye, and father though I be, it's only me kens how richt ye are."

"I hope, sir, to have the opportunity soon of paying my respects to Miss Elizabeth in a set of verses."

"There now, Eliza—that's a handsome tribute to you. Aye; and one the Ancients wad hae appreciated."

"Oh, I have done nothing to merit a poem, Mr. Burns."

Geddes said: "I know I can speak for Doctor Gregory, Elizabeth, when I say that Robert Burns will have in you a source of inspiration that could not possibly fail him—or fail to bring forth his sweetest and purest notes."

"Thank you, Father."

"Well, Eliza, if Mr. Burns writes a poem in your honour, I'll promise to mak' him give me a copy o' it—and I'll wear it next my heart." Gregory said this with conviction.

"Gentlemen," said Monboddo, much moved (for he doted on his daughter), "you have brought comfort to my grey hairs. Without my daughter's ministrations and companionship my life would be gey dreich. And in paying her thae compliments ye hae gladdened my heart. Eliza, my dear, fill up the beakers and we'll drink a toast."

Bishop Geddes and Professor Gregory lived in Saint John Street. The Bard bade them goodnight in the wind-swept darkness. They had promised to meet again round Monboddo's table.

Gregory reached out for his hand. "Damnit: shake hands, Burns. I did you an injustice—but I hope you'll bear me no grudge for that. And if there's onything I can dae for you—just come down and chap on my door: I'll consider it a pleasure. Good luck to you."

"You're very kind, Doctor——"

"No, damnit—begging your pardon, Father—I'm no' kind—that's half my trouble. But I've learned a lesson the nicht I'll no' forget in a hurry. And mind me wi' a copy o' your verses on Eliza Burnett."

And as he trudged home the Bard began to try over some verses in his mind. But the words refused to clink. His mind refused to leave the rut of stilted English prose.

There was no passion in his regard for Elizabeth Burnett—only admiration and much gratitude. She was not of the flesh and blood of his world. She was angelic: she belonged to another world. And he began to doubt if his muse could follow her there.

But if he did manage a set of tolerable verses Bishop Geddes would be the first judge of their merit. On such a theme there could be no appeal from the judgment of such a remarkable man.

HENRY MACKENZIE'S VERDICT

The following morning, Saturday, the ninth of December, he obtained his copy of *The Lounger* from Creech.

"There you are, Robert—and you can't say Henry MacKenzie hasn't given you a lift. Oh aye: he means every word o' it. You heard him yoursel'; but you'll find it interesting—aye, stimulating—to read it all in print. I thought it excellent in manuscript; but it's wonderful how print improves on a manuscript."

"I'll take another two copies to send to my friends in Ayrshire."

"Certainly, Robert: they'll be very proud to have it. . . I understand you were supping with Lord Monboddo last night. And Bishop Geddes and Doctor Gregory! How did you find them?"

"I found them most kind—and most interesting. Do you think, perhaps, that a set of complimentary verses on Miss Burnett might go into my new edition—if we have a new edition?"

Creech's eyes shifted cunningly.

"You are on dangerous ground, Robert. Very dangerous ground. . . Of course——"

"I had intended that Bishop Geddes would be the judge as to the propriety of my verses should I write them."

"Geddes . . .? No: Henry MacKenzie or Doctor Blair must constitute your appeal in all such matters. Father Geddes is somewhat out of touch with the sentiment of the Town now-a-days. But I would be discreet about any verses that involve any members of our society. I've already told you—

one false step and the prospect of a second edition may be ruined."

"Yes; but I cannot conceive that what I might write concerning Miss Burnett would endanger my edition. I have nothing but the most solemn and sincere admiration for Miss Burnett."

"Naturally, Robert: she is a very fine as well as a very handsome young woman. But if MacKenzie and Blair approve then I shall raise no objection."

Considerably depressed, he set off to keep his appointment for a midday bite with John Richmond in Forrester's Wynd. Richmond was not in the best of spirits either.

"Would you care to read what Henry MacKenzie says about my poems in The Lounger, Jock?"

Richmond raised his eyebrows. "Oh: so MacKenzie has put you in The Lounger, has he!" He took his copy at the opened page. He looked the review over. "Give you plenty o' space, Rab. What does he say . . .?"

Having read the review while waiting for Richmond, the Bard contented himself with watching the expression on his friend's face.

At first Richmond read with a puzzled frown. Then he said: "This man's a bluidy snob: 'What uncommon penetration and sagacity this heaven-taught ploughman, from his humble and unlettered station, has looked upon men and manners!' He must think you came out o' Poosie Nancie's howff. 'Humble and unlettered station!' No: I find that difficult to thole, Rab."

"Go on, go on, Jock! There's more to follow."

"There is! 'Against some passages of these last-mentioned poems it has been objected that they breathe a spirit of libertinism and irreligion.' I wonder who's objected? Oh, this has all been discussed and thought out before it was set in print. They've had a committee sitting on this for six months. Libertinism and irreligion! I'm willing to lay a wager that after the committee o' the literati wrote that they adjourned to some low brothel and got drunk. Imagine onybody prating about libertinism and irreligion in Edinburgh! If they'd

Daddy Auld in the High Kirk o' Saint Giles they'd ken a'
aboot it. Are you for taking this and saying nothing?"

"Read on!"

"Aye . . . of course—tries to blame it on the ignorant folks
in the country. That gives him a handy back-door. No: he
comes back again (and you think highly o' Henry MacKenzie!):
'In this, as in other respects it must be allowed that there are
exceptional parts of the volume he has given to the public
which caution would have suppressed or correction struck out;
but poets are seldom cautious, and our poet had, alas! no
friends or companions from whom correction could be
obtained.' (What about Robert Aiken and John Ballantine in
Ayr—what about Gavin Hamilton and Dr. John MacKenzie?)
'When we reflect on his rank in life, the habits to which he
must have been subject, and the society in which he must
have mixed' (There's more than Wee Smith and me libelled
here!) 'we regret, perhaps, more than wonder that delicacy
should be so often offended in perusing a volume in which
there is so much to interest and to please us!'

"Now listen, Rab. There were times when I thought that
you went over the score a bit . . . you ken fine what I mean.
But never in what you wrote out for Wilson to print. The
hypocrisy o' this stinks worse than the stinks o' Edinburgh.
What! Everybody in the Toon kens that MacKenzie mixes wi'
a' the low-life cock-fighting riff-raff such as Poosie Nancie
wouldna let lie on her midden. Cock-fighting, mark you; and
it's only the dregs that go in for that. What is it he says again
—'delicacy should be so often offended.' The Man of Feeling!
He used to be a hero o' yours—that's what tickles me. Wait
till I finish.

"'To repair the wrongs of suffering or neglected merit;
to call forth genius from the obscurity to which it had pined
indignant, and place it where it may profit and delight the
world—these are the exertions which give to wealth an enviable
superiority, to greatness and to patronage a laudable pride.'"

Richmond threw *The Lounger* on the table. His face was
white with anger.

In the past Richmond had ever been inclined to caution and

to canniness. He had never championed the Bard with the spirited fire that had always burned in James Smith. But not even Smith could have denounced MacKenzie as vehemently as did John Richmond.

"Has this damned condescending fiddle-faddle got under your skin, Rab?"

"I'm grateful for your defence, Jock; grateful for the friendship that prompts it. No: it hasna got under my skin. I think I know the minds of the literati—at least I have some little experience of them. And I had some more experience wi' Creech this morning. No . . . MacKenzie means well—and he praises highly—very highly—for MacKenzie! He kens nothing about Ayrshire, kens nothing about you or me or Gavin Hamilton or John MacKenzie. He thinks we're nothing but ignorant rustics. Weel, let him think. After all I'm a gey poor rustic, Jock. Not a penny to my name. Naturally men like MacKenzie think that they are the only folks who have read a book. I admit that bit's hard to thole. I suppose they are hypocrites . . . but they just couldna understand, Jock. We might as well be savages from Africa. So I'm a heaven-taught ploughman! That gives *me* a back-door. It saves me tedious explanations—explanations that wouldna be believed onyway. So I'll just play Henry MacKenzie and his like at their own game. You see, Jock: at bottom they mean well—generously well—as long as it's clearly understood that learning and taste and delicacy are their province."

"You think I havena had to suffer this in my own walk o' life since I came to Edinburgh? Ah, but then there's nothing heaven-taught about me—I give no enviable superiority to greatness. I've to write corns on my fingers. Listen, Rab: if this review will do you ony good then forget what I've said. Aye . . . I suppose it will help you. I suppose I should be congratulating you on a piece o' good fortune—and if it is good fortune you ken you have my good wishes. But I'm a better man than Henry MacKenzie ony day o' the week—and a better judge o' poetry—and *I'm* no' fit to buckle *your* shoon."

"Don't worry over me, Jock. I'll get back to my plough

one o' these days—and you'll win back to Machlin. And we'll look back and laugh at the whole bluidy lot o' them."

"I hope so, Rab. What would you and I no' give to be sitting in Pigeon Johnnie's back-room the nicht?"

"At least, Jock, if we canna be back in Machlin, we can get a measure o' Kilbagie."

"That's an inspiration, Rab. To hell wi' economy for once!"

THE OFFER OF PATRICK MILLER

"Sit doon, Mr. Burns, sit doon! Dinna stand on ony ceremony wi' me. It was verra kind o' you to come over and see me. . . Of course you ken why I sent for you?"

"No . . . but the fact that you wanted to see me was sufficient——"

"You ken my brother?"

"You mean the Lord Justice Clerk?"

"Sir Thomas Miller, President o' the Court o' Session, nae less. Of Barskimming and Glenlee. You ken Barskimming weel enough."

"More than well, Mr. Miller."

"I've no doubt you poached the ground mony a time."

"Not in that sense, sir. I was never that kind of poacher."

"Oh . . .? Are there other kinds? Weel, weel: we'll let that flea stick to the wa'. Aye: I'm interested in you, Mr. Burns. I'm a man o' many interests, I may say. Director o' the Bank o' Scotland—though dinna you think that because I sit on the Board there along wi' Henry Dundas that I'm ane o' his kept men. Na, na! And I'm in the chair o' the Carron Company. . . But I'm mair interested in the Ayrshire ploughman. I've heard plenty about you since you cam' to Edinburgh—a' to your credit, Mr. Burns. And though I havena had the good fortune to read your Kilmarnock volume I've read what Henry MacKenzie has to say in The Lounger. . .

"But poetry's a fickle business, Mr. Burns, as you nae doubt ken. There's nae siller intilt—is there?"

"I have hopes that there will be enough to cover my Edinburgh expenses and see me safely back to the plough. I'm not looking for any fortune."

"Aye, weel: you'll no' be disappointed. So you intend to resume the plough? You hae nae foolish thochts about setting yoursel' up in a literary way about the Toon?"

"I had thought, Mr. Miller, that I might try my hand at the Excise."

"In what way?"

"As a common gauger."

"A common gauger! Hae you nae ambitions?"

"To secure for myself an appointment that will give me a steady income, however small, in return for my labours is ambition enough for a man whose only talent is for verse-making."

"Na, na, na! Na, na, Burns: you maun cast aside ony notion o' being a common gauger. Before you were a poet you were a ploughman. Aye; and you're a wee ower modest about your ploughing. I understand you're a tenant-farmer?"

"In partnership with my brother. But a poor tenant-farmer has to plough harder than any ploughman hired by the term."

"Exactly so. But you ken plenty about farming—that's the point?"

"Well——"

"And you ken nothing about Excise work. Now I've been haeing a word wi' Willie Creech and Jamie Sibbald o' the Edinburgh Magazine—aye, and twa-three others—and they think—though this is for your private lug—that you micht turn a bawbee or two on your Edinburgh edition. Noo I wadna like to see you dissipate the bit pickle o' siller that micht be accruing to you. You maun hae a plan. A plan: there's nothing beats a plan. What money comes to you you should lay out in the stocking o' a tidy bit farm."

The Bard shook his head slowly—very slowly. Patrick Miller eyed him keenly. And it was a keen eye that glinted under his bushy grey eyebrows. He had come to the point quicker than he had anticipated and he began to fear that he had come to the point too soon: he didn't like the way Burns shook his head.

The previous year he had bought the broken-down estate of Dalswinton near Dumfries. He was planning to let out some of the land and have it broken into good farms. It was work for strong young men who were intelligent and ambitious. Patrick Miller knew that such men were not to be had merely by raising the hand. His head spun with ideas and inventions. He belied in many ways his coarse exterior, the harsh tone of his utterance, his long nose, his gross flabby cheeks and his cruel cod-like mouth.

He was in many ways a self-made man; but essentially he was an amalgam of idea and action. He had made money— so much money that he could afford to experiment in practice with his ideas.

The ploughman-poet was an idea to him. He liked the idea of a ploughman who wrote poetry—this represented a pleasant and judicious unity of idea and action. Such a man might make an excellent experimental farmer—and Patrick Miller was as full of ideas about agricultural improvement as he was about money-lending, iron-smelting or naval architecture.

But the ploughman-poet interested him in another sense. Money in itself was of little interest to him. What he could do with money was what mattered. And there was no reason why his money should not buy him the ploughman-poet. It would be but another of the many feathers in his cap if he could get him away from the Edinburgh drawing-rooms and place him on his estate.

And no reason why it shouldn't prove a good investment as well—Burns would make money out of his poems and he would make money out of Burns.

Aye; but he would need to move cautiously. This poet was no fool with a pale face and a wild-staring eye. He had an eye that defied analysis, an expression that could not be read at a glance and a cast of mind that suffered little from illusion.

"Oh, I dinna ask you to mak' up your mind on the spot, Burns. Far from it. After all you ken your own mind best.

It was just that I have lately bought the Dumfries estate o' Dalswinton. There's some grand holm ground about it on the banks o' the Nith. I intend to big a wheen new farm-steadings, drain and enclose—and let out to good men at verra advantageous terms. Aye—and seeing you are who you are, Burns, I half thocht o' letting you have the opportunity of doing yoursel' some permanent good."

"Your kindness is overwhelming, Mr. Miller: I wouldna like you to think I was without interest in your project. But I—and my father before me—have had a good deal of farming misfortune. We have always suffered the lack of the necessary capital sum to tide us over bad times and to develop our resources. This has meant that we have had to farm poor hilly ground——"

"And use the old-time methods. What's the farmer's greatest worry, Burns?"

"That he may fail to gather a sufficient harvest for the winter."

"Exactly! Fodder for his beasts in the winter. Do you ken ocht about fiorin grass?"

"No: I never heard of it."

"You will some day. My, Burns: you're wasting your time in Edinburgh. Good agricultural land: that's the kind o' ground should be under your feet. . . Ah weel: I've some business that will hae to be attended to afore I get to my bed, Burns. Another glass? Afore you go! We'll keep in touch. Are you ever doon about Dumfries?"

"I have never had the occasion, Mr. Miller."

"Weel, if you think o' looking round there, tak' a look at Dalswinton. Let me ken aforehand and I'll fix things wi' Cunningham my factor to show you the ground."

"You must understand, Mr. Miller, that I can in no way commit myself to the thought of a farm——"

"Unless you mak' a hantle o' yella Geordies wi' this book Creech'll bring oot. That's understood, Burns—I'm only trying to help you in a practical way."

"And for that, sir, I stand very humbly in your debt."

"It's nothing, my boy—nothing to Patrick Miller. And

stand your ground: you're doing weel—so far. And dinna let yoursel' be run into debt. There's plenty when they hear o' your success will be offering you a bit loan here and a bit loan there."

"Perhaps, sir, I value my independence more than I value good opinion. And having known poverty all my life it's hardly to be expected that I'll become a spendthrift now."

Patrick Miller saw him to the door of his fine house and let him out onto Nicolson's Square that stood back-to-back with Alison's Square in the Potterrow.

They shook hands warmly.

Patrick Miller went back to his fireside in a ruminative mood. He liked the Bard. He hadn't unbent much. He had stood on his dignity, polite and reserved to the end. Patrick Miller liked that. He jingled some coins in his pocket and edged a lump of coal into the fire with the point of his broad-toed shoe.

Poverty? A damnable thing poverty—especially for a man with the independent pride of Robert Burns. Damnit, what was ten guineas? He'd paid twenty-five thousand pounds for Dalswinton Estate! To a man like Burns ten guineas would be a fortune. Jamie Sibbald! That was the man: he would leave ten guineas with him to-morrow to pass on to Burns. Sibbald would know how to handle him without wounding his pride. Damnit, but a likely-like farmer to have about Dalswinton. A young farmer in the pride o' his years—and one with a poetical pedigree.

Patrick Miller stuck this feather in his cap and poured himself a generous drink. He would take the ploughman-poet from under their noses.

The Bard wandered slowly down Nicolson Street towards the Cowgate. He was flattered at the attention Patrick Miller had shown him. But though he was flattered he was far from elated.

So much hung in the balance. The *Roselle* still lay at Leith waiting for Jamaica. Creech was still dithering about issuing the prospectus for the second edition. His money would not

last much longer; and he could not face going back to Mossgiel. . . . There was no certainty anywhere. And there was no
certainty about a farm. There was no sweetness in the thought
of Mount Oliphant, Lochlea or Mossgiel. It was obvious the
man was no farmer and had only the haziest theoretical notions
about farming. It was obvious that he had plenty of money
and it was obvious that, like so many of his kind, he had been
seized with the fever of agricultural "improving"—based on
English experiments. But there were few districts in Scotland
where modern English methods yielded any prospect of
success. . .

No: he wanted above all to escape from the soil, from the
worry and slavery of farming life. The prospect of paying
rent to Patrick Miller rather than Gavin Hamilton offered no
allure. A common gauger *was* below his worth—he knew that
a damned sight better than Patrick Miller Esquire.

But there was certainty about the Excise: security there did
not hang on the weather and the quality of seed. And it would
give him the leisure—when his work was done—to apply
himself to his books and his verses.

The more he thought of the Excise the more he liked it—
and the less appealing was the thought of a farm.

LETTERS TO AYR

The Bard had never been able to forget a kindness.
Gratitude was one of his virtues which he often carried to
the point of over-gratitude. But certainly he owed much to
John Ballantine and Bob Aiken and Willie Chalmers in Ayr.

To Ballantine he wrote:

My Honoured Friend,
I would not write you till I could have it in my power
to give you some account of myself and my matters, which
by the bye is often no easy task. I arrived here on Tuesday was
se'ennight, and have suffered ever since I came to town with

a miserable headache and stomach complaint; but am now a good deal better. I have found a worthy, warm friend in Mr. Dalrymple of Orangefield who introduced me to Lord Glencairn, a man whose worth and brotherly kindness to me I shall remember when time will be no more. By his interest it is passed in the Caledonian hunt, and entered in their books, that they are all to take each a Copy of the second Edition, for which they are to pay one guinea. I have been introduced to a good many of the noblesse, but my avowed Patrons and Patronesses are, the Duchess of Gordon—the Countess of Glencairn, with my Lord and Lady Betty—the Dean of Faculty—Sir John Whitefoord. I have likewise warm friends among the Literati, Professors Stewart, Blair, Greenfield, and Mr. MacKenzie the Man of Feeling. An unknown hand left ten guineas for the Ayrshire Bard in Mr. Sibbald's hand, which I got. I since have discovered my generous unknown friend to be Patrick Miller, Esq., brother to the Justice Clerk; and drank a glass of claret with him by invitation at his own house yesternight. I am nearly agreed with Creech to print my book; and, I suppose, I will begin on Monday. I will send a subscription bill or two next post; when I intend writing my first, kind Patron Mr. Aiken. I saw his son to-day, and he is very well.

Dugald Stewart and some of my learned friends put me in the periodical paper called *The Lounger*, a copy of which I here enclose you. I was, Sir, when I was first honoured with your notice, too obscure, now I tremble lest I should be ruined by being dragged too suddenly into the glare of polite and learned observation. I shall certainly, my ever-honoured Patron, write you an account of my every step; and better health and more spirits may enable me to make it something better than this stupid, matter-of-fact epistle.

I have the honour to be, good Sir,

Your ever grateful humble Servant. . .

To Aiken he wrote:

Dear Patron of my Virgin Muse,
    I wrote Mr. Ballantine at large all my operations and

'eventful story' since I came to town. I have found in Mr. Creech, who is my agent forsooth, and Mr. Smellie who is to be my Printer, that honour and goodness of heart which I always expect in Mr. Aiken's friends. Mr. Dalrymple of Orangefield I shall ever remember; my Lord Glencairn I shall ever pray for. The Maker of Man has great honour in the workmanship of his Lordship's heart. May he find that patronage and protection in his guardian angel that I have found in him! His Lordship has sent a parcel of subscription bills to the Marquis of Graham with downright orders to get them filled up with all the first Scottish names about Court. He has likewise wrote to the Duke of Montague and is about to write to the Duke of Portland for their Graces' interest in behalf of the Scotch Bard's Subscription.

You will very probably think, my honoured friend, that a hint about the mischievous nature of intoxicated vanity may not be unseasonable, but, alas! you are wide of the mark. Various concurring circumstances have raised my fame as a Poet to a height which I am absolutely certain I have not merits to support; and I look down on the future as I would into the bottomless pit.

You shall have one or two more bills when I have an opportunity of a Carrier.

I am ever with sincerest gratitude, honoured Sir,

> Your most devoted humble servant. . .

SUBSTITUTES

He had seen her several times as he came and went to John Dowie's howff in Libberton's Wynd for a bite of food or a caup of ale. She had attracted him by her intense, almost splendid physical vigour. She was maid to two of the less-consequential members of the nobility who dwelt in a tenement at the corner of Libberton's Wynd and the Cowgate. She was tired of sleeping on her shake-down under the kitchen table. When the two old maids went early to bed it could be lonely enough; and it was a far cry from the Cowgate to the small clachan in Glen Nevis. Ten years ago, as a bare-footed Highland lass of fifteen years, she had tramped from the foot of the Great Glen with her uncle who, on his discharge from the army, was taking up a post with the Edinburgh City Guard. Ten years ago: her uncle was dead and she had never had a stocking on her legs yet. . .

She had had lovers for she was a comely lass. But who wanted a poor skivvy for a wife unless someone as poor as herself: someone who was desperate for an unpaid servant? She might come to that; but not yet. At twenty-five she was not desperate. . . There was plenty of red blood in her and she had a healthy lust for life. Morality, she had found, was something the gentry liked to hear preached about as long as they hadn't to practise it. . .

She was pleased when Robert Burns spoke to her. He was a gentleman and had a right to ask questions. But he was not too much of a gentleman; and in spite of his gentility he seemed a kindly good-natured fellow. There could be no harm in seeing him. If she didn't like him she knew what to do. The old maids went to bed at eight o'clock: provided he promised to come sober, the door would be off the sneck at nine o'clock.

It was an honest enough arrangement. She was a fine strapping wench and as honest as they came in Edinburgh. He was wearied with the gentry, wearied with their endless senseless chatter and empty pomposities. Not yet had he found male company in which he could relax and be comfortably at his ease. John Richmond was a good fellow; but he had his limitations. . .

Her name was Margaret Cameron. He called her Peggy for it was a favourite name with him. He told her a pack of lies. But they were romantic lies, lies that soothed his mind and fed her hungry fancy. She knew they were lies; but she was honest enough to pretend otherwise.

Had circumstances been different, they might have come to love each other. Though they grew fond of each other, the barrier of circumstance remained. There was a terrible strength to his passion; but he was always gentle and tender; and the hour with him on the shake-down mattress in front of the kitchen fire was the sweetest she was ever to know, and far sweeter than ever she had dreamed might be possible.

She came to know that he was Robert Burns the ploughman-poet; and she was proud that she had become his mistress. She could accept his poetry: she refused to accept his ploughing. He was too fine in the grain and too deep in his knowledge to be a ploughman; and he was too generous with his money. . .

She was never to know how much she meant to him: never to know how she saved him from the debauchery of the Town life.

She reminded him of Mary Campbell; but she was even more Highland than Mary; and, though her English was fair, she never ceased to attend the Erse chapel. All her instinctive thinking was done in Gaelic. She was more robust than Mary though she had few of her intellectual and spiritual qualities.

He kept the secret of Peggy and did not mention her to John Richmond. Maybe at last he was learning to be discreet. . .

It was to Peggy he could talk freely and without restraint. He did not talk about things that were beyond her understanding. He seldom talked about things he felt deeply. But he had never been able to cultivate silence with his love-making.

Even if the old maids did not sleep soundly, they were protected by their deafness; and as the door from the kitchen was barred from the inside, the lovers could not be taken by surprise.

Sometimes he talked romantically to Peggy, making love to her with words she understood, words that clothed the emotional bareness of their relationship. Sometimes he questioned her about her life: her life in the Highlands, her life in the city, her life as a servant, her life in the Highland community of the Town: her life in relation to other men: her life in relation to her prospects, her hopes and her ambitions. . .

He found that she was not without friends. She knew many other Highland servants. During harvest many of her kinsmen came down from the Great Glen to work with the farmers.

Here was a Highland life that was new and strange to him, though he had known Highland shearers in Ayrshire.

More and more she enjoyed her furtive meetings with him. Not only for the profound passion he stirred and so deeply satisfied but also for the quality of his human companionship.

She knew she could not be his wife. She did not wish to become his wife. Perhaps he had a wife already. She gave such thoughts only a superficial consideration.

She knew him as a strange man, kind-hearted, good-natured and curiously, if richly, satisfying to know. He owed her nothing; but she felt she owed him much. He seemed to give so much more than he received.

"You needna be worrying about me for I ken how to be looking after mysel'," she had reassured him.

His reply had worried her for a moment. "Just as well for you, Peggy lass, for it seems that I have a genius for paternity."

Christina Laurie and her minister-student brother Archibald lived in Shakespeare Square adjacent to the Theatre Royal. Children of the Loudon manse at Newmilns, they had met the Bard under their father's roof shortly after the publication of the Kilmarnock edition.

Christie had reached her twenty-first year and hoped to marry Alexander Wilson, the Glasgow bookseller, in the spring. Meantime she was keeping an eye on her brother and putting the finishing touches on her social education. She played the piano well and sang sweetly.

Christie knew the Bard was passionately fond of music—she had discovered that at Newmilns. Now that he was becoming the talk of the Town she wanted to see him again.

There could be no harm in that. He was a family friend: she was his countrywoman. She sent her brother, as ambassador, to seek him out.

Archie came back elated. He had seen the Bard in his unpretentious lodging up the dark and nasty Baxters' Close. But, pinned above the mantelshelf, he had seen the sheet of paper on which the Bard's engagements were listed. It was an impressive list, noting appointments to breakfast or to sup with half the nobility of the Town.

Christie was a handsome young lass. Perfectly mannered in accordance with the boarding-school code of the day, and superficially Anglicised, she was a gay heady passionate virgin.

The Bard came to Shakespeare Square, drank tea, talked of Gray and Collins, Beattie and Shenstone with Christie and her companion the staid Miss Irvin, and enjoyed the hour of ease and relaxation.

Christie played and sang and he was delighted. He agreed to accompany their party to the Saint Cecilia's Hall concerts and to the Theatre.

True, his heart beat the faster for the passion that simmered beneath Christie's politeness; but it was fine to sit in the snug well-furnished room at a good fire and talk of the West country.

Christie, attentive to the animation and cadence of his voice and watching the glint and glow of his great eyes, was strangely stirred and fascinated. She struggled hard not to betray herself.

In the bare brutality of Baxters' Close the Bard pondered the problem of Christie Laurie. He knew he was not in love with her: he knew she was not in love with him. But he knew he was by no means averse to physical contact and guessed that she was avid for it. If she did not distract him she intrigued him more than was good for his peace of mind.

Christie Laurie favoured the bare-shouldered low-cut gown of fashion. Her tight corseting upthrust her full breasts and she displayed more of her bosom than the Bard thought fitting —for he had the peasant's aversion to artificial aids to physical allure. But he would not have thought her indecent if she had stood naked on her bare feet.

As she fingered the tune he had asked her on the keyboard, she became conscious of the waves of his physical presence. Her fingers faltered. A deep flush spread over her fine features and dyed the paleness of her bosom.

Involuntarily he placed a hand on her bare shoulder. The contact sent shivering spasms through her.

She rose from the stool with a sudden movement. Her head was bowed and she turned to him. In a second his arm was strong round her waist. She flung her head backwards, their eyes fused in a smouldering flash; and in the instant their lips pressed together.

But only for an instant. Christie freed herself and was gone from the room with the alarm of a frightened doe.

The Bard cursed, snatched his coat from a chair-back and made rapidly for Bayle's Tavern in the Square.

Archibald Laurie met him in front of the house and turned with him into Bayle's.

He noticed that the glass shook in the Bard's trembling hand.

"You and Christie had words, Robert?"

"Words? No . . . no words, Archie."

"Your hand's trembling."

"A poet's hand may tremble whiles—without visible cause."

"You ken—Christie's—in—love wi' you?"

"What put that nonsense into your head?"

"She thinks she can do onything wi' you."

"And that I can do nothing wi' her? A lass like Christie doesna ken her own mind five minutes."

"Maybe she'd be better married."

"Maybe, Archie. You've gotten an auld head on your young shoulders: drink up!"

"I ken Christie a' richt."

"No: you think you do. The man's no' born yet that can fathom the mystery o' a woman's mind. But since you think Christie has silly notions in her head about me—maybe I'd better stay away for a while."

After taking his leave of young Laurie in Bayle's he could not go back immediately to Baxters' Close: he was too agitated. What an impetuous fool he had been! She might blab—and then the fat would be in the fire. His skin burned to the roots of his hair when he thought of the possibility of her father and mother getting any hint of his conduct. And he had still to answer her father's letter. What stupid bitches even the best of women could be at times. Christie had known what she was doing—just as he had known he was in danger of falling in love with her.

But she might not blab. Women rarely did—unless there was a third party. Then they would blacken you out of all recognition.

He would need to take a hold of himself—anchor himself with Peggy Cameron. Elegant manners and boarding-school politeness did not go with love-making—not as he understood it. But then honest lassies like Peggy didn't get the opportunity to play the piano: they had to scrub floors and peel tatties and carry water and empty slops. . .

Maybe it would be prudent if he wrote Christie a polite prudent note. My dear Christie. . . My dear Miss Laurie. . . No: too formal. My dear Countrywoman. . . Right! But what to say? If he took Jock Richmond's advice he would say nothing. Jock was set against putting pen to paper where a woman was concerned.

But he would need to think of some way of patching things up with Christie—and writing a letter might be the best way.

That night, slightly drunk, Archie said to his sister: "What went wrong wi' Robert and you?"

"What did Robert say went wrong?"

Lacking in guile, Archie answered truthfully: "He didna say onything went wrang. But *I* think something did."

Christie laughed nervously. "Oh you wise men! Of course nothing could go wrong between Robert and me. It was—just that I had a headache."

"Oh! I think he must hae had one too."

"Why yes: he often complains of headache—and *you'll* have one too in the morning."

The Bard stripped and got under the blankets with Peggy

Cameron. He seemed to shed his worries with his clothes—especially the worry of Christie Laurie.

Snuggling into him, Peggy said: "And whatna gentry hae you been seeing the day, sir?"

"You're desperate keen to hear about the gentry, Peggy. Why do they interest you?"

"Och, I hear plenty of gossip about yourself and the same gentry. Isna the whole Toon talking about you?"

"And what do they say?"

"They say you must be a verra clever ploughman."

"Well . . . they could say worse than that."

"Och, some say now that it was a Doctor Blacklock that wrote your poems for you."

"That's good, Peggy. I must tell that to the Doctor when I see him."

"And would the Doctor not be wanting to ken who told you?"

"Gossip never had a Christian name, Peggy. The worthy Doctor will know that as well as me."

"And some are saying that as like as no' you'll be sleeping wi' the Duchess o' Gordon—and a wheen mair o' their leddy-ships."

"Do they think I'm a stallion—and their ladyships but a stable o' brood mares?"

"Some o' the coorse weemin think there must be something aboot you that has naething to do wi' your verses. . . Och, but you ken, sir, I wadna be fyling my tongue wi' the things thae coorse weemin wad be saying."

"I like you for that, Peggy: that's the decent Highland upbringing you had. But are you never tempted to tell them what you ken?"

"And lose my position wi' the auld leddies here? I'd be biting oot my tongue first."

"But what d'you think they would say if they kent you and me were lying bare scud ablow the blankets?"

"Och they wouldna believe me—and you couldna blame them."

"No . . . I don't suppose I could. . ."

"Are you in a talking mood the nicht, sir?"

"I'm aey ready for a blether, Peggy. You're a good lass—as honest as daylight and twice as real. You've good tasty plump flesh on you—no' blown up wi' polite boarding-miss nonsense."

"You wad think you didna like the leddies."

"And I don't, Peggy. They're a sham—an illusion."

"Did you ever lie wi' the Duchess o' Gordon, sir—or ony o' the quality leddies!"

"God bless you, Peggy! The Duchess of Gordon has had six o' a family."

"But could she no' hae anither six? My mother had fourteen."

"Maybe she could and maybe she couldna. But as far as I'm concerned, Peggy, she'll hae none o' mine. I'm a wee bit particular wha I bed wi'."

"But wad a duchess no' be different?"

"Would you rather I was a duke?"

"Och, I could hae bedded wi' a rotten auld duke afore noo—had I been minded. And ye ken brawly, sir, I wadna allow anither man the things I allow you. I like you, sir—and when ye like a body it's different."

"Aye, lass—that's a deep saying. If folk would only act on their likings it would be a better world."

"I managed a wee taste o' brandy for you: it's on the dresser: will I get it for you?"

"Lie still, lass. What's a drop o' brandy when I've got you to warm my blood? But thank you for minding. I'll have it afore I face the cold winds that'll be piercing down Libberton's Wynd."

"Aye: there's sense in that. You hae a lot o' sense aboot you, sir."

"You ken nocht about me, Peggy. D'you think I'd be lying here if I'd ony sense?"

"Oh—you could be lying mony a waur place, I'm thinking."

"No, no; I didna mean ony insult to you, my dear. If I'd sense I'd be trying to marry into one of the rich families."

"You'll maybe do that yet."

"No: I think not."

"And what would hinder you?"

"There's such a thing as independence, Peggy. A man or a woman should be free to go their ain gait—and say what they want to say—aye, and say it in their own way."

"That's you being a poet. Plain folks dinna think thae things."

"What! Do you tell me you hae nae thochts about independence?"

"Dinna be havering, sir: ye ken fine a servant-lass canna be independent. You need to be having money—and you need to be born and bred to be independent."

"I suppose the Forty-five knocked a lot of independent spirit out o' you Heilan' folk. Your fore-folks didna think like that— or act like that either. Would you not like to be married and have bairns and a house of your own—and be independent o' thae twa auld bedlam hags up the stair?"

"Aye, fine that, sir. But where now wad I get a husband that could get me a hoose and keep me sitting like a leddy?"

"But you'll marry some day in any case."

"Aye—when I see there's nae betterment for me. I'm gey well off the now compared wi' a lot o' lassies I ken."

"Well, that's a form o' independence too, Peggy. But see and no' get married afore I leave Edinburgh. I dinna think I could thole it without you."

"And when d'ye think ye'll be for leaving the Toon, sir?"

"God alone kens that! But gin another month I may be able to win clear o' it."

"Ye'll no' be able to come here in the clear nichts, sir: I'll miss you then."

"Damn the clear nichts. Come on: they're a century away. Here and now time ticks awa' on well-oiled wheels. . ."

An hour later, as he climbed slowly and carefully up the middle of Libberton's Wynd, a drunken workman staggered out of a howff, and in a not-so-drunken voice sang to the world at large or the female companion whose arm was supportingly round his waist:

"Although the nicht be ne'er sae wet
  An' I were ne'er sae weary;
I'll lay thee ower the lea-rig
  Bonnie Anne, my dearie. . ."

The Bard slowed his pace that he might listen. God! Here in the dank evil-smelling mirk of an Edinburgh wynd was a queer place for a man to be singing *The Lea-Rig*. Aye, and a man who, by the stagger of his gait in a shaft of dim light, might have been a ploughman. . .

The pair lurched into an entry and were swallowed in the darkness: the singing ceased.

The Bard lowered his head and plodded steadily up the steep rough-cobbled wynd. And then the melody of *The Lea-Rig* slid quietly into the slow differently-accented strathspey that William Marshall had named in honour of Miss Admiral Gordon: the tune that always came into his mind whenever he thought of Jean Armour: the song she had crooned to him so sweetly under the shade of the green thorn tree.

And in the instant he was back again on the banks of the Ayr; and the mellow golden-green trance of the evening carried no heavier burden than the hum of bees and coo-cooing of a wood pigeon; and the nut-brown jig of a dozen may-flies was timed to a tune too soft for sound.

He groaned aloud in his agony. He would never know such bliss again, never tremble at the ecstasy of such a love. That love came to a man but once—and he was lucky if it came at all. A thousand women held in the arms for a thousand years could not weigh down those golden hours in the scales of experience.

A Christie Laurie was but the fragment of a memory out of the past—a fragment broken from the harmony of an image that had shattered from a blow of circumstance into the dust of morality. Out of the past, from the depths of his subconscious, he would clutch at such fragments of the image that had been. Even Highland Peggy was but such a fragment. She carried but a broken fragment of Jean Armour within her. It was deep within her—part of her essential unsophisticated womanhood. The fragment shone in Christie Laurie's eyes or sometimes trembled beneath her fingers on the ivory keys. Highland Peggy was an echo from the blood pulse: Christie Laurie was an echo from the refrain of a song.

Maybe someday he would find a lass who would carry the curve of the melody in her blood as Jean Armour had done before she herself had broken.

But maybe for him there was only one Jean Armour.

JAMES SIBBALD

It was Peter Hill who took the Bard over to Parliament Close and introduced him to the editor, bookseller and librarian, James Sibbald.

The Bard was at a loss to know why such a wide and spacious square, complete with an equestrian statue of Charles II, should be referred to as a close.

Peter Hill could not enlighten him. "I expect, Robert, that it would be a close at one time—I've never heard it referred to as ocht else but the Parliament Close—except sometimes the Parliament Yard."

In and around Parliament Close the diversity of life was intriguing; but then it stood within a circle (of some three hundred yards' circumference) that enclosed the Mercat Cross, the Luckenbooths, the Tolbooth, the Kirks of Saint Giles. . .

Parliament House stood in the west corner where once the Three Estates of Scottish government had deliberated and where now the highest law courts in the nation gave judgment.

But though the Close was famous for the law courts, it was also a hive of other activities. In the south-east corner was the General Post Office where postmaster Oliphant and his staff officiated. Adjacent to Parliament House was the Goldsmiths' Hall, which, apart from being a meeting place for the numerous corporation of goldsmiths, was also let as a meeting place for other bodies. Then there was the popular John's Coffee House (run by Mrs. Parlane)—a resort not so much frequented for the

nature of its refreshments as for the gossip of the day and the
latest intelligence from London and the South. Here, also,
James Sibbald had his well-known and equally well patronised
lending library (the bulk of it had been Allan Ramsay's) and
John Bell, William Gordon and Charles Elliot had their
bookshops.

But indeed the Close was infested with a wide variety of
petty merchants who erected small booths against any wall
or coign of vantage they could secure, and who managed to do
remarkable business.

Even within the precincts of Parliament House the
merchants had managed to secure lodging. And, apart from
the ubiquitous bookseller, coffee was brewed behind a booth
made of wooden strips and brown paper.

The Scottish Parliament, shamefully corrupted and shockingly unrepresentative, had been bribed into merging with the
English Parliament in 1707.

The odium of that unparalleled bribery enraged the Scottish
people at the time; and the stench had lingered in their nostrils
ever since.

"So that," said the Bard viewing the elegant Parliament
House, "is where we were bought and sold for English gold?"

"Well, I suppose we were, Robert—as they say, it was the
end o' an auld sang."

"An auld sang, eh? Glorious music to the Southron billies,
Peter. And they've been calling the tune and we've been paying
the piper ever since."

"And that—talking about English gold, Robert—is the
Goldsmiths' Hall—a bit of a meeting place now. There's an
incorporation o' the Goldsmiths for a' that—and maist influential too. That's why a' thae bits o' booths that are stuck
onto Saint Giles's at this end belong to the smiths and the
jewellers . . . do a roaring country trade in wedding rings and
bits o' knick-knackets."

"I see: my friend Richmond promised to show me the
interior of the Parliament House——"

"Well, you couldna get onybody better—though I thought
my Lord Monboddo, seeing he's a law lord, or Henry Erskine,

seeing he's Dean o' the Faculty o' Advocates, would have conducted you over the place."

"Oh, I havena presumed on their friendship to that extent, Peter. Between you and me, I have no great liking for the law —though I confess to having met wi' some lawyers who were excellent fellows in their own right. No: by God, I've no reason to have any affection for the law courts. My father was engaged in the maist damnably protracted litigation at Lochlea that brought him to his death-bed—aye; but that's a' past now. I mind o' one name from those days—Lord Braxfield. Do you ken ocht about him?"

"No' much. Mr. Robert MacQueen he was before he was raised to the Bench. A coarse violent-tempered man. They say he's the filthiest-tongued man in Edinburgh—of any class or condition. Only two things interest Lord Braxfield, law— and sculduddery poems and stories. I heard him once in Creech's shop. It was shocking to hear a man o' his position talking the way he did. Oh, and no' under his breath. Roaring out o' him like a bluidy bull. . ."

James Sibbald, for all his long years in the Capital, seemed as if he had lately stepped from between the stilts of the plough. His complexion was still that of the country-man— seemingly weather-beaten and vigorously red. Only his hands betrayed him: though not over-clean and with dirty finger nails, his flesh was soft and callous-free.

His speech had the burr of the Borders.

"Aye, Maister Burns—and how are ye liking the Toon? I got your letter—and verra nice too. Aye. . . Your edition wi' Creech coming forward to your pleasement?"

"I think so, Mr. Sibbald, I think so."

"You're a lucky man, Maister Burns: it's no' everybody that falls in wi' Creech's good graces. He'll make a job o' it . . . I've nae doubt."

"Yes . . . everybody's been maist kind, Mr. Sibbald—I owe so much to you for your goodness in printing——"

"Nothing, sir, nothing worth mentioning. You were news —and I was damned glad to get something worthwhile to fill up my space. It's me has to thank you. . . But what can I do for you the day?"

"Well . . . I would like to borrow Hugo Arnot's History of Edinburgh if I may."

"Certainly. Hugo Arnot! Aye: a good history Hugo's. Right up-to-date. How about Maitland's when you're at it? Of course Maitland's is no sae weel wrote as puir Hugo's. Pity ye never met Hugo Arnot. Heck, sir, but there was an oddity for you! Just a mere sparrow o' a man and that bad wi' asthma, he could hardly draw a breath on a windy day—and windy days are no' unheard o' in Edinburgh. Aye; but a grand writer and a great wit, a free-spirited and erudite wee sparrow was Hugo Arnot and wrote a thundering good history. Opinionated, though. Hugo had his ideas and wasna afraid to set them down—without fear or favour as the saying is. . . Are you specially interested in ony particular feature o' Edinburgh history, or do you just want to get a kind o' general historic view o' the Toon?"

"A general view first, I think, Mr. Sibbald. I am not entirely ignorant of the Toon's history—but I would like to know more of its buildings—and its places of interest. Even Parliament Close here—I find it maist interesting and yet there's little I ken about its history."

"Just so . . . just so. Oh weel, the Parliament Close has an interesting history. I'm not as well up in it as I should be maybe. . . Oh, but Hugo Arnot should be a great help to you, Mr. Burns, and if, after you've been through Arnot, you still feel there's something you'd like to ken—drap in and see me and I'll see what can be done for you."

"I'm greatly obliged to you, Mr. Sibbald."

"You can have the run o' my place here, Mr. Burns—any time you feel like it—don't stand on ony ceremony."

Peter Hill returned from looking over Sibbald's stock—there were a few items he wanted for himself.

"Well, then, Peter," said Sibbald, "how are you finding things wi' the great Mr. Creech?"

"We're just doing away, Mr. Sibbald—things have been falling off a little of late."

"Och aye—but Willie Creech hasna a' his eggs in the one basket—and if he's losing a penny the one road, he'll be making a pound the other."

VERDICTS

Mrs. Alison Cockburn, sitting snug in her flat in the dark grimness of Crichton Street in the South Town, heard all the gossip of the day—and of the night too. She was seventy-four now and not able to get about the narrow streets and steep closes. But she had her friends who moved in exalted circles who did not fail to keep her informed.

As the exalted circles were discussing the ploughman-poet it was only natural that Alison should be interested in the talk. Only her most intimate friends knew she had written a version of *The Flowers o' the Forest*. Alison had been a Border Rutherford and she had married a Cockburn of Ormiston. Doubly a lady, it was fitting that she should doubly guard against the vulgarity of her versifying being widely known.

But Alison, for all her age and her gentility, was no genteel dame withering away in social withdrawnness. She was totally unlike her sister versifier, Miss Jane Elliot, who frigidly gathered her sixty spinstered years about her in Brown Square. True, Miss Elliot's version of *The Flowers o' the Forest* was generally conceded to be the finer. But Jane, who was not only plain but downright ugly, was as haughtily highborn as she was ugly. Her tongue, for all her great gash of a mouth, was fearfully, awesomely Anglified—as she thought. Alison was as broad as Jane was prim. Her brogue was rich and couthy. Jane thought she had intellect: Alison knew she had shrewdness and wit. Jane sniffed at the vulgar manners of the modern age: everything was grist to Alison's mill. Her mind was as nimble as her nimble fingers on the knitting pins. The best wits of the older generation of men delighted to drink a dish of tea in her comfortable room—and the brightest and liveliest of the younger generation of society's young ladies delighted in her company. For Alison's wit was as broad as her tongue;

and she could regale the giggling misses with some rare bits of scandal.

So rare indeed was her zest for life and especially the gay busy life of the Town that her zest overflowed into her letters for she was as addicted to gossip with her quill as she was with her tongue. Even the great David Hume had not been ashamed to treasure her letters to him.

And so on the December evening she took pen and paper and wrote to the Reverend Robert Douglas of Galashiels:

"The town is at present agog with the Ploughman Poet, who receives adulation with native dignity, and is the very figure of his profession—strong, but coarse; yet has a most enthusiastic heart of love. He has seen Duchess Gordon, and all the gay world. His favourite, for looks and manners, is Bess Burnett—no bad judge indeed . . .! The man will spoil, if he can spoil; but he keeps his simple manners, and is quite sober. . ."

It was a shrewd estimate for an old woman who had not seen the Bard. It spoke well for the veracity of her informants.

But then, where Jane Elliot had written: "I've heard the lilting at our yowe's milking, lassies a' lilting before the break o' day; but now they are moaning on ilka green loaning—The Flowers o' the Forest are a' wede awa!"—Alison Rutherford had written: "I've seen the smiling of fortune's beguiling, I've felt its favours and found its decay; sweet was its blessing, kind its caressing—but now 'tis fled—fled far away." She could not but be intensely interested in the fortune that was smiling on the ploughman-poet. She had read some of his verses and they had moved her deeply.

But the fame of the ploughman-poet was spreading ever outwards from Edinburgh. The Reverend Alexander Carlyle, minister of the parish of Inveresk lying east outside the Town, had heard about the Bard. It is true that Alexander was little of a divine and very much a man of the world—and of letters. Like Alison Cockburn, though ten years younger, he was shrewd, witty and much given to the gossip of tongue and pen.

The minister drank deeply and laughed loudly with the best of the literati, the speculative eccentrics among the law lords, the dons of the University and the clerical dignitaries of the Kirk of Scotland. He was intimate with many noble families and was a staunch henchman of Dundas.

Though he did not write for publication, Jupiter, as he was known to his friends on account of his handsome bearing and appearance, wrote much for his private amusement. And his private journals, diaries, notes and sketches gave him genuine amusement for he had an etchy picturesque quill.

And so, in writing to his friend the Duchess of Buccleuch, he included his observations on the Bard.

"Nothing in the literary way has occupied Edinburgh for some weeks past so much as the poems of Robert Burns, an illiterate ploughman of Ayrshire. His poems are many of them extremely good, both those in Scots dialect and in English. He is thought to be equal, if not superior to Ramsay in original genius and humour. I am not certain of that. But he surpasses him in sensibility. We, you may believe, with the prejudices of the Scotch, are ready to believe that the productions of the milkwoman of Bristol are mere whey compared to Burns; and that the poems of Stephen Duck, the thresher, are but like chaff in comparison. Lord Glencairn is his patron. A new edition of his poems is printing. But I hear he has not been so advisable as to suppress some things that he was advised to suppress."

Before he was a man of God, Jupiter Carlyle liked to remember that he was a gentleman.

Andrew Dalzel, the Greek professor at the College, had none of Jupiter Carlyle's faults. He wrote, *inter alia*, to his friend Sir Robert Riston:

"We have got a poet in town just now, whom everybody is taking notice of—a ploughman from Ayrshire—a man of unquestionable genius, who has produced admirable verses, mostly in the Scottish dialect, though some of them are nearly in English. He is a fellow of strong common sense, and by his own industry has read a good deal of English, both prose and verse. The first edition of his poems was published at Kilmarnock, and sold in that part of the country very soon, insomuch that they are now not to be got. I, among others, have seen them, and admire some of them exceedingly. A new edition of them is now in the press here, and he is encouraged by a most numerous subscription. It is thought he will get some hundred pounds by it, which will enable him to take a small farm. He runs the risk, however, of being spoiled by the excessive attention paid him just now by persons of all ranks. Those who know him best, say he has too much good sense to allow himself to be spoiled. Everybody is fond of showing him everything here that the place furnishes. I saw him at an assembly t'other night. The Duchess of Gordon and other ladies of rank took notice of him there. He behaves wonderfully well; very independent in his sentiments, and has none of the *mauvaise honte* about him, though he is not forward."

Not only were the upper and middle classes discussing the Bard. In the socially inferior classes were many ardent readers of his verses—or such of them as had appeared in public prints. These were read and discussed with warmth and admiration. This new poet was a ploughman and this put him on a social footing with them—or maybe below them. But he was not one of the literati: he was not a gentleman: there was nothing of the gentry about him. Neither (which was what mattered) was there any genteel nonsense, social or literary, about his verses. Their appeal was immediate, direct, blazingly vivid. His verses did not require any critical dissertations to make them intelligible.

And so it came about that even as he was being discussed in the drawing-rooms, in the assemblies of the fashionable, and in the clubs, he was being pointed out in the streets and wynds and closes as the ploughman-poet. He became a figure of intense public interest. Folks who had never read a poem in their lives (and folks who couldn't read the alphabet) stopped to stare at him and whisper his name to each other. The street urchins got to know him and would shout after him or beg a coin from him.

He had to escape from the Landmarket, the High Street and the neighbouring closes before he could walk about in peace.

This overnight blaze of popular notice caused him some inconvenience—and some wonder. He knew that his verses had not circulated in any degree commensurate with this publicity. He felt it was not founded on any deep acknowledgement of his essential poetic virtues. Deep down he felt that this notoriety was as cheap as it was popular and that quick as it had blown up as quickly would it die.

But it would be in the interest of his second edition if he got it out before this wave of interest receded; and so he worked hard at the correction of his proofs in Smellie's office.

THE CADDIE'S ADVICE

One afternoon as he was emerging from Libberton's Wynd onto the High Street, the caddie, John Boyd, stopped him.

"I wonder, Mr. Burns sir, if I could hae the honour o' shaking you by the hand——"

"Oh! you're the caddie I met when I first came to Town?"

"That's me, sir. It wadna be ower great a liberty wad it, sir?"

The Bard extended his hand. "No, no: shake, my lad. I'm pleased to meet in wi' you again. You belong to an honest calling. What's your name?"

"Jock Boyd, sir. Thank you, sir. And I wish you a' the best. But ye ken, sir, caddies are no' what they were."

"Oh. . . And what's wrong wi' the caddies now?"

"Ah weel, sir, plenty are no' to be trusted—some o' the young anes. . . Mind ye, sir, I kent ye were nae ordinary ploughman that day I took ye up frae the Grassmarket."

"Aye . . . you're no' so slow either."

"I've read your poems, sir."

"You've read my poems, have you! I suppose you take a drink, Caddie?"

"Me, sir? Oh . . . weel . . . when I can afford it, Mr. Burns."

"Let's step into Mrs. MacPherson's in Gosford's Close here."

"I didna mean to presume, Mr. Burns."

"Dinna fash yoursel', Caddie—I'll do a' the presuming. . . So ye read my poems, did you?"

"I did that, sir. . . Ah weel, if you insist, sir, I'll hae a drap o' whisky wi' my ale. . . You're verra kind, sir. Ah, but a'bodies speak weel o' ye, sir."

"Do they?"

"Aye: that they do, sir. Oh, and they couldna do ither. I hear a' aboot ye, sir. The hale Toon kens aboot ye. Aye; and they a' hae the same guid word for ye. Well: here's my best respects to you, sir."

"Good health, Caddie—and long life to you."

"God bless you, sir."

"And which of my poems did you like best, Caddie?"

"There you hae me, Mr. Burns. I liked them a', sir. Maybe To a Mouse, sir, or The Twa Dogs. . . Ach, ye canna pick and choose, sir: they're a' guid. But—eh—is there onything I could dae for you, sir?"

"Well . . . and what could you do for me, Caddie?"

"I could put ye on to a fresh bawd or twa, sir."

"So you're a pimp as weel's a caddie?"

"Me, sir? Na, na, sir: dinna mistake me. It's juist that in the way o' my trade, sir, I've got to ken a' things."

"Aye, aye. . . But what makes you think I'd be interested in a bawd?"

"Nae offence, sir. But I mean. . . Weel, a guid fresh bawd's no' easy to come by in the Toon, sir. It was juist if you were interested. Mind ye: it's putting nothing in my pocket, sir. It was juist that I thocht. . ."

"I don't blame you—only I'm not interested in bawds."

"You'll no' think the worse o' me, sir, for mentioning it?"

"No: I don't think ony the worse o' you, Caddie."

"Ye see, sir, the gentlemen o' the Toon are aey on to me to direct them to ony fresh bit i' the Toon. Noo a guid caddie has to ken his business. And if I was to direct ony o' the gentlemen to a hoose or a bawd and he got the foul disorder—ye see whaur I'd be, sir . . . out o' a job. Mind ye, sir, you're the exception. Ye'd be surprised at the folk that come to me, sir—the clergy as weel. Ach, but since a' bodies are at it, what does it matter?"

"I think it matters a lot, Caddie. I'm no' preaching morality, and I'm no' setting mysel' up to be ony better than I am——"

"Listen, sir: believe me, you're better without them—if you can manage. But if you canna manage, then, sir, tak' my advice and watch your step. It's no' only the disorder you've got to watch: ye can be robbed too."

"Damn it, Caddie. You put a bad taste in my mouth—but I'm obliged for your good advice."

He had liked the caddie, had liked his clean sharp intelligence. Now he blotted the caddie from his mind even as he had tried to blot out the bawds. And yet he felt uncomfortable. He had received his sexual initiation from a bawd though she was an extraordinary bawd who took only love for payment. And what of Peggy Cameron? Maybe she wasn't a bawd; but maybe he was going a long way towards making a bawd of her.

If only Jean Armour had not turned against him. . .

With a vicious crack he brought his riding-crop across his booted leg. . .

CORPORAL TRIM'S HAT

Mrs. Carfrae entered the room and shut the door behind her.

"You'll excuse me, Mr. Burns; but that's a young leddy speiring for you. A Miss Laurie."

The Bard rose from his table where he was writing. He looked anxiously round the room.

"Oh, Miss Laurie! Show Miss Laurie in, Mistress Carfrae, like the good woman you are."

"I dinna approve o' young leddies visiting my boarders—unaccompanied."

"Now, now, Mistress: dinna wrong yourself. As you say, Miss Laurie is a lady. Indeed, she's the daughter of a very eminent clergyman in Ayrshire."

"A gey wheen o' thae shameless hizzies up the stair claim to be ministers' dochters too, Mr. Burns. I'll show her ben this time, though I canna be haeing a habit made o' it."

"That's a good woman—show the lady ben without more delay."

Christie Laurie came into the room in a high state of nervous excitement.

"Come in, Christie, come in! There's no' much o' a fire; but come in and make the best o' it."

"I brought you back your copy of Collins, Robert. I—I—— You never came back for it. . ."

"Tuts, Christie! I havena had time, what wi' one thing and another. But sit down . . . my dear."

"No . . . I darena, Robert. I shouldna have called on you alone. And I wouldna, except I had a call to make on Mr. Burline, the drawing master."

"Francis Burline o' the Close here? I see. Well . . . but you maun sit down and tell me your news—and what your news is from home."

"I got your letter, Robert. I'm sorry for what happened . . . I mean I'm sorry if I hurt your feelings. I wasna really angry, Robert."

"We'll say no more about that, Christie. 'Twas me was overbold. I forgot myself for the moment. I was falling in love wi' you, Christie. Oh, quite honestly and genuinely. . ."

"But you're cured now?"

"Cured?"

"You're in no danger now?"

"I'm aey in danger, Christie. And I'll aey be where you are concerned. Mind: I miss your playing. I couldna tell you how much I miss that. And I miss the bit hour's crack round your pleasant fireside wi' you and Miss Irvin."

"You never told Archie onything."

"Me? I never tell, Christie."

"Neither do I."

"There you are then!"

"But you said you wished to be with me ten minutes by myself. . ."

He drew his chair into the fire beside her, reached for her hand and held it.

"Yes, Christie Laurie: I wished to have ten minutes with you—by yourself. But I also wrote that I didna ken what I would say to you. . . My dear: I wanted to tell you how much I loved you and why I loved you and why I wished to make you happy. . . In a word, Christie, I wanted to blurt out all the usual lover's blethers—wi' this difference, that I would have meant every word I would have uttered. But that's bye, Christie my dear. You and me could never hae been lovers— you realise that now, don't you? Of course you do! But I mentioned the beaten way o' friendship. That's something that never passes, never alters . . . friendship! Now, now: I'm going to talk to you for ten solid minutes and you're no' going to get that wee red tongue o' yours in edgeways.

"You're betrothed to Mr. Wilson in Glasgow . . . I ken your father and your mother, your brother and your sisters. . . Now, just suppose that you and me had forgotten ourselves so far as to fall in love! You ken fine what that would hae meant sooner or later. I may believe in friendship—but I dinna believe in platonic *love*. And neither do you. Before long you would hae said farewell to more than your maidenhead. You micht hae enjoyed that and so micht I. But . . . what wad hae been the upshot? Suppose there had been a bairn. Would you hae married me—could I hae afforded to marry you? Would your family have allowed it? What would your brother and sisters have said? What would Mr. Wilson have said? What would Miss Irvin—what would Edinburgh and Ayrshire have said? It would hae meant ruination for you and me. . .

"Now what brocht you here this afternoon—Mr. Burline? No doubt . . . but something else as well. You're tempted, Christie—the same as I was tempted. You think you're in love wi' me—the same as I thocht I was in love wi' you. Hell, Christie, I'm still in love wi' you. Nothing easier in this world, my dear, than that you and me should lie down on the bed there. . . No' now; but if I hadna spoken the way I'm speaking. . .

"Now, Christie! you're itching to tell me that the thocht never entered your pretty boarding-school mind. Aye: that's only the superficial polish. You can polish away at the mind and the manners; but you canna polish away at the heart. Now I'll come back to Shakespeare Square and have tea wi' you and Miss Irvin as if nothing had happened. And you'll play to me and sing to me and pour me a dish o' tea . . . and I'll worship you as you've never been worshipped before! Now dinna think that I'm preening my fine feathers on being a fine fellow. If you dinna let me talk to you without interruption my blood'll maybe get the better o' me. . . I'll maybe forget the good folks at Saint Margaret's Hill—and Mr. Wilson. . .

"Ah, but dinna worry, Christie my dear: I can see I've talked you out o' a' danger: your blood's running cold in you. You want to withdraw your hand. You want to run away again. But no: you're going to get married in a few months. And we're going to be friends. God, lass: life's a queer thing; and men and women, when the blood runs hot atween them, are poor passion-swayed creatures. And by God, lass, I could hae loved you—and could love you yet. . .

"Now what are you crying for? Because I've talked brutally to you? You ken I havena talked brutally to you. You're crying, lass, because you're happy—happy that we didna make ony mistake that we would hae rued a' our lives. . ."

He freed her hand. She rose, searched for her piece of cambric and dabbed her eyes. He rose and took her in his arms.

"Dinna hold back the tears, Christie. Cry them out—and wash away the memory o' what micht hae been. And never say a word either now or hereafter. And pay no attention to what I'm saying to you. Maybe I'm beginning to blether. . . God damnit, Christie, I'm no' beyond greeting myself, if it comes to that. . .

"You and me's going back to Shakespeare Square thegither —it'll be dark in ten minutes and naebody'll see us. And what would it matter if they did?"

Christie quivered in his arms. But her sobbing had ceased. Her head still on his shoulder she said:

"Oh, what kind o' woman must you think me, Robert? Miss Irvin's across at Miss Baird's the dressmaker at the Bowhead. She'll be waiting for me now. I dinna want to let her ken I've been crying. Oh, Robert . . . I feel so ashamed o' myself. Dinna think bad o' me."

"Come on! Tidy yoursel' up. There's a wee bit shard o' a mirror that we use for shaving. I'll put a licht to the candle. D'you want the licht?"

But for answer she put her arms round him and held up her mouth. They kissed; and it was a long passionate kiss. His hands went over her body. Their blood leapt and sang. . .

The Bard freed himself and, seizing the candle, held the wick to the fire.

"Come on! Tidy yourself up! Quick now! Can you see?" He placed the lighted candle so that it shone on the mirror.

"You're fine, Christie! Miss Irvin'll notice nothing. Now come on! I'll see you across to the Bowhead. Right then: I'll convoy you to the head o' the Close. Let me see you? Touch up that curl. There now! Fine!"

"And you dinna think bad o' me, Robert?"

"For Godsake, lass, let's get to hell out of here."

"Maybe we should get married, Robert. Oh, God! Robert —but I do love you."

Her face that was still a young virginal face carried in its appeal the long-stoked fire of virginal passion. It was a look as old as the legend of Eve. It was the look that comes in a virgin's eyes when she no longer delays and dissembles but begs to be taken and deflowered regardless of any consequences. It was the look that springs from biological necessity, when the craving to conceive crushes morality into a bloody pulp and treats the holiest vows as nought.

Only for a second did the Bard waver. He strode to the door, lifted his hat from the peg, opened the door wide and said in a high matter-of-fact voice:

"Thank you for the volume, Miss Laurie. . . And will you please tell your father when you write him. . ."

And as she passed him going into the dark lobby he gave her bottom a pat that was more eloquent than any words he could have uttered, and better calculated to break the physical-emotional spell between them than any other action.

BALLOON TYTLER

Smellie nodded his head.

"You see that man there, Robert? Him like a bluidy scare-craw withouten a crown till his hat and his auld bachles o' cod-mouthed shoon? That's Balloon Tytler. By God, sir, and that's a character for you! Mad's a hatter—or he'd be the cleverest man in the world—aye, the cleverest man o' a' time."

"Him that went up in the hame-made balloon?"

"He didna go far, puir beggar! Aye; but he took on the Encyclopædia Britannica after me. Wrote on every bluidy thing that onybody ever thocht o' and a lot mair besides. Would you like to meet him? Mind you: he's gyte . . . but you'll get a guid laugh oot o' him if he's in form. I'll introduce you and leave you wi' him. Come doon and let me ken how you get on, afterhand."

There was certainly a mad glint in Tytler's eyes. He was poorly clad and dirty. His thin face was grey with under-nourishment as well as dirt. His black worsted stockings hung loose and wrinkled round his pathetically thin shanks.

"Aye, aye . . . so you're the poet Burns. The Ayrshire ploughman. Hoo're ye getting on? Liking the Toon? Bringing oot a new edition? Creech! Aye. Caledonian Hunt. . . Talk o' the Town. Aye. Poet mysel'—no' as guid as you. Aye, aye. Turn my hand to onything. I could write your life ower a glass o' ale. Ony time you like—if Creech would pay for it! Take's a poet to write the life o' a poet. Ploughman-poet. Toast o' the Town. Certainly, Mr. Burns, certainly: tak' a cappie ale onytime. Rich poet to a poor poet."

Tytler rubbed his long sharp nose with the back of his hand and then wiped his hand on the seat of his breeches.

They adjourned to Dawney Douglas's.

"Would you like a platter o' something, Mr. Tytler?"

"Aye, aye—onything tasty. The skirl o' the pan. Some days I dinna fash wi' eating. Nothing to bluidy eat—aha!"

He had a high-pitched maniacal broken-off laugh. It exploded whenever he wanted to underline a point.

"Here, Dawney: like a guid man! Bring Mr. Tytler the best you have. Now make it good, Dawney, for Mr. Tytler hasna eaten for a week."

"Decent o' ye, Mr. Burns. Ye'll be making plenty money?"

"Enough to provide you wi' a good meal, Mr. Tytler."

"Canna return the hospitality, Mr. Burns."

"Tuts, man—what's a meal atween bards?"

"'Xactly! 'Xactly! Atween bards—aha!"

"I'd like to see some of your poetry."

"Aye, aye. I work in ony style or metre. Oh, juist for my ain amusement."

"I'll warrant you get a lot o' fun out o' life."

"No! No fun. Leave fun to the idiots. Too much to read: too much to write. Experiments! Tak's a lot o' time— experiments. Chemistry—verra interesting."

"I heard you played the Irish bagpipe."

"Play yoursel'? No? A grand instrument—proper scale. Italian stuff—rubbish! Artificial. Tralalalala lalala—aha! Constipate a cuddy."

"But quietly, gentlemen," said Dawney, putting a great platter of mince collops and a dish of potatoes on the table.

Tytler shovelled the steaming hot food onto the floor of his mouth, breathed out steam and a jumble of indistinguishable words. He had a fantastic method of eating. He held the spoon level with his eyes, shot out his lower jaw, dumped the food onto it and shot it back again. He seemed insensible to the hotness of the food. After a quick rumble round his mouth he shot his neck forward, swallowed and repeated the performance without a pause.

The plate cleaned, he shoved it aside and grabbed a potato in his dirty hand.

"Grand food, Mr. Burns, grand food. Like to hear me play on the pipes? Sing to ye too. Dance if ye like: ony bluidy thing. Write your life in ten days. A month and I'll make it twa volumes: octavo. Bound in leather—if Creech'll pay. Cheap and accurate. My fee: twa yella Geordies per volume—best elegant style."

"Could you take another platter o' collops, Mr. Tytler?"

"I wadna say no, Mr. Burns. It's a guid plan to lay by for a rainy day—when ye get the chance. And seeing there's sae mony rainy days and sic few chances—— Aha!"

The hot food and the ale were beginning to take the nervous staccato from Tytler's speech. The Bard realised with a shock that the man was ravenous. Strangely enough he was entirely without self-pity. Indeed he seemed to consider himself fortunate.

It wasn't till he had wolfed down his second helping of mince collops that he began to slow up sufficiently for the Bard to hold a moderately reasonable conversation with him.

Gradually he began to tell his life story—or such tracts of it as he deemed tellable.

He was a son of the manse and had received as good an education as possible. He had made two voyages to Greenland as a medical assistant. He had studied both for the ministry and for medicine. He had abandoned both and had married Miss Young, the Writer to the Signet's daughter. He had set up as an apothecary and had experimented in chemistry. Madly he went from one failure to another. His wife took their five children away from him. Then she died. Next he married a butcher's daughter. She lasted about four years and died. Then he married Miss Aitkenhead. . . At the moment he was living with her in Hastie's Close off Adam's Square, close to the South Bridge with their four-years old twin daughters. . . And he was only in his late thirties!

But if Tytler's domestic life had been varied and stormy, his literary and scientific life was no less so.

He had accomplished the first aerial ascent in Britain; he had invented a chemical bleach of first-rate importance; he had made a printing press of his own design and printed his own

W.G.W.   F pamphlets and papers. . . He was presently working on a mechanical device for ensuring perpetual motion. . .

He had expanded the *Encyclopædia Britannica* from three volumes to eight volumes—quarto! He had published a translation of the Eclogues of Virgil and a first volume of a *History of All Nations*! He was presently engaged, among many other things, in preparing *A System of Surgery*!

It was a story of mad erratic genius triumphing over every conceivable obstacle and the Bard evinced a great deal of admiration for him.

When he accompanied him to his hovel of a lodging in Hastie's Close he realised as never before just what town poverty could be.

The entry to his workshop was by a back court; and there under a dark stair was his sanctum. His wife and daughters occupied a living-room on the top of the building. It was an untidy mess of papers, books and pamphlets. A small window in the door was all the daylight it admitted. The room was unheated. But apparently Tytler did most of his cold-weather reading and writing in what served as a bed.

"Aye, aye: no' much o' a place, Mr. Burns; but I lived in worse when I took sanctuary in the Abbey when I was avoiding my creditors. . . Here: sit down on this tub—mony a guid article I've written on that, Mr. Burns, aha! Whaur's my pipes?"

He got down on his knees and fished under the bed. He drew them forth gingerly. The Bard eyed them with interest. They were different from the Scots pipe in that they were blown with an arm bellows, and the drones, tied to a common stock, lay over the left forearm and not on the shoulder.

Tytler sat on the bed and buckled the bellows-strap round his waist and worked for a moment vigorously with his right arm.

The pipes came alive like a hive of honey bees, sweet and mellow.

"They're in grand order—I was playing them the ither nicht. Tricky in the tuning until ye get acquaint wi' them."

The Bard watched him fascinated. His movements were

quick and deft as he tuned his drones, never a skirl and never a groan. And under his turning and twisting the bee-like droning became incredibly sweet and infinitely mellow.

He started off playing jigs. The puckish notes danced about the room. Tytler was transformed in his playing. His head was cocked to the side and the mad glint in his grey eyes faded and grew almost child-like with wonder.

The draught that came in at the open door was devilishly cold but the Bard did not mind it. Here was a man who had music in him, a man with mad-merry music quivering at his finger-tips. Suddenly the jig-playing ended in a shower of grace notes and with a deft twist to his drones he began to play a slow melancholy air which he informed the Bard afterwards was the *Lament for Black Donald of the Battles.* . . .

The darkness came early to Hastie's Close. But Tytler played on in the darkness, going from one old tune to another.

Then he stopped suddenly, undid the waist strap and placed the instrument on the bed.

"Bad for me to play too much—puts me off my work. Could play a' day and half the nicht. But I maun get on wi' my work."

The Bard rose stiffly from the upturned tub.

"And just what is your work, Mr. Tytler?"

"My work, Mr. Burns? I never discuss my work wi' onybody that's friendly wi' Henry Dundas."

"And what makes you think I'm friendly wi' Dundas?"

"Creech is publishing your book, isn't he?"

"Well?"

"And ye liked my playing didn't ye, Mr. Burns?"

"Yes, Mr. Tytler. It was a grand experience sitting listening to you. You're a great musician—although it's no' an instrument I'm particularly acquaint wi'. Maybe I can come back some other time and hear your songs?"

"Aey an open door here, Mr. Burns—aha! I hope to enjoy a platter o' mince collops wi' you some ither day. And noo, sir, if you'll excuse me, I'll see if I can get my leerie lit and get on wi' my work."

The Bard stumbled and groped his way out of Hastie's

Close. He regretted he had not won James Tytler's confidence. A madman—maybe. And maybe not. And maybe there wasn't a man in Scotland could hold a candle to him. He regretted he had not met his wife and daughters. It would have been interesting (and perhaps enlightening) to have talked to the woman who had become Tytler's third wife.

THE PORTRAIT PAINTER

Peter Hill looked relieved: "I've got it, Robert! Sandy Nasmyth's the man. He usually has a bite in Johnnie Dowie's in Libberton's Wynd. He'll maybe be there now. Will we go over and see?"

On the way to Dowie's Peter explained what he knew of Nasmyth.

"He's a first-class painter—either portrait or landscape: just came back frae Italy about two years ago. A sterling-good fellow into the bargain. A bit wild in his politics—I think the foreign influence would account for that. And I ken he likes your poetry—in fact he's one o' your admirers for he's often talked to me about you in the shop."

"And why didn't Creech commission him to do the portrait?"

"There's two good reasons for that, Robert. First, as you ken, Creech doesna like parting wi' his money. Second, Nasmyth hates the sight o' him."

"That as good as ends the matter, does it not?"

"No: I wouldna say that. No. . . Nasmyth's peculiar. But him and me get on fine thegither. If he's in a good mood you never ken what'll happen. He's a wee bit worried the noo. You see, his wife's expecting her first in aboot a month's time. The first one's aey a wee bit o' a worry. Some women take bad wi' it. . ."

By good fortune Nasmyth was sitting alone at a table eating a hot bite when they entered. Hill immediately effected the introduction. Nasmyth lost no time in ceremony.

"You'll sit down and join me in a bite, Mr. Burns? I've been looking forward to this. . . I maun paint you: right away: while the mood's on me! If I could get your eyes—catch that light in them. No' so easy. No . . . no' so easy. I'm enjoying a platter o' ribs here—I can recommend them heartily. Peter: away and chase up Jean to serve the table. Aye. . . I've read your poems—revelled in them. But I canna tell you about them just now—this is no' the place. But you'll let me paint you?"

"Strangely enough, Mr. Nasmyth, Creech wants my portrait so that it can be engraved that I may sit facing my title page—like other fools."

"And why didn't the creeping louse speak to *me* about it?"

But Peter Hill had returned and he took up the case.

"It's like this, Sandy. Creech wanted some cheap-jack picture to cost next to nothing. I don't think Robert's poems should go out without his picture. But Robert, of course, has nae money to pay for a commission——"

"Who the hell mentioned commission—d'you think I'm some bluidy huckster?"

"Easy, Sandy, easy. *I* mentioned to Robert that you *might* do the portrait since Creech is only handling the sale o' the book—Robert's bearing a' the expense himsel'."

"The stinking, sanctimonious, snivelling, smirking hypocrite! That's settled then, Mr. Burns—I'll paint you. Aye—and Jock Beugo'll do the engraving on the same terms as me. We'll no' see your edition stuck for want o' a picture o' you. Whaur are you biding? Baxters' Close! That's beside me. I bide in the next close—Wardrop's. That makes everything simple. You can jowk down and see me—or I can jowk up and see you—when the mood's on me—or maybe when the mood's on you. . . God damned! I'm sick and tired painting titled nobodies and wealthy everybodies. . . Of course, I've got to live. Sometimes you write a verse or two out of compliment, Mr. Burns?"

"Well . . . not as a rule, sir. The poetry of patronage does not flow easily. But where the heart's involved it's easy enough. I dinna live by my verses."

"Aye—and that's where you're fortunate. Me—I've no other means o' earning the salt for my kail."

"I should have thought that would be easy enough——"

"No, sir, nothing's easy in this Dundas-ridden country. And I take it you're no' a Dundas flunkey?"

"No: I never was a Dundas man—but I must confess I've seen little evidence of his hand in Edinburgh."

"You havena seen much then. The poisonous influence o' that man is everywhere. His henchmen occupy every position of authority in kirk and state, law, commerce and learning."

"Some of them seem to hide their allegiance very well."

"They do. Dundas doesna pick fools and idiots to do his dirty work. You understand what Dundas is after? Power, privilege and position. Dundas runs Scotland for Pitt—and plunders it for himself and his friends. But you kent that, Mr. Burns."

"Yes. . . But personally I haven't suffered from Dundas. After all, there are few pluckings off a poor poet."

"Aye—but you're nae poor poet. Your quill has a point to it a damned sight more dangerous nor a dagger. A satire or two aimed at the wrong target and you'll damned soon feel the power o' Dundas."

"As a matter of fact, some of the verses I had hoped to include in my Edinburgh edition have not found acceptance with the literati—but Dundas can hardly have anything to do with that."

"Don't be too sure. MacKenzie and Blair are his men even though Creech is only an errand boy for him."

"But Henry Erskine——"

"Erskine will no' go far. Dundas'll draw his halter damn short one of thae days—just whenever it suits him."

"Yes, I suppose he will. Actually, Mr. Nasmyth, I'm under no illusions concerning either Dundas or his henchmen—only I'm not so familiar with the politics o' Edinburgh as you are— and maybe I've been too busy and too much involved in meeting folks to get my bearings. Edinburgh's a big change from my native Ayrshire."

"Edinburgh's changing . . . and I'm no' sure that all the

changes are for the best. We're living in a time o' great change. Everything's on the move—for better or worse. But folks are wakening up and beginning to challenge the authority o' kings and priests. Our American brothers, wi' Washington at their head, hae shown us a grand example. And in France and Italy men are writing and thinking in a way they havena done for centuries. Aye, things are ripe for change, Mr. Burns— haud on a wee while and you'll see things beginning to move. Damnit, your verses show that. Frae beginning to end they breathe a spirit o' independence and a love for human liberty and human happiness that hasna been in Scotland since William Wallace. What surprises me is how you got a' this in your native Ayrshire. The West Country canna be sae corrupted as Edinburgh."

"Corrupted enough, I'm afraid. Otherwise I wouldna be here. Indeed, so corrupted has Scotland become that I'm looking for a job as a gauger."

"A gauger—in the name o' God! You'll need to aim higher than that, Mr. Burns. Mind you, I have never been able to understand how you ever were a ploughman—and certainly I canna see you ever going back to the plough. But a gauger...!

"What else is there for me?"

"And here you are—the greatest poet we've ever had and you ask what else is for you! But dinna get me angry—I was enjoying my platter o' ribs. . ."

DUNDAS AND BRAXFIELD

The Lords of the Council and Session (to give them their full title) were headed by the aged Lord President Robert Dundas of Arniston. The Lord President's country mansion lay in a pleasant estate—an easy ride to the east of the Town in the parish of Borthwick. Dundas was coming up in years and he did not pay the attention to affairs of state or of session that formerly he had done with such skill and cunning. He was content to hold on to his position as the head of the justiciary while his half-brother, Henry, ran the nation and his son, Robert, held the key post of Solicitor-General.

The Dundas family held the affairs of the Scottish nation in fealty to their English overlords—especially as their overlords were represented in the person of Premier William Pitt. But they were no fools so far as Pitt was concerned: hence they were no fools for themselves. As Premier Pitt had enough on his hands to worry about Scotland, he was content to give Dundas a pretty full rein—as long as he secured for him in Parliament the votes of the Scottish members.

In place of the corrupt politicians of 1707 came the equally corrupt Scottish lawyers whose high legal decisions were meted out according to bribery and family influence. Sometimes, according to the amount of bribe-money involved or the relative strength of family connections, the bench of judges were thrown into variance and the dust and heat of legal warfare would be felt far beyond the confines of Parliament House.

And sometimes, since all men are not corrupt all the time, comparatively insignificant cases were settled almost entirely on legal merit—or at least on the strength of what was thought to constitute legal merit.

And always Henry Dundas was in the background, all mighty, seeing that in no case in which his manifold interests were involved did a miscarriage of justice involve him in any unfavourable decision.

Some of the Lords of the Session were quaint oddities. But on one thing they were not odd: they approved of the Union —and the Dundas family. For this absence of oddity they were amply rewarded. And, being rewarded, they could indulge their oddities to their hearts' content.

Robert MacQueen, as Lord Braxfield, could take a chair from Fortune's Tavern to his house as drunk as any lord of whatever degree; and he could curse and swear and roar bawdy jokes and sexual obscenities to his heart's content as long as the Dundas interest was assured that they had not a more valiant and ruthless defender of their interests.

And as Thomas Miller of Barskimming was Lord Justice

Clerk, it did not greatly matter that he was almost in his dotage, since he could be depended on to put his signature to documents he had not the mental grasp to understand.

Islay Campbell, on the other hand, was a keenly alert and vigorous Lord Advocate; and when Henry Dundas paid him a visit to his private study in his grand house in Brown's Square, he knew that he would have one of the best brains at his disposal.

With the entire legal and administrative superstructure of the nation in their hands, the Dundas family could move exactly in whatever direction they desired. True, they had always the fear that those they bribed might themselves be bribing. But this fear was relatively small and only concerned personal cases as they came before the Courts. Still, even in this respect, Dundas did not like to think that any of his paid men might accumulate wealth by hidden means: he liked to have his agents securely in his own grasp and confined to his own favours. But the ordinary day-to-day business of the Courts had to go on with as little interruption as was desirable considering the merits of each particular case; and the tradition of bribery and corruption was much too firmly established for Dundas to break it, or, indeed, become fully cognisant of its underhand ramifications.

Naturally the ordinary citizen was almost entirely ignorant of the true state of affairs. But he did know that the law's delays were interminable and that, if he wanted a settlement to be expedited and with the possible chance of the decision going in his favour, he had to be prepared to pay his lawyer sums that were out of proportion to the merits of the case.

Lawyers (and this term embraced, in the ordinary mind, everybody connected with law: advocates, attorneys, Writers to the Signet, and common writers) knew in general what was going on and what was required of them if they wished to succeed.

Local government representation was no whit behind the Law. The City of Edinburgh under the iron rule of the Right Honourable Sir James Hunter Blair knew exactly where it stood. The baillies and the ordinary council deacons did not need any second warning. The Lord Provost was not only a man of ability and ambition: he was a Dundas man to the last ounce of his energy. If the baillies and councillors did not toe his line, then there would soon be no line for them to toe. Only an odd rebel acted on his own behalf and tried to appropriate to his own interest something more than the drippings that fell with a slow but succulent sureness from the Dundas roast.

But if the civil arm was wielded by the Dundas interest, no less so was the religious arm. And in the General Assembly of the Kirk of Scotland the voice of Daddy Auld was no more heard than the voice of the Reverend William Greenfield.

The hierarchy of the Kirk, led by Dr. William Robertson, Principal of the University, and supported by sturdy henchmen like Dr. Carlyle of Iveresk and Dr. Hugh Blair, saw to it that nothing was done except in the Dundas interest, and that the democratic voice of the Kirk was effectively nullified. Even the revolt against patronage was successfully side-tracked by those clergymen who cared more for a good living than they did for the principles of Presbyterianism.

True enough, throughout the length and breadth of the land there were murmurings of revolt. Sometimes the murmurings broke out into open revolt as when, on this or that issue, the people acted in defence of what they considered to be their precious-won liberties. Not often did the clergy of patronage find that the congregations, upon which they had been foisted by the superiority of the local overlord, allowed them to gain easy access to their kirk; and many were the long and bitter fights that resulted from the ecclesiastical dictatorship of the General Assembly.

Even such innocuous officers serving the Customs and Excise had been secured. The Customs and Excise had, of course, a long tradition of service to the ruling interest. It was this body that had been ordered to secure the names and addresses and the extent of the crime of every man, woman and child who had participated in the Stewart side of the Rebellion of 1745. Even forty-three years after, the Excisemen (of whatever rank) were vetted in the interest of the Dundas family.

Of the behind-the-scenes facts concerning all this, the Bard knew little. And, at the moment, he cared less than ever he had cared in his adult lifetime. But there was much that he knew instinctively.

He knew something of the extent of the Dundas dictatorship; and he knew that corruption was rife in all the leading circles of administration. And there was no man, not even Henry Dundas himself, who was better versed in the significant trends of national and international politics.

Meantime Henry Dundas, who had all the politician's contempt for a poet who was still living and about whom he had not heard in his student days from his teachers, had heard of Robert Burns. . .

In this he was in advance of some of his stoutest supporters. When a lady at a card party asked Lord Braxfield what he thought of the ploughman-poet, he looked at the lady, whose face was shadowed, and said with brutal and inconsiderate coarseness: "And who the bluidy hell is the ploughman-poet? Goddamnit: hae we no' enough to thole without bein' speired siccan ridiculous questions?"

It so happened that the lady was none other than Lady Clerk Maxwell from Princes Street; and Braxfield had to apologise, stating that he had thought he was addressing his wife—an apology which was immediately accepted!

George's Square, the aristocratic centre of the South Town, was certainly its most handsome show piece. There lived such ladies as Miss Abercromby, Mrs. Dalrymple, Mrs. Douglas of Cavers, Lady Don, Lady Anne Duff, Miss Dundas of Dundas, Lady Elphinston, Mrs. Grant, Miss Hall of Dunglass, Lady Macdowall Hay, Mrs. Hay of Lawfield, Lady Henderson, Lady Philipshaugh, Mrs. Scott of Gala and many others. These gentle dames gave a tone of elegant decorum to the Square that could be felt the moment the stranger set foot on its plainstones.

Here Dictator Henry Dundas had his town house and his henchman Robert MacQueen lived hard by at Number Thirteen.

When he was in Town, Braxfield reported to Dundas with careful regularity.

Dundas, though physically a very different type from Braxfield and having a very different manner, had a genuine admiration for him. He had a mellow laugh for Braxfield's verbal brutalities.

"So you're no' taken on wi' the ploughman-poet, Robert?"

"By God, Harry, I'd be hard pressed for something to dae to tak' up wi' that clown."

"Aye . . . I'm wi' you there. A piece o' damned nonsense. Poetry's an auld maid's hobby at best—but a ploughman's poetry! Clean ridic'lous, Robert . . . Glencairn and Erskine hae taken him up, though."

"Aye . . . taken him up! He's aboot all they could tak' up. I never liked that Ayrshire crowd, Harry."

"No . . . I've no great liking for them mysel'."

"And what's Henry MacKenzie and Dr. Blair makin' sic a fuss o' him for?"

"Good men, Robert. Good men. They'll no' mak' ony wrang assessments. I've had a word already on the quiet wi' Blair. MacKenzie! He'll come in handy yet. No, no: this ploughman-poet is only a diversion wi' them. It's the way the women hae taken him up annoys me."

"Well, Harry, I blame Duchess Gordon as much as ony o' them. Ye ken how the women-folk try to ape her."

"Jane's a'richt. . . Likes her frolic and her fancy-men. But for a' that, Jane's the shrewdest woman in Scotland. Aye, or England! There's ae thing, Robert. It'll never be said that Harry Dundas ever stooped to flatter the ploughman-poet."

"Nor Robert MacQueen."

"But then you're incapable o' flattery, Robert."

"That's richt, Harry. Robert MacQueen flatters naebody. But he can be depended on to come down—and come down hard—on the richt side."

"And if he's ever in doubt as to what the richt side is——?"

"He kens whaur to speir."

"Anither glass, Robert. . . I dinna ken what I'd dae withoot you. Come on, drink up, damn you, and gie me your latest bawdy story. I want to forget a' aboot this bluidy ploughman. Oh, juist ae thing, afore I forget. If his subscription's being taken up in the best quarters put your name doon—it'll look better."

"Are you putting your ain name doon, Harry?"

"Me? I'll be verra much surprised at mysel' if I dae. But whiles I dae things that surprise mysel', Robert. That's what comes o' haeing an open mind."

Henry Dundas smiled very blandly at Robert MacQueen. The smile wasn't lost on him.

THE MEN OF LETTERS

At Creech's breakfast table one morning the literati met and discussed the Bard. It was Lord Monboddo who began the discourse.

He tilted his long pointed nose sideways and seemed to twitch it at the point. Then he clacked his toothless gums.

"Burns—*noo* what d'ye think o' him? I've had him to supper in my house and I maun say I find him prodigious interestin'—aye. A mind far above that o' a common ploughman. And extraornar level-headed: extraornar level-headed. His original parts I wad place verra high—in fact I can think of nane whae's natural ability I could place higher. But he wants a classical education—and he canna get that noo. That's a grave misfortune. . . His manners and breeding leave naethin' to be desired——"

"May I interrupt you, James?" broke in Blair with his harsh unmusical voice. "Burns is no rustic boor; but I confess he is somewhat forward in the expressing of opinion."

"What's that, Blair? Wad ye hae him backward?"

"I wad hae him circumspect, James: his opinions are no doubt original; but they are crude—not at all the ripe judgments of a trained mind. I think he sets too high a value on his uninformed opinions. His being a rustic rhymer of admittedly high talent need not obscure the fact that he is no philosopher—and his opinions, I submit, carry no more authority than those of a street caddie."

Monboddo clacked furiously; but Dugald Stewart stepped into the breach.

"I think you are a trifle austere there, Blair—and a trifle unjust. We all admit that Burns is no academic. But there lies his strength—not his weakness. I find his opinions verra interesting—on whatever subject he cares to venture them. Nae doubt he sometimes ventures them with a downrightness to the which we are no' accustomed—from *outside* our circle. But downrightness is part—and a large part—of his character."

William Greenfield said: "I find him unfailingly charming. He is modest in the extreme and over-grateful, I think, for the most trifling favours. He is a model of considerate politeness to the ladies. I think his natural charm—aye, and his natural easy gallantry—puts us all to shame."

"Fiddlesticks, my dear Greenfield—fiddlesticks!" But Blair's proud haughty features flushed slightly. "I know of no one at this table who need feel in any way ashamed of his manners and his breeding. Your enthusiasm has carried you away, Greenfield."

"Then, sir, I trust and pray I may never lose my enthusiasms."

The suave Creech was quick with the oil.

"I think, gentlemen, we have strayed from the intent of my Lord Monboddo's remarks. We were discussing the lack of a classical education—but is there, I venture to enquire, any other form of education worthy to be so called?"

Professor James Gregory rugged his pock-marked features across his facial bones with an extraordinary muscular gesture and mobility of lower jaw.

"Whatna bluidy cant is this we're jawin' aboot? Burns indeed made *me* feel ashamed o' my manners—and he's the only man that ever did that. The man's a genius. And he's a damned fine fellow."

The Man of Feeling had finished picking the remains of his breakfast from out the hollows of his decayed teeth.

"I think I put my opinion very clearly into The Lounger.

Burns is a genius—a genius of rustic sensibility. His parts may not be as profound as some of us could wish—nor as refined. There is, too, a measure of coarseness in his composition inseparable from his rustic environment. You see: he is heaven-taught—in the broadest sense, Blair. We can account for his inspiration no other way. But Burns, like the rest of us, is mortal: his inspiration often becomes sullied. But I must say that the regrettable expressions of coarseness and libertinism exhibited in the grosser moments of his verses are most pleasantly lacking in his conversation—and so far as I can gather—in his conduct. I confess that I trembled on this score when I heard he was come to Town—but I think we need not alarm ourselves."

Gregory thrust his hands deeply into his breeches pockets and permitted himself the outrage of a harsh horse-laugh.

"You're a lot o' bluidy auld wives! Ye wad think ye were sitting here in judgment to see gin Burns was fit to enter the Kingdom o' Heaven! Ye'd be a damn sicht better employed examinin' your ain souls. For mysel'—I'll awa' and set to on the dissectin' o' a stinking corpse. We *medical* men only cut up the dead—but, by certes, you literary folk tak' a hell's delight in cutting up the livin'. Leave the honest ploughman alane—the fact that he canna compose bad sense in worse Latin is nae handicap... Has it never struck ye what an ordeal it must be for the man—and him straight frae the plough— to mix and haud up his head wi' you flowers o' wit and wisdom? Aye—and haud up his head wi' credit! A lot o' his verses are gey crude—d'ye no' think you could help the man how to write better instead o' trailing his tripes on the table for inspection?"

James Gregory was one of the rough characters of the academic world. But so great was his ability as an academician and a man of medicine that his roughness was looked upon merely as an amiable weakness to be condoned rather than censured.

But though Dugald Stewart merely smiled tolerantly and William Greenfield nodded in sympathy, Dr. Hugh Blair shrugged his immaculate shoulders and Creech looked apprehensive. Lord Monboddo, clacking at a furious rate, was almost beside himself with excitement.

"Well spoken, Jamie Gregory—well spoken, Jamie! Now I maun awa' across till my pleas afore the Session. Gentlemen —Jamie, here, has spoken a true word. Gie Burns what help ye can—that's your privilege as literary men. I mak' an exception o' you, Henry—you did brawly in your Lounger. And dinna be frichted to hae the man at your tables—he'll no' disgrace ye—you or your weemin folk . . . and that's mair than I can say o' some folk that wear silks and fine linens. Come on, Jamie—I see you're impatient for the cutting-up o' your cadavers—I'll get you across to Parliament House, you'll be gaun doon the Steps till the College . . .?"

When the pair were gone, Creech said:

"Notwithstanding what my Lord Monboddo has just said, I wonder, gentlemen, if you have come to a decision about the use of his daughter's name in his Address to Edinburgh?"

Blair said (and it was obvious from his manner that he was more than a bit hipped): "Quite out of the question, Willie. I told him myself he might leave a blank. If we allowed Miss Burnett's name to be bandied about in the fashion suggested there is no saying where it would stop. This is but an example of Burns's lack of taste and discrimination."

From the corner by the fire where he had been sitting shivering in his two great-coats, Professor Adam Ferguson turned a walnut-wizened monkey face.

"I like the lad weel enough," he croaked. "But he's too much made o', too much made o'. A poet's a poet and nothing to get excited aboot. Leave poets to the weemin-folk. Men o' learning should hae mair important matters to concern them."

"Come now, Ferguson," said Dugald Stewart. "Life would be a dry business without poets. Maybe we have made too much of Burns—but has he any rival we could make half as much of?"

"Profoundly observed, Dugald," chimed Greenfield. "Burns is quite exceptional. And—though I say this with all deference —we are all his inferiors in the relationship of our natural parts."

But Greenfield's speech was received coldly. Blair eyed him for a brief moment with a very cold eye before he turned to Creech and deliberately changed the subject.

THE BUBBLE OF FAME

The Reverend William Greenfield sat in his snug kitchen in his house at the Bristo Port—at the junction of the Candle-maker Row and Bristo Street.

He lowered the sheet from his eyes.

"Listen to this, my dear," he said to his wife who was sitting by the fire sewing some baby clothes. "It's a letter from Robert Burns. 'Tis an extraordinary letter, my dear."

"Read it to me, William. But I do think you should have invited Mr. Burns before this."

Mrs. Greenfield was a very attractive woman with a very pleasant disposition. She was in love with her husband and he was in love with her.

Greenfield had the finest voice of a professional preacher in Scotland. His wife loved to hear him speak. Greenfield coughed professionally.

"I have invited him out to see us, my dear. 'Tother day I was asking him if there were any poets in Ayrshire apart from himself. He encloses me two songs, the compositions of two Ayrshire mechanics. But to his letter:

' Reverend Sir,
' On raking the recesses of my memory the other day, I stumbled on two Songs which I here inclose you as a kind of curiosity to a Professor of the Belles lettres de la Nature; which, allow me to say, I look upon as an additional merit of yours; a kind of bye Professorship, not always to be found among the systematic Fathers and Brothers of scientific Criticism. They were the works of Bards such as I lately was; and such as, I believe, I had better still have been.

' Never did Saul's armour sit so heavy on David when

going to encounter Goliath, as does the encumbering robe of public notice with which the friendship and patronage of some "names dear to fame" have invested me. I do not say this in the ridiculous idea of seeming self-abasement, and affected modesty. I have long studied myself, and I think I know pretty exactly what ground I occupy, both as a Man and a Poet; and however the world, or a friend, may sometimes differ from me in that particular, I stand for it, in silent resolve, with all the tenaciousness of Property. I am willing to believe that my abilities deserved a better fate than the veriest shades of life; but to be dragged forth, with all my imperfections on my head, to the full glare of learned and polite observation, is what, I am afraid, I shall have bitter reason to repent.

'I mention this to you, once for all, merely, in the Confessor style, to disburthen my conscience, and that— "When proud fortune's ebbing tide recedes"—you may bear me witness, when my bubble of fame was at the highest, I stood, unintoxicated, with the inebriating cup in my hand, looking forward, with rueful resolve, to the hastening time when the stroke of envious Calumny, with all the eagerness of vengeful triumph, should dash it to the ground.

'I am ever . . .' "

"Oh, poor fellow!" sighed Mrs. Greenfield. "How beautifully, yet how sadly, he writes. William, you must invite him to breakfast."

"My dear: everybody who thinks they are anybody is inviting him to breakfast. But you would like him, my dear. His modesty, his peculiar charm is in ratio with his genius. . ."

LOWLAND PEGGY

He first met her about the middle of January, when at long last he paid his duty visit to blind Dr. Blacklock in his upper flat in West Nicolson Street.

From the moment he saw her he fell in love with her.

His mind flashed and flared and his heart thumped in his breast. It was a long time since he had experienced such a direct assault on his emotions.

It was not that she was either a great beauty or was possessed of a strong personality. Indeed she was subdued—almost mouse-like in her demeanour. But she was young and fresh. Her eyes were a bright friendly hazel: her oval-shaped features were of an olive complexion: her lips, though small, were nevertheless full and red. When she smiled she revealed enough of her teeth to prove by their whiteness that they were still innocent of decay.

She dressed quietly as became her mood; and there was nothing of ostentation about her.

Finest of all was her voice. She spoke clearly and well but with a rich softness of modulation.

Dr. Blacklock introduced them: "Come Peggy, my dear, and meet Mr. Burns, your countryman. Robert, my boy, this is Miss Chalmers who is my angel of mercy. She comes and reads to me—and plays to me, aye, and sings to me. And does it all as if she had come directly from paradise."

For once the Bard was discomfited. He stepped forward and took her hand readily enough. But words fused and ran together in his mind and he found himself speechless.

Peggy Chalmers gave a slight curtsey. "This is truly a great honour, Mr. Burns. I'm glad you have managed to free yourself from the pressing engagements o' the Toon to pay kind Dr. Blacklock a visit. We had almost despaired of you——"

"Madam, I—I have already made my apologies to Dr. Blacklock. Believe me——"

"No more apologies, my boy—no more apologies. You have come to see me; and Peggy has come and . . . my cup is full. Come and sit down beside me, Peggy. Is Sarah busy with the tea-things?"

"Yes . . . tea will not be long now, Doctor."

"I'm afraid I drink as much tea now as Doctor Johnson. You drink tea, Robert?"

"A little, sir—on occasion."

"Ah yes. . . We Toon's folk are become gey intemperate wi' dishes o' tea. And how is your kind mother and aunt, Peggy?"

"As always, thank you, Doctor. They are in good health and spirits. Mamma sends you some herbs. I've told Sarah how they are to be brewed; and you're to tak' a wine glass of the brew when you retire."

"You see, Robert, how they nurse me? If only I could stop this palsy in my hands that I could play my flute. . . But no, no: I mustna complain. . ."

The unseeing eyes in the great white face of the Doctor, the trembling in his hands and the occasional convulsive spasms that shook his frame distressed the Bard. He felt the more guilty that he had not made his visit earlier. He felt even more uncomfortable when Blacklock asked him about Christie Laurie.

"She complains that you have deserted her, my boy. Christie and her brother are such good children."

"But you know, Doctor, that Mr. Burns has so many pressing engagements——"

"Ah yes, yes. I'm so glad for your sake, my boy, that your genius has been so quickly acclaimed in the Toon. Her Grace of Gordon and my Lord Glencairn—in addition to the literati. . . How glad I am to gather that all the praise has in no way turned your head."

"The only praise likely to do that, sir, is the praise of such as yourself who have written so much that is superior to my rustic muse."

"No, no, no, my boy: no, no, no! I am but a poor versifier —you are our only poet, our only true and genuine poet of nature. The promise you hold for the future is so precious that I—I almost said that I trembled for you did I not already tremble from old age and declining health. But we must have no dark thoughts! Peggy, you must play for Mr. Burns—and for me! But for Mr. Burns: yes, that he may know what a ministering angel you are."

"Madam, may I second our worthy host in this matter. I am, may I say, convinced of the angelic side of your ministrations—but I should be honoured to hear you perform at the keyboard."

There was no nonsense of false modesty about Peggy Chalmers. "Very well," she said. "Though I really should be assisting Mrs. Blacklock with the tea. I must warn you, Mr. Burns, that I am no musician such as you have lately been accustomed to hearing in Saint Cecilia's Hall. I play to please myself, knowing that I also please Doctor Blacklock. . ."

The tinkling melody and the soft fall of chords lingered in his memory until he saw her again.

He plagued John Richmond, who was intimate with the details of Gavin Hamilton's family, for more information about her and her mother.

But that she was a cousin of Gavin Hamilton: that her father, James Chalmers, had died some years ago near Machlin; and that she now lived with her mother in Edinburgh and occasionally with her widower uncle John Tait—who had the country residence of Harviestoun in Clackmannanshire and a Town house in Park Place—was as much as he could learn, except that her elder sister, Cochrane, had married Sir Henry MacKenzie of Gairloch.

Naturally, he determined to put his friendship with Gavin Hamilton to good use. His only regret was that he had not called on Doctor Blacklock earlier. It was obvious that he had lost some of her good opinion by delaying for so long his call on the old poet who, in his declining years, was having a struggle to eke out a living by tutoring some student boarders.

But only now was he beginning to find his feet in the Town, only now becoming familiar with its geography and the location of its personalities. It had been made clear to him that Dr. Blacklock was not held in the highest literary esteem either by Creech or Dr. Blair and his colleagues.

It was perhaps the thought of Blacklock's undoubted merits and the handsome generosity of his criticism that enraged him one morning when breakfasting with Creech.

There were several strangers at the table that morning;

but by far the most talkative was the Reverend Mr. William Robb (of Tongland and Balnacross) who seemed to think no end of himself as a literary critic.

When the Bard found himself next to him at the table he withdrew into himself. But the wizened chattering monkey merely used the silence to improve, as he thought, on the Bard's rustic ignorance.

The discussion had come round, via Dr. Blair, to the poet Gray.

At the mention of Gray the Reverend Mr. Robb almost jumped up in his seat.

"I never held wi' Gray as a poet! His Elegy, written in the Graveyard, is full of the maist obvious and glaring faults o' prosody. Consider now the opening lines: 'The bell hath tolled the knell of parting day; the ploughman homeward plods his weary way!' Nae better than honest doggerel! The ploughman homeward plods his weary way—wearily the ploughman plods his homeward way—homeward the ploughman plods his weary way—his weary way the ploughman homeward plods——"

But, by this time, the Bard's gorge had risen beyond the point of prudent caution.

Very red in the face, he turned on his neighbour.

"Sir," he said, in a tone of voice that boomed from the depths of his anger, "I perceive that a man may be a learned critic by square and rule—and for all that be nothing but a damned blockhead!"

In the pert proud face of Dr. Blair, beady eyes swivelled in amazement. Dugald Stewart lowered his gaze and bit his lip. Henry MacKenzie made a noise that might have emanated from an intelligent donkey. Creech coughed discreetly on an imaginary fish bone. . .

It was an awkward situation. Nobody came to his assistance. Indeed there were some at the table who felt he classed more than Mr. Robb as a damned blockhead.

Sensing the situation, the Bard rose to his feet and looked at Creech: "I regret, sir, the necessity that compelled me to upset your table—pray allow me to withdraw."

From Craig's Close he went straight (or as straight as the devious wynds and closes permitted) to Doctor Blacklock.

But Blacklock gave vent to a long palsied chuckle.

"Robert, my boy, I would that I had been there to hear you. . . But don't blame yourself—and don't do it again. Why! The Reverend Mr. Robb cannot do harm to Gray: Gray will never be forgotten: Mr. Robb will never be remembered. . . When I say you mustn't do the like again—I mean not in polite company. Polite company, my boy, will tolerate anything but the truth—that is why it is polite. And maybe that was why I was never fond of it—or it of me. . . But I am happy as I am—happier than most, despite my growing afflictions. My Peggy is better than all the polite company in Edinburgh——"

"With that sentiment, sir, I am in the happiest accord."

"Why, of course you are. And Peggy forgives you for not having come earlier to visit me."

"Then she was annoyed?"

"Annoyed? Well, she was annoyed—for my sake. And you can forgive her that, I'm sure."

"I forgive everybody but myself, Doctor. I sometimes feel I should throw everything to the winds and go back to the plough. The polite circles of Edinburgh begin to weary me out of all my puny stock of prudence and patience."

"A little discipline, my boy, will do you nae harm—taken in moderation. I hope you are attending, with assiduity, the preparation of your book. . . Ah yes, Willie Smellie is an excellent printer—and a maist learned fellow. Rough, of course, very rough and downright—but do not ignore his strictures or his advice should he offer any. Smellie is not only a man of learning—he is much experienced in the ways o' the world. . ."

But the Bard went away from Nicolson Street feeling depressed: Peggy Chalmers had not made an appearance. He would need to find an excuse to come back soon. And he must find an opportunity to speak with her alone. The old Doctor might not be able to see; but his hearing was doubly acute and he had an alarming faculty for sensing everything that went on around him.

The Bard buttoned up his great-coat for the winter wind was raw and penetrating. He found his footsteps taking him down Buccleuch Place, past the Assembly Rooms and out onto the grey wind-swept Meadows.

It was fine to get a breath of the fresh air and fine to get away from the overtowering presence of tenements and buildings.

He should be sitting on Smellie's office stool correcting his proofs; he should be writing letters; he should be soliciting the great ones to advance his case with the Excise Board of Commissioners; he should be doing anything but wasting his time striding the Meadows. . .

But he was in love with Peggy Chalmers. Here was a woman who would make a wife in ten thousand. A woman to love—and yet to admire in the loving. A woman possessed of every admirable quality; a woman of exquisite taste and high intelligence; a woman who moved in genteel and aristocratic circles and yet remained modest and unaffected. . .

He had never imagined such a woman possible. The fashionable young women of Edinburgh were intolerably affected with their damned boarding-miss manners. And brainless. There had been no alternative to them but Christie Laurie and Highland Peggy in the Cowgate.

But Christie Laurie had lacked real depth and understanding and poor Peggy for all her warm heart and warm flesh was but a serving-wench and would never be able to rise above her lowly station.

There were others who had tempted him—but tempted only. Peggy Chalmers was the fulfilment of all his ideals—and his longings.

He smacked his crop smartly against his booted leg.

His longing, yes. God damnit, was it unnatural that he should long for a woman with whom to share the burden of life—its ups and downs, its joys and sorrows? If he had but found such a woman earlier in his life and had had the wherewithal to ensure her physical comfort. . .

Jean Armour. . . But Jean had been tested and found wanting. Jean lacked that quality that would have bound her to him—and him to her—with bonds that neither time nor circumstance could have sundered.

Peggy Chalmers seemed to have all the essential qualities that Jean lacked—or seemed in retrospect to lack. To hell: why should he stride about here torturing his mind with comparisons. He wanted to see more of Peggy Chalmers—to explore the mysteries of her physical and spiritual being.

And why hadn't she been at Blacklock's—surely she hadn't decided to avoid him? But this thought proved so disturbing that he turned abruptly on his heel and headed for Dawney Douglas's tavern in the Anchor Close. . .

That evening lying with Peggy Cameron he said:

"Ye ken, Peggy, that one o' thae nichts I'll stop coming here?"

"I ken that, sir. But I'll be sorry. And ye needna . . ."

"You'll be sorry?"

"You see, I'm fond o' you in my own way."

"And is your own way so different from another's?"

"I'd rather no' be speaking about it, sir. It's no' a thing that should be spoken about."

"You've never objected to me speaking before, Peggy."

"I'm no' objecting to you speaking, sir, for you've the great tongue on you for words. It's just that I dinna like speaking about—about you and me, sir."

"I think I understand, Peggy lass. But maybe I don't. You see, whiles I think I understand mysel'—and then whiles I ken I dinna."

"D'you no' think that ye ask yoursel' ower mony questions? It doesna make ye ony happier, does it?"

"Is that why you don't ask yourself questions, Peggy?"

"I get feared when I ask myself questions, sir. Have you fallen in wi' a lass, sir, that ye dinna want to be coming back? I dinna mind you having a lass. Are you thinking o' getting married?"

"We'll say nae mair about that, Peggy—but you can rest content that I'm no' getting married."

"I'd like to see you married and settled down—and you

could come and see me once in a while and tell me how you were getting on."

"Listen, Peggy—do you believe there's any—reality—in love? I mean: do you think it's possible for a man and a woman to be in love?"

"Nae mair than you and me's in love, sir—if that's what you mean."

"No. . . I don't quite mean that. But maybe I'm only blethering—as usual."

"If you're fond o' a lass, sir, that's a' that matters. But there's plenty folks get married that are no' very fond o' each other—or they wadna do the things wi' each other that they do."

"Aye—all right then, Peggy: we'll forget about love and marriage and a' that kind o' romantic nonsense."

"It is nonsense, isn't it——?"

"No, by God, Peggy, it isna nonsense. It's the only sense there is in the world. It's the only thing that's worth holding onto in the world: it's the only reality in the world. . . It's the only thing that raises us above the beasts—though God kens just as often it lowers us beneath them. . . When I find the lass I really love—when I find the lass that really loves me —then, then I'll no' come here, Peggy."

"Do you mean you've found her and you're no' coming back?"

"No. . . I havena found her yet. And the damnable bit is that she may not even exist—except in my imagination."

"Then why worry aboot it, sir? Do you no' think it wad be far better to look out for a nice quiet lass—wi' some money —and get married decently and settle doon?"

"Aye—if I wasna a bluidy idiot that's just exactly what I wad dae, Peggy."

"You could dae a lot worse, sir. I dinna like to see a man wi' your intelligence worrying about things that dinna really matter. And ye micht get to be real fond o' her after a while."

"Aye; and when I wasna very fond o' her I could aey clash her ears and go out and get drunk."

"Och, I dinna think ye'd be hitting her too hard, sir: you've a richt kindly nature—even when ye hae a drink."

"By God, Peggy, but that's a testimonial would look well wrote out in a fair hand on a fresh sheet o' paper."

"Och now, sir, come and lie doon and dinna tease me ony mair—what's you and me to do with ony words wrote out on a bit o' paper?"

"You wouldna like me to write a song for you?"

"No, sir—it wouldna be true."

"Oh, it would be true enough, I'll warrant."

"Well now . . . then it wouldna be decent."

"And that's what really matters?"

"Och well, sir, ye ken fine that folk aey like to be thinking they're decent—even them that are na."

"I'll say nae mair to that, Peggy. For whether ye richtly ken it or no', there's nae mair can be said."

"I could hae been telling ye that lang ago, sir. Snuff the candle, sir—they're aey getting on to me up the stair about the wastry that gauns on. . ."

LETTER TO JOHN BALLANTINE

My Honoured Friend,

It gives me a secret comfort to observe in myself that I am not yet so far gone as Willie Gaw's Skate, 'past redemption,' for I have still this favourable symptom of grace, that when my Conscience, as in the case of this letter, tells me I am leaving something undone that I ought to do, it teases me eternally till I do it.

I am still ' dark as was Chaos ' in respect to Futurity. My generous friend, Mr. Patrick Miller, brother to the Justice Clerk, has been talking with me about the lease of some farm or other in an estate called Dalswinton which he has lately bought near Dumfries. Some life-rented, embittering recollections whisper me that I will be happier anywhere than in my old neighbourhood, but Mr. Miller is no judge of land; and though I dare say he means to favour me, yet he may give me, in his opinion, an advantageous bargain that may ruin me.

I am to take a tour by Dumfries as I return and have promised to meet Mr. Miller on his lands some time in May.

I went to a Mason-lodge yesternight where the Most Worshipful Grand Master Charters, and all the Grand lodge of Scotland visited. The meeting was most numerous and elegant; all the different Lodges about town were present, in all their pomp. The Grand Master who presided with great solemnity, and honour to himself as a Gentleman and Mason, among other general toasts, gave 'Caledonia, and Caledonia's Bard, brother B——,' which rung through the whole Assembly with multiplied honours and repeated acclamations. As I had no idea such a thing would happen, I was downright thunderstruck, and, trembling in every nerve, made the best return in my power. Just as I had finished, some of the Grand Officers said so loud as I could hear, with a most comforting accent 'Very well indeed!' which set me something to rights again.

I have just now had a visit from my Landlady who is a staid, sober, piously-disposed, sculduddery-abhoring Widow, coming on her grand climacterick. She is at present in sore tribulation respecting some 'Daughters of Belial' who are on the floor immediately above. My Landlady who as I said is a flesh-disciplining, godly Matron, firmly believes that her husband is in Heaven; and having been very happy with him on earth, she vigorously and perseveringly practises some of the most distinguishing Christian virtues, such as, attending Church, railing against vice, etc., that she may be qualified to meet her dear quondam Bedfellow in that happy place where the unclean and the ungodly shall never enter. This, no doubt, requires some strong exertions of self-denial, in a hale, well-kept widow of forty-five; and as our floors are low and ill-plaistered, we can easily distinguish our laughter-loving, night-rejoicing neighbours—when they are eating, when they are drinking, when they are singing, when they are, etc., my worthy Landlady tosses sleepless and unquiet, 'looking for rest but finding none,' the whole night. Just now she told me, though by the bye she is sometimes dubious that I am, in her own phrase, 'but a rough an' roun' Christian' that 'We should not be uneasy and envious because the Wicked enjoy the good things of this life; for these base jades who, in her own words, lie up gandygoin' with their filthy fellows, drinking the best of wines, and singing abominable songs, they shall one day lie in hell, weeping and wailing and gnashing their teeth over a cup of God's wrath!'

I have this day corrected my 152nd page. My best good wishes to Mr. Aiken—

I am ever, dear Sir,

Your much indebted humble servant. . .

THE FRIEND OF FERGUSSON

Though the Bard enjoyed the entertainment offered by the Edinburgh Theatre Royal he did not really thrill to the theatre until he witnessed the performance of plays and especially the performances of the Town's leading actor, the self-styled comedian, William Woods. On the night of 15th January he first saw him play. The play was *The School for Scandal* and Woods played the part of Joseph. . . After the performance the Bard met him, in company, at Bayle's Tavern.

Woods was a handsome man in his thirty-seventh year. He was talented, witty and an excellent conversationalist. The Bard had heard that he had been friendly with Robert Fergusson. . .

"Aye, Mr. Burns, I kent puir Bob Fergusson—he was one o' my best friends. You would have liked him, Mr. Burns. Aye; and he would have liked you. . . Oh, you're the better poet, without a doubt. But mind you: I like to hear you say that he was your model."

"My model and my inspirer. After I discovered Fergusson I never looked back, Mr. Woods."

"Aye, man; but you'd have liked him. The damned lies they've told about puir Bob. Those that kent nocht about him say he died o' drink, that he was dissipated. Ah, but they never daur to say that in the presence o' onybody that kent him. Oh, he could tak' a bit drink like the rest o' us. But I canna say

I ever saw him drunk. Damnit, he hadna the constitution to drink. 'Course, the gentry here didna like some o' his satires so they had to blacken him somehow. Man, Mr. Burns, it's damnable what they say about a man after he's dead—especially if he's onyway gifted above the lave."

"But he had a sore unhappy death, had he not?"

"As you say, Mr. Burns: a sair unhappy death. He fell doon the stair at hame and hurt his head. He never really got ower that. No' properly. Oh, wi' guid nursing and attention for a year or twa I believe he would've come roun'. Aye; but then his mither, puir body, was desperately reduced to beggary. Aye . . . when they put him in a cell in the Bedlam ablow the North Brig he was finished. Aye, a damnable business, Mr. Burns. He was very fond o' the Theatre . . . he was aey here when I was on the boards. The best o' company when he was at himsel'. And damnit, a likable lad at ony time—real likable. What a pity the pair o' you couldna hae met."

"There's no man in the Town I would rather hae met, Mr. Woods, as there's no man whose memory I cherish more——"

"Gie me anither shake o' your han', Mr. Burns. Sir, I'm real pleased to hae made your acquaintance—mair than pleased, sir: honoured! Ony time you want to come to the theatre, come and see me an' I'll get you a seat: I did the same for Bob Fergusson and I'll do the same for you. Not a word, Mr. Burns: I'll look upon that as a privilege. . . Now how would you like to try your hand at writing for the stage?"

"Indeed, sir, that has ever been an ambition of mine."

"There you are—the same as Bob Fergusson! Well, Mr. Burns, what's keeping you back?"

"Nothing—except that I have neither the talent nor the necessary experience for writing for the stage; and that's everything."

"A sensible enough attitude, Mr. Burns. Folks write the damnedest impossible rubbish for the stage, believe me. Aye: you need experience. But you'll get that by coming and watching the plays. Reading them's no' the same thing. You've got to see them on the boards. But you can write. What about trying out your hand on a bit prologue?"

"I would be glad to have the opportunity of trying out my hand on that species of composition—provided you would guide me."

"I'll tell you what I'll do! I'll be having a benefit night about the end o' March or the beginning o' April. You write me a prologue and I'll speak it. Think it ower and we'll hae a talk about it later on. Tuts, man, I want to see mair o' you. Noo, what about another drink? I want to hear how you're getting on wi' your second edition. . . I'm a wee bit o' a poet mysel'—just a bit rhymer-like. . . ."

The Bard agreed to the drink. He had the feeling that William Woods was as honest and as warm-hearted a man as he had met in Edinburgh. His heart warmed to him.

SAINT CECILIA'S HALL

The Edinburgh gentry sat in the elliptical concert room of Saint Cecilia's Hall situated almost on the corner of Niddry's Wynd and the Cowgate, and listened to the orchestra of the Edinburgh Musical Society playing the works of such composers as Abel, Haydn, Vanhall, Corelli, Geminiani, Bach, Handel, Stamitz, Arne.

Admission to the concert was strictly limited and every stranger had to be vouched for. The Bard's first sponsor was Henry MacKenzie.

The gathering was almost as fashionable as that of an assembly—indeed it was an assembly with the music tacked on instead of dancing. Four rows of seats curved round the west and east walls. The entrance was at the south and the organ loft and platform occupied the north end.

But the centre of the hall was open space, and formed the assembly floor. Only when Samuel Mitchelson appeared on the platform (after the orchestra had finished tuning) to announce the programme did the elegant gentry move to their seats.

But the Bard was not greatly impressed with the music.

Neither Abel nor Arne meant very much to him. But then the atmosphere of the Saint Cecilia's Hall was fashionable and artificial to an intense degree. The Bard's ear was tuned to the dominantly pentatonic folk-music of the Scottish country-side. Arabesques and geometric music-patterns for their own sake did not register greatly with him.

No doubt Signor Hieronymo Stabilini as first violin was a great player despite his feminine appearance and weak chin; no doubt Herr Johann Georg Christoff Schetky, sawing industriously at his 'cello, was as strong and redoubtable a musician as he looked; no doubt Signor and Signora Domenico Corri were talented vocalists—but they were certainly no folk-singers. Signor Pietro Urbani had a wonderful range of melody in his rich soothing voice; but it was difficult to appreciate his interpretation of the works of Guglielmi, Paisiello and Sarti. . .

Indeed the Bard was more interested in the personalities than the music at Saint Cecilia's. He got more thrill from watching Christie Laurie than listening to gut-scraped whorls of Corelli or Bassani; and he had more pleasure, during the interval, in speaking to her and listening to Henry MacKenzie's praise of her.

But perhaps there was only a handful of folks really interested in the music. The concert hall was a place to meet friends and display fashion and advertise wealth, power and position.

Here everything was grist to the Bard's mill. And even the dead-haddie face of George Thomson sawing industriously among the supporting fiddles held him by its sheer concentrated essence of musical flunkeyism.

Henry MacKenzie tried to draw a moral for him.

"You see, Robert, music in the Scotch dialect, like poetry in the Scotch dialect, is dying out. We must go to Germany and to Rome, to Paris and London, for our music and our musicians. As we become civilised and cultured we abandon our coarse native homespuns. I merely press this on you so that alongside your native muse you will cultivate elegant English that you may be understood and appreciated by the majority. Your work in Scotch is already not understood, or but imperfectly understood, by many of our best people. In ten or twenty years perhaps it will not be understood at all and spoken, if at all, only by illiterates. But with the cultivation o' an elegant English—such as you can speak—and with a growing familiarity with classical literature—yes, even in translation—your themes are boundless and there are no heights to which your music—with the widest possible appreciation—may not be able to soar. But tell me more, my dear Robert, about your very lovely and charming Miss Laurie. . ."

That night the Bard said to Richmond:

"By God, Jock, count yourself fortunate that you're no' a gentleman likely to be invited to a concert at Saint Cecilia's Hall. If I thocht the damned would have to listen to the likes of it for a' eternity I'd turn saint to-morrow and find myself a cave in the wilderness for the rest o' my earthly existence."

"Was it as bad as that, Rab?"

"You've nae idea, Jock! I begin to understand now how the Edinburgh gentry spend the feck o' their nights drinking and whoring. They're driven to it."

"But they're no' driven to go to the concerts——"

"Are they no'! Faith, they're driven! Fashion drives them. It's part o' the price o' living a fashionable existence."

"It seems to be the price *you're* paying for a fashionable existence."

"Maybe I'm vulnerable there, Jock. It's a good point."

"I meant nae offence, Rab. I mean——"

"I ken fine what you mean, Jock. However: my fashionable existence, as you call it, will be damned brief. Still, it's a great experience—if I'd time to absorb it all. And if I were really interested. They mean well by me, I suppose; and I just canna help it if they dinna understand me. The fact is, Jock, I just canna be bothered contradicting them. It would take too long to explain. Henry MacKenzie couldna have been kinder or more considerate to me. Yet when he lectured me about writing in elegant English I never said a word."

"Dinna mention that man to me. Are you coming to bed?"

"Yes . . . I'm coming to bed, Jock. Tramping thae bluidy causeways is mair tiring than following the plough. And it seems there's no' a Scotsman left can play a fiddle. . . No wonder Fergusson composed his lament for Scots music."

And yet, as he lay in bed, he could not help feeling gratitude towards many of the Edinburgh gentry. Many, too many of them, were unbearably silly and snobbish and ignorant either of art or of life to an astonishing degree. But they meant well by him. Six short but crowded weeks ago, if they had seen him ploughing the Mossgiel ridge or tramping down the hill to Johnnie Dow's, they would either have turned their heads on him or pretended not to notice.

Now they were tumbling over each other to be introduced to him, to shower invitations on him and to flatter and compliment him in the most extravagant fashion. . . So many of them indeed that he could not remember their names!

Aye . . . it was an amazing transformation from the hodden grey on Mossgiel to the blaze and glitter of the highest fashion in the land on the carefully guarded floor of Saint Cecilia's.

When he thought of the transformation it was almost stupefying in the violence of its contrasts.

But it would blow over. He couldn't stand for ever on the ground he now occupied. This was all very artificial and very temporary. It would come to an end all too soon. And then what ground would he occupy?

Oh, let to-morrow come and bring what it may! Once his edition was out it would be time enough to cast around him and plan for the future.

And the present constituted a great and wonderful experience. He had always wanted to see and taste life in all its phases. And now he was seeing it. Gilbert would never believe how the Edinburgh gentry had taken him up. Even Jock Richmond, lying by his side, seemed reluctant to believe it. Indeed, he had difficulty sometimes in believing it himself.

When the day came to leave Edinburgh he would be able to say that he had experienced its heights and its depths, all its moods and colours to the full. . .

A FRIENDSHIP IS BORN

William Nicol, Latin master in the High School, snapped across the desk at his lawyer, Alexander Young, who had not yet been a year admitted to the Society of Writers to His Majesty's Signet.

"And why, Mr. Young, do you think that I shouldna have this young thief pursued?"

"In the first place, Mr. Nicol, he isna a thief: he has merely returned to England and forgotten to pay your fee for tutoring and translation. In the second instance, he is the son of a very noble house; and I doubt if it wad be in your best interest to sue. Mr. Roscoe, the Liverpool attorney, also advises no action."

"Indeed! Hae you any idea what trouble I had trying to knock some learning into the blockhead's meikle skull?"

"That, sir, is beside the point; and I still think it is not in your interest to prosecute. There is no such objection to the others."

"I'll tell you this, Mr. Young, if it is of any interest to you. If Jesus Christ came back to earth and got me to translate a Latin thesis for Him and then refused to pay me the agreed-on fee then I would crucify Him upside down. Dinna ask me to hae any sympathy for a damned rotten dirty thieving bit o' useless trash like a duke's son. And I'll never admit to you or any other body that it is in my interest to lose guid money that I had to work damned hard for. If dukes want their bits o' brainless bastards taught Latin, then they'll just need to pay for it like the rest. Sae you can stop clawing your lug, Mr. Alexander Young, and remember that I'm paying *you* for a change. And if you dinna like the colour o' my money, then there's plenty o' starving lawyers in Edinburgh that will."

Mr. Young, in his twenty-eighth year, said nothing. But as a young lawyer and the only son of the Reverend William Young, minister of Hatton, he decided that it would be injudicious to act any further in the interests of William Nicol.

The classical master was in the prime of his forty-third year. A native of Dumfriesshire, there was something about his square tight-lined face that suggested the dour fighting expression of a black Galloway bull. He was quick in his speech and his actions, and had all that animal's sudden uncertainty of mood.

Born to poverty and hardship, Nicol had studied for the church and then for medicine. Finally he had won to his present position through open examination. He knew perfectly well that he was the finest classical scholar in Scotland, and of the first flight in Europe. For twelve years now he had held his present post; but he was beginning to realise that his inability to tolerate fools and to flunkey to the great would keep him there. . .

One day Smellie, having to consult him on a point of scholarship, introduced William Nicol to the Bard. Immediately they adjourned to Dawney Douglas's.

Nicol eyed the buff and blue in the Bard's dress.

"So you're a politician as well as a poet, Mr. Burns?"

"I have some first political principles, Mr. Nicol; and I make no apology for them."

"Then your friends must do that for you."

"Meaning, sir?"

"That nobody but a bluidy fool would go about Edinburgh sporting the colours o' Charlie Fox unless he was seeking trouble."

"So I'm a bluidy fool?"

"I should imagine you're that as weel as other things. But tell me who's no' a fool in this Town and I'll tell you otherwise."

Smellie intervened, for he saw that the Bard was becoming very red in the face.

"Pay nae attention to Willie Nicol, Robert: he's the thrawnest beggar in Scotland. Willie's never happier than when he's insulting folks right and left."

"I understand, sir, that you are the finest Latin scholar in Britain?"

"I have yet to meet a better."

"It seems a pity then that a man of so much learning should succeed so well in cultivating the manners of the more ignorant section of the noblesse."

"For Godsake!" cried Smellie. "Now I'm telling you, Willie, you've met more than your match here. . . And you ken damn well there's mair than a touch o' the buff and the blue about you."

Nicol grinned. "Aye, aye: I like a man to hae a bit o' spirit, Mr. Burns. In fact, I've wanted to meet you since ever I heard about you; and when I saw you in there wi' Smellie I thocht you looked ower good to be true. Only, don't expect ony flattery frae me."

"And who the hell would want *your* flattery, sir? I can well imagine that the only commodity of that nature having conceivable value would be your censure. And even that, since I don't happen to be in competition with you in the sphere of classical learning, would not interest me."

"I see you're about as pig-headed as mysel', Mr. Burns. But sit down, man: I had no intention of insulting you. And don't imagine that I care a fiddler's fart for my classical learning: it's a dead learning and only dead folk ever master it. Only there were some good bawdy poets among the Latin billies; and plenty o' grand sculduddery satire too: something after your own heart, Mr. Burns. I hope to have the pleasure o' translating some choice examples for you. You ken, of course, that you are a bluidy miracle? You came here to Edinburgh from the plough-tail and within a week you were the talk o' the Town! Open door for you everywhere in spite o' your Foxite livery. . . Aye, and they tell me that in spite o' their flattery you stood up to them and gave better than you got. . . And how d'you think that we on the outside o' things felt about that? We were proud o' you, sir! If I could hae gotten the jaw bone o' an ass I would hae sent you it wi' my best wishes. . . For by God, you're in the hands o' the Philistines here. . . And watch that crawling creature Creech, for he's lower than a snake's arse. . . Willie Smellie's all right; but he's one o' the few men you can trust——"

"Listen to me, Nicol, you ill-tongued bitch! First the

Caledonian Hunt were for subscribing for copies at a guinea; now it turns out to be the subscription price o' five shillings; the price to non-subscribers is six shillings. So what do you think? Willie Creech sets himsel' doon for five hunner copies as a subscriber so that he can make an extra shilling a copy . . . and Robert here sees nothing wrong wi' that."

"I'm indebted to Creech in many ways: so why should I grudge him his bit jobbing? He's gone out of his way to help me——"

"Aye; but only when he saw that by helping you he was helping himsel'. . . . There's no' a mair cunning man walks the causeway than Mr. William Creech."

"Yes, Willie, I have no doubt you are talking no more than plain truth. But it isn't a truthful world; and Creech is no worse than his kind. But don't think for a moment that I fail to appreciate what you and Willie Scott are doing. If you had asked for your money in advance—or a substantial sum of it—then there would have been no second edition."

"To hell wi' Creech!" cried Nicol. "I'm interested in Mr. Burns here. Aye, aye: I ken I've ruffled your feathers the wrong way; but you'll get ower that."

Smellie paused in sucking the knuckle of a bone and wagged it in front of Nicol's snub nose.

"Listen to me, you thrawn beggar: Robert here's no' the man to be won by assault and battery. I ken fine you've been itching to meet him this whilie back; but you're gaun aboot it the wrong way. Here, Robert: tak' this frae me: Willie Nicol's his ain worst enemy. He's on your side: mair nor you think. Nicol's gotten a heart like a wee lassie—and her awa' frae her mither for the first time. And he's ashamed of that. So he swears and rages and blusters in the hope that folks'll take him for a dangerous savage. But you'll get on fine thegither—when you get to ken each other."

Nicol blushed deeply. "And since when, Smellie, did I need ony damned school-marm's testimonial frae you? Burns here can see through the pair o' us like a bit o' clear glass. Mr. Burns, sir, would you like me to give you Willie Smellie's character?"

"No, sir: that I wouldn't. To hell wi' your characters, testimonials and a' siccan trashery. You have only one testimonial that interests me: you carry it in your face."

"And what may that be when translated into honest Scotch?"

"That you hae too good an opinion of your parts—too guid a conceit o' yoursel'."

"You wouldna be trying to insult me, would you?"

"You insult yourself too weel, Mr. Nicol, for me to venture in competition."

"Noo, for Godsake!" cried Smellie, "let's hae nae mair o' this: you're civilised men—no' a lot o' bluidy cannibals! God damnit! I never saw twa men mair determined to tear the tripes out o' ane anither. It was you, Nicol, who started this. You're damn near twice the age o' the Bard here—and you're supposed to be educated——"

"Supposed! To hell, Willie, Burns here is as auld as Methuselah—or Homer at least. A' day I spend my hours teaching—a man among weans. But here I sit at the feet o' a poetic Gamaliel. But I sit like an unruly child. Does that satisfy you? Damn you for a blind bitch, Smellie! Wi' a' your bluidy natural philosophy ye canna see that. You've read the man's poems, haven't you? You've heard how he has conducted himsel' afore God's anointed aristocracy o' Edinburgh. . .? You've heard how he's dealt wi' the Duchess o' Gordon and refused to lie wi' her when a' was said and done! Ye ken this man's the darlin' o' the Earl o' Glencairn and Harry Erskine an' a' the gilded peacocks o' the Caledonian Hunt and yet has retained a' the characteristics o' his native independence! God forgive you, Smellie, the brainless blind bat that you are! And you, Robert Burns, the *supposed* Ayrshire ploughman: don't imagine for one moment that you deceive Willie Nicol. You're a genius—a stark staring uncorrupted genius. An' if I havena tears to wash your bluidy feet I shed a' the tears a being can shed—as a laddie in Annan long ago. When Henry Mac-Kenzie said you were a heaven-taught ploughman, why didn't you kick his teeth in?"

"For Godsake wheest, Willie."

"Wheest yoursel', you lump o' useless blubber. I'd hae kicked his teeth in—the sanctimonious stinking hypocrite! The Man o' Feeling! I ken the kind o' feeling he went in for! The horse-faced hypocrite wouldna ken a poem frae a pot stick —I've seen a more intelligent arse hangin' ower a window sill——"

Nicol's face was livid: his small eyes were bloodshot with venom: he spat his words between clenched teeth. . .

The food on the platters grew cold and the grease congealed. Again and again Smellie combed his unkempt hair with his thick black fingers. . .

The Bard's staring eyes never left Nicol's face. He was scandalised, shocked and yet held by his obscene eloquence. He had never seen a man so raised in his life. It was something akin to madness. Yet the madness sprang from a fundamental integrity. This integrity appealed to him. However uncouth, however savage, however disordered, here too was genius— of a kind.

Of what kind he was not certain. It was sufficient, for the moment, that it struck a deep responsive chord within him.

When he found himself speaking he was surprised at the gentleness of his tone.

". . . so, since I have done you an injustice, Mr. Nicol, let me apologise with what honesty I can muster. I will not flatter you, for you are beyond flattery. I ask you—in all honesty of purpose and intention—to accept my hand in admiration, and in friendship, if you will acknowledge it."

They stood and clasped hands—in silence. Smellie was almost beside himself. "By God, sirs, I thocht you were for murdering ane anither. But sit doon, sit doon—and let's hae anither platter o' hot meat: mine's stane cauld. Are you frien's noo? I hope so; for I tell you I've never seen the like o' this—never! Never in a' my born days have I seen onything like this—— But, if you're happy, blessings on you. Dawney, Dawney! Come you Heilan' stot! Dawney, there's a guid man! Awa' an' bring us a hot platter o' somethin' tasty— collops or ony damned thing—an' a bottle o' claret, Dawney—

for this is a special occasion. How special you don't know, Dawney——"

"But quietly, gentlemen," said Dawney sadly. "Mr. Nicol, sir, I hope you are feeling well enough. Times are very trying, gentlemen—very trying."

"Go on, damn you!" roared Nicol. "You heard what Mr. Smellie said to you."

"You're the terrible man, Mr. Nicol—the terrible man. Aye: a hot platter o' something tasty. . . Aye, aye; but quietly, gentlemen, quietly. Like Mr. Burns who is always the quiet gentleman."

But as far as the Bard was concerned this interruption might not have taken place. He spoke quietly, though quickly, to Nicol, occasionally taking in Smellie with a glance of his eye.

"Mind you, you are wrong in many things, Mr. Nicol. You grossly overestimate my abilities—but just as grossly do you underestimate the abilities of others. Henry MacKenzie has his faults like the rest of us. But he has great merit— literary merit; and there is much kindness in the man. Aye, I ken what he did to poor Fergusson. It's hard to forgive him that. But he must not be judged on that alone. It's hard to forgive him his gluttony, his snobbery and his low brutish pastime of cock-fighting. No doubt he is as unlawfully lustful as he is lawfully lustful. . . All these things can be set down against Henry MacKenzie. But the man is streaked wi' genius and ability like a slice o' lean bacon for all that. And I would have his merits listed as well as his failings. MacKenzie has shown me much kindness—kindness that he need not have shown me. *And I shall not keep silent about that no matter whose company I am in.* And so with Glencairn and the others. These men have befriended me—without their personal interest in my welfare I would have sold myself to the plantations by now.

"As for the Duchess of Gordon—I know nothing, personally, of her morals. She may be a better judge, as you say, of the physical than the spiritual. I do know she's not a bad judge of poetry. She has wit and high intelligence. . . I resent—and very sharply resent—any suggestion that I might have bedded wi' her. And I am certain she would resent that suggestion as much as I do.

"Now I hope I'm making myself plain—now and for the future—if there's to be ony friendship between us. I reserve the right now, and I'll maintain it in the future as I've done it in the past, to honour whom I like—and for reasons best kent to myself. I'm no moulded saint—nor did I ever pretend to be —and I ken just how much weight to put on the patronage o' the gentry. But I have certain principles—and rough and home-made though they be I intend to stick to them. . . And I hope that I'll no' need to preach ony mair sermons about them."

"And by God, sir, I hope I'll never need to listen to them. But never mind: I accept the text—as it applies to you. But I ken you'll change the text o' your sermon afore you leave Edinburgh. . . I wonder what the hell's keeping Dawney?"

But when Dawney had served them a fresh dish, piping hot, and they had eaten it in silence, Smellie sipped a glass of claret and said:

"Aye: you'd grace a pulpit wi' the best o' them, Robert. You wadna think our friend Nicol here once thocht o' the ministry——"

"I wasna a big enough hypocrite. . . You'll come up to my hoose some nicht, Mr. Burns, meet the wife and hae a bit crack roun' the fireside when the bairns are bedded? I could translate some grand Latin verses for you—if you liked you could cobble them into guid Scotch. I mean verses that the literati ken nocht about. . ."

"Yes. . . I would be glad to enjoy a seat some evening at your fireside, Mr. Nicol."

"Right then: I live in Saint Patrick's Square—the Buc-cleuch Street pend—richt fornenst Buccleuch Place—you canna miss it if you travel straight doon the Potterrow. . ."

"Weel . . . my blessings on the pair o' you," said Smellie, raising his glass, "and the Beggars' Benison wi' it. And by the bye, Robert, I'll hae some sheets ready for you to correct gin Monday—sae dinna fail to look in."

CROCHALLAN CRONIES

The red wine sang in the big-bellied bottles; the malt-oily whisky coiled endlessly in the wide-mouthed quaichs; and the strong ale reamed and frothed in the wooden bickers.

The gale-gusts of laughter broke on the solemn walls of the Crown Room in Dawney Douglas's howff in the Anchor Close; but it surged back into the gasping lungs of the men who sat round the long table.

Over and above the strong liquors that heated the blood and fired the imagination stood the phallus—male set against female . . . life and death and eternal resurrection.

The laughter was male laughter; and it rioted at the glorious strength of the male phallus, strong against the submission of the female phallus, ever anxious that the fertile seed should be sown in the urgent furrow.

But there was also the madness, the incongruity, the basic ruthlessness to the phallus, knowing no conscience, no morality . . . answering to nothing but the surge and swell of life, seed-spumed and fertile-crested.

No tenderness here; and no compassion. For here there is no woman—only the female phallus. And this must be mocked and ridiculed as the holiest joke of creation, that man, for a brief moment, might know freedom from his sexual slavery to woman . . . the slavery, slobbering or sadistic, from which man can never free himself not even in impotence but only in death —or, momentarily, in drink.

In the ranks of the Crochallan Corps were many diverse elements; but in this they were united: they were glad to laugh their slavery to scorn and to mock that which held them in thrall.

But not all of them (or perhaps any of them) were intellectually aware of the significance of their mocking phallus-worship. Their basic instinct was to seek the sanctuary of male fraternity and rejoice in their spasms of freedom.

The Bard relished the bawdry of the male as a relief from

the burden of his sexual urges. His was the cross of tenderness in his passion for women. When his being was most charged with passion so his spirit was most charged with compassion. Only in the fraternity of his brothers could he find relief from his burden; and as his burden was greater than theirs so was his relief.

He did not need drink to liberate himself as so many of his companions needed drink. The bowl was as much a symbol of his bawdry as was the phallus. He did not drink so much to drown his sorrows as to liberate his laughter.

From the burden of Christie Laurie and Peggy Chalmers— aye, and of Peggy Cameron—he sought relief in the Crochallan Corps. But the burden of memory was also heavy with Jean Armour and Mary Campbell and . . .

Once inside the walls of the Crown Room they were shut out—out of the world of pain and travail and torment.

Into this stronghold of bawdy illusion he came like a giant refreshed. And the comrades rejoiced in him for his bawdry was sun-tanned and nut-sweet and vigorous as a young colt kicking his heels on a windy knowe.

Charles Hay, a lawyer who had been admitted to the Bar in 1768 at the early age of twenty-one, was Major (and Muster-General) of the Corps. His love was strong drink; and his regular consumption of five bottles of claret would have killed a weaker man. And Major Hay was driven to strong drink even as his father James Hay of Cocklaw had been driven before him. The Major frequented the brothels—and he had to wash the taste of them from his mouth.

His main driving forces in life were drink and bawds. He earned his living by the law for he was a clever, astute and conscienceless lawyer. He made an efficient major in his ruthless legal fashion. . .

But it was Smellie who was the spirit of the Corps. Smellie did not frequent the bawdy houses and Smellie drank only to free his wit from the shackle of morality.

Smellie and Willie Dunbar were the managers: Charles Hay was the titular head of the Corps.

They had many regular attenders: they had casual members who were not resident in the Town; and occasionally they had a visitor.

Alexander Cunningham, a sensitive but rather negative young lawyer, was then favourite tenor. He was well-connected, being a far-out relation of Glencairn and a nephew to Principal Robertson of the University. His favourite song, concerning the wildly unorthodox sexual conquest of a girl named Una, he sang with great feeling—and it was the bawdiest song the Bard had ever heard!

But there was no essential coarseness in Alexander Cunningham who was afflicted with a double dose of the century's philosophy of sensibility; and the Bard and he soon became firm friends. The Bard needed the companionship of many diverse characters. His many-sided personality needed many-sided contacts.

He could enjoy himself immensely, and with glorious gusto, with Willie Smellie. Yet Smellie only satisfied a part of his nature and occupied a fraction of his interest. With Dr. Blacklock he could sit calmly and come away from him refreshed after a long intimate discussion of the old poets and ballad-makers of Scotland. With Peter Hill he could relax into the small talk of the literary world and exchange with him certain confidences regarding their mutual ambitions. He could meet with William Greenfield for an intense moment on a level of intellectual friendship that Dr. Blair would not have understood and Smellie would have mocked in Gargantuan guffaws.

Strangely enough, it was with William Nicol that he was most at his ease. Nicol had fiery intolerance but he also had great understanding. Nothing escaped Nicol's penetrating eyes. He saw through all the shams and the illusions. . . He even saw through the sham and the illusion of the Crochallan Corps.

"What you've got to avoid, Robert, is getting tangled up wi' folk that canna do you ony good—and I don't mean in ony worldly way. Na, na: you're a poet and you mauna let folk drain away your inspiration like a wheen o' horse-leeches. . .

In the Crochallan Corps that's just what they're doing—sucking you dry to feed their own dry brains. Damnit, Robert, you're meat and drink to them—and if you dinna watch yoursel' they'll leave you nothing but the banes that hold you up."

The Bard realised the profound truth of this. But he had no intention of being sucked dry. He gave lavishly of the richness of his personality; but he absorbed plenty in return.

He needed this company. It was but an extension, though on a higher and more intense level, of the company that he had so often delighted in in the back-room at the Whitefoord Arms in Machlin and Jock Richards's howff in Tarbolton.

But he appreciated the fact that of all the Edinburgh men he had yet met, Nicol was the one man who considered first his own essential interest and his own essential well-being. Because of this he found himself warming to Nicol in a way he had never yet warmed to another man.

More than anything he enjoyed his odd visits to Nicol's fireside and the presence of his wife and family.

He warmed to Nicol's friends, his fellow teacher William Cruikshank and his wife—and Allan Masterton, the writing master. With these good folks gathered round Nicol's fireside he could enjoy an evening of real friendship. There he was not on show, there he did not need to pose unnaturally or watch the timing of his sallies. There he was a friend, accepted for his qualities as a human being and silently held in unquestioned esteem for his qualities as a poet.

Relaxed, at his own ingle-cheek, Willie Nicol was a very different man from the battling aggressive Latin master descending from the High School down into the Cowgate and up again into the howffs of the High Street.

The Bard had a deep sympathy for Nicol as he began to realise that the man had a giant intellect and was compelled by circumstance to confine it to the narrow confines of a class-room under the rule of a rector who was not only a sanctimonious humbug but a man of markedly inferior gifts. He also understood why Nicol drank fiercely, tossing back his drinks as if to quench a drouth that burned inside him.

But the Bard's weakness consisted of an over-consciousness

of the good qualities of every man he met. If a man had any real goodness and integrity in him he was quick to discover it. For little virtue he was inclined to forgive a man much unworthiness.

The one thing that Nicol, for all his massive intellect, was unable to understand was the fact that Robert Burns had never enjoyed a boyhood. At times he seemed to possess all the mature experience of an aged prophet: at others he seemed carefree and inconsequential as a callow youth.

So it came that one night a pretty callow youth came to Crochallan and immediately all the youth in the Bard went out to him.

Robert Ainslie, the callow youth, had good manners, good breeding and a smooth and admirable diction. His manners were easy and, where the Bard was concerned, diffident.

As he listened with open-eyed wonder to the Bard's devastating bawdy sallies, he formed an admiration for him that bordered on hero-worship.

The Bard, though he was not conscious of this, needed a measure of youthful hero-worship. Unlike the friendship with Willie Nicol that had matured slowly and was still maturing, the friendship with the lawyer's apprentice was immediate.

Robert Ainslie was no fool, though there was something of the fop in his character. He came from a worthy and respectable Border home where he had been brought up piously.

He had come to Edinburgh with good intentions. He still had good intentions. But life as a lawyer's articled clerk was damnably dull and circumscribed and the night life of Edinburgh swarmed lively like fleas on a warm blanket. Wine, women and music were easily come by and Robert Ainslie found that he came by them easily. He was pleasant, good-natured and he was not without wit. He knew exactly when to chip in—and, better, he knew how to let his elders and superiors take the floor.

That Robert Burns, the toast of Edinburgh's drawing-rooms, should condescend to take notice of him flattered Bob Ainslie —but he was astute enough not to show that he was overwhelmed.

Give him his due, Ainslie was perhaps the most attractive young man in Edinburgh—and the Bard found much pleasure in his company. His employer, Samuel Mitchelson, was a noted and enthusiastic musical amateur and, when Ainslie introduced him to his home, old Mitchelson was delighted and made much of him.

LOOK UP AND SEE

"There are two poems here, Mr. Burns, that in no conceivable circumstances must you print. I refer to your Love and Liberty, the very title of which is enough to render it unfit for publication. Another is The Prophet and God's Complaint. . . None, of course, are without some poetic merit. But I am afraid that here you have confused licence with liberty, love with—er—lust—and the Almighty with certain deistic heresies. . . I have already advised Mr. Creech. . . I take it that your Love and Liberty is a juvenile production?"

But the Bard was not to be drawn. He now realised that he had made a mistake in submitting these poems for judgment. Blair realised they went much deeper than anything he had yet written. Very well: he would not argue with him since by so doing he would betray too much of his real philosophy of life. If Blair liked to think of them as juvenilia so be it.

"You saw the notes I wrote out for Mr. Creech with the page references to your Kilmarnock edition?"

"I'm much indebted to you, sir, for the care and attention you have bestowed on my verses."

"I have no desire other than to assist you to the best of my ability. You see, Mr. Burns, you are stepping out of your rural shades—as you call them—and making your bow before the world of letters. I have had to bear this in mind very strictly. The rustic mind—here I refer to your rustic audience —is, I am afraid, inclined to a grossness and indelicacy and, I very much regret to add, a profanity altogether shocking to the world of letters—and polite society generally. . .

"I have tried to indicate best where such blemishes may be removed—and in cases where the blemishes pervade the entire poem, why that poem may not be printed.

"In addition to this, however, two of your songs have lately been submitted for my opinion. These I have advised against on quite other grounds. I refer to your song on Miss Peggy Kennedy of Daljarrock and your song on Miss Alexander of Ballochmyle. Both of these ladies I had occasion to meet when I was staying at Barskimming. Now the sentiment that inspired you to their production is in a high degree honourable. But the intimacy of the phrasing is quite injudicious. Decorum demands their exclusion from print. A lady of quality, my dear Burns, must not be addressed with that homely familiarity which is only in place when addressed to the denizen of the humble cottage. Here the question is one solely of propriety —and not, I am glad to add, of poetic merit.

"It is always distasteful to administer admonishment— especially to a sensitive poet. I trust, Mr. Burns, that you will receive these—ah—strictures of mine in a spirit of under-standing. I have no wish other than to enhance the value of your second edition, and to ensure that its subsequent reception will in no way be marred by the presence of—ah—er— blemishes. I may add that Professor Stewart and Mr. MacKenzie are fully in agreement with me on the issues I have raised. . . But you would be well advised to pay strict attention to such individual points of criticism as they may care to raise with you."

The Bard thanked Dr. Blair, took his leave (without betray-ing anything of the emotion that was beginning to boil up in him), and made straight for Smellie's printing office.

Smellie was out on some business. He strode up and down the office and occasionally cracked his whip in the air or slapped it across the leg of his boot. . .

Damn the Edinburgh literati and the pedant, frigid soul of their criticism for ever and ever! Why had he always to be at the mercy of other men's minds and other men's ideas? Why couldn't he be allowed to publish what he wanted, how he wanted? Smellie had a better brain than any of them; and he

saw nothing wrong with his verses. But he couldn't afford
to send them to hell because he was a poor man; and though
he might be heaven-taught *they* were better taught than
heaven. . . It was the same wherever a man went: money and
privilege counted more than honest worth. Maybe honest
worth counted for less in Edinburgh than anywhere else. . .

The printers, busy setting up his verses, eyed him askance.
This ploughman-poet could be a dour, uncertain beggar when
he liked. When Smellie was about he was all laughter and
sallies. When he wasn't, he was like a bear broken free from
its chain but still irking at the shackle on its leg. . .

So many members of the Crochallan Club had turned up,
whether by design or accident, at the Anchor Close tavern, that
it was decided to hold an informal meeting in the Crown
Room.

Smellie, Nicol and the Bard had been first on the scene.
Smellie had roped in Nicol on a discussion of verses of the
Bard that had been rejected by the literati as unsuitable for
inclusion in the Edinburgh edition.

They were joined by Robert Cleghorn, Sandy Nasmyth and
Jock Beugo, Alexander Cunningham and Bob Ainslie. It was
then that Smellie decided to adjourn to the Crown Room where
they would have peace and privacy for their discussion.

"Sit round, lads," said Smellie, "and form a quorum.
Robert and me hae been weighing up some o' his verses that
hae been rejectit by the literati. Noo, in my opinion, some
o' the rejections are just damnwell intolerable. There's a
cantata on the subject o' Love and Liberty that I hae nae
hesitation in declaring the Bard's finest effort to date—in fact,
I doubt if there's a finer set o' verses on the like theme in ony
language. . . What I suggest is that the Bard, here, should do
us the honour o' reading his rejectit pieces——"

The Bard interrupted: "That's too long a job, Willie."

"Well, I'll read out some and Willie Nicol can read out some
—and what aboot you, Sandy Nasmyth?"

"I'll read the whole bluidy lot, Smellie. In ony case we can
sit here a' nicht, can we no'?"

"That's very generous o' you," said the Bard. "But to do my cantata on Love and Liberty justice I need a wheen o' guid singers."

"Cunningham here'll sing."

"Aye—but I need women too. I need a martial chuck and a grand Highland widow. . . No: you can read my Love and Liberty from the manuscript. What I was arguing about wi' Willie Smellie this afternoon concerned some strictures on the life o' David o' the Psalms—King David o' poetic brief. Smellie said I had been too harsh on Royal Davie—and that I had been unjustly savage on the Old Testament. With your permission I'd like to borrow a Bible from Dawney Douglas and read you a lesson—and then, and not before then, I'll read you my verses."

There was a roar of approval at this. But the Bard went on in a serious tone:

"Some folk accuse my verses o' being indecent and irreligious——"

"Aye—but they're a' the better for that, Robert."

"I'm going to surprise you, Sandy. I think my verses neither indecent nor irreligious. But then my notions o' decency and religion differ from the notions o' the reverend and the right reverend divines of Edinburgh and of Ayrshire. If the Christian religion bases itself on the Old Testament— then I am not a Christian. If atheism bases its claim to our attention on the non-existence of the Godhead, in any shape of form, then I am no atheist. My own views I've expressed in my verses again and again. He that hath eyes to see let him see! I'm not going to expound my views to you here and now. . . But bring ben the Book and then he that hath ears to hear. . ."

Smellie rose and left the room and returned presently and placed a Bible before him.

The company was strangely silent. This was an utterly new Robert Burns who confronted them. He was deadly calm and completely unemotional.

The Bard opened the Book and read in a calm voice:

"Now there was long war between the house of Saul and

the house of David; but David waxed stronger and stronger, and the house of Saul waxed weaker and weaker.

"David was thirty years old when he began to reign; and he reigned forty years.

"In Hebron he reigned over Judah seven years and six months; and in Jerusalem he reigned thirty and three years over all Israel and Judah. . .

"And David perceived that the Lord had established him king over Israel, and that He had exalted his kingdom for His people Israel's sake.

"And David took him more concubines and wives out of Jerusalem, after he was come from Hebron; and there were yet sons and daughters born to David. . .

"And David did so, as the Lord had commanded him; and smote the Philistines from Geba until thou come to Gazer. . .

"And David danced before the Lord with all his might; and David was girded with a linen ephod. . . And as the ark of the Lord came into the city of David, Michal, Saul's daughter, looked through a window, and saw King David leaping and dancing before the Lord; and she despised him in her heart. . .

"Then David returned to bless his household. And Michal, the daughter of Saul, came out to meet David, and said: ' How glorious was the King of Israel to-day, who uncovered himself to-day in the eyes of the handmaids of his servants, as one of the vain fellows shamelessly uncovereth himself. . .' And David said unto Michal: ' It was before the Lord which chose me before thy father and before all his house, to appoint me ruler over the people of the Lord, over Israel: therefore will I play before the Lord. And I will yet be more vile than thus, and will be base in mine own sight; and of the maidservants which thou hast spoken of, of them shall I be had in honour.' Therefore Michal, the daughter of Saul, had no child unto the day of her death.

"And it came to pass, after the year was expired, at the time when kings go forth to battle, that David sent Joab, and his servants with him, and all Israel; and they destroyed the children of Ammon, and besieged Rabbah. But David tarried still at Jerusalem.

"And it came to pass in an eveningtide, that David rose from off his bed, and walked upon the roof of the king's house: and from the roof he saw a woman washing herself; and the woman was very beautiful to look upon. And David sent and enquired after the woman. And one said: 'Is not this Bathsheba, the daughter of Eliam, the wife of Uriah the Hittite?'

"And David sent messengers, and took her; and she came in unto him and he lay with her; for she was purified from her uncleanness; and she returned unto her house. And the woman conceived, and sent and told David, and said: 'I am with child.'

"And David sent to Joab, saying: 'Send me Uriah the Hittite.' And Joab sent Uriah to David. And when Uriah was come unto him, David demanded of him how Joab did, and how the people did, and how the war prospered. And David said to Uriah: 'Go down to thy house, and wash thy feet.' And Uriah departed out of the King's house, and there followed him a mess of meat from the King. But Uriah slept at the door of the King's house with all the servants of his lord, and went not down to his house.

"And when they had told David, saying: 'Uriah went not down into his house,' David said unto Uriah: 'Camest thou not from thy journey? Why then didst thou not go down unto thine house?'

"And Uriah said unto David: 'The ark, and Israel, and Judah, abide in tents; and my lord Joab, and the servants of my lord, are encamped in the open fields; shall I then go into mine house, to eat and to drink, *and to lie with my wife*? As thou livest, and as thy soul liveth, I will not do this thing.'

"And it came to pass in the morning, that David wrote a letter to Joab, and sent it by the hand of Uriah. And he wrote in the letter, saying: 'Set ye Uriah in the forefront of the hottest battle, and retire ye from him, that he may be smitten, and die.'

"And it came to pass, when Joab observed the city, that he assigned Uriah unto a place where he knew that valiant men were. And the men of the city went out, and fought with Joab; and there fell some of the people of the servants of David; and Uriah the Hittite died also. . .

"So the messenger went, and came and shewed David all that Joab had sent him for. And the messenger said unto David: 'Surely the men prevailed against us, and came out unto us into the field, and we were upon them even unto the entering of the gate. And the shooters shot from off the wall upon thy servants; and some of the King's servants be dead, and thy servant Uriah the Hittite is dead also.'

"Then David said unto the messenger: 'Thus shalt thou say unto Joab: Let not this thing displease thee, for the sword devoureth one as well as another; make thy battle more strong against the city, and overthrow it; and encourage thou him.'

"And when the wife of Uriah heard that Uriah her husband was dead, she mourned for her husband. And when the mourning was past, David sent and fetched her to his house; and she became his wife, and bare him a son. But the thing that David had done displeased the Lord. . .

"And again the anger of the Lord was kindled against Israel; and he moved David against them to say: 'Go number Israel and Judah.' For the King said to Joab the captain of the host, which was with him: 'Go now through all the tribes of Israel, from Dan even to Beer-sheba, and number ye the people, that I may know the number of the people. . .'

"So the Lord sent a pestilence upon Israel from the morning even to the time appointed; *and there died of the people from Dan even to Beer-sheba seventy thousand men.* . .

"And it came to pass, that after the year was expired, at the time that kings go out to battle, Joab led forth the power of the army, and wasted the country of the children of Ammon, and came and besieged Rabbah. But David tarried at Jerusalem. And Joab smote Rabbah, and destroyed it.

"And David took the crown of their king from off his head, and found it to weigh a talent of gold, and there were precious stones in it; and it was set upon David's head; and he brought also exceeding much spoil out of the city.

"*And he brought out the people that were in it, and cut them with saws, and with harrows of iron, and with axes. Even so dealt David with all the cities of the children of Ammon.* And David and all the people returned to Jerusalem. . .

"Now the days of David drew nigh that he should die; and he charged Solomon his son, saying: 'I go the way of all the earth: be thou strong therefore, and shew thyself a man. . .

"'Moreover thou knowest also what Joab the son of Zeruiah did to me, and what he did to the two captains of the hosts of Israel, unto Abner the son of Ner, and unto Amasa the son of Jether, whom he slew, and shed the blood of war in peace, and put the blood of war upon his girdle that was about his loins, and in his shoes that were on his feet. Do therefore according to thy wisdom, *and let not his hoar head go down to the grave in peace.* But shew kindness unto the sons of Barzillai the Gileadite, and let them be of those that eat at thy table; for so they came to me when I fled because of Absalom thy brother.

"'And, behold, thou has with thee Shimei the son of Gera, a Benjamite of Bahurim, which cursed me with a grievous curse in the day when I went to Mahanaim. But he came down to meet me at Jordan, and I sware to him by the Lord, saying: "I will not put thee to death with the sword."

"'Now therefore hold him not guiltless; for thou art a wise man, and knowest what thou oughtest to do unto him; *but his hoar head bring thou down to the grave with blood.'*

"So David slept with his fathers, and was buried in the city of David."

As the Bard had read he had watched the company seated round the table. In his younger days he had memorised much of what he now read. Smellie's face was graven; Nicol's eyes held a deadly concentrated look; Nasmyth was frankly cynical; Beugo's eyes were far-away and dreamy; Alexander Cunningham seemed uneasy; and there was a white glint of fear in the young eyes of Robert Ainslie. Only the calm open eyes of Cleghorn seemed completely unaffected; but his mouth betrayed his anticipation.

"And there endeth the reading," said the Bard. "Now it so happens that an Ayrshire friend of mine, David Sillar, himself a poet and a fiddler, took exception to certain of my remarks concerning this self-same Royal David. And in a set o' verses to me reproved me as follows—and I quote you what Davie Sillar wrote because Willie Smellie is seemingly of the same opinion as Sillar was.

"' O, Rabbie Burns, I'm wae to think, that in your rage for names to clink ye sud hae daured sae ill to link, King David's name, and tried to spatter wi' your ink his haly fame.

"' As I a Davie am mysel' sic things I say ye sudna tell, nor rax an inch until an ell ye mak' it look; tak' my advice, ye infidel, and read the Book.'

"But I've yet to meet in with the man or woman who has read the Book more assiduously than I have. And so I replied to Davie Sillar as follows—Look Up and See!

"Noo, David Sillar, that's the plan, quo I, last night, when in my han' I gaed your latest screed a scan rebukin me about your model name-sake man,—look up and see!

"Altho it may be unexpectit, an' few the facts hae yet detectit, my Bible hasna been negleckit sin I was wee, and nae sma' lore I hae colleckit—look up and see!

"Bad as I am, or hae been ca'd by jauds that lang hae at me jawed and priests that fain my pash had claw'd, I winna lee, King David's life ye less can laud,—look up and see!

"Gin I had but a Gowdie's airt at treating him to his dessert, this saintship after God's ain he'rt, as said to be, I'd prove a villain maist expert—look up and see!

"Aye, though that Jesus styled Divine is shown to be o' David's line through mair than ae poor concubine, the pedigree has plaiguit ither heids than mine,—look up and see!

"I'm sure, my frien', ye never heard that I, although like him a Bard, wi' daft, unseemly dancin' garred my shanks to flee, till a' the decencies were jarred—look up and see!

"His wife, at least ane o' the lot, since by the score he had them got, for thinkin' him a filthy snot—Saul's dochter she—a cruel curse at her he shot—look up and see!

"And neist his tricks wi' Abigail: her man or lang begood to ail and was as ye may read the tale alooed to dee; syne David did the widow nail—look up and see!

"And wha his conduct could defen' when like a coward as

we ken, he sacrificed sae mony men upon the plea God banned
the Census Takkers pen?—look up and see!

"He was a cruel Man o' War and for his plunder traivelled
far defenceless fowk to mash and mar and spill their bree in
bluidy streams amang the glaur—look up and see!

"And some for unco little cause he cut wi' harrows and wi'
saws: wha likes for that may shout huzzahs, I'll never gie sic
fiendish deeins my applause—look up and see!

"None spared he in his anger wild; not age itself, nor
yet the child, although upon the sword it smiled or crowed
in glee—— How *can* the texts be reconciled?—look up and
see!

"For David, as the Scriptures say, as black a rascal in his
day as ony Tyrant noo we hae or e'er may dree was God's
especial protégé—look up and see!

"Can parsons, think ye, close the lid and keep the awfu'
story hid on hoo the rascal—God forbid we ere sud pree what
he to puir Uriah did—look up and see!

"And since the Psalmist, as we learn, gat stown Bath-Sheba
twice wi' bairn he must hae had a hert o' airn to shut his e'e
to Nathan's reprimandin' stern—look up and see!

"Fine stock they were we maun aloo! Himsel'—we ken
wha he cam through—and Solomon they'd gar us true bore
Wisdom's Key, but here's my best advice to you—look up
and see!

"Foul-mouth'd auld Davie also was and mony proofs your
Bible has o' his inspired profaneness as ye maun agree if 'tis
as in my copy 'twas—look up and see!

"E'en lyin' on the bed o' Death the scoundrel, bent on
spreadin' scaith, kept up his cursin' tongue, in faith ne'er
stoppit he till Cloutie chokit aff his breath—look up and see!

"And yet in face o' a' his record, his lang career sae vilely
checkered, and hoo his licht sae aften flickered, in Heaven hie
nae angel's seat is better siccared—look up and see!

"I've read my Bible, Davie man, and that's the reason hoo
I stan' opposed to a' the pious ban' that bow the knee to saints
o' royal David's clan—look up and see!

"Should a' be true the prophets tell, if I the lines am fit to spell, King David mair o' dirt should smell than Deity; and gin there's sic a place as Hell—look up and see!"

He paused. "There you have it, friends. I stood by that then and I stand by it now; and let him who dares say I've raxed an inch until an ell. And now, Willie Smellie, what have you to say for yourself?"

Smellie held out his great blackened paw: "Put it there, Rab: I retract everything I said—if onything you've been too lenient on royal Davie——— But, by the holy, I'd liked to hae seen Blair's face gin you had read him."

Nasmyth roared: "Let's hae Dawney ben for the drinks— that's a poem mak's you dry doon to your big taes. . ."

The truth was that *Look Up and See* was too much for most of them. Only when the drink had circulated did they begin to talk. After some desultory conversation Smellie again took the chair.

"I've admitted my error; and you've a' expressed yoursel's as greatly taken on wi' the poem. Noo the question is: had the literati ony right to ban this poem—amang a wheen ithers —frae the Edinburgh edition? Noo I'm in the chair here. I ken you're bursting to say plenty, Nicol—but wait your turn. You, Nasmyth: what hae you to say?"

"Print the poem and be damned to the literati! Anything the Bard writes should be printed. There can be nae argument aboot that."

"Aye, but what about the literati? D'ye think there's ony reasonable grounds for suppressing the poem?"

"None! D'ye expect a stinking hypocrite o' a priest to allow onything in print that exposes his hypocrisy? You canna be a priest unless you are a hypocrite—and the bigger the thundering hypocrite, the bigger and better the bluidy priest! Mankind will never be free till it disposes o' a' its priests—regardless o' denominations. As the Bard's no' in favour o' the priests, why the hell should he bother to consult wi' them . . .?"

"Noo, noo, Robert: just bide a wee: you'll get your turn to speak after. Cunningham! What hae you to say?"

"Me? I've nothing to say. Except I wouldna exclude the

verses. If Look Up and See offends, the Holy Fair should offend. But I understand there's nae objection to the Holy Fair. I see no reason why the verses shouldna be published."

"Mr. Ainslie?"

"I think it would be better if Look Up and See was excluded. It will offend a lot o' folk that needna be offended. I'm not sure that it gives a true picture of David's life. I . . . mean: well, he repented of his sins. I understand Mr. Burns's argument—though maybe not for the same reasons. I mean: it would be safer to exclude the poem—excellent though it is for private circulation. I hope you don't misunderstand me, Robert?"

"We'll see about that later, Mr. Ainslie. You, Beugo?"

"To tell the truth I've never been able to tak' the Bible seriously. Certainly the Bard has made out an unchallengeable case. You canna dispute it: look up and see! Still, if the Bard's depending on the patronage o' the Edinburgh gentry, then young Ainslie's point here may be worth considering. If it was left to me it would go in along wi' the rest."

"Noo, Nicol! And dinna tak' a' nicht; for I've something to say mysel'."

"The poem shouldna go in. The poem canna go in—not yet. Why? Because the Edinburgh edition would never see the light o' day. Blair and company are no' bluidy idiots even if they are bluidy hypocrites. If that poem could be published and read in every Scottish home, what would happen? The clergy would be out o' a job. Every line o' that poem's a fully loaded carronade. . . The time for such an assault on the citadels o' theological humbuggery is no' yet. Later on, when the Bard has won to an unchallengeable position, he can publish what he fancies—like Voltaire. The issue's as plain as the nose of your face. Either David was a bluidy rogue or he was God's anointed. And either God anoints bluidy rogues or He doesna. But why should the Bard raise that issue—at this juncture? Noo, there's no argument. Look Up and See nae mair goes in than Holy Willie's Prayer—or Love and Liberty! Unless the Bard wants to be a martyr and end up wi' being burned at the end o' the Tolbooth. Of coorse: I'm speaking in the *interests* o' the Bard. For mysel', I found oot lang ago that the Bible's a collection o' tales and fancies belonging to the Jews. The old Jews werena idiots: far from it. There's a lot o' wisdom aboot them—but a lot o' bluidy murderous morality too——"

"Well—the verses dinna go in—that's what it amounts to, Willie?"

"You heard me!"

"Oh aye—we heard. But you, Captain Cleghorn: I damn-near forgot aboot you. Hae you an opinion?"

"If Willie Nicol will allow me an opinion."

"I'll no' allow you an opinion, Saughton—but speak your mind for a' that."

"Thank you, Willie. I'm for the verses being included; and I'll tell you why. Nocht that the Bard puts down is put down in malice. There's nae spite nor hate nor ony bad efter-taste o' bitterness aboot it. Damnit, the Bard could write a verse or twa about the Almichty Himsel'; and gin he did there's naebody would laugh heartier than God Himsel'. Sae gin God could laugh at the Bard's glorious wit and humour, what way should ony pigeon-chested little scart curl up his lip? Mind you: there's things in Look Up and See that, if I took literally, would offend *my* religious principles. But I find the whole thing maist refreshing and invigorating. God meant us to laugh as well as greet. And there's mair to greet than laugh aboot in the world. So I say print, Robert—and print it richt at the start o' your book; and onybody that's offended's better offended. A damn sicht! Gin there's sic a place as Hell—look up and see."

Smellie took a good drink of his whisky and smacked his lips.

"Well, frien's, a grand discussion! Noo, if I were to tak' some time and go deeper into the theological niceties o' the auld Hebrews——"

"Damn you and your auld Hebrews, Smellie—come to the point!"

"I gave *you* plenty rope, Nicol, you thrawn beggar. Howsomenever, I'm no' gaun into the niceties o' auld Hebrew theology. I just want to take up the point so well made by Saughton here. It was a point I was for making mysel'—only no' as weel, I'll say that for you, Saughton. It's a point, howsomenever, that requires a wee bit o' elaboration. I agree you canna tak' offence at onything the Bard writes—provided you're smit wi' the way the Bard looks at things. *I* think the Bard's way's the right way—so I laugh when he laughs. But that's only *me*. The world's no' composed o' Robert Burns and Willie Smellie. Nane o' your pig's grunting, Nicol: I'm no' comparing myself wi' Robert Burns. What I'm telling you is that I think alang the same lines—especially on this question o' the auld Jewish theology. But there's the point I want to mak'."

"How mony points d'ye want to mak'?"

"As mony as I think necessary, Nicol. . . When I read Look Up and See I thocht it went ower the score in so far as it was libellous—an exaggeration. But when I heard the Bard give chapter and verse, then, damn me, it doesna go hauf far enough. I never thocht that David o' the Psalms was half the blackguard he was. In fact I never thocht he was a blackguard at a'! And this brings me to the crux o' the matter. How mony folks ken just what David's character was? Naebody but the Bard here. So what effect will it hae on the folk? A shocking effect! I doubt if they'll laugh, Captain Cleghorn. They'll say what I said (even them that wad laugh)—you've gaun ower the score, Rab. You're exaggerating, Rab.

"Am I richt or wrang? If I'm richt, then the poem shouldna appear in print unless chapter and verse goes in along wi' it. And that's my verdict. Noo: you've a' had your say. I want to hear what Robert, here, has to say in reply. After that we can argue till the cock craws for a' I care. Come on, Robert!"

"Gentlemen: the literati of Edinburgh are not honest men —as I understand honesty. But they are, in effect, the sponsors of my Edinburgh edition. However much I may disagree with them, and however vehemently I choose to argue my disagreements with them, the fact remains that there is no appeal from their verdict. And that's that!

"As for my own position. I must make this as clear as I can. I accept no absolutes. Mankind is compounded of good and evil. There are good priests and evil priests as there are men of other ranks and occupation. The Roman Catholic Bishop Geddes is a good priest; the Presbyterian Reverend William Greenfield is a good priest. But even in them, as in all of us, is the admixture of evil—however little it may be. Now I would not offend a man who holds to his opinions and beliefs honestly. I would not wittingly offend the good that is in any man. But neither will I compromise my beliefs for any man—or woman. Captain Cleghorn thinks that nobody can take offence at what I write. Alas—that is far from being true. Yet if offence there must be, then that offence must not be the offence of meanness. At least I pray I shall ever be spared the sin of meanly offending for the mean sake of offence. . .

"My quarrel with organised religions is that they dare not laugh. Laughter dissolves conceit. And organised religion is nothing but organised conceit—the terrible conceit of thinking that priests can interpret the will of God and the purpose of creation. A man may, with some justice, claim to be a man of feeling, a man of war, a man of love, a man of this or that qualification. But there is no conceit to equal the conceit of a man who claims to be a man of God.

"Either we are all God's children or we are orphans of blind chance. I think we are all children of God. And if this raises the question: Who or what is God, then I am content to risk eternal damnation by stating that I do not know.

"But this I do know: God does not make His eternal presence felt only to those who gather round the Ark of the Covenant, the Pope of Rome or the General Assembly of the Kirk of Scotland. Jew, Catholic, Protestant, Mohammedan, Philistine, Heathen, Infidel, Atheist—these are but names, but labels signifying belief or unbelief according to the label. And whatever label a man has hung on his neck by his parents matters only in so far as he is true to his label—true to his belief or his unbelief. For if, as I think, we are all children of the one almighty and inscrutable Father—or Force—then we will be dealt with each according to his deserts—either here or hereafter.

"Or if blind chance has cast us fatherless upon the earth, then equally blind chance will destroy us. Either way there is no room, no justification for conceit. . .

"But, gentlemen, you have driven me to a lanthorn-jawed solemnity that ill becomes a session at the board so long associated with care-defying mirth and social glee. I am deeply grateful to all of you for expressing your opinion so frankly and so freely. What the hell does it matter here and now that the literati rightly or wrongly have rejected some of my verses? I am thankful that they have accepted any. And now I ask you, Captain Cleghorn, and you, Ensign Cunningham, in the absence of our Colonel, to sing—and sing as you have never sung before—and for the love of whatever God, or gods, we swear by, let us push about the jorum!"

Smellie crashed a fist on the board.

"No! By God you don't—not a one o' you! I'm in command here! And I'll court martial and punish the first man that opens his mouth. Fill your glasses, gentlemen! Full bumpers, full bumpers! And when I tell you—and not before—drain them to the lees. Gentlemen: you've listened to a sermon this nicht, in this room of a' places: a sermon that should put us a' to shame—that's what it does to me. This is no' the time for me to mak' a speech—I'm no' adequate to this occasion. But, Robert, my lad, every bluidy man-jack o' us will now rise to our feet—be upstanding there!—and every man o' us will drink a bumper to you. Gentlemen: to the health and happiness, to the long life and every joy that's dear to the heart o' man—this we wish to our comrade, our brither and our peer, the Bard o' Caledonia—Robert Burns!"

Willie Nicol, his glass drained, smashed it on the table. The others followed his example. Robert Ainslie's was the last glass to break.

But the Bard's open palm was across his eyes and his thumb and forefinger, spanning his brow, were deeply pressed into his temples.

THE FORGOTTEN GRAVE

The beadle showed him the grave, pointing to it with a swollen-jointed dirty finger. He said nothing but shuffled away on his rheumaticky shanks.

There was no grass on the grave, though some withered weeds still lingered on the grey-black earth. There was nothing to mark the spot, nothing to indicate that here lay the mortal remains of a man whose verses were nevertheless immortal.

And as he stood there bare-headed beside the Canongate Kirk and the cold raw wind tossed back his black hair, the Bard felt raw and cold in his emotions.

He remembered the dark days he had spent in Irvine's gloomy vennel and how the verses of Robert Fergusson had warmed and heartened and elated him. Many a heart-warming, heart-lifting hour his poetry had given him. He had borrowed from him richly and freely and the bright flame of the poor scrivener's genius had indeed lighted him the way to the Kilmarnock edition—had now lighted his steps to his very grave.

He sighed; but it was a bitter sigh. And he cursed the Edinburgh gentry, cursed them deeply and silently for their cruelty in letting their finest poet rot to death on the sodden straw of their madhouse.

They had murdered him. And yet some food from their overburdened tables and a small percentage of the cash they threw away at cards would have preserved his health and supported him in comfort.

What indeed had been his crime? That he was too generous in his spirit; too free in the free-flowing spirit of his genius. He had mocked them: he had laughed at their pride and their pretensions. He had not bowed down before their empty and glittering hours. He had praised the simple and enduring elements of life. His heart had sung at the sight of a butterfly in a city street; he had derided the solemn, lanthorn-jawed gentility of guid braid claith. . .

He had addressed himself to the honest folks o' Auld Reekie

that he had loved so deeply. . . 'Whan big as burns the gutters rin, gin ye hae catcht a droukit skin, to Luckie Middlemist's loup in, and sit fu' snug o'er oysters and a dram o' gin or haddock lug. . .'

Ah well: if there was anything of an after-life, poor Fergusson would have all the gin, oysters and haddie lugs he could stomach—and nae drookit skin but the warmth o' Lucky's eternal ingle. . .

The raw wind blustered and moaned amongst the tombs. . .

Eternity could arrange matters to suit eternity. Here and now he must do something that folks to-day, and the generations yet unborn, might be directed to one of Auld Scotia's sweetest singers. . .

' In troth, my callant, I'm sae fain to see your sonsy, canty strain, you write sic easy style and plain, and words sae bonnie, nae suth'ron lown dare you disdain or cry fy on ye.'

At his own expense he would have a headstone erected on this sacred and beloved spot—and damn Edinburgh's gentry and Edinburgh's literati. . .

So he penned a note to the Baillies of the Canongate seeking permission to erect a memorial stone and the worthy baillies passed on the request to the Managers of the Kirk who granted him the necessary permission "in consideration of the laudable and disinterested motion of Mr. Burns, and the propriety of the request."

Then over a tavern table he discussed details with Robert Burn, the mason.

The mason, white with chiselled dust, was unemotionally practical.

"So you want to put a bit stane on poor Bob Fergusson's grave—and pay for it yoursel'?"

"Who else would pay for it?"

"There you are, sir, there you are! That's the whole case in a nutshell."

"Are you feared for your money?"

"No . . . no: I'll do you a cheap job—leastways, I'll dae you a good job cheap—seeing how it is."

W.G.W.   H

"You knew Robert Fergusson?"

"I mind seeing the lad."

"You were never interested in his verses?"

"I canna say that I was. I've read some o' yours, though. Aye . . . and I suppose it's natural for poets to hang thegither like ither tradesfolk. I suppose making poetry's a trade like ony other. Aye. . . And this is what you want chiselled on the stane? That's a wheen letters, Mr. Burns."

He spread the paper on the table.

HERE LIES ROBERT FERGUSSON, POET
Born September 5th 1751—Died 16th October 1774

No sculptured marble here, no pompous lay,
 'No storied urn nor animated bust';
This simple stone directs pale Scotia's way,
 To pour her sorrows o'er the Poet's dust.

"Still, that's verra nice, verra nice. And then you want this on the reverse side:

By special grant of the Managers to ROBERT
 BURNS, who erected this stone,
This Burial-place is to remain for ever sacred
 to the memory of ROBERT FERGUSSON.

"Aye: in the coorse o' my trade I carve a lot o' gey rubbish on guid stane—and maist o' it the damndest lies . . . speak nae ill o' the dead, ye ken. Still, mind you, Mr. Burns, I wadna like a lot o' damned lies put on my headstane when I'm dead. Aye, you never ken what micht be held against you in the next warld. But I suppose Bob Fergusson was a guid enough poet for a lawyer's clerk."

Robert Burn, mason and architect, was oblivious to the fire that smouldered in Robert Burns's eyes; nor did the curtness of his tone in any way perturb him.

"I only hope, sir, you're a good enough mason to execute his headstone."

The mason dusted the front of his waistcoat with a broad hand.

"We'll see, Mr. Burns, we'll see—an' a hunder years after this it'll mak' the same odds to you an' me as it's makin' to puir Fergusson the day."

ALL THE BLUE DEVILS

Of the New Town, with its wide spacious streets and large elegant blocks of dwelling houses and business premises, the Bard was little enamoured. After the High Street and the Landmarket he favoured the South Town with Brown Square, Argyle Square and George Square. The South Town, unlike the New, had diversity and character. The main streets that led through it all tended to merge at a point beyond George Square on the main road south, going past the Meadows. These main streets, Bristo Street, the Potterrow, Nicolson Street and the Pleasance, though comparatively modern, had a settled air about them and were warm and homely. . .

From the Grassmarket he could make his way to Dr. Blacklock or Willie Nicol by way of the Candlemaker Row and the Bristo; from the Canongate end of the Town he could proceed by way of the Pleasance. From Baxters' Close he nearly always went down Libberton's Wynd along the Cowgate and up the Potterrow.

Every step he took and by whatever street, brought different angles of interest; and everywhere the streets and closes and wynds swarmed with interesting folks. In the New Town there were the gentry and their servants, much space, good clean air and a raw spiritless uniformity.

Sometimes he regretted it was winter with short days and long dark nights. Especially did he regret this when he enjoyed a morning or afternoon walk with Peggy Chalmers. The greyness of the days and the rawness of the weather mitigated against the pleasure of those rare jaunts. . .

"You know, Peggy—this is when I miss Ayrshire. When I think of the walks I could take you there."

"But Ayrshire can be gey bleak and bare in winter, Robert."

"Ah, but never as bleak and bare as this and seldom so raw and cold."

"You've been out on the Braid Hills wi' Professor Stewart, have you not?"

"Yes—and enjoyed every step of it. But then he's a very pleasant man to walk with, is Dugald Stewart—he's the most interesting talker I've ever met with. But you ken fine what I mean, Peggy. If you and me were walking down by the Ayr at Barskimming or round by Ballochmyle and Catrine . . . or round by the Fail at Tarbolton. . ."

"It wouldna make ony difference atween you and me, Robert."

"I think it would, Peggy."

"You're a persistent man, Robert."

"Can you blame me?"

"Robert: you ken fine there can never be onything but friendship between us."

"Friendship's a very great deal, Peggy. . . Can you be sure you can set rigid limits to it?"

"I'd be sorry to lose your friendship, Robert. But it'll be your fault if I ever lose it. . . Now, tell me what progress you are making with your proofs . . . and tell me the latest gossip about the literati."

"In short, my dear, you want me to talk to you about anything except what I want to talk about? Well. . . I'll give over. . . I'd rather talk to you about nothing than not talk to you at all."

"But really, I am interested, deeply interested, in your news; and Doctor Blacklock is aey asking me for news of you. I sometimes think if I absented myself from him you would do likewise."

"Now, Peggy, be honest! I admire Doctor Blacklock greatly. I esteem the privilege of his friendship above that of the literati. The Doctor is the only poet in Edinburgh. But if I do find my visits to the Doctor more pleasant because you are there, can you blame me?"

"No . . . I dinna blame you, Robert. If you would only be

sensible. . . If men would only be sensible; but men must aey be protesting their love. Where a woman's concerned men are never content wi' friendship—and you are no exception . . . which is a gey pity."

He had spent a hard morning correcting his proofs in Smellie's office. His craving for the company of a lass was an agony. And he desperately wanted to make love to Peggy Chalmers—without any thought of sex at all. Indeed, and this was the strangest thing about his love for Peggy, it was almost completely sexless, almost idealistic. This made her refusal of his advances so bitterly, frustratingly disappointing. He wanted to put his arms round her and kiss her and whisper to her . . . whisper poetry and whisper of his ambitions for her; whisper just how deep and intense yet unsexed and unselfish was his love for her. The real things he wanted to say to her were things that could not be shouted, could not be talked about in casual conversation. The physical link would first have to be established—and then softly he would unburden the weight of verbal intimacy upon her. . .

But no matter how near they came she would not allow that physical contact to be made. Her denial hedged her about. . .

The winter dusk came down on the town and lum reek hung about the chimney pots and a wet raw haar was trailing in from the sea. Lights began to show, weak and half-hearted, in the small square windows.

They came in through George Square, lonely and withdrawn in the winter twilight. The great wax candles were not yet lit though here and there a ghostly flame flickered from a fire and danced dully on the dank window panes.

They did not hurry their step. Rather did he feel that Peggy lingered in her step. From some window came the strain of a fiddle and the slow rhythm of the melody hung listlessly on the air.

She allowed him to take her arm and yet somehow not quite take it.

For she sensed something of his mood. And she felt for him. He *was* a genius and he was sincere and he was attractive. But—but he was a ploughman and would carry the stamp of the ploughman on him for the rest of his life. He had nothing to offer but his fame, his poetic genius and the social and economic status of a ploughman's wife: at best the wife of a small tenant-farmer. Peggy knew too well from observation what that meant, exactly what it signified. . . The pity of it—for it would be so easy to let Robert Burns take her in his great strong arms—and lose everything that she wanted from life: a rich husband, leisure, books, music, entertaining, splendid parties, hostess in a fine house, travel on the Continent—London and Paris. . . What a world to exchange for love and poverty and the slavery of a farm kitchen!

He could have wept when he parted from her. The loneliness in his heart, the grey weary emptiness in his emotional life consumed him like a grey cancerous growth. His need for the love of a lass was terrible in its intensity; and Peggy Chalmers with her denials, her withdrawnness, had increased that intensity to such a degree that he doubted if ever again he would be able to make physical love to a girl. His blood was completely drained from him: the grey dank haar seeped into his veins and lay cold in the chambers of his heart.

The lights that began to appear in the tavern windows glowed pale with a phosphorescence as from the grave. The citizens that shuffled past loomed out of a dead world. And all the ghouls that ever were breathed the dank haar of their deadness into every neuk and cranny of the dead town.

The dull echo of the Bard's steps sounded deep in the hollow of the earth.

He was in the grip of a ghastly attack of melancholy—the blue-devilism he had such good reason to fear. . .

BEGINNING TO DRIFT

After an evening spent in the riotous atmosphere of the Crochallan Club the mornings dawned raw and cold and unbearably empty.

His heart ached for Peggy Chalmers.

If only he could get a job, earn enough money to support himself and a wife (with Peggy as wife), how blissful would life be! There would be no need for taverns then and no need for any bawdy bravado. With a girl like Peggy to grace his home and warm his bed there would be no need for any outside distractions.

No . . . he could not remain in this loneliness much longer. He must win Peggy Chalmers.

During the early months of 1787 he applied himself diligently to his proof-correcting in Smellie's office; and for the rest he divided his time mainly between Ainslie and Nicol. He did not consume his time in friendship. When John Beugo engraved his portrait he worked from Nasmyth's portrait and from his subject direct. Beugo was interested in acquiring the French language. As the Bard had always wanted to improve on the scant knowledge Murdoch had imparted to him, he eagerly fell in with Beugo's scheme and they arranged to have lessons from Louis Cauvin who was delighted to have them.

The Bard knew that he had to make the most of his opportunities. Soon he would have to leave Edinburgh and return to Machlin.

To go back to Machlin was the last thing he wanted. There was no place for him now at Mossgiel—as it was, it provided a bare enough living for Gilbert and the family.

Besides there was Betty Paton's child—and Jean Armour's twins! He must continue to help in their maintenance.

Yet no one here in Edinburgh would take him seriously on the matter of the Excise. They dismissed the very mention of it with an airy hand. They advised him to wait till his new edition came out, and, with the return it would bring him, to invest in a small farm.

He began to realise, not without bitterness, that they were prepared to honour his poetry but that they were not prepared to assist him to earn a living. He was to go back to the plough —and write poetry as and when he could. Wasn't it sufficient for him that they had acclaimed him as Caledonia's Bard?

Even Glencairn, though he had made him the present of a

silver snuff box on his birthday, did not seem to worry about the problem as to how he should live. Nor was Glencairn prepared to offer him the hand of social equality. His was the hand of patronage. Only to those of rank would he offer friendship. And yet again and again he gave proof that his patronage was no formal thing but a protecting warmth that went further than a peer was entitled, by social law and custom, to extend to a poet who was also a ploughman. It was this knowledge that saved the Bard from going sour.

He realised, as he had long realised on the rigs of Lochlea and Mossgiel, that he would have to work out his own salvation, that only by his own efforts would he ever extract himself from the down-sucking bog of poverty.

One night at Nicol's fireside he confessed to his deepest worry.

"You see, Willie: it's very comforting to talk about poetry as if all I had to do was fill up sheets o' paper wi' it. Before I was acclaimed as a poet I wrote freely enough—some o' my best efforts were written clean offhand.

"But, now that I have been acclaimed, the position is different. I canna write ony longer as a ploughman. My productions are now scanned wi' a critical eye. I must take a thought as to what I write. Aye . . . and that's no' the only trouble. Poetry doesna come to me ony mair—and this worries me. They all want me to give up my Scotch verses and concentrate on the English. And though I can write an English piece without much trouble, my heart—and this means the best o' my inspiration—lies in our native tongue."

"I can understand that—but what's your real difficulty?"

"That I've lost my aim and purpose, Willie. I'm beginning to drift again. The future's as black as the back o' the lum there."

"You're no' the only one wi' a black future afore you. But —wait till you get the money in frae your new edition. That should be enough to settle you for a while."

"Settle me where—and how, Willie?"

"Wherever the hell you want! You canna teach blockheads

Latin, can you? Weel then: what can you do? You can work a farm——"

"God damnit, Willie, the very word farm strikes a coldness into my heart."

"Aye—the farms you've been used to. But now you look about you and *pick* your *own* farm. I'm nae farmer, Rab; but I ken plenty that mak' a good living frae the land. There's our friend, Robert Cleghorn, out at Saughton: he does weel out o' it—aye, bluidy weel. Cleghorn's never doon to his last bawbee."

"I know, I know—but I canna hope to rent—far less purchase—a farm like Cleghorn's—that wad take a couple o' thousand pounds—fifteen hundred maybe. Smellie and Creech and Peter Hill think I micht clear three to four hundred pounds for my second edition. Even at that I've got to pay back something to my family in Mossgiel."

"Why should you?"

"Because I owe them that at least."

"You owe naebody a penny—dinna be a sentimental idiot."

"No, I dinna think I'm a sentimental idiot, Willie. But I know the extent o' my obligations—and nobody can decide for me what I'll do to discharge them. But, in any event, and taking things at their best, I'll have twa-three hundred pounds at my disposal by the summer. My problem is how to put the money to the best use as an investment against the future."

"You dinna want to go back to the plough—and you dinna want to settle in Edinburgh?"

"That's right."

"You dinna ken what to do?"

"I don't."

"And yet you hanker after this Excise job?"

"It spells security."

"A poet has nae right to hope for security."

"Listen, Willie—a poet's a human being—isn't he? He's got to eat and sleep. He's got to have a roof to cover his head and clothes to cover his nakedness. This is the bare demand that the human being asks of life. But even the poorest of our human kind, like the beasts of the field, demand something more of life. They hunger for love, for parenthood—and some measure of security for their young against the hunger of the day. But surely, Willie, the poet—if he be a true poet—longs for something more than a mere humdrum level of existence. He has, for one thing, a keener experience of life. He gives more to life than ordinary mortals—and so he demands more from life. He but rarely gets it. The world is too busy grubbing a living for itself to pay much attention to her poets. Yes: the world in its odd moments of ease will harken to us. But in the busy morning we're forgotten. I want to get married; and I want to settle down somewhere where I can rest my head—and fulfil my manhood. I don't want to wander on the face of the earth like an Ishmaelite—cursed because I'm a bluidy poet. Am I asking for something unnatural, unheard of —something preposterous and absurd——?

"Listen: I've had all the poverty a man can thole and no' go bitter black wi' the bile o' discontent. By God, I ken what poverty is—not poverty in idleness, but poverty yoked in slavery. Aye: you've kent poverty, Willie: heart-breaking poverty. But you havena tasted *physical* slavery along wi' it. I've hauled and dug and sweated in the wet glaur till I was more like a beast than a human being—and the Black Bonnets tell us that God created man in His own imagine? I watched my father die—— No, no, Willie, a thousand times no . . . I canna bear the thocht o' it. I keep it choked down within me and then when the fits o' melancholy come ower me. . . Like a lot o' folk you think I'm a gay hearty laughing fellow seeing only the sunshine o' life and nothing o' the shadows. God damnit, it's because I've lived so long in the shadows that I revel in the sunshine. Maist folks ken beggar-all about poetry —beggar-all. . . Besides, what is a poet? A being more sensitive to life than his fellows. It's as simple as that. But don't think that's simplicity. A poet is a complex many-sided individual— or at least let me speak for myself. Or why the hell should I speak at all. Maybe I don't know the first bluidy thing about mysel'. But I can speak about the things I'm conscious o'. I ken what hurts me and what fills me wi' joy, pleasure, exalta- tion. And I ken I dinna tak' things as calmly—as judiciously—

as other men do. Maybe in all this I am a fool—but then that's
the kind o' fool I am. And I canna change. Time and again I
keep repeating: on reason build resolve—that pillar of true
majesty in man . . . like a priest repeating a prayer. I have a
brain and I have a heart—and a powerful set o' organs o'
generation: if this holy trinity—but then there's no trinity. . .
Instead there's a conflict o' the parts. And yet, is the war within
me—or without me? God knows, I ask little from life and less
frae mankind. A' I really crave for in life is a wife and weans
and a but and ben and the wherewithal—earned by my own
labours—to keep them frae hunger and cauld. Maybe for
luxury I ask for a glass o' honest nappy and the music o' a
sang. And maybe as richness to a' that I ask for a secluded
romantic bit o' countryside wi' woods and shaws, the green
swell o' a hillock and the drumlie waters o' a bit burn . . . and
birds and beasts. . . And yet I might as well be asking for the
moon and twa stars or the key to the gates o' heaven. Oh—
don't think I'm ungrateful for your fireside, Willie, and the
great comfort o' talking to you. Sometimes I lie wi' a wench
i' the Cowgate that gives me her body as you give me your
mind. . . No: dinna think me ungrateful, Willie. I wad never
like it said o' me that I was ungrateful, say what the hell else
they like—and they'll say plenty; but—you see how different
life would be if only I had a small measure of security?"

Nicol was awed by the Bard's intense seriousness.

"God, Rab, if I could provide you wi' this security that you
want—aye, and need—I wad do it willingly. Man, Rab, your
greatness lies precisely in the fact that you are *normal*—you're
flesh and blood and not just a wheen senseless words wrote
down on paper. Maybe I'm no' making mysel' plain. What I
mean is: you're normal in the sense that every man and every
woman can recognise immediately and instinctively that
you're expressing the instincts of the normal. You're no' awa'
up in the bluidy skies—your twa feet are on the solid ground.
And because o' this you protest at everything that degrades the
fundamental decencies o' life. That—and a lot more, Rab:
I'm not so good at putting it into words. Aye . . . so I think
I can understand what you mean when you ask if you're

human. That's just the point I've been trying to mak': you're the maist human poet that ever wrote. Naturally you want to get married and hae a family and enjoy some reasonable kind o' security. That's what I meant when I said earlier that you owe naebody a penny. Everything that's owing is owed *to* you and no' *by* you—and get that firmly into your mind! Scotland's in your debt, head ower lugs, for your verses—that means every man and woman in Scotland, whether they like it or no'; whether they ken it or no'. And the big thing about your verses as far as I can judge, Rab, is that folks tak' to them on first sight."

"My second edition will prove how far that is generally true, Willie."

"You needna worry on that score. What you've got to worry about is the money. You've got to see that you get every penny that's due you. I tell you, Robert, I dinna trust Creech —you can say what you like about taking folks as you find them; but unless I'm mistaken—which, for your sake, I hope I am—you'll find Creech will do his damndest to defraud you. Still . . . this is no' helping you in your present difficulties. Sooner or later you'll need to get some kind o' employment that'll bring you in a steady income. For wife and weans you canna do much on a pound a month—you're mair needing a pound a week."

"A pound a week wad be a fortune to me."

"Aye—on a farm where you hadna to pay for every bite you put in your mouth, the way we have to do in the towns. But . . . I'm thinking you wad need to choose your wife gey canny to get one that wad be content on a pound i' the week. You'll get nane o' your Edinburgh dames to jump at that."

"That's another o' my worries, Willie. I hae an Edinburgh dame in my mind—an' I wadna tak' her into poverty even if she wad come wi' me."

"She's no' gentry?"

"She's no' *that* kind o' gentry. But gentry enough to be familiar wi' the best in the land—she's a sister married on Sir Henry MacKenzie o' Gairloch. But she's nae snob——"

"To hell, Rab: forget her. Even if she did settle her fortune on you, would you like that?"

"As far as I can find out, Willie, she's got little fortune."

"That mak's it worse. The proudest damned vermin in Scotland are the poor gentry—what they lack in money and gear they mak' up for in stinking pride."

"You don't know the lass, Willie—or you wadna say that."

"You're in love wi' her?"

"Most damnably."

"There you are! No doubt you think she's an angel."

"Angel enough, Willie. Only I don't expect you to believe that."

"No: nor ony other body. You may be interested in the theological aspect o' the matter—angels belong to the masculine gender. There's nae female angels in theology—and there's nane in real life—only to mad beggars o' poets when they're in the demented passion they ca' love. In ony case, they tak' aff their wings alang wi' their stays when they gan to bed. Aye—marry your angel, Rab, and you'll wake up like as no' to find you're tied till an ill-tongued ill-natured jad o' a she-devil. For God's sake, keep awa' frae the Edinburgh gentry, or you'll be ruined beyond redemption. . . Of course, I ken nae mair than what you've told me; but I still think the richt lass for you is your Machlin Jean."

"God damn you, Willie: why had you to mention Jean Armour! You ken nae mair aboot Jean than I've told you—and that's little enough compared wi' what I *could* tell you. Hell, Willie, I never loved a woman as I loved Jean Armour—and never will again. If you'd seen her the day I first met her! On the road to Mossgiel. I could hae gone down on the stour and kissed her feet; I could hae ryked up and kissed her hair! I can see the sun snared in its meshes even now. God, Willie, I've kent women—dozens o' them. There's not a dame in Embro, gentle or simple, could haud a candle to Jean Armour —afore she denied me! I could knock my head agin the wa' there just thinking on the Jean Armour that was. You see, Willie—— Oh, I canna tell you about Jean: you would need to see her."

"And yet you tell me you're in love wi' your Edinburgh angel?"

"No! No! I loved once. I loved Jean Armour. No: twice! After Jean I loved a Highland lass—and she died. And her memory will torture me to the grave—and beyond it maybe."

"Steady, Rab—you'll wauken the weans inbye. What the hell's the matter wi' you? Will we go doon to Lucky Pringle's? It looks to me like you could be doing wi' a guid dram."

"Beggar you and your drams. No: I want nae Lucky Pringles. No' the nicht——"

"Beggar you, Rab. What's the matter wi' you? What *dae* you want?"

"I've told you a thousand bluidy times what I want! Don't be so thrawn, Willie."

"Me thrawn? God Almighty! You're the thrawnest beggar I've ever met in wi'. Listen, Rab: draw your heels thegither for ony sake. What I said was that I thocht your Machlin Jean was the richt lass for you *and I still say that*—and you can threip doon my throat to the contrary a' the rest o' your bluidy life—and I'll still say it. And if you smoked I'd tell you to thoomb that doon into your pipe and to smoke it till you were blue, black, yellow and green in the bluidy face."

"Oh, I've had a draw at a pipe o' bacca afore now, Willie. . . No: forgive me, I got excited there for the minute. Jean Armour, Jean . . . there'll never be a lass again like Jean Armour —in many ways. But . . . there's things hae happened atween Jean and me that you ken nocht aboot, Willie—or could ken ocht aboot. The lass I'm after hasna even the reflection o' the radiance Jean Armour had—and maybe still has. But then, Willie, I dinna love Jean Armour now the way a man should love the woman he ettles to marry. And this lass has brains, accomplishments and a deep and delicate understanding."

"Oh, well then—if it's a paragon o' a' the virtues you want, Rab, I suppose you'll need to get it. And who am I to understand a poet in love?"

"Where is the man that understands love, Willie? I havena met him yet—and I've never read o' him."

"The Latin billies thocht they kent something about the

subject. Horace could even tell you how to pick a bawd in a brothel—but you're richt enough, Rab: naebody has ever been able to tell a man how to pick a wife—successfully. And I doubt very much if there's meikle chance o' success aboot it."

"But the wife and you get on well enough——"

"Aye: weel enough. What the hell's the use o' getting on ony ither way—once you're married!"

"Well . . . I don't know. I know what my heart, my instincts, my blood tells me—and the only thing that stands atween me and the answer is the security o' a reasonable job——"

"——and a heap o' siller i' the bank?"

"That's about it."

"'It's no' in wealth; it's no' in rank——'"

"Don't quote me, Willie—no' against myself. You see: I hae a wisdom as poet that I canna be expected to hae as a lover. For when you view him in cold light a lover's a puir bluidy gull—and everybody can view him in a cold light—but himself."

"Oh, you're richt enough there, Rab. . . And what's the upshot then?"

"Not much o' an upshot, Willie. But I haven't despaired yet—and I'm no' poet enough to pine away and die of unrequited love."

"Thank God for that. Here: what about a real hot toddy for the road—I'll see ye doon the length o' the Tron . . .?"

ROBERT CLEGHORN

The learned critics might reject his *Love and Liberty*: the Crochallan cronies welcomed his bawdy songs.

And in faith they did. When Farmer Robert Cleghorn of Saughton Mills came along he was at him immediately for copies.

"By the Lord, Robert, but you have a poet's taste all round. Nothing seems to hae missed you. You maun hae had some thundering nights in Machlin?"

"Weel, Saughton, it's like this. Folk have to escape from the black denials of the Kirk here as weel as onywhere: maybe more so. In the country folk take their bawdry as simply as they take everything else. In Edinburgh it's only natural that things have to be organised. It's the age-long battle between the flesh and the spirit. I don't think there should be ony battle. The flesh and the spirit are one: at least they both live under the same thatch and within the same walls."

"You're right there, Robin!" cried Smellie. "And the Latin poets kent that as weel as ony. Though I never heard the point put so well before."

"Damn you and your bluidy literature!" roared Charles Hay. "Can we no' enjoy a sang without ye hae to jaw about literature?"

"Go on, Robert," said Cleghorn. "Charlie's at his third or fourth bottle. To hell, man, we hae to learn the theory as well as the practice o' your art. I think you've hit something there. Damnit, a guid sang does ye as much guid as a gill o' whisky... I'll tell ye what, lads: we've never had a song-book. I think we should appoint the Bard here to compile one for us."

"Moved and carried!" roared Willie Dunbar. "Captain Cleghorn: that's the best idea we've had for a while. Now push about the jorum, boys, push about the jorum, for the night's wearing on and I want to hear Ensign Cunningham in another sang. Let's hae The Yellow Yorlin'. And to wind up, I want Mr. Burns's Corn Rigs frae you, Captain."

But long after the Crochallans had officially broken up for the evening, Robert Cleghorn and Robert Burns sat discussing the old free songs of Scotland. They compared notes and reminiscences. It delighted Cleghorn to find someone with whom he could discuss the subject seriously. And when Dawney Douglas finally told them that he must now lock up the premises, they went out into the street and discussed the subject for another hour.

"Some day, Bob, I hope I'll be able to publish my songs with the music: that's important. Words without music are less than half the song; for the words canna be properly understood unless you have the melody that determines their value.

I couldna write a good song unless I had the music in my mind first; and if I can work in a lass so much the better. . . And then, you see, the best o' our auld tunes are the ones that hae the bawdiest words; and I'm thinking that for general purposes I might clean them up a bit. What d'you think?"

"Now that's another capital idea, Robin. I'm aey humming thae auld tunes about the hoose; and if you could fit some words to them that wouldna offend the womenfolk, then, damnit, you would be doing a national service."

"I did that with Green Grow the Rashes; and I think I made a tolerable job of it."

"A capital job: couldna hae been better. . . But, for Godsake, what are ye going to do wi' yoursel' when ye hae finished bringing out your new edition?"

"I wish I knew, Bob: the future opens before me like a bottomless pit. . . But let the future be as black as the Earl o' Hell's waistcoat! D'ye ken Andro and His Cutty Gun? Now there's an auld sang o' the kind I mean. Bawdy; but honest as the day. Some nameless country bard now forgotten, alas, made it up round a common-enough experience. But think o' the poetry that's in it. ' When a' the lave gaed to their bed and I sat up to clean the shune. . .' A simple opening; but perfect in its simplicity—hitting the right note on the opening. ' The bawsent bitch she left her whelps and hunted roon' us at the fun. . .' That's poetry, Cleghorn—the stuff o' genius is there . . . and the words so blended with the melody that the word and the note melt, then fuse in immortality. And there's the glory o' song-making, Cleghorn. The most difficult art in the world—to wed words to music in imperishable harmony. But it's been done again and again by an odd man here and an odd woman there. True, their names have perished in the dust; but their songs remain. I mind a lass in the town o' Irvine telling me years back how a guid sang can outlast the hills. And she could mak' a song hersel'. . ."

The moon was sitting flat-faced above the aircock of Saint Giles's. The night was calm; the rain had ceased and the sky was washed clean and clear. The moonlight was cold and remote where it touched the lands on the north side of the street; and a swathe of throbbing stars glinted up the Land-market and throbbed above the Castle on the Rock. Across the dark shadowed street an occasional shaft of moonlight lay gently on the causeway. The Auld Toon was silent and deserted: the ten o'clock drum had sounded and the company of the Town Guard had marched down from the Castle. An odd bawd coming from a late appointment slunk across the shadows and disappeared down one of the gushets that led to her lodgings, or her home, in the Cowgate. But the Town seemed as remote and as unreal as the moonlight that lay so softly along its roof-tops.

On such a night the same moon would be shining on the ridge of Mossgiel; and the wide rolling farmlands would be bathed in stillness and soft shadow.

And in Machlin Cowgate Jean Armour would be sleeping under the deep thatch of the attic room with a bairn in either arm. . .

He turned to Robert Cleghorn who was watching him even as he watched the night. "There's one thing I sometimes regret: that I canna drink. I haven't the stomach for much drink or, by God, I would drink myself into a blind stupor."

"Aye: there's a lot to be said for a guid drink whiles. But it's a pity you canna get relief in drink, Robert. Man, a guid drink and a guid feed and a guid sleep and you waken the next morning to a new world. Ah, but nae mair than once a week —and if you can haud out for a month, sae much the better."

"And you can rise fresh the next morning?"

"Fresh and renewed, Robert! Of course, if I let myself go I could be topping every night like maist o' the Corps. But the work would soon suffer."

"Ah yes; but you've got something to work for. You've got a good farm—from what I hear—and you've got a good wife."

"A widow wi' a son to her first husband and a son to me —one o' the verra best."

"The tone o' your voice tells me all that and more. You're settled in life—and see something for your labours. You're a happy, fortunate man, Bob; and drink and bawds are no' in your line. But for all that, there's a something that unsettles you. Maybe your life's too settled, too secure, too humdrum —else why would you come about Crochallan . . .?"

"I never thought on't that way, Robert."

"What other way is there, sir? The road o' life is full o' heights and hollows. We don't fly from the cradle to the grave as the crow flies—or is supposed to fly. We canna always be on the heights: we canna always be in the hollows. And, in our ignorance, we dinna ken what turn on the road lies ahead —whether to right or to left. . . In fact, how many of us can be sure we are on any road and not wandering aimlessly in the wilderness. . ."

"You couldna put it truer, Robert. Damned—there's nae escaping it. I do well enough at Saughton Mills—and mind you, that's a promise that you'll come out and see me and the wife. . . Aye, I do well enough—and better than most; but, as you say, it's no' enough. Sae I come into the Town when I canna thole it ony longer—and if Crochallan's in session, then I'm there. But d'you no' think that for a' that, the town men live a maist damnable unnatural life?"

"When man divorces himself from nature he divorces himself from the sources o' life . . . from . . . from the natural rhythm o' life. There's no' a more learned man in the Club there than Willie Smellie, unless it's Willie Nicol. And yet— of what interest to either o' them is the fertility o' the soil— seed-time and harvest? They live wholly by their brains—and man wasna made to live that way. The hands need to work as well as the brain. And I don't mean work with the hands like a mechanic—damnit, man, I've seen weavers i' Kilmarnock that were sae bent wi' their looms that they didna even look like human beings. But . . . you and me, Cleghorn, we're lucky; for the nearer to the soil, the nearer to life."

"Aye. . . I'm wi' you there, Robert . . . every time. I wadna live my days in one o' thae lands for a king's ransom. And yet, as you said, nae matter where or how we live we itch to be thegither round the bottle wi' a sang and a jest—and nae womenfolk."

"And nae womenfolk—and us hankering after them a' the

time! Sometimes I think a good marriage would anchor me in life. Other times . . . well, maybe the ideal would be a sensible wife with plenty o' understanding—and then you could hae a mistress as you fancied."

"Aye—but where would you get such understanding in a wife?"

"Where indeed, sir! And maybe that's why I'm still a bachelor."

"Ah, you'll fa' in wi' the richt lass yet, Robert. Only dinna be in ony hurry. I put dozens through my hands when I was your age—but I got the richt ane in the hinderend. . . But afore we go: you were talking about your songs. Hae you met in wi' James Johnson? The last time I spoke to him he was working on a collection o' Scotch sangs—to be printed wi' the music. He's discovered a new way o' printing music. Speir Willie Smellie about him—I think his place is in Bell's Wynd. A richt decent man, Jamie Johnson—and maist knowledgeable about the auld sangs. . . And mind you come oot to Saughton Mills—there'll be a richt hamely welcome waiting on you."

As he stretched himself out in bed beside his wife, Cleghorn said: "I'd another grand crack wi' Robert Burns in the Toon last nicht. . ."

"Oh! And just what is the attraction aboot Robert Burns apart frae his poetry?"

"God! Now you've asked me! You would like him—you couldna help liking him. A big strong fellow wi' a good strong face and a good strong voice; wi' a pair o' eyes i' his head the like you couldna describe. But God, Barbara, if you heard him speak. . . Oh, a poet: every inch and bit o' him— and a *man* every inch and bit o' him. I'll take my oath, as straight and honest a fellow as ever set foot on the High Street o' Embro. I've invited him oot here again and I only hope he'll come. I've never met a mair interesting man. A genius . . . but, damn it, modest. Nae bluidy airs and graces aboot him at all. I'm taken wi' him—even more than I was taken by his poems."

"Ah weel, Bob: *they* went to your head."

"Aye . . . and they went to yours too, Barbara. Come on: admit it."

"I never denied it. Aye . . . and how did you fa' in wi' Robert Burns this time?"

"Oh, I met Smellie the printer."

"Oh aye—ye'd be at mair o' your coarse songs."

"That's the strange bit, Barbara. I've nae doubt Burns kens mony a rare sang. But no: I'd a lang talk wi' him. As a matter o' fact we were talking about the merits o' the toon against the country. . ."

"Aye. . . I'm sure you were!"

"Ah, you'll need to meet him, Barbara—and then you'll understand what I mean."

Robert Cleghorn found it impossible to tell his wife exactly how Robert Burns had impressed him. But as he lay by her side he tried to re-live every moment of their meeting and recall every word of his conversation. And, strangely, when some of his remarks were analysed they were commonplace enough—though full of common sense. There was a something else about Robert Burns he was beginning to realise. He had two extraordinary qualities that, either singly or in combination, were irresistible—his eyes and his voice. His eyes were uncanny and the light that glinted in them or suffused them was damn-near no' human. But the voice! Here was a voice that could impart to the most ordinary sentiments the most extraordinary nervous fluency—so that you could sit or stand for half the night just listening to it.

Robert Cleghorn was a lusty singer and had a rare mellow baritone range. It seemed strange to him that Robert Burns was no singer for he had the most musical voice he had ever heard in a human being, a voice that could phrase, pitch and modulate itself in a manner that any singer worth his salt would give his right hand to possess.

Cleghorn wondered if he had hit on the secret of the Bard's fascinating conversational charm.

SPRING SUNSHINE

William Creech shifted a trifle uneasily on his chair.

"Of course, you ken that your money will not come in for some time—say six months?"

"Six months!"

"Not earlier, I'm afraid."

"But . . . how am I to live for six months? It's been difficult enough up till now. But for the generosity of some patrons in paying for their copies in advance——"

"Quite so, my dear Robert. But I think I warned you that the financial side of poetry—and indeed all subscription authorship—is attended with much vexatious delay . . . and uncertainty."

"But surely you dinna think there's any uncertainty about my money?"

"No . . . not in any large measure. As your agent I shall see that copies go only to reliable booksellers—and against a firm order."

"Then . . . I must . . . hang on here for another six months?"

"Not necessarily, Robert. Not after the edition is out. Unless, of course, you canna find a better or more convenient place—er—to hang on."

The Bard felt he was trapped.

He still had no prospects of settled employment and nothing at all regarding the Excise. Yet he must get back home if only for a brief visit; and he could not go home penniless. Ainslie had talked of a visit to the Borders and he had promised Patrick Miller to go home by Dumfries and have a look at his Dalswinton farm proposition.

The cautious Creech let the gravity of the position sink home. Then he coughed discreetly.

"There is, of course, a way out of your present difficulties, Robert. I have every mind to be generous with you."

"If you can help me in any way, Mr. Creech, you would earn a grateful bard's eternal thanks."

"Aye. . . Well now. Your poems will be out any day and with a bit of luck the edition, though somewhat larger than public demand and prudent caution would warrant, may—eventually—be sold. In a word, Robert, their market value is exhausted. However, I think—for your sake—I might be prepared to risk a very long-term investment by making you an offer for your copyright."

"My copyright!"

"Yes: your copyright. Not that it's likely to be of any value for many a long day. Meantime, it could earn you some ready cash and you would be foolish not to take advantage of it."

The Bard looked glum and Creech began to think he had pressed his advantage too far.

"Perhaps you would like time to think it over, Robert? After all, I can't be in any hurry about it. Perhaps you would like to consult with—eh—Mr. MacKenzie?"

"You wouldn't mind if I did?"

"Not by any means. In fact I could think of nothing better. We might well agree to allow Mr. MacKenzie to act as—er—assessor in the matter."

"Have you any idea of what you might be prepared to offer for my copyright?"

"No . . . I hadn't considered the offer, Robert. I merely made it on the spur of the moment from a desire to help you —if I could. But let me see . . .? Oh, maybe something in the region of, say, fifty pounds sterling."

"Fifty pounds! And for this sum my poetry would become yours?"

"Not quite, Robert, not quite! Nobody, for any sum, can take away your poetry from you. No . . . no; but against a possible future market I would have the right to publish—all at my own risk."

"I see! Don't think me ungrateful, Mr. Creech—these are matters I don't fully understand."

"That's all right, my boy, there's mair in this business than meets the casual eye. A publisher runs many grave risks with his capital. But—eh—consult with Henry MacKenzie and take his advice. Or do you wish me to arrange a meeting between us?"

"Yes—if you would be so kind. I can at least take Mr. MacKenzie's views into my consideration."

"And there need be no worry as to your immediate needs. Many of the subscribers are paying in advance. Very many will pay on the day of publication. They ken the situation—how the edition is being published solely for your benefit. Some of the noblesse have indeed paid more than the face value for their subscription copies. Have no fear: in the first week of publication there will be enough money coming in to last you for a month or two . . . until the final settlement. . ."

He left the gloom of Creech's private sanctum and emerged slowly into the noise and bustle of the High Street. The April sun had begun to warm the ancient stones and the promise of better days was in the air. Folks about the Cross seemed cheerier than he remembered seeing them. There was much laughter; and a barber's boy carrying a pair of freshly trimmed and curled wigs whistled blithely as he threaded his way through the crowded street.

The Bard halted on Creech's outer steps and surveyed the gay scene.

Aye, there was indeed the promise of a fine summer in the air. But not a summer he could spend in Edinburgh. He had had his fill of the gay world of fashion and folly, of pride and poverty. A fresh wind would be blowing in from the sea across the Ayrshire uplands—the caller air about Mossgiel would be clean and invigorating to the nostrils. How he would appreciate that now since his nose had become inured to the stinks of the Town. . .

Fifty pounds! What could he not do with fifty pounds? Buy a horse and ride off to the Borders with Bob Ainslie! See much of the Scotland celebrated in song and story. He would never have such an opportunity again. What though his Poems never sold and he had to go back to the plough! What if he never saw Peggy Chalmers again. . . What in hell—or out of it—did it really matter?

A man might winter in Edinburgh snugly enough. But the summer! No: it was not to be thought of. And, in any event, he was duty bound to have a look at Dalswinton Estate. God knows: it might be the very spot for him to settle on. . . There would be a braird on the corn and the grass would be green again.

Aye: fifty pounds! And all his own to do with as he liked. Half to Gilbert and that would still leave him twenty-five. He'd get a horse for five—a horse that would do him bravely enough.

And he could take his Poems into the Border country and introduce them there! Already he had names of folk he could call on—Mrs. Scot o' Wauchope House for one! Patrick Brydone of Lennel House for another. In any case, he would be meeting new folks and seeing new country—fine romantic country by all accounts.

Why not? He had spent . . . December, January, February, March . . . the big half of April . . . almost five winter months in Auld Reekie. He was due a change: a break from the monotony of city life. . .

He was unaware that he was wandering aimlessly down the Canongate.

Five months in the Capital and any day now . . . April 21st . . . would see his second edition on the market.

Five months since he had cantered out of Machlin—after kissing Jean farewell. . .

Five months; and he had made many friends in that time. Closest and dearest of all friends: Willie Nicol—sharp, uncompromising; but with a heart of gold and a brain of the first quality. Square-faced snub-nosed pock-pitted jaw-jutting Willie Nicol. The first Latin scholar in Edinburgh—which meant the world. Maybe the finest Latin scholar who had ever lived—a scholar to whom Latin was no more a strange tongue, or a dead tongue, than the Scottish tongue he had imbibed at his mother's knees in Annan—thirty-odd years ago.

Willie Nicol . . . who had, at their first meeting, outraged almost every sentiment his bosom had ever known. Crude violent disdainful abrupt contemptuous sarcastic bloodshot-eyed obscene vitriolically vindictive . . . Willie Nicol; who had calmed down into gentle solicitating kind-hearted Willie Nicol. A man who had suffered much—even as he himself had suffered—born into poverty hardship and neglect. And yet by his own efforts, his own dynamic will, had raised himself out of the damp biggin of the Annan mason, out of the cold poverty-stricken biggin of the Annan mason's widow . . . raised himself by his own herculean efforts from the ministry, from the faculty of medicine into the foremost Latin scholar of his day. . .

Well . . . that was much more than he had been able to do.

He had ploughed soil and carted and weeded and hoed, in season and out of season, in all weathers and on a diet of thin and watery gruel. *And* he had read books . . . he had argued and debated . . . he had pondered over the mystery of the universe . . . and he had written poetry and songs.

He had written poetry—and poetry that had found an echo and a response from all kinds and conditions of men and women. . . Robert Aiken, John Ballantine . . .

John Rankine—dear good-hearted rough rude ready-witted Rankine. With some of his fifty pounds he would buy John Rankine of Adamhill a worthy present from Auld Reekie that would be a token of their long friendship.

John Rankine—and his daughter Annie! It was upon a Lammas nicht. . . Annie Rankine—Mrs. John Merry that now was. The dance at New Cumnock . . . and the fiddler stroking the green rashes from his strings. . . How heartily had they sported in that long low room and the sweat blinding them—or blinding him.

Aye: John Rankine and his daughter Annie that he had first danced with in the Tarbolton barn and the bare feet of them licking the stour from the earthen floor.

The hoot of an owl in the gloaming . . . sitting on a knowe and the call of the herd-laddies coming to them shrill on the golden gloaming—and the soft-spun darkness whispering to them from the hollows of the green land. . .

The voice of John Rankine: ". . . hold your head high—haud it heich. . ."

John Rankine . . . and all the green heights and hollows twixt Lochlea and Adamhill, twixt Lochlea and Tarbolton.

How long ago? Seventeen eighty-seven! Seventeen eighty-three—four. . . God Almighty! a mere matter of four or five years ago . . . and it seemed like a century.

And Davie Sillar scraping the thairms . . . long, long ago that was—but only yesterday by the almanac.

It was time—long past time—that he was back in his native Ayrshire; in that green swelling land of whitewashed farms and smoking cot-houses. . . Auld Ayr . . . Auld Killie . . . snug Tarbolton crouching down to the warm earth under its low thatching and Willie Muir o' the Mill grinding corn below the Beltane Tor where the Fail wound leisurely to join the Ayr at Failford. . .

The Ayr at Failford . . . and further up where the Machlin Burn joined the same Ayr fornenst the Stairaird Bluff. . . One Sunday in the green month of May long ago when Mary Campbell had lain in his arms . . . for the last time. Oh, Mary . . . Mary. . .

A whore from Hyndford's Close (from whence the Duchess of Gordon had often sallied on a pig-riding expedition) leered at him, her face twisted against the slanting rays of the April sun. But he was oblivious to her.

It was time he got out of Edinburgh. There was much he had to forget for his own peace of mind. Highland Peggy—her bare flesh roseate in the glow of the fire. No Jean Glover . . . no Annie Rankine. By God, and no Jean Armour. Just the bare flesh of a young healthy lusty lass—and thatched wi' glory. A lass wi' a name who might nevertheless be nameless; a homely lass lying by the winter's fire, happy that her desires were gratified and thankful when all was done for the warmth of his companionship. No doubt he owed her nothing—neither in cash nor in kind. There was no love between them, no vows—and she knew to a hair what risks she was taking. Maybe there were others besides him. She was too lusty a wench to go long without a lover.

But it was time he forgot her. Once or twice lately he had got the idea that she might be pregnant. . .

And Peggy Chalmers: maybe he would need to forget her too. She was going to some friends at Harviestoun in Clackmannanshire for the summer. Edinburgh without Peggy Chalmers was not to be thought of.

Yet Dr. Adair, who had once been a visitor to Crochallan, was much interested in Peggy's cousin, Charlotte Hamilton —Gavin's stepsister. He wouldn't lose sight of Doctor Adair: any link that connected him with Peggy was valuable. And Adair wasn't a bad fellow: they got on well together.

No: it was too complicated. He had no money and no job. To hell with them then. He would take Creech's fifty pounds and ride down into the Border country with Bob Ainslie.

He could relax with Ainslie—and he could laugh and sing and do or say whatever came into his head. Ainslie was a gay young fellow—and he could be doing with some gay youthful company. . .

Having made up his mind, he realised that he had wandered down to the foot of the Canongate; and as he turned abruptly and made to climb back on his steps he realised that the sun had gone down and that a sudden chill had come into the air. High up on the washing poles, jutting from the windows, rags of clothes fluttered in the evening breeze. . .

It was a droll place Auld Reekie—a gay mad scramble of a world all on its own. Well . . . he had strutted across its stage. He had explored the heights and the depths of it. He knew what it could offer and what it could withhold; he knew what it valued and what it disdained.

It was time to say goodbye. Apart from the cash that lay in Willie Creech's canny grasp, it held nothing for him now.

The hour chimed from the Tron steeple. If he hurried he would get Ainslie before he left Carrubber's Close. . .

A QUESTION OF FAITH

Bishop John Geddes shook his hand warmly. "Congratulations, Robert, on the successful publication of your Edinburgh edition. You have every reason to be proud——"

"I suppose I have, Father—at least I'm grateful."

"I know you maun be. But every subscriber and every subsequent reader will be grateful too. I've sent off the copies abroad. They'll be deeply appreciated by our Scottish students there. But—there's something you might consider doing for me. Do you think you could fill in the full names against the blanks and the initials in my own volume? You see, a dedicatory poem to G—— H—— would mean a lot more to me if I knew who G—— H—— was. If you could possibly find the time—I know it's asking much from you, Robert."

"It's nothing, Father—I am much in your debt. Let me have your volume as soon as you find it convenient and I'll fill in the blanks with pleasure."

"I shall be ever grateful to you, Robert. And what are your plans for the future? I hope you can see your way to accept Patrick Miller's offer of a farm."

"So you too, Bishop, think I should embark on a farm?"

"Yes. . . I think you should—though I have not the townsman's illusions about farming. I shouldna think there's onything for you to do in Edinburgh. Or is there? Or am I being too inquisitive?"

"There *is* nothing for me in Edinburgh—and maybe there's nothing for me in the country."

"This will never do! Surely your many worthy and wealthy patrons can do something for you."

"And maybe I don't want to be indebted to them. Oh, I'm far from complaining, Father Geddes—very far from complaining. . . But, as for my future? Well, it's always been dark as chaos—and dark as chaos it remains."

"A dark outlook, indeed, Robert."

"But—for a' that, Father, I'll laugh and sing and shake my leg as lang's I dow."

"You've a wonderful spirit, Robert."

"Why not, Father! It's either that or sack-cloth and ashes and, with no offence to your cloth and your office, I think it a miserable alternative."

"Well . . . maybe your only real sin, Robert, will consist of abusing the gifts God gave you."

"And there, Father, I seem to hear an echo of the voice o' Daddy Auld, the parish priest o' Machlin."

"Should that surprise you?"

"There's a lot surprises me, Father Geddes—especially where clergymen are concerned."

"A quality of surprise that is no doubt reciprocated, Robert."

"Life consists of surprises."

"You're not disillusioned with what you have seen in Edinburgh?"

"I came wi' few illusions, Father: if possible I'll leave wi' less. But then it does a man good to shed his illusions."

"Provided he doesn't lose faith in the process."

"Faith? It's a wonderful word, faith. It means everything and it means nothing. Unfortunately for theology, only death reveals whether faith is justified or isn't the greatest of our illusions."

"You have faith in your fellows, Robert?"

"Some of them."

"Even if you have faith in only one of them, does that no' prove something to you? We have never discussed this question of faith, Robert. I think maybe we should have done so before now. You have a wonderful faith in your fellow-man, Robert: it shines through all your poetry. By implication, then, you must have a wonderful faith in God."

"Well, Bishop, that may be so—I hope it is so. But to have faith in God and to have faith in Kirks—whatever the denomination—represents two different faiths to me."

"What you mean is that you feel in yourself that you have no need for ritual."

"Neither for ritual nor for dogmatism, Father; and the two go hand in hand."

"But then, you surely realise that men are weak? They must be tended like a flock of sheep: they must be shepherded, brought to the fold, guarded against straying——"

"And what prevents the shepherd from straying?"

"There are other shepherds——"

"Aye . . . there are other shepherds, Bishop. There's no lack o' shepherds—that's what's wrong: the shepherds canna agree among themselves."

"In the Roman Catholic faith, Robert, there is no disagreement."

"Ah weel, Father, that could be gey monotonous too. But you and me hae got on weel enough together because we respected each other's opinions—and there we'll need to leave it."

"Oh, I'm content to leave it there, Robert. The world moves slowly but surely towards the adoption of the true faith, the only possible faith. A thousand years hence you may be canonised and take your place with the Saints. Ah . . . stranger things have happened, Robert."

"A thousand years hence, Bishop, onything may happen. It's what happens here and now that matters to you and me however much we may deceive ourselves otherwise. If posterity makes me the Patron Saint o' Ploughmen at least my bones winna agitate themselves in the grave."

"And your immortal soul, Robert?"

"My immortal soul, Bishop, will be attended to by immortality—that's one thing at least I'll have no say about. . . But send me your copy, Bishop, and I'll say a' that need be said about the blanks."

"Thank you, Robert, thank you indeed! Ah, you're young in spiritual experience. I have no fear but that you'll come out right in the end. . . I'll call at your lodgings with the book. If not before your tour of the Border country, then when you come back. . ."

SALE OF A BIRTHRIGHT

Henry MacKenzie took a mouthful of claret and then cleared his throat authoritatively.

"The position then, I take to be as follows: you, Robert, are willing to dispose of the copyright of your poems—that is—let us be perfectly clear on this—the poems as published by Mr. Creech here. You, Willie, are prepared to purchase Mr. Burns's copyright. You are both agreed on this . . .? Good! Now we can proceed a step further. At what figure are you prepared to sell, Robert?"

"I had thought, Mr. MacKenzie, we had met here to-day to discuss the terms. In the matter of money I am in your power, gentlemen, and I take it that you will trade with me on honourable terms."

MacKenzie's horse face took a judicial cast.

"Quite so, Robert, quite so. But you are not in anybody's power. Far from it! You are perfectly free to sell—or refrain from selling—just as you think fit."

"May I ask then, sir, if you approve of my selling?"

"I am not here to approve—or disapprove. But since you ask my advice—and I give it solely in my personal capacity—I would be inclined to say—considering your circumstances—yes."

"Then, gentlemen, I am prepared to accept the best offer Mr. Creech cares to make. I have not the nature of a huckster, neither have I the stomach for niggling and haggling. I have never considered my verses in terms of hard cash—grateful as I am for any cash they have brought and may yet bring me."

MacKenzie looked at him in admiration: even Creech shifted uneasily in his chair.

MacKenzie took another mouthful of claret—and coughed.

"Mr. Burns's sentiments are becoming in a poet of nature. But as I'm here solely in a business capacity I canna allow myself to be swayed by ony sentiment. Willie, are you prepared to mak' Mr. Burns an offer for his copyright?"

"Yes—yes, I am prepared to make an offer, Henry—eh—in the spirit Robert, here, has just indicated. I will double my original tentative offer. If Mr. MacKenzie, Robert, is prepared to draw up an agreement, I'm prepared to pay you a hundred pounds!"

The Bard felt the blood rushing to his face. A hundred pounds! This was indeed a fortune. . .

"I think, sir, Mr. Creech's offer errs on the side of generosity——"

"You are prepared to accept a hundred pounds then, Robert?"

"If you, sir, do not think it too much."

"It is indeed a generous offer—but I'm in the mood to be generous too. Willie! Mak' the pounds guineas—and I'll draw up the agreement now."

"It's nice to be generous wi' other folks' money, Henry. But having consideration of the fact our young friend is, as you say, a poet of nature and not a sharpening professional author, I'll increase my offer from one hundred pounds sterling to one hundred guineas."

"Very generously spoken, Willie. Now we only need a simple clause or two and we can have the document signed and witnessed while we finish this excellent claret."

But Creech, though willing enough to sign the document, still had reservations. He would have to write to his London associates, Messrs. Cadell and Davies, in order to ascertain if they would relieve him of part of the cost.

MacKenzie thought this reasonable since Creech agreed to pay in full should Cadell and Davies not enter into his scheme. Accordingly, he sanded and folded the papers away. . .

"So you're going off on a tour of the Border country, Robert—with young Ainslie, I understand. Yes; an amiable fine fellow."

"My tour will not wholly be a pleasure jaunt, sir. I hope to lay in a stock of poetic ideas—my jaded Pegasus finds little nourishment about the planestanes or the causeways—and I hope to inspect a farm Mr. Patrick Miller would like me to rent. The place is on the banks of the Nith—Dalswinton is the name of the estate."

"Aha! So Patrick Miller has been interesting you in a farm, has he? Well . . . Patrick Miller is a man of many interests— and most of his interests have a habit of prospering. Yes: an original man. I didna ken you knew him, Robert?"

"I wasn't long in the Town till Mr. Miller sought me out —and extended great kindness to me."

"And very glad I am to hear that, my boy. So you intend setting up as a farmer?"

"I didn't say that, sir. Successful farming is no easy matter in these days. I had hoped for a commission in the Excise——"

"No, no! Farming's your bent. Poetry and ploughing— they have brought you fame. I think it would be inadvisable for you to turn aside from them now. . . Well, I wish you good luck on your expedition—shall I call it—to the Border country. You will understand—or I've no doubt young Ainslie has told you—that there is much wild and unimproved territory in the Borders—not much different I'm afraid from our own wild Highlands. You are riding horse-back . . .?"

But the Bard was paying little attention to the loquacious MacKenzie—the Man of Feeling was evidently putting the top on a drinking session: he was talking because he enjoyed the sound of his own sonorous voice.

The Bard was wondering when he would receive his hundred guineas. It was difficult to be angry with Creech. After all, he owed him more, perhaps, than he owed any man. It was no doubt true, as his friends were always telling him, that Creech was interested only in making money out of him. But Willie Creech was the best man he could find to make money out of him—and the more money Creech made for himself the more would eventually accrue to him. It was sheer nonsense to expect Creech to do all he had done for nothing. Had not publishers, like poets, to live? He would need to be on his guard to avoid being uncharitable to him.

With a hundred guineas in the offing, it did not occur to the Bard that he might just as easily err in over-gratitude towards his publisher.

GOOD-BYE TO PEGGY CAMERON

It was on an April Sunday night that he said good-bye to Peggy Cameron. Peggy was strangely sad. She seemed troubled; though, to his questioning, she replied that nothing troubled her.

". . . it's only that you're going, sir. I'll never see you again."

"I'll be back in Edinburgh—in a month or two maybe."

"No. . . I dinna think I'll see you again, sir."

"I'll miss you, Peggy."

"No' as much as I'll miss you, sir. You've got everything before you. For me, I hae little to look forward to—and only you to be looking back on. You wouldna hae an address you could be leaving me?"

"An address? You canna write, lass: what good would an address do you?"

"Och . . . just, it would be making me feel that . . . you . . . were somewhere I could be thinking aboot."

"That's a kindly thought, Peggy. But—well, I couldna rightly say where I'll be. I'll be travelling a lot of strange country—and every nicht laying doon my head on a strange pillow——"

"But will you no' be going hame, sir?"

"For a nicht, maybe. No' that I have a real hame, Peggy. I said farewell to my hame for ever when I came to Edinburgh. No. . . I'll no' be staying long in Ayrshire."

He kissed her; and she clung to him desperately.

"Why, Peggy—what's the trouble, lass?"

"Oh, I'm fond o' ye, sir. . . I'm fond o' ye."

"Well, so am I o' you, Peggy—but you mauna fa' in love wi' me."

"You'll come back and see me—soon?"

"I'll be back afore the summer's spent . . . maybe gin the end o' July."

259

"I'll just need to be contenting myself till then . . . but it will be a lang time."

"Noo listen, Peggy. You and me came to a bargain at the beginning. We hae nae claims on each other—you ken that."

"No. . . I ken we canna be married. . . But I micht be needing your help some day—in a way."

"Help what for? You're no' pregnant?"

"No. . . No. . . I dinna think so. But you can never be sure, can you, sir?"

"Damnit, Peggy—either you're pregnant or you're no'."

"I dinna think so, sir. . . But if I was . . .?"

"I thocht you told me that you kenned how to look after yoursel'?"

"Och, there's nothing maybe to worry aboot, sir—it's only if there was . . . I . . . would need to be depending on you."

"On me?"

"And who else, sir, would I be looking to for help?"

"Well, Peggy, lass, I never promised anything as you ken. And I'm damned if I'm for promising onything now. I've made no promises and I admit to no responsibility. Only . . . if the worst has happened . . . and by God I'll blame you if onything *has* happened. . . I'll do what I can in the circumstances. No: damnit, if you're pregnant you'll damnwell need to face it as best you can. You canna expect me to acknowledge anything, to admit to anything. If there's ony danger why don't you see some auld wife aboot the Toon that can put you right?"

"I have heard aboot a Mistress Hogg, a shoemaker's wife in the Landmarket, where you bide, sir."

"To hell, Peggy—I maun say you disappoint me. I thocht you knew better what you were up to?"

"Maybe a lass can sometimes be foolish."

"Foolish! Listen: I want a straight answer, here and now. Are you pregnant or are you no'? If you are, how long are you —and why the hell do you leave it till now to tell me?"

"I dinna ken, I dinna ken . . . maybe I'll be all right in another month."

"How long are you past your time?"

"I dinna richt ken . . . maybe a week or twa . . . maybe a month."

"You've been late afore now?"

"A wee while . . . yes. Och, sir, I didna mean to worry you or to be upsetting you . . . it's just that you're going away."

"Peggy: make up your mind that there's nothing I can do for you——"

"Nothing, sir? Oh, I wadna have expectit this from you. I had aey hoped that if onything did happen that you would have stood by me."

"In what way?"

"Well, sir, I wad be losing my job . . . and what wad I do for shelter and a bite o' food?"

"You never thocht o' this before now?"

"Did you, sir?"

"Did I . . .? You assured me there was no reason for thinking onything, Peggy: you maun understand that you canna depend on me. If I hae a pound or twa I'll see what can be done to tide you past the worst o' your trouble. But you maun understand that I havena many pounds—and I hae plenty roads for them—aye, and mair deserving roads than yours maybe."

"I'm sorry I've angered you, sir: I've never seen you angry afore. It was just that I had to be knowing how you would stand by me . . . and I just canna bear to think that you wadna."

"Damnit, I'll stand by you—as far as my means will allow me. Dinna let that worry you too much. But if you are going to have a bairn then you'll need to think what you're going to do—you'll need to make plans—you'll need to think. There's surely some woman-body o' your own kind you can turn to. . ."

But the Bard was at his wits' end. He had never for a moment envisaged the possibility of Peggy being pregnant. When the time came for him to part he had reckoned they would part without fuss or ceremony—least of all without tears.

He was angry. But more angry with himself for having walked so simply into a trap. . . And how easy it had been to walk into the trap. . . Peggy, after all, was just a silly lass who thought she knew what she was about. Now she was going to throw herself at him.

But not if he could help it. He'd be damned and doubly damned if he would allow himself to be made responsible for any woman's foolishness—or stupidity. Peggy had consented to become his mistress—on the terms of the moment. Each moment, each encounter, had stood by itself. Time had added familiarity—but it had added no responsibility. . .

His anger cooled and he looked down at Peggy sitting before the fire, her eyes gazing into the embers with a sad far-away look.

He pulled on a boot with a vicious tug and his heel hit the flooring with a thud.

Peggy looked up: her tone was flat. "You're making a lot o' noise, sir!"

"Damnit, Peggy, what's a bit o' noise atween you and me now?"

Peggy resumed her fire-gazing. He buttoned up his great-coat and turned away his gaze.

But already his heart was beginning to melt in pity for the lass.

He put his arm round her neck and tilted back her chin.

"There's something to keep you going for a while, Peggy —and dinna worry ower much. Shake yoursel'—and see what Mistress Hogg can do for you . . . and it'll no' be long till I'm back. . ."

He had arranged to meet Ainslie in John Dowie's howff. After a quick drink they issued out into the dark street.

"You know that lass I told you about?"

"Your Highland Peggy?"

"Aye. . . I've just left her. She fears that she may be pregnant. The good old cause, Bob . . . the curse of Adam and the sin of Eve . . . or anything else you like to think on."

Ainslie entered a forefinger between his elegant (if somewhat dirty) cravat and his neck and tried to ease the stricture that seemed of a sudden to compress his throat.

"I've knocked the bung in the barrel myself, Robert."

"No? Robert Ainslie, the most eligible bachelor in Embro? Who's the lucky lady?"

"Lucky. She doesna think so. A mistress, my dear Robert, much like your own—shall both be innominate?"

"You're a damned cautious chiel, Bob . . . just like my good friend John Richmond. I suppose it's your legal training——"

"Isn't it common sense too, Robert? A man should ever be on his guard where a maid is concerned, especially if he's running ony risks. Is your girl likely to prove troublesome?"

"I'm not even certain that she's couped yet. Maybe she's only trying to get round me. . . I don't know, Bob. . . I just don't know. . ."

"Maybe there won't be any need to worry——"

"Worry! Do you see me worrying? I've a damned sight more to worry me. Maybe I'm worried about her being so bluidy stupid—since at the commencement she was so wise and knowing. . . But, we'll cross our bridges when we come to them. . .

"I was speaking to MacKay o' the White Hart and he thinks he has the beast for me. She's an auld mare that threw a reverend Episcopalian gentleman and broke his collar bone—so he sold her cheap to MacKay. She's hired out the now but when she comes back—in a day or so—he'll give me the first chance o' her."

"Did he mention a price?"

"Aye, he hinted something about fifteen pounds——"

"You'll get her for ten . . . if you hold out. Much depends on her condition, of coorse."

"MacKay assured me she wasna much to look at but that she would suit my purpose weel enough—if I didna drive her ower sair."

"We can tak' it easy. The first day'll be the worst. If we get away early in the morning and meet wi' a fair day on the hills we'll manage my home at Berrywell in time for a good supper."

"A good supper! Damnit, Bob, I believe I could tak' a bite now—I feel easier in my mind. . . And that's a brave fresh wind

that's blowin' in frae the Firth. You're coming to the Theatre
to-morrow night?"

"Oh, Woods is speaking your prologue? I'll be there,
Robert."

"No' for my sake. But it's Willie's benefit and he deserves a'
the support we can give him. A grand fellow, Willie Woods."

"Yes . . . and a good actor. But I'll be on tiptoe to hear
your prologue."

"Ah, it's no' what it should be, Bob. Damnit, I just canna
write in Edinburgh. I get plenty ideas, but I never seem to
be able to settle down properly and get them down on paper."

"I don't know how you can bide in Baxters' Close, Robert,
far less write poetry there."

"Baxters' Close is fine. A poet should be able to write
anywhere. No: I'm unsettled within mysel', Bob. Maybe after
my jaunt round the Borders I'll be able to settle down somewhere . . . somehow. Come on: let's get that bite o' supper."

PURPOSE

At first glance James Johnson was a smaller and quieter
edition of William Smellie. Certainly he was neither so
forceful nor so learned.

The Bard met him one day in the company of William
Tytler, an elderly lawyer dilettante and antiquarian, who was
interested in music and especially Scottish folk-song. With
him was Stephen Clarke, the organist of the Episcopal Church.
It so happened that Johnson had perfected a new process of
engraving from pewter plates. As this process greatly reduced
the cost of music publishing, he had embarked on the venture
of publishing the music, as well as the words, of all the Scottish
songs he could lay hands on. Yet, though he was interested in
the words, it was the melodies he was most anxious to preserve.

Old Tytler, who had written a disquisition on music for
Hugo Arnot's *History of Edinburgh*, had conceived a high
opinion of the Bard's gifts as a song-writer and he had effected
the introduction over a bite in Fortune's Tavern.

Fortune's being one of the select howffs, Johnson had come to the meal in his best coat and breeches. For all that he looked poorly and it was obvious that he had little of the world's gear about him.

The Bard expressed his disappointment that, as he would be leaving Edinburgh by the beginning of May, he had not met the engraver sooner.

"Faith, an' I would have liked to hae met in wi' you, Mr. Burns. But then, sir, when I saw how you were being taken up by the gentry and the nobility, I didna see my way to intrude mysel' on you."

"Well, sir, more's the pity. From what I have heard from Mr. Tytler here about your projected volume of Scots songs, there's no man in the Town I would rather have met sooner. But tell me, sir—you are not an Edinburgh man?"

"Weel . . . no: I'm native to Ettrick—but I cam' here as a young man and here, like as no', I'll remain."

"Then it was in your native Ettrickdale that you first formed your love for our native melodies?"

"Aye—that'll be true enough, for my mither—God rest her—was a grand singer o' auld ballads and sangs."

"So was mine, sir. There is no doubt that it was from our mothers we first inherited our love of melody."

"I'll grant you that, Mr. Burns—but my difficulty is that a melody is but half a sang wanting the words! And we hae lost the words—or at least a decent set o' them—for mony a grand auld tune."

"And here," broke in Tytler, "is just where Mr. Burns can be of greatest service to you, Jamie. Mr. Burns may be willing —for I have no doubt as to his ability—to furnish you with the maist excellent words for your tunes."

"Wad that no' be asking ower much frae a man o' Mr. Burns's eminence?"

"Eminence! My dear sir, what is my eminence—a mere seven days' wonder and the seven days are past. Talk no more of eminence. If I can be of any assistance to your publication —command me! I assure you I have never been more en- thusiastic about anything in my life. I shall deem it a high

honour to be associated with you in however humble a
capacity."

"There now, Jamie: I told you how Mr. Burns would
respond to the suggestion of contributing to your Musical
Museum. And I have discovered that he knows dozens of old
tunes that are quite new to me——"

"That's maist gratifying news, Mr. Tytler. I wonder, Mr.
Burns, sir, if you hae onything that micht still be included in
my first volume?"

The Bard's eyes glowed. "You mean, sir, that you are
prepared to include a song or two of mine in your first volume
—but I thought that was ready for the press?"

"Well, it is—and the plates are nearly finished. But if you
could give me twa songs—that's aboot a' I could mak' space
for——"

Tytler said: "What about Green Grow the Rashes, Robert?"

"Yes: I would like that. But you are too kind, Mr. Johnson,
in making room for me at this late hour."

"Man, Mr. Burns—if you only kent how pleased I am to
have your sangs . . . and how mair than pleased I am to think
that I'll have your support. . ."

The honest face of James Johnson was incapable of register-
ing the extremes of emotion; but now it did register a pleasure
and a gratitude that was unmistakable. Even old Tytler's
frosty countenance seemed to thaw.

But the Bard was elated. Here was an opportunity he had
long wished for. At long last he would see some of his songs
published with the music that belonged to them. After that
he might have the opportunity of seeing some of the grand
old tunes rescued from the oblivion that was fast overtaking
them. But then the possibilities for the future were manifold.
There were so many tunes falling into neglect because the
words had been lost; and there were so many old song words
fermenting to decay through lack of a good tune to hold them
green. And here was modest James Johnson, an Edinburgh
engraver, prepared not only to recognise him as a song-writer
but as a song-smith of old words and melodies.

"There's only one thing, Mr. Johnson: I'm no' very good

at noting down a tune. I wonder if Clarke, here, would care to help me in this?"

Hitherto Clarke had said nothing. He was a lank lazy devil of a man but highly gifted as a musician.

"Oh . . . I'll do what I can, Robert. Hum your tunes ower to me and I'll soon set them doon for you. You read music?"

"I can *read* song music well enough: my difficulty is in writing it."

"Nothing to it. I'll give you a few simple points to keep in mind."

"I take it you're keen on the project, sir?"

"Keen? I'm enthusiastic. I'm bluidy near mad about it. Why, our folk-tunes *are* our only tunes. Nine-tenths o' the stuff they murder in Saint Cecilia's is just ornamental rubbish. But our auld Scots tunes, sir—there's simplicity and a clean enchanting bewitching melodic line . . ."

"And why didn't we talk o' this before, Stephen?"

"I never knew you were interested till Mr. Tytler raised the matter. God damn my soul, Robert, I've come into this glorious venture as musical editor. I know how to set a tune out for the voice; I know how to free a melody from those insufferable Italian shakes and trills that pass for embellishment at the Gentlemen's Concerts. And I know many of our old tunes. But you, Robert, if you can provide tunes *and* words— why the project is certain to be a success. If I can help you in any way—but then we're all here to help each other. I maun say, Mr. Tytler, that Johnson and I are overjoyed at your bringing Robert in."

"Thank you, Clarke: it was really my son Alexander who first drew my attention to Robert's interest—and knowledge o' the subject. Well . . . as you say, Clarke, this is a verra fortunate meeting for a' concerned. . ."

Deep in the creative well of his being the trickle of inspiration began to flow again. From henceforth he would write new songs and collect old ones. There were dozens of songs waiting for him to write.

This was something for the future, something to sustain him richly in the days that lay ahead. Once more he had been given an aim and an object—and one that lay to his heart warm and snug.

He raised a buoyant arm and beckoned on the lass to bring a last round of drinks to the table.

MRS. CARFRAE SAYS GOOD-BYE

"So you're for awa', Mr. Burns."

"Yes, Mistress Carfrae—but I'll be back."

"I'm glad to hear that, sir. My! and to think that when ye cam' here I wisna verra sure o' ye. And noo you're leaving me the maist famous man in Edinburgh."

"Hardly that, Mistress Carfrae. But I must thank you for the comfort of your lodgings——"

"Nae thanks, sir. It's been a real pleasure, to say nocht o' the honour, haeing ye. Aye; an' ye've been a guid-living sober decent lodger: I couldna ask for better. You're maybe no' juist as strict a Christian as I wad like to hae ye, Mr. Burns. Aye, I'll say that. But I could wish that a' Christians were hauf as guid and kindly as you, sir. Noo, God's blessing on you and a safe journey—and—and haste ye back, sir."

And with that, honest Mrs. Carfrae softened her landlady's heart sufficiently to shed tears. She hastily dabbed her eyes with the hem of her apron and left the room.

GRATITUDE

Now that he was leaving Edinburgh, he realised that he had a lot of ends to tie up. There were many friends he had not— and would not—be able to see in the flesh before he left. He must write them a good-bye note. Courtesy also dictated writing his thanks to some others. Dr. Hugh Blair, for example, and members of the literati. They had befriended him; they had gone out of their way to help him; and no doubt their intentions had been good. . . Sometimes he had been angry and hurt and baffled by their academic obtuseness and their social snobbery (which conditioned their literary affections). But that part of them that had been actuated by a sincere desire to help, he would do well to acknowledge. It wouldn't matter if he never saw one of them again: he had nothing in common with them and there were no bonds of social friendship. James Gregory had sent him a copy of an English translation of Cicero's select orations—the tribute had touched him deeply. It showed that Gregory had not forgotten him. Maybe the others had not forgotten him either. . . But then there had ever been an almost brutal forthrightness about Gregory that had been lacking in the others.

He had made many friends in his six Edinburgh months—more than he had made in his life before. Maybe, as he had once written to Mrs. Dunlop in Ayrshire, few would survive the distance of a carriage drive.

Among the noblesse he could rely, he felt, on the patronage of Glencairn and his family, the Duke and Duchess of Gordon, Lord Maitland, Harry Erskine and his titled elder brother, Lord Buchan.

Among the literati, Dugald Stewart, William Greenfield, Henry MacKenzie and Lord Monboddo could be appealed to, as occasion might arise, with the knowledge that his appeal would not fall on unresponsive ears.

But his real friends lay further down the social scale. Among the artists he had forged common bonds with Sandy Nasmyth and Jock Beugo; and Louis Cauvin, the French master, had given of his time in friendship and not for money. And Willie Woods, the actor, was a man whose friendship he could claim without any stand-to of formality.

Among the lawyer class he had not a few acquaintances. Willie Dunbar, Charles Hay, Old Mitchelson, and, most intimate of that lot, Bob Ainslie and Alexander Cunningham. . .

And with Ainslie and Cunningham he had to add in the category of intimate boon companions, Willie Nicol, Willie Smellie, Peter Hill and Robert Cleghorn—though he valued Nicol's friendship above the others.

But there were other men who came close to the boon companions, such as the sweet singer Allan Masterton, the writing master. . . When he reviewed them in his mind he realised that he had made many interesting contacts in Edinburgh. Turn where he would in the Town, he was known—from the college professors to the caddie boys in the streets.

There was nothing he could complain about—not even with the women. He was more friendly with Dr. Blacklock's wife Sarah than he was with the Duchess of Gordon; but he was as friendly with his landlady Mrs. Carfrae as he was with the Duchess. He had never set his heart on Eliza Burnett; but he had spent many a happy hour with Christie Laurie at the Concerts, at the Theatre—and in Shakespeare Square. Christie had passed out of his life and she meant nothing to him now— but once he had been glad enough to spend an hour in her company.

With Peggy Chalmers he hadn't been so successful. He had almost lost his heart to her and he had not given up hope that he might yet win her affections. Aye . . . Peggy was an exceptional lass whatever way he tried to view her. He could leave Edinburgh gladly enough as far as the others were concerned—but he was loth to think that he might never see Peggy again.

But of course he would need to come back to Edinburgh in order to settle accounts with Willie Creech. Creech was away to London, leaving Peter Hill in command. . .

Now that he was away to London he was beginning to realise how much Creech meant to him. Smellie could talk as he liked, but Creech had the business brain that could see exactly what was needed to be done and had the energy and authority to see that what was needed was in fact done.

No: he had had his angry moments with Creech; he had had doubts and disappointments and often a galling sense of frustration . . . but in the end Creech had emerged with credit and he felt little but warmth towards him.

But then, as always, when things were going well he was filled with warmth towards everybody. His only fear now was that he might leave Edinburgh and forget to acknowledge that warmth.

When John Richmond came home he was still busy writing. He explained what he was doing.

"I'm trying to clear up some arrears, Jock—trying to overtake the thanks I owe so many folk i' the Town for so many kindnesses——"

"You're forgetting the unkindnesses?"

"They were few and far between, Jock—and I doubt if folk really meant to be unkind——"

"You're as variable as the women's minds you talk about."

"I suppose I am. I hope I've never yet forgotten any o' my real friends, Jock—and I'm in a generous enough mood to forget—if not forgive—my enemies."

"If you can afford to be as noble as a' that, Rab. . . You're for off on Saturday?"

"Saturday morning, Jock—at the crack o' dawn—all on a fine May morning."

John Richmond tried hard not to be envious—but it was difficult. The edge of bitterness was in his tongue. Not that he was bitter at the Bard—not deep down. He was bitter at life. The Bard would return to Machlin crowned in success and glory. There was nothing Machlin admired more than success. The Machlin folks would forget all about Rab the Ranter: they would be falling over each other to shake the hand of Scotland's Bard. Maybe they would ask about him— and how would the Bard answer? That he was still toiling in a lawyer's office writing corns on his fingers. Jenny Surgeoner would be sure to ask of him—and Gavin Hamilton.

"I suppose when you get back to Machlin, Rab, they'll be asking about me?"

"Of course they will. I ken what to tell Gavin Hamilton, Jock. Gavin'll be pleased to hear how well you're coming on with Wilson. But . . . eh . . . what am I to tell Jenny?"

"Tell her what the hell you like!"

"Oho! Well . . . I'll tell her that you're coming back one day—and soon—to marry her."

"You'll tell her damn all o' the kind."

"Damn you for a thrawn beggar, Jock. You ken fine you hope to do that some day."

"Aye . . . but when? That's what galls me, Rab. God kens when I'll get back."

"You don't want me to sound Gavin, do you?"

"No. . . I want to come back and settle down for mysel'. Gavin Hamilton is no' the man to share ony o' his real business wi' me. But if I'd some money behind me I think I could settle down for mysel'—and do weel enough. Hamilton's lazy, Rab. I'd make it my business to go out and get work. I've learned a few tricks in Edinburgh Gavin Hamilton kens nothing about. Only, Rab . . . put a good face on things."

"What the hell d'you think I wad dae? Damnit, Jock, you give me little credit whiles——"

"I know I do. I'm sorry, Rab; but you ken how it is. I left Machlin under a cloud . . . and if they thocht I wasna doing well . . . You ken how they would lick their chops. As for Jenny . . . I'm damned sorry about Jenny. I've sent her an odd pound—for the bairn's sake. If I ever come back to Machlin I'll marry her."

"Your fortune'll tak' a turn, Jock. I thocht you were getting mair work about Parliament House?"

"Aye . . . but it's slow, Rab: hellish slow. There's hundreds o' young lads like me scrambling for ony extras that are going. You need money and influence."

"Well, you know how I spoke to Colonel Dunbar and Charles Hay and Mitchelson. I even mentioned you to Henry Erskine. If there's anything else you think I could do that would help——"

"Oh, you've helped me, Rab: I ken a difference. But folk are no' in law for charity. No . . . as long as you put up a front for me in Machlin. . ."

"I understand, Jock."

"I'll . . . miss you, Rab. We've had many a fine night here —and you've brightened mony a long dull Sunday. I hope you have a good jaunt round the Border country."

"Thanks, Jock. . . Give me half an hour to finish my letters and we'll go down to Dowie's for a bite and a drink. It's damned dry work writing polite screeds. And Jock! It's been a great privilege living wi' you here a' those months and you never questioning my outgoings or my incomings——"

"I couldna question you, Rab."

"Maybe no'; but many another wad hae tried. But we'll hae a drink ower it a', my trusty friend. A good drink and a good bite. . ."

MAY MORNING

The city was early astir. In the Grassmarket where Jenny Geddes, as he had christened his mare, was stabled with Francis MacKay, there was much bustle and activity.

Carters from outlying farms were driving in milk, butter, cheese and eggs for the early delivery and against merchants' orders. Carriers were already loading their vehicles against various country journeys. . .

There was much laughing and jesting between men and maids and much ill-natured swearing between man and beast.

The Bard, who had never yet been so early in the Grassmarket, found the scene much to his interest. He led Jenny out onto the causeway and showed her to Ainslie who was already mounted on a black hack that had seen better days. Jenny moved slowly and awkwardly. Ainslie was no judge of horse-flesh but he voiced his disappointment.

"If she carries you to Dunse to-night, I'll be surprised, Robert."

"Oh, she'll warm up, Bob, she'll warm up. Sure you will, Jenny? Your joints are stiff wi' the night-damp. Ah, but gin breakfast time and the sun weel up i' the lift, you'll be kittled up fine. God help me if you're no'."

He examined his girth: saw that his saddle-bags were balanced and secure: put his foot in the stirrup and mounted clumsily.

"Steady, lass—dinna get frichted! Damned, the night-damp's been getting into my banes too. Ah . . . but that's better. It's six months since I've been in the saddle, Bob—and I fear my rump's fully tenderer nor I wad like it. Ready, Bob? Lead on then and I'll bring Jenny in ahint till we get clear o' this infernal rabble."

"Feel all right, Robert?"

"A bit like Sancho Panza on Rozinante—but never felt better."

Bob Ainslie looked every inch the young gentleman. His nag had the better of Jenny by a couple of hands and Ainslie sat on a well-padded high-moulded saddle. His yellow riding-coat buttoned back at the knee-flaps displayed his highly polished boots to advantage and there was a dashing and debonair curl to the wide brim of his hat.

But the Bard was well put-on himself, in his brown coat with bright metal buttons—and his elegant walking boots were safe in his saddle-bag. The eye that flashed beneath the brim of his hat told the world that he didn't give a damn for man or beast.

And so they picked their way out of the Grassmarket, up the Candlemakers' Row and out the Bristo Port. . .

On the 28th of November he had ridden in by the West Port in low spirits with much trepidation as to his reception and ultimate fortune.

On the 5th of May he turned his back on the West Port and rode out of Edinburgh with a light heart and a few copies of his Edinburgh edition in his luggage—and he rode out as Scotland's Bard . . . and the wonder of all the gay world that was Scotland's capital.

Part Two

THE LONG WAY HOME

OVER THE LAMMERMUIRS

ALL MORNING they rode steadily out of Edinburgh passing carriers and pack-horses going from and to the landward districts. By the time they reached Gifford the road was much quieter and they decided to have a meal before they faced the long climb through the Lammermuir hills by way of Longformacus.

While they rested their beasts they refreshed themselves with ale and cheese, bannocks and butter. The Bard was in high spirits.

"This is just what I need, Bob, to put me in good heart. Good fresh air, a good appetite—and plenty o' good meat and drink. I know I'm going to enjoy this tour. Aye: every mile o' it."

"We've a long sair ride ahead o' us, Robert."

"Jenny Geddes is bearing up brawly. I could have done a lot worse for my money. If she jogs along no worse than she's done I'll be more nor satisfied."

"She's surprised me. I must say that I didna like the look o' her when you mounted in the Grassmarket. But I must warn you about what lies ahead."

"Warn away! Any country would be a joy after the causeways o' Edinburgh—and the smells! You have no idea what the taste o' good country air in my nostrils does to me. I was beginning to feel my head singing wi' it. And talking about singing: I'm full o' music. Tune after tune has been going through my head. I must have made a start on at least a dozen songs. But then I'm bluidy near gyte wi' Johnson's idea of a collection of all our Scots songs. It's the greatest idea I've ever fell in wi'. And there couldna be a worthier one. Think, Bob: a' the sangs o' Scotland wrote down correctly—words and music."

"It's a grand idea—if Johnson has the ability to carry it

277

out. Anyway: you've had the idea yourself for years, have you not?"

"I've had the idea; but what's an idea if you canna carry it out?"

"True enough. But I've the fear that it may take you off your real job of writing poetry."

"What could be finer poetry than the words o' a sang wrote down so smoothly that the words damn near sing themselves? That's real poetry; and difficult. I'd sooner face a dozen ballads than try out a four-line verse and chorus."

"You are a man of enthusiasms, Robert. I suppose you'll just have to wait till this song-writing fit wears itself out."

"Na, na, Bob: you dinna understand. I was always a sang-writer. My first effort was a sang and as like as no' my last effort will be the same. I hope so anyway . . . However, I'll no' deave you wi' my sang-writing. I'm here to enjoy every minute of this and I don't want to miss anything . . . not a hill or a bird or a blade of grass . . . or a burn. There should be burns in the hills—and the music o' running water does more to me than a' the shakes and trills that were ever heard in Saint Cecilia's Ha': aye, a thousand times."

"But you heard some fine music there——"

"No: it would be wrong of me to say that I did. I'm a man o' simple harmony. A' yon contrapuntal stuff weaving out and in wi' little sense and less passion seems gey artificial to me. Nae doubt it's difficult and highly diverting to those whose ears are deaf to the rhythms of nature. In any case, it's the music for folk that live in the towns and think their sweetest hours are spent in a parlour or on the plush chairs of an assembly. But sitting out here on a plank seat at the gable-end o' a change-house in the month o' May. . . Just listen; and look while you listen."

Robert Ainslie both looked and listened. But it was with an unhearing ear and an unseeing eye. He did not see the globules of green life that tipped the hawthorn across the yard. He did not hear the linnets that bobbed and sang in the branches. He saw bushes beginning to burst into leaf and he heard the inconsequential chatter of birds. It was all very pleasant, no doubt. It was the country; and it did not seem to him that there was anything very remarkable in the country being so characteristically itself. . .

The Bard realised that Ainslie was paying little attention to the scene around him. He said nothing. He had not chosen him as a travelling companion for his love for or interest in nature. He had chosen him because he was a light-hearted fellow full of fun and high spirits and in revolt against the sanctimonious humbug of the unco guid.

A barefooted serving-lass, a splendid specimen of the barn-yard beauty, came out of the change-house and, skipping across the yard, called to a hen and her chicks and threw them some scraps. Ainslie sent a gloating lecherous eye over her prime physical proportions.

"It's a fine leg that, Robert. I suppose you would call her a thumping quean? Did you see what her face was like?"

"I did not; but her legs could do wi' a taste o' soap and water. . . ' But gin you meet a dirty lass, fye gae rub her ower wi' strae.' "

"I never suggested——"

"I never said you did. Come on: let's push into the hills that you talk so much about. Time enough for the lassies when we get to Dunse."

As they plodded up out of Gifford the sun went into a bank of clouds and the clouds began to bank up on the sun. It became colder as the wind came in from the Firth of Forth and swept over the bare moorland. They plodded up the incredibly rough and rutted track in single file. It led through long slow-sloping rounded hills of indefinite character. All around them was high moorland: coarse grass, moss, bracken fronds and heather. Stonechats, whinchats and wheatears abounded: and whaups. There were whaups everywhere. And they filled the air with their long spiralling melancholy notes.

They had passed the last cot-house miles behind and they had seen the last lamb and heard the bleat of the last sheep as they rose onto the fourteen hundred foot ridge of the Redstone Rig.

They rested their beasts for a while on the crest of the hill and looked back over the ground they had travelled. The Bard thought that he had never looked down on a scene so desolate, so remotely isolated and withdrawn. There was no sight of human habitation. Nothing but a wilderness of hills falling in ever descending slopes to the lowlands around the direction of Dunbar. He did not respond to the scene though Ainslie assured him that, on a hot summer's day, it was not without its own wilderness-like charm.

"And on a winter's day?"

"It depends on the winter. If there's no snow you can just manage. I've never done it in the dead of winter myself. But my father has. There's a change-house at the Fasney Water. That helps in the winter or when there's a mist on the hills. But every time I cross the Lammermuirs I thank God for the High Street o' Edinburgh."

"I dinna doubt that for a moment, Bob. There are some wild parts in Ayrshire, but nothing to equal this. Damnit, this *is* the wilderness o' Scotland."

"Wait till you get to the Fasney Water and then you'll ken what a wilderness is like."

"And who in God's name ever made a road here—such as it is?"

"It's a busy enough road in the season when the drovers are bringing over the cattle for the winter. But for myself I never feel happy till I get to Langton Edge and can see the Merse lying below me. . ."

As they rode into the hills the day became greyer and rain threatened. They descended steeply to the Fasney Burn, gave their beasts a drink before splashing through the ford and then dismounted at the pathetic little change-house that stood crouched into the hill on the other side. Even the dogs that barked round them seemed to be outlandish curs. The landlord who came to the door of the house might never have seen a barber in the course of his uncertain lifetime. But he received them civilly enough. On Ainslie telling him who he was he enquired for his father and made some show of concern to produce them his best ale which was of indifferent quality and his best cheese which was vile.

"If this hovel in this benighted hollow hasna yet been christened the Arse-hole o' Creation, I hereby christen it so now."

"It couldna be better named. What kind o' a sang you could make about a place like this, Robert, baffles my poor imagination. But since you consider yourself the Bard of Nature no doubt you could think of something. For myself I've had all the nature that I can appreciate in my own home at Berrywell. I don't like to be out of sight of a tavern or a tempting piece of ribbon. . ."

Ainslie spoke the truth as he knew it. For him life was study—and relaxation. He studied in order to be a successful lawyer. For relaxation he wanted no more than wine and women. He liked wine because he liked the mellow company of wine-bibbers. Besides, wine fired his blood—and fired blood sent him chasing after the lassies. . . In Edinburgh he knew where to find the girls—when he had money.

Not that Ainslie revealed any of this to his companions: the darker his deeds the darker he kept them.

But Robert Burns knew little and guessed less of this side to Ainslie's character. There was no sentiment in his relationship with girls. He would no more have thought of making love to them than of marrying them. Even his tentative thoughts on marriage were practical if not cynical. Someday in the distant future he might get married. But if he did it would be for money and social position. He regarded men who fell in love with women as dangerously weak and unstable. If he made an exception of poets it was because poets made falling in love part of their trade.

It was the mask of his youth and the cloak of good-fellowship that protected Ainslie from the analytical penetration of the Bard. . .

A horseman, trailing three diminutive pack-ponies, came from the Border side towards them. Ainslie hailed him. "Good day to you, pack-man: what like is the weather on the Merse side?"

"Guid day to you, sir. It was a fine morning when I cam' in by Dunse; but it's gotten gey dreich and cauld i' the hills for the time o' year. Aye; and there was a lot o' mist on the Wrunk Law as I cam' ower. . ."

The pack-man had dismounted and had allowed his beasts to go forward to the water. He cursed the barking dogs and went inside.

"You notice," said the Bard, "that he didna think it worthwhile to ask us about the weather on our side?"

"They never do. These fellows can tell the weather by a sniff o' their noses. If you're ready we'll jog on—for I want you to see Berrywell afore the sun goes down and the supper's cleared off the table. . ."

"How many hours' riding do you think lie afore us?"

"Oh . . . maybe three or four. After we win through Longformacus there's a good stretch o' road for a bit . . . and after we get to Langton Edge it's downhill a' the road hame."

The Bard was glad when they wound into Longformacus. Not that it was much of a place. But at least there was smoke coming from some of the miserable roof-trees; and there were dogs and goats and cattle and sheep—and children. There were a few trees and some scrub bushes. In every other respect it was a cold god-forsaken hole; but after the bleak hill track over the Wrunk Law it was almost civilisation. As the dogs barked and the children ran into their miserable dwellings, the guidwives of Longformacus poked their thin noses out of the doors to view them up. It was obvious that they did not like strangers in their midst.

They trotted out of the village with a crowd of ragged children shouting after them and a pack of yelping curs barking and snarling at their heels and gurling and growling at each other.

"Well: I'm glad I'm out of that," said the Bard when they were past the last cot-house. "Why folk want to keep so many hungry mongrel curs about them, I don't know."

"Oh, there's naebody'll slip into Longformacus in the dark and steal a fowl: he'll be lucky if he's no' eaten alive."

"I suppose you canna blame the folk either. It'll be a' the

protection they can afford—and maybe they'll need a' the protection they can get."

As if to mark the passage through the gloomy village, the sun began to break through the clouds and immediately they could feel the warmth of its rays. Their spirits brightened.

"That's us past the worst now," said Ainslie. "Or very nearly. There's a bit o' a climb till we get to Harden's Hill—then you'll see something o' the Border country as you should see it."

For quite long stretches now they were able to ride comfortably abreast and converse at their ease. Both were anxious to get to Berrywell and see what reception awaited them. Ainslie's father could be a thrawn devil when he liked.

The Bard, too, was anxious. He was venturing into strange land and was throwing himself at the mercy of strange people. He did not know that he would like Ainslie's family. He had learned by experience that a man can be very unlike the stock he springs from. His fears were not deep-seated or else he would never have ventured to accept the invitation. But he would feel happier when he had met Ainslie's folks and had had a meal with them.

They trudged up the last half-mile of Harden's Hill to spare their tiring mounts.

"Mind you, Bob, Jenny Geddes has done better than I expected."

"My father'll have a better beast for me: he has aey prided himself on his mounts. This damned hack can go to the grass till I take him back to Town."

"Ah well: Jenny'll need to bear me through mony a shire before I see hame again."

"Aye; but a good beast can save you an hour's riding at the end of a day. . ."

They had reached the top of Harden's Hill. The Bard stood transfixed: seemed suddenly to have become drained of life—except that he still held Jenny's bridle in his hand.

Below them lay the Merse: the great broad scooped Border

valley through which ran the Blackadder Water and beyond that, on the English border, the glorious Tweed. The May sun, as it sank into the west, set out against its far-caressing every ridge and knoll, every height and hollow. None but the dullest brute could have failed to respond to something of its nerve-tensing beauty. Ainslie, though he was no clod even if he was no poet, hesitated to advance his pace. Yet the scene, in some strange way, embarrassed him.

That which had seemed to drain away the life of the Bard was no more than the draining away of his consciousness. He was intellectually inactive. Only his senses were alive. Every pore in his body, every nerve-end seemed to be tautened in its response to the beauty that lay before him; and towards this heightening even the faculty of breathing seemed to be suspended.

He said nothing. Words, and the faculty of thinking in terms of words, had deserted him for the moment.

The southward low-lying land seemed incredibly green and miraculously prosperous—as the Promised Land must have seemed to Moses. Soon the Bard would find, on closer inspection, what its flaws and faults amounted to. Here in the sunset, and at the height of a thousand feet and the distance of a score of miles, the Merse looked like a land that might well flow with milk and honey—and give the shelter of warmth and plenty to a contented peasantry.

Perhaps his senses were heightened coming upon the scene so suddenly from the bleakness of the Lammermuirs. But, however this may have been, he could not remember, afterwards, a scene more impressive.

They moved down the hill slowly; and neither of them made to mount. Ainslie had the good sense to realise that this was not his moment; that he would have to be guided by his companion. They walked a good mile down the steep and uncertain road before the Bard broke silence.

"There's something about a scene like this that means more than a woman could mean. That, Bob, is what the Craft means: the Divine Architect of the Universe. . . At least I can think of no other meaning. . . And even at that it's only

something that we put words on—in the infinity of our
ignorance. By God, but we're a poor lot o' beggars when you
come to think on't; given an infinite awareness and a finite
understanding: often enough no understanding at all. At
least nothing that we could build a foundation of belief upon
. . . No: for me, Bob, Nature is supreme. And if you ask me
what I mean by Nature, I can only take you back up the hill
and say: ' Look! ' If you don't know what I mean by that,
then I've nothing more to say. . . But maybe I shouldna have
said anything when I canna put in words what I mean ony
better than I'm doing!"

"I think I've a glimmer of your meaning, Robert. I'm
inclined to accept things as they are without too much
questioning. The way you put it in Green Grow the Rashes
is the way that appeals to me: ' Dame Nature swears the
lovely dears, her greatest work surpasses O. . .' But if you
like to prefer a sunset, it's no' for me to criticise. . ."

"But you're criticising, nevertheless. And in a way you're
right. Man is Nature's greatest work because Man has the
brain to understand, has the moral sense—or at least has the
possibility of understanding. . . But as I've told you before,
Bob, I have a few first principles I'm prepared to stand by
through thick and thin: for the rest I just don't know. As
for the lassies: Nature wi' a' her manifold creations has
created nothing finer than the swell o' a lassie's breast: there's
no' a sweeter shape in a' Nature. . . And that shape, that
sweet curve, holds the very milk of human existence. . . Think
that over at your leisure and see if you can hit on the answer
—if there is an answer that you and me, to say nothing o'
the Faculty o' Advocates, can understand. The reverend and
right reverend divines don't even know that there is a question.
The root o' a' wisdom is not the presumption of knowing the
answers to questions—but in knowing the questions that need
answering. . ."

"That's a very profound statement, Robert—though, con-
versely, you'll agree that any fool can ask a question?"

"Aye: and, by the same token, I've known a fool ask a
question that no Professor of Knowledge could answer."

"But then you make a distinction, do you not, between a fool and a foolish person?"

"Exactly! And then there's the kind o' fools you and me are at this minute."

"Meaning?"

"That even a wise man will talk sense into nonsense provided he talks long enough. And, little claim though I have to any wisdom, I ken I can talk more bluidy nonsense than is good for me."

"But you were very far from talking nonsense—even though you were beginning to talk me out of my depth. You know, Robert, you have a tremendous capacity for metaphysics."

"No: that's just a polite and learned way o' saying that I'm a bluidy blether."

"I must protest that I never thought, far less hinted at, anything of the kind."

"Dinna let it worry you, man. Some o' my jokes hang off the plumb. But what about mounting our naigs and taking the weight off our feet . . . ?"

They were past the steepest parts of the hill and were beginning to come in among trees and bushes and cultivated strips of land. Slowly, almost imperceptibly, the gloaming crept downwards from the soft far-away hills and the blushing sunset died away in the western sky. Jenny Geddes snorted, tossed her head and rattled the bit against her teeth as if anticipating the corn that awaited her at Berrywell. . .

The pleasant township of Dunse lay below the Law, and straggled around the edge of the Dunse Castle estate. Only at the cross were there any signs of congestion; and since the evening was Saturday there was something of evidence of a congestion of folks—for Dunse. The Bard liked the look of the place. It was quiet and sleepy and seemed detached from the world. And yet he could easily understand why it held little attraction for the young and eager Ainslie. It was a place a man might well retire to when he had come to the evening of his days and wanted to doze away without interruption or distraction. It was an unlikely place for a venturesome spirit to begin the battle of life. But for all that, after the long bare bleak ride across the hills, it was a very welcome place to ride into.

When Ainslie informed him (but without any seeming pride) that the town was the birthplace of "the Angelic Scholar," John Duns Scotus, and also of the Reverend Thomas Boston, author of *The Fourfold State*, the Bard's interest quickened. He knew only of John Duns Scotus by repute: Thomas Boston, by his works, he knew only too well.

"Old Boston! Did you ever read him, Bob?"

"I was supposed to have read him. But, to tell no lies, Robert, I found him infernally dull."

"I wish I had a penny for every hour I pored over *The Fourfold State*. There was a time when I knew it nearly by heart. Not that I ever agreed wi' it. But, by God, sir, that was the basis of my early theological reading. It was something you could get your teeth into. A lot o' folk broke their teeth on him. So Thomas Boston was born in Dunse, was he?"

"He was that."

"Well, Bob: I've travelled a long road, mentally, since I first opened his pages. Though I must say in all fairness that he gave me a taste for heavy reading that has stood me in good stead."

"Heavy reading—and light women, eh?"

"Where a lass is concerned I'm vulnerable. But there isn't always a lass available; and the lover, like the warrior, needs his moments of relaxation. . . Sometimes, Bob, the moments of relaxation are the finest moments in life. . . If I could have devoted my life to a lass I would have done it long ago. . . But a lass only engages me for the moment . . . even though the moment is for ever recurring. . . And almost any lass frae a barn-yard beauty to . . . a lass like Peggy Chalmers is good enough for any moment. . . In Peggy Chalmers I thought I saw a lass that would last a lifetime. . ."

They went sharp right off the main Berwick road through a wooden gate and entered the wooded policies of the small

estate-cum-farm of Berrywell and arrived at the front door
of the substantial house as the last reflected rays of the dying
sun went down over the rolling lands of the Merse.

The sound of the horses on the gravel was heard by the
inmates and they came rushing out to meet them. Douglas
was first: a sturdy boy of some twelve years; then Rachel, a
stout though very comely lass of some nineteen summers. Old
Mr. Ainslie followed; and behind him, in the doorway, her
face wreathed in happy smiles, stood Mrs. Ainslie. Sam, an
old negro servant, held the horses and, after enquiring civilly
for Ainslie's health, led the beasts to the stables at the back
of the house. . .

Ainslie patted his brother's tousled head, kissed his sister
and then shook hands with his father. Only then did he
introduce the Bard. The children smiled happily; but the old
man took a good look at the Bard when he held out his hand.
There was no doubting the warmth of his grip. . .

"You're verra welcome to Berrywell, Mr. Burns—indeed
we are honoured to have you."

"And I am equally honoured to be here, Mr. Ainslie: I
trust, sir, that I find you and your family well?"

"We have nothing to complain aboot, Mr. Burns: what
kind o' a journey had ye ower the Lammermuirs? It was a
blessing that ye got a good day for it. There was a while i'
the forenoon I thought the weather might break. . ."

Meantime Ainslie had met his mother and had told her
what news she needed to know. The Bard found her quiet and
self-effacing, but kindly and sweet-natured for all that. It
was with genuine heartiness that she welcomed him ben the
house to have a meal.

The table was set in the long rectangular dining-room
with the large window looking onto the fields that belonged
to Berrywell farm. There was a good braird on the corn; and
the lapwings tossed above it, having been disturbed by their
arrival.

In the dining-room the Bard was introduced to an elderly
man of quiet demeanour: he was introduced as a poet.

"I'm nothing much of a poet, Mr. Burns," said William

Dudgeon modestly. "Juist a bit country-rhymer and in no way to be compared to yourself. But I would like to pay my respects to you, sir, for I have waited thir wheen o' days for just this opportunity."

"I am honoured, Mr. Dudgeon. There is nothing to apologise for in being a country-rhymer. I am no more myself though circumstances have elevated me——"

"Na, na, Mr. Burns: we ken your worth; and we ken that Edinburgh has elevated you nae higher than the rest o' Scotland. Indeed, sir, ye canna be elevated ower high for our way o' thinking. Remember that you are the Bard o' Caledonia and nae langer the Bard o' Ayrshire."

Old Ainslie said: "Willie Dudgeon's speaking nae mair than the truth, Mr. Burns."

The Bard was fully conscious of his welcome. But he was equally conscious of the glowing brown eyes of Rachel Ainslie —and of her full bosom and voluptuous figure. Ainslie had not told him that he had so charming a sister.

When the pair retired to wash up from the dust of their journey, Ainslie was in good humour. "I never had any doubts, Robert; but I can see that you've made a hit with the family: especially my father. . . And Rachel tells me she thinks you no end handsome and romantic. So: there you are! We're in for the time of our lives. . ."

"You never told me about Rachel. . ."

"Oh, she's a wanton-tailed wee bitch: I suppose she's gotten the usual Ainslie blood in her: don't be putting her in the family-way whatever you do."

"Surely you don't think——"

"Robert: I dinna think where women are concerned. All's fair in love or war—or politics. I ken fine you'll respect Rachel . . . Only: if she wants a kiss and a cuddle—and she wouldna be human if she didna—you won't find me keeking ower the hedge. But watch your step! The old folks are damnably strict. If they knew I was going to be a father in August . . . d'you think they'd be roasting the fatted calf? Robert Ainslie would be more likely to cut me off without a shilling. That's why I want some money to settle with the Edinburgh maid.

Above all things that must be buried. By God, if old man
Ainslie knew what went on in Edinburgh. . ."

The Bard was somewhat disturbed at Ainslie's levity. He
was also disturbed about Rachel. The girl had fired his blood
the moment he had clapped eyes on her. He had seen the
answering look in Rachel's eyes. She had bloomed like a blood-
red rose when he had taken her hand. And she had known
how a hand should be taken . . . the slow subtle caress: like
a female Mason's grip—if such a thought could be entertained.
Rachel Ainslie, for all her nineteen years, knew what she was
about. . .

He slunged the warm water about his face and then dried
himself briskly with the towel. It was good to feel clean. His
tiredness seemed to have left him. He was ready to have a
gloaming-walk with Ainslie's sister. . .

During the meal, while Mr. Ainslie discussed agriculture
and William Dudgeon tried to get a word in edgeways about
poetry and Mrs. Ainslie saw that his wants were attended to,
Rachel never took her eyes off him. And when their eyes met
she lowered them with a much too maidenly blush—and a
coyness that was older than her years. It was with some
difficulty that he managed to give his replies as intelligently
as he did. . .

And then, all too soon, it was time for Rachel and Douglas
to say good night and the four men were left to themselves—
and the port.

The host poured a generous glass. A log fire burned in the
grate and they gathered round it. They wanted to hear what
the Bard had to say on this topic and on that. He did not
disappoint them. Now that Rachel was out of the room he
was no longer troubled with the chemical reaction she set up
in his blood. But the excitement she had given him added fire
and eloquence to his tongue; and he delighted his hearers.
Ainslie held his peace. But he marvelled, as he had often
marvelled in Edinburgh, how it was that Robert Burns could
so easily throw aside the mask of boon companion and launch
forth into the poet and the philosopher. He had the capacity
of suiting himself to whatever company he found himself in

without ever sacrificing anything of his essential individuality. He was always and unmistakably Robert Burns. But one had to know Robert Burns well not to be misled into thinking that (maybe) he was playing a part.

Ainslie listened with half-parted lips and wondered at the manner of man who was his travelling companion. And sometimes he doubted that he was any nearer to him than his father or old Dudgeon was. There was so much of him that was beyond understanding. . .

"Politics, Mr. Ainslie? I am a ploughman and a poet— and my ideas as a ploughman do not basically conflict with those of the poet. Therefore in politics I speak as a ploughman —and for those depending on his industry. Then, sir, what connection, what similarity of views, what common bond of sympathy and interest links the poet, the ploughman and the politician? Can you expect me to approve of the politics of Mr. Pitt—or his Scottish henchman, Henry Dundas? On the other hand, what is the alternative to the Pitt administration —Charles James Fox? It is the *only* possible, feasible, sensible alternative. And what of interest can there be between the ploughman and Fox? Very little, I am willing to admit. But at least Charlie Fox has a greater—and therefore deeper and broader—conception of human liberty and human welfare. Therefore, I support the buff and the blue—in terms of party politics. But then, I am under no illusions about the intrigue, the place-hunting, the jobbery and corruption that constitutes the daily bread of party politicians. The whole corruption of our present-day society is caused by politicians. And yet if we are to be wise and sensible, we must realise that reform can only come through politicians—but politicians of a very different kind from the creatures who strut about Saint Stephen's Ha'——"

"And just what kind of politicians have you in mind, Mr. Burns?"

"Honest men, sir. Men who will put the welfare of their country and the people of their country before any private personal gain. Politicians who are, at heart, poets—and maybe ploughmen. Indeed, sir, though you may think me out of my sober senses—a parliament of ploughmen may be the only parliament to bring our nation to the full measure of its greatness—and happiness. But whether ploughmen or poets —they must be honest men. I never tire of quoting Pope's line ' An honest man's the noblest work of God.' Yet, sir, I am only too willing to admit that, reformer though I am, I have little hope in my lifetime of seeing the destiny of my country determined by the deliberations of my country's native rustic sons—and so, for the moment, I give my support and allegiance to Charles James Fox."

" You have studied the classical philosophers—the sages of antiquity, Mr. Burns? Your philosophy—or I mistake it, derives from the ancient Greeks——"

" No, sir: I have some small knowledge of ancient philosophy—but so small that it wouldna bear me from this chair to your privy. I am willing to believe that the Ancients —as my friend Lord Monboddo affectionately calls them— have much to contribute to the living waters of human knowledge. But just as willing am I ready to believe, sir, that an honest ploughman may recognise an honest fact when it stares him in the face."

" But it is hardly to be expected, Mr. Burns, that a plough-man's honesty alone fits him to express judgment on the intricacies of human society. Man must be guided by funda-mental principles, both secular—and theological. The mere instinct for good is not enough—there maun be learning— and understanding of high affairs of state——"

" And yet, sir, without this instinct for good, of what use is all learning and all state-craft? As a ploughman I *may* bow to your learned politician—as a poet I know that mere learning availeth nothing. And if I am not to mistake—or misread— the signs and portents of my generation—here and abroad— America and France—then the common man—embracing in this larger generality the common ploughman and the common poet—may decide to take his fate into his own hands and on the principle of a common humanity determine his own destiny."

" I confess it's a highly poetical if not highly practical idea,

Mr. Burns. And your eloquence fairly carries your ideas along. No', mind you, that I have any objection in principle to your ideas—far-fetched though they may sound. But, mind you: it's difficult to see how the cobbler is no' best employed at his last—and the ploughman at his plough—and, of coorse, the poet at his poems—it's difficult to see how a man not born and bred to the art of civil government can be trusted in that capacity——"

"It is difficult to see that just such men lost us the American colonies."

"That's a point, Mr. Burns: that's a point. But what kind o' job will the colonist make o' things across the Atlantic?"

"They, and not us, will be the better judges of that, Mr. Ainslie—as I think you will allow. Far be it from me, sir, to sit in judgment on my fellow men, be they politicians or ploughmen. Doubtless here and there, if we could find them out, there are honest politicians. And doubtless there are dishonest ploughmen. But I know something of the common people of my country—especially the West country. I know something of the history of my country—especially the history of the glorious William Wallace—and I cannot remain dumb in the light of my knowledge. Do you not find, sir, that the truths of this world are simple? It is only the lies and the evasions, the cant and the humbug that are difficult and obscure? And I must confess that I'm more than a trifle impatient with those who seek to darken the sun with counsel of doubt and ambiguity. This winter I have had the honour —for honour indeed it was—to meet many of the great ones in Edinburgh. I found them prone to haggle in learned jargon over points, obtuse and metaphysical, that to my simple and direct mind were utterly *beside* the point. That point being, sir, that poverty and ignorance are no crimes to those who are poor and ignorant, but that the crime—and crime it is— lies in there *being* poverty and ignorance. And yet, such is the glory as well as the contradiction of life—the poor and ignorant have in their hearts and all the instincts that abound therein, a greater and deeper understanding of the problems of life and the divisions of right and wrong, than have the learned. I hope, by the bye, on my tour through your Border country, to visit many places sacred to the Caledonian Muse. Cowdenknowes and Traquair, for example. Why? Because I lately met an enthusiast in Edinburgh who will shortly issue his first volume of Scottish Songs. Now, sir—if I may appear to digress—in the Songs of Scotland do we not find enshrined in words and in melody something of this essential goodness, simplicity and harmony that is essential to the ordinary, unlettered folks of our country? Our national songs have not been written and composed by the learned and the mighty, but by the humble and the unpretentious—by simple men and simple women— rude at the rustic plough or simple and unaffected by the spinning-wheel as it sat in the sunshine of their cottage doors or beside their simple ingle-lowe. . . And what do these songs express if they do not express the love of country, the details —the affectionate details—of what Gray describes as ' the simple annals of the poor '; of the joy in the simple uncorrupted loves of the human heart; aye, of the humour, the jollity, the abounding merriment taken in the gift of life itself. And, sir, I have taken upon myself to gather together as many of the old songs of Scotland as I can find . . . and if necessary to cobble the broken uppers of the words and even, should that be necessary, to provide fresh words for old melodies. And this I gladly undertake—and with heart-felt joy embrace—because I feel that in our old songs are to be found the old truths and the old satisfaction of living. Not, sir, living in terms of slavery and bondage—but in the old free terms of free men, in a free society. . ."

Old Mr. Ainslie leaned back in his chair. "Ah, weel, Mr. Burns, you hae me beat. But I agree wi' your sentiments— though maybe I'm too auld to follow you in the words wi' the whilk you express them. Aye, man: there's a lot we hae lost in our auld sangs. Nae doubt about that: nae doubt at a'. Still and on, I think you should study mair o' the ancient times, and you'll see that in thae far-away aulden times the folks then had their bits o' problems and their bits o' worries. The country's been in a sair mess this while back—since ever the Union in fact. And what wi' the upset o' the late Rebellion we've had our difficulties. But I think we're getting ower our troubles. And maybe I'm wrang; but I pin my faith to good and intelligent husbandry. Folks can say what they like; but without the country linked up in prosperous well-doing farms there's nothing but poverty and hardship afore us——"

"Well, gentlemen," said Willie Dudgeon, "I'm inclined to agree wi' the baith o' you. I'm no' so sure that I understand you fully, Mr. Burns, and there's a wheen o' points I'd like mair time to tak' up wi' you. Onything I ever heard about the auld days was bad—maistly consisting o' ignorance and naked want. But however that may have been, I canna deny that the auld folks i' the auld days wrote and sang our best sangs. . . I mean sangs that go further back than Robert Fergusson or Allan Ramsay—I mean sangs that were sung aboot the firesides when I was a bit laddie and fit for nothing mair fatiguing than keeping the kye frae the corn."

"Such are the songs I am interested in, Mr. Dudgeon—and indeed, sir, I beg of you to recall as many of them as you can—especially the melodies."

"I'll think oot what I can for you, Mr. Burns—and I'll be honoured to do so—but I was never ony great shakes wi' a tune. In fact, I might as weel confess that I hae nae lug for music at a'! No', mind you, that I dinna like to hear a guid sang weel sung. And a stout lass wi' a good pipe and her binding after the shearers on a braw hairst morn. . . Man, I can appreciate that. But for keeping mind o' a tune after I've heard it . . . weel I've never had the occasion to mind them——"

"Nevertheless, anything you can recall, either words or tune, will be a service to me."

Old Mr. Ainslie put his pipe up on the mantelshelf: "You hae made a study o' music, Mr. Burns—where did you get the time for that?"

"My mother, when we were younger, was a fine singer and the song was ever on her lips. . . Then I got a fiddle and some fiddle music—Craig's Scots Airs and the like . . . and I fiddled ower the notes till I got the tune in my head. Once I had it there it never left me. Then I made a habit, as I had the money, of making the purchase of as many books that contained music for words as I could find. . . And then in the West, wherever folks gathered together—especially young folks—there was fiddling and song-singing. . . And it is my hope now that James Johnson in Edinburgh has started on his Scots Musical Museum not only to do my part in preserving for future generations our musical heritage—but to see my own words printed against the old notes to which I composed them. What is my song Corn Rigs, for example, without the glorious melody that goes with the words?"

"Mr. Burns—I want to say this." And his host adjusted himself in his seat to say it. "From a close reading o' your poems I gathered you were nae ordinary ploughman—but a child could hae told that. What I didna expect to find was a ploughman—and I maun grant you that since you insist—a ploughman wi' such an extraornar range o' interest. And while, Mr. Burns, I dinna want to belittle ony o' your genius —for that's what it is—I would like to say that you're a great credit—no' only to Scotland or to your native Ayrshire—but to your father and mother. . ."

An owl hooted softly in a near-by tree and the summer's night lay sleeping in the corners of the big room; the candles burned, one on either side of the fireplace, in a steady draughtless glow. The port had sunk far down in the bottle—the second bottle that had been opened.

After the torrent of talk the two old men sitting across the fireside and the two young men sitting between them gazed with quiet eyes into the dying logs and the dull red glow in the heart of the silver-grey ashes.

Each was separate in his own thoughts but united in a common bond of sympathy. And young Ainslie, who had spoken not at all, thought that someday he would let the world know of his worth and ability. If a ploughman from the West could conquer Scotland in a few weeks with his genius, what might he not do in a few years with—with what? Bob Ainslie was ambitious; and listening to Robert Burns and thinking of the Edinburgh he had laid at his feet, found his ambitions fortified. . . Someday his name would be as famous as that of Robert Burns—even if it had to be famous in a different capacity.

But young Bob Ainslie, sitting in his father's house in the presence of Robert Burns, did not know, and could not know, the role that Fate had reserved for him.

He was not to be blamed for what no man ever knows regarding his future—or can, in any point of the present, know of the future. . .

Rachel Ainslie, as she undressed, thought: Robert Burns is in love with me. He must be in love with me. Every time I raised my eyes. . . But I watched him all the time and in spite of all the talk he noticed me. Oh, he did more than notice me. From the moment we shook hands. . . How delightful if we could only be together—alone. Of course I wouldn't need to allow him any liberties . . . any familiarities. But why not! With such eyes, and with such a beautiful voice, why shouldn't she allow him liberties? But perhaps he would not be content with liberties?

Rachel Ainslie had been kissed and cuddled many a time. But until now she had never fallen in love. She felt it must be love that made her tremble so, that made her blush, that made her feel faint, that filled her mind with urgent pulsating images—frightening because she had so long forbidden them any deliberate lodgment in her consciousness.

Rachel Ainslie, virgin, with a quivering sensitivity to the physical overtones of passion, battled with the mental images that wrought havoc with her composure. . . Excited, tormented, elated, she at last got into bed. She snuffed the candle; but immediately the soft summer's darkness enveloped her with an overpowering, blood-lapped bewilderment. . .

She was an Ainslie—blood sister of her brother Robert: she was passionate in her physical make-up. . . And so Robert Burns, the elemental tone of life burning and suffusing his great eyes, had done something to her that no man had ever done before. He had made her conscious that she was a woman —made to receive with an all-embracing urgency and avidity the impact of male passion. . .

Long into that May night Rachel Ainslie tossed and tumbled on her bed. The frenzied tumult of creation beat against the walls of her blood; and the pitiless urge of the lover for the mate, of the mother for the child, smashed down every mental barrier so that she bit into her pillow and wept in her hysteria for what she knew not. . .

And so in a night of soft throbbing stars and the hoot of an owl in a leafy bough and the leap of a stoat on a dew-wet mappy, the hymen of Rachel Ainslie's psyche was torn to shreds. . .

Sitting on the edge of his bed, in a room that backed on Rachel's, the Bard took out his Journal and made the following entry:

"Lammermuir hills miserably dreary but at times very picturesque. Langton Edge a glorious view of the Merse. Reach Berrywell. Old Mr. Ainslie an uncommon character —his hobbies agriculture, natural philosophy and politics. In the first he is unexceptionably the clearest-headed, best-informed man I ever met with; in the other two, very intelligent. As a man of business he has uncommon merit, and by fairly deserving it has made a very decent independence. Mrs. Ainslie an excellent, sensible, cheerful, amiable old woman. Miss Ainslie an angel—her person a little of the embonpoint but handsome, her face, particularly her eyes full of sweetness and good humour—she unites three qualities rarely to be found together, keen, solid penetration; sly, witty observation and remark; and the gentlest, most unaffected female modesty. Douglas, a clever, fine promising young fellow. The family meeting with their brother, my companion de voyage, very charming, particularly the sister.

"The whole family remarkably attached to their menials. Mrs. Ainslie full of stories of the sagacity and sense of the little girl in the kitchen. Mr. Ainslie high in the praises of an African, his house servant. All his people old in his service. Douglas's old Nurse came to Berrywell yesterday to remind them of its being Douglas's birthday.

"Mr. Dudgeon, a Poet at times, a worthy, remarkable

character—natural penetration, a great deal of information, some genius and extreme modesty."

He closed the book and put it away in the bottom of his saddle-bag. These notes would come in useful in the years that lay ahead—by their aid he would be able to refresh his memory at any time.

But there were many things he would not need to refresh his memory about. That first view of the Merse from Langton Edge would always be with him. And the impression Rachel Ainslie had made on him—he would never need any notes from a journal to remind him of her.

Grand folks, the Ainslies. Berrywell was a grand house—and this was a grand bed. Maybe he would dream about Rachel—but if he did it would be a sweet dream, flowering from the depths of a sound sleep. It was many a day since he had felt so honestly tired. . .

SUNDAY AT BERRYWELL

The next morning, being Sunday, the entire family set off in the morning to attend the Kirk in Dunse that was ministered to by the Reverend Doctor Robert Bowmaker. Dunse was plentifully supplied with kirks: besides the Relief Kirk there were two houses that catered for the Secession congregations.

Dr. Bowmaker was of the kidney of Black Jock Russell of Kilmarnock—but lacking that worthy gospeller's sledge-hammer righteousness. In the douce Dunse kirk he roared and bellowed like a bull too long kept from the gospel heifers. Nor did he for a moment seem to be conscious of his short-comings. Far from that: Dr. Bowmaker believed that whether he was the Light of the Holy Writ, he was the Authority of the Kirk of Scotland in Dunse; and he was determined that no one should be in any doubt as to his authority. A couple of sinners, guilty of the sin of houghmagandie, he rated as if no man had been born with the physical attributes of Adam and no woman endowed with the attractions of Eve.

During this blustering tirade (lacking the cold West-country fury of Calvinistic convictions) the Bard noticed that Rachel (who had contrived to be at his side) sat with head bowed. But when she raised her head at the end of the admonition, he was not slow to observe that her eyes were troubled with an emotion that had little to do with Christian piety. She fumbled with her Bible, looking for the text. . .

Quickly, but unobtrusively, the Bard took out his pencil and wrote on the fly-leaf of her book:

> Fair maid, you need not take the hint,
> Nor idle texts pursue;
> 'Twas guilty sinners that he meant,
> Not angels such as you.

Rachel read the lines—and rewarded him with a look more expressive than any words could have been.

The Berrywell household held the Sabbath strictly. There was little the Bard could do but fold his hands and join the family circle round the fireside. The day had turned out surprisingly cold. . .

Only in the late evening, after family prayers, did he manage to escape with Ainslie into the fields. Here they planned their escape in the morning. They would ride to Coldstream; and since the Bard had evinced a desire to see England they would have that opportunity by the simple expedient of crossing the Coldstream Bridge. . .

"Of course you know what a Sunday is like in the country," said Ainslie. "That's why I did my best to escape from it. It seems to be the same wherever you go: in the country they observe Sunday in a way that would not be tolerated in Edinburgh. . ."

"And yet," replied the Bard, " a Sunday here is like the levity o' the damned compared wi' Ayrshire. Doctor Bow-maker can roar bluidy near as loud as Black Jock Russell o' Kilmarnock—but it's the roaring o' a sucking dove as you quickly realise when the waft of his words goes past your ears.

But who is this fellow Cimon Gray who came forward after the service this morning and pressed on me a couple o' sheets o' damned doggerel?"

"Tut! Forget about Cimon Gray. He's no more a poet than I am. I suppose he's eccentric . . . maybe mad, for all I know. He's got some ability, I suppose. Lately retired from London where he was some kind o' bookseller. Ah well, Robert: to-morrow's Monday and we can get away bright and early and see something of the Border country. You'll want to cross the Tweed at Coldstream into England. We can call in on Mr. Foreman and you can pay your respects to Patrick Brydone at Lennel House—it's no more than a mile east of the town—if it's that. I've arranged for us to sleep at Coldstream and then we go off to Kelso. . ."

And so they planned their future journeys as they wandered round the edge of a belt of trees, eased their stiffened muscles and breathed the cool evening air. Ainslie was impatient for the morrow. He found that being too long in his father's company imposed a nervous strain on him. The Bard wanted to make the most of his holiday; but he was in no hurry to leave the comfort of Berrywell and the intriguing company of Rachel Ainslie.

It soothed his nerves walking around the Berrywell policies and along the edges of the fields. And it was equally soothing to look forward to a night's rest in an airy room in a comfortable bed with no alien noises coming through from Lady Stair's Close and no strains and stresses coming down from the bawds and their customers above the ceiling.

But then it was deeply soothing to be back in the country and picking up again the sounds of the countryside. And almost like a wine to his head were the scents from the woods and the hedges—of briars and woodbines budding green. . .

After the long months of the sounds and smells, the jostling and crowding of Edinburgh, the peace that nestled in the hollows of the Merseland was almost physical in its intensity.

The Bard sighed lightly: there was nothing of this he could share with Robert Ainslie. . .

ON ENGLISH SOIL

Monday the seventh of May—and they cantered through the still sleepy streets of Dunse, wheeled to their left and came through undulating leafy country by the old village of Swinton down into Coldstream and beheld the glorious river Tweed. . .

They had taken the ten-odd miles, over tolerable roads, at their ease: they were on holiday: there was nothing to hurry them. The Merseland through which they had passed was undistinguished except that the Bard had never seen so many patches of turnips laid out as a general crop. Nor had he ever seen so many well-built substantial farm-houses, golden-grey in the May sunshine against the sweetness of the summer's early green of grass and shaw.

And then the glorious Tweed, broad and majestic, making her way calmly to the sea between rich rolling banks. . . The far-famed Tweed that here marked the frontier of the Auld Enemy. The Tweed at Coldstream across which, from either side, had ridden innumerable armies . . . across which the remnants of the Flowers o' the Forest had retreated from the Field of Flodden but a few miles away. . .

The Tweed, the Borders of Scotland and England. . . The Bard was moved and moved deeply. But he did not let his feelings betray him nor his emotions overcome him.

Instead they rode across the magnificent bridge and trod the English soil to the mile-distant village of Cornhill just as they had trod the soil of Scotland. . .

Fresh from his travels on foreign soil, he dined with Ainslie's friend Mr. Foreman, vanquished him in a discussion on Voltaire, and in the afternoon, still very much the traveller, rode to Lennel House and paid his respects to the celebrated traveller and author of *Travels in Sicily and Malta*.

He had already in Ayrshire in his poem *The Vision* paid poetic respect to his host as "Brydone's brave ward," for Brydone had conducted his Ayrshire patron, Colonel Fullarton of Fullarton, on a continental trip . . . . and Fullarton had been loud in his praise.

Now Patrick Brydone was at the height of his fame, and having married the sister of Principal Robertson, the famous historian, and having rented the magnificent Lennel House from the Earl of Haddington, he was basking in the sunshine of success and modest fame.

He proved a kind and well-meaning host, even if he could not resist showing to the rustic bard of Scotland the elegance of social snobbery; even though in doing so he was unaware that he threw into relief the natural elegance of mind and of manner that so truly distinguished his wife.

The first thing the Bard did as soon as the formalities of introduction were over was to thank Brydone for subscribing for six copies of the Edinburgh edition (from his Princes Street address) and to enquire if they had safely come to hand.

"We must encourage real talent, Burns, wherever it may be found—and you have more than talent, my boy."

"Very much more than talent," said Mrs. Brydone softly.

The Bard bowed.

"Yes—I think—speaking not only as an experienced author —I think it no more than a duty of all gentlemen in Scotland to follow the example of the Caledonian Hunt. Think no more of it, my dear fellow—I am sending copies abroad to friends in various parts. . . And how is my friend Colonel Fullarton doing in your part of the country . . . ? I understand he has quite an estate. . ."

Mrs. Brydone said (when she got an opportunity): "I'm so glad you managed to call on us, Mr. Burns—is your tea to your taste? But I'm so much more pleased that you are managing to make this tour of our Border country. You have earned it and I do so hope you'll enjoy it. Perhaps it will give your muse a fresh inspiration."

"Yes," boomed Brydone, "nothing like travel—*nothing* to equal it for broadening the mind. Pity you couldn't travel abroad—if I hear of any gentlemen going abroad and in need of a secretary I'll advance your candidature, my boy. Travel is the great coping-stone to a liberal education. Most essential, I think. . ."

"Well, sir, I have this day commenced travelling—having ventured a mile upon English soil——"

Brydone's not unhandsome face broke into a hearty laugh.

"Damn good beginning—damn good, my boy. . . But of course you are very sensible in making a tour of the Border district. I suppose you'll find inspiration for your gifts in our native land. Yes, indeed, there are many fine seats of the Scottish nobility scattered about—you would do well to note their magnificence and pay them fitting poetic tribute. Lennel House now——"

That night before he slept the Bard noted in his Journal: "Mr. Brydone a man of quite ordinary natural abilities, ingenious but not deep, cheerful but not witty, a most excellent heart, kind, joyous and benevolent but a good deal of the French indiscriminate complaisance—from his situation past and present an admirer of everything that bears a splendid title or possesses a large estate. Mrs. Brydone a most elegant woman in her person and manners, the tones of her voice remarkably sweet. My reception from Mr. and Mrs. Brydone extremely flattering. Sleep at Coldstream."

MELTING PLEASURE

But if the Bard was pleased with Coldstream and the Tweed there, he was even more delighted with Kelso when he rode west the some nine miles to breakfast there on the following day. If possible Kelso was even more charmingly situated, and the bridge over the Tweed almost as fine as that at Coldstream. The town square was the largest he had ever seen in a country town; and he was struck by the excellence of the shops there. He visited the vast mansion of the Duke of Roxburghe and was duly impressed with its grandeur and the fineness of its situation. The ruins of the Abbey excited more his curiosity—especially the holly bush that marked the spot where James II had been accidentally killed by the bursting of a cannon. He was particularly incensed to learn that the fine old Abbey garden had been rooted out and destroyed by a servant of the Duke—'An English Hottentot' as he was afterwards to describe him.

They dined in Kelso with a farmer friend of Ainslie's, MacDowall of Caverton Mill, and he learned that the farmer had sold his sheep, ewe and lamb together, at two guineas apiece. But he was beginning to realise that the Border farmers were no small crofting-men but more of a rank with the Ayrshire bonnet-lairds—except that they had none of the poverty that so often went with that species of gentry in the West.

Having dined, they crossed the bridge into Maxwellheugh and took the road for Jedburgh. This road proved to be extremely bad and their progress was slow. They touched the Teviot where it absorbed the Water of Kale—a bare and barren countryside—and still heading west and south came to Jedfoot. They came up the Jed in the gloaming to the rude and ancient gauntness of Jedburgh, partook of a late bite and went straight to bed.

In the morning they had an appointment to breakfast with a blind lawyer who was, nevertheless (as Ainslie assured him), the first business man in the town. Not only was Mr. Fair blind, he seemed to be a trifle deaf; for breakfast was hardly over than his wife and her old maidenish sister began to squabble about some minister who had recently been in the town. Mrs. Fair went so far as to accuse her sister, Miss Lookup, of 'laying snares' to entangle the said minister, then a widower, in 'the net of matrimony.'

The Bard was amazed that such an abusive personal altercation should have arisen in the company of two strangers like Ainslie and himself. When the old lawyer suggested that they might care to ride out to a sale of grasslands some two miles out of the town, he was only too glad to escape from the house.

Once outside, in the morning air, he was able to get something of the feeling of Jedburgh. More than Coldstream or

Kelso it breathed the spirit of that rude romantic grandeur he had associated with the Border towns. But the Jeddart folk had taken full advantage of their situation and the town was pocketed and surrounded by gardens and orchards. Many of the fruit trees still carried late blossom.

The Jed itself, though nothing like as broad and majestic as the Tweed, pleased the Bard more by its character. Its waters seemed crystal in purity and at times it twisted and turned and dashed over its rocky and boulder-strewn bed very happily.

When they got back to Jed (after having dined with a Captain Rutherford) they found that the Fairs had arranged an afternoon walk for them to visit Love Lane and Blackburn, two of Jed's famed beauty spots. It was quite a party—Mr. Potts, a fellow lawyer of Mr. Fair, and the Reverend Thomas Somerville made up the escorts. The ladies consisted of Mrs. Fair and Miss Lookup—and the thought of their being in the company almost reconciled the Bard to a dull afternoon.

As they came out into the sunshine he reckoned he had rarely seen a more ugly or more stupid pair of women. The two Fair daughters were only tolerably agreeable. The Bard could not help noticing that they had too much of their mother's half-ell mouth and hag-like features. The party was brightened, however, by the presence of a Miss Hope, a girl who was not only pretty but bubbled over with good humour.

And then there were the two sisters of Doctor Lindsay! Isabella, the elder, was captivating. She was, perhaps, a little on the plump side to merit classical award for beauty. The Bard found her, as he had found Rachel Ainslie, none the worse for that.

And when he had the opportunity to survey Peggy, her sister, in the flush of something (though he did not know it) that was more dangerous than her twenty-one years, he realised that, had Isabella not been present, Peggy would have captivated him almost as much.

Ainslie, seeing Isabella and the Bard's mutual interest, was torn between Miss Hope and Miss Peggy—and prayed that he wouldn't be involved in any professional conversation between Messrs. Potts and Fair.

But both of them—especially the Bard—reckoned without Mrs. Fair and her sister.

Immediately they sensed what was afoot and immediately they set about their campaign of action. They out-flanked the Bard and lost no time in insinuating that Isabella Lindsay was not all that she might appear to be. . .

"A young man like you, Mr. Burns, who's become sae famous should watch himsel'," began Mrs. Fair.

"Aye, certes," cut in Miss Lookup, her lean jaw jutting out sharply, "there's a wheen young jads now-a-days oot to hook a young man. Shameless young hizzies withouten sense o' decency or shame——"

"Brazen Jezebels," augmented her sister, "forward and impudent—and nae modesty where showing aff their figures is concerned. A wheen lemans that wouldna be oot o' place in an ill-house. . ."

But the Bard was in no mood for their spleen. At the earliest opportunity he shook them off, and, by a series of masterly movements, soon found the arm of Isabella Lindsay. In fairness to Isabella it must be said that she anticipated the Bard's tactics and by an adroit (though cunningly dissembled) movement or two placed herself in a most advantageous position.

And it was a position that resulted in much pleasure for both parties. It was indeed the most exhilarating experience the Bard had known since he had left home. Isabella Lindsay reminded him of Peggy Chalmers—but she had none of Peggy's cautious resistance. And he found her company, and the intimacy of physical contact, too pleasant to consider if she had anything of Peggy's character.

Indeed, the thrill of fresh conquest had swept away all the cold prudence of assessment and comparison.

The Bard was almost prepared to swear that he had never spent a more enjoyable afternoon. The weather was perfect and no more pleasant spot could have been chosen in Scotland than the sun-dappled banks of the Blackburn.

He was beginning to realise that his fame as Scotland's Bard was a tangible asset. That an attractive young lass like

Isabella could quote his verses and speak softly of his greatness flattered his vanity and sweetened his ego. He had flattered himself that he was too deeply experienced in the ways of the world ever to be unsettled by a roguish smile and a dimpling cheek. But Rachel Ainslie had caused his pulse to quicken; and now Isabella Lindsay was already beginning to play ducks and drakes with all his sober-headed coolly-calculated resolutions.

Already he began to make alterations in his plans. To-morrow he was due to ride out to Wauchope and spend a couple of days with Alison Cockburn's niece, Elizabeth, wife of Walter Scot.

He supposed, now that he was here, that he was honour bound to pay her a visit. She had written him (and before his Edinburgh edition had come out) a kind and couthy poetical address; and he had written her an equally kind and couthy one back. Yes: he would need to pay his respects at Wauchope House. But there was no good reason why this should occupy him overnight. He would pay his respects, make his excuses, and hasten back to Jedburgh. Isabella was a poem in flesh and blood: the words dropped from her lips like the cadence of a fine song. . . He needed closer contact with such a model.

And this was their first meeting! Then by all that was holy, this must not be their last. . . But why was he allowing his mind to wander? Her soft rounded arm was snug and intimate in his; and she returned his pressure that was the more doubly assuring because it was so infinitely prolonged and gentle.

But they were with a party—and certain proprieties had to be observed. Ostensibly they enjoyed the scene . . . the young green of the beech leaves; the low singing of the Blackburn water; the sweet monotony of the cushat's cooing in the hidden branches; the bob of the wag-tail as it flitted among the burn-boulders; the flash of the water-ouzel as it arrowed against the sunlit bank already rich with the promise of a dank harvest of autumn weeds. . .

They did admire the scene; but admiration seeped softly into their senses and their eyes held a dreamy far-away focus.

In the condition of physical intimacy their blood beat in a common harmony and in a unison of physical vibrations they became as one in their responses. . .

But that melting moment, though it belonged to eternity, was framed in Time's mortality.

They separated. Others wanted his company, were greedy for his conversation or were jealous of their happiness. . .

Maybe he groaned inwardly—but he bowed to the inevitability of circumstance. So he shared among the company, talked sober sense and listened to dull observation. And the soft distant dreaming vanished from his eyes and the world was itself again. There were the magnificent ruins of the Abbey to inspect, there was this fine house and that fine garden to enthuse about; and there was the hard, inviolate core of the old Jeddart tenements that housed the ancient worthies of Jeddart, the weavers, the smiths, the wrights, the masons, the saddlers, the souters, the tailors—the essential men and their wives and children who clung resolutely to the grim tenement-rock fastness of their community, lived a life of their own dictated rhythm and spurned the blandishments of an alien world.

As the Reverend Thomas Somerville said: "Yes, Mr. Burns, the old townsfolk of Jeddart may seem lazy and indolent—they may even seem bold and defiant. In truth I must confess that I neither know them nor understand them and—though I confess I do not exactly mean this in a Christian sense—I'm not sure that I want to know them."

"That I can understand in your sense, Mr. Somerville. But aren't they the direct descendants of our Border heroes—haven't they in the past fought and forayed, known siege and starvations, victory and defeat?"

"Well, yes—there is that aspect to be considered. After all, Mary of Scots came here—and nearly died. Plenty of folks here at this moment remember well the Highland Host—Charles Edward slept the night in the Canongate. But we live in a peaceful age now, my dear Burns—and this they ought to recognise. No: I would ask you to think of Jedburgh in terms of its quiet houses and gracious gardens—these, and not the rows of grim gaunt tenements huddled on the hill here, most truly represent our town."

But to all this the Bard said nothing. He would always think of the Jed Water, of the Blackburn—and Isabella Lindsay. He knew only too well why the Jeddart worthies refused to mix with incomers; and he did not blame them.

In the evening in his small Canongate room he wrote calmly in his Journal:

"Miss Lindsay a good-humoured amiable girl; rather short et embonpoint, but handsome and extremely graceful—beautiful hazel eyes full of spirit and sparkling with delicious moisture—an engaging face and manner, un tout ensemble that speaks her of the first order of female minds—her sister, a bonnie, strappan, rosy, sonsie lass. Shake myself loose, after several unsuccessful efforts, of Mrs. Fair and Miss Lookup and somehow or other get hold of Miss Lindsay's arm—my heart thawed into melting pleasure after being so long frozen up in the Greenland bay of indifference amid the noise and nonsense of Edinburgh. Miss seems very well pleased with my Bardship's distinguishing her, and after some slight qualms which I could easily mark, she sets the titter round at defiance, and kindly allows me to keep my hold; and when parted by the ceremony of my introduction to Mr. Somerville she met me half to resume my situation. Nota Bene—The Poet within a point and a half of being damnably in love—I am afraid my bosom still nearly as much tinder as ever.

"The old, cross-grained, whiggish, ugly, slanderous hag, Miss Lookup, with all the poisonous spleen of a disappointed, ancient maid, stops me very unseasonably to ease her hell-rankling bursting breast by falling abusively foul on the Miss Lindsays, particularly my Dulcinea; I hardly refrain from cursing her to her face. May she, for her pains, be curst with eternal desire and damn'd with endless disappointment! Hear me, O Heavens, and give ear, O Earth! may the burden of antiquated Virginity crush her down to the lowest regions of the bottomless Pit! for daring to mouth her calumnious slander on one of the finest pieces of the workmanship of Almighty Excellence.

"Sup at Mr. Fair's—vexed that the Miss Lindsays are not of the supper party as they only are wanting. Mrs. Fair and Miss Lookup still improve infernally on my hands."

THE GUIDWIFE OF WAUCHOPE HOUSE

On the morning, they rode out of Jedburgh by way of Bedrule since Ainslie desired to make contact with a Doctor Elliot who lived in that neighbourhood. They set off early. The distance to Wauchope was reckoned by Mr. Potts to be no less than fifteen miles—whatever more. No one in Jedburgh could tell them exactly how they might reach Wauchope other than that it lay immediately beyond Bonchester Hill. . .

It was a bad road and a slow climb to Bedrule; and even then they had some difficulty in finding out the house of Doctor Elliot. But their search was rewarded. Elliot turned out to be something of a character. He served them up an excellent breakfast for it was now about nine o'clock of the morning. After the dish of fried trout which, he assured them, he had caught himself but an hour before, he produced some excellent whisky which he likewise assured them was from his own still.

This might well have been true for his place was isolated; and his waste could easily be disposed of in the Rule Water that ran conveniently past his door.

Doctor Elliot did not know the Scots of Wauchope personally; but he did know where Wauchope House lay and offered to accompany them as far as Bonchester Hill from whence he said they could obtain "commanding views" of the district.

As he looked down from Bonchester Hill the Bard found the land lying beneath him at Hobkirk pleasant enough; but when they made the ascent of Wolfelee Hill a mile to the south, and overlooking Wauchope, they found a different prospect.

True, there were some beeches round Wauchope House and there were traces of boskage in the banks of the Wigg and the Wauchope Burns; but otherwise the land was bleak and bare even in its summer scad of green. Indeed, he felt there was something sinister about the landscape and he had never had that feeling about any landscape before—not even amid the bleakness of the Lammermuirs. The ground rose into bare featureless hills and great characterless humplocks—and these extended without relief into the far horizon.

But there, immediately below, set in all its lonely isolation, stood Wauchope House, substantially grey. He guessed (and guessed correctly) that the main agricultural wealth of the district lay in sheep and hill cattle.

The day was wearing on and they had had enough of commanding prospects that commanded little more than a coarse and heathy wilderness. They descended the hill at a steep and not too comfortable slant, forded the burn and rode up the avenue of beeches to Wauchope House.

For once Ainslie was unsure of himself. "I hope the Scots make us welcome, Robert, for I canna say that I warm to the look of the place."

"Nor me, Bob; but the Guidwife canna be an uncivil woman or she wouldn't have written me as she did."

But when they rode up to the front door of Wauchope House their worst fears seemed to be confirmed. It was a long square stone building, damnably substantial and damnably forbidding. The front door itself was mean and narrow—a mere rectangular hole in the grey wall.

The usual dogs barked around them before they could dismount; and there was an unwelcome note in their barking. Walter Scot came to the door, called off the dogs, and greeted them not too uncivilly. He called a servant in a hectoring tone and had their mounts led to the stable with instructions to give them a feed of corn.

If the goodman of Wauchope House was something of a boorish oddity—(the Bard could not help thinking that he exactly fitted his conception of Sancho Panza)—his goodwife was a terror no words could adequately describe. She had a face like a horse: big-boned, bold and extremely critical. The Bard grued inwardly as he shook her powerful hand.

But she was pleasant in her masculine (or rather equine) manner.

"Weel, Maister Burns: so you've managed to pay me a visit! Staying in Jedburgh, are you? In the Canongate! What number? Humm! twenty-seven: that'll be just above Dean's Close? Aye, I ken it fine: I have friends bide there. Did you see my Auntie Alison Cockburn before you left Embro? A fine woman: a remarkable woman—in fact there's no' her like in Scotland. Aye: come awa' ben, Maister Burns: you'll be tired after your lang ride. Michty me! ye were up the Bonchester Hill *and* Wolfelee, were you . . . ? What took ye up there?

"We had a taste o' sheep's-heid broth for the dinner: ye'll tak' some gin the lass heats it up for you . . . and Mr. Ainslie? Mmm! frae Dunse! Oh weel: we're glad enough to have you: the baith o' you. And you're gaun back to Jeddart the nicht? Oh weel: if you maun, you maun. I canna stand in the way o' Scotland's Bard.

"And what are your plans for the future, Maister Burns? I see, I see! Oh, but you'll be making plenty o' money out o' your Embro edition. . . William Creech is the man to see that he gets a return for his bawbees—so you'll get yours. Patrick Miller: that's the brother o' the Lord Justice Clerk: my Auntie kens him well. . . So you're thinking maybe you'll rent a farm from Mr. Miller?

"Mr. Scot'll tak' you a turn round the steading when you hae a sup o' the broth. . . Of course you canna expect me to believe that you were just a ploughman in your native Ayrshire. Na, na: that'll no' digest in my stammick. . . Ah weel: I suppose we are a' self-educated if it comes to that. For myself I just write a verse or twa now as the inspiration comes over me. Of course I've that much work to supervise and attend to that whiles I never get the opportunity to put pen to paper. The men-folk have mair time on their hands than the weemin. . . 'Course, I never thocht o' setting mysel' up as a *professional* authoress—or I could have done a lot more than I have. . .

"And you're coming out for a lawyer, Mr. Ainslie? Just so. A Writer to the Signet next year, eh! You have no ambitions to be a poet? No: I didna think so by the look o' you: I can see you're made for a gentleman. And whaur did you fa' in wi' Maister Burns . . .?"

The guidwife of Wauchope House had a tongue that never ceased to clack in her great gash of a mouth. Her tone was not so harsh as it was shatteringly powerful—her words flailed on their ears. But she was oblivious to their discomfort.

Maybe she was lonely: maybe she knew that her sands were fast running out: maybe she had never recovered from the loss of her young lover by drowning long ago. She was coming up on sixty and her late marriage to Walter Scot had not been a happy one. Maybe she missed the long years she had spent in Edinburgh and the company of her aunt Alison Cockburn (they were both Rutherfords) and literary friends such as Doctor Blacklock. . .

What it was the Bard did not know and was never to know; but he had never before set foot in such a gloomy unhappy house. Even in the big upstairs room, in which they now sat on moth-eaten tapestry-covered chairs and amid her books and portraits, there was an atmosphere if not of tragedy at least of deep unhappiness.

She must have been a powerful-willed, strong-charactered woman in her day. Now, with a wisp of reddish-white bristles about her creased upper lip she no longer had any element of womanly grace or charm to soften the impact of her personality.

And yet, without any trace of self-pity, she was desperate to impress the Bard of her antecedents, of her wide culture and her poetic ability. But for a move of impatience from her husband she would have read some of her English verses—as she called them.

"Though I can scribble away bravely enough in our Scottish dialect, I prefer the classical muse, Maister Burns. You must understand that I was thoroughly grounded in Latin and French and introduced to a wide range of literature.

I was writing poetry before I was eleven years of age. Doctor Blacklock and many others thocht very highly of my gifts . . . If I were you, Maister Burns, I'd turn my attention to the classical muse. She will be more difficult to woo. But then she is the scholar's muse as well as the poet's. She would extend your range, Maister Burns—and at the same time refine it. You dinna mind taking advice frae a woman who has seen much of literary life in Embro? And dinna think I'm casting ony slur on your hamespun efforts. Na, na—it's just that you're young and have plenty o' time before you——"

Her husband said: "Awa' doon and hurry on the lass wi' the broth, woman: thir lads are bound to be starvin' for a bite."

When she had excused herself and departed, he continued: "Aye, aye, Maister Burns, just that noo! You'll no' worry if I dinna fash aboot poetry and sic-like. I never much held wi' it for a man-body. But damnit, I will say that you hae naethin' o' that humpty-backit, ghost-glowering, ditch-delivered look aboot you commonly connected wi' your kind. You're a weel set-up fellow, sturdy-shankit and wi' a guid strong grip till your hand. Man, I wonder that you fash wi' the bluidy pen: the stilts o' a plough's mair like you. Ah, but you're a wise man for to settle yoursel' doon in a farm— that's the honest countra sense coming oot in you. Far better than gittering oot and in the Embro howffs knocking yoursel' sick wi' bad drink and blin' wi' reading and writing. It's different wi' Maister Ainslie, here: we can get on without poets but we canna dae withouten lawyers—eh, Maister Ainslie?"

"I'm afraid, sir, we lawyers *are* a necessary evil—but we do our best——"

"Aye, and ye ken fine how to charge for your best! Ye tak' a damn lang time to render your bills; but, by certes, when ye do, folks ken a' aboot it. . . Ah weel then, Maister Burns, I'll show ye roun' my steading when ye've eaten. . . What's that? Aye; just that—sheep and hill-cattle. Ah, but we plough a bit too; and I hae a wheen pigs and goats to say nothin o' the midden-fowls. Damnit, we maun eat whatever else we dae. . . Dishorning cattle, did you say? Saw the bluidy horns aff and stop the hole wi' a handfu' o' cobwebs. There's nae need to waste pity on a beast or a servant. Dinna you start wasting your sympathy on your servants when you get your farm, Maister Burns, or, by God, they'll damned quick tak' advantage o' ye. Give the beggars their meat—and then see that they work for it——"

Mrs. Scot came in and announced that their meal was ready. She led them downstairs to a dining-room as large and lugubrious as the parlour upstairs. Mr. Scot was a man of gigantic proportions and it was obvious that Wauchope House, square solid and barn-like in its spaciousness, had been built for a family of such men.

They sat into a long massive table to a meal of broth and bannocks. Scot poured them another glass of whisky. The whisky tasted raw and crude and the sheep's-head broth had a bitter burned taste.

Though the day was warm and clear it was cold and forbidding inside. Hungry though they were, they made a short hasty meal and were glad to get outside into the sunshine and to view the substantially built and well-planned steading buildings.

Walter Scot of Wauchope certainly had his limitations, but he certainly knew how to conduct his farm.

Both the Bard and Ainslie pleaded the long ride ahead of them and the urgency of affairs to be settled in Jedburgh. Nor did Scot attempt to detain them. Mrs. Scot was more reluctant to see them go. She made the Bard cool his heels at the doorstep while she delivered a harangue consisting of what she thought was excellent counsel and advice.

Plodding home the long fifteen miles—and it felt more like twenty—he said to Ainslie:

"God preserve me from all female authors, Bob. That woman would make me throw myself into the burn, head-first; and if I dinna manage to knock my brains out on the boulders I would at least have the sense to keep my head under till I was safely in the next world."

"I dinna ken much about poets, Robert, and less about female authors; but God preserve me from any of the kind if Mrs. Scot o' Wauchope is any likely sample."

"And yet—she means well. But married to a complete Hottentot like Walter Scot and living in a meikle dungeon o' a house like that, what can you expect? It's a wonder after the life she lived in Edinburgh that she's got ony sanity left in her. But what a pair! And how in the name o' God did they ever come thegither . . .?"

In the fullness of the evening, with the mist lying in the bed of the Jed Water, they came to the Canongate, supped with Mr. Potts and did more than justice to the bottle he had uncorked for them. . .

But the Bard had already forgotten about the guidwife o' Wauchope House. He was thinking about Isabella Lindsay.

SWEET ISABELLA LINDSAY

The next morning they were up betimes to keep a breakfast appointment with the Reverend Mr. Somerville.

Somerville was already drinking claret when they arrived and the Bard was shown into his sanctum. He was not the man to let the morning go by without feeling the warmth of alcohol stimulating his fancy. This morning the reverend gentleman was certainly in a merry mood.

"Mr. Burns, Mr. Burns! And how do I find you, sir, this fine morning? Excellently well, I hope, and ready for a bumper before breakfast!"

"A bumper is something I could not well carry before *supper*, Mr. Somerville. For a poet I'm a sober man to the point of being poor company."

"Poor company, did you say? Hark you, Mr. Burns: if honest claret is too much for your fickle stomach, what say you to the company of a fair maid?"

"What fair maid would you have in mind, sir?"

"What fair maid would I have in mind! What fair maid

would *you* have in mind? The fair, the dear, the charming Isabella Lindsay?"

"Miss Lindsay, sir? I doubt that you do Miss Lindsay an honour."

"And would you do her an honour, my boy, and she desperate to sample a kiss from Scotland's Bard? No, no, Mr. Burns: you can deceive yourself but you canna deceive me. I have too long an experience with such affairs. The heart, my dear sir, the heart determines such matters. Come, confess: tell me honestly that you would not rather see Miss Lindsay—that indeed you would rather see the devil—and I'll tell you what a liar you are. Think not of my cloth, sir. Or rather think kindly of it. An unfortunate devil of a clergyman, sir, is still a son of man however he may attempt to disguise that fact in the pulpit and before the multitude. Sir: God knows my virtues and my weaknesses; and I wish harm to no man or woman. I may not have much of a conscience left me; but what I have left that I will answer for. . . My sins are not many. A little wine for my stomach's sake . . . but then you see what a stomach God has given me! You see: I should have been a scholar. Well, then: while my good lady (and she is the very best o' wives and the most understanding even if she is expecting her sixth in a few days) . . . while my good lady entertains Mr. Ainslie in the next room let you and me drink an honest glass of claret. And then allow me to send for Doctor Lindsay and his sisters that we may eat together and be merry. The Doctor and I have many a glass together. An excellent fellow. The Doctor won't come, of course: he's a busy man. But I'll send word privately that Miss Isabella is to come no matter what betide. Aha: I see that that warms your heart, Mr. Burns. Sir: it is not every day that we have a poet in our midst—and especially such a poet! Sir, I am taken with you: I like you. Robert, my boy, you have lightened my long and dreary hours here. And there is nothing gladdens my heart more than seeing the young folks happy and enjoying themselves. The other day when we were walking in that romantic glade by the Blackburn I was only too conscious of the happiness that reigned in the heart of Isabella and yourself.

When I saw you link arms my heart softened. Why, I said to myself, should not I join in holy matrimony my dear, sweet Isabella and the Bard of Scotland! Believe me, my dear Burns, nothing would give me more happiness. . . And why not? You like the lass?"

"Sir: there are few lassies I like more. But there are degrees of familiarity in these matters I would have observed. After all: the young lady may have her affections otherwise engaged . . . But I'll join you in a glass of claret; and I shall ever be in your debt if you can so arrange it that Miss Lindsay and myself are as much together as propriety will allow."

"Well spoken, my boy; and it shall be done immediately. I'll send my serving-lass round to Doctor Lindsay with a message. . .

"May I confess to you that I have ambitions to come before the public as a writer of history? I am specialising in the reign of Queen Anne. A most interesting period. What age do you think I am? Just coming into my forty-seventh birthday! And you thought I was at least ten years older. . . Still, I have twenty years more experience of the world and its ways, my dear Burns, and, believe me, that is a real advantage. . . Now if you will go through and keep my wife and young Mr. Ainslie company while I write a note to Doctor Lindsay. . ."

"I am in your debt, Mr. Somerville. How comes it, sir, that the Border clergy—presumably trained in the same school of theology—are so different from their brothers in the West? Yes, sir, I know that the West Country was the real home of the Covenanters. But is that the whole explanation?"

"Yes . . . and no, Mr. Burns. Yes and no. Yes, because the dour aggressive spirit of the Covenanting times still lingers there. No, because in the Borders here, though we are equally zealous in our faith—we are not so bigoted. For myself, my dear boy, I like to take a man's good intentions for granted . . . We have our bigots, of course. But they are in a blessed minority. We clergy as you wisely remarked are of the same theological school—rather we are of the same theological *year*. Some of my brothers in orders belonging to a much older year than myself, I find very trying. My boy—clergymen, like poets, differ. But as long as we are Christians, what does it matter?"

"You don't know the West Country, sir. There a man is not a Christian unless he subscribes to the doctrines of the Old Light party. There, sir, a rigid, narrow, intolerant, inhuman Calvinism alone is equated with Christianity—though even the very word Christian has a certain heretical sound about it... But forgive me, Mr. Somerville. When on the rare occasions I drink in the morning, my mind takes a theological bent. If you will pardon me, I'll join Bob Ainslie—and your good lady."

What it was that Somerville wrote to Lindsay no one but he and Isabella ever knew. But it had the effect of bringing her along to join the breakfast party before the party had properly commenced.

Her dissimulation was perfect; and on this account she gave the Bard no cause for embarrassment. But though she had "just dropped in" she was able to convey to him the real reason for her presence.

There was nothing the Bard wished more at that moment than to be alone with her. He knew that Isabella was his—granted the time and place. But he doubted if Somerville's experience of life extended far enough to agree with this.

In this he was right. Somerville was keen that there might arise a love-match between them. In addition to his wretched addiction to puns he was the great match-maker of the parish and liked to think that he had a hand in many discreet matrimonial affairs... Nothing would have pleased him more than a marriage between his best friend's loveliest sister and the Bard of Caledonia... The fact that he had arranged that the Bard be given the freedom of the Burgh by the magistrates later in the day was all part of his scheming and planning...

As it would not be possible to arrange an excursion such as they had enjoyed to the Blackburn—for time was wearing on—Mr. Somerville had hit on a plan that they would all go and visit the local fortune-teller, Esther Easton, who had a cottage and a lovely garden just on the skirts of the town.

". . . Esther we call her in Jeddart. Her history need not be gone into for the moment. But there is no more remarkable woman in my parish. True, she is no longer young; and, since we are all gentlemen, we will not examine her years too closely. She writes verses——"

"But they are not very good verses, Mr. Somerville——"

"They are not, Isabella . . . but they are very remarkable, coming from Esther. We must be charitable to all God's creatures; and I dinna think that Mr. Burns will object to Esther's verses——"

"I will gladly accept your charity, sir, if you will allow me to accept Miss Isabella's literary judgment."

"' They say! What say they?' *Lind*say. . . Ha, ha, ha! Excellent, my dear fellow! Excellent! Well, well: Esther we go and see Esther or Esther we don't——"

"La, Mr. Somerville, please!"

"Ah, you never do appreciate my wit, Isabella. But seriously for the moment; and to return to our muttons as it were: Esther is a most remarkable woman. Just how remarkable I'll tell you in your private ear afterwards, Mr. Burns—now, now, ladies: there are confidences that may be exchanged between a clergyman and a poet that may not be exchanged between others. You shall be the judge, Mr. Burns. She can repeat Pope's Homer from first line to last. I admit that not only would I not care to do so, but that I would not care to *read* Mr. Pope from end to end. After all, man's chief end is to glorify God. . . But she has studied Euclid by herself. Euclid hardly expect more from a professor of mathematics. . . Ha, ha, ha!"

Underneath his breath Robert Burns execrated the Reverend Mr. Somerville's pathetic propensity for punning. But his execration was short-lived. He was more than delighted by the signs that shone in the eyes of Isabella Lindsay. Her eyes told him more surely than any words could have done that she agreed with him; that she shared his sentiments; that her dearest wish was that they might be alone together. . .

They escaped from Esther who was all (and very much

more) that Somerville had indicated. . . They were at the bottom of her garden while the others were still indoors listening to her sibylline utterances—and skilfully detained by Mr. Somerville.

"Isabella—and I may call you Isabella . . .?"

"Gladly you may, Robert."

"My dear, my dear . . .! I'm leaving Jeddart to-night: may never see you again. . . Will you accept this engraving of my likeness. . . It will give me more than a heart-throb when I am back in my native West to know that you have it in your possession. . . Isabella: I'm a man of the simplest words. . . I am a ploughman before I am a poet . . . though I think I was always a poet too. . . Isabella: I love you. . . Oh, not in any genteel fashion. To hell with that kind of mawkish sentiment. I could put you down behind that bush there and father twins on you quicker than it would take time to tell. . . And if I did it *would* be twins: or triplets. I am incapable of fathering any solitary child on you. . . No, no, my dear: you have no idea how safe your virginity is from me. . . I only tell you what is in my heart. . ."

But by this time his hand was in her bosom and his lips on her lips.

It was the Bard who broke himself free. He sensed that Isabella's defences were down; her most inviolate citadel become violate. . .

"Robert: I do love you! I loved you from the moment I saw you. What can we do about it . . .?"

"Beggar-all, my dear: that's the hell and the fury of it. I leave Jeddart to-night. . ."

"Must you . . . must you . . .? I'll wait, Robert: I'll wait . . . even if it were ten thousand years, I'll wait. . ."

"No: you won't wait, Isabella. The stuff of waiting's not in you. . . No more than it is in me. . ."

Her breasts were sweet and yielding to his hand that had grown soft with the months of manual idleness in Edinburgh. He knew that Isabella Lindsay was his to the uttermost ends of the earth. . . But even in the heat of their passion he knew that theirs was not the love that would go to the ends of the earth. Isabella was but another lass who was made for love, for passion, for the excitement of the passing lover. There was not the slightest excuse for him to prolong his stay in Jeddart... If he did he would have to marry her...

It was a pity. Yet it was but part of the pity of life. Two met in the passion of love and affection. Passion flared on the fusing of their mutual desire. But time and circumstance were against them. They could do no more than acknowledge to each other their awareness of the attraction before they parted.

Or so it was with Robert Burns and Isabella Lindsay. At the base of their attraction lay the magnetism of desire. This was the base of all attraction between a man and a maid. But desire writhed and coiled from the base in an infinite variety of pattern. There was no resemblance in the pattern of his desire for Isabella Lindsay and his desire for Peggy Cameron: only the stuff of which the pattern evolved remained constant.

Thus every new love was as fresh as the morning dew. They were standing even as the eternal lovers had stood in the garden of Eden . . . only the Angel of Time with the flaming sword of Circumstance was about to separate them.

Knowing this they could afford to be frank with each other. There was no time for the dallying foibles of suspension in delay. Had there been time how different might that moment in the garden have been. So in five minutes they achieved an intimacy that otherwise might not have been achieved in as many weeks—if ever.

The Bard took a quick look round. Then they embraced on that unspoken knowledge. There was a sudden frenzied strength in Isabella's embrace and a flaring passion in her kiss. Perhaps it was that she had subconscious fore-knowledge of the sudden flaring consumption that was soon to destroy her sister Peggy and that would all too soon cast herself into an early grave. . . And maybe it was that the consumption in her blood gave an added fire to her passion.

They walked up the garden in time to meet the party coming to seek them out.

He returned to the Canongate, was received by the provost who made a flat speech, presented him with his burgess ticket, shared in a riddle of claret, shook hands with him and wished him good luck and a speedy return to Jedburgh.

But the honour and the ceremony had curiously little effect on him for he was emotionally depressed. It was unlikely that he would ever be back in Jedburgh. He would remember the Jed and all the fairy romance of its setting. And he would never forget Isabella Lindsay. . .

The candle guttered by his bedside and Ainslie snored lightly as he wrote in his Journal: "Took farewell of Jedburgh with some melancholy disagreeable sensations. Jed, pure be thy crystal streams, and hallowed thy sylvan banks! Sweet Isabella Lindsay, may peace dwell in thy bosom, uninterrupted, except by the tumultuous throbbings of rapturous Love! That love-kindling eye must beam on another, not me; that graceful form must bless another's arms, not mine!"

GILBERT KER OF STODRIG

The farmers' club at Kelso (where they lunched the next day) was no mean circumscribed affair. By now he was used to the opulence of the Border farmers and noticed how sharply they were divided from the small tacksmen of the remoter areas. The farmers who met in the Kelso club were the pick of the parish—if not the Borders. Each of them boasted at least one hunter at a value of around thirty to forty pounds; and they rode to the hounds as part of their social activities. In such company the Bard was but small fry and poor Jenny Geddes not to be mentioned. Not that the farmers snubbed him: most of them condescended to show him a mild and passing interest.

And yet it was in the Kelso club, through Ainslie's introduction, that he met one of his best Border friends. He was Gilbert Ker who owned the farm of Stodrig that lay a mile out of the town on the far side of the Roxboroughe estate; Ker was a widower with a small family. This did not inconvenience him in any way, however, since he was wealthy enough to provide himself with a housekeeper and servants aplenty.

His demeanour was mild and his mind inclined to the serious side of life. Yet no one in the Borders had so far approached the Bard with such intelligent understanding.

"I'm indeed honoured to have made your acquaintance, Mr. Burns. I'm yours to command in any way that may help you in your travels. Bob Ainslie (I ken his father well) and you will stay with me for a few days: for as long as you care! I ken you will want to see as much of the country-side as you can. The weather could be better: I dinna like the look o' things in the west. Aye: May can be a cauld wet month. . ."

"Mr. Ker, sir, I shall be only too grateful for your hospitality. Not that I will impose on it. To-day is Friday: I should like to set off for Selkirk and Ettrick and Yarrow on Sunday morning since Sunday seems to be a favourite day of travel in this country-side. Very different, I assure you, from the West, where our Calvinist clergy do not hesitate to bring you before the Session for such an offence. . . To-morrow I should like to pay my respects to Lady Henrietta Don—the sister of my honoured Patron, the noble Earl of Glencairn. Her ladyship would count it an offence if she knew I had been in the district and had not paid my respects. I understand that her seat, Newton-Don, is convenient to Kelso."

"Couldna be more convenient. Just aff the Embro road: a mile out o' the town you haud right for Newton-Don; and left for Stodrig. . . I'll show you as we ride out to my place. . . You dinna ken Sir Alexander Don . . .? Oh, a nice enough fellow in his way. His lady is a particularly fine woman. You're verra lucky to have a patron like the Earl o' Glencairn. . . When some o' the folk hereabouts get to ken that they'll cock their lugs. . . Aye; and what are your plans for the future, Mr Burns? Have you been able to make enough from your Edinburgh volume to enable you to settle down comfortably

—or are you looking round you for a bit before you make up your mind?"

"I'm forced to make up my mind, sir, whether I would or no'. Presently I shall have to resume the plough. Some of my friends think I should make the purchase of a small farm. But of course you can have little idea what farming means in the West. I'm afraid it's a poverty-struck business compared to the opulence I see hereabouts. . ."

"What's your rents in the West?"

"A pound the acre will rent but indifferent sour land."

"You could get the best o' land hereabouts for sixteen shillings the acre. But you need a good wheen o' acres to make farming pay. You need a big outrun for your sheep . . . and plenty turnips for them in the hard back-end. You get a lot o' snaw here and it lies a lang time. You can lose a wheen o' beasts gin you canna winter them on the low ground. A sma' farmer never gets his head up; and a bad season can finish him. Dinna start on a sma' farm, Mr. Burns: if it doesna break your heart it'll break your back. I've an idea from your verses what you've been through. I'd try and look for something more congenial to the poetic temperament—something that'll give you life a bit easier than you have had it. Man, you ken: a' the time I was reading your verses I couldna help saying to mysel' that it was the damndest pity that a lad like you should have had to slave so hard and for so little. Could some o' your Edinburgh friends no' see their way to place you in a bit office o' the Government? There's plenty folk getting a bit pension for doing nothing."

"That I know, sir. But I dislike the practice. I did learn that Adam Smith, the distinguished author of The Wealth of Nations, interested himself in my welfare to the extent of suggesting that my name should go forward for an appointment in the Salt Office—which, as you doubtless know, is a sinecure. But Doctor Smith was in failing health and gone to London and as a consequence unable to press the matter with more resolution. But, much as I appreciated the venerable author's interest, I doubt if I could have accepted such an appointment—had it been made. What I would like is an appointment with the Excise. There I could *earn* my money. I have made some study of the work that is wanted; and in such a capacity I would not be beholden to any man as long as I did my duty."

"There's some sense about that—though I would never have thought on't mysel'. That shouldna be hard to get frae your Embro friends."

"Much harder than you think, sir. Everybody seems to think that a rustic bard should work nowhere else than on the land: what kind of land does not seem to matter. I'm glad to see that you ken better. I've to look at a farm, the property of Mr. Patrick Miller, brother to the Lord Justice Clerk, on my way home to Ayrshire. It's in Dumfriesshire— somewhere about the banks of the river Nith—Dalswinton is the name of the estate. . . I was thinking that I might take a trip into England and return by way of Carlisle to Dumfries when I'm here anyway."

"You werena thinking of going as far as Newcastle, were you?"

"Maybe. . . I could pick up the Carlisle road from there."

"Well, I was thinking of a journey that length mysel': I have business takes me there; and there's no reason why I shouldna tak' a bit holiday-like jaunt when I'm at it, provided we didna taigle too long on the road. I could weel enough come by Longtown and doon Saint Mary's Loch back hame."

"Sir: if there is any possibility of having your company on such a tour I would be delighted; for it is not a journey that I would care to undertake alone."

"No, you want a bit o' company on the road—and if the company is congenial, it halves the miles. Aye, I'm taken on wi' the idea. Of course I couldna set off for a week or ten days yet. . ."

"Ten days would just about suit me as I shall have the company of Mr. Ainslie till the twenty-first of the month."

"That's a bargain, Mr. Burns: I'll look into my affairs and let ye ken the maist convenient date about then; but a day back and forward winna matter for me, once I see my way clear. . ."

It did not surprise the Bard to find that the exterior of Stodrig House appeared in its grey stone and square proportions to be as substantial as any farm-house he had seen in the Borders. It stood back from the steading buildings; and the fine windows of its principal rooms looked out into a grand park of trees where cattle grazed.

What did surprise him was the elegance of the furniture and the decorations. It was obvious that no money had been spared to fit out the house in a style that would not have disgraced George Square in Edinburgh. But there was no vulgar display of wealth. The elegance was that of a fine taste and a nice discrimination.

When he went next day to dine with Sir Alexander Don he found a very different atmosphere. The estate was a lovely one and the mansion-house all that a Border baronet could have wished. But everywhere there was mean pretence and shabby vulgarity. Sir Alexander Don was a man of shallow airs and empty graces. How Glencairn's sister, Henrietta Cunningham, could have married such an empty upstart and borne him children, was something he could not understand. But the Bard admired Henrietta and she fully reciprocated the admiration. Could they have shared the meal together, they would have both relished the pleasure. As it was, the petty snobbery of the squire and his endless shallow small talk forced the Bard to depart as soon as he decently could and return with thankfulness to the solid homeliness of Stodrig and the quiet intelligence of Gilbert Ker. . .

WILLIE'S AWA'

When they left Stodrig the following Sunday morning some rain was falling. They had not gone many miles till the heavens began to open and pour down on them. Ainslie was in a mind to turn back.

"Time's wearing on, Bob, and I would like to see Melrose and Dryburgh . . . and this rain canna last. I'd like to push on to Yarrow. . . We may be sodden wi' rain; but this whole country-side is sodden wi' history and legend and song. And rain or no rain, mist or no mist, I'm getting the feel o' the country—and that will stand me in good stead when I'm settled down and my wandering days are over. You've a good coat on you and a grand pair o' boots—and you can lay in some good whisky punch when we settle for the night."

Ainslie agreed. He was always hoping that he would fall in with a likely-like serving-lass at some inn or other. Stodrig was a dull place for him and Gilbert Ker much too solemn: he did not share his companion's extraordinary capacity for getting the most out of every situation. . .

The bad weather held. But they took time to view the ruins of Dryburgh Abbey. Ainslie kept his patience and the Bard kept his peace. They crossed the Water of Leader, and came down the Tweed which they forded above Melrose. Here Ainslie flatly refused to visit the ruined abbey until he had eaten and warmed himself.

"I'm damned, Robert, but I'm no' used being out in a' weathers like you. And I must eat a warm bite of some kind."

"Well, well: lead on to the inn and see what we can get. I dinna care for this kind o' weather mysel'; but somehow, Bob, I feel I'll never be here again. I felt that when I left Jed——"

"You mean you felt that when you left Isabella Lindsay——"

"One and the same. If I had felt I would have seen Jed again I would have felt I might see Isabella again. You see:

I've read about the Border abbeys and the history of this part
of the country . . . it means far more to me than it means to
you . . . you can come here any time you like: or damn near
it. But once I get settled in the West. . ."

"But you will always manage a holiday from the West."

"I wish I could hope so. No: if I get tied up in a farm my
jaunting days will be over. As a matter of fact, I never should
have had jaunting days: I was never meant to. All this I owe
to Willie Creech. If Creech hadna taken me in hand. . ."

"If Glencairn hadn't told him to take you in hand. . ."

"I'm no' likely to forget Glencairn. . . But Willie Creech
was the man who carried through my Edinburgh edition;
and I've never shown enough gratitude to him. Whiles he
annoyed me; whiles infuriated me. But Willie Creech had
the right ideas—and he managed to get my book out. Without
the book and the subscription I wouldna be here to-day in
Melrose. More than likely I would have been in the West
Indies . . . or lying rotting wi' fever somewhere. So lead on
to the inn, Bob, and I'll drink a glass to Willie Creech even
though he is in London. . ."

And despite a comfortable room at the Melrose inn, and
despite a good fire and a glass of hot punch, and despite Melrose
Abbey, a ravishing ruin in the rain, he could not get the
image of Willie Creech out of his mind.

Even as he rode up the Ettrick, red with the swollen waters
and the red-clayey soil, he still pondered on Willie Creech.
And then he knew that as soon as was convenient he would
take pen to paper and write to Creech . . . and . . . and thank
him. Show something of his appreciation. Creech had his
faults; and plenty of his Edinburgh friends had never tired
dinning his faults into him. But the hard rock of truth per-
sisted and could not be worn away with criticism. Without
Creech he would have been lost. . .

They rode into Selkirk like drowned rats. Ainslie led the
way to Veitch's Inn, his heart in his boots for he was miserable.
The Bard and he hadn't exchanged words for over an hour.

Unfortunately for them a Doctor Clarkson and a Selkirk
baillie were occupying the best room of the inn with a couple

of friends, and though they requested that they might join them at the fire, the Doctor, on being informed that they were not quite gentlemen, refused to share the comfort of the room. Why should he, indeed, when he was busy telling his friends about the marvellous book of poetry that had just come out of Edinburgh, written by an Ayrshire ploughman?

Ainslie cursed and groaned. They were shown into a wretched room in which there was no fire and less comfort. He insisted that a fire be put on for them. But this was going to take some time—and, as it turned out, the fire smoked damnably for about an hour after it was lit. What annoyed Ainslie even more was that the Bard did not seem to care what happened to him. Finally he agreed to accompany Ainslie to the kitchen, there to dry themselves at the fire till their own room was heated.

Once seated at the fire, the Bard closed his eyes and seemed to go to sleep though Ainslie knew that he wasn't sleeping. . .

And then a servant-lass came in to stir some broth for them. Ainslie began to brighten. The lass had possibilities. Ainslie lost no time in discovering that she would need little coaxing. He jingled the cash in his pocket and began to feel better. . .

While Ainslie amused himself with the lass, the Bard sat alone in the bare room and began to put pen to paper. Soon he forgot all about his discomfort. And while, in the next room, Doctor Clarkson quoted extracts from his poetry, he proceeded to write a poetical address to Willie Creech. At long last the words were skelping rank and file—almost before he knew. He dashed off a rough draft and with few corrections copied it onto a fresh sheet for Creech. Then he added a short letter, turned it over and sealed it. No more than a couple of hours' work and he had discharged a debt that had been hanging over his head since ever Creech had issued his subscription bills in Edinburgh more than six months before. . .

Aye: *Willie's Awa'* was a good effort: something like his vein of Westlan' hamely jingle. . . And Willie would appreciate it. Willie Creech had never been a fool. . . If he had flattered

him it was because the man was worthy o' a bit flattery—
here and there: it was a damned poor man who wasn't. . .

When Bob Ainslie returned from his session with the
servant-lass he carried a measure of hot toddy in his hand.
He slumped himself down on the chair.

The Bard cocked a critical eye at him. "Enjoy yourself?"

"I've had worse, Robert; and you?"

"I'll let you be the judge. I've just penned off a poetical
address to Willie Creech. Maybe you're ower tired to be
bothered?"

"No, no: my ears are cocked, Robert; and ready to tak' in
onything that fa's frae Caledonia's Bard. And I'll be more
than interested to see what you make o' Creech."

The Bard took a sip of his whisky and read without more
ado:

"Auld chuckie Reekie's sair distrest, down droops her ance
weel burnished crest, nae joy her bonnie buskit nest can yield
ava: her darling bird that she lo'es best, Willie's awa'.

"O, Willie was a witty wight, and had o' things an unco
sleight! Auld Reekie aey he keepit tight and trig an' braw;
but now they'll busk her like a fright—Willie's awa'!

"The stiffest o' them a' he bowed; the bauldest o' them a'
he cowed; they durst nae mair than he allowed—that was a
law: we've lost a birkie weel worth gowd—Willie's awa'!

"Now gawkies, tawpies, gowks, and fools frae colleges and
boarding schools may sprout like simmer puddock-stools in
glen or shaw: he wha could brush them down to mools,
Willie's awa'!

"The brethren o' the Commerce-Chaumer may mourn
their loss wi' doolfu' clamour: he was a dictionar and grammar
amang them a'. I fear they'll now mak' mony a stammer:
Willie's awa'!

"Nae mair we see his levee door Philosophers and Poets
pour, and toothy Critics by the score in bloody raw: the
adjutant of a' the core, Willie's awa'!

"Now worthy Greg'ry's Latin face, Tytler's and Greenfield's modest grace, MacKenzie, Stewart, such a brace as Rome

ne'er saw, they a' maun meet some ither place—Willie's awa'!

"Poor Burns ev'n ' Scotch Drink ' canna quicken: he cheeps like some bewildered chicken scared frae its minnie and the cleckin by hoodie-craw. Grief's gien his heart an unco kickin' —Willie's awa'!

"Now ev'ry sour-mou'd, girnin blellum, and Calvin's folk, are fit to fell him; ilk self-conceited critic-skellum his quill may draw: he wha could brawlie ward their bellum, Willie's awa'!

"Up wimpling, stately Tweed I've sped, and Eden scenes on crystal Jed, and Ettrick banks, now roaring red while tempests blaw; but every joy and pleasure's fled: Willie's awa'!

"May I be Slander's common speech, a text for Infamy to preach, and, lastly, streekit out to bleach in winter snaw, when I forget thee, Willie Creech, tho' far awa'!

"May never wicked Fortune touzle him, may never wicked men bamboozle him, until a pow as aul's Methusalem he canty claw! Then to the blessed new Jerusalem fleet-wing awa'!"

Ainslie bounded up and shook the Bard's hand.

"That's glorious poetry, Robert—just glorious. Effortless. And you dashed that off when I was ben the house? It beats me, Robert. There's no point in me even pretending to understand how you do it. Was that what was in your mind a' the road down frae Melrose?"

"Something like it, maybe."

"Of course, I don't know Creech as you do. And I know a lot o' folk don't like him. But you've certainly anointed him in that poem."

"I mean it, Bob—dinna think I wrote it wi' my tongue in my cheek. But it seems that nobody but myself kens the debt I owe Willie Creech. But—that's the debt paid now, Bob. Paid in full. It's up to Willie Creech now."

"I hope he appreciates it, Robert. There's plenty in Edinburgh would give their right hand to have a poem like that wrote on them."

"Aye; but a poet has to have the same philosophy as a prostitute."

"And what's that?"

"Never look for appreciation and you'll never be disappointed."

"Well, I never heard a poet compared to a prostitute afore."

"When a poet starts selling his wares to the public at large —what's the difference? Think it ower, Bob—at your leisure."

ELIBANKS AND ELIBRAES

Despite the poetical address to Willie Creech (and, for Ainslie, the accommodation of the serving-lass) they spent a miserable time in the Selkirk inn. Monday morning found them only too willing to depart. They crossed the Ettrick and went up the opposite bank from that down which they had come, joined the Tweed just below Fairnilee, came round an easy road by Caddonfoot and then proceeded to climb up the stony valley of the Tweed.

There was still some rain and the day was not of the best; but they were climbing away from the bad weather and they had left Selkirk behind them. They were making for Innerleithen, a famous spa and holiday resort of the Edinburgh gentry, and they hoped for better treatment there than they had known in Selkirk.

Ainslie had already spent several holidays at Innerleithen. He knew the road well and was acquainted with several families on the way. For the first time since they had left Stodrig, Ainslie was in good spirits and ready for any sally or adventure.

"Take a good look across the Tweed," he said when they had topped the hill at Thornylee. "The sight of that place should cheer your heart, Robert. What you see there is nothing less or more than Elibanks and Elibraes."

Simultaneously the pair of them broke into the first verse of the old bawdy ballad of that name: "O Elibanks and Elibraes my blessings aey befa' them. . ."

"Steady, Jenny my lass, and hae a look along wi' me! And when you get back to Machlin you can tell your stable-mates what you hae seen. . . Weel, Bob, I never thought I would look upon Elibanks and Elibraes! And a fine romantic spot—if the weather was better. . ."

Actually there was little to be seen across the Tweed that was so very different from what they had been seeing all day. There were the ruins of Elibank Keep high above the belt of green shaw. Behind the trees the ground rose in a slow-slanting slope to the seventeen hundred feet of Elibank Law. But the memory of the old song invested the place with a tenderness and a deep emotional quality.

The Bard took off his hat: "Damnit, I hae taken off my hat in Dryburgh and Melrose; but there's even more reason why I should pay my respects to this soil that is sacred for better reason than any other soil in Scotland. I would give my right hand to have written Elibanks and Elibraes. . . Yes, and when I take off my hat I take it off to the nameless bard who wrote it. May his soul be in whatever heaven he fancied and his bones be rotting in peace; for his was a noble effort. ' Green be the broom on Elibraes, and yellow be the gowan! My wame it fistles aey like fleas, as I come ower the knowe, man. My blessings on that bonny knowe, our bed amang the heather, where sic a tup to sic a ewe, was never matched thegither. . .' I wonder, Bob, if folks will remember this place long after you and me are under the green sod? I'm loth to think that folk may yet come to pass it by without feeling a quickening o' the pulse for what it once meant to a bonnie lass—and should mean to ilka bonnie lass that comes into the world and hopes to ken something o' its joy as weel as its sorrow before she has to leave it. . . I wonder; but it's an idle wonder. Yet I'm certain there'll aey be an Elibank and an Elibrae somewhere for every bonnie lass that has the red blood o' life in her."

"Robert! I think you get more out of these auld sangs and ballads than onybody else."

"Even than the folk that wrote them? Dinna hold the sense o' life so cheap, Bob! It's just that folk are getting damnably polite the more they get damnably corrupted. Notwithstanding: I suppose the puritan will always be with us. And the hypocrite. . . And this leaves folk like you and me and Smellie and Willie Nicol and Robert Cleghorn—and countless thousands that we ken nothing about. But we'll no' mourn about that if we're wise. Folk maun aey be some way, as the auld wife said."

"I've no reason to complain. . . But I still think that you get more out of life than anybody I've ever known; and not only because you are a poet——"

"Because o' what, then?"

"If only I knew! You're so many different men—rolled into one, as it were. And yet no' that either since they're a' separate. You're one man when you talk to my father—another when you talk to Gilbert Ker—still another when you're in company as you were wi' Somerville and Potts and Fair and the ladies. And I'll warrant you were an extraordinary different man when you had your arm round Isabella Lindsay——"

"And what's so strange about that?"

"I ken it's difficult to explain—and you're aey Robert Burns no matter where you are. I've told you all this before; but I don't know that I have been able to make myself understood."

"You've gotten a flea in your lug: dinna let it worry you . . . or maybe it does worry you. . . Maybe you think I'm aey acting some part or other?"

"No, no, Robert: dinna get that idea into your head. You're always Robert Burns: always sincere and always true. The last thing your worst enemy could accuse you o' is hypocrisy . . . if you dinna mind me talking in this strain?"

"Of course I mind. We're here on a holiday: no' to talk about our virtues and our failings. How the hell would you like if I started dissecting you and telling you what a fine open-hearted considerate fellow you were? Let's accept each other for what we mean to each other . . . then jouk and let the jaw gae by. . ."

"I'm sorry——"

"And whatever you do dinna apologise: you've nothing to apologise for. . ."

And so they talked and laughed and reminded each other of bawdy ballads, boasted of former loves and talked solemnly and soberly about matters of literature and philosophy. In short: they spoke whatever came into their minds. Or they remained silent; or pondered their own thoughts; or viewed the country-side.

This was what the Bard valued most about Ainslie. Ainslie had a good head. But he could talk nonsense to him as much as he liked. It is true he was careful not to reveal *all* he thought. Ainslie had indeed a good head; but his understanding, like his experience, was limited. To offset this there was much in him that was fresh and virginal. Yet he was vigorously bawdy. In many important ways he was as yet uncorrupted by the endless compromises of society and the vicissitudes of life. His essential uncorrupted instincts were decent and kindly. His laugh was spontaneous and his smile infectious. Women thought him a very handsome and well-mannered young man: men thought he had ability and would get far in his profession. He had already all the easy assurance of the successful lawyer: only to Robert Burns did he dare to reveal some of his weaknesses for the Bard never mocked him. And if in the fullness of time Ainslie was to betray his friend more shamefully than he was ever to be betrayed, no thought of that was in his mind or his heart as he rode the hilly Border roads with him. His mood was still Elibanks and Elibraes my blessings aey befa' them. . .

They came round by Hollowlea and then by Pirn (where they were soon to be entertained), and into Innerleithen which they found a pleasant place well-spaced out and gardened with shrubs and trees.

In the evening they walked out in the pleasant air, crossed the pleasant Tweed where it was little more than a broad stream gurgling over some bleached boulders, and came to Traquair House, as old and ancient-looking a mansion as they had ever clapped eyes on. Beyond this they came to the "Bush aboon Traquair" that the poet Crawford had sung so sweetly about near the beginning of the century.

And indeed there was much that a poet might sing about

around Traquair apart from the bonnie bush that had bloomed so fair in that distant May. It was pleasant and pastoral, a green and fertile oasis after the stony hill-sides they had travelled along all day.

In the evening light and in the soft air the Bard had pleasant thoughts of it and was to remember it with quiet affection. He walked back contentedly with Ainslie to have an enjoyable meal with Farmer Horseburgh of Pirn.

BACK TO DUNSE

The next morning they retraced their steps to within a mile of Caddonfoot on the Tweed. Then they debouched by Clovenfords, came round by the pleasant heights of Torwoodlee down onto the sweet banks of the Gala Water and so into the rude village of Galashiels. The Bard liked the Gala Water: it had about it the intimacy of an Ayrshire stream.

But they had a long ride before them; and there was little time to pause for admiration or reflection. Ainslie was determined that they reach Earlston in time for the midday meal.

The Bard gave Jenny Geddes a playful slap on the neck and urged her on. Earlston was the birthplace of Thomas the Rhymer and he did not want to miss the opportunity of paying the memory of True Thomas his respects. And close by there was Cowdenknowes of the broom—the bonnie, bonnie broom. . .

Back at Dunse, after sixteen days of travelling, they stopped in at the Farmers' Club to have their evening meal. Ainslie had promised that he would be back in time for this Wednesday event: he had kept his promise.

The Bard was grateful: he had had a surfeit of scenery and places of historical and antiquarian interest. Now he was in need of good company. This the Dunse Farmers' Club liberally supplied.

But if he had winced at the punning of the Reverend Somerville of Jedburgh, he had more to endure from the punning of the Reverend Smith who had come to the Club specially to meet the Poet—and as the poet feared—in order to display his wit to what he doubtless considered the best advantage.

If Mr. Smith was thought to be famous for his peculiar wit, Mr. Meikle was no less famous for his inventive genius, having lately devised and brought to considerable practical usefulness a threshing machine in the form of a mechanical mill. . .

They were not stupid men those douce Merse farmers. They farmed well and they talked well; and they ate and drank sensibly. They did not ask him foolish questions and showed no surprise that a ploughman should be a poet. Indeed they seemed to accept his ploughing and his poetry as natural if not inevitable concomitants. But, by this time, they had learned that he was also a tenant-farmer in the West; and this, perhaps more than anything else, clinched his credentials.

Andrew Meikle was an old man of much experience; but, though he was coming up on seventy, he was still hale and hearty and looked like living well beyond his allotted span: the Bard and he exchanged much quiet information.

"Ah weel, Maister Burns, I hae enjoyed our crack. Ye see: you work awa' wi' words and rhyme—and I've nae doubt ye'll invent a bit word back and forrit as ye fin' the need—an' I work awa' wi' bits of machinery. . . An' whiles ye'll fin' things coming to your han' an' sometimes ye winna: I ken fine how it is. . . Oh aye, man: I've worked awa' the best years o' my life on my thresher. . . Exactly: ye've juist to wark awa' till things come richt wi' ye. . . Aye, aye: the idea juist comes till ye. How, ye dinna richt ken. My son, Geordie, has the same kinna bent as mysel': rins in the bluid—as the auld sodger said about his wooden leg. Here's your verra guid health, Maister Burns: and a' guid things attend you an' yours. And see and come awa' soon wi' another bit like your Cotter's Saturday Nicht—aye, or your Twa Dogs. We can dae wi' a sheaf o' your verses ony time. . ."

And when Farmer Hood heard that he intended making the journey into England he immediately expressed a desire to accompany him.

"I hae business on the way, Mr. Burns. We Merse farmers do a lot o' trade back and forrit wi' the Cumberlan' men—baith in cattle and sheep. Aye, man: it can be a dreich enough journey wanting company. But wi' Gilbert Ker and you it should be a grand ride. Aye . . . and what think ye of our Border country?"

"I think very well of it, Mr. Hood. It's different from the West—almost like another country. I am much taken with your methods in farming—and I'm much taken with your hills and rivers. I hope to celebrate some of your scenic charms in verse some day."

"That's nice o' ye, Mr. Burns—I'm glad to hear you've enjoyed yoursel'. We've a' enjoyed meeting in wi' you. Folk speak highly o' ye, sir. And damned! We Merse folks are no' given to saying much either one way or the other. Come ower and see my place, Mr. Burns—get young Ainslie to fetch ye: ye'll get an honest welcome."

As he came out of the Farmers' Club and was about to mount Jenny Geddes, Cimon Gray, the Dunse poet, came forward and handed him a packet of his manuscript verses. He was a small man with a big head (crowned by an unusually large bonnet) and it was difficult to assess his age. But he spoke with some assurance and no little civility.

"Maybe you'll excuse a liberty, Mr. Burns. I wonder if you'd care to glance ower my poems. You will have it, Mr. Burns, that I'm dull—but I think you'll change your mind when you read my Rejoiciad."

The Bard took the packet and thrust it into his pocket—Ainslie was already mounted.

"I'll give your verses another ca' through, Mr. Gray——"

"You'll just say what you think, Mr. Burns? I dinna want ony flattery."

"Very good, Mr. Gray: I'll try not to disappoint you."

"Thank you, Mr. Burns."

Cimon Gray raised his hand in salute to his outsize bonnet and, making something of a bow, shuffled back to the foot-walk.

They rode home to Berrywell in good spirits. They had eaten well, drank no more than made them happy, and the Bard's mind was filled with mellowed memories. Rachel was there to smile on him very much as Isabella Lindsay had done: indeed they were very much of a kind. He went to bed in a contented mood. Ainslie promised that to-morrow Rachel would be in the company as he proposed to ride out with them to see an old flame of his that had recently married. . .

The Bard was too pleasantly tired to remember the packet of poems that Cimon Gray had handed to him.

THE NYMPH WITH THE MANIA

Ainslie was determined the Bard should see as much of the Borders as his time permitted. They had made a tolerable exploration to the south and west of Dunse: it was now time to see what the north and east looked like.

To this end they rode out on Friday the eighteenth of May to Berwick lying at the mouth of the Tweed. From Berwick they went up the coast to the congested if important fishing village of Eyemouth, there to be the guests of Ainslie's friends, the Grieves.

The next day being Saturday, and the Grieve brothers being keen Masons, the Bard and Ainslie were made members of the Royal Arch. Ainslie was a little piqued that he had to pay a guinea fee. The Bard was treated differently. "On account of his remarkable poetical genius," as it was recorded, "the encampment unanimously agree to admit him gratis, and consider themselves honoured by having a man of such shining abilities for one of their companions."

After dinner they enjoyed a sail in a fishing boat. But the

Bard found that the salt waters of the North Sea were in no way different from the equally salt waters of the Firth of Clyde. It interested him more to note that tithes had to be paid for any fish landed on the Eyemouth pier.

But most of all, perhaps, he was interested in Betsy Grieve. Though neither an Isabella Lindsay nor a Rachel Ainslie she was a good-natured good-looking lass. And she didn't hide her interest in him. Betsy was sorry to learn that he was setting out for Dunbar the following morning.

As the Bard caught her eye across the supper-table he experienced a twinge of regret. It was a stimulating adventure this touring the country-side and being acclaimed everywhere as Caledonia's Bard. But the glare of publicity had its disadvantages. As far as the lassies were concerned (and they seemed to be as much concerned as he was) it was fatal to any amorous ploys. And the routine of here to-day and gone to-morrow could be tantalising and frustrating—and more so for the lassies than for him.

Isabella Lindsay slept with his engraving under her pillow —when she managed to forget him long enough to sleep.

But it was time for Ainslie to get back to Dunse: he was due to ride back to Edinburgh on the next day. He had promised, however, that he would introduce his companion to his night's lodgings which he had arranged with Farmer Sherriff—a tenant of Sir James Hall of Dunglass who had a fine estate on the Dunglass Water some seven miles below Dunbar.

He saw Ainslie to his horse in the court of Dunglass Mains, and expressed his gratitude to him.

". . . a never-to-be-forgotten jaunt, Bob. But I'll write you from England and give you my news. You can write me to Dumfries—or safer still, to Machlin. And be sure and let me know as soon as that lass drops her bairn."

"I'll let *you* know—but you'll be the only one. After this I'll keep to the whores o' the High Street. . . Well . . . watch your step wi' Nancy: I can see she's mad about you. And . . .

good luck, Robert. I hope everything turns out well for you. I hope your English journey will prove a success—though, mind you, I canna say that either Hood or Ker would be my fancy for travelling companions——"

"All right, Bob, I'll miss you—more than I can say. But I'll write you . . . and give you all the news. And if onything good turns up in the way of a skirt, I'll give you full details. Good-bye, Bob . . . and the Beggar's Benison accompany you wherever you go. . ."

The hoof-beats of Ainslie's horse sounded quietly among the trees and gradually faded into the golden glow of the early evening. The Bard turned slowly on his step, walked over the shadow-softened cobbles of the court-yard.

Meeting him in the door of the farm-house, full-breasted, eyes heavy-lidded, was Nancy Sherriff.

The Bard had never before seen in the eyes and general expression of any woman such a suggestion of milk-curdled cream-lappered passion. His step faltered and he wished he could have made his escape.

The lowering intensity of her expression seemed to lift as he came forward. But when she spoke he realised that the tone of her voice had altered. She spoke thickly and the bass undertones vibrated from her midriff.

"I see you hae got rid of Mr. Ainslie."

"Mr. Ainslie had to get back to Dunse—I got rid of him no more than he got rid of me."

"Oh—I just thocht you would be glad that he was gone. . ."

"I don't see that I should: he's my best friend——"

"I didna think he would mean a' that to you."

The Bard was nettled. "Yes—Mr. Ainslie means a' that to me and a lot more. More than any woman means to me. Don't you think we should go in and join your brother and his friends upstairs?"

"His *friends*! Well . . . maybe we should. It'll no' be long till he's convoying them doon the road. After that he's to call on Sir James, the Laird. We'll hae the place to oursel's."

"He'll maybe want me to go with him."

"Na. . . Why should he? Or d'you want to go? Maybe you don't like me, Mr. Burns?"

"Of course I like you—Miss Sherriff. Is there any reason why I shouldna?"

"I was just wondering, Mr. Burns . . . just wondering. . ."

It was a hallan-door that gave access to the farm-house. Nancy's heavy breasts bulged over the bolted lower half as she pressed tightly against it, barring his entrance. She had never moved since she had taken up that position in order to watch him taking his leave of Ainslie.

The Bard began to feel uncomfortable.

"If you don't want to join the company, maybe you'll excuse me while I do."

Nancy slipped the bolt and, leaning back, took the half door with her. She allowed him sufficient entry to squeeze past—and unavoidably squeeze her in the passing.

"I'll come and see you, Mr. Burns—after they go."

Her great coiled masses of copper hair, rather coarse and wiry, caught the light as she swung back. For a second it flashed and burned in the slanting sunlight and seemed vividly, startlingly alive.

Sherriff bored him intolerably. He was ignorant; and he had as much conceit as he had ignorance. But fortunately he was just about to go off with his friends.

The Bard was glad to be rid of him; but he wasn't so sure of his sister. As soon as her brother was gone she came into the room and found the Bard standing at the window. She invited him to sit beside her on a great broad settle that was drawn up before the blink of fire.

The Bard could do nothing but comply. Nancy's manner had changed. Her voice was natural again and she had lost the heavy brooding look. She was altogether lighter and more at her ease. Maybe he had been mistaken in her. And she was no longer in outward appearance the barmy quean of a farmer's daughter.

She had changed her dress. Her bodice was low-cut, in the best fashion, and her pretences to a boarding-school-miss education was much in evidence. She had used the half-hour since he squeezed past her at the hallan-door to good advantage. If he had any criticism it was that she had used the scent-bottle too lavishly; and Edinburgh had taught him to be suspicious of over-scented dames.

She talked of love. Poets must know everything about love; and she was certain from his poetry and from his appearance that Robert Burns knew more about love than any other man in Scotland: certainly more than any other man she was likely to have to herself on a long May evening. . .

"But you maun have made love to many lassies in your day, Mr. Burns—I'm just goin' to ca' you Robert: we canna sit here a' nicht Mistering and Missing. . . Maybe you've made love to more than you would like to own up to. . . I dinna mind: I ken fine men mak' love to lassies when they get the chance. . ."

"I'll warrant you could give *me* a few lessons, Nancy: I'm certain many a wooer comes to Dunglass Mains. . ."

"Oh, no' so many: my brother chases them aff: I'm too guid a housekeeper for him. . . But if it came to lessons I dinna think I wad be a bad pupil. I think it's a shame that men should hae a' the best o't. Of course, I dinna expect you to agree wi' that."

"Are you so certain men have the best o't?"

"I'm sure you ken that better than me. It's the lass that gets the pain and the man that gets the pleasure."

"If you believe that then I dinna see that you should be keen on . . . love-lessons. Where love's concerned there's little need for lessons. Nature gave folk a natural aptitude for love. . ."

"But what's the good o' a natural aptitude when you have to sit maist nichts by your lane . . . knitting or sewing."

"Damnit, Nancy: lovers canna be as scarce as that about Dunglass."

"Oh, but I'm particular: I wouldna let just ony man put his arm round me! Ach, but come on, Robert, and dinna talk daft-like: you ken fine what I mean."

"You're no' suggesting that you and me go to bed the-gither? I dinna think your brother would like that."

"And d'you think I would? The only man I'll go to bed wi' will be my husband—and no' until we're married."

"I'm glad to see you're a sensible lass, Nancy."

"But you would like to come to bed wi' me—if we were married?"

"I wouldna like *no'* to come to bed wi' you if we were married: that's expected from married folks, is it not?"

"You're a terrible tease, Robert: you twist everything I say round about. Maybe you're betrothed to a lass and just waiting the chance to get married: some fine Edinburgh dame, I've no doubt."

"I'm sure you ken that poets canna afford to get married."

"Ah weel: the man that gets me will get a decent dowry. I've a good penny laid by that my brother kens nought about —as weel as what he does ken about. Of course, I wouldna just let a man tak' me for my money. . . I feel I can be frank and open wi' you Robert: I feel I can be intimate wi' you the way I couldna be wi' ony other man."

"Now be honest wi' yoursel', Nancy: what the devil do you know about me?"

"Och: you dinna need knowing. The moment that Mr. Ainslie introduced you I felt that I had kent you a' my days. But maybe that's you being a poet and me having read your verses. You see: you're just what I pictured you: a fine big strong man with a kind face. . ."

The Bard felt himself blushing. He supposed he would need to humour Nancy before the night was out: otherwise she might unsheath her claws. . . Yet there was something attractively simple in the way she talked. If there was evil in her then she took a dangerously frank way of showing it. If she was foolish then she was truly to be pitied. That she was desperate for love was only too obvious. Either that or she was setting a trap for him and he had better watch every move she made. . .

On the other hand, she was not unattractive in a physical sense. Maybe she had more physical experience than he knew. Maybe this was her way of forcing the pace, of making him realise that there was no time for foolish dallying. . .

"I suppose your brother will be back soon?"

"He'll no' be back for hours. Besides, we'll hear the dogs barking and the sound of his horse; and then he's to stable the beast: you needna worry about my brother."

"It's a comfort to know that you won't be caught in a love-lesson, Nancy. Your brother might not think it a lesson. Or do you really think he would mind?"

"Och, he's stupid in some ways. The lassies dinna mean a thing to him or he would have more sympathy for me."

"So you lead a quiet life here and nobody comes to roll you in the hay?"

"Is it nice being rolled in the hay?"

"If it's dry and the day's warm there are worse things you could be rolled in. . ."

"But would it no' be more comfortable . . . where we . . . like where we are . . . ?"

She had moved ever closer to him as they had talked. Now she leaned her head quietly on his shoulder and vented a long low sigh.

The Bard could not get her measure. When he had been introduced to her in the afternoon she had been quiet and efficient and almost self-effacing. At the hallan-door she might have been a witch or a fury in disguise. Even while they had sat here talking she had changed. Maybe he was changing with her. Damnit, the lass was but human—and he was no less so. It was a pity to see the lass fidging at the end of her emotional tether. . .

He put his arm round her shoulder. His touch seemed to electrify her. In a flash she had turned her head and fastened her lips on his.

In the morning Sir James Hall came to breakfast. He was delighted to welcome the Bard to his estate. As soon as breakfast was over he hied him off to meet Lady Hall and to view the picturesque wooded and watered glen famed far and near as the Deane of Dunglass. He even pressed on him a strong invitation to dine with him. But the Bard made his excuse. The memory of Nancy and the previous evening was too much for him. He was determined to get away from Dunglass with all the speed he could decently muster. He had no objection to an hour's daffing with any likely lass. But Nancy had other ideas. And her ideas (to do her the least injustice) were far from maidenly albeit she was maiden enough for any man. Only by deploying every stratagem he knew, and many that he never imagined he knew, had he saved himself from the horror of violation. And this, he congratulated himself, he had achieved without brutally offending her.

But he had under-estimated the stratagems of Nancy. When he returned for Jenny Geddes he found Nancy all ready to ride with him into Dunbar. As he described her afterwards to Ainslie: "She was *bien poudre bien frise* in her cream-coloured riding clothes, mounted on an old, dun cart-horse that had once been fat; a broken, old side-saddle, without crupper, stirrup or girth; a bridle that in former times had had buckles, and a crooked meandring hazel stick which might have borne a place with credit in a scrubbed besom. In the words of the Highlandman when he saw the Deil on Shanter-hill in the shape of five swine—' My hair stood and my ***** stood, and I swat and trembled.'"

But indiscretions that might take place behind locked doors could not be permitted in the high noon of a summer day and on the broad highway. He realised only too well that long before they reached Dunbar she would have him compromised and paraded for all to see that she was his sweetheart.

In such a situation it is not to be wondered that he sweated. He wiped his forehead and insinuated that their position might not do her any good in a district that was bound to be full of malicious gossip. But Nancy was too far gone to heed gossip: the blood in her body burned like a hot wine.

"In any event, Nancy, I'm in the devil of a hurry. I should have been in Dunbar by now to keep an appointment with Mr. Fall there; and I'm given to understand that he is the first man in East Lothian. Sir James with his palaver about his estate has already kept me late. By far the most sensible thing for us to do is to part here and let me ride as fast as Jenny will take me."

"But if you're late for Mr. Fall, you're late; and if you ride in with me it will give you a good excuse: I can back you up in how Sir James delayed you. Provost Fall wouldna dream of taking offence at anything Sir James did."

"Ah, but my business wi' the Provost is of too desperate a nature for me to delay. If you are determined to ride wi' me, Nancy, and no' listen to good advice, you'll need to shake up your mount and get him into a gallop."

But Nancy, God help her, was desperate enough to risk a gallop on old Jolly. She cursed her brother inwardly for refusing her a decent mount and brought her hazel wand down with a vicious swish on the flank. The old brute shambled into as wild and erratic a canter as the Bard had ever seen. Nancy was bounced into the air; her fat hips came smack down on the saddle and the feathered hat came down on her brow. So desperate was she to maintain her seat that she could not spare a hand to adjust it. She continued to thump down in the saddle till the Bard was frightened she would break the beast's back. He was sure she wouldn't be able to sit on anything harder than a down pillow for at least a week.

He eased Jenny. At any moment the pillion girth might give way under the strain and Nancy would be pitched into the road. He could see in the distance a party of riders coming towards them. . .

But Nancy had had enough. Not only was she frightened: she was quite sure that her bottom was in red flesh; and the moment they eased into a walking pace she knew that it was. She was almost ready to cry with the pain and discomfort. At the next loaning she stopped, having by this time recovered her breath and adjusted her hat.

"My uncle's place is just around the bend of this loaning, Robert, please call in wi' me for a few minutes."

"I'm sorry, Nancy woman: that's quite impossible. Listen to me. You canna ride into Dunbar on a mount like that. Damnit: you're risking your neck."

"You care a lot about my neck. I'm disappointed in you, Mr. Burns: I thought at least that you were a gentleman."

"Now, now, Nancy: we'll be sorry for this after——"

"Well: thanks for doing your best to kill me."

All element of sexual desire had been shaken out of Nancy. She had at last come to her sober senses. In the realisation of her shame her face burned with a brutal intensity.

"I suppose I made mysel' too damned cheap to you last night for you to have any respect for me . . . ?"

"Forget that last night ever happened, Nancy. It could have been a damned sight worse: that's the only thing I would ask you to remember."

"As for you and your trash o' poetry,"—and here she spat in front of Jenny's nose, "—that's a' *I'll* remember."

Before the Bard could say a word she pulled savagely on the bit and turned her cumbersome mount into the lane.

The Bard sat in his saddle and watched her disappear round the bend. It was a pity for the woman; and there was no good blaming her for realising, in effect, that she had been scorned. It was a damned poor woman that wasn't woman enough to resent that.

He took out his napkin and mopped his brow. A timely deliverance nevertheless! If he'd made a mistake last night he would have paid for it for the rest of his days. Nancy would have seen to that even though she had had to commit murder. There was no getting away from it: women were a problem and the man who could swear that he understood them was a much wiser man than Solomon. . .

"Come on, Jenny," he said to his mare; "you're a woman too . . . and certes, lass, ye're seeing things since you came to me that must be giving you plenty food for thought. It's a pity about Nancy: it's a pity for ony woman that doesna get the affection she hopes for in this life. . . Though if she only knew she's maybe better without it. Aye; but pity or no pity, I canna let myself be nabbed by a scheming woman like Nancy. I'll admit in your private lug, Jenny, that I'm as fond o' a lass as the next man; but I draw the line at being seduced and then trapped into matrimony. Now had it been Isabella Lindsay! Ah, but you never got a richt look at Isabella, did you? There was a lass! There would have been no seduction about Isabella: it would just have been a natural as well as a divine consummation. Aye; and I believe I would have been willing to enter the matrimonial state, as they ca' it, wi' the Joy o' Jeddart. Or Miss Ainslie, now? The sweet Rachel! Just another Isabella: only no' as experienced in the ways o' love. . . But a sweet lass. . . If only she wasna an Ainslie! Maybe I was too long shut up in Edinburgh to pree the lassies in the way I should. . . Ah, there's nothing to equal the freshness o' a young lass and her in love. But Nancy there wasna a young lass in the first flush o' love. She was a desperate woman looking for a man . . . a husband. And when she does get a man, by certes, she'll comb his hair for the years she has lost. It's a damnable thing the lost years, Jenny: you can never win them back nae matter what you do or how you mourn. . . Come on, lass: we canna blether here a' afternoon. I'll no' gallop you the day; but let the folk see what you can do by way o' a brisk canter.

"D'you see the rigs there on either hand beginning to wave wi' the young green corn? That's a sight for you! There'll be some braw oats there gin the harvest. Damned, I don't think I have ever seen such glorious corn country in my life: glorious! Rig after rig on either hand stretching away as far as we can see. . . That's real scenery for you—scenery that warms a farmer's heart and the heart o' a' country folks. What finer could you see than a rig o' corn or a rig o' barley and it waving in the wind. . . ? And bien country cot-houses and tidy weel-doing farms . . . and the sea out there to bring you a good blaw o' air when you need it—and maist likely when you dinna. . . I reckon you and me hae little sailor's blood in us. The sea's like the wilderness: you canna get intimate wi' it no matter how you may try. And treacherous. . . Aye: whatever we may think about mankind, of this we can be certain: man may be a poor enough fish but he's no' a salt-water fish. Onyway, we'll stick to dry land as long as we can. . ."

He found Dunbar a neat little town built of hard stone on hard rock. Otherwise he found little to interest him in the town. So he wrote in his journal that night:

"Dine with Provost Fall an eminent merchant and most respectable character but undescribable as he exhibits no marked traits. Mrs. Fall a genius in painting, fully more clever in the fine arts and sciences than my friend Lady Wauchope without her consummate assurance of her own abilities. . ."

And then he remembered Nancy—the sweat broke on him. By all that was holy he had had a narrow escape. It wouldn't even be safe to mention her name to a living soul.

DOCTOR BOWMAKER AND CIMON GRAY

The next morning he retraced his steps for some three miles till he reached Skateraw inn where he breakfasted. John Lee, the landlord and farmer, was a happy host: he had no difficulty in getting him to turn Jenny out to grass and to relax himself for the rest of the day. . . The Bard felt he needed a day to relax himself. Mr. Lee was a subscriber to his Edinburgh edition.

But by evening a goodly company had gathered for a meal in his modest inn. Chief among them was Doctor Robert Bowmaker, the parish minister of Dunse, who had been present at the Dunse Farmers' Club with the Reverend Mr. Smith when he had come back from his first Border tour.

It was interesting to see how Doctor Bowmaker behaved himself when he was out of his own parish. It was obvious that he had every intention of enjoying himself. Already he had a goodly cargo of liquor laid in about the holds of his vast innards against the eventualities of the evening.

The company was completed by the presence of two naval officers, young Doctor Brown from Dunbar, David Lee, a cousin of the landlord and a dashing young blade, and his companion, Clarke, who, if not quite so dashing, was a much cleverer and more responsible fellow.

Doctor Bowmaker boomed from the depths of his great barrel chest: the man's whisper could have been heard through a barn wall.

"I'm real glad to hear that you're still having a successful trip, Mr. Burns. Next year I suppose we'll be honoured wi' a new book of verses on your tour. You maun have seen everything that was worth seeing—which is more than I have. Gentlemen, as you no doubt know, this is my friend, Robert Burns, Caledonia's celebrated Bard; but you all know that. Don't let my cloth restrain you, gentlemen: a clergyman has as much right to eat and to drink and to be merry as any other man. And more so; for he is ever in the company of those who have cause to be sad . . . or who think they have. . .

"You haven't found a wife for yourself, Mr. Burns? Poets maybe dinna like the idea of a constant love? At least that's what we're led to believe. May I put in a word for my dear little angel, Rachel Ainslie?"

"If you think this is the moment to do so, sir. . ."

"Why, any moment is good enough to advance the claims of an angel. . . And, believe me, they are not so common on earth; and I'm not certain that poets have much chance of making their acquaintance in the hereafter; but no more than clergymen! Come now, gentlemen, we are all good Christians: drink up! The day is far spent and we have much to drink before the evening shadows tell us that the time has come. . . Drink up!

"I understand that you are no great drinker, Mr. Burns. I should have thought you would have found great inspiration in the bottle. Indeed, sir, when I have a bottle or two laid in me I feel I could compose a verse or two myself. Oho! but not like poor Cimon Gray of Dunse.

"Attend, gentlemen! It is a well-known fact that every parish in Scotland has its poet. Indeed I have kenned of parishes to have had more than one—to their sorrow. I have one in my parish. 'Pon my unworthy soul, he is the plague of my life—always seizing me by the button-hole and thrusting some of his unceasing efforts on me. . . Not, mind you, that Cimon Gray is any unlettered village idiot. Far from it! Cimon might well be described as an extremely lettered idiot. Anyhow: to my story. When Mr. Burns came to Dunse what think you but that Cimon must send him some of his verses.

Mr. Burns, who is the soul of polite consideration, read his effusions; and in the metre adopted by Cimon—and perhaps invented by him—replied briefly: 'Cimon Gray you're dull to-day.' Nothing daunted, Cimon sent out another parcel to Berrywell which elicitated the reply: 'Dullness with redoubled sway has seized the wits of Cimon Gray. . .'

"But was the good Cimon deterred from further importuning our friend here? Not a bit: Cimon was highly flattered that he had become the subject of two little verses— or epigrams as I think they are called. He placed in Mr. Burns's hands his two major compositions—the Jasperiad and the Rejoiciad. The packet was handed to Mr. Burns when he came back from visiting Tweedside and joined us in Dunse at our Farmers' Club. But when he did manage to look over Cimon's masterpieces he wrote him as follows. Actually, gentlemen, he gave me his reply to pass on to Cimon—if I thought fit.

"I have not yet done so. Some day, when Cimon has tried my patience beyond limit, I shall take great delight in doing so—even at the risk of swelling Cimon's head (and it is a cranium of noble proportions) beyond the possibility of his getting a bonnet to fit it . . . except of his own weaving."

Doctor Bowmaker was meantime searching in the pockets of his short jacket and presently produced the folded sheet.

"Allow me, gentlemen, to read you this delicious trifle. It will be the more interesting to those of you who have already met Cimon in the flesh as I know some of you have: 'Dear Cimon Gray, the other day when you sent me some rhyme, I could not then just ascertain its worth for want of time; but now to-day, good Mr. Gray, I've read it o'er and o'er: tried all my skill, but find I'm still just where I was before. We auld wives' minions gie our opinions, solicited or no'; then of its faults my honest thoughts I'll give—and here they go: such damn'd bombast no age that's past can show, nor time to come; so, Cimon dear, your song I'll tear, and with it wipe my bum.'"

Doctor Bowmaker, now roaring drunk, did more justice to the piece than it merited. The Bard said nothing to contradict the reverend Doctor of Divinity. But, in point of fact, he had

had a word with poor Cimon and had told him exactly what he did think of his efforts. Cimon had nodded wisely and had begged that he might be written something that he could circulate round the parish . . . and the more severe it might be the better. As Cimon shrewdly remarked, it was good for a poet to get noised about, and in any case he only wrote for amusement since that was all the world was fit for. So he had written out the verses and given them to Bowmaker to pass on to Cimon after he had left the district; for he did not want to be troubled with him again. Now he could see that Cimon was about to have his desire fulfilled. In the capable hands of Doctor Bowmaker his name would be noised about to an extent he would probably find uncomfortable.

But Bowmaker having set the ball rolling and the drink going round the table with a rapidity that startled the Bard, the night was set for merry tales. For the most part the Bard remained a spectator—only replying to direct questions. There were few things he enjoyed more than observing a general company thrown together round a tavern table. At the meal he had made an instantaneous assessment of each individual character. It was absorbing to see how these assessments worked out as the night wore on and restraint gave way to loquacious unburdening through alcoholic release. . .

That night, before retiring, he took a walk down to the Skateraw shore. It was a calm evening and the sea lay quiet and as motionless as a pewter plate.

To-morrow he would be back in Berrywell. He would ride into Kelso to find what arrangements Gilbert Ker had made for their English jaunt and generally find how the land lay. . .

All day he had idled at Skateraw. Idled physically. But his brain had been working. He had taken stock of the present and mapped out a plan of campaign for the future.

Only there was no future he could plan for. He would call on Patrick Miller at Dalswinton. But he doubted if Dalswinton was the answer to the future: his heart did not lie to farming. At least not the farming his limited capital would allow him.

In the background was Mossgiel. Again and again he had tried to forget about the home he had left on that bare wind-swept ridge—the home he had said good-bye to on that windy November morning six months ago.

But he had never been able to forget it for long. He had sent Gilbert an odd five-pound note as he had found one to spare. . .

What would he find when eventually he did get back home? But that was the rub: it was no longer home—for him. He had wiped the glaur of it from his boots. Never again could he take up where he had left off. Not that Gilbert would want him to do so. Gilbert had enough on his hands. . .

And there was Dear-bought Bess and Jean Armour's twins. . . God, but it was bitter, too: he couldn't get rid of Jean's image. She had plagued him enough in Edinburgh. Whiles he had been able to forget she had ever existed. But when the memory of her came back it came back with a blow to his heart.

What in heaven's name was there about Jean Armour that was about no other woman he had ever known? Maybe he had loved her too much, too deeply, too completely. Maybe that was why she had so cruelly wounded him—that he had felt the wound so cruelly.

Ah, hell roast Jean Armour! She had played him double—and repaid him double. Damn the black bitch! But she had given him a son—and a daughter! A son Robert. He just couldna wipe the boy off the slate. No: nor had he ever intended he should. He had promised Jean Armour he would bring up the boy in Mossgiel—and, when he got back, he would need to see about honouring that promise. No son of his would be brought up under the roof—and the influence—of James Armour. Not that, by God——

Aye: he would have some problems to face once he got back to Machlin. But then when had he not had problems to face? His whole bluidy existence from the moment he had reached consciousness had been a series of hard difficult problems.

He turned about on the shore. Maybe now that he hadn't

Ainslie to chaff and banter with, his accursed melancholy would settle on him. . . If so he would beat it back. This was no place to be seized by melancholy. . . It would be better when he got back to Berrywell. Rachel Ainslie would help him to forget.

Women, women: there had always to be a woman. Impossible to live without them—and bluidy near impossible to live with them. What a time he'd had with them, Rachel, Isabella —and Nancy Sherriff. Fundamentally they were the same problem. You fell in love wi' them and couldna possess them —or they fell in love wi' you—and you didna want them! And yet, try to live without them and what was the upshot?

What was the upshot anyway?

One immediate upshot was that he wouldn't need to go back to Berrywell by way of Dunglass. The bold Nancy might be waiting for him. Or he might run into her—and that would be just as painful.

He would speak to Farmer Lee before he retired.

But when he got back to the inn Doctor Bowmaker was staggering about in the gloaming rifting and belching and cursing creation.

"Robert, my boy. Ro-bert. . . Listen: my auld guts are giving out on me. Wise—boy—not to drink too much. But to-morrow I'll drink and—the—next day I'll drink. Then some day my auld guts will rot and burst. And Robert, my boy, there'll be a hell of a stench. I know, I know—better than any o' your medical bunglers. I've been at a man's death-bed when his guts burst. Not even a man of God can pray after that. . .

"Give me your arm, my boy, and walk me along the road. . . I'm beginning to feel better. Talk—that's the antidote. A drunk man always talks—even to himself. That's why we drink—so that we can talk. You don't think me an auld fool? No . . . you wouldn't think me that. But of course, that's ex-actly, exactly what I am . . . an old fool. But, my boy, tell me the man who isn't a fool. . . You don't mind me talking? And on Sunday—on Sunday I'll talk so well I'll have the beggars weeping. They like to weep—and God knows they have much to weep for. God be praised that the wind's beginning to break on me. . .

"Now believe me, Robert Burns, I'm sane and sober. . . The strange thing, y'know, is that nae matter how drunk I get I always remain sane—oh, just damnably sane. Only that I must talk . . . and break wind. My auld guts make enough wind to drive a ship from the pier o' Leith to Rotterdam. . .

"What's that? You dinna want to go back to Dunse by way of Dunglass? You met Sir James Hall. Fine chap, Sir James—damnably learned, damnably learned. About the earth and rocks—and geology. Maist damnably scientific. Crony of old Hutton of Edinburgh. Theories about the earth . . . rocks and strata . . . and . . . minerals. But a decent chap. Oh—and quite modest. Damnably in love with his fine wife. . .

"You dinna want to go back to Dunglass. Why should you? You're going back to Rachel Angel. Angel . . . not Ainslie. You go the quickest road. So you go up the Elmscleugh Water, come round by West Steel and Bransby Hill . . . and then down the Monynut Water. There's a young exciseman—Lorimer—going that way in the morn. Rode in when you were out. See him in the morning. He'll see you back to Dunse.

"But now . . . take me back to the inn. You'll join me in a bottle of brandy before we get to bed? Don't talk rubbish, my boy. I'm as sober as a corpse. Remember—last thing at night, brandy. First thing in the morning, claret. Port in the middle of the day. After that you can drink what you like. . . Yes—a bottle of French brandy—that puts you to sleep. And no dreams. No dreams—sleep. . .

"You won't write a poem on me, Robert? Don't write a poem on me, because. . . Well: write what the devil you like, my boy—write whatever the devil you like. I'm going into my brandy. But—whatever you write tell them that Doctor Robert Bowmaker, minister in Dunse, was an honest good fellow—and say that when my auld guts burst the stink will be felt over half the country. . . Yes, sir, even at the Cross o' Edinburgh."

SWEET RACHEL AINSLIE

He arrived at Berrywell in the late afternoon of the following day to find that the only Ainslie present was Rachel. . . She made no attempt to disguise her welcome.

"How glad I am to see you back, Robert. How hungry are you and I'll see what can be brought in from the kitchen? The family are all out on a visit and have left me to keep house. . . I thocht you'd be back this afternoon. . ."

"You waited in for me, Rachel? No wonder everyone calls you an angel."

"Indeed nobody ever thocht of calling me that till you came . . . till you wrote thae precious lines for me in the kirk. But wait till I see what I can get for you to eat. . ."

When she had tripped out of the room the Bard took a seat by the big window that looked out across the fields to the low distant Cheviot hills across the Merse. This was a greater temptation than he should be suffered to endure. What was the matter with him? If he had no lust for Rachel Ainslie what was it he had for her? Love? It could hardly be that. She was nine years younger—though this was difficult to realise from her looks and her behaviour. What was it, then, that caused his heart to flutter and an agitation to rise in his breast . . . ? Maybe it was lust: clean healthy lust; the clean lust for a maid that was the stirring and source of all life. Yes: maybe that's what it was. Only he was too much the coward: he could not expose his lust to Rachel. He had too great a respect for her, maybe too great a fear for her. . . And maybe there was a code of decency that operated in such cases, a code that had its origin far back in human society. She was the sister of his friend: she was the daughter of his friend. Not for any lust that ever blinded a man's judgment and sent the red waves of unreason blinding behind his eye-balls could he betray his friends. And yet: if only he did not know her father and her mother and her brothers!

She had waited in for him. Now they were alone together.

Damnit, hadn't he known before this that women had a wisdom in such matters that made men, by comparison, seem the most ignorant and brutish oafs? Of course Rachel knew *what* she was doing even if she didn't know *why*. Nature may have given men brains; but she had given women an intuition that went deeper than brains could go. Women had an extra sense that men had not...

He looked out across the shimmering Merseland. The crops ripened. Women in the ploughed patches were busy thinning the long drills of turnips; cattle grazed contentedly at the sweet grass; rooks winged back to the Berrywell trees to feed their voracious young; a field cart creaked and rumbled in a near-by loaning... The land was incredibly fresh and green; and burgeoning growth was everywhere in evidence...

Never had the green of early summer seemed so sweet and fair. Never had it seemed so distant and remote. For the first time in his life he had watched a spring coming and going and he had done nothing to help in its essential husbandry. For the first time in his life he had not toiled on the land and carried its soil-grains embedded in the pores of his toil-calloused hands. He looked at his hands. The first time he had realised they had grown white and soft was when he had fondled Isabella Lindsay. Now he realised why. He was no longer a farmer, no longer a ploughman, no longer a worker on the land... Now a field was a scene he looked at over a hedge or a dyke: a scene of labour that knew him no more...

All this drifted into his mind with the slow rhythm that came to him across the soil of the Merseland. And he was drifting in another sense: he was refusing to face up to the reality of his position, he was running away from his responsibilities. He didn't want to go back and face Jean Armour and Gilbert. Sending Gilbert money wasn't enough. And his mother and his sisters ... and Jean's twins: his twins... God damnit, he was only laying in a stock of poetical scenes and ideas against the future... Laying the foundations for his future work with James Johnson and his *Musical Museum*... Why the hell had he ever to be making excuses for himself, justifying himself? Here in Berrywell life was slow and quiet and easy. Nobody was in want; and no one strove against the universe as if it were an implacable monster. Here they lived a calm and gracious existence. And Rachel Ainslie bloomed, sheltered from the cold winds and the storms without. . .

If Jean Armour or Betty Paton had lived such a life. . . If his father had been allowed to ripen towards the grave in the peace that old Mr. Ainslie enjoyed maybe his laughter would have sounded about the walls of the homestead; and maybe his mother would still be singing.

But Rachel was back in the room and the impact of her maidenhood blinded the backward-looking in his mind. She was there smiling . . . bringing with her into the room the feeling that the world was just and gracious; that life was kind and gentle and that harshness and sorrow, cruelty and tears, despair and longing had no part in it. And so, like the sun bursting from a cloud, the greyness of his mind was instantly transformed into golden light; and the light danced and shone in his great eyes—and Rachel felt she was walking on a carpet of sun-sodden air. . .

She set the tray of food on the table and poured him a glass of milk: "It's not much, Robert; but I didna want to keep you waiting. Won't you sit into the table and eat a bite?"

"Yes, Rachel: I'll eat a bite. I doubt if manna ever tasted so good——"

"Robert: it's not true that you were ever a ploughman?"

"And why should it not be true, my dear? Do you think I couldn't handle a plough?"

"But not a ploughman like my father's ploughman! I ken you say that your father was a farmer upon the Carrick border; but you also say in your poems that you were a ploughman."

"My father was many things in his day. But it's true that he was a farmer upon the Carrick border—though a poor rent-racked tenant-farmer—nothing like what you have hereabouts. And it's equally true that I was a ploughman and did all kinds of labour about a poor farm. But why do you ask?"

"I just canna think of you as a ploughman—though I ken

there's nothing dishonourable in being a ploughman. Please don't think I——"

"Rachel: the world's all before you. You find it a very comfortable place, don't you? I mean: you have nothing to worry you?"

"I've plenty to worry me, Robert."

"For instance?"

"You're my worry at the moment. I want to make your stay here as comfortable as I can: my brother told me I was to be good to you."

"And you always do what your brother tells you?"

"I'm very fond of my brother."

"So am I, Rachel: very fond of him. He gladdened what would otherwise have been many a dull hour for me in Edinburgh; and he has been a great strength to me on this jaunt of mine. I couldn't have undertaken it without him——"

"Robert worships the ground you walk on. And I'm glad of that. I think you are a good influence on him."

"Nonsense: your brother can well look after himself."

"Then why is he always in debt?"

"Did he tell you he was in debt? If he did, don't believe a word of it."

"We have no secrets from each other. He told me he'd need a lot of money. He told me about the girl who was going to have a baby——"

"He told you that?"

"We have no secrets. . . Father would be terribly angry if he knew; and it would break Mother's heart. . . I gave him what I'd saved."

"Rachel: you know what you are talking about? Or rather, do you know what your brother was talking about? You know what all this means?"

"Why shouldn't I? I'm a woman."

"No, no: you're far from being a woman. You're still a wee lassock. You'll be a woman time enough, Rachel. Now I won't have you worrying about Bob: he's well able to look after himself. And I'm much annoyed that he told you anything about his troubles—and I'll tell him so when I get back to Edinburgh."

"Then I'll never forgive you! Besides: isn't it natural for young men to sow their wild oats?"

"Rachel: you haven't the least idea what you're talking about. Who's been filling your head wi' this nonsense about wild oats?"

"You can't treat me like a child, Robert. I know all about such matters: at least I know all about the consequences. You forget that I sit under Doctor Bowmaker every Sunday."

"All right then: Robert has put an Edinburgh servant-lass in the family-way; and you give him money—and think nothing about it. I suppose that that's a' a servant-lass is fit for?"

"I gave my brother money so that he could provide for the unfortunate girl. But how am I not to know that she isn't a bad woman?"

"I don't know, Rachel, I don't know! I refuse to sit in judgment."

"You don't think my brother deceived her?"

"I still don't know, Rachel; and I would rather we didna discuss the matter ony further. In fact I refuse to discuss it any further."

"But I thought you'd understand better than any other person I could talk to: you see, there isn't any other person I could talk to. . . Are there really bad women in Edinburgh? My brother told me there were houses that a man could pay to go to and pay for the favours of bad women; but this girl he had got into trouble is not that kind. I would like to know about such places. . ."

"When I was in Edinburgh, Rachel, I stayed below a bawdy house, a brothel, a house of ill-fame. I got to know many of the girls who traded there. And, but for the fact that they sold their bodies, they were all good girls who had been unfortunate. I mean, Rachel, they were good in the sense that they were kindly and good-tempered and law-abiding. Many of them I understand marry and make decent wives to decent men and bring up their families in the fear of the Lord. There are women, on the other hand, who frequent the closes and wynds and waylay men; and maybe they are not so honest since they are often diseased and pass on their disease. And then there are honest lassies who give themselves to men for a wide variety of reasons . . . and they have a child . . . and maybe they are ruined as a consequence. . . The world isn't an easy place, Rachel, as you know if you listen to Doctor Bowmaker. . . No: the world isn't easy. But there are, in the main, two kinds of women: angels and the others. You are an angel: so we will say nothing about the others. As for your brother: he has made a mistake and the lass has made a mistake; but I know he will do the best for her. Won't you be satisfied with that?"

"I'm not worrying, Robert: not now. . But it must be awful to be a woman who has to sell her body."

"Just as awful for the man who buys her body."

"I know you've never done anything like that."

"I've many things on my conscience, my dear; but that's not one of them."

"I'm glad of that. And because of that I can speak to you frankly."

He looked into her eyes where she sat beside him at the table, resting her chin on the palm of her delicate hand. Her eyes had a wisdom and an experience that was not in her mother's. What kind of brain lay beneath those bright auburn curls, he could only guess. For himself he was a turmoil of emotions. He was fired by her beauty and her amorousness: he knew that he had only to coax her and she would submit to him; and there was nothing at the moment he would have liked better. Knowing this he suggested that they might walk into Dunse as he had a letter to post.

Rachel Ainslie would have given herself to Robert Burns willingly. But she feared him; and she wished to retain his respect. Mentally she compared herself to the girls he must have made love to; and she found herself wanting. She agreed to walk into Dunse with him.

That night he recorded in his Journal:

"Found Miss Ainslie, the amiable, the sensible, the good-humoured, the sweet Miss Ainslie all alone at Berrywell. Heavenly Powers who know the weaknesses of human hearts support mine! what happiness must I see only to remind me that I cannot enjoy it . . . ! I walk in to Dunse before dinner and out to Berrywell in the evening with Miss Ainslie—how well-bred, how frank, how good she is! I could grasp her with rapture on a bed of straw, and rise with contentment to the most sweltering drudgery of stiffening Labour. . . Charming Rachel! may thy bosom never be wrung by the evils of this life of sorrows, or by the villainy of this world's sons!"

ENGLISH JOURNEY

The Bard was all set for his journey into England when he went down with a high fever that burned itself out in twenty-four hours. But it gave him a fright. It reminded him that he was subject to such fevers and that maybe he would die in one. So scared was he that he determined to mend his ways and (as he recorded) "to live in such a manner as not to be scared at the approach of Death."

This illness took place in the house of Farmer Hood who was to accompany him and Farmer Ker on his journey across the Border.

After a day's rest he went out with his host to see the roup of a farmer's stock in the neighbourhood. The spectacle of the farmer's belongings going up for sale affected him almost as much as his recent illness. He wrote in his Journal a note that did scant justice to his feelings: "Rigid economy and decent industry, do you preserve me from being the principal Dramatis Persona in such a scene of Horrors!"

Not only did the scene remind him of the fate his family had narrowly escaped at Lochlea: it warned him of the uncertainties that would be his if ever he took up farming again. . .

On Sunday the twenty-seventh of May he rode out with

Hood and Ker and crossed the Border into England at Coldstream for the second time. This time he rode on. And as they passed the field of Flodden where, in 1513, the Scots had suffered such a mortal defeat at the hands of the English no one said a word. Yet each one of them thought of that day when the Flowers of the Forest had been mowed down like a crop of thistles in a grazing park. . .

But he found his companions had very little to say when they were travelling. They had set themselves a hard day's riding and the road was not of the best: sometimes it was no more than a rutted track. Indeed once they had traversed the flat ground that bordered the Tweed and had mounted into the uplands, there was little difference between the Alnwick hills and the Lammermuirs. The country-side was wild in the extreme; and the poor folks that lived along the way were as beggarly as any to be seen in Scotland. . .

His companions were each of them very different from Bob Ainslie. He could say whatever came into his mind to Ainslie. With Messrs. Ker and Hood he had to be circumspect. They were men of a sober cast of mind and they were not given to levity in any shape or form. . .

The country they crossed into Alnwick continued wild and uncultivated. There was only coarse pasturage for sheep and hill-cattle and there seemed few of either.

As they came into Alnwick the road skirted the seemingly interminable policies of the Duke of Northumberland. As it happened, Gilbert Ker was known to the Duke's agent, Mr. Wilken, and at Ker's request (the Duke being absent) Wilken showed them something of the palace-magnificence of Alnwick Castle. They all agreed that in this quality of magnificence there was nothing in Scotland to equal it.

But though the town of Alnwick was a compact mass of history in stone, there was little of history in his English tour that really held the Bard. And there was little in the scenery to make him hold his breath. The highways and by-ways they travelled to Warkworth were pleasant enough. At Warkworth the River Coquet, though small, was ' romantic '; and the village itself not lacking in scenic charm. But against the scenic charm stood the gaunt and squalid figures of unrebellious poverty.

They slept at Morpeth (a pleasant enough village dozing in peace and reasonable comfort) and continued the following day to Newcastle.

Newcastle was a disappointment to the Bard. It was an untidy township of little character scattered about the banks of the Tyne—a river he thought sadly unromantic. As a market town, however, it was by no means to be despised and both Hood and Ker were well satisfied with the business they transacted.

But by now he was anxious to turn Jenny's head north-west and to incline for the Border. He felt he had seen enough of England. Not that he was foolish enough to think that a short tour of the extreme north of England was sufficient to enable him to form a picture of the Kingdom of "the dominant partner." He had read enough to realise that the broad rolling acres of England were something very different from the hilly land of Northumberland, Cumberland and Westmorland. But at least he had had a look over his neighbour's garden wall.

At Wardrue (heading north-west) he wrote in his Journal: "Left Newcastle early in the morning, and rode over a fine country to Hexham to breakfast—from Hexham to Wardrue, the celebrated Spa, where we slept."

At Longtown they were almost back in Scotland. It was feeing-fair day and crowds of young folks, hoping to sell their labour for the next year, thronged the streets and haunted the market. If some of the older and less readily employable men and women were anxious and worried about their prospects of employment, the young folks didn't seem to care much either way. For them the day was a holiday; and, as they wouldn't have another for a long time, they decided to make the most of it.

As he sat down in a crowded eating-house with Hood and Ker for a farewell meal, the Bard could not help commenting on the high spirits of the young folks.

"Damnit, it does a body good to see sae mony cheery good-natured youths taking the world i' their stride."

"Ah weel," said Thomas Hood soberly, "maybe aye . . . and maybe no. There's too much light-headedness aboot the young folks now-a-days. A' they can think aboot is pleasure. Work's a thing o' the past. They'll only work when they're driven to it. D'ye no' agree, Stodrig?"

"Man, Tam, I wouldna be too hard on them, either. You were young yoursel'—aince. But I agree that there's no' the same tendency to work. Na: they're shy when it comes to hard work. . ."

The Bard did not contradict his sober companions. But he was glad to hear that the rising generation were not so keen on hard work as their fathers had been. Having known for too long what physical slavery to the soil meant, he could sympathise with them.

Gilbert Ker changed the conversation. "Weel, Robert, this is where we part company. I dinna ken about you, Tam—but I've enjoyed your company. It was a privilege to ken you, Robert—a great privilege; but this jaunt has made it a pleasure as weel."

"I'll back you up in that, Gilbert. Aye . . . we Border farmers are supposed to be a douce lot an' no' given to saying much—especially in the way o' compliments. But I couldna dae ither than fully endorse a' that you say, Gilbert. I hope you didna find us ower dull, sir . . . ?"

The Bard had found his companions very dull. Neither of them possessed any wit or levity or much of innocent merriment. Sound solid common sense and rock-like integrity were their dominant characteristics. But he had learned much from them in relation to farming and the sober science of agricultural economy; and withal, he had formed a great respect for their characters. Above all, he could not hurt them.

"I've learned mair on our jaunt frae Newcastle than I ever learned before on twa days' riding. . . Believe me, gentlemen, I'll benefit greatly from what I've learned."

"D'you think, then, you'll settle on the Dumfries farm, Robert?"

"I canna say. I'll need to see the place first . . . and there are many factors to be considered. If I had the necessary capital to set myself up with adequate stock and buildings on good land, then there is nothing I would like better than to settle down on some pleasant bit of country and begin farming. A working farmer of course. I have no wish to be of the gentleman variety."

"Ah damnit," said Hood, "you'd mak' a braw gentleman-farmer riding roun' your march dykes on a guid day and sitting snug at your fireside on the lang nichts writing oot your verses. Though I agree, mind you, that a spell o' guid hard work never did man or beast ony harm."

"It'll be a big enough change for me to turn farmer on modest terms without that, sir. In fact, I hardly dare to hope to become Mr. Miller's tenant however reasonable his terms may turn out to be. But if hard work will ensure my success then I have no fear on that score."

"Ah—but you'll need to watch your health, too, Robert. Man, I didna like yon fever you had wi' me."

"No. . . I didna particularly like it mysel'. But. . . Well, I'll cross my bridges when I come to them. And if ever I come back to the Borders I'll count it a privilege to call on you. And if I do settle about Dumfries and you're ever my way——"

"Oh we'll no' gae by your door, Robert. Dinna fear on that score. . . Dinna fear on ony score: a lad wi' your abilities needna fear what he puts his hand till. Only Robert—and I said this before in Kelso—it's a damned pity some of your Embro patrons couldna fix you in some office or other that would let you write to your heart's content. . . Aye: a damned pity."

They were douce farmers by any reckoning; but they wished him more than well.

He parted with them (when it came to the moment of parting) with genuine regret. He felt he would never meet them again.

When the two farmers rode up the street, heading for the Border, he felt suddenly empty and sad. Here he stood, still on English soil, with Machlin two hard days' riding away.

His deepest promptings urged him to mount Jenny Geddes and to ride north-west day and night till he reached the Machlin Cowgate. But prudence, which is ever a thin veneer, prompted otherwise. He was on English soil; and he might never stand on English soil again. Besides, Jamie Mitchell, a good Ayrshire friend, had a printing and dyeing establishment in Carlisle, less than two hours away.

THE LASS AT LONGTOWN

Maybe he refreshed himself too well or maybe his thoughts burned too intensely of Jean Armour. But when a lass smiled at him he gave her a nod of recognition that brought her sidling, with a sway of her plump hips and a twist to her lustful lips, to his side.

Her sister who claimed to be a sober married woman, though she was no more than a year older, held the fort in the window recess.

The sidling whore, for whore she was, pleaded ignorance of the road to Carlisle. She was travelling—the unblushing liar that she was—with her sister to Carlisle on a mission of mercy.

She was just the kind of diversion the Bard needed after the days he had spent in the company of Thomas Hood and Gilbert Ker. But he had no intention but to divert himself. He assumed the role of innocent country farmer on a business jaunt to the feeing-fair on the look out for a couple of labourers. No sooner had he admitted that he was a bachelor than the whore played all her cards, quickly and expertly. The Bard admired the skill of her manipulation. There was no man she admired more than a farmer. She had been brought up on a farm. She could milk and churn, and mend and sew and set a hen on a dozen of eggs with the best.

The Bard decided that English whores worked with a speed and skill that left their Scots sisters far behind.

The following day, in Carlisle, he told James Mitchell of his adventure.

"I arranged to meet her in Carlisle. And though she had never been here before she was able to mention a tavern by name. Her mission of mercy over in Carlisle, she was prepared to return to Scotland with me by way of Gretna Green. At least she had all her plans made for a Gretna Green affair."

"And she turned up in the town?"

"That she did, Jamie—and without the married sister. But I couldna keep the farce up ony longer. I gave her a bit tousle in the back room—harmless enough for I was still the innocent farmer and green bachelor. And I stood her a bottle o' cyder.

"The cyder did it. I drank nothing stronger mysel'—and she couldna very well object to that. Clever, Jamie; and no' a bad lass at bottom. But a whore for a' that. As soon as she saw she was wasting her time she cut her losses. The mission of mercy became desperate in its urgency. Needless to say, I didna offer to detain her."

"God, Rab, but you're the boy for fallin' in wi' the dames . . . eh? Sir, an' I'm telling you there's a wheen o' toppers in Carlisle. Oh aye—juist the same in Edinburgh. Damnit, Rab, the weemin noo are getting fair outrageous. Oor mithers wadna believe what gans on noo-a-days. Juist wadna believe it. High kilts and powder and paint and rouge and what-not. I hae them in my works here. Bairned time and again—but aey manage to get rid o' them afore their time. An' the young lassies i' their teens waur nor a'. I'll show you them when I tak' you roun' the place. Man, Rab, morals is a' to hell the-gither the noo—I kenna what's come ower folk. Of coorse, since the American war things haena been the same."

"I misdoubt, Jamie, but onything's ever the same. Times change—a' the time. Nothing remains constant. And yet, deep down—if you read the Auld Testament—nothing changes. Manners, speech, dress, food and drink—even the weather—change; but no' fundamentally."

"I dinna ken, Rab. I've seen a heap o' changes in my time. But och, things maun aey be someway—so what's the odds? When are you getting married? But I'll tell you what. If you

need ony bed furnishings at ony time, drap me a line. I'll see
you accommodated wi' the best stuffs at the cheapest prices.
Nae mair nor the cost price to me. 'Coorse, that applies to
yoursel' and only yoursel'. Your friends I'll quote as cheap
as onybody—and supply superior goods to onybody in the
trade, Scots or English. . ."

The Bard's fame may have reached Carlisle. But if so he
managed to ride out of the town on the first day of June
without anyone but James Mitchell seemingly aware of his
presence.

Not that this worried him in any particular. He was
Scotland's Bard—not England's.

He shook the reins on Jenny's neck. "Come on, lass, and
let me see how you can throw the miles ahint you twixt here
and Annan. You've cantered nobly since you left the Grassmarket in Edinburgh. But I promise you a lang rest and a park
o' sweet green grass when you get to Machlin. No' too fast,
noo! You'll no' be there the nicht—and you've mony a sair
mile to hoof yet. Aye; but every mile's a mile nearer hame
—is that it? Damnit, you're a wise beast too, Jenny. If only
your master was as wise. That's better noo: juist an easy
trot—and we'll win Scotland a' the quicker. . .

"Aye, aye, Jenny: it's been a wonderfu' trip when you
think it ower. You'll no' forget your lang, sair drag ower the
Lammermuirs in a hurry. A pity you didna see some o' the
lassies though. Sweet Isabella Lindsay o' Jeddart—I wonder
how she's feeling now? A fine lass, Jenny—and a rare sweet
armfu'. I'll maybe no' get my arms round a sweeter for a
while. An' willing! Nae haudin' back in the yoke but coming
into you a' the time. . .

"And Betsy Grieve yonder at Eyemouth! Another topper.
Hingin' like a ripe plum—just ripe and ready for a lusty lover.
An' I could hae been the lover, Jenny—to our mutual satisfaction. I'll guarantee that bit o' it. Aye, but maybe better
the way it was. There's nae lass i' the Borders wondering
whether or no' she's couped to me—and I've nae worries on
that score either. It wadna be a nice feeling noo to think that
my sweet wee angel at Berrywell was beginning to boak her

kail. But, by certes, if she doesna watch her step she'll boak her kail ain o' thae braw mornings. By God, Jenny, but I should be patting mysel' on the back. There's no' a man in a' Scotland fonder o' a lass than your master. And damn few can enjoy them to better purpose. There are four lassies i' the Borders I could hae coupit without ony deception on my part. Aye, and when I think on Nancy Sherriff, at Dunglass, I remember that I had to use a' my wit to prevent mysel' being seduced and raped in the maist thorough-going fashion.

"But there you are now—I resisted a' temptation. Keep min' o' that, Jenny, when folks run me doon for a conscience-less fornicator. I wonder how mony reverend and right reverend divines could hae resisted a' I hae resistit on this jaunt? Or in Edinburgh, either. Ah, but I made one slip in Auld Reekie—or did I? I wonder. Aye, I wonder how Peggy Cameron's getting on? No' that Peggy was exactly a slip either. You see, Jenny, the difference—or one o' them— betwixt a man and a beast is juist this. The notion o' a mate only comes ower you when Dame Nature decides you need a foal—and you ken how seldom that occurs in a twelvemonth. But the human being needs a mate or mates a' the time.

"If love-making could be separated frae procreation then it would be easy enough. But Dame Nature didna mak' things easy for folks. Na, na: she laid doon the consequences and the penalties. And so, when a man and woman come thegither, sooner or later, the bill has to be paid. But there you are, folk canna live separate so folk are aey paying the consequences. Yet, Jenny, when you're weighing me up in your auld head there and wondering juist what kind o' a man I am, remember that I aey hae a thocht for the consequences as far as the lass is concerned. It's juist a wee bit point o' the compass i' my favour. For if I didna think on the consequences, by certes, but I could have had the lassies by the dizzens—aye, by the score. No' that I'll get ony credit for that, Jenny—so I'm juist for taking the credit to mysel'. But, mind you, maybe I'm wrang. Maybe Isabella and Rachel and Betsy would rather hae run the risk o' being couped than preserving their maiden-heads for some future occasion that may neither promise nor turn out to their better advantage. You can never be sure where a lass is concerned.

"No: you can never be sure, Jenny. So maybe, a' things considered, I was better to play safe. And if I havena played safe wi' Heilan' Peggy, then damnit, she needed me juist as desperately as I needed her. An' if she ran ony risks then she ran them wi' her twa e'en as wide open as ever a lass's e'en were open. An' there you hae the whole position in a han'fu' o' corn—an' you can bruise it atween your auld teeth to your heart's content."

NATIVE HEATH

There was nothing but a stone on the side of the road to indicate that he had crossed from English soil to Scottish. It seemed an arbitrary place to fix the Border. At Coldstream, crossing the Tweed, he had felt that there indeed Scotland stood separate from England. But on the Carlisle to Annan road there was no such feeling.

But he noted the stone and felt happier that he was back again on his native heath. And when he rode into Annan he knew unmistakably that he was back in Scotland. He called at the inn and ordered a meal.

After the meal he felt better. Feeling better, he began to think better. He would ride into Dumfries. The next day he would ride on to Miller's estate at Dalswinton. The next day he would ride to Machlin.

His heart jumped a beat at that. Machlin! Jean Armour and Gilbert . . . and Mossgiel . . . and Johnny Dow and Eliza Miller. But no Richmond and no Jamie Smith. . . No . . . it wouldn't be the same Machlin he would ride into. But damnit, it would still be Machlin. There was no escaping Jean Armour —not for long. And there was her double throw of twins! By certes, but he was an adept at deceiving himself. He wanted Jean as much as ever he had wanted her. There wasn't anybody anywhere who could take her place. Not so completely, so easily, so naturally.

Almost he felt like dismissing Dalswinton from his mind and his itinerary and riding post-haste for the Machlin Cowgate. . .

He was wearied with travelling. It would be a great relief to come to rest with Jean. She was stable and enduring. Somehow he felt that no matter what came or what went there would always be Jean Armour.

But a shock awaited him as he came in the Annan Road and down English Street into the Royal Burgh of Dumfries. He stabled his horse at the King's Head Inn and walked up the sunlit street to the post office.

A few letters awaited him. There was one from Ainslie, one from Willie Nicol, one from Gilbert, one from Peter Hill . . . and one written by a Mrs. Hogg on behalf of Highland Peggy Cameron.

Peggy was definitely with child; and as she felt she wouldn't be able to hide her condition much longer she begged that he come to her assistance.

His emotions boiled in a stew of anger frustration fear and pity. God roast and damn the stupid bitch! All along she had been too confident, too cock-sure of what she was about. But that last time he had seen her . . . ? She must have known then. So: she had deceived him from the beginning and now she was desperate—and had taken her case to this Mrs. Hogg and got her to write to him. . .

He would need time to think. Plenty of time. He wouldn't rush into any commitments. Maybe this was a trap. Maybe she had been pregnant before he had known her. That seemed possible, looking back on it, for she had never given him a refusal . . . not once. And this in itself was damned suspicious.

But there was an element of pity too in his reaction. Now she was fearing what would happen when her pregnancy could no longer be concealed. And she'd reason to fear, no doubt of that. The two old bitches would throw her out. She would lose her bed beneath the kitchen table; she would lose her bite of food; she would lose the twa-three bits o' bawbees she got half-yearly by way of pay . . . !

Damn the doubt, Peggy Cameron was in for a hard time. And if she went about Edinburgh proclaiming to all and sundry by the swell o' her womb that he was responsible for her condition it wouldn't do him any good.

Not, deep down, that anybody in Edinburgh, or Scotland, gave a cadger's curse for a bastard bairn. Every man of the least consequence had twa-three to his name and thought nothing of it. The Edinburgh gentry would sneer to think that anybody lost a night's sleep for the sake o' an odd get here and there.

But then he wasn't one of the Edinburgh gentry. He was the heaven-taught ploughman. And that title carried no rights in the trade of illegitimacy. They would laugh at him. Maybe they would sneer at him. Maybe they would turn their backs on him.

Then let them! He'd been a damned fool—and he would need to pay for his folly. . . But Peggy—she too would need to pay for her folly. Pay a sore price. He would need to do something about her. Send her some money. Advise her to seek refuge among friends in the country till her trouble blew over. He couldn't just leave her to her fate—even though she had brought that fate on herself. After all—it wasn't easy to forget her. Many a cold bitter night in Edinburgh, lying in front of the fire in the warm glow, she had been something more than a physical solace to him . . . something a lot more, the poor unfortunate, silly, warm-hearted, sweet-fleshed, soft-spoken jad. . .

He must write Ainslie immediately and enclose this letter from Mrs. Hogg and arrange for him to call at Hogg's and leave some money for her.

He took a sheet of paper from his pocket and, on the edge of the tavern table, with no one else in the room, wrote to his friend and fellow sinner:

My Dear Friend,

My first welcome to this place was the inclosed letter—

I am sorry for it, but what is done is done. I pay you no compliment when I say that except my old friend Smith there is not any person in the world I would trust so far. Please call at the Jas. Hogg mentioned, and send for the wench and give her ten or twelve shillings, but don't for Heaven's sake meddle with her as a *Piece*. I insist on this, on your honour; and advise her out to some country friends. You may perhaps not like the business, but I just tax your friendship thus far. Call immediately, or at least as soon as it is dark, for Godsake, lest the poor soul be starving. Ask her for a letter I wrote her just now, by way of token—it is unsigned. Write me after the meeting.
Dumfries, 1 June 1787.

Despite the blow of his Edinburgh news, the Bard recovered his outward calm sufficiently to appreciate something of the burgh of Dumfries. He eyed it keenly enough. If he settled somewhere on the Nith with Peter Miller of Dalswinton, Dumfries would then become his Ayr or Kilmarnock.

It wasn't a bad town either, as he surveyed it in the June sunshine. It had a good broad High Street, a tolerable Tolbooth and some well-built if not very imposing public buildings. Off the High Street ran some narrow vennels giving access to the sands on the bank of the broad Nith where it roared over the caul just below the eight arches of the fine old bridge.

Many women had their tubs down in the Nith and were busy tramping their washings. . .

But though Dumfries dozed sleepily away under the June sun and nobody but the washer-wives seemed busy, his fame had reached the town and a messenger came to him requesting his company at the provost's house.

There the Bard was introduced to a company that included the Reverend William Burnside, the young minister (he was thirty-six years old) of the New Church, and Anne, his extremely beautiful wife who was the same age as the Bard.

Provost William Clark, a burly heavy-drinking pot-bellied shallow-pated merchant, welcomed him in the semi-sycophantic egotistical tin-pot-lord-of-all-I-survey manner so characteristic of provosts.

"Welcome to the Ancient and Royal Burgh o' Dumfries, Mr. Burns. Sir: seeing how your fame has been gien—as it were and so tae speak the—er—hum—haw—authority o' the Capital o' Scotland to wit, Edinburgh . . . myself as Provost o' the Town—the Council agreeing wi' me—thocht we could dae nae less than confer on you the high honour o' making you a freeman o' the Ancient and Royal Burgh—ahem—ahem— the whilk ceremony and honour will tak' place on Wednesday. This honour, Mr. Burns, we are confident will be duly appreciated by you for its great worth. Edinburgh of course is a great Town and, speaking personally, I hae nae desire for to cast ony slur on the way it conducts its civic business— ahem—ahem—but we here in the Ancient and Royal Burgh o' Dumfries are no' in any way behin' han' wi' the way *we* conduct oorsel's. And in my capacity as Provost—ahem—ahem —an honour, I may say, thrust on me by my fellow citizens and worthy burghers—in my capacity, as I was saying, as Provost o' the Ancient and Royal Burgh——"

But the Bard had long ceased to listen to the pompous and fatuous provostorial mouthings of William Clark. He knew his type only too well—and he bored him intolerably.

But he was not wholly bored. Anne Burnside's beauty overcame the profitless platitudes of Provost Clark. The Bard eyed her whenever he got the opportunity—and she was not slow to respond. Her husband was a lusty red-faced clergyman addicted to his food and the bottle with no more than a hasty though hot-blooded interest in his pretty wife. And yet Anne had longed all her young life for a love that would satisfy her romantic cravings: she had never thought she might become a perfunctory bed-mate. Her secret longing as she looked at the Bard welled to over-flowing in her soft brown eyes. . . What a glorious sensation it must be to be loved and not merely made love to. . . But how was a girl to know what a man was like until she had married him? And Anne Hutton, since she had married William Burnside in 1778, had borne him six children; and she wasn't a day older than the Bard. . .

The Bard rode out of Dumfries on the afternoon of June the 4th with mixed feelings. In Dumfries, folks had treated him well. He had his burgess ticket in his pocket and the idea of Anne Burnside in his heart. Her husband had turned out much better than he had hoped: he had shown him much intelligent consideration and had, in every respect, been a model host. If only he hadn't been married to Anne. . .

Still, he was doing not badly. A month since he had left Auld Reekie—and in addition to much lavish and varied hospitality he had been given the freedom of Jedburgh and Dumfries and made a Royal Arch of St. Abbs. . .

And he liked Dumfries. He could settle down near many a worse town; and if he liked the town he liked more the country-side about it.

As he rode up the left bank of the Nith that was finely wooded and looked across and beyond to the hills (green and pleasantly contoured) he felt that here was as romantic a district as could be found in Scotland. By the time he had ridden the six miles into Dalswinton he was completely in love with it.

Patrick Miller was in residence and though busy with a dozen schemes and worried how to get his great rambling house into decent repair, he dropped everything to attend to the Bard.

He had fitted up a great barn of a room for himself and it was cluttered with plans and papers and piled high with books.

"You'll excuse the mess I'm in here, Mr. Burns? I hae mair to attend to than I hae *time* to attend. But I hae time to attend to you—dinna worry. I'm glad to see you again, Burns—glad that you hae had the intelligence to realise that you can do nothing better than invest your money in a farm. . ."

"You have been very generous in your offer, Mr. Miller— and if it can be arranged—nothing would please me better than to settle in this part of the world and to have you as my landlord."

"And I'd be damned glad to have you for a tenant, Burns.

But drink up and we'll tak' a walk down by the Nith. There's some grand holm ground on the ither side o' the Nith frae here—and that's where I thocht wad be best for you to settle —of coorse, I'm no' rushing you. There's other possibilities about Dalswinton. Hae you got a' your money frae Creech?"

"No: that I canna well expect, Mr. Miller. The money has still to come in from the subscribers. It will be August or September before I'll be able to settle accounts with Mr. Creech. Until I know exactly what money I have in hand, I winna be in a position to fix definitely on a farm here. But at least I'll be able to know my mind when I do get my money."

"Weel, that's sensible enough, Burns. Though, mind you —you'll maybe hae a bit bother getting your money out o' Willie Creech. Howsomenever—he canna keep it frae you indefinitely or you can hae the law on him. August'll do me fine—I'll be back in Auld Reekie gin then—so you'll look in on me when you get back? Weel—if you're ready then, Burns, we'll view the land——"

Patrick Miller was in a friendly—almost a genial—mood. He was always at his best when he was parading his abilities and the evidences of the wealth he had managed to amass. His long nose twitched as he sniffed at the sweet summer air so different from the foul stenches he was familiar with in Edinburgh.

They went round by the loch and Miller became almost eloquent about its possibilities.

"Juist a pleasant stretch o' cauld water, Burns, wi' a wheen wild deuks and cootes sooming aboot on it. Oh, a pleasant enough loch, I'll agree. But wait you, Burns—when you're settled doon here you'll see a difference. By the time I'm done that'll be the maist famous stretch o' water in the world. Aye: you may look as if I didna ken what I was talking about. Keep a' this to yoursel' the noo—but it's my intention to sail a steam boat up and doon Dalswinton Loch. A boat, let me impress on you, wi' nae sails and nae masts—but for a' that driven wi' a mechanical device—or rather, an arrangement o' mechanical devices, for it's a complicated and highly ingenious invention——"

"Such an invention would revolutionise navigation—would it not?"

"Certes, it'll revolutionise navigation. Ships'll be able to make way *against* wind and tide and currents. Ships'll be able to go just where they like—and be damned to the elements. And that's whaur this useless deuk-pond—for that's a' you can richtly ca' it—a magnified deuk-pond—that's whaur *that* comes in. Folk think that I've retired frae Edinburgh to live the life o' a country gentleman. Ah weel, Burns, the life o' a country gentleman'll no' tak' up much o' my time. . .

". . . and there, just fair across the Nith, there—that's a bit kent as Ellisland. Juist a bit tumbled-doon place as you can see frae here. Well, I'd build you a new house and steading and give you a generous allowance for enclosing. The stuff's there all right. The best o' agricultural land. Richtly treated and cultivated it'll yield the best crops in Dumfriesshire—and that's saying something. D'you like the look o' it?"

And that was exactly what the Bard did like. It was a spot that for scenic charm couldn't be improved on. They traversed about a mile on the Nith's pleasant banks and every yard of it seemed more pleasant than the other. But at Ellisland he was persuaded it was more attractive. The holm ground—though it was hardly of the holm variety—consisted of a long plateau shelving steeply and at parts precipitously into the river. To the east however the land did run down to the water level and this no doubt gave it the name of holm ground.

There were some trees about the place and plenty of scrub bushes which, in their fresh June greenery, decked the river banks with a beauty he could not resist. If only he could settle here—if only fortune could see her way to lavish such fortune on him.

Miller could see that the Bard was impressed; and he listened to his enthusiasm for its attractions with a satisfied twinkle in his usually cold glassy eye. But the poet was becoming much too enthusiastic.

"Weel, I'm delighted that you like the place, Burns. As I told you from the start, I thocht it was a venture that would please you—I'd never ony intention other than to see you

settled doon on a guid farm—I was loth to think you micht
hae been tempted to settle doon in Edinburgh and waste your
substance at garret scribbling. But—and here I maun warn
you—you canna live aff a grand view and an acre or twa o'
romantic scenery. Na, na . . . farming's a serious business and
needs a' your energies to mak' a success o't. Dinna let the
view carry awa' your poetic fancy, Burns. You've made a
handfu' o' money wi' your verses—but you canna dae that
every year. No' that I want to stop your verses. There'll be
plenty o' time for that—especially in the lang dark nichts o'
winter—but you'll ken a' that better nor me."

"I appreciate everything you say, sir—and I bow to your
superior wisdom and sterling common sense. I know only
too well what successful farming demands—and I know just
how much poetry can be written after a hard day's labour at
the plough."

"I ken, I ken, Burns. I've nae fear o' you."

"I hope not, sir, for I have long wanted just this opportunity of settling down quietly—something indeed I have ever
dreamed about. . ."

"Of course you'd be the better o' a wife coming into a
farm—a good wife that knew how to assist you—wi' milking
and dairying and the like. And you'll want to bring up a
family that'll be able to come in and help you——"

"Yes. . . I suppose it would be foolish to think of turning
farmer without a wife—a wife brought up to the farm-kitchen
and the dairy. But a wife is hardly to be picked up at a feeing-
fair like any other servant—unless a man places no higher
value on her——"

"Damned, Burns, but I think sometimes there could be
waur ways o' coming by a wife. But dinna think I mean anything personal. You'll marry wha you fancy—I ken that fine
enough. Only I'm damned glad you didna marry an Embro
dame. The toon kind wad never settle hereabouts. I've a bit
bother wi' my ain—but that's in your private lug, too. Aye:
weemin are no' logical, Burns—that's the difficulty wi' them.
They're no' like men. A man can think logically and think
towards a given end. But a woman acts and doubles on her

tracks so that you can never depend on her. Aye—we canna well do without them; but, by God, sir, they gie us mony a thocht—and mony a jolt when we're least expectin'."

The Bard found Patrick Miller less formal, though more garrulous, than he had found him in Edinburgh. And he sensed that he was genuinely friendly towards him, that he wanted to help him all he could. He thanked Miller and took his road north-west by way of Sanquhar and Kirkconnel to New Cumnock.

He called at the New Cumnock Inn hoping to see Annie Rankine. But both she and John Merry were out visiting friends in the district. So he said farewell to the Nith he had followed from Dumfries; and, since night was coming on, he pressed Jenny Geddes forward to Machlin where he promised her a good feed of corn and the freedom of a grass park.

He was tired with his long day's riding; but the thrill of being back in Ayrshire buoyed him up. It had been a long journey and he had travelled a full circle. From Machlin to Edinburgh; from Edinburgh to Newcastle; from Newcastle to Dumfries; and from Dumfries . . . home. The sweetest country-side in all Scotland was Ayrshire. Especially Ayrshire in June. . . The June gloaming . . . and it creeping softly over the green swelling land. . . He could not hold back the moisture that gathered in his eyes.

The thought that within less than an hour he would be greeting his old Machlin friends and seeing his old Machlin enemies was deeply, but richly, disturbing. . .

Part Three

JEANIE'S BOSOM

LASSIE, MY DEARIE

DARKNESS HAD begun to fall as he turned Jenny's head into the Machlin Cowgate. In such a poor light no one would recognise him. Maybe he would be the last person anyone would expect to meet there. As he passed the Armour house all was quiet: not even a light glimmered in the windows. He guessed they were all abed.

But Johnnie Dow was at his back premises; and as he dismounted the landlord came forward to take the horse, recognising that the traveller would be staying the night. Then he fairly let a roar out of him:

"God Almighty, Rab! It's no' you!"

"It's no' my ghost yet, Johnnie: can you give a weary traveller a nicht's lodging?"

"Gie me a shake o' your han'. Damnit, man, Rab, are you hame at last?"

Johnnie Dow hustled him into the inn, calling loudly for his wife and making haste to fill out two generous measures of his prime Kilbagie.

"Michty bless and keep us a'! Rab Burns!" Mrs. Dow was plainly flabbergasted. "Gilbert said you would be hame ane o' thae days. . . How are you keeping since ye went to Edinburry and became sae famous . . . ?"

"You're richt there, wife: the maist famous man in Scotland! What did I aey tell ye? I kent it, Rab. When ye went awa' that morning I said to them that cam' in afterhan': 'There's Rab Burns awa' till Edinburry; and mark my words,' said I, 'he'll be the talk o' Scotland afore ye'll can say knife. . .' Didn't I, wife? If I should be struck doon dead this verra minute, Rab, that's exactly what I said."

"Aye, aye, Johnnie; and what's fresh aboot Machlin since I left? How's everything at Mossgiel?"

"Fine, fine; but ye'll be gaun up there the nicht?"

"No' the nicht. I'm tired; and I dinna want to upset them: I'll mak' a surprise visit in the morning."

"Juist as you say, Rab. Wife: awa' and see the bed ready. What hae ye a notion o' eating? Mind, we canna gie ye what ye hae been in the habit o' eating in Edinburry."

"A bit cheese and a bannock is a' I want the nicht, Johnnie. And I hae enough Kilbagie here to wash it ower."

"Aye, man: eh . . . ye'll hae heard frae the Armours?"

"Why should I? But how's . . . Jean?"

"Couldna be better . . . and twa bonnie bairns, Rab: twa o' the bonniest. . . I could still slip the ladder agin the back window? But maybe no' . . . eh?"

"Maybe no', Johnnie. She can wait till morning—along wi' the lave."

"Juist whatever you say, Rab. Juist whatever you say. Mind ye: she's still doted on ye. Oh, damned aye. Aey speiring for ony word about ye . . . even ony word i' the public prints. God, Rab, but she's keen on ye. 'Coorse, mind ye, that's atween our twa selves: if ye dinna want ocht to dae wi' her you can lippen on me never to say ocht."

"We'll see, Johnnie, we'll see. . ."

This news that Jean was still in love with him, that she hankered after news of him, gave him deep pleasure. Maybe he should risk the ladder against the gable window. . . If it got known, that would give Machlin something to talk about! He began to tremble. But whether from fatigue or emotional strain he didn't know. He was sitting alone in Johnnie Dow's kitchen. Dow was seeing to Jenny Geddes. His wife was seeing to his bed. The embers in the fire had burned very low. A strange mellow peace lingered about the corners of the room, a peace that he had never known elsewhere. Behind the wall of that peace lay Jean Armour and his twins.

He rose suddenly to his feet. He must make an attempt to have a word with her. But even as he did so the door opened and there stood Jean herself.

"I . . . I heard you had come back, Rab. . . I wasna sleeping and Mrs. Dow told me. . . You're no' angry . . . Rab?"

He stood staring at her, paralysed by the sudden onslaught

of emotion. The candle light flickered slowly across her features and glistened for a moment in her black hair. She stood in her bare feet. He noted the small well-spaced toes even as he had noticed them on their first meeting. The scarlet fringed shawl draped her shoulders lightly. She was more Jean Armour than ever she had been and a thousand times more desirable. The wave of passion that surged through him rendered him completely inarticulate. He could only hold out his arms.

In a flash Jean was being crushed in them. Their embrace was long and ardent. He was conscious of the warmth of the bed that was still about her. Never before, perhaps, had two lovers clasped and kissed each other with such strength and longing and passion. Jean gave a quivering strangled sigh that seemed almost to split open her midriff. . .

"I left the bairns sleeping, Rab. . . I'll need to slip back in case they wauken. . . I dinna want onybody to ken—and you'll come and see me in the morning. . . Oh, Rab: it's been a lang weary time waiting. . ."

Long into the night he paced his narrow room. He was back in Machlin and he was back where he began with Jean Armour. Worse than he had ever been: or better. God Almighty! what kind of woman was she that the mere presence of her could work physical annihilation on him, devastate him emotionally. He could be tempted by a thousand women. But the mere touch of Jean Armour's lips could do more to him than all the love-making of all the women he had ever known . . . aye, or all of them fashioned into one. And yet he had determined he would never get himself entangled with her again. . . As if that was a matter that could be determined upon by mere reasoning. He might as well face up to it: he had always wanted Jean and his life was lost and empty without her. Maybe if he got his farm. . .

But he was much too upset to reason about the future. The impact of Jean was still with him and the flood of his passion had not ebbed. In the morning he would reason things out and decide on a plan of action. Jean had assured him that there would be no difficulty now as far as her parents were concerned. But he wasn't sure about that and he wasn't certain he wanted to be sure. He would be damned if he would bow the knee to the Armours under any circumstances; and if James Armour thought that he would ever eat humble pie in his presence then he would damned soon learn his mistake. . .

FAMILY FAVOURITE

He rose tired in the morning though he was grateful to Johnnie Dow that he had let him sleep till the sun was well up in the sky. He washed and shaved, put on a clean shirt and had his best boots given a high polish. He made a light breakfast, and, despite the news from his landlord that the half of Machlin was waiting to see him, had Jenny saddled and brought round to the front door.

He pulled his hat well down on his brows, strode to the door, mounted Jenny and, without giving as much as a look round, turned down into the Backcauseway and went up the Kilmarnock road at a brisk canter to Mossgiel.

His brothers must have seen him approach for they came down to the road-end to meet him. Gilbert ran forward and grasped his hand even before he could dismount. Willie took Jenny's bridle. Beneath the simple words of greeting emotions ran deep. Gilbert's lip trembled.

The Bard did his best to break the tension as much for his own sake as for theirs. "Well, here I am, lads, as large as life I hope . . . and how is everybody? You've grown into a fair man, Willie, and you, Gibby, you're looking well: crops coming on all right?"

But even as he was talking, and they had turned into the Mossgiel loaning, Isa came running down to meet him, shouting and waving her hand. He lifted her up in his arms and gave her a hug. Everybody seemed to be talking at once and his head began to spin with the questions Isa kept firing at him. And then there was Bell, the tears running unashamed down her cheeks. She shook his hand; and before he could say a word she turned and ran back into the house.

Nancy received him at the door; and she was, outwardly at least, the most collected of the family.

"So you cam' back, did you? Well, we're richt glad to see you. And a great swell you are too. Come ben and see your Mither."

Mrs. Burns rose slowly from the fireside and held out her thin work-worn hand: "Weel, Robin: I see you've managed back . . . are you a' richt?"

"As richt as could be, Mither. You're keeping no' sae bad yoursel'?"

"I'm daeing awa', son. But sit doon: you'll be tired after a' your stravaiging aboot the country-side."

Nancy said: "You'll tak' a glass o' milk and a bannock till the dinner's ready?"

At long last he managed to escape into the steading with Gilbert. He mopped his brow with his napkin. It had been a nerve-shattering ordeal.

"Well, thank God that's over, Gibby: I've been dreading that since ever I left Edinburgh. But I'm glad to see everybody looking so well—including my wee lass Betty. You'd notice naebody said a word about her. . ."

"We're a' glad to see you back, Robin; and nobody wants to rake up the past: that's a' forgotten about. Mother doesna say much; but she thinks plenty. She canna just grasp the fact that you're as famous as you are."

"That's wise enough: there's bluidy little in fame, Gibby."

"Weel: you hankered plenty after it, Robin."

"Aye: an honest poet's fame—in so far as I was worthy of recognition. But it makes nae difference as far as the family's concerned. But tell me how things are doing wi' you, Gilbert. . . ?"

"Just doing away, Robin. . . Have you managed to make any definite plans for your future?"

"Plans? It's difficult to plan, Gibby, when you havena got anything to plan for. The money I sent you wasna very much,

maybe, but it was all that I could spare. I havena been paid for
my second edition. Not that I can expect that yet: it takes
time for the money to come in. But if it does come in I'll no'
forget you—though I'm hoping I can settle somewhere
modestly in a bit farm myself. I looked at Patrick Miller's
place at Dalswinton. I'm taken wi' it. . . But I would need
Auld Glen—or somebody like him—to come down and look
it over. I don't want to repeat the mistake we made when
we took Mossgiel. Not that we had any choice then. . .

"No, Gibby: I'm no' much further on than I was when I
left. . . I mean as far as a settled way of life is concerned. . .

"My immediate plans? Well, I've some money to collect
in Paisley and Glasgow. . . Then I'll need to be back in Edinburgh for August and try to settle up my affairs wi' Creech
and Patrick Miller. . . Oh aye: I'll be here for a week at least.
I'm sleeping at the Whitefoord Arms: you'll understand that,
Gibby? I mean: I canna come back and settle in here. There's
too many complications, wi' . . . one thing and another. . .
And I've so many folk to see. . ."

"I understand, Robin; but we could still make room for
you. . ."

"Thanks, Gibby; but you know how I left. What am I
for doing about my verses, did you say? As far as my verses
are concerned, I've made one decision that'll keep me going
for a while. I confess that I'm desperately keen about it. I'm
going to collect all the auld sangs o' Scotland that I can lay
my hands on—supply verses where verses are missing and so
preserve our ancient melodies. The first volume came out
when I was touring the Border country: James Johnson's
Scots Musical Museum. I've twa sangs in it: Green Grow the
Rashes and my verses on Peggy Kennedy o' Daljarrock. . .
I'll send you a copy. . .

"Aye, but your corn's coming on, Gibby. . .

"Jean Armour? I'll be seeing her, I suppose. We made a
bargain that we would take Robert to Mossgiel: I don't suppose onybody wants to go back on that. You ken I'll make
what payment I can. If you get a good harvest this year it
should make a big odds to you.

"Edinburgh, Gibby? It's a wonderful place—in its way; but it's no' the place that I would like to settle in. I met some sterling good fellows there; and I met plenty just the very opposite. It's a place of great contrasts. . .

"Marrying? No: I'm no' thinking about it, Gibby: no more than you seem to be. Maybe neither of us can afford that luxury. . . I met Gavin Hamilton's cousin, Peggy Chalmers. A fine lass Peggy: I'd marry her if I got the chance. . . But even although I sink whatever money I make into a farm, you ken as well as me it will mean slavery for the rest o' my days: at least it'll mean damn hard work."

Gilbert saw that he was restless and ill-at-ease. He gave up asking him interminable questions. No doubt he would be seeing a lot of him while he was in Machlin. He had changed: he wasn't the Robin who had rode away that November morning. But Gilbert didn't know how to assess the change. He was quieter, more sober, older, altogether more subdued. But he was harder to pin down, more elusive: the old bond of deep confidence between them seemed to have gone. Maybe he had acquired some of Edinburgh's ways and manners. And yet, if anything, he was more modest than he had been just before he left: the bold reckless defiance was gone. Maybe a good thing too: mixing wi' the gentry and the literati was bound to have rubbed some of the hard corners off him. But it was difficult to realise that here, standing on the Mossgiel ridge, with his hands in his pockets, was the same Robert Burns who had lately been the wonder of the gay world that was Edinburgh.

JAMES ARMOUR FORGETS

Later in the evening, when he could contain himself no longer, he knocked on James Armour's door in the Cowgate. His knock was answered by Mrs. Armour.

"Guidsakes it's yoursel', Mr. Burns! Wad you be pleased to step ben into the room?"

James Armour, rather shamefaced, rose and offered him his hand. "I'm verra pleased to welcome you, Mr. Burns. I hope, sir, that I find you well?"

"Well enough, Mr. Armour; and how are things wi' you?"

"Canna complain, Mr. Burns, canna complain. You'll have a drop o' spirit just to oil the welcome as it were?"

"Thank you, sir: I had called to have a word with Jean . . . and to see the twins."

"Certainly, Mr. Burns, certainly! I fully understand. Jean'll be verra pleased to see you and show you the bairns— and fine bairns they are, Mr. Burns, fine bairns. The wife and her are juist tidying the room upstairs; it'll be mair private for the baith o' you: I've nae doubt you'll hae private matters to discuss that's no' for our ears. Oh, I understand perfectly, Mr. Burns. I needna say how highly the wife and me regard the honour o' this visit. You've nae idea what a great pleasure it has been for us here to follow the success you hae made i' the Capital. Everybody in Machlin has got a lift through your success. We're a' verra proud o' you, sir. . . And, of coorse, ony wee bits o' differences we had in the past . . . weel, we never think about that noo. Juist a parent's feelings getting a wee thing upset as it were. Happens in the best o' families, Mr. Burns. But we'll say nae mair aboot it. Ah weel: here's the wife an' Jean wi' a bairn apiece. . ."

The sycophancy of the Armours disgusted him. But for the sight of his children he would have excused himself and fled from the house. . .

Upstairs, in the attic bedroom, he said to Jean: "What the hell's come over everybody? You'd think I'd come into a fortune?"

"It's juist that my folks are sorry for what they did, Rab: they're doing their best for to make amends."

"I was going to get angry, Jean lass; but I canna get angry wi' you: no' when I see the job you've made o' the bairns."

"They're our bairns, Rab. . ."

"Our bairns, Jean. . . I was speaking to Gilbert to-day

about taking Robert to Mossgiel as soon as you hae him richt weaned. . ."

"They're just aboot weaned noo . . . anither fortnicht, maybe. But I wouldna like to part wi' him afore the back-end."

"Aye: that'll be time enough, Jean. Now sit doon here on the bed beside me and tell me a' that's happened since I left Mossgiel. A' the news about Jeannie Smith and Eliza Miller and Jean Markland. . . But put the bar on the door first. I don't suppose we need fear ony interruptions?"

"We hae the place to oursel's, Rab, for as long as you like to stay."

"So your parents dinna mind you being locked up wi' a bachelor? I've a good mind to go now, Jean."

"If you want to gang, Rab, you ken fine I'll no' keep you. I dinna look for you to tak' up wi' me after the fame that's come to you in Edinburry. But I thocht after last nicht. . . You ken fine I wouldna haud you to onything that you didna want to be hauden to. But nae matter what happens you're still the father o' my bairns."

"Come and sit doon, lass, and dinna worry your head about the things I say: it's just that I'll never be reconciled to your parents whatever happens. . ."

He had come prepared to argue a very different case. He had come in a turmoil of emotion. There was the intense, almost unbearable physical desire that Jean had re-awakened in him—and there was the anxiety not to be caught in any compromising position. The Armours had relinquished any claim on him. Rather they had spurned him in the most contemptuous manner. He was determined they would never get the opportunity of humiliating him again, or of getting their clutches on him again. As for Jean: Daddy Auld had given him a bachelor's certificate. And a bachelor he would remain until such time as he decided of his own accord to surrender in marriage.

But he reckoned without Jean Armour and his deeply-founded love for her. He reckoned without that other force that was born between them the moment they came into contact—a force greater than any force of resistance either of them singly could command.

And so, even as he thought to argue with her, coolly and naturally, all the longing and love and passion that had ever been between them flared up in unbearable tension, a tension that snapped as rotten threads the bonds of restraint, prudence and caution. Caught in this elemental force they were helpless.

Downstairs, Jean's parents were congratulating themselves. Mrs. Armour had warned Jean on the lines her husband had indicated. Among other things, she had told her, that, if she watched herself, there was no reason why she should not secure the Bard for her husband. Jean had said nothing to all this. She loved the Bard so deeply she was prepared to let her love be her guide. She was desperately anxious to have him as her husband. But she was not prepared to intrigue towards that end. Well she knew he would be bound by love and only by love.

Jean was fundamentally fatalistic in her philosophy. What was to be would be. If Rab Burns wanted to marry her he would marry her: if not she would just have to dree her weird as best she might. Cunning and scheming and plotting were not parts of her make-up.

When Adam Armour came in with some of the younger children he was immediately packed out to keep them in amusement so that the couple upstairs might not be disturbed. Adam guessed what was going on. He grinned broadly and did what he was told. His admiration for the Bard was still as great as ever. . .

FRIENDS AND ENEMIES

That night he did not pace his room. He went to bed and enjoyed as sound a sleep as ever he had known.

In the morning he wakened late to find the June sun blazing

in at the window. When he got downstairs he found Johnnie
Dow very excited:

"The hale toon's asking for you, Rab. Damned if I've ever
kenned it to be sae set-up about onything. Baith Gavin
Hamilton and Doctor MacKenzie hae been asking about you.
Even Holy Willie was roun' snooping to see what he could
find out. Asking maist politely for Maister Burns! By God,
sir, it's changed days. I'm expecting Daddy Auld in ony
minute to gie you his blessing and the blessing o' the Session.
Nothing would surprise me noo, Rab. God! Jamie Humphry
was in the room last nicht telling a wheen o' them that you
had aince ca'd him a bletherin' bitch. Damned he was prouder
o' that than he'd gotten a gowden guinea frae you. But you
lay into your plate there and mak' a guid breakfast."

"Ah weel, Johnnie, I ken who were my friends before I left
for Edinburgh; and just as weel do I ken who my enemies
were. So it'll mak' nae difference to me what they think.
Though it seems a strange thing that a man has only to get
patted on the head by the Edinburgh gentry for everybody to
come crawling round about him."

"Crawling's the word, Rab. Their only fear is that you'll
no' recognise them. Aye; and that's no' the warst o't. There
was wee Tobaccy Ronald sitting ben there last nicht telling
the crowd that he had as guid as written some o' your best
verses. Ah, but some o' the lads werena for having that. And
they were a' asking where you were. 'Coorse I wasna lang
putting them aff the scent."

"To hell wi' them, Johnnie! I want nothing from them
and I hae nothing to give them. I'm damned if I'm for having
my private life snooped into as if I was up for a cutty-stool
offence. When they ask for me, tell them to go to hell wi' my
best wishes. Except my friends, of course; and I think they
are as well known to you as to me."

"Aye, certes: an innkeeper kens a' sides o' a' bodies' characters. And because you never gied a damn for the unco guid
you made some bluidy bad enemies as weel as loyal friends.
But if you were to ask me, Rab, I would say that you hadna
a better friend in Machlin than Wee Jamie Smith."

"I'm glad you ken that: I canna tell you how much I miss Wee Jamie's company."

"Aye; and he was as true a frien' to her across the 'Gate there as to you. An' it's no' often you can trust a frien' where a lass is concerned—especially the lass we're talking about."

"You dinna think. . ."

"Dinna mistake me, Rab: there's no' a truer lass in Scotland than Jean Armour. I should ken for I've had my eye on her here since she was born. Jean's as honest and clean as a drink o' spring water. But, by the Lord, she's a thundering topper —and there's been a gey wheen after her. Ah, but Wee Smith and her were mair like brither and sister. They used to play roun' the back when they were bairns. . . Aye, aye; and what d'ye think o' Machlin noo after the steer and bustle o' Edinburry?"

"I never realised before it was such a low-built place. I feel I could look over the biggins. But I suppose that's after the ten storey lands I hae been used to in the Capital. It's no' the place I thought it was, Johnnie: it's meaner than I thought. I canna right describe it; but the warmth seems to have gone out of its stones. Maybe it's me that's changed. And with Smith and Richmond away that does make a difference. . . When did you see John Rankine last?"

"Adamhill? He hasna been in this while back. But he's doing away from a' that I hear."

"Well, if you saddle up my mare and bring her round to the door, I think I'll ride up and see him now. Maybe you could send word over to Gavin Hamilton that I hope to pay my respects there in the evening?"

PRESENT FOR JOHN RANKINE

John Rankine nearly wrung the hand off him. "Man, Rab, and am I glad to see you! Let me hae a richt look at you. By God! but you're looking real handsome. Edinburry maun hae agreed wi' you: it's weel seen that you managed to steer clear o' the pox . . . or did you?"

"The only way you can steer clear o' that, John, is never to take ony risks. As usual, I took none."

"Aye, damn you; but sit doon on the plank here and enjoy the sun while I enjoy your crack. How lang are you hame for? For good, I hope."

"I micht be here for a couple o' weeks. . ."

John Rankine was insatiable for knowledge and information. He wanted a verbatim report of what had happened since the day and hour he entered Edinburgh.

"And so you didna get tied up wi' ony o' thae Edinburry Jezebels! That's a God's blessing onyway. Mind you, I feared for you, Rab: wi' the weemin, I mean. Oh, I never had ony fear o' you otherways. I canna say that I juist expected you to be hailed as Caledonia's Bard the moment you put your foot on the plainstanes. Damnit, that was a bit sudden. But it says a lot for the folks i' the Capital: the beggars there canna be sae blate after a'. Aye; and what you say aboot the whüres and the ministers is mair nor interesting. By God, sir, but there maun be some wicked places aboot Auld Reekie—and us puir gowks i' the country never as much as hearing a cheep. Ah, but ye did wise to steer clear o' the whüre-shops. Man, there's a lot to be said for the country wenches even when they are clarted up to the houghs in coo sharn. Coo sharn's clean dirt compared wi' the clart o' pox ye'd get aff a rotten whüre. . .

"So you're thinking, maybe, you'll tak' a farm frae Bar-skimming's brither? Weel, you micht dae weel enough aboot Dumfries. But see that Miller gies you the richt kind o' lease: drive the best bargain you can at the commencement. Yet I'm sorry to think you may be gaun out o' Ayrshire. By God, you've nae idea, Rab, juist how I've missed you. The place is no' the same! I hae a crack whiles wi' Gilbert when I fa' in wi' him. Ah, but Gilbert's getting gey sober since you left. 'Coorse he was aey a bit that way. And, mind you, I like Gilbert: a guid steady lad and nae nonsense about him. Only: what's life without a bit o' nonsense back and forward. . . ?"

As the Bard was about to leave his friend he produced a

present for him: "Just a wee bit minding I brought you from Edinburgh."

Rankine examined the silver snuff-mull with a thistle design on the lid and bearing an inscription. It flashed in the sunlight.

"Damn you, Rab, for a silly clown! What did you do this for? To hell, man, this is far ower kind o' ye."

"There's naebody I would rather mind than you, John: it's but a small token for all the many kindnesses I've had at your hands."

John Rankine was deeply moved: "This'll be handed doon the Rankine family till the Last Trump, Rab. By God, sir, and ye didna mak' a fool o' me. Come on in the hoose and hae a dram. . ."

DALJARROCK PEGGY

Gavin Hamilton had visitors that night. There was his wife and her sister Margaret Kennedy from Daljarrock, Doctor John MacKenzie and Robert Aiken the lawyer from Ayr.

They made a great fuss of the Bard; and between Hamilton and Aiken there was some show of rivalry as to which of them had contributed more to his initial success. MacKenzie was much quieter; but then there was little of boasting ego in MacKenzie. His keenness in the Bard's welfare was entirely disinterested.

Robin could not help but bask in his fame. It was very pleasant to find so many worthy folks—and folks for whom he had a great regard—pay him so much court. The Kennedy sisters went out of their way to pay him flattering compliments. But then Peggy Kennedy had always had a fondness for him even when she was but a blushing young beauty of seventeen summers. Now, at twenty-one, she had grown into a very lovely lass, possessing all the social grace and consideration—without any of the social snobbery—of the young dames who graced the drawing and assembly rooms of Edinburgh.

As soon as the congratulations and the cross-talk had died down and he was able to find his feet and compose himself to a rational remark, he produced his copy of *The Scots Musical Museum*.

"I'm sorry, Peggy, that I wasn't able to get my verses in compliment to you published in my second edition: the Edinburgh literati are touchy about compliments paid to unmarried ladies: they may even be more critical of compliments paid to married ladies——"

"Don't worry about that, Robert: it was more than compliment to me that you wanted to include them in your volume. Gavin told me at the time how disappointed you were. But then Edinburgh does do silly things at times."

"Still, it's an ill wind, Peggy; and what my second edition lost by way of a good song has been the gain of this new publication which has just been issued from the Capital. Perhaps the company will allow me a little explanation . . . ?"

And when he had explained to them the significance of Johnson's publication, and how much its future success meant to him, it was with considerable pride that he turned up the volume at the seventy-eighth song and handed it to Peggy Kennedy.

Immediately the company was all agog to see the song. Peggy herself wanted to know how the tune went. Although she could read music at the keys of her spinet, she was an indifferent sight-reader.

No one knowing the tune, *Loch Errochside*, she begged him to hum over the first few bars. They listened to his quiet unstrained crooning till he had gone through the air, verse and chorus.

"Why," said Peggy Kennedy, genuinely moved, "that was very sweetly rendered, Robert. I'm surprised you dinna sing."

"No, no, Peggy: I dinna mind humming through a tune; but I have no voice for singing."

"Well, I must thank you again, Robert, for choosing this lovely air for my verses: I think it fits them beautifully."

The company was unanimous in agreement. But it was MacKenzie who put the position clearly in words; and possibly he alone of the company, realised the full significance of the Bard's enthusiasm for Johnson's venture.

"I think I understand what you're after, Robert. I think we've discussed something like this before. But only now do I realise what it means to you. How much richer does a song become when you can have the melody to go with the words: the enjoyment is increased rather more than twofold."

"Much more than twofold, Doctor: I would go so far as to say that a song without its music isn't a song at all. . ."

"I suppose, Robert, that you write the words first and then search round for a melody to fit them?"

"No, Peggy: it's quite the other way round. I must have the melody first. When the rhythm of the melody and the balance of its notes have been fully absorbed then I'm ready to write. But I must have a model for my verses too."

Bob Aiken was thoroughly interested in this aspect of song-writing. "I can see that we're to be treated to a rare harvest o' new words to auld sangs; and I'm maist interested in the idea. But I dinna want you to gie up other pieces, Robert. You mauna desert your descriptive pieces and your satires. Man, your Address to the Haggis, and the Unco Guid, are twa thundering performances: I misdoot nor you've written better. . ."

But it was time for the ladies to retire. With her hand on the door Mrs. Hamilton said: "Peggy will be staying with us for a day or two yet, Robert: I hope we'll see more of you before she goes. Come round in the afternoon and drink a dish of tea with us . . . we've *our own* questions to ask you about Edinburgh."

When she had gone Gavin Hamilton rose and filled up the glasses: "Aye, aye, Robert: sae you won the heart and the good opinion o' the Capital, did you? Weel, that's a gey big achievement; and you have every reason to be proud o't. What I hope is that you're for making plenty o' guid siller out of the venture."

Aiken agreed: "That's a good point, Gavin. You made damn little out o' your Kilmarnock edition. And though I ken fine that Willie Creech doesna sell ony hens on a rainy day, I would like to think he took equal care no' to sell yours on a rainy day either."

Hamilton pressed the point: "Just what do you hope to make out of this second edition: has this Creech come to ony definite terms wi' you?"

"I have no reason to doubt that Creech will play fair with me. It takes time for money to be collected. . . But I've every reason to suppose that I'll clear some four hundred pounds by the venture."

Hamilton raised his eyebrows. "That's a tidy sum to rake in by way o' a book o' poems! A tidy sum, Robert. That would put everybody on their feet in Mossgiel."

"I hope it will help to put me on my feet too. I'm thinking of leasing a small farm from Mr. Patrick Miller, brother to Barskimming."

Hamilton's face betrayed some apprehension. "Oh you are! I thocht your interests would hae lain up the hill. Are you thinking o' getting married to some Edinburgh lass?"

"I may be able to take a modest farm, Gavin, but even a modest wife is a different proposition."

MacKenzie said: "Quite so, Robert. . . But I think it would be a good thing for you to get into a place of your own."

"Actually I would rather go into the Excise. Farming without sufficient capital is a heart-breaking business at best. At worst it's plain murder."

But none of his friends could countenance the idea of the Excise. They thought it was completely beneath him. A poetic farmer was one thing: even a heaven-taught ploughman could be tolerated; but an Exciseman-poet was not to be thought of: it was socially absurd.

All this Robin realised quite clearly. But he said nothing. These three men had been among the first to acclaim him and extend to him the hand of friendship. If they did not like to think of him as an exciseman earning an honest if prosaic livelihood, he would think no less of them. There was much they did not understand: there was much they could not be expected to understand.

But he was puzzled at the tone of Gavin Hamilton's voice when he had mentioned the four hundred pounds. Did Gavin honestly expect him to invest it in Mossgiel? Why should he expect him to do so? Surely it wasn't that Gavin Hamilton was thinking first of his own private interest? It was a chilling thought and the Bard dismissed it as an unworthy one.

The conversation shifted back to Edinburgh: to Sir John Whitefoord, the Duchess of Gordon, Henry Dundas, Dr. Hugh Blair. . .

And when the Bard had retired to Dow's, Aiken said to his host:

"He seems to have met a'bodies that matter aboot Edinburgh, Gavin. It's the maist extraornar thing I hae kent happen."

"It certainly is, Bob—I doubt we've mistaken our profession. We should hae taken to scribbling verses."

"Ah, but damned, Gavin, ye canna but admit that Rab Burns is a genius?"

"A poetical genius—yes. Dinna think I grudge him his fame, Bob. Maybe I think poetry can be over-rated. It cost him nae effort to write his verses—no more effort nor it costs him to breathe. You and me hae to work a damn sicht harder to earn our money—and Edinburgh gentry wouldna mak' a sang ower us gin we were in Edinburgh the morn."

"I see your point, Gavin—it's a thocht, aye, it's a thocht. But then lawyers in Scotland, and mair sae in Edinburgh, are as common as dogs gaun barefit."

"Maybe so, Bob—but there are breeds o' dogs—just as there are breeds o' lawyers—as weel you ken."

MacKenzie, who had left with the Bard, said as they walked slowly up the Bellman's Vennel to the Sun Inn: "Failure mak's a man a lot o' enemies, Robert. It's a sad fact; but there are folk that delight in kicking a man when he's lying doon. Plenty folk in Machlin thocht you o' little account when you first cam' frae Lochlea to Mossgiel. They found it gey hard to thole your verses—to say nothing o' your independent spirit. But success brings a man enemies o' a different kind. Envy and jealousy are ugly sins, Robert, and unless I've misjudged the world badly you'll meet wi' plenty. Oh, dinna worry—folk'll be nice enough to your face. Plenty that didna look the road you were on will be breaking their shins to get near you now. But behind your back they'll be misca'ing you for everything."

"I think I ken something o' the ways o' the world now, John. At least I've had plenty experience. I'll admit that I've been pretty well put out of conceit wi' my species since I came back to Machlin. It's the sneaking servility of people that sickens me. Only my best friends treat me like a human being. The rest. . . Well, what with insincere flattery and injudicious cross-questioning. . ."

"You mauna let it worry you, Robert: that's an attitude you'll meet wi' through life; and the more you succeed the more you'll meet wi' it. There's just one other bit of advice I would like to offer you and I do so in all friendship, Robert. Hang on to whatever money you make from your Edinburgh volume. It'll be a while maybe before you get the chance of earning so much again in such a short time. And in money matters never let your heart rule you: always your head. I don't mean by that that you should ever be mean. Indeed, I ken fine that that's something you could never be. But I can see you being foolish where other folks are concerned. And whatever you owe our good friend Gavin in friendship, dinna think that you owe him, or anybody outside your family, anything of a monetary consideration. And though I wouldna presume to pry into your family affairs I would even go the length o' adding a word o' caution there. Now I ken verra weel, Robert, that I've nae richt to be talking to you in this strain. But maybe you'll look ower my rashness for the sake of our friendship."

"I think I understand, John; and I dinna think I'm liable to take ony offence from you. Indeed, I'm more than grateful to you for your good advice. I see the value of it and I'll do my best to keep it in mind. Of course, I havena got my money yet: except what I collected before I left Edinburgh. And I'm hoping to keep living by what I can collect here in the West until I get back to Auld Reekie and settle up wi'

Creech. You see, John, I'm still as far as ever from settling myself down anywhere. Though I keep this to mysel' I'm desperately anxious to secure an Excise commission so that if I do finally settle wi' Patrick Miller, and my farm under him doesna prosper, then I'll have something to fall back on."

"There's sense in your scheme, Robert, and quite good sense. I can see your point, that, wi' small capital on a small farm, the margin o' security maun be verra narrow. And the continual worry o' insecurity would kill a horse far less a sensitive poet. However, Robert, I can only wish you the best of success and I hope that it'll no' be long till a' things come richt wi' ye. . ."

A SNUB FOR HOLY WILLIE

Willie Fisher thought it his duty as the Reverend William Auld's leading elder to acquaint him of the latest news.

"And now, Mr. Auld: what d'ye think? Burns is back frae Edinburry . . . bolder than ever, Mr. Auld, ooooh aye: bolder than ever."

"I'm fully aware that Mr. Burns is back among us, Mr. Fisher: you're fully late wi' your intelligence. Maybe ye think I go about Machlin wi' shut een and deaf ears?"

"Ah, but surely, Mr. Auld, you ken that I think nae siccan thing."

"I'm glad to hear that, Mr. Fisher. But allow me to tell you, Mr. Fisher, that Mr. Burns is now a verra distinguished man. Mr. Burns, Mr. Fisher, is now the celebrated Bard o' Caledonia."

"I'm aware o' that, Mr. Auld. Ooooh aye: the Bard o' Caledonia nae less! But begging your pardon, Mr. Auld, I dinna ken that I particularly agree wi' siccan a title. . . No', Mr. Auld, that I'm ony critic o' poetry; but—eh—I think wi' your guidance, Mr. Auld, that I ken something aboot a man's duty to God and His Kirk. Nor am I juist likely to forget on

a sudden the trouble Burns gave to the Session afore he went
to Edinburry."

"Ah weel, Mr. Fisher, your forgetting o' a' that will need
to be verra sudden: verra sudden indeed. As I told ye afore,
Mr. Fisher, Mr. Burns left our Parish free from ony scandal.
And so, while Mr. Burns is among us again, I trust, sir, that
you'll treat him wi' every respect and consideration. I hope
I'll hae nae reason to be disappointed in you, Mr. Fisher."

"Ah weel, Mr. Auld, ye ken fine that Willie Fisher has aey
been willing to be guided by you. But there are wee bits o'
principle that an Elder o' the Kirk has a richt to maintain as
ye weel ken, Mr. Auld——"

"And juist exactly what are thae wee bits o' principles
that are worrying you, Mr. Fisher?"

"Ooooh, naethin' much, Mr. Auld: naethin' that need
cause ony difference atween us. It was juist that I thocht I
wad mention my richts as it were."

"As it were. Indeed now! Go home, Mr. Fisher, and pray
for strength—and for some little enlightenment as to what
a principle may be. It so happens that I'm expecting Mr. Burns
here at ony minute."

"If everybody prayed as much as me, Mr. Auld, it wad be
a better parish; but I'll no' intrude on you ony langer, Mr.
Auld."

"It's no' how much a man prays that matters, Mr. Fisher:
it's the fervour and the *humility* that he brings when he *humbles*
himsel' afore his Maker."

But Willie Fisher slunk down the Bellman's Vennel muttering under his breath. It was a queer thing and a highly unfair
thing that he aey got the wrong side of Mr. Auld whenever
he mentioned the name of Burns. He had just to mention
the blackguard's name and immediately Mr. Auld was on his
stiffest dignity. And, danged, Mr. Auld had been verra stiff
the night: verra stiff. Verra dry in his manner, too: verra
dry. Aye; and he was having Burns up to the manse no less.
To hear a' the gossip o' Edinburry at first hand. Aye: Mr.
Auld's mind was a deep one to fathom. Right from the beginning he had had a soft side for the blackguard in Mossgiel.

It was all very difficult to understand; and Willie's understanding was limited. What he did not understand was Mr. Auld's attitude to him for he had tried to serve him with unswerving loyalty since ever he had assumed the duties of eldership. It never crossed Willie's mind that Auld might despise him.

But then it was quite impossible for the most despised man in the Parish of Machlin to believe, far less understand, that he could be despised.

DADDY AULD IS TROUBLED

The Reverend William Auld extended a thin bony claw towards his late parishioner. As he did so his great wrinkled forehead was lifted as if he were lifting, specially for the occasion, great heavy spiritual and mental cares from his consciousness.

"Well, Mr. Burns . . . I'm verra pleased to see you again and to welcome you back to Machlin and to the manse. May I congratulate you on the success, even fame, that you hae achieved in the Capital?"

"Thank you, Mr. Auld. I trust I find you in good health and spirits?"

"Fair enough health, Mr. Burns, a' things considered. The cares o' this parish advance wi' my advancing years. But wi' the strength that comes only from the Lord, I think I'll manage to wear out my time in His service."

"I can only hope that is so, Mr. Auld. But no one, I think, could grudge you a respite from your labours."

"Na, na, Mr. Burns: the Lord's work is never done until you lay down your burden in His bosom. But . . . eh . . . sit down, Mr. Burns, sit down. I'm interested in your success in Edinburgh. I spent many happy days there myself. Where were you biding? In Baxters' Close? Would that be the one below Lady Stair's Close? I see: oh, I ken the Landmarket as weel as I ken Machlin. A grand place, Auld Reekie. But a

Toon, unfortunately, no' lacking in wickedness either. There's much temptation aboot the Capital. I understand, Mr. Burns, that ye met everybody of ony consequence. And I'm verra proud to learn that you proved a great credit to your parish. I got my intelligence frae the Capital verra regularly. 'Coorse, Mr. Burns, ye ken that I was never under any doubt aboot your genius. It's a while noo since I talked to you aboot the gifts the Lord had bestowed sae lavishly on you. And I think you'll realise that ony chastisement I had to mete out to you was for your good. What I was wondering, Mr. Burns, is if you were thinking o' settling down again in my parish, or if this is only a passing visit o' yours?

"Juist a passing visit! I see, I see: I can understand that there'll be a lot o' ends o' business to be tied up in Edinburgh. . . Oh yes: a verra distinguished man, Mr. Miller: a verra successful man too, from what I gather. You couldna be in better hands. I understand you're for taking Jean Armour's boy to your mother at Mossgiel. That's verra worthy o' you, Mr. Burns: I would be maist happy to think that you were reconciled to the Armour family. It's a pity that you and Jean were ever guilty o' the sin o' fornication. It's a sin that has the way o' haunting a man and a woman long afterwards. But by easing Jean o' the burden o' the boy you're doing much to mitigate that. . . No', Mr. Burns, that I'm attempting to catechise you. That would be altogether outside my province here the nicht. It was juist that I could see a lot o' guid in the baith o' ye and I was sorry that it had to turn out the way it did. But the Lord's ways are inscrutable, Mr. Burns: sae we maun juist keep His commandments and seek His guidance and His mercy. . . And how was Mr. Richmond when you left him . . . ?"

Auld spoke quietly and sincerely. But he had mellowed. The light of Jehovian righteousness no longer flashed in his eyes and the thunder of damnation was no longer in his voice.

Or so it seemed to the Bard. Actually Mr. Auld was troubled; and he was human. He was troubled for he was by no means certain that Robert Burns was a reformed character; but he did not want any more scandal in his parish on his account. He was human in that he wanted to see him again and to learn from him how he had succeeded in Edinburgh. It was true that Auld had thought highly of his gifts; but his sudden and meteoric rise to fame in the Capital had surprised him as much as it had surprised any of his parishioners. And from every point of view Daddy Auld thought it best to be on good terms with Robert Burns. The Lord's ways were indeed inscrutable; and strange things could happen any day. . .

LASSIE, LIE NEAR ME

Jean Armour lay on the bed with him and the soft warm gloaming was all the blanket they needed.

"And what did Mr. Auld say about you and me?"

"What could he say, Jean? He hoped that I was reconciled to your parents and he admired me for taking Robert to Mossgiel. But what was there to say after that?"

"He didna say that you and me micht come thegither again?"

"For your sake, Jean, I can only hope that he never gets to ken how close you and me are thegither just now."

"You ken fine what I mean, Rab."

"I ken fine what you mean, lass. God knows: I suppose we're as much in love as ony twa ever were. But I doubt that we were ever meant to come thegither as man and wife. Even Daddy Auld never thought that."

"And are we never to come thegither, Rab? Are we to part again——"

"You ken I'm in nae position to get married, Jean. It'll maybe be long enough before that can happen. And by then you canna guarantee how you'll be feeling. You micht be married yoursel'!"

"No . . . I couldna marry anither man after knowing you, Rab; and you ken that weel enough. I'm making nae claim on you——"

"You've nae claim to make on me, Jean; and it wasna me broke up our marriage."

But even as he spoke he knew that he lied. Lied in a sense that had nothing to do with morality. He lied in a deeper sense. He should have done something for Jean when the trouble broke. And the fact that he was not in a position to do anything did not help him. The fates were against him; but they were against Jean in being against him. But for that, she would not have acted in the way she did. . .

"All right, Jean, we'll no' argue the rights and wrongs o' what happened. Maybe I was as much to blame as you were."

"But whatever happened, Rab, I should never hae denied you: that's the thing I can never forgie mysel': that's why I wouldna make ony claim on you. An' I've paid for my mistake, Rab . . . and I suppose I'll pay for it till the end o' my days. But nae matter what happens, Rab, I'll still love you."

"And I'll still love you, Jean: whatever happens . . . and whether we ever get married or no'. After a', you ken as weel as me that you canna bind love wi' a marriage ceremony. I ken the winter must hae been gey lang for you. Sometimes I felt it gey lang mysel'. It can be lonely in Edinburgh, Jean. You could be lonelier there than in the middle o' Machlin Moor. And many's the time in the closes and wynds o' Auld Reekie I had mind o' you and the tune you gave me ablow the green thorn tree. And sometimes, Jean, the memory o' you cam' ower me like a fever, like a madness. . . But then you've aey affected me like a madness. Mind you: I never thocht that you and me would ever lie thegither again. I knew I would see you again; and maybe I hoped that we micht manage a walk down by the banks o' Ayr. And yet I couldna see that happening either. You wi' the bairns on your hands. And then folks seeing us. I knew they would be watching every step I took. But I never expected this. Maybe we're fated never to lie thegither till we waken in the morning but must forever be parting when the hour's sweetest. . .

"When I was visiting Willie Muir o' Tarbolton Mill yesterday he was telling me that you sometimes managed out to see him and the wife: you could hae worse friends, Jean."

"Sometimes, Rab, when I couldna stand being here ony langer I used to get my sister Jenny to look after the bairns and I'd trek oot the road to the Mill. They baith think the world o' you; and they used to give me hope to carry on. Sometimes, Rab, I needed to meet folk that didna sneer at me; folk that had a kindly word for us baith. . ."

"A kindly word for us baith, Jean: that's real friendship. There's no' sae much honest friendship in the world. You ken that once you're out and about. I gathered from the Muirs that they had taken to you; and I would expect them to do that. Naebody that kens you could be angry wi' you: no' even me. . . Ah, but, Jean lass, I'll need to be on my way again: in a couple o' days. I've money to collect in Paisley and Glasgow and Dumbarton. I micht even take a turn up the length o' Ben Lomond when I'm there. Money's the curse, Jean: I canna dae without it now. And Gibby's looking for something to help at Mossgiel. . . Gibby and you never got on weel thegither?"

"It's no' my fault, Rab: I would speak to Gibby if he would speak to me. But he never looks the road I'm on . . . at least he pretends never to see me. Your sisters, if they see me, give me a nod in the passing. I suppose they think I'm at fault juist as my folks thocht you were at fault. . ."

"Aye, families can be the devil at times wi' their false notions o' loyalty. I'm no' surprised at Gibby. Gibby's rotten wi' respectability. He should hae been a Calvinist minister. He'd have made a good one . . . a modern Daddy Auld. There's plenty Gibby doesna understand in life. Gibby's foot will never slip wi' a lass: he's too bluidy decent and upright to have ony natural feelings or failings.

"I've arranged wi' Jeannie Smith and some o' the lassies we used to run about wi' to hae a wee bit party when I come back from my Glasgow visit—and you're to be there. Oh, I didna even hint that you and me had met much. I just told her I'd called—as it were. But Jeannie Smith has a lot o' understanding."

"Aye. . . Jeannie has been good to me. . . But you ken what her stepfather's like. An' ever since my trouble he's refused to let me come near the house. And he forbade Jeannie to come and visit me—though she cam' in a hidlin way when she could."

"You were more or less an outcast then—was it as bad as that?"

"It was as bad as that, Rab. Mony a time, if it hadna been for the bits o' bairns, I wad hae run away."

They lay silent for a while in each other's arms. The Bard's mental vision was terribly limited and it ended in a wall of utter darkness. He saw no road ahead for Jean and himself. There wasn't even a glimmer of light in the darkness.

And yet in Jean's arms he lay passive and contemplated the darkness. He was fatalistically calm. It was easy to lie calm and quiet in Jean's arms, easy to be silent in her presence at any time. Yet his relationship with Jean intrigued him. He had married her—his marriage had been "torn up"—she had borne him twins—and now he was back with her after six months' absence. Viewed calmly—and he was capable, lying quietly by her side, of viewing her calmly—she was a remarkable person. She was without anger; incapable of hating anybody; fatalistic—yet she was, deep down, the happiest and most contented being he had ever known. A strange mixture, Jean Armour; but a complete woman. Lacking in a knowledge of literature and philosophy, perhaps. But perhaps not. Jean didn't need books for her happiness—and she had her own philosophy and was not likely to change it for any brand that could be argued in words.

He had never met a lass like Jean Armour; and he doubted if there was another lass who had, in like measure, her total of excellent qualities and quiet virtues.

Maybe if he got a farm soon he would take Jean with him. Maybe. . . Yet, why was he not enthusiastic about the prospect of doing so? In some ways he was raving mad about Jean—in other ways he was coldly impersonal. Maybe the deep hurt of her denial still troubled him. Maybe this was why he could not think about re-marriage with her. Maybe that was why he hankered after a fresh wife and a fresh marriage. Maybe that was why he hankered after Peggy Chalmers. . . And yet, he couldn't see Peggy in a farm kitchen—at least not in his farm kitchen. She could grace any drawing-room in Edinburgh—something Jean Armour could never do. Unlike Jean, she could hold converse with any of the literati—and it would be fine to have a wife who could do that.

But, once away from Edinburgh, what drawing-rooms would any wife of his have the opportunity of gracing; and who of the literati would she be likely to meet?

Ah well: the problem of marriage would have to solve itself—and that wouldn't be to-morrow . . . or the next day. . .

THE FAIR ELIZA

He met Eliza Miller and they walked down the Barskimming road in the June dusk towards the banks of the Ayr.

Eliza was bright and her conversation sparkled.

"I thocht you would hae forgotten us plain maids o' Machlin after the fashionable dames o' Edinburgh?"

"Oh, they're no' that fashionable, Eliza. And after all: what difference do clothes make? It's hard to tell the difference atween one lass and another i' the dark."

"Aye . . . but you were never i' the dark where a lass was concerned."

"On the contrary—I was gey often in the dark."

"But no' that kind o' dark, Robert. In daylight or in dark nae lass ever deceived you—however many you may hae deceived."

"Oh—and d'you think me capable o' deceiving a lass?"

"You'd deceive ony lass—if she was fool enough to let you."

"In that case, Eliza, I'll never deceive you."

"That you—or any other boy—never will, Robert. . . But that's no' to say I'm stuck up."

"You go so far . . . is that it?"

"I'd hae gone ony length *you* wanted, Robert—you ken that."

"Aye—we did no' bad as it was, Eliza."

"D'you think I'm likely to forget . . . ? D'you remember yon night doon the Catrine Road . . . ?"

"D'you mind yon night in Ronald's stable?"

"Oh . . . Robert: you and me should hae been married."

"Think so, Eliza? I dinna think I'm the marrying kind."

"You dinna think——? You'll marry Jean Armour—despite a' you say—and a' you have said."

"And what makes you think that?"

"A woman kens thae things, Robert—and so do you. You've gotten a woman's understanding as well as a man's."

"You're no' suggesting I'm ony kind o' a Jenny Willocks, are you?"

Eliza went into a high-pitched giggle. "What! You—a Jenny Willocks! God forgie you, Robert. For a man, I dinna suppose there's anither man like you in Machlin Parish. That's what makes it sae hard to forgie you Jean Armour."

"And what harm has Jean Armour done you?"

"Ach, Robert. . . Jean Armour kens what you're like better than ony other lass—and I havena seen ony o' your Edinburgh dames."

"But I assure you, Eliza—Edinburgh was a Greenland Bay of Indifference to me."

"Robert! How can you say siccan things. You ken fine you couldna live a week without some lass or anither. I wouldna be surprised to learn ye'd had hunners in Edinburry."

"Oh, you wouldna—would you no'? Well, for once, Eliza, you're mistaken—sorely mistaken. I saw mony a damned fine lass in Edinbro—baith o' high and low degree. . . But why should I tell you things you wouldna believe onyway . . . ?"

"That's richt, Robert, dinna you tell me anything I wouldna believe—for I wouldna believe it."

"What about you and me going down the banks towards Stairaird?"

"Let's—only you canna get round me now the way you used to, Robert. But I'll go onywhere wi' you. . . Tell me—

and I'll never breathe a word to onybody—tell me honestly, Robert—how mony dames did you make love to in Edinburry?"

"You want an honest answer, Eliza?"

"That means you're no' going to gie me an honest answer. No: dinna tell me: I dinna want you to sin your soul on my account."

"You're a hell o' a lass, Eliza. But you're far off the mark —indeed you're no' in the same field as the target. And I'm sorry, Eliza, after a' that's been atween you and me that you should think me a common whoremaster."

"Oh, I never thocht onything like that, Robert—never! I wouldna be walking out wi' you now if I thocht onything like that about you. It's just, Robert, that I realise fu' weel that the woman isna born that could hold you for hersel'. And, of course, some women would rather hae a share o' a good man than hae an indifferent man a' to themselves. . . But siccan women are in the minority. I wouldna share you wi' onybody. Yet if I married you that's just what I'd hae to do—nae matter what you promised."

"Weel. . . I must thank you, Eliza, for your high opinion o' me. You're the first lass who has ever stated her case so clearly. Only, why the hell should I be faithful—as you call it—to one woman? Did you ever hear o' such a gowk before?"

"Aye, plenty—but that was because they never got ony other opportunity. Either that or they were frichtened."

"So that's what you think o' men, is it?"

"Listen, Robert, the man—if he is a man and no' a monkey —who can be trusted wi' a woman hasna been born yet."

"And what about the woman—provided she's a real woman —as far as men are concerned? After a', Eliza, it tak's twa to mak' a bargain."

"Aye . . . but women are weak creatures in the hands o' an unscrupulous man. You ken fine—naebody better—that after a wee while a woman has nae resistance left. That's how men tak' advantage o' lassies."

"Just like that? Women hae nae moral sense? They dinna ken when they're doing wrong?"

"Oh! I thocht you were the man that didna believe in

moral sense. You said you were the kind o' man that didna believe in religion. . ."

"Listen, Eliza: you've become a bluidy blether since I left Machlin. You didna walk doon here wi' me to talk a lot o' damned rubbish and to get me talking rubbish in reply. We're baith daft."

"Maybe we are; but dinna think that I cam' doon here to do onything else but talk. I've grown up since you went awa' to Edinburry——"

"So you have grown up, Eliza, and I didna notice that. Aye: you've grown up into a fine woman. You'll damn soon be a matron if you go on the way you're doing——"

"Are you trying to joke wi' me?"

"I wouldna try to joke wi' a grown-up woman like you, Eliza. That would be very foolish o' me, wouldn't it? Especially since you canna be deceived ony langer by a glib-spoken infidel like me. So I think we'll better turn and haud awa' hame——"

"Och, the night's young yet. . ."

"Aye, the night's young yet, Eliza . . . and you're young and all nature's young. And even the month's young, the month o' June. The month o' June, Eliza. It's a month that would break your heart wi' its beauty. As it has broken mine mony a time. You see the leaves on the trees there? Where did you ever see a green like that? If ever virginity had an emblem, had a colour, then that's it. . . God Almighty, Eliza, the freshness o' it is like a breath o' paradise. I wonder if we'll ever see sic a place—supposing there is sic a place? There's one thing, Eliza, we'll never hear music like that either in this world or in the world to come. The birds singing. . . True, they're past their best. You hear the best o' them in the early spring . . . wi' a smirr o' rain drifting across the ploughed land. But then it's so perfect that you juist canna bear it. I've listened to a mavis singing till I could hae grat like a great blubbery bairn . . . aye, and maybe I did greet. . . But, come June, the pathos is worn off the sangs. The birds hae mated and their brood is out and it's only at the end o' the day that they can spare the time for a sang o' rejoicing . . . a thanksgiving sang. . . A sang wi' joy in it and a lilt in every note. And yet whatna bluidy fools are we human beings gifted wi' sic superior wisdom and understanding? When do we sing? And the month o' June may come for us but once in a lifetime . . . and maybe it may never come. But when it does come, by certes, and we can sing too. That's the strange thing about life, Eliza: it's a great contradiction and never twice the same. Yet maybe we can recognise the general pattern: the mixtie-maxtie o' pain and pleasure and birth and death . . . and the only certainty is that having been born we die . . . some day sooner or later. And that's true o' everything that has life in it. And yet the birds sing and human beings sing as if death had no place in the scheme o' things at all. Oh, there's plenty to wonder at, Eliza; and for myself I never tire o' wondering."

"And I suppose, Robert, you could lie here wi' me a' nicht and wonder. And I believe I could lie a' nicht and listen to you. Nae wonder you mesmerized the folk in Edinburry. . . Are you in love wi' an Edinburry lass, Robert . . . ? Tell me what she's like? No, I'm no' jealous. I suppose I'm like the rest o' the Machlin lassies: I loved you and lost you. But I could love you still, Robert, if you would let me . . . if you would like me to. . ."

"You ken damn-well I love you, Eliza——"

"The same as you love the rest?"

"No' quite the same. Everybody has their own measure o' love. If a' love was the same there would be no point in loving ony particular lass: just ony lass would do."

"Sometimes I think just ony lass would do you, Robert. No: I dinna mean that: no' really. . ."

"So you dinna think I'm a libertine?"

"No, Robert, I dinna think that . . . no' now. I dinna think you would deceive a lass. You're no' deep enough; no' cunning enough; no' wicked enough. And then you would need to tell the lass what you were doing . . . you couldna keep your mouth shut, Robert: that's part o' you. . . You maun aey be speaking no matter what happens. But mind you, I like to hear you speaking. I dinna think onybody ever spoke like you afore. . . I mean . . . och, I dinna ken what I mean: you've got me fair daft wi' that tongue o' yours. . ."

They lay on the bank of the river Ayr where it murmured and gurgled its way to the sea. Not so far away he had courted Jean Armour; only a little further away he had courted Mary Campbell. . .

God's curse on him! Why had Mary Campbell to come back to him now? He had buried her deep, deep below his consciousness. Or he thought he had. . . And the night had been so perfect, perfect as only a Scottish June night can sometimes be perfect. . .

"You're shivering, Robert: surely you're no' cold?"

"Aye . . . it's getting a bit damp now: let's walk back. . ."

But Eliza Miller felt he was cold in a way that was far from physical. It worried her; for it had come over him suddenly and there was no explanation she could think of. Even his voice had grown cold and she thought she detected a trace of fear in it. . . Fear or sadness: she didn't know which. She had known Robert Burns in many moods. But usually she was able to find out what lay behind his moods. But not to-night. . .

And then his mood changed as suddenly: only there was desperation in him now. . .

"Listen, Eliza! We'll no' go home. It's no' so long ago that you were saying the night was young. Damnit: it's no' so much older now. You were aey a good walker. What d'you say if we walk down to Failford, up the Fail, and come doon the back road to Largieside and hame that way?"

"And how long would that take us, Robert?"

"No' that long; and maybe we'll no' go as far: we'll see. Only dinna let us go back to Machlin yet. You see, Eliza: I'll be leaving Machlin maybe to-morrow or maybe the next day. . . I'll maybe no' be back for a month . . . maybe longer: I don't know. . ."

There was no denying the urgency of his pleading. This was a mood in which Eliza could never resist him. Maybe it gave her a sense of importance; for it did seem that Robert Burns depended so much on her, needed her so much. And she liked to think that he needed her. . . Had he wanted her on the bank of the river she would have given herself to him willingly. Indeed she had been disappointed that he had not seemed to want her that way. Now it was different. If he wanted her now—and in whatever way he might want her—she was his.

It was the gloaming hour when the softness of the shadows smoothed away all harshness from the world and all hatred from human hearts. A gloaming night such as God chose to walk in the garden with Adam. A night when the shadows were softer than the softest hair that a summer's wind ever tossed on the brow of a dark beauty . . . the hour in which the lover walked with his beloved in silent ecstasy and the hush of immortality, quieter than the wing-beat of a tawny owl, was over all the land. . .

And in that twilight of all the Gods that had ever been or ever would be, the Bard held to the arm of Eliza Miller and fought desperately not to remember the touch and the accent of Mary Campbell now gathered to a gloaming that was indeed eternity, that was indeed the vast nothingness that had existed before the creation, that would exist again for every individual. . .

But no matter how he clung to Eliza Miller he could not keep the memory of Mary Campbell out of his mind. . .

Eliza behaved nobly. It seemed that she understood all that was wanted from her; and even though she did not fully realise what she was doing, she gave more of herself to the Bard than he gave her. . .

Maybe it was the night that did more for the Bard than Eliza. It was a night in which darkness never came. But about midnight there was a pause in the turning of the world; when the world seemed to stand still and when all nature was hushed, if not asleep; when a leaf turning on its twig could be heard from afar. . .

That night he lay with Eliza Miller at the back of a hedge and listened to her heart beating and heard the turning of his own thoughts. There was no difficulty in hearing Eliza's heart beating: never had her blood surged so riotously.

So still was the night and so still did they lie that rabbits came close to them; and they could hear their teeth tearing at the sweet dew-wet grass.

And when Eliza asked him why he did not marry her, he replied truthfully enough: "I canna marry you, Eliza, because I canna marry anybody. The God's truth is that I could marry—— Oh, maybe I could marry every likely lass that crossed my path who would give me something of her love in return. . ."

INQUEST ON MARY CAMPBELL

He had told no one about her; and he had given no hint that he was going to Greenock. But in his last days at Machlin the memory of Mary Campbell worried him deeply.

He rode into Greenock in the hope of learning something about her. . .

MacPherson's wife received him in a dither of excitement. She left him alone in the high bare room with Mrs. Campbell.

"God knows, Mrs. Campbell, what has brought me here. Your daughter Mary was my wife——"

Mrs. Campbell, very pale and emotionally taut to breaking point, could not prevent her lips from trembling. She was a small white-haired body—the Mary Campbell he had known grown old and grey with years of worry and poverty and hardship.

"You were never a husband to my dochter—and you should be kenning better than come here to torment me."

"I dinna ask forgiveness, Mrs. Campbell. Only God can forgive—now. But I didna come here to torment you. Aye, though you canna believe it, Mary and me were married—in the way we both acknowledged before . . . God . . . and man. Mary loved me—and—I canna tell you how much I loved Mary. I didna ken she was ill wi' the fever. The only word I ever got was that she was dead. And then it was too late."

"Then it was too late! And what aboot the bairn? That never gave ye a thocht?"

"Thocht! Oh well, Mrs. Campbell, maybe a husband, a father and a lover has no right to mention his grief in front o' a mother. But if Mary's death gave you a sorer heart than mine——"

"Dinna blaspheme, sir, and dinna deave me wi' your fair words and lang-winded explanations. Maybe God will be forgiving you what you did to poor Mary—but neither me nor onybody belonging to me ever will. I'd be obliged to you if you'd mak' your stay short."

"I canna mak' you believe what you dinna want to believe, Mrs. Campbell. But . . . you saw the Bibles I gave to Mary— you could read what I wrote on them? Maybe you saw some o' the letters I wrote her? D'you think—honestly, Mrs. Campbell—that the man who wrote what I wrote was a blackguard or a deceiver? If my only concern had been to deceive Mary, did I need to carry my deception to that length? D'you think now that Mary's dead and buried a deceiver would come back to plead wi' her mother?"

"And what are you pleading for?"

"Aye, what indeed? I dinna ask for my letters back: I dinna ask for the Bibles back. I came to see you, Mrs. Campbell, because—because you're the next best thing to seeing Mary. Because you're her mother and I thocht above onybody you would maybe understand. If only I had the chance o' explaining. . . But if I maun plead, Mrs. Campbell, it would be for some wee bit minding o' Mary, some wee bit memento."

"You didna try very hard to cadge some minding o' her after you ruined her and sent her awa' that May morning."

"And if Mary had been spared, what d'you think wad hae happened?"

"Ah, but then poor Mary couldna expect to be spared whan she let hersel' be ruined. No: Mr. Burns, looking at you and listening to you I canna say that you strike me a'thegither as being the blackguard I had thocht you. But I ken noo how you hae a saft tongue on you—and I think I ken how the saft words o' you got round my Mary. Oh, but I canna change— and I canna saften my heart to you. No' after what happened; and you canna expect me. You maun juist be going the way you cam'. The Lord'll deal wi' you in His ain time and in His ain fashion. I hae cursed you and a' that belongs to you—and I ken my curse'll be answered. You may mak' a name for yoursel' as a poet. But you'll never—and yours'll never—ken happiness this side o' the grave. What waits you after that I'm content to leave in His hands. And if I'm doing you an injustice, may He forgive me."

"And that's your last words to me, Mrs. Campbell?"

"I've naething mair to say—laddie. Except that if you did love my lassie you loved her without God's blessing. Sae your love wasna a clean love. . ."

Mrs. Campbell sat into the window. As she spoke she looked out from the high window across the shimmering firth to the great Highland hills. Her thin blue-veined hands clasped and unclasped on her lap. Her profile in the light seemed thin and sharp and unusually pale as if drained of blood and emotion.

Yet the Bard realised how distraught, how deeply agitated she really was. There was no point in his staying and there was no point to his pleading.

"I'm sorry if my coming here has upset you or caused you distress in ony way. And if I canna accept your censure, Mrs. Campbell, neither for mysel' nor for Mary, I think I can understand how you feel and why you feel the way you do. And, in bidding you good-day, I can only hope that time will soften your judgments—and ease the burden o' your grief."

If he rode out of Greenock a wiser man (making along the banks of the River Clyde towards Paisley and Glasgow) he was also a much sadder man.

Life was a tragedy; and part of that tragedy lay in the fact that a man could love—and love sincerely—more than one woman. For if he had gone to the Indies with Mary he would have left a heart-broken Jean Armour in the Cowgate. And it wouldn't have lessened Jean's heartbreak any to know that she had brought it all on herself. . .

CAMPBELL COUNTRY

He rode into the weavers' town of Paisley, saw bookseller Alexander Pattison and his friend Cowan, and spent a friendly, hospitable night with Cowan and his family.

On Friday morning, 23rd June, he rode out from Paisley into Glasgow. Glasgow he found a pleasant town of fine broad streets and low buildings, many good orchards, fine gardens and meadows. He had no occasion to make contact with its striking backlands. His business done with Smith the bookseller there (and he was annoyed to discover that he had been under-supplied to the extent of fifty copies for the subscribers) he went early to bed. There was nothing to hold him in Glasgow, no more than there was in Paisley; and he intended next morning to ride into Dumbarton and make contact with John MacAulay and the good citizens of Dumbarton who had subscribed so liberally to his edition. If he did not manage to collect money there he would at least determine whether or not they had got their subscription copies.

When he arrived at Dumbarton John MacAulay was absent; but on Mrs. MacAulay advising him that there was a good inn at Arrochar, he determined, the day being Sunday, to push into the Highlands and see Loch Lomond. Assuring the guidwife of Levengrove House that he would return in a couple of days, he thanked her for her hospitality and rode on.

He had become restless and ill-at-ease ever since that interview with Mary Campbell's mother. He had been unable to relax; and as he rode on into the Highland hills he found his restlessness increasing. Not even the beauty of Loch Lomond, glinting beneath the watery sun, arrested his attention. The whole countryside and its inhabitants seemed somehow savage and barbarous.

The rain had ceased that morning; and everywhere great burns came tumbling and roaring down the mountain-sides, a cascading of brown peaty waters and tawny foam. It was a tortuous road with many rude crooked-backed bridges; with a scrubby vegetation of heather and bog-myrtle, alders, hazels, birches and oaks. Down below, the loch lapped into small shingly bays; and across the water the great rugged base of Ben Lomond dropped steeply into the loch while the cone-top seemed to thrust towards the white low-hanging clouds. But all around there were mountain tops stretching into the horizon. What animal life there was consisted of wild lean sheep and wild lean cattle. Of Highlanders there were few; but the few he saw were the most wretched beings he had yet seen on his travels. They were poor and dejected. The imprint of a dour and sullen rebellion was on their unwelcome unsmiling faces.

With every mile that Jenny Geddes carried him into the hills, the countryside became wilder and more desolate. How the ' Wild Highlands ' had been subdued was a mystery. Surely if the Highlander had stayed in his rocky fastnesses he could have defied any conqueror . . . ?

At Arrochar, on Loch Long, where he found lodgings for the night, he fell in with Dr. George Grierson who intended travelling the next day to Inveraray on a small matter of business. The Doctor suggested that the Bard might accompany him. . .

Inveraray was the seat of the Duke of Argyll. The Duke had subscribed to his Edinburgh edition and had expressed himself to Creech as being interested in the Scots Bard. There seemed no reason why he should not find a welcome on the shores of Loch Fyne.

But it was a long sore road to Loch Fyne; and an incredibly rough and steep road led them through Glen Croe. As they ascended into the glen, the Bard thought they would have to go over the mountain tops to get out of it. And that was what they had to do. They reached the top of their perilous climb with difficulty. At places the track was washed away with the rush of the mountain tarns—sometimes they seemed more like waterfalls, so steep was their descent. At the top they rested beside a large stone which, the Doctor told him, was known by the name of Rest and be Thankful.

And they rested and were thankful. In the shelter of the stone they were warm in the sun. For all that the wind swept through this high pass in the hills. In its sound was the sadness of many centuries.

Behind them rose, in rocky ledges, the Hill of the Lochan: in front was massed the great bulk of the Butter Hill, its summit more than three thousand feet high. Looking down into the glen from which they had climbed, they could still see the hill-tarns pouring down from the steep shoulders of Ben Dorrich, the Brack and the Cobbler, making the Croe Water churn over the boulders like an endless flow of buttermilk.

It was a scene of Ossianic grandeur; but the Bard did not respond to it as he responded to the Ossianic saga. Maybe it was that he missed the great mythical figures of the Ossianic God-world. Or maybe it was that, in the Highlands, his heart was still in the Lowlands.

Outwardly, as he rested his back to the stone and Jenny Geddes recovered her wind and cropped the tops of the coarse mountain grasses, he appeared to the observant Grierson as calm and unemotional a fellow as he had ever met with.

"Is this your first time in the Highlands, Mr. Burns?"

"Yes."

"You're not impressed, I take it?"

"Impressed? I don't know. I'm afraid I'm not in the mood to appreciate scenery, Doctor. Oh yes: it's an impressive scene —in a savage, barbarous way."

"More so than Loch Lomondside?"

"Much more so. Especially to be within a day's ride of Glasgow. Had this been the far North I wouldna have been surprised."

"Just what is it that surprises you, sir?"

"That the Highlands were ever conquered. Especially by South'ron billies. One sturdy fellow with a battle-axe should have been able to hold this pass."

"Yes . . . but what about the Campbells in the rear?"

"Maybe I was forgetting the Campbells."

"That's one clan you canna afford to forget, Mr. Burns—not when thinking of the Highlands."

"Maybe I have good cause to remember the Campbells."

"Meaning?"

"Meaning just what I say, Doctor."

"I didna mean to be inquisitive, Mr. Burns. There is much Jacobite sentiment still flourishing in Scotland—aye, and in England and in France."

"And I take it that you are no Jacobite, Doctor Grierson?"

"Nor, do I take it, are you, sir."

"What the hell does it matter—now? There are more desperate problems facing us to-day."

"Agreed. Most heartily agreed. But how many of our present day problems arise from the effects of the late Rebellion?"

"Sir: I have little patience for quibbling. I own allegiance to no king. But I own less to Royal Geordie. And if you want to report me as being disaffected——"

"No, no, Mr. Burns. Dinna think that whatever you do. Your sentiments are indeed very near my own. True enough I own allegiance to Royal Geordie as you ca' him—but merely out of necessity. But I don't know that I would have been any more loyal to Charlie Stewart. We are many of us, my dear Burns, in a like dilemma. We have lost our nationhood. But I doubt if we ever had a real king to lose unless we go back to Bruce——"

"Or Wallace?"

"Ah, Wallace. Yes. Guardian, not king, of Scotland."

"Hum! Well, let's get on our road to Inveraray, Grierson—now that we understand each other a bit better. Or do we?"

"What exactly do you mean?"

"Nothing. Indeed, sir, I havena a mind the now to discuss affairs o' state. You'll need to pardon me if you find me dull—and impatient."

"You're needing a holiday."

"I've been on holiday since the beginning o' May. Maybe I'd be the better o' some good hard work."

"Yes. Work can be a wonderful specific."

"Aye; but it doesna stop you worrying either. Come, sir: let's mount."

They continued their journey and made tolerable progress down Glen Finglass where height alternated with hollow, like the waves of the sea, between Binnein an Fhidhleir and Beinn an t-Seilich, till they came round by the Kirk of Kilmorich and Cairn Dhu and so to the head of Loch Fyne.

The Bard found the long narrow arm of the sea more attractive than he had found either Loch Lomond or Loch Long. The shores of the Loch were pleasantly wooded and they were sheltered from the sun, while a cool breeze blowing up the water took the edge from the day's heat.

They were now approaching the very heart of the Campbell country. Here the native Highlander, if as poor as his Loch Lomondside neighbour, was much more arrogant. However heavy was the hand of Argyll on the land, it was *his* land; and no stranger—from wherever he came—would dispute with that. Inveraray was the last place for anyone to come to pick a quarrel with the Great Argyll.

For his own part, the Bard had no quarrel with Argyll; and as Caledonia's Bard he had no reason to suspect that his welcome might not be a friendly one. But then he reckoned without the temperament of the Duke's vassals. Edinburgh might have proclaimed a ploughman from Ayrshire as the Bard of Caledonia; but what cared the Campbells for that! It is true that the Duke had lent his distinguished patronage to the same poet; but then the Duke did many strange things in Edinburgh...

For all that the Bard entered Inveraray with a light heart. It was little more than a cluster of mean thatched houses clustering round the Kirk and the Courthouse beside the gates of the Duke's estate. There was indeed an inn of sorts in the village and to this they repaired.

The landlord kept them waiting his pleasure; and when he did come to his door it was to inform them, with little ceremony, that he had no pleasure for them at all. He was full up. He had no room for strangers. The Duke, his Lord and

Grace, had many guests at his Castle, and he had enough to do attending to their servants and followers. He might, indeed and whatever, give them a kind of a meal that would take them back the road they had come, or forward the road they might be going. But it would be but a poor meal for he needed all the scanty food he had for the Duke's visitors.

Never before had the Bard met with such contemptuous incivility. Ever quick to react to the effect of boorishness, he rashly asked if he could be directed to someone who could offer them hospitality. At this the foxy bloodshot eyes of the landlord hardened.

"I am the only man who will have the authority to be putting up any strangers about Inveraray; and if there is no room at my inn there is nobody hereabouts that will be as much as giving you a corner to lie in with some bodach. . ."

And with that the surly Highlander returned to the depths of his inn. The Bard and Grierson, rudely shaken by their reception, sat into a table. Grierson was the first to speak.

"I'm sorry for your sake, Mr. Burns, that this should have been our welcome; but in truth I should have expected something of the kind; for here there is but one authority and that is the authority that comes from His Grace, the Duke, through his servants. My business in Inveraray will not take me long. I suggest that if you care to wait for me, we will return to Arrochar immediately. We at least are promised a bite of food. Our poor nags will have to content themselves with what grass their miserable sheep and goats have left them on the roadside. At the same time, Mr. Burns, I would not have you think that all Highlanders are like the Inveraray Campbells; and if we return by Loch Lomondside I hope I shall have the pleasure of introducing you to some Highlanders who have at least civilised notions of hospitality."

But the Bard was listening with only half an ear. He was planning his own form of revenge... And when Grierson was gone he took out his diamond-pointed pen (a present from the Earl of Glencairn) and wrote on a window pane:

Whoe'er thou art that lodgest here,
    Heaven help that woefu' case;
Unless thou com'st to visit Him
    The Lord *their* God—His Grace.

There's Highland greed, there's Highland pride;
    There's Highland scab and hunger;
If heaven it was that sent me here
    It sent me in an anger.

With that the Bard felt mollified. He had to leave some record of his treatment here in the miserable clachan the Duke of Argyll kept within the circumscription of his sporran.

When Grierson returned he was delighted with the epigram and pencilled it down in his leather-bound notebook.

Presently a slatternly pale-faced pock-marked Campbell wench appeared and unceremoniously pushed two bowls of cold mutton broth towards them. Neither Grierson nor the Bard, ravenously hungry though they were, could make much of it. They agreed to return to Arrochar.

"In any case," said Grierson, pointing to the inscription on the window pane, "there'll be the devil to pay for that when our scurvy landlord sees it. It may, however, take him a while to spot it. Prudence, I should say, dictates that we put as many miles between us and Inveraray as our jaded nags will cover."

They rode out of Inveraray seeing nobody but some small ragged children chattering in Gaelic. Folks were trained to keep indoors when strangers passed through the village— though they could peer at them through the rags that covered the small ventilation holes in their dry-stone walls—the rude apertures that served as windows to let in the minimum of light and emit the minimum of foul air.

And as he rode past the Duke's gates, the Bard remembered how James Armour from Machlin had once worked as a mason on the Duke's castle. It would be interesting to compare notes with him when he got back—provided he had then the stomach for such a conversation.

HYMN TO THE SUN

At Arrochar they rested in the inn where the landlord was much more pleasant—though whatever he may have thought about the Campbells he was careful to say nothing that could be quoted against him.

Here the Bard availed himself of the opportunity to write a letter to Bob Ainslie who was back in Berrywell and had recently sent him a letter dated from Innerleithen.

It was pleasant, after the inhospitable wildness of the Argyll country, to cast his mind back to the pastoral greenness of the Merse and to brood again on Rachel Ainslie.

But it wasn't so pleasant to think about Peggy Cameron. The news Ainslie had sent him concerning Peggy hadn't been too good. It seemed, indeed, that she dated her conception from April. . . According to Ainslie she bore no external evidence of being pregnant. . . It was all very disquieting and he began to think that Peggy had tricked him. She hadn't seemed that kind of lass. But then, why had she complained that the two old women had discovered her condition?

April to May; May to June—she could have held on for another month at least. . . But that was the damned thing about women: you never really knew how you stood with them.

Maybe she had battened onto his fame with the idea of making as much out of it as she could . . . !

And yet, maybe not. Maybe he was doing Peggy an injustice. Maybe; but the seed of doubt was there. And now he would never know for certainty that her child would indeed be his. Neither Betty Paton's lass nor Jean Armour's twins bore any resemblance to him that he could see. Dear-bought Bess was her mother all over. And if Jean's twins weren't Armours in appearance he'd be damned to know what they were. . .

But he hadn't long to brood over his worries in Grierson's company. The Doctor was anxious he should join a party that

431

was planned to pass the night in a gentleman's house on Loch Lomondside. It was to be a mixed party and there was to be singing and dancing and general merry-making.

The Bard welcomed the idea. He was desperately in need of a night's social fun.

So they rode down the Lochside to Bannachra, near Arden. Here their host, Mr. MacLauchlan, his son Duncan, and his daughter Mary, made them very welcome. They had as guests a MacFarlane from Jamaica, merchant John Sheddan and his daughter from Glasgow, Mr. Gardner from Ladykirk and the two Misses Butter from Edinburgh.

If the Highland welcome at Inveraray had been an occasion for cruel satire, Bannachra proved the opposite. They danced and sang and drank until three in the morning. The fun was often fast and sometimes furious. When they relaxed the ladies sang songs, good honest Scots songs, and sang them very sweetly. When they had recovered from the strenuous vigour of throwing themselves into *Bab at the Bowster* they set to on *Tullochgorum* or *Loch Errochside*.

At three o'clock the ladies retired; and the men gathered round the punch-bowl. The Bard found that the Glasgow men could drink as hard and tell as merry a story as the men of Edinburgh.

At sunrise they all followed their host out to the lochside and waited till the sun came over the top of Ben Lomond. Maybe they were drunk; but they were far from being beastly drunk. They were sober enough to drink to the sun and drunk enough to realise that the sun was worth drinking to. While Duncan MacLauchlan kneeled down on the earth and held the bowl towards the light, the Bard pronounced a benediction in the form of an incantation: a mumbo-jumbo that might mean nothing or might mean anything—according to the state of mind of the hearer. . .

FREEDOM OF DUMBARTON

It was difficult to believe that only a few miles and a hilly pass separated the wildness of Argyll from the happiness that breathed so joyously around lower Loch Lomondside. . .

Yet when he, Grierson and Gardner went down the lochside making towards Dumbarton some time later (having previously dined and wined with Mr. Buchanan of Arden) they were confronted with tangible evidence that a native life, however barbarous, existed independent of the big houses of the Glasgow merchant princes.

No sooner were they on the road that led from Arden than a Highlander passed them riding a horse without saddle or reins or anything that usually harnessed a mounted horse. The rider was a kilted Highlander and he held onto the mane of the horse and didn't seem to mind that his bare backside might be rubbed into quick-flesh—either that or his hindquarters had been worn by usage into a hide as tough as saddle leather.

Be that as it may, the Highlander constituted a challenge to Lowland horsemanship. The Bard drew his crop along Jenny's flank and urged her forward. But after a chase, during which the Highlander proved himself to be a tolerable bareback rider, he suddenly drew his mount across the road with the object of blocking the Bard's path. But the movement was much too sudden. Down came his horse and a second later down came the Bard and Jenny Geddes on the top of them. But not before the Bard had a vision of the Highlander's bare hurdies go sailing through the air to land in a clipped hedge.

His companions came to his rescue. But apart from some bruises and a few cuts he was little worse for his fall.

Jenny Geddes escaped with the least hurt and the Bard was able to mount her and ride on, having ascertained that the galloping Gael had suffered no more than a bottomful of petty lacerations that would prevent him riding bareback for at least a month.

At Dumbarton, a couthy township sitting on the banks of the River Leven where it joined the River Clyde, the Bard was royally entertained by the Town-clerk, John MacAulay, and some of his friends at Levengrove House. He had many admirers in Dumbarton and not a few of them had subscribed for his Edinburgh edition. The next day he attended a Masonic meeting and the next he was presented with his burgess ticket and given the freedom of the town. The Bard noted with satisfaction that Provost James Colquhoun gabbered and habbered much less than Provost William Clark of Dumfries.

But though the magistrates presented him with an attractive folded burgess ticket, he reckoned without the Reverend James Oliphant, minister of the town—and late of Kilmarnock.

Oliphant had been satirised unmercifully by the Bard when he had been inveighing against the narrower of the Old Light Calvinists—and the Reverend James had not forgotten.

The next day being Fast-day in Dumbarton, he fairly let himself loose and denounced the magistrates for their heinous crime of honouring the author of vile, detestable and immoral publications—the Reverend James not deigning to refer to such a grossly secular subject as poetry.

The magistrates, who were present in force (Oliphant was their nominee) writhed under his thundering invective. Afterwards they decided to withhold minuting the freedom cere- mony and conveyed their decision to Oliphant, who, though still breathing fire, brimstone and eternal damnation, was somewhat mollified. The magistrates (including their clerk, John MacAulay) decided to communicate nothing of this to the Bard.

And so he said farewell to Doctor Grierson and Gardner and took a very cordial goodbye with John MacAulay and his family at Levengrove House.

Having been ferried across the shallow Clyde at Dumbarton he proceeded home to Machlin by way of Johnstone and Kilmarnock.

COWGATE NIGHTS

Back at Johnny Dow's in Machlin he completed a letter to Jamie Smith at Linlithgow, drank a pint of ale and reviewed his position.

His week's jaunting hadn't been wholly in vain. He had renewed some valuable acquaintances, made some new friends and had collected a few much-needed pounds of subscription money.

He was glad to be back in Machlin—glad that once more he would be seeing Jean Armour and Jeannie Smith and Eliza Miller . . . and Gibby and Willie and . . .

Aye: he was glad enough to be back among them again for this was indeed the only place he could call home.

And yet it was no longer home. No matter what happened he could never settle again in Machlin. He would have to make a home somewhere for himself.

To-morrow was the first of July. Time passed quickly nowadays. But not quickly enough so far as his settlement with Willie Creech was concerned.

The noises of Machlin—drowsy human noises—cut across every now and then by the shrill cries of bairns at play—came in at his open window. His window looked straight into the Armours' house: maybe Johnny Dow had been cunning enough to give him a back room.

He could feel Jean's presence across the narrow gap. But then he had felt her presence in Edinburgh and in the Borders. There was nothing to surprise him here. Jean was ever in the topmost layer of his thoughts just as Mary Campbell was in the nethermost layer. He needed but to go downstairs, cross the gap, and in a minute he would be in Jean's arms.

He might write to Jamie Smith or Willie Nicol or he might conjure plans concerning Creech; he might think of the songs he would send to honest James Johnson and his *Museum* . . . but always mixed with his plans was the voice of Jean Armour and the taste of her flesh. . . .

435

Damnable the way the dice-box of fate threw her verdict. He had drawn to Mary Campbell in an attempt to heal the wounds Jean Armour and her family had so grievously inflicted on him. And now—for it was as much for this as for anything else—he was flying to the arms of Jean in order to staunch the flowing wound that Fate—through Mary Campbell—had inflicted on him.

Was he never to be rid of the deep agony of Mary's cruel death? Reason told him he had nothing to do with her death while something much deeper than reason told him he alone was responsible. If, somehow or other, he could have got to Mary's side maybe she would not have died. . .

He went down to Johnny Dow's kitchen for a drink. It was still too early to visit Jean—he would wait till the gloaming had blurred the outline of his movements.

The gloaming—and the blurring . . . a fit atmosphere. Everything was blurred now and the gloaming was over against his future.

Ah well: to-day was to-day and to-morrow would need to look to itself. Hell roast anybody that thought he was doing wrong in going to Jean Armour's bed in the darkness. And hell roast them if they thought he was going there for sex alone. Sex there was with all the sweetness of honey; but there was something more substantial and more sustaining than honey. There was love and understanding, the complete acceptance of one human being by another—and no questioning, no recriminations. The memory of Mary Campbell might haunt him to the point of making his conscience stampede; but the personality as well as the flesh of Jean Armour signified deep fulfilment.

That night he said to Jean:

"Sometimes, Jean lass, I think I just canna do without you, I'm so fond o' you . . . aye, and the bairns. . . But I canna settle down here again in Machlin. I'll never be able to do that—never! Mind you: I'm no' denying that I had many a happy day here. But the heart's gone cold on me now. Davie Bryce is away, Richmond's away and Wee Jamie's away. And maybe I miss Wee Jamie most of all. Machlin's no' the same

without him.   Even Daddy Auld's no' the same—nor even
Holy Willie.   Mossgiel's no' the same either.   Six months—
and I'm a stranger in my own home.   Of course my mother
says I was aey a stranger at my own fireside.   That's a queer-
like thing for a mother to say.   But it's true enough in a way.
For years I spent my nights onywhaur but at my mother's
fireside.   It's no' that I hae ony unnatural feelings towards
them—the very opposite.   I bought them a' dress lengths o'
mode silk when I was in Glasgow. . .   But it's one thing liking
folk—especially your ain folk—and it's another thing living
wi' them.   Mair so round a crowded fireside.   Maybe things'll
be different gin I manage to rake in a' my money from my
Edinburgh edition. . .   But just when that'll be, Jean, is mair
nor I can say.   Aye, fegs, it should be a simple enough matter
taking in the bits o' bawbees.   But nothing's simple, lass, when
you come to deal wi' the lang-headed business chiels o' Embro.
Nothing's simple and everything's cent per cent and a wang
o' profit here and a kebboch o' expense there, till the cheese o'
your endeavour's whittled away. . .   I can see I'll no' get my
money this side o' the back-end.   So I'll need to make Embro
early in August, to catch Willie Creech, my publisher, when
he comes back frae his holiday—the Embro folk usually holiday
about the month o' July.

   " God, Jean, you'll never ken the nichts I lay in Auld Reekie
—and it's well named—and thocht on you and the twins lying
ablow the thack here.   Especially on a moonlicht nicht—I aey
seemed to think on you when I saw the moon on the tops o'
the high roofs. . .   God damnit, lass, mony's the time I ate
my heart out thinking on you. . .   Oh, dinna worry: the
Embro dames are ten-a-penny and frae what I hear aey have
been.   But what's an Embro dame?   No, Jean: you ken I've
had mair nor ae lass in my day—and I'm no' promising that
I'll no' hae a wheen mair afore I'm finished. . .   I micht as
weel be truthful. . .   Oh, you've aey kent that, have you?   Oh
weel, you'll ken I'm telling you nae lies.   But I'm telling you
nae lie, Jean, when I tell you that I've kent nae lass that could
hold a candle to you.   Somehow, Jean, I think o' you as I
think on the lass in Elibanks and Elibraes (and I saw Elibanks

and Elibraes when I was on my Border tour wi' Bob Ainslie)
. . . the lass that would let the Deil rive her to candlewicks if
ever she refused her Joe. . . Or am I flattering myself, Jean?

". . . oh, I ken fine I'm a terrible man—they're aey telling
me that. But is your motto, as far as I'm concerned, no' the
same as the lass o' Elibraes . . . ? Aye, of course it is—and you
wouldna be Jean Armour if it wasna. God damn you: I kenna
where you got it, but you're the sweetest-fleshed lass I've ever
known. Green Grow the Rashes contrasts the lassies wi' the
widows. But there was never ony gash about you, Jean. And
you were aey weel-thatched wi' glory. . .

"It's no' blood you've gotten in your veins, Jean: it's
molten lead. . . Me? What did I write to John Rankine?
' And by my gun, o' guns the wale. . .'

"Aye . . . and it's the best blood that's in me that you get,
Jean: I couldna give you better. You can do to me what nae
other woman's ever done—draw the marrow out o' my bluidy
bones. . ."

A few more weeks of idle vaiging, visiting friends in Ayr,
Maybole, Girvan, Daljarrock, Glenconner, Ochiltrie, Kilmarnock, Craigie, Tarbolton—and sometimes working on the
hay at Mossgiel—and he was saying goodbye to Jean Armour
once again.

"I must go to Edinburgh, Jean. A letter from Creech
decides that. . . It's time I was away. I'll go by Paisley to
Glasgow for I've business to do on the way. . . You don't
know Mrs. Dunlop of Dunlop House, Stewarton? But you
ken o' her . . . ? Aye: sent her servant twenty miles to enquire
for my health—a great woman, Mrs. Dunlop. I went and saw
her the other day. A fine family . . . the finest. I've written
a long autobiographical letter to a relation o' hers—a Doctor
Moore that now bides in London—oh, a famous author in his
way: according to some, at the very top o' the ranks o'
authorship. Damnit, Jean, the amount o' recognition I've had
for my poems is nothing short o' extraornar. No: I'm no'
exaggerating. Why should I exaggerate? Dinna worry, lass:
I ken my ain worth far better than ony o' thae folk. But it's

nice to get their recognition for a' that—and I'm far from insensible to their notice. . . I mean: among literary folk there are degrees o' recognition and degrees o' indifference. . ."

But Jean, though she listened to his literary and philosophical talk with surprising understanding, was to-night impatient of his enthusiasms. She had enough to worry her. And yet it was with extreme reluctance that she did worry him.

"I dinna want to frichten you, Rab—but I think I'm awa' again."

"You're no'?"

"I—I think so, Rab. . . God kens what I'll dae if I am."

"For God's sake, Jean, hae I but to rub myself against your thigh and you're in the family-way?"

"I just . . . I just canna help it, Rab. It must be the way I'm made. . ."

"And what chance d'you think I hae? Surely to God, Jean, there's *something* you can do about it."

"Dinna get angry, Rab. . . I'll see what can be done. I'm no' ony mair anxious than you are. . ."

He knew she was bound to be worried and worried far more than he was. But there was little he could do about it. . .

"But what can I dae, Rab—if it's true?"

"*If* it's true. God damnit, Jean, either it's true or it's no' true. You women when you think you're in the family-way become the damndest dithering bitches———"

"I shouldna hae telt you———"

"Who else could you tell? Who has a better right to know?"

"Weel, you ken noo—and you ken I'll no' expect you to do onything for me. If I hadna listened to my mither———"

"Oho: so your mither's in this, is she? A bluidy trap, eh?"

"No: nae trap. Juist that she tellt me I was safe as lang's I was nursing the bairns———"

Suddenly he was sensitive to the note of asperity in Jean's voice.

"I'm sorry, Jean. I'm sae damned touchy nowadays. Listen, lass: I maun go to Edinburgh. God kens when I'll get back. But I'll no' stay ony langer than it tak's Creech to settle wi' me."

"I didna mean to worry you, Rab."

"But I've got to worry, Jean. And I'm wi' you, lass, to the bitter end. Dinna think I'll desert you. But I canna dae onything till I get fixed on my farm. As soon as I dae get settled I'll tak' you away oot o' here. And the further frae Machlin the better."

"And you really mean that, Rab?"

"Every word o' it."

"In that case, Rab, I'll tak' what's coming to me."

"Dinna worry: I'm no' awa' for six months this time. I'll be back just as soon as I can manage. . ."

They took a long and ardent farewell of each other.

Gibby said: "Away again, Robin . . . ? Well, I hope you manage to collect your money from Creech, and . . ."

But Gilbert couldn't say that he hoped he would soon find himself settled into a farm. This prospect for Robin chilled Gilbert. He was hoping that some of the Edinburgh money would be sunk into Mossgiel even though he realised that never again would Robert be back to work on it.

The family knew this as well as Gilbert. Their emotions were torn. They loved him very deeply as a brother; they were proud of the fame he had achieved; but somehow all of them knew they had lost him—that he would never really be their brother again.

Of them all, Willie was the most anxious to spread his wings and take flight from Mossgiel. He again pressed Robert to seek out some kind of suitable berth for him.

Robert promised. He wasn't happy leaving Machlin; but neither was he happy looking forward to Edinburgh. The thrill of his first journey there was over. Edinburgh held little for him now.

The more he pondered his future the more necessary did it seem to him that he would need to settle with Patrick Miller —as soon as he had settled with Creech.

Part Four

OSSIAN'S COUNTRY

HEAT WAVE IN AULD REEKIE

AULD REEKIE lay burnished and golden-grey beneath the blaze of the summer sun—and she stank abominably. Flies in myriads feasted on every bit of filth and rubbish. Great blue-bottles, green-bottles, brown-bottles and golden-bottles, gorged to bursting with garbage, buzzed lethargically or settled on window panes and ledges in sun-sickened satiation.

The Town crawled under the heat. Half-naked youngsters and three-quarters-naked children stirred in the gutters or crept about the stairs. Their mothers sat out of doors, some beaking contentedly in the sun, others content to seek the coolness of the shade from the high lands. Groups of folks of all ages gathered about the Town wells awaiting an opportunity to cool their parched tongues.

In the Grassmarket, carters' horses stamped their feet on the cobbles and tossed their heads in irritation at the clouds of pestering flies that settled on them. The urgent work of the day had to go on, heat or no heat; but men and women went about it languidly. The rich merchants, the literati, the clergy, the aristocracy—all who could afford it (and many who could not but owed it to their social positions) had gone ' out to the country.'

In that sense the Town was empty. But with so many folks sunning out of doors it seemed to the Bard that it was crowded to suffocation.

In one way he was glad that he would not be lodging with John Richmond. Richmond had gone back to Machlin since the death of his employer in July. As it was, the heat and stench in Baxters' Close would be intolerable. If Willie Nicol's house in the Buccleuch Pend was more crowded, at least it was lighter and airier. And coming from his long stay in the country he felt he could do with all the air he could get. It was only the beginning of August; and though June and July were gone, in all probability there would be much heat yet to come in August and September—and certainly the grain (from what he had seen on his journey) could do with all the heat it could get. The crops looked like being backward because of the late spring sowing. . .

BED AT WILLIE NICOL'S

Willie Nicol said: "I'm damned glad to see you again, Robert. Damned glad. . . I've missed you—though maybe you wouldna think I could miss onybody. Man, I wish I could get away to the country—it would be fine on the Solway sands on a night like this! But I've some pupils to coach in their Latin afore I can have a break. Och, you'll stay for a week or twa when you're here. What the hell's to tak' you back to Machlin—unless it's your Jean—eh? And you'll need to settle that writ your Heilan bitch got served on you. Tach, man, you're safer wi' the bawdy-house. But you wad be sae damned infernal particular. And noo you'll need to pay for't . . . but maybe she was worth it—I wouldna ken. No, I wouldna ken: what's one man's meat's another's poison—and that applies mair to women than what you ladle into you wi' a horn spoon. But I suppose you canna mak' up your mind till you've seen your precious Creech—the creeping bastard. . . Aye, there's a bed for you as lang as you like to stay—provided you can thole the gabble o' Latin conjugations and bear wi' the steer o' the bairns."

INTERVIEWS

William Creech, more dapper, more pert, more suave than ever, polished the nails of his right hand against the inside of his left forefinger.

"Ah yes: you've certainly travelled, Robert, since you left Edinburgh. Yes. . . I think you have pushed forward the business of the subscription—John Smith in Glasgow *should* have had his copies: Hill must have slipped up somewhere. . .

"The reason I sent for you to come to Town, Robert, is just this. There is some money due you from incoming subscriptions. But before I make any settlement—of a temporary nature, of course—I must know just exactly how much money you have drawn on your travels. . .

"Ah, you have prepared a statement. Fine, my boy, fine. Splendid indeed! I'll get Peter Hill to check up on the figures. By the end of a week—or a fortnight—I should be able to make some kind of temporary, to-account settlement with you.

"A final settlement, Robert? Ah, that takes time. These matters canna be hurried. Yes, yes—I'll do all I can *on my part* to expedite matters."

The Bard thought that behind Creech's suave assurance he was worried and that he was not telling him all that was in his mind. He pressed him for a statement as to what he hoped the final sales might be.

"Final sales, Robert? That's very difficult. If we are fortunate we may sell up to three thousand—and that would be a very good sale indeed. For safety we may put the figure at two thousand copies."

"That would give me a figure of £500 to work on; and out of that I still have to pay Smellie for the printing and Scott for the binding. I cannot reckon that on less than a couple of hundred pounds. So that by settlement date, Mr. Creech, I may hope to have some £300 of capital; and then there is the matter of the hundred guineas for the sale of my copyright?"

Creech nodded but said nothing. With the possibility of the Bard earning £300 against his own £100 for commission on the sale, he did not think he should be rushed into payment.

"And of course, Mr. Creech, in the meantime I have got to live; and I have to contribute something to the support of my family in Ayrshire."

"But you are thinking, are you not, of investing your money in a small farm under Mr. Miller at Dalswinton?"

"Such is my plan should I fail absolutely in securing an Excise commission; but I cannot very well fix on Mr. Miller as a future landlord until I have the £300 in my hand. In the meantime, Mr. Creech, I shall be in your debt if you can let me have as much of the money against the subscription as you can spare."

It was quite true that the Bard had to live. His Border tour and his West Highland tour had cost him money. Even the humblest innkeeper did not give Jenny Geddes a corner of his stable and a feed of corn without charging him; and every day he stayed in Edinburgh Jenny Geddes would cost him money. Nor could he accept Willie Nicol's hospitality for nothing. Everywhere he turned, indeed, he had to dip his hand into his pocket. He did not tell Creech about Peggy Cameron. Creech was not the man to understand such things or to condone with them even had understanding been his.

His interview with Peggy Cameron had not been a happy one. He had not managed to see her except in the presence of Mrs. Hogg and she was obviously under Mrs. Hogg's influence. Whether or not he was the father of her child was, legally, beside the point. He had consorted with her; and he would be unable to prove, in law, that he was not the father. It had been distasteful for him to haggle with Mrs. Hogg as to the price at which Peggy would agree to withdraw her writ; and if the writ were not withdrawn, very soon the whole of Edinburgh would be discussing the affair. On one thing he had remained adamant. If he was to pay Peggy Cameron he was determined that she must leave Edinburgh until her trouble was over. Though Mrs. Hogg had demurred at this Peggy herself had readily agreed. She had no more wish than the Bard to have the scandal noised about the closes and wynds. She would go to friends in the country provided the settlement was satisfactory. Finally he had agreed to a payment of £20 provided Peggy withdrew her writ; and there, for the moment, the matter rested.

Apparently he had to pay for his follies both in cash and in kind.

WHAT OF THE FUTURE?

He moved idly and uncomfortably about Edinburgh. His uncertain position made him quite incapable of settling down anywhere. And the more he considered his position, the more futile did his plan seem of visiting Patrick Miller at Dalswinton at the end of the month—as he had promised. He could tell Miller no more now about his plans than he had been able to do at the beginning of June.

He did visit his old acquaintances: Smellie was still the same rough rude-witted kindly-hearted Smellie. Robert Cleghorn was as glad to renew his acquaintance as he was to renew his. He discussed the second volume of the *Museum* with James Johnson and old Mr. Tytler of Woodhouselee; and he paid an odd visit to Balloon Tytler's wretched dwelling in Hastie's Close and listened to his singing of his own songs: *I Canna come ilka day to woo* and *The Bonnie Brucket Lassie.*

Of the literati, Henry MacKenzie, Lord Monboddo and Doctor James Gregory welcomed him as much as ever they had done; but he could see that the interest in his Edinburgh edition was dying. They were anxious to know what new work he had written, what new verses had been inspired by his tour of the Borders and what his literary plans for the future were. It seemed strange to him that they did not share to any marked degree his interest in Johnson's scheme for preserving the songs of Scotland. It was clear that the literati of Edinburgh had roots that spread no deeper into the Scottish soil than the whinstone Edinburgh causeways permitted.

The only bright light on his horizon was Peggy Chalmers. He paid her as much court as she would allow; and he had every reason to believe that this was considerably more than mere acquaintanceship decreed. After a walk with her in the warm shadows of Hope Park in the gloaming hour of evening he believed that it might still be possible to win her in marriage.

The something that attracted him to Peggy was something

447

he had found in no other woman. She had an intellectual quality that flowed harmoniously with his own; and he could discuss books and music, philosophy and religion with a basic sympathy that seemed to stem from the same spiritual soil; and yet with all this she was a woman and aroused in him a passion that was not alone of the intellect.

Yet of all the women he had known she was the one least likely to be won by direct assault; and though she was open and frank to an astonishing degree there was that about her personality she never exposed: the inner core of her personality remained inviolate. Such revelations of her character as she gave, she gave in small portions at a time. So it was that the more he talked with her, the more he saw of her (and she was still a regular visitor to Doctor Blacklock), the more enraptured and entranced did he become with her.

Her mother and her sister, Lady MacKenzie, had gone to Harviestoun and she planned to join them later in the month. Because of this she probably had more time to give the Bard: time she might otherwise not have had.

But again and again the question arose, black and threatening: what of his future? How could he settle in a farm and hope to take Peggy Chalmers with him; and would she take more kindly to the thought of being a gauger's wife? As Peggy came more within his grasp the possibility of marrying her seemed more remote.

HURRAH FOR THE HIGHLANDS

Towards the middle of the month Willie Nicol proposed that they should tour the Highlands together.

"It's a project I've long had in mind, Robert. I'm needing a complete change of scenery; and going south into Dumfriesshire is no' the kind o' change I have in mind. Besides you'll see enough of the south before you're finished. A visit as far as Inverness would be a guid tonic for us both; and to tell you the truth, Robert, if I don't do it in your company I'll never do it."

The Bard welcomed the suggestion. Despite Peggy Chalmers he found that his days in Edinburgh were becoming intolerably burdensome.

"If we go by Inverness, Willie, would there be anything to hinder us coming back by way of Aberdeen so that I might call on my cousins and my father's people about Stonehaven and Montrose?"

Nicol spread the map over the Latin grammar and the Latin exercises that lay scattered on the table.

"There's no reason at all, Robert, why we shouldna come back by Aberdeen. In fact it would suit our purpose very well. There's a good road here, along the Moray Firth, through Nairn, Forres, Elgin, Fochabers, Cullen, Banff and doon here to Aberdeen. Then we could come by Stonehaven, Montrose, Arbroath, Dundee, back to Perth, doon by Loch Leven here, Dunfermline, across the ferry and back to Auld Reekie."

The Bard followed Nicol's ink-stained forefinger. "And how do you propose to go?" he said.

"We'll go by Stirling," said Nicol, "Linlithgow, Falkirk and Stirling. Then we could hold up by Dunblane to Crieff, Aberfeldy on to Dunkeld, up there across the high hills, then to Killiecrankie, Blair Atholl—— This is General Wade's road, you know. Up to Dalwhinnie, Pitmain, Aviemore and on to Inverness, coming round by Culloden."

Each place Nicol named awoke memories of Scotland's history.

"If Jenny Geddes could take me triumphant over the Border hills, and all the way frae Newcastle back to Machlin, I see no reason why she shouldna tip-tapper along General Wade's road."

But to this Nicol immediately objected. "You're hardened to Jenny Geddes by now, Robert; and the long years you held the plough in all weathers has nae doubt rendered you impervious to our out-door climate. But from all the reports I ever had from the North, there is just the possibility that we could be washed from the saddle. No, Robert: nae horse-back jaunt for me. We'll take a chaise and ride in comfort."

The Bard raised the question of expense. "Oh damn the expense," said Nicol. "We can hire a chaise and a guid man from the Pleasance that'll work out as cheap as the hire o' a horse; and in ony case, I'll be only too glad to stand the expense of the chaise provided you will bear your expenses for your keep on the journey."

"And how long do you reckon we'll be away?"

"Well, to do it in comfortable stages it would take, now let me see. . . Yes, we would be best to allow ourselves a good three weeks, allowing, that is, for bad weather and a chance to see round us. If I know you right, you'll no' want to go hurtling through Bannockburn and Stirling, or the Field of Culloden. Damnit, there should be something of interest to us on every stage of our journey. . ."

A CLASSIC TEXT

The Bard's mind was fired by the prospect of a visit to the North. He would be glad—more than glad—to meet his relatives around Stonehaven, to meet his uncles and the men and women who had known his father. He would be interested, too, to call on some of his Edinburgh patrons on the way. Josiah Walker, whom he had met so often at Doctor Black-lock's, would be sure to give him a welcome at the Blair of Atholl. The Duke and Duchess had shown themselves much interested in his Edinburgh edition. He might even call at Castle Gordon for the Duchess had always assured him that if ever he was in the North he would be welcomed there.

When he mentioned the venture to Peggy Chalmers she gave him a hearty invitation to visit Harviestoun. Willie Dunbar, Muster-General of the Crochallan Corps, immediately wrote him out a letter of introduction to Baillie Inglis of Inverness. Henry MacKenzie gave him a letter to the chief of the Grants and to Mrs. Rose of Kilravock, his cousin. Every-body, indeed, seemed most anxious to render what help they could either by way of advice or introductions to ensure the success of the tour. And this was the more surprising since neither Henry MacKenzie nor Willie Dunbar looked with any favour on Willie Nicol.

So fired with enthusiasm was he that when news came to him from Robert Ainslie, still at Berrywell, that his servant-lass had given birth to a boy, he took up a sheet of paper and wrote:

> As I gaed up to Dunse
> To warp a pickle yarn,
> Robin, silly body,
> He gat me wi' bairn.—

From henceforth, my dear sir, I am determined to set off with my letters like the periodical Writers, viz., prefix a kind of text quoted from some Classic of undoubted authority, such as the Author of the immortal piece of which my text is a part. What I have to say on my text is exhausted in a letter I wrote you the other day, before I had the pleasure of receiving yours from Innerleithen: and sure never was anything more lucky, as I have but the time to write this, that Mr. Nicol on the opposite side of the table takes to correct a proof-sheet of a thesis. They are gabbling Latin so loud that I cannot hear what my own soul is saying in my own skull, so must just give you a matter-of-fact sentence or two, and end if time permit with a verse de rei generatione.

To-morrow I leave Edinburgh in a chaise: Nicol thinks it more comfortable than horse-back, to which I say, Amen; so Jenny Geddes goes home to Ayrshire, to use a phrase of my Mother's, "wi' her finger in her mouth."

Now for a modest verse of classical authority:

> "The cats like kitchen;
> The dogs like broo;
> The lasses like the lads weel,
> And th' auld wives too.

Chorus

> An' we're a' noddin
> Nid, nid, noddin,
> We're a' noddin fou at e'en——?"

If this does not please you, let me hear from you: if you write any time before the first of September direct to Inverness, to be left at the Post Office till called for; the next week at Aberdeen; the next at Edinburgh. The sheet is done, and I shall just conclude with assuring you that I am, and ever with pride shall be. . .

A LOVELY MORNING

On a busy Saturday morning a sound and serviceable chaise from Duncan MacCulloch in the Pleasance drew up at the Buccleuch Pend. Willie Nicol and the Bard packed their luggage into it, and, surrounded by a yelling horde of children, drove off over the North Bridge and along Princes Street, en route, by way of Corstorphine, Kirkleston and Winchburgh, to Linlithgow where they hoped to dine with Wee Jamie Smith, late haberdasher of Machlin.

It was a glorious morning with the red ripening August sun promising to beak its beatitudes on yellow-green crops; the rankness of growth everywhere in hedgerows and dyke-sides; a riot of flower blooms in the many gardens that boasted the extravagance of herbaceous plants; a glorious morning with the dust still dew-laid; and the nut-brown complexions and tanned arms and legs of the country maids betokening health and vigour and physical ripeness. . .

The sight of the waving grain or the curve of a berry-brown calf (even if the owner were no more than the humblest of clytrie-maids returning from the midden with her odorous pail) was enough to set the Bard's blood atingling with heightened desire. No man's blood ever responded with such

sensitivity to nature when she called forth the limitless glory
of blood-drumming designs in shape and colour and smell;
for here all earth was round and swelling in the bursting
pregnancy of autumn—and everywhere was the lapping
warmth of mellow sunshine. . .

And how glorious it was to rock and sway in leather-
cushioned ease and absorb the slow-passing scene in relaxed
cosy comfort. The fantastic luxury of it! And day after day,
for three whole weeks, time stretching ahead with the careless
random-flung miles. . .

And what a companion to travel with: Willie Nicol! True,
here was no blood tingling in response to nature's aphrodisiacal
overtones. Maybe Nicol was not yet beyond the urge to
wrestle a servant-lass on a bed of straw; but no neighing
trumpets would call him to the combat. For the idea of Nicol
in love was at once ridiculous and highly incongruous.

How different from the gay sex-avid Bob Ainslie who had
accompanied him on his Border Tour. Yet how satisfying the
difference. Ainslie had been much his junior; and despite his
bold boyish audacity he had been glad enough to be sub-
servient to the Bard. And the Bard, though he was fond of
him and responded to his gay care-free nature, treated him as
his junior. When he cared to give his thoughts a French cast
—which was often enough—he summarised him—*avec un
pechant pour les dames adorables.*

Not that the pug-nosed savagely pock-pitted Nicol was
staid and stagnant and incapable of response to the challenge
of the wine and women of life. But he had no softness in him.
The marrow of his responses did not melt and run down his
nerves in quivering ecstatic agony. The only quivering agony
Nicol knew was when the black drunk-inflamed bile of his
hatreds churned up his innards and narrowed his eyes to
bloodshot slits.

For Nicol's rages bordered on insanity and were fearful to
behold. And when the black bile was bubbling and frothing
he could rage and fulminate for days on end.

Nicol was a man whose intellect rumbled like a thunder-
storm lit by flashes of dazzling lightning. He was possessed

of tremendous mental audacity coupled with profound erudition. He was a scholar who tore learning apart with urgent fingers and consumed it reeking raw. No diet was too tough for his intellect and the knowledge he had digested in theology, philosophy, medicine, natural history, geography and, of course, the classics of Greece and Rome, would have stuffed to bursting point the capacity of any dozen of Europe's leading professors.

And yet his learning could be dry and arid and irritating as a diet of powdered glass. Nicol, coming into contact with the sensuous flesh-flaming genius of Robert Burns, sensed this. The dead weight of his dead learning weighed on his fiery spirit. He could do nothing with it but pour it into deaf ears, ladle it into vacuous mouths or ram it down rebellious throats: the ears, mouths and throats of the children of his enemies.

For Willie Nicol was an enemy of society. Stylistically he was a snobbish and sarcastic anarchist. Politically he belonged to the party of Willie Nicol. His experience of life had been embittering. On all sides he had seen men of quite inferior merit leaving him behind through the shallow opportunism of superior social connections. And so he came to hate all such.

On the other hand, his bare-fisted learning and indefatigable industry induced in him a snobbish superiority to the vast uneducated mass upwards from which he had hacked and hewed and torn his way.

He was, socially, a lonely misfit born into a society that but grudgingly recognised his merits. Hence his position in society produced an almost uniform irascibility of mood that only too often accumulated till release was found in an explosion of temper, dire and demoniacal in its effect.

Not that Willie Nicol was without friends and good and loyal friends at that. To them Willie revealed in generous measure the other side of his crabbed genius. To them he was kind, generous and witty—and strangely, almost embarrassingly, forbearing.

To Louis Cauvin, the French teacher, Johann Georg Christoff Schetky, the musician, and his teaching colleague, Willie Cruikshank, he was a loyal friend and something of a boon companion. To know Willie Nicol at his own fireside, relaxed and at his ease, was to know a man completely unrecognisable to the Edinburgh of the High School.

There was no man he admired more than Robert Burns. He had admired his poetry before he had met him. But after their first wild meeting he admired the man even more than the poet. Here was a man he could learn from; here also was a man he could teach!

By degrees their friendship ripened. In the Bard's case it ripened into an admiration softened with real affection. In Nicol's case it ripened into an affection that was protective. There was something in this protective feeling of the guide-philosopher-and-friend complex—and something of the kindly benevolent father. Only there was a growing tendency on the part of the father to decide and determine what was best for the son. Being fifteen years older than the son and in his forty-third year, Nicol was of an age to develop this father complex and at the same time young enough to enjoy his companionship.

But though they were to have many wordy battles and their temperaments were to clash in furious conflict before they saw Edinburgh again, they rode into Linlithgow and sought out the Avon Printworks, with no diminution of the high spirits that had accompanied them along the rattling cobbles of Princes Street and out by the sun-basked braes of Corstorphine.

THE OLD BLUE WHINSTONE

The following night in Stirling the Bard wrote in his diary against the date of Sunday 26th August:

"Falkirk nothing remarkable except the tomb of Sir John the Graham, over which, in the succession of time, has been four stones laid. Camelon, the ancient Metropolis of the Picts, now a small village in the neighbourhood of Falkirk. Cross the grand Canal to Carron—breakfast. Come past

Larbert and admire a fine monument of cast iron erected by Mr. Bruce, the African traveller, to his wife. N.B.—he used her very ill, and I suppose he meant it as much out of gratitude to Heaven as anything else. Past Dunipace, a place laid out with fine taste—a charming amphitheatre bounded by Denny village; the pleasant seats of Herbertshire, Denovan and down the way to Dunipace. The Carron running down the bosom of the whole makes it one of the most charming little prospects I have seen. Dine at Auchenbowie. Mr. Monro an excellent, worthy, old man. Miss Monro an amiable, sensible, sweet young woman, much resembling Mrs. Grierson. Come to Bannockburn. Shown the old house where James III was murdered. The field of Bannockburn—the hole where glorious Bruce set his standard."

Aye: Bannockburn. He would write a worthy poem on that subject someday. Oh, the poems he was going to write someday. . . Pen in hand—and the point but freshly cut—he thought of Robert Muir of Kilmarnock. He set aside his diary and took a sheet of paper and wrote to him:

I intended to have written you from Edinburgh and now write you from Stirling to make an excuse. Here am I, on my way to Inverness, with a truly original, but very worthy man, a Mr. Nicol, one of the masters of the High School in Edinburgh. I left Auld Reekie yesterday morning, and have passed, besides by-excursions, Linlithgow, Borrowstounness, Falkirk and here am I undoubtedly. This morning I knelt at the tomb of Sir John the Graham, the gallant friend of the immortal Wallace, and two hours ago I said a fervent prayer for Old Caledonia over the hole in a blue whinstone, where Robert de Bruce fixed his royal standard on the banks of Bannockburn. . .

STIRLING CASTLE

Stirling, as the Bard and Nicol knew from history, was an important centre: in many ways it had been more important to Scotland than Edinburgh had been.

Like Edinburgh it had decayed and declined—and for the same reasons. The loss of the Court and then the loss of Parliament. . .

But nothing about Stirling drove home to the Bard the neglect and distress of Stirling more violently than the condition of Stirling Castle standing like Edinburgh's on its great bastion rock. Here Scottish kings, the great Wallace and most of the Jameses, had sojourned. There was scarce a great figure in Scotland's history who hadn't known the inside of the Castle.

And what a situation for such a castle. Below the rock lay the carse of the Forth bounded to the east by the Ochill Hills, Dumyat, tubby and green, bold on the flank. To the north and west, blue and fantastic, stood the great Highland peaks Ben Chonzie, Ben Vorlich, Ben More, Ben Ledi, Ben Lomond . . . and all the many folded ridges and spurs, the great corrugations of which made up the seemingly endless and eternal fringe of the great Highland bastion—black, blue, blue-black, smoke-blue; in shadow and light; cloud-capped, mist-capped; ethereal but enduring; dissolving in shade; disintegrating in the corridors of distance and yet cored from the earth's hardest rock. . .

The great green sea of the carseland lapped the foothills. . . Immediately below the Castle, winding and twisting through the carseland in enormous doubling-back loops, the silver ribbon of the River Forth. . .

High upon Highlands and low upon Forth! And Stirling Castle guarding the plain against the north and securing the rear-guard in retreat from the south. Guarding the only bridge that crossed the Forth from Edinburgh to Kincardine and Menteith.

There, on the flank of Dumyat stood the Abbey Craig from whence Wallace had charged on the forces of Edward, Hammer of the Scots, and had hammered and harried and ham-strung his forces across Stirling Brig and beyond—harried them into wretched defeat and disorder.

And then Bannockburn and the final utter rout of Edward —south over the Border not to return for two hundred years. . .

And for Nicol, Stirling had the added interest of being the spot where the Romans had crossed and had returned from their defeat by Calgacius at Mons Grampius—or so he assured the Bard.

But the Bard soon forgot all about the Romans and the serrated horizon of high Highland hills.

Viewing the wanton disrepair of the Castle, in the company of Captain Gabriel Forrester, officer in charge, his anger mounted and he vented himself explosively.

Captain Forrester listened with a sardonic grin on his tough lean features. He had never formed any opinion of poets before now—except that in a vague general way he regarded them as half-mad and half-female. That so robust and manly a fellow in command of such a splendid voice and flow of invective should also be a poet surprised him most agreeably. If his poetry (of which he had heard) reflected in any real way his personality then it should be worth reading.

It was Nicol who, for all his Jacobite leanings, tried to restrain him.

"What the hell are you getting excited over an auld biggin for—however historic it may be. None o' your ranting and raving'll do ony good—far less bring back the Auld Stewarts."

"And who's wanting to bring back the Auld Stewarts? But when you're on the subject o' the Auld Stewarts, let me remind you—though you shouldna need reminding—that whatever faults they had—and I'm no' saying but what they had many—they were a damned sight superior in every way to the Hanoverian clowns and idiots that have since occupied the throne. And I'll be damned either for you or ony other body if I'll stand on this sacred spot—sacred not for the Auld

Stewarts but for the Auld Scotland they represented—without raising my voice in protest."

"Protest then till you're blue in the bluidy face, for a' I care—as long as you can afford to tak' the consequences."

"Gentlemen," said Captain Forrester, drawing himself up though unable to douse the twinkle in his grey eyes, "you will please to remember that no more loyal subject of His Majesty, King George, ever wore his uniform than your much obliged and humble servant. And if you want to put that loyalty to the test of the sword-point or the open end of a pistol you have only to say the word and the ravens can feed on your rotten carcases to-morrow. But—eh—among ourselves, I may say that I have some sympathy for your views, Mr. Burns. I have myself often thought it was a damned disgrace to let Stirling Castle rot the way it has. But I'm a sodger; and damn me if it matters a musket-load of damp powder who's king, provided I hold my rank and draw my money!"

This speech mollified the Bard and broke the tension between him and Nicol. He guessed that the Captain spoke no more than the truth and that he would make a good mercenary under whatever flag he might choose to serve. Having made the army his career he was fit for nothing else. . . .

Back in the inn, and still smouldering, he took a sheet of paper and dashed down his reactions:

> Here Stewarts once in glory reigned
> And laws for Scotland's weal ordained;
> But now unroofed their palace stands,
> Their sceptre fallen to other hands:
> Fallen indeed, and to the earth,
> Whence grovelling reptiles take their birth!
> The injured Stewart line is gone,
> A race outlandish fills their throne:
> An idiot race, to honour lost—
> Who know them best despise them most.

Pleased with his effort, he took his diamond pen and

transferred it to the window-glass. He knew there was a risk in stating his opinions so boldly; but he was too angry to care.

ON DEVON'S BANKS

On the Monday morning they rode out by Causeway Head and crossed the Forth. At the Abbey Craig they took to the right and, avoiding the steep climb to Blair Logie, came round by Tullibody and up to the pleasant hill-foot weaving town of Menstrie.

The Bard thought he had never seen greener or more gently contoured hills than the Ochills. They overhung the hill-foot villages. Indeed the villages seemed almost to be burrowed into their flanks, taking the opportunity of every stream and cleft in the hills to do so.

Travelling very pleasantly along the hill-foots they came by Alva and Tullicoultry and a mile and a half beyond that, nestling below King's Seat, to Harviestoun.

He found it all that Peggy Chalmers had said it was—and possibly more. But it took the Bard some time to explain to Nicol the intricacies of the relationship between Peggy Chalmers and Gavin Hamilton: the stepmothers, half-sisters and what-not that made up the Machlin-Harviestoun relationship.

"It's simple enough if you take it this way, Willie. There were three sisters of the name Murdoch: one sister became Gavin Hamilton's stepmother: another sister married a Chalmers of Fingland—that was the father of Peggy Chalmers. The other sister married this Mr. Tait on whom we are about to call. Mrs. Hamilton, I should have said, has her daughter Charlotte—a half-sister to Gavin Hamilton—staying with her here. I have met Charlotte and her mother and Peggy Chalmers and her mother and Peggy's sister, Lady MacKenzie; but I have yet to meet Mr. Tait."

"And what the devil are they all doing here?"

" Mrs. Tait died not so long ago; and Gavin's stepmother, together with her family, is acting as housekeeper to this Mr. Tait who's her brother-in-law."

" You canna expect me to keep mind o' all that rigmarole, Robert."

" Nobody will expect you to, Willie. All you need to do is to remember that they are all related through each other."

" And to remember that the three original Murdoch sisters are all widows?"

" No—only two, Willie. One of them is dead—Mrs. Tait; and that is one point you would be as well to get clearly into your head."

But Nicol decided that he would say nothing: he would speak if he were spoken to. For the rest he would address them as ' Madam ' and leave it at that.

Actually Nicol would much have preferred that they had pushed into the Highlands and not wasted a day that promised to be, for him, infernally dull.

But the day turned out to be very far from dull. They were given the warmest of welcomes at Harviestoun and, though Peggy Chalmers was absent, Charlotte Hamilton proved so gracious as almost to win Peggy's place in the Bard's affections. Mr. Tait, though a man of somewhat melancholy disposition, was neither too positive nor too negative to obtrude his personality.

After breakfast and an inspection of the grounds of Harviestoun, a party was made up and they drove off to spend the day at the far-famed Rumbling Bridge, some four miles away, and inspect the Caldron Linn and the Devil's Mill.

The country-side around Harviestoun and along the course of the winding Devon was as pleasant as the Bard had ever seen. Even Nicol, who was not prone to be impressed by mere scenery, had to confess that it was well worth the deviation from their route.

The Bard paid as much attention to Charlotte Hamilton as he could manage; and Charlotte, although she was in complete control of herself, was secretly much flattered by the attentions he paid her.

In the early evening they went up the steep path into Dollar Glen and visited the grey and gaunt ruin of Castle Campbell. . .

Driving home along the hill-foots against the wall of the Ochills, Nicol said: "I havena got the genealogy of all this worked out yet, Robert; but I must say the folks I met at Harviestoun to-day are as pleasant a lot of people as I have ever met with."

"And not an ounce of false pride among the lot of them! I must write to Gavin Hamilton and tell him of my visit. I cannot understand why Gavin neglects them. You would think with such upstanding brothers and sisters, even if they are his stepmother's, that he would at least write them from time to time and not let the connection die."

"You think very highly o' Gavin Hamilton."

"I've every reason to think highly of him, Willie. He has been a good friend to Gilbert and me."

"If your Gavin Hamilton's onything like the Harviestoun folk, he'll pass muster. But you'd better get your letter written to-night for to-morrow we'll need to push north and win Taymouth before supper."

On their return to Stirling, however, there was no time for writing letters.

INSTINCTS OF A GENTLEMAN

Captain Forrester from the Castle and David Doig, the Rector of the Grammar School, and others, were present for a night's talk and drinking.

"——Stirling," roared the Bard above the din of the smoke-thick drink-heavy yellow-ceilinged room. "Stirling—that saw Wallace and Bruce and damn-near a' the Jamies—what do I care—or what should you care—sitting here in Stirling that was one time Capital o' Scotland——"

"Sit doon, Robert—you're drunk!" growled Nicol.

"Drunk? Let naebody be deceived into thinking I'm drunk.

But dinna think to put me off the track o' my discourse, Nicol, by irrelevant interjections."

Rector Doig raised his thin eyebrows at the unexpected Latinisms of the heaven-taught ploughman. "And what *about* sitting here in Stirling, Mr. Burns?"

"Just this, my right worthy reverend doctor. Just this: sitting here, why should I care what I say in defence o' the ill-fated house of Stewart? As for those who usurped the place of the Stewarts, why should I be too white-livered to say what I think o' them?"

Mr. Doig's eyebrows shot upwards on his narrow brow.

"You know the meaning of the word sedition, Mr. Burns?"

"Aye—among enemies and crawling creeping weevil-kneed traitors to their country, fine I ken the meaning o' the word sedition. If onybody here cares to denounce me—then let them denounce. My fathers died in the Stewart cause——"

"You'll die in your own cause, Mr. Burns, if you dinna learn to put a bridle on that tongue o' yours—and your diamond pen." Captain Forrester threw a pistol with a heavy clatter onto the table. "Oh, I read your inscription on the glass, sir. Only"—and here he looked with a stern eye on Rector Doig— "I read it in my *private* capacity. Otherwise if I didna ken you to be as fine a gentleman as ever livened the company of an officer I'd blaw your bluidy brains oot against that wa'. But at least, Mr. Burns, unlike so many men I've shot, you have brains to blaw out. And now, gentlemen, to restore order in the ranks and harmony in the mess, Chris Bell will sing us The Plenipotentiary—the work of another Captain, gentlemen—a rattling fine fellow too—Captain Morris."

"I am unacquainted with the military gentleman's work, Captain Forrester," said Doctor Doig.

"By God you are, sir—but you won't be for long!"

But between drinks and Bell's bawdy song-ballads (Rector Doig was now too drunk to remember he had once taken orders) there were arguments and cross-statements.

Gradually Doig relaxed in his chair till finally, and with hardly any noise, he slipped dead drunk under the table. When he noticed this Captain Forrester bent down and loosed his cravat. "I dinna want the auld runt to choke," he explained.

"Let him choke!" cried Nicol. "He's gotten the damndest dog-Latin for a rector ever I heard barring Adam o' the High School in Edinburgh. And it might be a bluidy sicht better if he did choke—for the Bard's sake."

"You dinna suggest, gentlemen——"

But the Bard pushed the bottle towards him: "Drink up, Captain—we dinna suggest onything—and I'm more than able to tak' care o' myself. The pen—if you will allow me, Captain—is a more powerful instrument than the sword."

"I'll allow you, sir—seeing as you wouldna ken a sword frae a cutlass. What I do know is that a dozen lawyers sitting in Edinburgh can, with their quills, undo the work of an army."

"That they can, Captain. Take a note of that, Robert— that's an epigram."

But the Captain waved this aside: "And—Mr. Burns—you are proceeding to Inverness! Then let us drink now to General Wade. For without Wade's military road, gentlemen, you might as well try to take your coach up the Castle rock."

"It's a good road then, Captain?"

"It's a military road built by the first military gentleman of this or any other century."

"Hannibal," began Nicol.

"Hannibal, my dear dominie, was a cannibal! No foreigner, sir, is to be mentioned in the same breath as a Britisher, be he of the North or South, so long as he wears or has worn the King's uniform."

"A damned narrow insular prejudiced view, that, Captain."

"Mr. Nicol, sir, I am asking you to drink to the respect due to General Wade."

"I'll drink to the health of no anti-Jacobite," said Nicol. "Besides, he was an Irishman."

The Captain's jaw fell. "Mr. Burns: was General Wade an Irishman?"

"Yes, Captain, General George Wade was an Irishman— and dead these forty years. But why let that disturb you? He was a good soldier though he couldn't stop the Scottish Army,

sir. But in victory as in defeat, sir, a Jacobite can be mag-
nanimous. I shall drink with you to the memory of General
Wade—road-builder!"

"You may be a poet, Mr. Burns—but you have the instincts
of a gentleman. . ."

"The instincts of a gentleman," sneered Nicol, when they
got to their bedroom. "You're a blasted bluidy eediot, Robert."

"In what way precisely, my learned Latin Willie?"

"Doig, damn you! How d'you ken he isna a spy for
Dundas's men?"

"What of it, man? The authorities dinna pay attention to
Jacobite sentiments nowadays—they've more to worry
them."

"Maybe. But they dinna hold wi' onybody that's disaffected wi' the present monarchy. It may be true they're an
idiot race—it's in the nature o' kings to be idiots. But, whether
or no', they can damn soon tie you by the heels. . . And try
and mind I hae a wife and weans—if you havena. . ."

"I've three weans and will soon hae a fourth—and nae
wife! Nae wife! But, if I had as many wives as Solomon and
every wife had a baker's dozen and the whole bluidy battalion
dependent on me, I wouldna barter my opinions or the right
to say what I think—in company o' my own choosing. Come
to that, I've never known you to keep your learned jaw shut
when you wanted to open it."

"Oh, you havena, have you no'? You're mighty brave and
bold of a sudden to criticise my doings——"

"Well: don't criticise mine."

"It's for your own guid——"

"No: it's for your own guid, Willie—you canna deceive
me."

"I take that ill from you, Robert."

"That's no' half o' what you'll take frae me before I'm
finished. Being the first Latin scholar in Europe doesn't
entitle you to read me curtain lectures. I'm no bluidy half-
witted bairn in the High School to be bull-dosed wi' your
medicine whenever it comes up your learned humph——"

"God's curse that I ever set out wi' you as a travelling companion! But I'll look over it: you're drunk."

"*I'm* drunk? I could swim in the whisky *you've* drunk. Get to your bed, man, and no' haver."

Surprisingly enough Nicol growled under his breath—and did as he was told. But maybe he was too drunk to do otherwise.

The Bard was a bit drunk himself—but he hadn't drunk a quarter of what the others had done.

As a consequence, he was able to get up in the morning and write to Gavin Hamilton.

By the time he had written his letter, and entered his diary, Nicol was up, red-eyed—and growling about his headache.

THE BOB O' DUNBLANE

At Dunblane, where they stopped for their late breakfast, the Bard struck up an interesting and enlivening conversation with the landlady who served them in the kitchen.

This landlady was a miniature Martial Chuck and being in the fat forties was a woman to make his teeth water. He liked the company of big sonsy cheery women who were long and deeply experienced in life. He could enjoy a rare freedom of conversation with them.

She too had heard of Caledonia's Bard—or at least of the Bard of Ayrshire. And she was a bit of a bardess herself. Her sonsy well-padded sides quivered with song-rhythm. Her eyes sparkled to the old melodies of Scotland. And she was alive to history in so far as it could be popularised and humanised.

"Aye," she said sinking down on her ample hurdies on a chair at the table and displaying two hefty red brown-freckled arms, "you're no' the only famous man who has sat at this table, Mr. Burns. The Duke of Argyll sat in the very same seat as you're sitting on."

"Which duke was that?"

"Him that fought at Sherramuir. But I'm no' that weel-up in dukes to ken his name."

"That was Archibald—the third duke. But your memory doesna go back to 1715 and Sheriffmuir, landlady!"

"No, hardly. But it was in my auld Mither's day—and I've heard the tale mony a time."

"Let's hear your story, guidwife—for I've the notion it'll be worth the hearing."

"Ah weel, you ken what happened at Sherramuir—' Some say that we ran and some say that they ran '——"

"' And some say that we ran awa' man '—aye, fine."

"Weel, this was where the Duke o' Argyll rested after the fight. And he was telt that the result o' the fecht wasna too weel settled—a kind o' half and between affair as it were. ' Ah weel,' says the Duke, ' if they think it na weel bobbit we'll bob it again.' He was thinking on the auld song the Bob o' Dunblane. And I wondering if you kent *that* sang, Mr. Burns?"

"I ken Allan Ramsay's version—have you got a better one?"

"I ken nocht about Allan Ramsay—but I ken the sang that's been sung about here for long enough."

"Let's hear it then, guidwife—I'm aey glad to hear an authentic auld sang."

"Aye. . . I thocht you wad be. Here's how it goes then—but mind you, my voice is no' what it was."

And after a bit crooning as if to refresh her memory of the air, the landlady sang softly but with feeling:

"Lassie, lend me your braw hemp heckle, and I'll lend you my thripplin-kame; my heckle is broken, it canna be gotten, and we'll gae dance the bob o' Dunblane.

"Twa gaed to the wood, to the wood, to the wood, twa gaed to the wood—three came hame; an' it be na weel bobbit, weel bobbit, weel bobbit, an' it be na weel bobbit, we'll bob it again."

But the Bard had his pencil out before she was finished.

"Come ower the first twa lines again, landlady, till I get them right—I like the flavour o' that. . . Aye fine: I've got it now. I'm much obliged to you. . . And gin my learned and worthy friend, Mr. Nicol here, wasna in sic a hurry to make Crieff afore we bed the nicht I dare say you and me could gang to the woods."

"But I doubt nor three wad come hame!"

"Ye never ken your luck, wife—and ye wadna come hame empty."

"God help you, Mr. Burns—you're an affa' man."

"Ah we'll maybe gang to the woods yet, guidwife. I'll warrant there's naebody in Dunblane kens their way about them better."

"I've seen the day——"

"And you'll see a wheen mair yet."

"Will you be back this way again?"

"Dinna tempt me, now!"

"Oh, you're no' the man to need ony tempting, Mr. Burns. You'll be doing a' the tempting. What say you, Mr. Nicol—you're no' saying much?"

"Madam: I'm a man o' few words and I keep my observations to myself. Especially where a man and a woman's concerned."

"Aye . . . now I wadna say that *you* went much to the woods."

"Mr. Nicol prefers to go to bed—wi' a big-bellied bottle."

Nicol scowled at the landlady's rich laughter and then scowled at the Bard. He knew perfectly well that he was only joking with the landlady—but he was not so sure that the landlady was joking. She might tell stories about them that would not be to their credit. At the same time he could not help but marvel at the way the Bard got round folks. A few minutes in their company—especially the company of women —and he had them eating out of his hand, had them warming to him.

And the Dunblane landlady had certainly warmed to Robert Burns—even though she was but joking with him. Yet, at her heart, there was the regret that she was not of his age. For, with the instinct nearly all of her sex had, she knew that he would be a superb lover, a lover to remember. . . But she was also a realist. She knew that she could do nothing with him but enjoy his company—and look quizzically and nostalgically into his great glowing pools of eyes.

He had tried to get away from it often enough; but even as he took in the ample proportions of the landlady as she sat into the table he realised that he liked stout well-proportioned women; even honest-to-goodness (and good-natured) rolls of fat he did not find in any way repulsive. This he had now come to realise was almost a second law of his nature . . . until he met with a slim slip of a maiden with good looks and a good nature—and then her very lack of plumpness seemed to accent her charms.

He pushed back his plate. Perhaps he had a soft side for all of them—provided they were none of your simpering haughty dames poisoned with pride and rotten ill-nature. He could abide almost anything in a woman but pride and ill-nature and that peculiar haughtiness that goes with that combination of character defects.

As he rose he caught a look in the landlady's eyes that went back twenty or thirty years: he put his arm round her shoulder and gave her a kiss on the cheek. Simultaneously he placed some silver in her hand.

"That's for your sang, guidwife—and that's to settle the lawin, though you needna count it."

"My blessings on you, laddie—even if you are the great Scottish Bard . . . and I think I ken how you cam' to write that sang on Annie o' the Corn Rigs. . . Guid luck to you on your journey."

Back in the chaise Nicol relaxed his scowl and permitted himself a queer affectionate grin. "You're a deil's buckie, Robert. Damn you, you've given that woman the thrill o' her life. She'll carry the imprint o' that kiss to her grave."

"Just a fleeting gesture, Willie. But I'd rather a woman like that appreciated my sangs than a' the literati in Edinburgh: that's the greatest reward a poet can experience."

"Aye, I believe I can understand that, Robert. . . I believe I can. Mind you, there's times when I have a reunion dinner in Edinburgh——"

"——dinner on the table at 3 p.m. prompt—go on, Willie."

"Aye—that was the time we had the dinner. There young men come and tell me just how much they appreciate my tutoring. Mind you, that's what makes teaching worthwhile —wipes out the scores o' the ungrateful duffers—aye, and the superior eediots who wouldna deign to thank those who battered the education into them. Aye: I believe I can understand what that wife's appreciation meant to you. It must indeed be a grand thing to be a poet."

"It has its compensations, Willie. Mind you, I appreciate my responsibilities too."

"What responsibilities?"

"My responsibility to the folk who have acclaimed me poet. They expect a certain standard from me and I must try not to lower that standard."

"You'll no' lower ony standards. You please yoursel' wi' what you write. If you do that you'll please maist folks. Remember: you're your own best judge."

"In a sense yes, Willie. But there's another sense. There's a collective wisdom and judgment of the common folk from which there's no appeal. You canna be a poet o' the people until the people acclaim you as such. Then if you accept that acclamation you must accept the responsibility. For myself I'm humble enough about it—but proud enough too. In fact, Willie, I couldna be prouder for I've achieved my highest ambition; and no man can achieve higher than that."

"Aye—but you've been acclaimed, Robert. That's the difference atween you and me. I've achieved my greatest ambition. I set out to be the best Latin scholar of my day. Maybe I'm no' as good as I think I am; but I havena met onybody to equal me. But then I havena been acclaimed—and that mak's a hell o' a difference. Oh, they ken damned weel they canna come near me on the Classics—but I've still got to thole that bluidy useless auld wife Alexander Adam. That galls me, Robert, and galls deep into the quick."

"It must, Willie—but will your time no' come?"

"I doubt it—aye, and it would come too late if it came now. No, Robert, I'll just need to dree my weird—and fight to maintain my position. For mind you: Adam would get rid o' me —if he dared. Of course if he hasna got the scholarship he's got the style to impress the parents and the magistrates. And that, I'm afraid, is what counts."

"And what about his Roman Antiquities?"

"*His* Roman Antiquities? A mere compound o' other men's brains—the damndest plagiarism, the very damndest. . ."

But seeing that Willie was about to enter upon his now familiar tirades against Rector Adam, the Bard quietly let the subject drop (his private belief was that nobody could be as black as Nicol painted Adam).

As usual when they were silent, or Nicol was sleeping, he concentrated on the scenery and the passing scene from whichever window presented the more interesting picture.

NORTHERN SCENES

Everything interested the Bard—especially the rivers. Water always had fascinated him—except the open sea—and he took note of every river they crossed or bordered: the Devon, the Forth, the Teith and the Allan. He knew from his wide knowledge of Scottish song that there was hardly a river but had a song—and invariably a good song—written in its praise.

As they proceeded, the country-side grew more rudely picturesque; but the Bard, who was still the practical peasant, noted with regret that the land was sadly unimproved. It offended his idea of agricultural economy to see so much potentially first-class ground lying barren and waste.

This aspect also appealed to the Latin master—but in a purely academic sense. Yet in the back of his mind he planned against the day when he would have saved enough money to purchase a small estate for himself and his family.

But essentially Nicol was a Latinist. His interest was not only in the language: he was also intensely interested in everything that pertained to the Romans. He knew all the historic camping places of the Roman armies of occupation. He thought nothing of halting the chaise and trudging a mile or two over rough ground in order to inspect some ruin, bridge, road or camp. Thus they had to halt at Ardoch and inspect the groundwork of the famous Roman camp there. . .

They dined at Crieff, which was their halting place for the day.

In the afternoon the Bard, who had an introduction to Aberuchill House, some eight miles west along the Strath of Earn, set off with Nicol in good spirits. They had made enquiries at the Crieff inn; and though they learned with regret that Sir William Murray of Ochtertyre—about a mile and a half off their route—was absent, they decided to take the road that passed Ochtertyre House since the Bard, if he could not visit Murray, was at least determined to see his residence.

Of all the roads the Bard had travelled in Scotland he was inclined to give the palm to the road that led from Crieff round by Ochtertyre to Comrie and Aberuchill. And though both he and Nicol were somewhat depressed by the cold reception they received at Aberuchill, yet the romantic nature of the country-side compensated for that.

Here the Bard felt he was truly in the Highlands. Everywhere the eye was held and enchanted by the hill contours and by the fact that every turn of the road presented to them new vistas and mountain-mass formations to claim their attention.

"Personally," he said to Nicol, "I prefer the pastoral Lowlands; but then I'm native there. But I can't deny, Willie: there's something about the Highlands and the Highland scenery that's more romantic and inspiring than anything to be found south of Stirling."

Nicol agreed; but he agreed as a traveller. Both of them had the traveller's approach to the problem of scenery. It was a pleasant change from the land they had known, from the country that had been familiar to them from birth; and their rapture at the contrast was none the less genuine despite the fact that neither of them would have dreamed for a moment of settling anywhere in the Highlands.

Indeed this was their uppermost feeling as they continued their journey!

Vista upon vista of hills, stark and grim; hills, grass-green and purpled with heather; hills folding, crease upon crease, fold upon fold, crest upon crest of ancient enduring contours. And yet, though they were to travel in the presence of the high Highland hills for at least a fortnight (often in their shadow) it was not the hills that held and fascinated the Bard so much as the rivers that flowed through the glens and straths and gathered volume from every burn and tarn that tore and leapt from the hill-sides.

And sometimes, as when they spoke to an innkeeper, the Bard regretted he had no Gaelic. The soft tongue of the Highland people, as of the Irish, was more foreign, more alien and strange than the tongue of France or the dead words that had once lived in Rome. He regretted this; for the place names sounded strange to him and he could not get at the poetry they expressed. But sometimes he would hear a Highland lass singing softly the soft rising and falling Gaelic songs; and he would listen bewitched and enchanted. He did not know the words that accompanied those strange lilting melancholy airs; but at the first opportunity he was determined to prick down the notes, however crudely, so that with good Scottish words he might be able to preserve the airs in Johnson's *Museum*. With the spirit of the music he felt himself in harmony. No music other than Gaelic music could so poignantly express the sadness, the wildness, the utter desolation of the country-side.

And yet much as he admired, much as he responded to this main pulse of Highland life, the more he realised the tragedy that had befallen Scotland as a result of the defeat of the Highland Host at Culloden. And the more did he understand why it was that his fathers, under the Earl Marischal, had joined with the Stewarts—to maintain and defend the way of life that had been theirs since that day when "Old Time was still young."

There was not much of this he could convey to Nicol. Nicol was no poet. As a scholar, with his roots in the Annan soil on the Solway Firth and his brain sodden with the classics of Greece and Rome, he had no enthusiastic response to offer to the barren poverty-stricken Highlands. Nicol was interested in the scenes through which they passed; but he was incapable of enthusiasm. To Nicol, as to nearly all Lowland Scots, the Highlands presented a strange stern savagely-romantic scene.

Yet the Bard was more than thankful that he travelled in Nicol's company. From Crieff they went up the Sma' Glen on a dull morning; and the desolation and utter waste of bare hills would have depressed him to the point of deepest melancholy—but for Nicol.

At Amulree they turned sharply to their left, went up Glenquaich and climbed by the barren shores of Loch Freuchie; up into greater barrenness by the one thousand seven hundred and twelve feet pass of Meall A'Choire Chreagaich—and so by the steep descent into Kenmore at the foot of Loch Tay. . . Here the Bard realised that this multitudinous sea of petrified waves could not have been borne without company.

God! but the Highlands were dreary and desolate—barren beyond belief. And growing more barren every year. There was much evidence of this in ruined houses and farm-steads and patches of land that had once been cultivated going back to the wilderness of bog and heather and coarse grasses.

True, there had once been good healthy life here. The Highland Host had not been recruited out of the wilderness. It was obvious that the wilderness could not have supported so many thousands of brave and stalwart men. Maybe in the company of men and women and laughing children these gaunt mountains might be borne with fortitude—and even with favour.

It wasn't that Robert Burns was unused to loneliness and a measure of desolation. His early years on Mount Oliphant had been lonely and desolate. Maybe his reaction to the Highlands arose from his horror of all human isolation and loneliness. . .

The loneliness of the Lowlands was, at worst, a bleak and

bare loneliness—a moorland monotony. Here, rising above the bare moorland monotony, were the desolate and domineering mountains.

He would have spoken to Nicol about them; but the scholar protected himself from such scenic impacts by the simple expedient of closing his eyes and going to sleep—or pretending to do so.

The mountain torrents were no streams along whose banks a lover and his lass might wander. They were fit only for the mountain goat and the small hill sheep with their sure feet and small bleating black faces. . .

But at Kenmore they found a comfortable inn close to the waters of Loch Tay where the River Tay flowed eastwards from the loch. All melancholy thoughts were drowned in good drink, ballasted with good food and dispersed in the good company of the landlord and landlady. All around were gaunt savage hills; but Taymouth itself was peaceful and pastoral: a small northern Eden set in the wilderness.

It was not surprising that, after a walk around Taymouth, and before going to bed, the Bard took his pencil and wrote on the whitewashed wall above the chimney-piece:

Admiring Nature in her wildest grace,
These northern scenes with weary feet I trace;
O'er many a winding dale and painful steep,
Th' abodes of coveyed grouse and timid sheep,
My savage journey, curious, I pursue,
Till famed Breadalbane opens to my view.
The meeting cliffs each deep-sunk glen divides:
The woods, wild-scattered, clothe their ample sides;
Th' outstretching lake, embosomed 'mong the hills,
The eye with wonder and amazement fills:
The Tay meand'ring sweet in infant pride,
The palace rising on his verdant side,
The lawns wood-fringed in Nature's native taste,
The hillocks dropt in Nature's careless haste,
The arches striding o'er the new-born stream,
The village glittering in noontide beam—

Poetic ardours in my bosom swell,
Lone wand'ring by the hermit's mossy cell;
The sweeping theatre of hanging woods,
Th' incessant roar of headlong tumbling floods—
Here Poesy might wake her heaven-taught lyre,
And look through Nature with creative fire;
Here, to the wrongs of Fate half reconciled
Misfortune's lightened steps might wander wild;
And Disappointment, in these lonely bounds,
Find balm to soothe her bitter rankling wounds;
Here heart-struck Grief might heavenward stretch her
     scan,
And injured Worth forget and pardon man.

THE BIRKS OF ABERFELDY

After Taymouth greater glories awaited them—and they took the time and the trouble to sample them. They visited Glenlyon House—where once the most gallant and most persecuted of the Highland clans, the MacGregors, held sway; paused at Fortingal, an old capital of Gaelic culture; called at Castle Menzies; and crossed the River Tay to see for themselves the famous birch-trees of Aberfeldy.

They clambered up to the Falls of Moness and there and then the Bard took pencil and paper and wrote his first draft of *The Birks of Aberfeldy*.

Here even the prosaic Nicol was somewhat moved.

"I'm beginning to understand a poet a bit better now—now that I see you in the throes o' inspiration. And damnit, Robert, there's something here to inspire the dullest o' mortals. What is it? The thundering o' the waters, boiling in their bottled wrath; or the sun coming in through the birken branches? But, of course, *you* had to bring a lass into it!"

"Aye, Willie; and if I had the lass here I would show her that I meant every word I've written. There's a conjunction o' scenery—however wild and awe-inspiring—and the love o' a lass that aey comes over me. Maybe because heightened feelings need a lass to relieve them. I canna pour out poetic vapours to you, Willie. Nor do I feel like it. But wi' a lass—the things I could say! So—for want o' a lass I maun just invent one . . . and then sing to her! That's a' the secret about sang-writing. If folks could only be made to understand that, it would save me answering—or evading the answering—a lot o' damned silly questions. . . But one o' the great solaces o' the poet lies in the fact that what he canna experience in the flesh he can experience in the imagination. . ."

"Quite so, Robert. . . I'm no' such a bluidy ignorant gull as you sometimes seem to think I am. But you hae a bluidy realistic imagination. You beggar: it's little wonder nae woman can resist you! But come on: we'll be here a' day—and you can write a thousand sangs if you like in the long winter nichts——"

"But you ken what the poet Gray said?"

"I ken plenty; but I'm cocking my lug to you."

"Gray said that a word fixed at or near the spot was worth a cart-load o' reflection."

"Aye—but he didna say onything about a whole bluidy poem fixed at, or near, the spot—especially when a pair o' guid horses were champing at their bits—and a driver getting restless. I thocht you were anxious to see Niel Gow?"

"Niel Gow? I'm anxious: more nor anxious. So I'll need to come back here wi' my bonnie lassie some other day—or nicht! Oh, damnit, I must see Gow, if it can be arranged. This Doctor Stewart at Inver will maybe be able to help me. Do you want to see Gow?"

"I've heard him in Edinburgh—and he's worth hearing, the same Niel Gow. Someday his son Nathaniel will ding him to rotten sticks. But, by certes, Niel Gow can fairly kittle the hair on the thairms."

"I don't know about his playing, Willie—except what I've heard about it. But he's done some fine work and composed some fine airs: genuine Scots airs, Willie. They follow in the great tradition. Mind you, as a composer for the fiddle I think there's nothing to equal the Duke o' Gordon's butler, William

Marshall. Nae doubt about it, Willie: Marshall's the daddy o' them a' when it comes to composing a reel or strathspey. But if a' I hear's true, Niel Gow's the greatest fiddler Scotland has ever heard. And while I'd like to hear him play, I'm mair anxious to hae a crack wi' him. I don't know whether I told you before—but I'm mad on the fiddle. More than onything I would like to hae been a great fiddler. But a' I ever managed to do—though I can still do it—is to finger out the notes of a new tune——"

"And what good does that do you? Do you need a fiddle for that?"

"I use the fiddle as a student would use a Latin dictionary —maybe you ken the uses o' one yourself?"

"Damn you: I've thumbed half-a-dozen to tatters in my day. Go on: I'm interested. I'm a sicht mair interested in music than you think."

"Aye; but our native Scots airs, Willie. There's nothing to equal them. And if my musical ear's rude and unlettered, like my poetry, then I intend that it should remain so."

"Aye—your blood's at the dancing stage still."

"And aey will be. But can you no' see that our dance music—especially our slow strathspeys—if taken a shade slower still—are full of a fine melancholy—a deep heart-core melancholy—a truly pathetic quality that reaches deep down?"

"Maybe. . ."

"I've been through every bit o' Scottish music that's been published. Take Oswald's Caledonian Pocket Companion— there's a vade maecum for you!"

"I like a good fiddler, Robert—preferably a merry-going one. But you want to mak' sangs . . . is that it?"

"Yes: I want to make songs—that's the true work o' a poet. I canna write my own tunes—or, by God, I'd write both the words and the music. But the music comes first. Folk may forget the words o' a song—but seldom the melody."

"There's something in that. But how comes it, Robert, that since you can neither read music at sight nor compose it yoursel' you should hae such a nicety o' musical under-standing? You're forgetting that I've heard you discussing this with Schetky. I mind ae nicht after you'd left us, Schetky told me that you'd the maist acute ear for the turn o' a tune that he ever heard in a layman."

"Schetky's a grand fellow. But you'll no' deceive me in a Scots air, Willie—aye, nor an English, nor an Irish one either. I've studied them a'—or a big lot o' them. And if I hear a song sung, even on one hearing it'll come back to me—sometime. But then I was brought up on native Scots tunes; and I suppose they've got into my blood. . ."

And that indeed was where the time and the rhythm had entered. It was part of his being. And Niel Gow, for all his fiddling and composing, was not half the musician the Bard was.

A FIDDLER FROM THE NORTH

After coming down the River Tay to Inver and Dunkeld and spending the night with the hospitable Doctor Stewart, Niel Gow himself came and played to the company.

It was a grand moment when the Scots Bard met the Scots Fiddler. And Niel, though he was getting on in years and his hair was grey, had the healthy complexion of a young man.

What struck the Bard most was Niel's honest social bearing. Though he had been much flattered and lionized he was, like the Bard himself, entirely uncorrupted. His expression was strong honest and friendly. There was no guile about the man—except perhaps that he thought more of the Duke of Atholl than he did of King George.

He played some of his own compositions and then he played some of the Bard's favourites—*Tullochgorum*, *Loch Errochside*, *Invercauld Reel*, *Monymusk*, *The Cameronian Rant* and many others—though he pretended not to know *Miss Admiral Gordon's Strathspey*.

The Bard was delighted. Gow's upward bowing was unbelievably powerful, and his broad strong fingers worked with amazing accuracy on the thairms. But it was in his bowing that his genius lay. In the downward stroke especially he could nip in an octave grace note even in his quickest fingering when the notes flew from the fiddle like sparks from a stick-fire attacked by the bellows.

Between tunes they would talk of Scots music.

"Yes, indeed," said Gow in his soft sure voice, "there's just no other music. Indeed, yes . . . and good, mind you, though some of our tunes are to-day, the old ones were far better. Och, grand tunes they used to have—and many of them. And words to them too . . . in the Gaelic, yes. But there have been many sore and sad times in the Highlands since. Yes, yes: many a good fiddler as weel as a good soldier went down in the Misfortune."

"Aye . . . Culloden was a bad day for Scotland."

"Terrible, Mr. Burns, terrible. Yes, yes: a sad day and the end's not all told yet. . . But you're a fiddler yourself, now?"

"No: not even a poor gut-scraper. My fingers were too stiff and broken on the plough-handles ever to have done much——"

"Yes . . . I've heard the pipers talking about it too. Och, but mind you, good hard work can be a good thing for giving strength to the arms and fingers. Och yes . . . it's wonderful. . . And you're wanting some of my tunes for this Mr. Johnson's Musical Museum—and you to be putting words to the tunes! Indeed and you are welcome. It's the wonderful gift you have of words, Mr. Burns, and to be putting them to the music is a grand idea. In the old days it was always done—each district would be having its own set of words—and the tune would be altering here and there . . . and that's how there'll be so mony different tunes, as it were. . ."

"I agree," said the Bard. "But whether like the hen and the egg—whether the words or the melody came first, I doubt if there is any knowing now. What does matter, I think, is that a good tune never lacked words for long—nor did good words long lack a tune to fit them. But since there is no substantial difference between us, Mr. Gow—and as Mr. Nicol and I maun be moving on to the Blair of Atholl—maybe you would honour me—and I'm sure I speak for Doctor and Mrs. Stewart and the company—with another of your own compositions. . ."

CUMHA CHLAIBHERS

From Dunkeld they went north to the Blair of Atholl where Josiah Walker was tutor to the Duke of Atholl's young heir, the Marquis of Tullibardine. Here they hoped to spend at least a night and a day. Walker had assured him of a welcome at Blair. . .

But their journey north continued through romantic scenery—the apparently endless masses of heathery hills and tumbling rivers.

When the scenery was not romantic the Bard described it as of "crude grandeur."

But, as always, they noted everything en route—even Faskally House was noted in his diary as "a beautiful romantic nest."

Before Faskally, in the Pass of Killiecrankie, down by the rocky bed of the river Tummel they visited "the gallant Lord Dundee's stone."

Here again the Bard gave the cynical Nicol evidence of his protean qualities.

If ever a man was a protestant that man was Robert Burns. Or so reasoned Nicol—and he saw in him the epitome of all rebels who are in revolt against the soulless challenge of Authority.

By all the rules the Bard should have had little sympathy for Viscount Dundee who, as Bloody Claverhouse, had visited so much brutality on the Covenanters.

But it was not as the butcher, the torturer and the murderer of the rebel protesting Covenanters that the Bard now saw Dundee. He saw him as the Jacobite leader fighting gallantly for James and, at the moment of his victory over the enemy, falling mortally wounded.

The stone that marked the spot where Dundee had fallen marked a greater tragedy than concerned Graham of Claverhouse. The stone was symbolic of national defeat. Yet what nation was defeated? And was there indeed a Scottish nation in existence to suffer defeat or victory from an English nation?

The Bard had a clear answer to such questions. Catholics and Protestants had joined together (to say nothing of Episcopalians and a muster of nondescript faiths) to fight for the Stewart cause. Had there been no "alien race to fill the throne" he would have been as contemptuous of the Stewarts as he was of the Hanoverians and all the kith and kin of the Wee German Lairdie. But "a race outlandish" did fill the throne; and some forty years after the defeat of the Stewart cause, he felt, even as his ancestors had felt, that the Stewarts were symbolic of Scotland as a nation; that the defeat of the Stewarts was the defeat of Scotland. . .

And thus, standing by his stone beside the roaring Tummel river in the wild pass of Killiecrankie, the imagination of the Bard fashioned Graham of Claverhouse the killer of Covenanters, into the gallant Lord Dundee, symbol of his nation. . .

Here the Bard of Ayrshire transcended the boundaries of Carrick, Kyle and Cunninghame and became truly the Bard of Scotland.

Nicol learned much from the Bard in this; and his admiration for his genius grew deeper. But this admiration Nicol kept to himself—except in odd spasms when he was carried away by the enthusiasms of the moment.

WORTH GOING A MILE

Toward evening they arrived at Blair Atholl and put up at the inn. Josiah Walker had given the landlord instructions that he was to be informed of the Bard's arrival. Walker came down to see him shortly after they had settled in.

But Walker was troubled. He knew (for he had already sounded his employers) that the Bard would be more than welcome to Blair Castle: both the Duke and Duchess considered themselves his patrons. But Willie Nicol was another kettle of fish. Walker didn't like him; and he knew that he would never be tolerated for a moment inside the House. But—as he also knew of Nicol's violence of temper and his general irascibility—he realised, as much for his own as for the Bard's sake, that he would have to be very tactful.

At the inn, Walker drew the Bard aside.

"I have arranged, Mr. Burns, that you will sup this evening with the Duchess—the Duke and other members of the company, Sir William Murray of Ochtertyre, Mr. Graham of Fintry, General and Captain Murray and others being out on a visit, will not be back till night—they are indeed expected late. But the Duchess asked me to inform you that she expects your company to supper. But . . . there is the . . . slight difficulty of Mr. Nicol. I have not informed the Duchess that Mr. Nicol is travelling with you. Ahem. . ."

"Mr. Nicol is not invited—is that it?"

"After a manner. . . Of course the Duchess does not know he is here."

"I suppose I should resent that, Mr. Walker. But I ken well that Mr. Nicol has little interest in some of my friends and patrons—and some of them have less interest in him. But though I will not be dictated to in the matter—and manner —of the company I keep, I will not have Mr. Nicol slighted or offended."

"I understand, Mr. Burns: indeed I have been exercising some thought on the matter. To-morrow, I have no doubt, you will be invited to spend the day at the House and mix with the company . . . and I need not tell you how it would be very much in your interest to do so. I wonder . . . does Mr. Nicol care for fishing?"

"Mr. Nicol is very keen on fishing—a cruel cold-blooded sport; but there you are!"

"Excellent! In that case, Mr. Burns, I'll arrange for Mr Nicol to be supplied with rod and line and directed to one of the best stretches of the river. . ."

"You are well acquainted with Mr. Nicol?"

"No. . . I can hardly claim acquaintanceship, Mr. Burns. On the other hand, it would be idle for me not to admit that I am well acquainted with his reputation."

"An unfavourable reputation?"

"So much so, that I confess I'm rather surprised to find him in your company—but I mean no offence, Mr. Burns."

"No, no: no offence between friends, Mr. Walker. You're not the only one who has misjudged Nicol. We all have our failings. But the only failing I find in Mr. Nicol is that he has a damned in-kneed kind of a soul. . . But a heart of gold —and a mighty brain."

"I'm willing to accept your judgment, sir—more than willing. And I'm much relieved to know that you appreciate the delicate position Mr. Nicol places me in."

Nicol was delighted with the arrangement even if he wasn't overjoyed at the thought of the Bard hob-nobbing with the Duke and Duchess and their friends. He conceded, however, that it might be in his interest—in so far as that interest lay in selling out his Edinburgh edition.

For two days the Bard enjoyed the company at Blair. The company was highly distinguished as company distinguished by social rank goes. The Duchess, who was a daughter of Lord Cathcart, had the company of her two sisters, Mrs. Graham and the seventeen year old beauty Miss Cathcart who had been born in Russia when Lord Cathcart was ambassador there. Unfortunately, Miss Cathcart, like her sisters, was tainted with consumption. Like her sisters, she was doomed to an early grave. Then there was the family: the Marquis of Tullibardine, Lords James, Edward and Robert Murray, Ladies Charlotte and Amelia and the youngest, Lady Elizabeth, a mere five-months old.

The Bard had a genuine liking for the family—especially the younger members; and he could never resist a bairn. They were well-mannered and of an open friendly disposition and utterly lacking in social snobbery. They liked the Bard and delighted in his company.

Blair Castle was not an imposing house, viewed from the grounds, being little more than a plain square block with plain square windows. But such of the public rooms as the Bard had access to were splendidly furnished—even if the windows were confined to one wall.

From riding in the company of Sir William Murray of Ochtertyre, and viewing the Rivers Tilt, Tummel, Garry and Bruar; talking with the ladies; reciting to the children; and discussing public affairs with men like Graham of Fintry, he put in some agreeable hours.

But though he was pressed to stay, and though it was suggested that he might like to be presented to Henry Dundas (who was visiting the next day), he had to tear himself away. Nicol wouldn't have minded another day at the fishing; but they had their itinerary to watch and already they were a couple of days behind schedule. Besides the Bard had no wish to meet Henry Dundas, Dictator of Scotland. . .

GHOSTING THE GLOAMING

As they travelled up by the banks of the River Garry next morning to Pitmain Inn by way of Dalnacardoch and Dalwhinnie, Nicol quizzed him about the company.

"And why didn't you tackle Graham of Fintry about the Excise?"

"To be frank, Willie, I forgot about the Excise; but even had I minded I doubt if I'd have said a word. There's no pleasure in cadging a job at any time—but some times are worse nor others. There's something incongruous about asking a duke, when you meet him socially, if he could find you employment as his footman—so what more me asking a Commissioner for a post as a humble Exciseman?"

"Damn you, Rab, you're far too touchy and finicky about things. But maybe meeting so many gentry has put you off the notion o' being a gauger?"

The Bard did not reply, though he could have cut Nicol to the bone with the rejoinder that almost sprang from his lips. He regretted Willie's attitude at times—there was so much he could have discussed about his reception at Blair Castle. But he didn't even mention that Sir William Murray had pressed on him an invitation to Ochtertyre and had expressed his disappointment at being absent from home when he had been at Crieff.

There were so many things that Willie did not understand and so many things to which he was hostile. And yet such was the dialectic of their friendship that they were drawn to each other as much by their opposites as by their affinities. . .

At Pitmain Inn, in the Badenoch district, where they bedded that night, they experienced once more the strange feeling that though they were still in Scotland yet it was a Scotland into which they could not fully enter. There was a darkness about Badenoch and a loneliness that was foreboding. The country-side was here more open—the hills seemed to lie further back; and yet, beyond them, seemed to be interminable wastes of mountain and moorland and desolation.

And in the deep tangible darkness that lay thick in the glens and crept up the hillsides to meet the pall of grey-white mists that crept down from the hill-tops, the two travellers clung to each other for company.

For here indeed was the very country-side of James MacPherson whose translations and recreations of Ossian had, in the far Lowlands, so captured their fancy. Ossian's country or MacPherson's country, it mattered little: it was only too easy to imagine how the old Celtic heroes had lived out their heroic days against this sombre background of the terrible and awful.

Yet out there, in front of the inn, running north-east through the strath, was the River Spey. The Spey signified Strathspey; and Strathspey signified the flaming vitality of the dance music that had come to be known by the name of the district. There was nothing here at the head of the strath to suggest the bounding leaping heart-joyous pulsating strathspey music; no fingers cracking on the chanter; no fingers nipping neatly on the thairms. Maybe as the strath opened out to the sea they would find evidence of a landscape more in harmony with the music: here, despite the Spey, was the mood of Ossian and the Fingalian fantasy of far-off things ghosting the gloaming. . .

Next morning the white lazy mists still hung on the brow of the braes and the burns boiled in a tawny foam. The spirit of Ossian still brooded over the land, brooding from behind the ghost-white mists. And the land crouched under the brooding, bare and barren and heathery-brown—apart from the rich holms that bordered the river.

Still following the Spey, they travelled in silence the thirteen miles into Morayshire to breakfast at Aviemore—as wild and withdrawn a spot as they had yet touched.

But here, even as at Pitmain, the Bard was not wholly overpowered by Celtic gloom. There were rich patches of land on either side of the Spey—richer than they had yet seen around any truly Highland river. And rich or bare, and despite the corries in the high hills holding through the summer their eighteen feet of snow, the whole country-side was undeniably romantic. Towering mountains, snow-pocketed or mist-shrouded; cascading falls and swift tumbling boulder-strewn rivers—these were the hall-marks and high-lights of scenic romance.

Romantic but not homely; romantic but not pastoral; romantic but not warming to the heart. Romantic as the Lowlands were not romantic. Maybe there was nothing romantic about Ayrshire—the Ayrshire he knew from Daljarrock in Carrick to Dundonald in Cunninghame. Maybe behind those far-off hills where Stinchar flowed there was more than a touch of the romantic—and not solely because of Peggy Kennedy. . . No: in the Lowlands as in the Highlands there was barrenness and poverty and want and suffering; but there was, too, a bienness, a couthieness, a throughither warmth and richness of men and women, bush and brae, ploughed rig and delved kail-yard, market cross and clachan howff, that was absent from the Highlands. The Lowlands were home-spun, hand-knitted; hemp-heckled and thrippling-combed; but not, in any large way, romantic. The landscape there swelled and curved like a woman's body—sweet-breasted thigh-lissomed, buttock-rounded; bosky-delled with briar and woodbine-twined. . . Homely as home is ever homely; but not romantic.

The Highlands were romantic. Cold, stern, wild; grand, terrible, sublime; a primitive wilderness; a barren waste; land of brown heath and shaggy woods; land of fantastic mountains ever towering peak on peak; cascades. . .

The Highland scene completely overshadowed the poor remnants of the harried Highland clansmen. The Clan system was destroyed and there was no system to take its place. There was only drifting and withering away. Deadness and defeatism ate into what vitals remained of the old Gaelic economy. And though the Bard was not economist enough to make this analysis, he was poet enough to sense and assess the results in terms of human relationships.

NEVER AT THE CENTRE

They came up Speyside in a jig of slurs and dotted rhythms to Castle Grant, the home of Sir James Grant to whom the Bard had an introductory letter from his good-brother Henry MacKenzie.

But though Lady Grant proved both sweet and charming (and sweetness and charm in a woman ever captivated the Bard), the dullness of Sir James and his heterogeneous company of religiously ordained bores jaded him with their table-talk— to say nothing of Sir James's Oxford accent (where he had been an unofficial prize-winner in Sensibility). By the time they had emerged from the grand old house and the beautifully laid-out grounds the mist had come down again and with it a wet penetrating smirr of rain.

Presently darkness came down; and Johnny Fleck, the driver, had the devil's own job making the ten twisted miles on the deeply rutted military road to the inn at Dulsie, on the rocky banks of the River Findhorn.

It was darker inside the chaise than out. The travellers leaned their heads against the leather cushions of their respective corners and maintained a deep silence.

Nicol thought: just what was to be expected from any

relation of Henry MacKenzie's—damned proud ignorant upstarts. It would have been showing Robert Burns little enough hospitality if they had even made the offer to put them up for the night.

What the Latin master did not know was that MacKenzie's letter of introduction had warned the Grant chief against him. Had he known that MacKenzie had written: "Mr. Burns is accompanied in his Northern Tour by Mr. Nicol, with whom I have not the honour of being acquainted, but Louis, I presume, has a very feeling remembrance of him. . ." he would not have been surprised; but his temper would have known no bounds and he would, in all probability, have returned to Edinburgh to threaten Henry MacKenzie with even more physical violence than he had already threatened Rector Alexander Adam.

The Bard thought: Well, that's another company of dull conceited hashes to add to my collection. Deadly dull and insufferably conceited—especially the clergymen. Lady Grant excepted. Aye, a real nice body, Lady Grant. He could have enjoyed a long evening's crack wi' her at her fireside—alone. A woman of sense, sensibility and understanding.

What was wrong with him that the gentry could both humour and flatter him and yet, even at the height of their hospitality, treat him as an outsider, as someone who, however gifted, remained outside the pale of their suffrage. Always and ever inside the perimeter but never at the centre. . .

Ah well: he would live to fight another day. . .

His arm was sore hanging onto the strap in the chaise. It swayed and rocked, tilted and heaved, plunged and reared and betimes came to a juddering stop as a wheel sunk into a deep rut and Johnny Fleck had to lash the tired sweating horses into giving the extra lift necessary to pull them out.

Yet Johnny had to be careful how he used the beasts. Nicol was hard enough of heart to let him have his head but Robert Burns was a different type. He could fly into a white-raged fury at times when he thought the beasts were being over-sorely pressed; and on many a hill he had insisted that Nicol and he walk and that the beasts be led by the head. A strange man, this poet Burns, thought Johnny. But as strange a pair of travellers as he had ever driven. Sometimes their talk droned with a lazy rhythm, sometimes they seemed to be raging and quarrelling and sometimes they laughed uproariously and seemed to be in great high spirits.

God, aye: a mad pair, thought Johnny; but damnit, despite their faults, a likeable though ill-matched pair. . .

And so they came to Dulsie on the rocky banks of the Findhorn river, in the wet misty darkness, to lights, a fire, a hot supper and a warm bed.

SCENE OF A MURDER

A pleasant ride of eight miles brought them the next morning to Cawdor Castle which they were both keen to explore.

The Bard of Scotland was a keen student of the works of the Swan of Avon: Nicol, too, was something of a Shakespearian. But for Shakespeare they might have known little enough of MacBeth and Duncan. And at Cawdor the Red River (the Allt Dearg of the Gaels) and the River Avon met and commingled below Cawdor Castle.

And here, though modern extensions had been added, stood the old battlemented tower of MacBeth's days. They were shown not only the room wherein Duncan had been murdered but the very bed on which he had slept that fatal night—all as chronicled by Holinshed and dramatised by Shakespeare.

Even the cynical Nicol raised no objections for he was anxious to believe what he was told. And the worthy pair, having evinced their keen interest in Scottish history and paid their respects to Shakespeare's memory, moved on the few miles to Kilravock Castle.

At Kilravock they found Mrs. Rose (to whom, as his cousin, Henry MacKenzie had written a letter introducing the Bard) and her mother and the Cawdor minister, Mr. Grant: an odd trio. The mother indeed from the point of view of character was the most remarkable of the three. If she was full of Highland pride, she was also full of Highland hospitality and had all the robust common sense that usually accompanies an active managing woman. Her widowed daughter, on the other hand, was more accomplished. She entertained the Bard by singing—and playing her own accompaniment on the guitar.

Mr. Grant, the Cawdor minister, had imbibed some of the grimness—without any sense of the history—of Cawdor Castle. He was an opinionated man holding to his opinions with the greater strength because they were so few.

But Nicol was damned if he would listen to any widow singing—however accomplished she might be and however charmingly she might pluck at the strings of her guitar. He was anxious to reach his journey's end. Having seen the bed whereon Duncan was murdered he had no patience for braxie-brained clergymen.

Mrs. Rose, however, made the Bard promise that he would return to Kilravock on his journey from Inverness and with this promise Nicol escaped with him.

They reached Inverness by way of Fort George and found the Highland capital as dull and lifeless and uninteresting as the bare barren moors that surrounded it.

They put up at the Eccles hotel; and though the Bard was jaded to death by the journey he took time to scrawl a note to Baillie Inglis and enclose the letter of introduction Willie Dunbar had given him. It was up to the Baillie to decide on the next move. In his present jaded mood he was beyond worrying about meeting a leading citizen of Inverness.

He wrote also to his cousin, James Burness, a lawyer in Montrose, and told him he expected to be in Stonehaven by Monday the tenth of September (in six days' time) and asked him to meet him there that he might be his guide to meet his father's relations.

That done he went to bed for it was his intention to ride west in the morning and to visit the Falls of Foyers on Loch Ness-side some twenty miles away. . .

A HIGHLAND BAILLIE

He found William Inglis, Baillie of the Royal Burgh of Inverness, a kindly man some twelve years his senior and still on the sunny side of forty. Besides, he had a pleasant wife. . .

The Baillie liked his food and his supper-table was a generous one.

". . . just that now, Mr. Burns; and you were greatly impressed with the Falls of Foyers?"

"I was indeed greatly impressed not only with the Falls but with the whole journey, Mr. Inglis. I have now seen a large part of Scotland both in the south and in the north—and Scotland is indeed a gloriously romantic country in her scenery—even as she is in her history——"

"You find the history of Scotland romantic, Mr. Burns?"

"Indeed I do, sir. Dark and bloody as many of its pages are, yet I find a broad red ribbon of romance runs through it all."

"Aye, weel . . . poets may see things that way, of course——"

"And you don't, sir?"

"Well . . . to be quite frank, Mr. Burns, it's a thing I never thocht aboot much. Ye see my wark on the council. . ."

The Bard allowed the Baillie to habber and gabber about his work on the council and the burden of local administration and how he had little or no time to devote to the study of anything that did not directly contribute to the well-being of the town.

The Bard had heard the same story often enough before: indeed, he could have made the speech for the Baillie. But for all that, the man was well enough intentioned and he felt no anger at him.

What impressed the Baillie—and he was very much impressed—was the number of nobility and gentry who had dined and wined the Bard. It seemed that a poet could draw in his seat to the drawing-room fire of a lord where a worthy baillie (and of a Royal Burgh) might do no more than stand in the servants' hall with his bonnet in his hand.

"Aye . . . you seem to have travelled around, Mr. Burns, and met a' the folk that were worth meeting—you must feel very proud o' yoursel'. I gather you're no' without a pride in your independence."

"Indeed, sir, there's little more a man can be proud of. . . But to-morrow morning I should like to make my way eastwards from Inverness by way of Drummossie Moor. I should think that even yet the tragedy that befell——"

"Ahem . . . we dinna talk aboot Culloden now-a-days, Mr. Burns. We let that flea stick to the wa'—as it were. We're a' guid Hanoverians in the North now."

"I had not intended to raise the matter politically——"

"Ah weel . . . there's rightly nae other side to it, Mr. Burns. Either a man's a guid Hanoverian or else he's a disloyal subject. Though I've nae doubt ye see your red ribbon o' romance there as weel."

"Yes . . . even on Culloden Moor, Mr. Inglis. For there was courage there and high ideals; and I shall ever regret that Scotsmen were butchered and drowned in their own red blood on that sorry day."

"Aye . . . there were some puir misguided callants paid a sair price for their folly that day. But then that's the price a' fools maun pay sooner or later."

The Bard did not reply. He noted the consternation that was beginning to show on Mrs. Inglis's face and the alarm that excited the eyes of the three young ladies at the table.

He had hoped that a baillie of Inverness might have some pity for the Jacobites if only in the secret chambers of his heart. But like most men who aspire to govern their fellows the secret chambers of the Baillie's heart resounded only with the echo of his own ego.

So he returned to his lodgings and Willie Nicol, with little to show for his evening but advice about the best road to take for Culloden Moor in the morning. . .

THE LONG GRAVES

By the time they reached Culloden the sun had absorbed the last wreath of mist. He walked bare-headed about the long mounds of graves where the clansmen had fallen. How often had he raged and mourned, fretted and fulminated about the defeat of Scotland on Drummossie Moor? But a different pain came to him as he stood on the ground which, less than fifty years ago and but a dozen-odd years before he was born, had been soaked in the blood of Scotland's finest sons—the bravest of the brave.

Here on this sad lonely moorland Scotland's independence had bled to death.

Even Nicol was affected by the scene and by the Bard's mood. There were times when Nicol knew how to be silent—and to feel humble in his silence. And Willie Nicol was not a humble man. But when the Bard was in the mood; when all unconsciously the emanations of his feelings overran his physical boundaries, then Nicol knew to withdraw in himself and preserve a discreet and reverend silence.

Nicol's personality was aggressive. Never, in his spirit, had he genuflected to any man or any institution. But there was much essential humility in Nicol's make-up. And Robert Burns was one of the few men, who, on occasion, could make him aware of it.

Nicol wandered about the site of the battlefield; but he kept his physical distance from the Bard. He kept his silence. But occasionally, from under his jutting eyebrows, he watched him and wondered.

He loved that lad—for he was still a lad to him—loved him as a father might love a worthy and favourite son. Loved him to the point where he thought he had the right—born of unsentimental affection—to guide him, upbraid him, defend him, counsel him and rage at him.

Aye: God damnit, he loved him—and yet would never be

494

able to tell him so; even hint at it; would never be able to tell him of the pangs of jealousy he suffered when men and women utterly beneath him in every consideration but that of social rank exploited his company. The Bard thought that gentry like the Duke and Duchess of Atholl, Sir James Grant and his kind were interested in him for his own intrinsic worth and merit. But if his poems hadn't made a fuss in Edinburgh, would they have taken any notice of him? Not they; and though he knew this, the Bard didn't. Oh, he was no fool: he had damned few illusions about either fame or fortune. But he was weak in the face of their blandishments. A duke had but to treat him like an equal and immediately he accepted the duke as an equal—an equal in fellowship, if not in rank.

But—and here Willie Nicol girned and spat—if the gentry had any real regard for him they would place him in a good job. There were few jobs, aside from the teaching o' Latin and Greek, that Robert Burns couldna do gin he was given a bit smattering of instruction. . .

And so, on the Field of Culloden, Willie Nicol stood apart and watched his companion and clarified his feelings towards him.

As the Bard had pointed out to him: Scotland had perished with the Jacobite forces (Prince Charlie was but another useless head for a useless crown); and yet now, strangely enough, there stood on the graves of those dead clansmen the one man who might yet save Scotland and burn the consciousness of her wrongs into the hearts and minds of generations yet unborn.

One man. That was a thought. This burning-eyed boy was only on the threshold of his genius. But he would live down the ages, damn the doubt. Aye: when a' the dukes and gentry were clean forgotten. Aye; and if there was to be ony revenge for the horrors that Butcher Cumberland had visited on the defeated clansmen and their helpless dependants then young Robert Burns was the lad who would bring it about.

What could be more contemptible than a Highland duke whose father—or maybe himself—had led his clansmen to the field of slaughter and himself had escaped to France only to come begging to the Hanoverians to be allowed back his lands —that he had but shared wi' his clan—and in his miserable begging promising to be more loyal—to creep lower and crawl more abjectly—than the worm that wriggled on the damp earth. And to treat the remnants of his clan like pariahs!

The Ayrshire ploughman, become Caledonia's Bard, knew that better than most. And yet a German-Geordie-crawling duke had but to show kindness to him and he was ready to swear that he was one of the best of fellows. . .

What Willie Nicol could not appreciate was the Bard's longing for friendship, his desperate need for good-fellowship. His whole being longed to be at peace and friendship with all mankind. Man, in the abstract, he could detest as much as any: one men in the gross flesh of actuality he could equally detest. But the honest social friendly man, no matter who or what he was, he could not resist. And in judging a man's honesty he was only too prone to give him the benefit of the doubt, and to keep giving him the benefit until definite proof of his dishonesty had been driven home to him.

It was a serious flaw in the Bard's nature this inability to apply his otherwise sharply-critical eye to a man's character when it was cloaked with kindness and proffered friendship. It was this that caused him to extend the fullness of his personal warmth to men—and occasionally women—who were entirely unworthy of it. But occasionally he erred in contradiction. Beneath the mask of incivility and apparent enmity he sometimes judged a man—and more often a woman —too harshly and unfairly. But then it was difficult for him to feel in half-measures.

And he gave himself in no half-measure to the Field of Culloden. He offered up a prayer to the dead clansmen and their shattered ideals.

His prayer was genuine. He had a habit of praying when under deep emotional stress. But his prayers were not the prayers that would have won recognition from the Kirk of Scotland. Could they have been submitted for the learned theological criticism of the General Assembly of the Kirk they would have been found strangely rationalistic or pantheistic and strongly laced with all manner of heresy. . .

But he offered up his prayer in deep humility and deeper sorrow. It was not possible to believe—spiritually—that the men who lay under those long green mounds had died uselessly, had been mown down and butchered in vain. Surely there was some recompense—somewhere, somehow. They had died not for themselves but something greater than themselves; and they had died because their belief was stronger than their disbelief. . .

A cool analytical brain might say that they died in vain because they died for the vainest of all human vanities—the abstractions ossified in such words as nation, home, race, truth and honour. . .

But wherein lay the abstraction when men did in fact die for so-called abstractions? Did dying for an abstraction make it less abstract? Did dying for a lie convert a lie to truth? Or were truth and untruth abstractions also?

As the Bard raised his head and his eye caught a glimpse of the sunlight reflected on the clear waters of the Moray Firth, he was conscious of the limitations of his knowledge and of all knowledge. But his consciousness of the knowledge why the clansmen had fallen at Culloden was deeper and keener. And thus he dedicated himself—in spirit—to the fight that had been their fight, to the cause that had been their cause.

And why should he, an Ayrshire ploughman become Caledonia's Bard, weep unseen tears for MacIntoshes, Camerons and Frasers?

There was no answer from the glinting waters, no answer from the vacant moorland, no answer from the silent graves.

But there was an answer in his heart; and the answer in his heart assured him that an abstraction ceases to be an abstraction and becomes a burning, living and livid truth when the heart so determines.

And what determines the heart? If there were questions the wise men were too ignorant to formulate there were answers the poets were too wise to ignore.

As he entered the chaise, Nicol, from under his beetling brows, shot a quizzical glance at the Bard and was surprised but consoled at the look of concentrated resolution that burned in his eyes.

BONNIE CASTLE GORDON

From Kilravock (where the charming Miss Ross sang Gaelic songs that blended deeply with the carry-forward of his mood from Culloden) they journeyed onwards by way of the pleasant fishing village of Nairn, where they dined, to the ancient seat of Brodie of Brodie to pass the night.

The Bard found James Brodie (as he recorded in his diary) " truly polite, but not just the Highlander's cordiality." What the Bard did not realise was that Brodie's young wife, with whom Brodie had eloped, had been burned to death in Brodie House the previous year.

Brodie was still brooding over his loss. But in the morning he thawed sufficiently to tell them that MacBeth's Moor (in the vicinity), where Shakespeare had laid his witch meeting, was still haunted—according to the country-folks of the district who refused to traverse it after dark. . .

But by this time Nicol was itching for the road home. He had had enough of travelling in the Highlands. He wanted to meet some kindred spirits. Brodie of Brodie bored him. He was anxious to breakfast with the Elgin schoolmaster to whom the Bard had an introductory letter from Willie Dunbar.

But the Bard was still enjoying his journey and he cared more for the sight of the ruins of Elgin abbey than he did for the pleasant and insipid conversation of the Elgin schoolmaster.

And why should he bother with a schoolmaster nonentity when but eight miles onwards on their route stood Castle Gordon? An hour spent with the Duke and the Duchess would be much more stimulating. He knew he would be welcomed and he was keen to see how the Duchess looked in her Highland home and removed from the glitter and affectation of an Edinburgh assembly room.

But the eight miles' drive from Elgin to Spey Bridge at Fochabers were driven in a sulky mood by Nicol.

"So you insist on visiting Gordon Castle, do you?"

"If you like to put it that way, Willie, I insist. I'll no' spend much time there and you can dine at the Fochabers inn while I'm away."

"You ken, Robert, how I dislike the Gordons—aye, and the Atholls. But the Gordons! Damnit, the Duchess is nothing but an aristocratic whore—and you ken that——"

"No, Willie, I don't—and that's flat! Both the Duke and the Duchess went out of their way to give me a lift in Edinburgh. Neither o' them are ignorant—as I've told you. D'you remember me telling you that night at Pitmain Inn how Grant o' Rothiemurchus's poetry was told me by the Duke o' Gordon?"

"Telling *you* poetry. Huh! Bluidy impudence—aye and ignorant conceit. Telling you poetry?"

"Yes, telling me poetry. And the Duke's no mean poet himself, not to be a poet . . . if you understand me."

"Huh!"

"What are you huh-ing at, man? What have you got against the House o' Gordon? Nothing but idle gossip."

"Oh, go and kiss the Duke's **** for a' I care—and the Duchess's too, when you're at it. Kiss a' you can get frae here to Edinburgh. But there's no' one o' them has lifted a wee finger to help you—or ever will. You that wrote o' puir Fergusson and the Edinburgh gentry. . ."

With that Nicol grunted and turned his head to the window. But though the Bard regretted Nicol's attitude he wasn't put out by it. He knew his companion too well to let him get very deep under his skin.

Nicol glumphed at the inn while he spruced himself up. He walked the mile from the great gate to the palace of Gordon Castle. Unlike Blair Castle (the lay-out of which he thought had been spoiled by bad taste) the grounds of Castle Gordon were in every way delightful. The Castle itself with its modern

improvements (the Duke was raking in much money from the
Yorkshire company to whom he had sold his enormous forests
on a twenty-six years' contract) looked, for magnificence,
second only to the Duke of Northumberland's palace at Alnwick. Only here, beside the Spey and in the setting of distant
hills, the situation was superior.

He had some misgivings as he approached the great door;
but his feet crunched manfully enough on the gravel.

He announced himself to the liveried door-keeper and
waited in the magnificent hall with its great stairway and
marble busts. . .

To his surprise (and the servant's) it was the Duke himself
who came down the great stairs to welcome him.

"Ah, Burns, my dear fellow! How are you? Travelling
the Highlands, I hear. How kind of you to give us a call.
Come upstairs and meet my friends—and my family. My wife
will be delighted to meet you again. She's never done telling
our friends about you. Naebody like Robert Burns! And
damnit, Burns, that's true—there's naebody just quite like
you. Na, na: you're no' interrupting us. We'd be damned
annoyed if you'd passed by Castle Gordon on your journey—
and you but a mile frae the door. Oh aye: it's a grand place
in the summer—but a beggar to keep warm in the winter—
that's when we appreciate George Square and Auld Reekie.
I miss the Town, Burns, for a' that I like the country. You'll
dine wi' us—and tell us a' about your tour? Getting plenty
o' inspiration, I'll warrant! You maun do us a piece on
Castle Gordon if you catch ony inspiration. No: unfortunately Marshall's no' here the noo. A wonderful composer
in our native idiom—nobody better. But you maun meet
my secretary, James Hoy. A grand fellow: you'll like
him. Daft on our poetry and music too. A great admirer
o' yours. You'll need to spend to-morrow in the library wi'
him."

"To-morrow! Much as I would like that, your Grace, I
must not delay my departure beyond an hour or so—I lie
to-night in Cullen."

But by this time they were in the great drawing-room and

the Duchess was coming forward to meet him. She extended her hand and smiled on him:

"How nice of you to call, Mr. Burns—we're maist delighted to have you—come and meet the company——"

"Jane—Burns tells me he proposes to lie in Cullen to-night and that he can spare us no more than an hour of his company."

"Nonsense—you'll stay the night—stay for a day or two—for as long as you like. There's to be nae question of your lying in Cullen. Cullen indeed!"

"Much as I would like to accept your kind hospitality, your Grace, 'tis quite impossible. I have a very tight programme for my itinerary—and my travelling companion is waiting for me at the Fochabers inn with the chaise——"

"Do we know your companion?"

"Mr. Nicol, Latin master of the High School——"

"But what nonsense, Mr. Burns. I'll send immediately for Mr. Nicol. I have not the pleasure of knowing him—but your friends are welcome to Castle Gordon. You didna think we would turn them away at the door, did you? Excuse me for a minute and I'll have Mr. Nicol brought up."

She turned on her heel before the Bard could protest.

The Duke smiled at his discomfort.

"Na, na, Burns; you canna escape frae Castle Gordon so easily. Jane'll fix everything afore you can say knife. Now come and meet my daughters, Charlotte and Madelina. . . Colonel Abercrombie. . .

The company paid him every deference—a visiting prince could not have expected more.

But it was James Hoy, a mild-mannered though physically burly man, still this side of forty, who held his attention. Hoy took the Bard to see the library which was immediately above the dining-room. Here was the finest library the Bard had ever seen in a private house—indeed he had never seen a finer anywhere.

Here, chatting to Hoy, he forgot about Nicol and their decision to make Cullen that night—after all, Cullen was but at most a four hours' journey away. . .

"The Duke, as you may know, Mr. Burns, is something of a poet and a musician himself."

"Yes . . . but though he told me of the poetry of others he never told me any of his own."

"That's like him. Aye, and he favours our Scots dialect. I think his lines to Cauld Kail in Aberdeen are of some merit."

"I should dearly like to hear them, Mr. Hoy, for I already know of two versions that are presently sung—not forgetting the Reels o' Bogie, not quite a ladies' song."

"No: not quite a ladies' song—but I think, mind you, I could give you a version of the Reels o' Bogie less o' a ladies' song than the one you ken. The Duke, like the rest o' gentlemen, is fond o' a good bawdy song. But here's his version o' Cauld Kail—it reverses the coggie you ken and puts the lassies first. ' There's cauld Kail in Aberdeen, and Castocks in Stra'bogie, gin I hae but a bonnie lass you're welcome to your coggie. And ye may sit up a' the nicht and drink till it be broad daylicht; gie me a lass baith clean and ticht to dance the Reel o' Bogie. In Cotillons the French excel, John Bull in Countradances; the Spaniards dance Fandangos well, Mynheer an All'mand prances. In Foursome Reels the Scots delight, the Threesome maist dance wondrous light—but twasome ding a' oot o' fight, danced to the Reel o' Bogie——'"

But they were summoned to dinner. And, with much regret, the Bard had to quit the library and join the company at the table.

They weren't long seated when the servant returned from his mission to Nicol. The servant whispered the message to the Duchess—and the Duchess blushed. She turned to the Bard who had the seat of honour on her right hand.

"Your friend seems to be in an unconscionable hurry—he has had the horses harnessed and is waiting at the inn for you."

The Bard's face drained of colour.

"He proposes to proceed without you—but need that worry you?"

"I'm . . . I'm afraid it must, your Grace. . . I'm afraid I must go now. But I cannot tell you how much I regret this and how your kindness to me——"

"Not a word, sir; not a word. If you must, you must—and that is an end to it. It's a pity——"

The Duke raised his mild eyebrows. "Must you go, Burns?"

"I . . . I . . ."

He literally tore himself from the table after stammering his apologies and saying what good-byes he could muster. Humiliation and rage battled in him for supremacy.

Humiliation won. He trudged down the long avenue almost afraid to lift his eyes from the toes of his boots.

God damn Nicol now and for evermore! But he was almost crying with vexatious disappointment.

And then there was Nicol storming up and down in front of the inn. He set to on the Bard the moment he came forward.

"And what the hell d'you think you're up to sending a bluidy flunkey doon here to ask me to dinner. Ye ken fine *I* don't want ony o' *their* damn left-over invitations—you ken fine——"

But the Bard, noting that his luggage was safely aboard, opened the door of the chaise and took his seat. Nicol, maddened at this fresh insult, clambered aboard like an enraged bear.

"Noo listen here——"

"Noo listen here, beggar-all, Nicol. You want to get to Cullen the nicht—well, you'll get to Cullen the nicht. And frae here to Cullen clinch your ill-gotten tinkler's jaws thegither. I'm in nae mood to tak' ony o' your damned ill-natured jealous snash."

Nicol almost foamed at the mouth as the horses started forward.

He lowered his voice; but his bitter sneering had an edge to it like broken glass.

"Hae you nae manhood left in you? I've to kick my heels in Fochabers till you persuade the dirt o' gentry to send one o' their liveried flunkeys to me wi' a command to dine at Castle Gordon. Command me? They can command you, the independent Bard o' Ayrshire—o' Scotland; but by God, sir, the duke or the duchess's no' born that can command Willie Nicol——"

Yet all the time what Nicol really wanted to say was: Rab, I'm sorry if I've spoiled your visit with my headstrong irascibility. I didna really mean to do it. But I lost my temper —as I'm aey losing my temper——

But of course Nicol couldn't say this; and the more he raged and fulminated the more he increased his violence.

The Bard said nothing. Indeed he very soon ceased to hear what Nicol was muttering. After all, Nicol was in the right —and he had arranged to see his cousin James Burness at Stonehaven on Monday and since this was Friday it would take them busy to make it. Indeed he ought to be thankful to Nicol for dragging him away. He could quite easily have been tempted to stay the night at Castle Gordon—and then his cousin could have whistled for him at Stonehaven.

Suddenly his mood changed. Of course Nicol was right. It was quite useless for him to run with the hare and hunt with the hounds. Willie Nicol meant more to him than Duchess Gordon. Nicol was a dear companion: Duchess Gordon was but a patron. She was a fine patron and a fascinating personality—it was always a stimulating pleasure to meet her. And the Duke was, in himself and in his own right, a pleasant fellow. But both Duke and Duchess remained patrons. He might visit his patrons by himself; but he had no right to visit them in the company of his friends.

Having come to this decision he felt much better. He turned his attention to the passing scene and soon became entirely absorbed in it. He noted the poor unimproved state of the country-side and the primitive carts whose unshod disk-wheels juddered and lumbered in the ruts.

Half-way to Cullen, on the coast, he suddenly turned and laid a hand on Nicol's knee.

"I'm sorry, Willie, damned sorry. You were quite richt: we had to make Cullen the nicht. Only, Willie, believe me, you wrong the Duke and Duchess. They didna ken I had a travelling companion waiting for me at Fochabers. But the moment they heard, the Duchess insisted on sending for you."

"Dinna apologise to me, Robert: dinna apologise, damn you: dinna apologise."

And in that moment Robert Burns knew that he was a thousand years older than Nicol and ten thousand years older than his ancient knowledge. Yes, Nicol might be able to give him an odd scrap from his junk-load of classical learning; but in the ways of the world, the flesh and the devil, he could give Nicol more than he was fit to absorb.

. . . but the pity of it that he couldn't have stayed on at Castle Gordon; the pity that Nicol had to send that damned arrogant message so that he had had literally to tear himself away. For the Duke had made him happier than ever a great man had—noble, princely, yet mild: condescending and affable, gay and kind. The Duchess charming, witty, kind and sensible. . .

The pity that things had aey to be someway and never exactly how one wanted. . .

ABERDEEN AWA'

The following day they did some good travelling. Break-fasting at Banff, they left the coast and going south by the parish of Gamrie and through rough wild hilly country by Newbyth, came into Old Deer where they slept the night.

Sunday morning saw them up betimes on their way to Peterhead on the coast and taking in the famous Bullers of Buchan on the way south to Aberdeen by way of Ellon.

Although the Bard found Aberdeen an easy-going lazy town (taking advantage of a touch of late sun and the unusual absence of a knifing wind from the North Sea), he was delighted to meet with some excellent fellows who, for wit and worth, brought back to him memories of some of his Edinburgh cronies.

These cronies he met at the office of James Chalmers the printer of *The Aberdeen Journal*. That Chalmers was also a subscriber to the Edinburgh edition gave an added interest to the call. But though he found Professor Thomas Gordon from King's College, John Marshall, a minor poet, and Andrew

Sheriffs, a major poet (in his own opinion) interesting enough, it was Bishop Skinner who most delighted him.

On learning from Chalmers that the Bishop was the son of the author of *Tullochgorum* he insisted that they adjourn to the inn near by and celebrate the occasion by drinking a glass of wine. Here to his chagrin he learned that in passing through Peterhead the previous day he had passed within four miles of old Skinner's dwelling, Linshart, where he was Episcopalian minister.

"I'd have gone twenty, aye, fifty miles out of my journey to have paid my respects to your worthy father, Bishop. I regard the man who wrote Tullochgorm and The Ewie wi' the Crookit Horn as one of our finest song-writers."

"My father will be delighted to hear of your high opinion of his song-writing merits—though I wouldna say that he puts too high a value on them himself. He is an exceedingly well-grounded scholar in the Classics—as Mr. Nicol would have discovered had you visited him."

"That I dinna doubt, Bishop. But dinna you—or your father either—put too low a value on song-writing. From what I can gather there are many excellent Latin and Greek scholars in Scotland—but good song-writers you can count on the fingers o' one hand."

"A not unfair way of putting it, Mr. Burns."

"Aye. . . I'll write your worthy father and ask him for his songs that they may go into the next volume of Johnson's Museum—so that they may occupy a place of honour in what will be a national gallery of honour."

"Write to him, Mr. Burns! It will cheer his heart. I'll write him myself and tell him of our meeting and of your disappointment at passing so close to Linshart without knowing of his whereabouts—— And what has been the highlight of your tour, Mr. Burns—you'll have seen plenty to interest you?"

"Yes, Bishop, the more I see of Scotland, the more I realise what a wonderful country is ours. I have laid in a stock of poetic materials to last me a lifetime. Yet who but Ossian can do justice to the Highlands? My homespun muse does very well for homespun themes—and for nature in her quieter and more pastoral moods. But the Highlands, Bishop. . . Ah, the Highlands: there you have me! A lonely girl by the track singing to herself an old Gaelic melody—that I can appreciate; that I could hit off in a song myself. But mountains, range upon range, mountains whose names I do not know—there is nothing by which I can fix them. There must be some human incident, some immediate human emotion before such a background—or even foreground—can be used. Yet when I said I had laid in a stock of poetic ideas, I did not exaggerate. I have seen nature in many phases—to a lesser extent man and woman too—so that I can bring in a stroke from here and a colour or shade or fragment from there. . . I trust, my friend, I don't weary you——?"

"No, no, Mr. Burns—I am sorry you interrupted yourself. You have made clear so much that has been a deep mystery to me——"

"There is only one mystery, Bishop—life itself."

"Revelation aside—I suppose it is. But poetry is part of the mystery of life."

"In that sense, yes. I was thinking of the mystery made of it by the schools and the professors—and the critics. All nature is poetry. Show me what in nature is not poetry."

"The hawk that tears apart the harmless linnet pouring forth its melody from the leafy spray—would you call that poetry?"

"Yes. There is poetry in the hawk that swoops on high. Cruel poetry, dripping with blood, if you will; but poetry, Bishop. I see you're doubtful! Per contra, then, where is the poetry in the slaughtering gun of the so-called sportsman mutilating the muir-cock or the mountain hare? Besides, my dear Bishop, there's the morality of the business. The hawk swoops to death from instinct; from the iron law of cruel necessity; from its need to survive. But the sportsman and his gun? Here we have the perversion of natural—or divine —impulse. . ."

"But what has this to do with poetry, Mr. Burns?"

"Precisely this, Bishop. Poetry must be directed not to

the perversion of human instincts—but to uplifting and purifying—and liberating."

"You believe in the natural goodness of man then, Mr. Burns?"

"Not so to believe is to despair."

"Yet you are no moralist, sir, if I read your poetry aright."

The interruption came from the twinkling-eyed professor of philosophy.

"A much stricter moralist than the worthy Bishop here, my equally worthy and learned Professor. But my morality is the morality of freedom, independence. Liberty, sir, is the most glorious theme to which the human mind can address itself."

"But liberty for what, and for whom?"

"Ah, there you strike to the heart of the matter, Professor. I do not mean liberty in the abstract—that is every whit as impersonal and meaningless as scenery in the abstract. No, sir: what I have in mind is human liberty. Liberty for every man, woman and child under the canopy of heaven. What liberty has a starving man? Is a man tied to a thowless shrew of a wife free? Can a man build resolve on reason if his mind is shackled in superstition? I'm a bard whose morality proclaims the end of all man-made moralities and sets over against them the superior morality of nature; who proudly proclaims that the only law is Nature's law and that anything else is both a conceit and an impertinence. . ."

Against the Bard's sweeping eloquence Thomas Gordon did not advance the claims of academic philosophy, nor did John Skinner advance the claims of Episcopalian theology. They were much too captivated to do other than listen, occasionally interjecting a question in order to hear the reply rather than to engage in debate.

Both were very pleasurably astounded. The heaven-taught ploughman spoke as one having authority and not as any backward rustic. Both, of course, considered the views he advanced as untenable. But they were novel views and given rigorous and delightful exposition. There was nothing arrogant or dogmatic about the man. His most audacious utterance was charged with his personal charm and expressed with a magnificent modulation of voice.

From discussing poetry (or rather listening to an exposition on poetry) they passed to a discussion of Scots songs. This incensed Willie Nicol who was anxious that they should continue their journey. The Bard had expressed his desire to spend as much time as possible with his relations about Stonehaven. This seemed to Nicol reasonable enough even though it would probably mean that he would need to kick his heels in some lousy village inn the while. But it seemed unreasonable that so much time should be wasted in Aberdeen blethering to the son of a man who had written a couple of not very interesting old songs.

"We canna sit here a' day, Robert: we'll need to be pushing on to Stonehaven."

But nobody took notice of him. This increased Nicol's rage. He disliked being overlooked. But the greatest Latin scholar in Europe was a mere nobody in Aberdeen—at best he was the travelling companion of the Scots Bard and only as such was he to be tolerated. Indeed, the mild-mannered Skinner was somewhat shocked to find him addressing the poet so brusquely. . .

As Nicol and the Bard travelled south Bishop Skinner wrote, among other things, to his father. . .

". . . whom should I meet but the famous Burns, the Ayrshire Bard! And on Mr. Chalmers telling him that I was the son of ' Tullochgorum,' there was no help but I must step into the inn hard by and drink a glass of wine with him and the printer. . .

"He was collecting in his tour all the ' auld Scots sangs ' he had not heard of, and likewise the tunes, that he may get them set to music. ' Perhaps,' said he, ' your father might assist me in making this collection; or, if not, I should be happy in any way to rank him among my correspondents.'

"As to his personal appearance, it is very much in his favour. He is a genteel-looking young man, of good address, and talks with much propriety, as if he had received an academical education. He has, indeed, a flow of language, and seems never at a loss to express himself in the strongest and most nervous manner. On my quoting, with some sentiments of praise, the Ayrshire ploughman, ' Well,' he said, ' and a ploughman I was from my youth, and till within these two years had my shoes studded with a hundred *tackets*. But even then I was a reader, and had very nearly made all the English poets familiar to me, not forgetting the old bards of the best of all poetical books, the Old Testament. . .'"

FATHERLAND

The grey fishing township of Stonehaven clung in the rock-cleft by the harbour. The fisher-biggins were low and dour and sturdy and strong in order that they might brave the gales that swept in from the sea. Behind the fishermen's houses a scatter of biener dwellings gave to the place something of the air of a market town, which indeed it was to the surrounding country-side.

It was bare hard-bitten countryside. But the Bard noted its every shade and contour with deep emotional interest. Here was the land of his fathers. How often had he listened large-eyed and lip a-tremble, at Alloway, Mount Oliphant and Lochlea, to his father telling of those bitter hunger-harassed days at Clochnahill? Would he ever forget his father's description of that day he had stood on a bare knowe and had taken in in his outward as well as his inward eye, and for the last time, the scene of his birth and childhood? Clochnahill— his father and brothers and sisters standing at the door waving the half-hearted heavy-handed wave of sorrow. . .

And when, later in the day, he rode up the four miles to Clochnahill, on a borrowed pony, and found the steading deserted and the roof-tree fallen in, he could not hold the tears back.

Clochnahill was so pitifully like Mount Oliphant. The resemblance was overpowering. Here his father had laboured as a boy before he had apprenticed himself to Monboddo estate gardens. And gardening at Monboddo had meant no lessening of his labours—apart from the addition of a dozen miles of daily tramping. . .

His father had left Clochnahill because of a poverty that could no longer be endured, and had taken Mount Oliphant as his first farm. William Burns had been broken in Mount Oliphant even as his father had been broken in Clochnahill.

As the Bard's eyes searched the horizon he could hardly realise that the difference between Mount Oliphant and Clochnahill was but the difference of the miles that separated them. But the difference between himself and his father was greater than the years that separated them.

William Burns had been moulded by Clochnahill. If Mount Oliphant had moulded the Bard to an extent, he did not realise that he had reacted against that moulding process. . .

It was so much easier to understand his father now that he stood on the ground that had defeated him. Only the other day he had stood on the Field of Culloden. . . Now he stood on another but more intensely personal battlefield. But Clochnahill or Culloden, the results were the same: defeat. Defeat for the nation, defeat for the individual. . .

He let his eyes search south to the far horizon of smoke-blue hills. North, east and west the prospect was unbelievably bare and uninviting. But southward, down the Howe of the Mearns, down towards those far faint hills, lay promise. He could understand now why his father had gone south: it alone beckoned and gave promise of hope. . .

And here, by the throw of the dice-box of fate, the son returned, not trudging foot-weary in home-made brogans, but travelling in comfort and boasting the luxury of a chaise; not travelling unknown and unbefriended, but coming as the celebrated Scots Bard!

Aye: he had been born out of this hard-bitten, hard-driven wind-swept mist-shrouded clay-stony northern soil. A half of him. For at least half of him was his mother, born of the more prosperous Lowlands. And yet what was the difference here between Stonehaven and Tarbolton?

He could not express his thoughts to Nicol; he could not put down his emotions on paper. Someday he might express himself in a song. For the moment he could only endure the impact on his emotions. . .

Later that evening he spoke to his cousin James, the Montrose lawyer.

"I find it difficult to express myself, James. You see, I canna forget that my father was born here. I canna forget that he never lived to see it again."

"He never lived to ken o' your fame either, Robert. And I think that's the greatest pity o' a'."

"There's that to it too, James. But what I'm trying to say is this. My father left here in poverty and died in poverty. And now, but three years after his death, I come back. But no' in poverty——"

"My Uncle William would hae been proud o' that, Robert. Aye: as we're a' proud."

"It touches me to hear you say that. Touches me more than a' the praise I won in Edinburgh. I made this journey for a variety o' reasons. But in the forefront o' my mind I wanted to come here and see you a'—and see my father's countryside."

"And what d'you think o't now that you've seen it?"

"Well. . . I've seen some wonderful stretches o' Scotland since I left Edinburgh. Mile after mile o' the maist romantic scenery in Scotland. But, by birth and upbringing, I'm Ayrshire. There's no altering that: nor would I wish to alter it. No . . . but I couldna ca' this land romantic. It's cauld bare land, James—and a cauld bare coast."

"Och aye . . . but it's nae sae bad either, man: fowk get used till it. And when it's your hame-country what's the odds? You saw your aunties Jean and Isabel? Living hale and hearty and as like the world as you and me. And their guidmen, John Caird and Willie Brand, dinna look like deeing, do they? Of course your father, my Uncle William, frae a' I can hear, was an exceptional man. . . Aye, an exceptional man. Things are better of course than they were in your father's time:

that's admitted on a' hands. . . But what are you planning to do wi' yoursel' noo, Robert?"

"I suppose I'll turn farmer one o' these days. . . Somewhere in the south. . . But tell me more about my cousin Robert— and about yoursel'. . . My brother Gilbert is maist interested in a' our relations here and I'll need to take home a full account. . ."

He would liked to have spent more time with his relations; but not only was Nicol irking at the delay: their itinerary was also in danger. So missing a last breakfast meeting he scrawled a note of apology to James Burness and rode out of the North-east and down into the Howe of the Mearns.

They were now on the homeward journey and though there was still much interesting country to see and many interesting folk to meet, the highlights of the journey were over.

After Montrose (and a sail along the coast to Arbroath); after Dundee and Perth, after four days of travelling, they arrived at Kinross.

Here the Bard was seized with a violent attack of colic. He retired to his room in a melancholy mood.

BACK TO AULD REEKIE

On Sunday, his fit of the colic better, they rode across Fife and down to Queensferry. The silver Forth was a welcome sight in the glow of the watery afternoon sun. But, as soon as they had crossed, the sky became overcast with dull grey clouds and they rode into Edinburgh and down a deserted Princes Street in a drizzle of cold rain.

But Willie Nicol was obviously delighted at being back home.

"That's us back in Auld Reekie again, Robert. I'm damned glad to see her. We've had a grand trip. Damnit, it couldna have been better. Nothing to mar it barring that touch o' the colic you had last nicht. . . Aye: nothing to mar it. . . Ah damnit, there's something about Auld Reekie that canna be beaten. She tops every place I've seen yet. There's just nothing to compare wi' her—though you've got to travel to find that out. But I suppose Edinburgh's home to me now and that's a' that's about it. . . You'll be glad to get back yoursel', Robert?"

"Glad enough, Willie: though it's no' home to me."

"No: I was forgetting that, Robert. You've no home now. Except, mind you, that as lang as I have a bed you can make your home wi' me. Only I've thae bastards o' boarders to tak' in and batter Latin intil. . . And I'm no' looking forward to that. But when I canna put you up, Willie Cruikshank'll be able to give you a bed—and you couldna ask for better. Willie hasna the family I have and he doesna tak' in boarders. Dinna worry: between us we'll see you richt for as lang as you need to put up in the Town. . . But—you enjoyed your journey, Robert?"

"Why should you think otherwise? Of course I enjoyed my jaunt. If I have any regret it's the regret that I'll never have the opportunity o' enjoying one like it again."

"I wadna say that——"

"I'm saying it, Willie. As soon as I see Creech and get my money I'll need to return to Ayrshire. And I'll need to settle wi' Patrick Miller—if I'm no' too late. And then hard work again, Willie. In a way I'll no' be sorry. I was never meant for a life o' idleness."

Part Five

THE DIALECTICS OF DESIRE

END OF AN IDYLL

THERE WERE three major problems worrying Robert Burns that autumn in Edinburgh. The first concerned the question of settlement with Creech: the first step towards a settlement with Patrick Miller. The second concerned his prospects of securing an Excise commission. The third concerned Jean Armour and Peggy Chalmers.

Creech did nothing but make promises. And though they were infuriatingly vague there was nothing he could do about them. Hence there was nothing he could do about offering for Patrick Miller's farm at Dalswinton.

Jean Armour was pregnant again. James Armour, for all his lick-spittle fawning, might well issue another warrant against him. As for Jean: well, she wouldn't mind another bairn; and she knew she would be provided for. . .

Peggy Chalmers was a different proposition. But Peggy wasn't in Edinburgh. She was at Harviestoun and likely to be there for some time. There was nothing to hold him in Edinburgh. After the lapse of a week the Town couldn't hold him. And the news (which came to him in a roundabout way) that Peggy Cameron had given birth to triplets, and that they had died within a few days of birth, didn't help to make Edinburgh any more attractive to him—even though Peggy hadn't yet shown her face back in the Capital.

It was Doctor James MacKittrick Adair who, indirectly, came to his rescue. Foregathering one night at the Crochallan Club, they agreed on a tour, the main purpose of which suited them both. Both had invitations, for different reasons, to visit Harviestoun. The Bard was anxious to see Peggy Chalmers. Adair had notions about Charlotte Hamilton.

The Bard had also pressing invitations to visit Sir William Murray at Ochtertyre and John Ramsay at Auchtertyre—both houses within striking distance from Harviestoun.

The plan was so agreeable to both parties that no sooner

settled than they were off on horseback—Jenny Geddes having been brought back to Edinburgh the way she had left—by carrier Patterson.

For sixteen days the Bard enjoyed perfect relaxation. At Stirling he took the opportunity of knocking out the window with his "offending inscription": gladly paying the landlord for the damage.

At Harviestoun he enjoyed long walks and talks with Peggy Chalmers. Never had Peggy seemed more desirable, never had she given him so much of her confidence or received, with obvious sympathy, so much of his. The weather was delightful and the countryside a lovers' Eden. Darkness came down early enough to allow an hour by the fireside in the chilly evenings. And always the green soft swell of the Ochills soothed and caressed.

The Bard well knew that Peggy could not be taken by storm. His love-making, in its physical aspects, was gentle and reassuring. Then he proposed marriage. That was the end of the idyll. Peggy refused him with a delicacy that matched his proposal. But there was no more kissing, no more waist pressing, no more breast caressing. Physical intimacy was dead. Peggy offered her friendship. She loved the Bard too deeply to wish to hurt him.

Accepting the inevitable (no sooner had she refused him than he realised how inevitable the refusal was) he mounted Jenny Geddes and rode up into Strathearn to visit Sir William Murray. Here Sir William and Lady Augusta treated him with perfect understanding. He was free to come and go exactly as he pleased. . .

When he rode back to Harviestoun in a few days, Peggy was relieved to see that he was his old gay self again—at least to all outward appearances.

So gay and spirited did John Ramsay of Auchtertyre find him that he took notes of his conversational sallies—and Ramsay was something of a connoisseur in recording aspects of character.

Even Lady Bruce of the old Tower of Clackmannan, though having topped her ninetieth year, took to the Bard. Lady

Bruce was as worthy an ancient as Scotland had ever seen. She did not claim that she was descended from Robert de Bruce. She maintained that de Bruce was connected with her family. Being in the royal line, if not indeed of the blood royal, she took the Bruce's meikle sword from the wall and, making the Bard kneel on one knee, tapped the blade on both shoulders and knighted him there and then.

"Aye, aye, Maister Burns," she said. (She spoke with some difficulty, having lately suffered from a paralytic stroke.) "Aye . . . ye may weel be prood o' yersel': I dinna knicht a'bodies I meet wi', though I hae a better richt to confer that honour than onybody else I ken ootwith or inwith the realm. But gin ye hae won till the title o' Bard o' Scotland, and sin' ye be a guid Jacobite, ye micht as weel hae a bit knichthood to gae alang wi' it. I'd like fine to hae bestowed on ye a wheen merks o' land to gae wi' the title—but then a' Scotland's yours —which is mair nor ony o' German Geordie's cleckin o' gulls and gowks'll be able to claim. . ."

But nothing could daunt the Bard's spirit and even in Dunfermline Abbey he mounted the pulpit, and, while Doctor Adair mounted the cutty stool, delivered a mock harangue on the sin of fornication (after the style of Black Jock Russell of Kilmarnock) that astounded Adair and made the ancient mortar trickle in crumbs down the ancient walls.

But the Bard was enjoying his last fling, his last care-free holiday. He was in high spirits because his heart was heavy and the burden of his worries almost too heavy to bear.

Peggy was not for him—only her friendship. He might never even see her again. He was no longer a ploughman-poet: he was a poet who no longer had a plough to lay his hand to. How different with Adair. Adair was a doctor. He had money, address and an assured income. There was no doubt but that he would marry Charlotte Hamilton. Peggy? Ah, she would marry some well-doing professional man. She might even marry into the nobility.

No matter : he couldn't think ill of her. He would carry her name engraved on his heart till the day he died.

And so well did he hide his real feelings that James Adair never for a moment thought there was anything but the warmth of friendship between Robert Burns and Peggy Chalmers.

REASON FOR LIVING

Back in Edinburgh, and lodging in the attic of William Cruikshank's house, number two Saint James's Square, the Bard found himself stricken with his old trouble: a rheumatic feverish chill. But chill or no, he had to attend to immediate business. Here was a letter from Patrick Miller assuring him that he had not disposed of all his farms and would still be willing to entertain an offer from the Bard.

To this he replied:

Sir,

I was spending a few days at Sir William Murray's, Ochtertyre, and did not get your obliging letter till to-day I came to town. . . I want to be a farmer in a small farm, about a plough-gang, in a pleasant country, under the auspices of a good landlord. I have no foolish notion of being a Tenant on easier terms than another. To find a farm where one can live at all, is not easy. I only mean living soberly, like an old-style farmer, and joining personal industry. The banks of the Nith are as sweet, poetic ground as any I ever saw; and besides, Sir, 'tis but justice to the feelings of my own heart, and the opinion of my best friends, to say that I would wish to call you landlord sooner than any landed gentleman I know. These are my views and wishes; and in whatever way you think best to lay out your farms, I shall be happy to rent one of them. I shall certainly be able to ride to Dalswinton about middle of next week, if I hear you are not gone.

I have the honour to be, Sir,
        your obliged humble servant

That was as much as he could do about Miller—and his
future as a farmer. . .

Next he turned his thoughts to Johnson's *Museum*. The
farm and the Excise were problems of bread and butter, of the
need to live. The *Museum* constituted one of his strongest
reasons for living.

He must see more of his songs in Johnson's next number.
But Johnson was no Creech. He was a poor engraver and an
honest enthusiast. He must do everything he could to ensure
that Johnson's venture would be a success. He must get as
many folks interested in it as possible.

In any case he was due a letter to Castle Gordon. So he
took another sheet and wrote to James Hoy there. He had
written a song in honour of Gordon Castle and the sending
of it to Hoy might help to atone for his hurried parting that
day.

Sir,
I will defend my conduct, in giving you this trouble,
on the best of Christian principles—' Whatsoever ye would
that men should do unto you, do ye even so unto them.' I
shall certainly, among my legacies, leave my latest curse to
that unlucky predicament which hurried me, tore me away
from Castle Gordon. May that obstinate son of Latin Prose
be curst to Scotch-mile periods, and damned to seven league
paragraphs; while Declension and Conjugation, Gender,
Number and Time, under the ragged banners of Dissonance
and Disarrangement eternally rank against him in hostile
array!!!!!!

Allow me, Sir, to strengthen the small claim I have to
your acquaintance, by the following request. An engraver,
James Johnson, in Edinburgh has, not from mercenary views
but from an honest Scotch enthusiasm, set about collecting
all our native songs and setting them to music; particularly
those that have never been set before. Clarke, the well-known
musician, presides over the musical arrangement; and Drs.
Beattie and Blacklock, Mr. Tytler, Woodhouselee, and your
humble servant to the utmost of his small power, assist in

collecting the old poetry, or sometimes to a fine air to make a stanza, when it has no words. The enclosed is one which, like some other misbegotten brats, ' too tedious to mention,' claims a parental pang from my Bardship. I suppose it will appear in Johnson's second Number; the first was published before my acquaintance with him. My request is; ' Cauld kail in Aberdeen' is one intended for this Number; and I beg a copy of his Grace of Gordon's words to it, which you were so kind as repeat to me. You may be sure we won't prefix the Author's name, except you like; tho' I look on it as no small merit to this work that the names of many of the Authors of our old Scotch Songs, names almost forgotten, will be inserted. I do not well know where to write to you, I rather write at you; but if you will be so obliging, immediately on receipt of this, as to write me a few lines; I shall perhaps pay you in kind, tho' not in quality. Johnson's terms are: each Number, a handsome pocket volume, to consist at least of a hundred Scotch songs, with basses for the Harpsichord, etc.; the price to Subscribers, 5, to non-sub. 6sh.; he will have three Numbers I conjecture.

"My direction for two or three weeks will be, at Mr. William Cruikshank's, St. James's Square, Newtown, Edinburgh.

I am, Sir, Yours to command. . . .

THE ROSEBUD

In a few days the climax of the fever passed from him and though limp and exhausted he was able to get about the house in a normal fashion.

Mr. and Mrs. Cruikshank had much sympathetic understanding of him. Both were quiet reserved middle-aged folks happy though undemonstrative in their love for each other and utterly devoted to their lovely daughter Jenny who, at the age of twelve, was quite an accomplished player on the spinet.

In his passion for his *Museum* work the Bard found her a ministering angel. Every opportunity she could spare him, he sat beside her at the keyboard and got her to play over Scots tunes. As soon as he heard the melody once or twice it was fixed indelibly in his memory. And when she wasn't playing to him he was humming over the tunes or marking tunes in his music books for her to play over at the next session.

As Cruikshank said to his wife: "I've never seen the Bard in better spirits—and Jenny's gotten a new interest in her playing."

"Aye . . . it's a real pleasure to see the pair o' them busy at the instrument. My, but he kens a heap o' tunes—is there ony money in this work he's doing for Jamie Johnson?"

"It's a labour o' love, wife. Nae money could pay for it. And it's no' likely Jamie'll get ony money either."

"Weel . . . he maun hae a great love for thae auld tunes for he spends hours over them. . ."

But the hours that he spent seemed to the Cruikshanks more than amply fulfilled when he asked Jenny to sing and play a song he had written in her honour.

And the tears were in her mother's eyes as she sang her silvery piping notes:

> "A Rose-bud, by my early walk
> Adown a corn-inclosèd bawk,
> Sae gently bent its thorny stalk,
>   All on a dewy morning.
> Ere twice the shades o' dawn are fled
> In a' its crimson glory spread
> And drooping rich the dewy head,
>   It scents the early morning.

> "Within the bush her covert nest
> A little linnet fondly prest,
> The dew sat chilly on her breast,
>   Sae early in the morning.

She soon shall see her tender brood,
The pride, the pleasure o' the wood,
Amang the fresh green leaves bedew'd
    Awake the early morning.

"So thou, dear bird, young Jenny fair,
On trembling string or vocal air
Shall sweetly pay the tender care
    That tents thy early morning!
So thou, sweet rose-bud, young and gay,
Shalt beauteous blaze upon the day,
And bless the parent's evening ray
    That watch'd thy early morning!"

"That was awfa' nice, Robert," said Mrs. Cruikshank, unashamedly drying her eyes. "You're a witch, laddie, to mak' up a sang like that."

"It's mair nor an honour, Robert," said Cruikshank. "It's something we'll treasure a' our days—and sae will Jenny."

The Bard was touched that his friends were so genuinely affected. He was also touched for another, deeper and private, reason. He had just learned that his daughter Jean had died in the Machlin Cowgate. The news of her death—she had caught a chill that had developed into pneumonia—both saddened and infuriated him. Strangely enough he did not blame Jean—he blamed her mother.

Wee Jean might have grown up into another Rosebud. . .

"It's poor payment for all your kindness to me that I can only repay you with a song. But there'll be others; and since you like this one it shall go into Johnson's next number."

". . . and where did the tune come from, Robert?"

"The tune was composed by my old Ayrshire friend, Davie Sillar—you ken my Epistle to Davie? I could hae wished for a better; but until I hit on a better it'll do. I'm glad to be able to pay a compliment to so many good friends wi' the one song."

But for all his activity he was deeply worried. Creech was

still hedging. And he would need to put in an appearance at Dalswinton if only to convince Patrick Miller that his interest in the farm there was genuine.

And there was Jean. He would need to find out more about his bairn and how she herself was faring. He would have to stall the Armours if they contemplated any action against him. He would have to reassure Jean that she would be provided for. . .

Besides there was a letter from Gilbert. Things weren't going too well at Mossgiel and Gilbert was hinting that some financial aid was necessary.

He would ride Jenny Geddes back to Ayrshire, go down to Dalswinton, leave Jenny at Mossgiel and return to Edinburgh by the fly.

By that time he would tell Creech he would damn-well have to settle accounts with him.

AYRSHIRE INTERVIEW

Gilbert looked melancholy sour as he stood in the barn and kicked the chaff with his worn brogue.

"Damnit, Robin, you never seem to learn from your mistakes."

"As long as *you* benefit from them, Gibby——"

"Oh, dinna get on your high-horse, man. Jean Armour'll need to go on the cutty stool again. A fine exposure that'll make. I micht hae kent when you didna come hame but bided at Johnny Dow's what was keeping you."

"Very well, Gilbert—we'll let it rest at that. I can see you've infected the rest o' the family wi' your sour-whey disposition. Let's get down to practicalities. I'm taking Miller's farm. At least I've told Miller that I'll offer as soon as I get my money from Creech. And if I settle on Ellisland I'll tak' Jean Armour wi' me out o' your road—and she'll stand on no bluidy cutty stool to your pious discomfort. I'll pay what I can afford into Mossgiel here. I'll certainly pay you for Betty and Robert—I'll aey do that no matter what happens."

"And d'you think you'll have enough money to settle into Ellisland?"

"That I don't know for certain. I think there should be enough. But if this scheme falls through then the next best thing will be to look out for a better farm than Mossgiel and for the pair o' us to go into partnership again. That'll discharge my obligation to the lot o' you."

"D'you think so?"

"Well, what the hell *do* you think?"

Gilbert shrugged his shoulders. The prospect didn't thrill him. With two of Robin's illegitimate children on his hands and Jean Armour pregnant again it was difficult for him to think otherwise.

"Maybe you don't think we're entitled to ony claim on you?"

"Damnit, Gilbert, how can you stand there and talk like that? I've been as generous wi' you as funds will permit. I've sent you money back and forwards as I was able to come by it. You ken by now that I dinna answer to you or ony other body for my actions—at least I dinna apologise to you for them. God damnit, man, I'm worried to distraction wi' things. I want to do everything for the best. You canna accuse me of wanting to do ony harm."

"No . . . but you act very queerly at times—nearly a' the time. Since ever you left hame at least. Mind you, Robin, I'm no' taking Jean Armour's next bairn off her and you. There's a limit to that—and the limit's been reached."

"I'll provide for Jean Armour. And when I get settled down in Dumfries I'll take my two bairns off you——"

"If and when! I don't understand how Creech is keeping your money back—there must be something wrong somewhere—something that I don't understand. And the family doesna understand it either. I've got to make a' the excuses for you."

"Ah, you're a poor lot o' gulls too. Of course there's something wrong wi' Creech. He's too bluidy mean to pay out what's

owing me. But unless I take a court action how am I to get
the money out of him? And a court action would cost all the
money that's left. But I'll promise you this, Gilbert: I'm at
the end of my tether as well as you. I'll see Creech when I get
back to Edinburgh and I'll force a settlement óne way or
another. I'm not going to be kicked about like an auld shoe
ony longer."

"I hope so, Robin. And I hope you understand the way I
feel about things."

"Oh yes—Gilbert. I've enough imagination to realise how
you feel about things—supposing I needed ony imagination. . ."

NO ESCAPE

His interview with the Armours in the Cowgate was no
more satisfactory.

As he entered, the Bard was in no mood, after his interview
with Gilbert, to stand any nonsense.

But James Armour was absent on a building job and the
mother was too despondent to have any fight in her. Besides
she was still hoping that he would marry her daughter.

He interviewed Jean in the attic. At first there was no
demonstration of any affection between them. He asked for
her health and then he asked how the bairn had died. And as
she told him between her tears he softened.

"All right, Jean. What's done canna be undone. And now
for the future. Have you ony plans?"

Jean looked at him in soft-eyed wonder.

"Whatna plans could I have, Rab?"

"Juist what I thought. Everybody seems to be waiting on
me. I've got to plan and provide for everybody, when I canna
even plan and provide for myself."

"Are you no' for taking that farm?"

"You want a farm, do you? Just like that!"

"No, Rab . . . you ken I dinna want onything but you.

It was what we talked about in the simmer when we were lying here."

"And you were busy conceiving."

"Am I to blame for that too, Rab?"

"No . . . you're a woman and you canna help yourself. What attitude are your parents taking up? I've seen your mother wi' mair fight in her. Am I to suppose there'll be another warrant?"

"Oh no, Rab: dinna think that. Never as lang as I live."

"But what's their attitude?"

"Weel . . . they think you're for taking a farm."

"And taking you wi' me?"

"And would you no' tak' me, Rab?"

"Damnit, Jean, it's no' as easy as a' that. I'm in a bluidy fankle o' worries the now. Everything's going wrong that can go wrong."

"If there was onything I could do to help——"

"Well, what's going to happen if I dinna get the farm?"

"I juist . . . I juist dinna ken, Rab. I juist dinna ken. I dinna ken how I'm to face Mr. Auld and the Session. And my father . . ."

"What about your father?"

"He's in a terrible state, Rab. If he thocht you wouldna tak' me awa' I dread to think what he micht dae. But I'll no' let him do onything to hurt you, Rab."

"Jean, lass, life was never meant to be lived this way— tortured at every turn. Dinna worry: I'll see you right some way or another. But I dinna just see my road out the now. I'm waiting on money for my Edinburgh edition. It's no' to hand yet. But I'm going back to Edinburgh to-morrow to see what I can do about it. Whenever I get it, I hope to offer for that farm in Dumfries. Once I get that fixed there'll be nae need for you to worry about Daddy Auld and the Session. . ."

The November wind tore and battered at the Cowgate thatch; the light wavered from the smoky candle; from downstairs came the noise of the children gathered round the fireside.

Jean shivered where she sat on the edge of the bed; but she shivered more from apprehension and worry than from physical cold.

The Bard, who had been pacing up and down the narrow attic, slid the door bar silently into its socket and came towards Jean.

She knew by his action and by the tension in his gait what was coming; and even as she knew her legs trembled and they turned to water. It had always ended thus; always it would end thus. Neither of them could escape it.

MORE PATIENCE

William Creech began to get a trifle flushed.

"I must say, Robert, that I resent your attitude—I have other matters to attend to other than totting up the accounts of your edition. I have already assured you that just as soon as I find it convenient I shall settle with you. But you must not press me. My money is laid out in a number of ventures and there are still a number of booksellers and agents who have not yet settled accounts with me over your subscription."

"Sir—I have heard all this before. I must have a settlement as quickly as possible. I have responsibilities at home. I have responsibilities here. I have made plans for my future and they are in hourly jeopardy for lack of my due money. I have been patient——"

"Then you must have more patience."

"*More* patience!"

"Now you must excuse me—for I have much important work on my hands. Believe me, Robert, it is a waste of time to call here until I have communicated with you. I promise you I'll not delay: the moment my accounts are balanced I'll let you know."

"And when in God's name, sir, do you think that may be?"

"It's extremely difficult to put a date to such matters. But I hope by the end of the year——"

"By the end of the year! I shall be back here, sir, at the end of the week."

Smellie said: "Ye can dae nothing about it, Robert. Ye canna tak' the great Creech to law. And there's mair nor you in the same boat. Don't be a bluidy bit surprised if the great Creech goes bankrupt. I ken naebody that's getting their money out o' him the noo. I ken, I ken—I ken fine how ye feel. But it'll dae ye nae guid knocking hell out o' Creech. If you could choke gowden guineas out o' him I'd come up now and give you a hand—and by God, sir, but I'd chirt him. . ."

This news sent the Bard chasing after Peter Hill.

"No, I wouldna think that Creech'll go bankrupt," said Peter. "Mind you, that's just what I think. I'm Creech's manager and I ken mair about his affairs than maist—but I dinna ken everything. Creech keeps plenty to himsel'—and has private accounts naebody sees but himsel'. I reckon there's about £400 coming to you, Robert—and what about the hundred guineas for your copyright?"

"All I've got's a promissory note in his hand that's worth no more, it appears, than the scrap o' paper it's written on."

Peter shook his head. "I ken he's tight the now, Robert—and truth to tell, I never knew him tighter. Damnit, your account could hae been settled a couple o' months ago—the end o' August."

"Listen, Peter, I'm no' joking. If I dinna get that money frae Creech I'll do something desperate. And if he goes bankrupt . . ."

But here words failed him and he fumed with impatient rage.

Many a weaker and less resolute man would have broken under the strain. He could have been excused if he had taken to the bottle. But he thrust the bottle from him impatiently.

His head must be clear for thinking. There must be a road out somewhere. Supposing the worst, the unimaginable worst happened to Creech? What then? To whom could he turn?

There was only the Excise. Then by hook or by crook he

must get his name entered as a candidate and arrange for immediate training.

But how? Hook or by crook was all very well—but how? The question beat incessantly against the walls of his mind. He knew several Edinburgh cronies who were in the Excise. But there was nothing they could do for him. . .

Nothing. . . Except, perhaps, William Nimmo, an Edinburgh supervisor, a man who sometimes came to the Crochallan Club and who was a mutual friend of Peggy Chalmers. . .

He would need to try and see Nimmo sometime. . .

Not sometime: he would need to see him immediately. Nimmo was a bachelor living with a sister, if he remembered aright, in Alison Square off the Potterrow.

He tried to recall Nimmo. A quiet man with a quiet sardonic humour and a quiet but effective turn for a bawdy tale. . . They had been as friendly as casual acquaintances could be amid the noise and bustle of the Crochallan Club—especially when his immediate friends were Willie Dunbar, Willie Smellie, Willie Nicol, Charles Hay, Robert Cleghorn and, latterly, honest James Johnson. . .

HISTORY OF A YOUNG WIDOW

William Nimmo made him welcome. His house consisted of the first floor of a tenement on the north side of Alison Square leading off the Potterrow.

He soon stated his business.

"I am anxious to secure an Excise commission, Mr. Nimmo. I was wondering if you could help me?"

There was not much that Nimmo could do to help—at least not in a practical way. But he could tell him about the duties of an exciseman and what the prospects of employment were.

Nimmo, to do him justice, did not think that the Excise offered the Bard much beyond a minimum of subsistence.

"It all depends on where you might be situated, Robert—

and a great deal depends on your immediate supervisor. Aye
. . . and it's hard work, ye ken. Dinna flatter yourself that
you'll hae much time for writing verses. Unless you get an
easy division. . ."

The Bard thanked him politely. But William Nimmo was
an honest man; and he was a brother fellow-craft: his advice
and counsel were absolutely genuine. He liked Robert Burns,
liked him for himself apart altogether from his fame or his
poetry, though he deeply admired that too.

His sister, Miss Erskine Nimmo, was highly flattered that
the Bard had sought out her brother. To serve tea to a man
who had known the drawing-rooms of the Duchess of Gordon
and the Dowager Countess of Glencairn (to mention no others)
was indeed a thrill and an honour. It would provide her with
many a day's gossip among her friends. . .

And indeed she could hardly wait till the following afternoon till she put on her bonnet and sallied diagonally across
the Potterrow to General's Entry where one of her closest
friends lived, Mrs. Agnes MacLehose. . .

Agnes MacLehose had had what was known as a chequered
career. Daughter of a Glasgow surgeon—Andrew Craig—she
had at seventeen years of age married (rather than burn) a
Glasgow lawyer, James MacLehose. Her widowed father
hadn't been too happy about the marriage. But Nancy was
flaming with desire and she reckoned that James MacLehose
was the man to cool her blood.

MacLehose did what he could towards that end for he was
a passionate man himself. But Nancy was not easily cooled.
In addition to passion she had a gay high-spirited nature and
liked the social round. MacLehose was five years her senior
and he didn't like a young high-spirited wife gadding around
especially when she was in an almost permanent state of pregnancy. From time to time he exploded in jealous drink-
disordered paroxysms. Then he would beat the young Nancy
sadistically and finish up by ravishing her brutally.

By the time she was pregnant with her fourth child, and
had reached the age of twenty-one, Nancy was so degraded

by and disgusted with married love that she left her husband and went back to her father.

But her husband wasn't so easily put to defiance. Their first-born child was dead; but he took away the other two children; and as soon as Nancy was delivered of her fourth he deprived her of him too.

Nancy had enough maternal instinct to feel this separation from her children. But she preferred separation to returning to the tender mercies of James MacLehose.

Two years later her father died. He left his property so that Nancy would have a small annuity. Unable to bear Glasgow unprotected from an irate husband, she retreated to Edinburgh. Shortly afterwards MacLehose threw in his hand and went to London before finally settling in Jamaica. But he left in such a way that Nancy had to take over the children and provide for them.

To do this she applied and got small grants each from the Glasgow Writers' and Surgeons' Societies. . .

To her financial assistance also came from her cousin William Craig, an advocate-depute, who, by steady plodding, was keeping on the right side of Henry Dundas. . .

But Nancy needed something more than financial assistance to make her life in the dingy flat at General's Entry tolerable. This assistance she got in large measure from the Calvanistic Reverend John Kemp, minister of the Canongate Kirk where she worshipped.

John Kemp was in his prime. He enjoyed preaching; but he enjoyed more the "confessional." Kemp liked to encourage attractive women of his congregation to come to him privately, to his office, and unburden themselves of their troubles and anxieties—especially if they were of an emotional or sexual nature. Kemp had a sensual nature and a strong bent for fornication. As a Calvanistic minister of the Gospel he had to be careful—but as a minister he had many opportunities for familiarity with his female parishioners. . .

Destined to marry three wives and end up in a divorce suit, Kemp, while still enjoying his first wife, bore every indication of his future. . . But only to those who could pierce the sanctimonious veil of his Calvinism. This the impressionable Nancy could not do; and to her Mr. Kemp lavished much attention. The more she filled him with desire, the more he exhorted her in the ways of Fundamentalism.

Nancy had lost her mother at the early age of eight. But her mother had been a Fundamentalist, too, being the daughter of the Reverend John MacLaurin of Luss.

In her trials and tribulations Nancy remembered her mother and her piety. Under Mr. Kemp's lascivious eye it was not difficult for her to become a convert to pietism and to the luxurious belief that she had suffered in order that she might the sooner be brought into a state of Grace. . .

Being in a highly emotional state of Grace, it was easy for her to become a victim of sensibility and to take her sensibility as emotionally as she took her Calvinism.

But for all that she was very far from being a fool. She had the elements of a good brain; and knowing the terrible strength of her sexual passion she sweated and groaned and prayed in order to divert it into less dangerous channels than bedding with a lover.

Yet the need for male company could not be denied: it was ever clamorous.

At twenty-six years of age and with her two surviving boys, Andrew aged eight and William aged six, Nancy was pretty desperate for a lover.

She had heard much concerning Robert Burns and she was deeply stirred by his poetry. She had heard above all that he was a consummate lover and that no one, high or low, to whom he had been attracted had been able to resist him.

Nancy was pretty sure of herself—surer still of her physical and mental attractiveness. She was full-curved, plump to the point of voluptuous perfection. Mentally she was charged to load-line with sensibility. She knew her poets by the yard: she could even write an odd stanza herself. She had a voice that was pollen-honeyed with sex. Her soft eyes could swim in mists of heaven-or-hell-knew-what desire.

Nancy felt that she had only to meet with Robert Burns under circumstances that would display her to advantage and he would be hers. Had she ever known a man yet who wasn't desperate in his advances? Did not even Mr. Kemp's large white hand sometimes reach out in the zeal of holy rapture . . . ?

She would of course prove to the Ayrshire poet that there was at least one attractive woman who could not under any circumstances be seduced by him. Ah! but just to have the opportunity of putting him to the test. . .

And here was Miss Nimmo in her ripe middle age fairly loosening her elongated jaw on her.

" . . . and who d'you think we had to supper last night, my dear?"

"But how should I know whom you had to supper—unless it was Mr. Fordyce, perhaps?"

"Mr. Fordyce! Nancy, we had the celebrated Ayrshire Bard."

"Not Robert Burns! Erskine, my dear, not him!"

Miss Nimmo basked in her triumph—though she dearly would have liked to have had the courage to delay the disclosure. . .

She was not slow to observe that Mrs. MacLehose blushed like a naughty schoolgirl; that her bosom rose and fell in agitation.

Nancy turned to the window.

"You know how I admire his verses, Erskine—you might have invited me."

"Ah, but he called unexpectedly on Willie. I was so agitated I could hardly serve supper. But he soon put me at my ease. Really, my dear, he is the most charming and cultivated of men. Not at all the rustic one might have expected —had one not known about Duchess Gordon."

"Stuff, my dear Erskine—the Duchess Gordon could well be his mother. But I thought your friend Miss Chalmers——"

"Oh yes, my dear, Peggy told me quite a lot about him. But she didn't tell me he was so attractive."

"And he is attractive?"

"Terribly so. I canna understand how that girl in Ayrshire that had the twins to him refused him in marriage."

"Ah yes . . . a Miss Armour, was it not?"

"Yes, Jean Armour. Peggy used to speak of the Poet's Jean. Of course, maybe the Poet didna want her."

"That's much more likely. Will Mr. Burns be coming back to visit Willie?"

"Yes: he said he would come again."

"You must arrange a tea-party, Erskine. I'll never forgive you if you don't. You know I admire his genius so greatly."

But Miss Nimmo sensed that the lively Mrs. MacLehose with her husband in Jamaica was interested more in the poet than in his poetry.

MISTRESS AND MAID

Nancy did not leave anything to chance: she gave Miss Nimmo no rest until the day came when she was due to meet Robert Burns.

Nancy took great pains with her toilet. She warmed her room, heated two great pans of water and, defying the coldness of December, stood in a wooden tub and gave herself a good wash. This she did with all the secrecy of some mystic rite, for her friends would have thought her mad to be so foolhardy at such a season of the year. But then Nancy knew how easily her sweet curves sweated—and to use too much lavender-water would betray that fact.

She was determined to run no risk. Nancy fully realised what a fine body she had and she adorned it with taste and care.

Fashion favoured her figure. A woman with a fine bust displayed it to advantage. Plump hips enabled her to add only the lightest of artificial bums in order to display that part of her anatomy to advantage.

Even Jenny Clow, her occasional-maid and twice-weekly help, could not resist (as she pulled in her stay laces) expressing admiration for her figure.

"You're a fine figure o' a woman, ma'am."

"I'm well aware of that, Jenny—a little tighter, please.

You've got a good figure yoursel', Jenny. You ought to be thinking of getting married."

"Me, ma'am? Wha wad hae me?"

"There ought to be some young man in your own class— some decent labouring fellow."

"Plenty time for that, ma'am. Ye ken ye canna get a hoose the noo for love or money. Ye can har'ly get the share o' a room. My wee corner in the Potterrow'll dae me fine till I see the man I fancy. . . I hope the Poet Burns is ta'en wi' you, ma'am——"

"That's quite enough, Jenny. I've told you before that Mr. Burns will only be one of a most select company. As a married woman you must know that I have no interest in men as such."

But Jenny knew better. She had seen Mrs. Mac, as she called her, with Mr. Kemp . . . and others. Jenny who was man-conscious herself had long realised that her mistress was the more man-conscious of the two. And she knew she wasn't dressing from the skin out on this December day merely to impress Miss Nimmo.

Nancy's deep chestnut hair was frizzed in tiny curls on her forehead. A brown velvet bandeau was knotted above this and held in place a white gauze headdress that fell down her back and wisped round her shoulders giving to her bulk a magical lightness. . .

She tripped and tiptoed across the street to Alison Square as if she carried no more weight than her fringed satin-lined cape.

THE ONSLAUGHT

Immediately he clapped eyes on her the Bard was captivated. The suddenness of his physical response almost embarrassed him. He had to pull himself together in order to effect the formalities of introductions. But this over, he had eyes for no one else.

His first glance had told him everything. Here, if ever there was one, was a woman desperate to be seduced. And what an armful for seduction! What a gloriously fine woman!

". . . and when did you come to Town, madam?"

"*Come* to Town, Mr. Burns? I've been here these five years!"

"Impossible, my dear madam, or I should have known of your beauty before this."

"No flattering speeches, Mr. Burns. Don't forget I'm a married woman."

"I should have been shocked to find you anything else, madam. But MacLehose is not too common a name. Should I know of your husband?"

"My husband has been in Jamaica some years now, Mr. Burns."

A fresh glint, as of understanding, seemed to flash in the Bard's great burning eyes. And Nancy, with relief, read the meaning only too clearly.

But she was almost beyond realising, intellectually, what she read.

Her physical reactions were becoming as embarrassing as the Bard's had been. She had expected much from Robert Burns. She had never anticipated a physical engulfing such as this. It was a new and overwhelming experience. And yet not a word, not an action, not a hint had been out of place. It was not that his look, his eyes, were sensual or lecherous. There was nothing of the hard cynical look of the lecher in him at all. And yet his personality possessed her utterly and to a degree she had never before imagined possible.

Miss Nimmo's worst fears were confirmed. As she was hostess she had to prevent the situation from becoming socially embarrassing. It was clear to all that the Bard and Mrs. MacLehose were completely absorbed in each other to the oblivion of all else.

But before the tea-drinking was over Nancy had courage enough to ask the Bard if he would drink tea with her—and a Miss Mary Peacock—in her own flat on the coming Saturday.

To this the Bard agreed with the utmost enthusiasm.

"I shall be leaving Edinburgh any day now, madam. Once I am gone 'twill be a long time before I am back. I should be vexed past all enduring if I did not have the opportunity of seeing you again—and paying my respects to your literary taste and judgment. . ."

When the party had broken off, and Nancy had gone home, Erskine Nimmo could not refrain from speaking of Mrs. MacLehose.

"Well, Mr. Burns—and how do you like Mrs. Mac?"

"I think, madam, that she is a fine woman. I am at a loss to know why her husband does not send for her."

"Poor Nancy! I'll tell you her story some other day, Mr. Burns. By the way, she's a cousin of Mr. Craig, the advocate. Maybe you ken him?"

"Is she a Craig? I have heard of him."

"Aye . . . if it wasna that she was a married woman, Mr. Burns, I think you'd maybe be losing a bit o' your poet's heart to her."

"The heart, madam, is a small organ—and it is best kept whole."

"Aye: so you say, Mr. Burns."

"In any case, my dear madam, rest assured that Mrs. Nancy shall not occupy that ground of grateful regard in my heart that you occupy."

Though she poo-poohed the compliment, she was pleased with it nevertheless. Now that Mrs. Nancy was gone the Bard was impatient to be gone too, in order to luxuriate in his own thoughts concerning her. But he now realised that he had given himself away to Miss Nimmo and he lingered in the hope of covering his tracks. And yet he wanted to learn more about this wonderful Nancy. What Miss Nimmo told him fired his imagination the more. She wanted to show Mrs. MacLehose off to some advantage in order that he might be the more impressed with the friends that visited at Alison Square.

It was Willie Nimmo who saw him out to the Potterrow. He spoke quite plainly about Mrs. MacLehose. "She's needing a man, Robert—and whiles I think she has one when she gets

the chance. But man, wi' it a', she's maist damnably religious
—at least she's never done talking about her minister—Kemp
o' the Tolbooth."

"I don't know about you, Willie; but I think I ken what
conclusion to draw from that."

"Aye, I think you will. Oh, but min' ye, she's a great
credit to herself. She's nae whore; and by the Lord Harry,
considering a' her circumstances, she keeps a brave respectable
appearance. Aye, a brave appearance, Robert. Damned, and
clever too—a menace in some ways for she's gotten a man's
brains."

"Aye . . . she's certainly a clever woman. Your sister
wouldna be joking when she said she's a bit o' a poetess?"

"Oh no . . . she can write a bit verse off and on, I understand—daft about poetry onyway, if that's ony indication.
Spends half her time reading—of course she's been kept in wi'
thae twa bits o' laddies. . ."

He went home in a lather of nervous excitement and Nancy
went home feeling she was now more in need of a bath than
when she had set out.

He knew beyond the shadow of a doubt that he had made
a conquest—and a conquest he very much wanted to make.
If only this meeting had taken place earlier in the year—even
this time last year! What a glorious woman. Just his own
age—and his own type. Made for him! And been lying in
storage for four years . . .! The woman was made for love—
the kind of love he could give her in full measure.

It was difficult to believe there wasn't a flaw somewhere.
Of course: the husband in Jamaica—and her two children. . .

A fine glorious amiable charming cultured woman! One
of the middle strata of life. That kind, in her position, were
usually hard, dry and intolerably affected. But there was no
affection about Mrs. Agnes MacLehose—Nancy, as her friends
called her. Nancy Craig: that was better than MacLehose.
He could write a song on a Nancy Craig when he couldn't on
an Agnes MacLehose.

Aye, but this was better than writing a song—this was the
very stuff of which songs were made.

God knows—but he needed just such a woman. Even just to talk to her—to be in her company. A woman who understood with delicacy and with penetration a poet's feelings—something of the lady poet in her at that. Maybe something really good.

And what a turn for conversation—and in what a voice! All the softness of the West country in it. Damnit, there was no getting away from the West. The frozen Edinburgh dames couldn't hold a candle to them—not a farthing taper. This glorious woman was worth the whole bluidy Town. She had more voluptuousness in the curve of her little finger than all the golden guinea courtesans of Edinburgh. . .

But why, damnation why, had he to meet her when he was hourly expecting to leave the Town? Creech had promised to settle by the end of the year and he had promised Miller that he would, as like as not, arrange to take over Ellisland in the Spring—Whitsunday at the latest.

As always, this was just his luck: he had never known it better. True enough that Nancy Craig was there for the taking. But she couldn't be taken on the run. She was a cultured woman: she would expect a little finesse in the taking. She would need to be wooed—but what glorious wooing! This was a woman who couldn't be rushed. Not that he wanted to rush. She was like a fine port—one didn't gulp her down like a pint of ale. She was to be fondled—decanted gently. . . Just a sip! Then another sip! Each sip rolled round the tongue. The flavour extracted from every minute drop—and even then held as long as possible. . .

As he traversed Auld Reekie from the Potterrow over the North Bridge and up behind the Register House to Saint James's Square, lying bleak and bare and open to the dribbly December blasts, the Bard had the entire geography of his assault on Nancy Craig fully and intimately mapped.

He was an expert in this business by now: he knew every line of defence, every coign of vantage, every channel of attack. And he hadn't learned his art from the text books. Every woman he had known had taught him something—even Peggy Cameron. And Peggy, wi' her three bastards at a birth

—puir unfortunate bitch—had taught him plenty, taught him more about the female mind especially in its relation to simple physical elementals than almost any other had done. Of course Peggy had been simple; simple and utterly unsophisticated. Yet nearly all women, however simple, had some degree of sophistication. But Peggy had given herself as if her only function in life had been to do so without question.

Here the Bard did not stop for a moment to consider the effect he had on simple Peggy. For Peggy, the Bard had the quality of inevitability about him. He couldn't be denied. Whenever she had felt his strong warm flesh enveloping hers she knew that life held nothing more inevitable or more natural. She became mindless and only knew that her blood flowed like warm cream. How different, how harsh and momentary it had been with other men. If Robert Burns had sown the seed of twins in her she had added a third from herself as good measure. . .

No: he rarely considered what effect he had on women except in an intimate and personal physical sense. He was more concerned with the effect women had on him; and the only rational element all the surgings and billowings of his thoughts could bring him here was that Nancy Craig had had an immediate physical effect on him such as few women had ever had—or at least keener in the instantaneous quality of its intensity.

For there was no love for Nancy Craig—not the faintest flicker.

He could love no woman more than he had loved—aye, and despite everything did still love—Jean Armour. The memory of Jean's short evenly-spaced toes in the dust of the Machlin road meant more to him than Nancy Craig's voluptuous curves could ever mean. He loved Jean Armour—something in their love went deep into him.

But Nancy Craig was such a gloriously fine woman and his blood responded to hers with such unpremeditated instantaneousness that it was just a matter of time—if time there would be—for him to be lying in bed with her even as he had lain—but with the difference experience brought—with Jean Glover in Irvine long ago—or what now seemed long ago.

And yet (as he was soon to learn) when he had lain with Jean Glover, the first time he had ever lain with a woman, Nancy Craig, who was of his age, had had four children, the eldest of whom was then six years old!

THE FIRST LETTER

Before going to bed that night he sat down and drafted some notes to Nancy Craig.

He took some pains with the letter so that his way would be prepared for the coming Saturday. But though he composed with skill he did not compose without sincerity: he most definitely meant what he wrote.

He read over the finished letter with some satisfaction.

Madam,
I had set no small store by my tea-drinking to-night, and have not often been so disappointed. Saturday evening I shall embrace the opportunity with the greatest pleasure. I leave town this day se'ennight, and probably I shall not return for a couple of twelve-months ; but I must ever regret that I so lately got an acquaintance I shall ever highly esteem, and in whose welfare I shall ever be warmly interested. Our worthy common friend, Miss Nimmo, in her usual pleasant way, rallied me a good deal on my new acquaintance, and in the humour of her ideas I wrote some lines, which I inclose you, as I think they have a good deal of poetic merit; and Miss Nimmo tells me you are not only a critic but a poetess. Fiction, you know, is the native region of poetry; and I hope you will pardon my vanity in sending you the bagatelle as a tolerable off-hand jeu d'esprit. I have several poetic trifles, which I shall gladly leave with Miss Nimmo or you, if they were worth house-room; as there are scarcely two people on

earth by whom it would mortify me more to be forgotten, though at the distance of ninescore miles.

I am, Madam,

with the highest respect,
Your very humble Servant. . .

Yes—the letter together with the poetic trifle would impress Nancy Craig—if she could be impressed in this way. He had little doubt about the matter.

EVIL STAR

The intervention of Nancy Craig in the Bard's Edinburgh tarrying came in time to save him from despair over the dallying of Creech.

He waited impatiently for Saturday to come, not with the impatience of a lover but with the impatience (he couldn't find a better expression for it), the gloriously fine impatience of waiting for the company and for the further exploration of the personality of a gloriously fine woman.

But for the hundredth time he reckoned without the baleful influence of his evil star.

Coming back to Saint James's Square with Cruikshank after a visit to Willie Nimmo, the drunken coachman took the corner too quickly at the foot of the Register House Brae. The horse, taking fright, swung round. The coach overbalanced and crashed on the road.

The Bard gave a yell that frightened Cruikshank more than the fall, for he escaped unhurt. But the Bard had injured his knee somehow and lay groaning in terrible agony.

"My knee's broken, Willie," he groaned. "For Godsake dinna try to move me."

With the aid of some neighbours they carried him up to his bedroom and laid him on the bed.

Cruikshank undid the buckle-strap of his breeches and gently exposed the knee. It was shockingly swollen. Either the knee-cap was broken or the joint was dislocated. The Bard was in fearful agony and suffered excruciatingly when they pulled off his top boot.

"We'll better get a doctor," said Cruikshank to his wife— "I dinna like the look o' Robert's knee. The best man would be Sandy Wood since the Bard kens him weel."

So Cruikshank wrote a note and got a caddie to run with it to the Exchange below Baxters' Close.

Lang Sandy Wood read the note and, as his coach was standing by the door, he came immediately.

Lang Sandy (as he was universally known) had met the Bard on several occasions and they had a high regard for each other's worth.

Sandy was not only the most famous and popular surgeon in Edinburgh—not to mention his being the most highly respected—he was one of its most worthy characters. Tall and angular of body and with a long sharp face and a highly quizzical eye, he had a tongue that was as sharp and incisive as any lance he carried in his case. But there was no malice in the man.

When he saw Scotland's Bard lying in such agony he immediately set about an examination of the knee. By this time it was so badly swollen that it was difficult to diagnose the exact nature of the injury. But Sandy reckoned it was dislocated.

There was very little he could do about it. He suggested applications of hot and cold cloths.

And he prescribed rest. The limb was not to be moved under any circumstances until he gave permission. Sandy owed much of his reputation to the simple fact that he let nature do most of her healing with the minimum of interference from himself.

Seeing the agony in which the Bard lay, he placed a pillow under the knee and prescribed an immediate dosage of laudanum.

"Aye . . . it's a fell sair knee, Rab—aye, and ye'll no' put your fit ablow ye for a month or mair. Thae damned coaches are gaun to be the ruination o' folk. If they'd invent one that could go doon closes and up turnpike stairs. . . Aye . . . but we'll see your knee richt for ye, Rab, dinna worry. Aince the swelling gangs doon I'll ken mair aboot it. Noo get your laudanum doon ye and a guid gill o' reekin' hot whisky and that'll ease the pain for ye and ye'll get a nicht's rest . . . and I'll come and see ye the morn. What day's this? Damned, it's Saturday morning! Aye . . . I'll come in and see ye later on. Noo dinna worry . . . ye'll be sitting up and writing a blistering bluidy plaister o' a poem on drunken coachmen the morn. . ."

Morning came—and it seemed damnably long in coming —and the pain, though less excruciating, was hardly bearable.

And through the long dark December morning he lay and groaned and cursed his fate. Sometimes, if he lay perfectly still, the pain almost dwindled to the point where he could think rationally. And this was the day he was to meet that gloriously fine woman—Nancy Craig. God! and if Sandy Wood was to be trusted he was here for a month. A month! Prisoner for thirty days up an attic stair. . . Something would need to happen before then. He would never be able to stand a month of this. He'd go mad. This would mean good-bye to Nancy Craig. It might mean good-bye to the Excise for he could do nothing about it lying here.

It only needed Creech to go bankrupt and he was completely finished. . .

LOVE LETTERS

Nancy had prepared everything for the tea that night with taste and care. She had been at fever point since Tuesday. But now that Saturday had come and the appointed hour drew near she felt calmer. She had rehearsed everything she would say—the significant sentences. . .

Right from the beginning she would tell him of her devotion to religion—the Calvinism of the Reverend John

Kemp. This was important. This would provide the safe solid basis for their conversation. And it would prevent him from making—or attempting to make—urgent physical love to her.

In this Nancy was perfectly sincere and deeply serious. She had to have some claim to superiority over this amazing man of genius. She would advance her Kempish Calvinism as superior to his anti-Calvinism. She would plead and coax and cajole with him—show him the error—but gently—of his ways in the light of Divine Revelation. Of course he could never oppose her in that. He would have to bow before the inevitability of Revealed Religion, of Divine Love. Nancy's religion was saturated with this sublimated Divine Love. Mr. Kemp had assured her—his thick-knuckled large white hand reaching out—that the Divine Love was all-embracing; that the Father of Mercies would enfold her to His bosom—just as Mr. Kemp's ample arms reached out and enfolded . . .

How delicious it would be for her to act the part of Mr. Kemp with a man like Robert Burns. Her sensuous Calvinistic cooing would fire him with Divine Love like the *Song of Songs*. . .

She would talk of poetry too. And she would laugh and be gay. Oh, she would reveal to him many sides of her nature and prove beyond any doubt that Calvinism was not the sour-faced hypocritical bigotry he had found it to be in Ayrshire.

And then . . . when all her plans were completed, and she had rehearsed her exits and her entrances, a porter came and delivered her a note. Her heart sank; her ample bosom seemed to shrivel and dry up; an agony of emotional sentiment coiled and uncoiled sickeningly in her stomach.

He wasn't coming. He wasn't coming. He was probably leaving Edinburgh for good. . .

Very pale, and with a trembling hand, Nancy broke the seal and opened the sheet and held it to the candle flame.

As she read the sheet a curiously pleasant sensation pervaded her, and a ripple no grosser than the flutter of a butterfly's wings disturbed the plexus nerve centre so that her diaphragm contracted and expanded in involuntary ecstasy and the flesh on her arms and neck and thighs rose in a thin porridge of goose pimples.

Transfixed, she read the sheet again and again.

"I can say with truth, Madam, that I never met with a person in my life whom I more anxiously wished to meet again than yourself. To-night I was to have had that very great pleasure. I was intoxicated with the idea—but an unlucky fall from a coach has so bruised one of my knees, that I can't stir my leg off the cushion. So, if I don't see you again, I shall not rest in my grave for chagrin. I was vexed to the soul I had not seen you sooner; I determined to cultivate your friendship with the enthusiasm of Religion; but thus has Fortune ever served me. I cannot bear the idea of leaving Edinburgh without seeing you. I know not how to account for it—I am strangely taken with some people; nor am I often mistaken. You are a stranger to me; but I am an odd being: some yet unnamed feelings; things, not principles, but better than whims, carry me further than boasted reason ever did a Philosopher.

Farewell! every happiness be yours!"

When she had dried her tears Nancy sat down and wrote:

Enured as I have been to disappointments, I never felt more, nay, nor half so severely, for one of the same nature! The cruel cause, too, augments my uneasiness. I trust you'll soon recover it; meantime, if my sympathy, my friendship, can alleviate your pain, be assured you possess them. I am much flattered at being a favourite of yours. Miss Nimmo can tell you how earnestly I had long pressed her to make us acquainted. I had a presentiment that we would derive pleasure from the society of each other. To-night I had thought of fifty things to say to you; how unfortunate this prevention! You shall *not* leave town without seeing me, if I should come along with good Miss Nimmo and call for you. I am determined to see you; and am ready to exclaim with Yorick, ' Tut! are we not all relations?' We are, indeed, *strangers* in one sense; but of near kin in many respects: these ' nameless feelings' I perfectly comprehend, tho' the pen of a Locke could not define them. Perhaps *instinct* comes nearer their description than either ' Principles or Whims.' Think ye they have any connection with that ' heavenly light which leads astray '? One thing I know, that they have a powerful effect upon me; and are delightful when under the check of *reason* and *religion*.

Miss Nimmo was a favourite of mine from the first hour I met her. There is a softness, a nameless something about her that, was I a man, old as she is, I should have chosen her before most women that I know. I fear, however, this liking is not *mutual*. I'll tell you why I think so, at meeting. She was in mere jest when she told you I was a *Poetess*. I have often composed rhyme (if not *reason*), but never one line of *poetry*. The distinction is obvious to everyone of the least discernment. Not one living has a higher relish for poetry than I have; and my reading everything of the kind makes me a tolerable judge. Ten years ago, such lines from such a hand would have half-turned my head. Perhaps you thought it might have done so even *yet*, and wisely premised that '*Fiction* was the native region of poetry.' Pardon my little freedom I take with you; if they entertain a heavy hour, they have all the merit I intended. Will you let me know, now and then, how your leg is? If I was your *sister*, I would call and see you; but 'tis a censorious world this; and (in this sense) ' you and I are not of this world.' Adieu. Keep up your heart, you will soon get well, and we shall *meet*. Farewell. God bless you!

The effect of this on the Bard was devastating. But then it was a devastating letter written by a woman of near-genius whose instincts were keyed to their highest pitch. He read it over and over, put it down and picked it up and read it and re-read it till he almost had it by heart.

' Tonight I had fifty things to say to you '—what things? *Anything* this woman said was of first importance. This woman was . . . was without peer, without rival—beyond comparison. God Almighty! A gloriously fine amiable woman who could write like this!

' You shall *not* leave town without seeing me, if I should come along with good Miss Nimmo and call for you. I am determined to see you.'

Determined to see him! This was conquest with a sweetness of vengeance that brought tears to his eyes. Determined to see him! Nancy, Nancy, if only you were beside me now. . .

' If I was your *sister* I would call and see you. . . Keep up your heart, you will soon get well, and we shall *meet*!'

Before God they would meet! Oh . . . this woman was beyond anything in a woman he had ever imagined. But then he'd known from the moment he clapped eyes on her—and heard her speak. . .

The truth was that never before had a letter from a woman so overwhelmed and devastated him. It was hardly credible that such a letter could have been written by a woman. And extempore: she couldn't have wasted a minute in replying. . .

'And we shall *meet*.'

And why in hell's name had she to be tied to a husband in Jamaica—of all places? He might, had Mary Campbell not died, have met him instead of Nancy. . . But he would need to be on his tiptoes to deal with her. He would need to use every weapon of art that he knew—and every ounce of artifice. . .

Damn this knee. . . He doubted if a bottle of laudanum would blank off his mind sufficiently to give him a night's sleep. He was in no physical or nervous condition to give this letter the reply it merited. . .

Maybe that was just as well, for by the time he did take up pen and paper he was in no state to write to anyone.

What he did write was plain and prosaic enough:

I stretch a point indeed, my dearest Madam, when I answer your card on the rack of my present agony. Your friendship, Madam! By heavens, I was never proud before! Your lines, I maintain it, are poetry, and good poetry; mine were indeed partly fiction, and partly a friendship which, had I been so blest as to have met with you *in time*, might have led me—God of love only knows where. Time is too short for ceremonies.

I swear solemnly (in all the tenor of my former oath) to remember you in all the pride and warmth of friendship until —I cease to be!

To-morrow, and every day, till I see you, you shall hear from me.

Farewell! May you enjoy a better night's repose than I am likely to have.

THE WEAKEST LINK

But Nancy had had time to think things over. And in her excited state (the very remembrance of his physical being coupled with the sight of his handwriting could induce repeated orgasms) she was as unfit to think rationally as was the Bard. Of one thing (as she had gathered from Miss Nimmo) she had been careless. She had left herself vulnerable. She was a married woman: maybe she had written too freely to him. And maybe (Miss Nimmo had again sown the doubt) maybe he was but philandering with her. After all, he was Robert Burns—Scotland's poet and the toast of the drawing-rooms of the highest in the land. He knew she was a married woman. Then he could want her for one thing only. He wanted to take her to bed—the thing no woman had ever been able to refuse him. Not even (so vulgar rumour had it) the Duchess of Gordon. . .

Oh, how difficult to refuse him. But, oh, the consequences if she did not? If she conceived she would be irretrievably ruined. Of course she was no silly inexperienced virgin. . .

But suppose she obeyed her blood? Suppose she allowed him? He had known many women and, no doubt, many seductive courtesans. . .

Suppose she let him? He was still a bachelor—and this was the most ominous sign of all. No woman had been able to secure him. If that meant what she thought it meant, then physical intimacy was the weakest link in his binding chain. Once she granted that the chain would snap—he would no longer be interested in her. He was not like John Kemp, already married. . .

No: she must put herself right with Mr. Robert Burns. If (and this *was* a possibility) he was making a fool of her (banking on easy seduction—though it was flattering that he *wanted* to seduce her) she must defend herself: she must disillusion him.

Oh, but why must she do this and run the risk of offending him—of chasing him off? He was the one man—above and beyond all others—she wanted. She had never believed that a man like Robert Burns could be possible. He was nothing less than a young god—and a young god who was acclaimed on all sides and by all ranks as a heaven-taught genius. There wasn't another man in Scotland—in the world maybe—to equal him.

And he was used to women yielding to him. What then if he flew off at a tangent and decided to leave Town without seeing her again?

Nancy was in a cruel dilemma. She had no independent means and she had two boys of whom she was very fond. It was all right for Mr Kemp to call on her He was her minister; and no breath of scandal could attach to his visits. But if her cousin, Mr. (advocate) Craig, got a breath of any scandal he would withdraw his financial support. He had warned her solemnly about that. No breath of scandal could be attached to his name. . .

But if she were independent! She would visit him now and put all convention at defiance. What was good enough for the Duchess of Gordon would be good enough for her.

But she was not free; and she was terribly vulnerable in her economic dependency. She would need (if she didn't want to lose Robert Burns *and* her little security) to watch every step she took. Wasn't she perhaps taking too much of Robert Burns on trust? Maybe he would show her letters to some of his companions and she would be talked about in the Town. If this correspondence was to be continued until his knee was better then they must not sign their letters—they must develop a code. She would sign herself Clarinda and suggest that he signed himself Sylvander. That would effectively put anybody off the scent who might happen on them.

Passion gave point to her cunning even if it injected folly into her prudence. All she knew was that she was beginning to fall hopelessly in love with this man. She was even beginning to turn over in her mind the possibility (with the help of Cousin Craig) of getting a divorce from the wretched MacLehose. . .

She composed her next letter with care:

How could you tell me that you were in ' agony '? I hoped you would swallow laudanum, and procure some ease from sleep. I am glad to hear Mr. Wood attends you. He is a good soul, and safe surgeon. I know him a little. Do as he bids, and I trust your leg will soon be quite well. When I meet you, I must chide you for writing in your romantic style. Do you remember that she whom you address is a married woman? To be serious, most people would think, by your style, that you were writing to some vain, silly woman to make a fool of her—or worse. I have too much vanity to ascribe it to the former motive, and too much charity to harbour an idea of the latter; and viewing it as the effusion of a benevolent heart upon meeting one somewhat similar to itself, I have promised you my friendship; it will be your own fault if I ever withdraw it. Would to God I had it in my power to give you some solid proofs of it! Were I the Duchess of Gordon, you should be possessed with that independence which every generous mind pants after; but I fear she is ' no Duchess at the heart.' Obscure as I am (comparatively) I enjoy all the necessaries of life as fully as I desire, and wish for wealth only to procure the ' luxury of doing good.'

My chief design in writing you to-day was to beg you would not write me often, lest the exertion should hurt you. Meantime, if my scrawls can amuse you in your confinement, you shall have them occasionally. I shall hear of you every day from my beloved Miss Nimmo. Adieu! Be patient. Take care of yourself. My best wishes attend you.

Probably (considering all the circumstances) no more diabolically clever letter had ever been written before by a woman to the man she hoped would become her lover.

He had proof now that Nancy was more than a match for him at epistolary love-making. Much more than a match since she had a keener singleness of purpose and passion; and she fought from the more difficult ground.

Certainly the Bard's physical discomfort was to his immediate disadvantage. But it took him longer than it should have to compose his reply. It seemed to him as he read over his letter that something of his physical lameness had got into his English style. But it was the best he could do; and he could not keep her waiting indefinitely.

Your last, my dear Madam, had the effect on me that Job's situation had on his friends, when ' they sat down seven days and seven nights astonied, and spake not a word.' ' Pay my addresses to a married woman! ' I started as if I had seen the ghost of him I had injured: I recollected my expressions; some of them indeed were, in the law phrase, ' habit and repute,' which is being half guilty. I cannot positively say, Madam, whether my heart might not have gone astray a little; but I can declare, upon the honour of a Poet, that the vagrant has wandered unknown to me. I have a pretty handsome troop of Follies of my own; and, like some other people's retinue, they are but undisciplined blackguards: but the luckless rascals have something of honour in them; they would not do a dishonest thing.

To meet with an unfortunate woman, amiable and young; deserted and widowed by those who were bound by every tie of Duty, Nature and Gratitude, to protect, comfort and cherish her; add to all, when she is perhaps one of the first of lovely Forms and Noble Minds, the Mind too that hits one's taste as the joys of Heaven do a Saint—should a vague infant-idea, the natural child of Imagination, thoughtlessly peep over the fence—were you, My Friend, to sit in judgment, and the poor, airy straggler brought before you, trembling, self-condemned; with artless eyes, brimful of contrition, looking wistfully on its Judge—you could not, My dear Madam, condemn the hapless wretch to ' death without benefit of Clergy '?

I have written you this scrawl because I have nothing else to do, and you may sit down and find fault with it if you have no better way of consuming your time; but finding fault with the vaguings of a Poet's fancy is much such another business as Xerxes chastising the waves of Hellespont.

My limb now allows me to sit in some peace; to walk I have yet no prospect of, as I can't mark it to the ground.

I have just now looked over what I have written, and it is such a chaos of nonsense that I daresay you will throw it into the fire, and call me an idle, stupid fellow; but whatever you think of my brains, believe me to be, with the most sacred respect, and heart-felt esteem,

My dear Madam, your humble servant,

WOMEN MUST WAIT

From now on the fat was in the fire and sizzling beautifully. They vied with each other in epistolary love-making, all the time denying it was love-making as such—each protesting to high heaven and calling the Almighty to witness that their motives were so noble and pure as to be brought before the Throne of Grace without fear.

But the Bard had other things to do than write tortuous and wholly artificial love-letters. James Johnson's second volume was in the press. He was calling regularly with proof-sheets for correction. As he hoped to have some thirty songs in the second volume and as publication was fixed for the middle of February, he had plenty to do.

Ever since he had rode out of Edinburgh on his Border tour that May morn, he had reviewed tune upon tune in his mind; and at every opportunity he had collected airs or scraps of old tunes. Since he had come back to Town he had worked like a Trojan on them.

As James Johnson said, sitting beside him in Cruikshank's attic.

"I dinna ken how I ever got on without you, Robert. Man, some o' your sangs are juist perfect—juist perfect."

"Damned, Jamie, some are no' what I'd like them to be. I havena been able to give them the polish I would like. But we're preserving the tunes—the tunes *are* perfect; and that's the main thing. If we preserve the tunes for another day then the poets o' another day will put better words to them."

"Ah, man, you're far ower modest—far ower modest. The Birks o' Aberfeldy or MacPherson's Farewell wad grace ony collection. Or Whistle and I'll come to ye my lad! Juist perfect! Man, ye've gotten a wonderfu' ear for a tune. I've seen Stephen Clarke and me puzzling ower ane o' your tunes. I've seen us thinking you were wrang; but when we persevered and got the line o' the tune then, damnit, the words juist fitted in perfect. Clarke says to me ae night: ' Mr. Johnson, sir, if Robert Burns picks on a tune then you can let it go without question! ' And, mind you, that's a big tribute frae Clarke."

"Clarke's a professional musician, Jamie. He can set out a tune to a nicety—when he kens the tune. But when I've had him up here at times I've had literally to thump the tune into him. The natural turn o' the rhythm often escapes him till it's been pointed out several times. . .

". . . but there's a lady i' the Town, Jamie, who is a firstclass poetess—she shall be nameless—and I should like at least one of her poems set to music and published in the present number. Look over her lines here: To a Blackbird. I think they would go well to The Scots Queen. I showed them to Doctor James Gregory when he was up seeing me the other day—and he refused to believe any woman in Edinburgh could have written them; and Doctor Gregory's nae fool, Jamie. . ."

There were days when the Bard got little rest. Now that he was lying bedridden—or at best confined to his room with his leg lying over a cushion along a chair—he realised how many friends he had in the Town. Willie Nicol, of course, was constant visitor. But many of his Crochallan comrades came to see him, including Willie Dunbar (who urged him to write an elegiac on the recent death of Lord President Dundas, which, backed by Sandy Wood, he did—to his lasting regret). Robert Cleghorn came, Smellie came and Peter Hill; (but Creech never even wrote him a line). Willie Nimmo came often and just as often came Bob Ainslie.

He liked to see Ainslie alone for there were certain things he could discuss with him that he couldn't with any other man—Nicol not excepted.

Yet he liked Willie Nicol's visits best. One night he came with Schetky and Allan Masterton. Cruikshank came up and made the quintet. They drank several bottles of port and the attic room rioted with song and story. The incomparable Schetky was, of course, incomparable—as a professional musician. And he was full of wit and merriment and indifferent English. But Allan Masterton, the writing master, was a native amateur musician of great merit. Allan could compose in the native idiom very sweetly.

Nicol, of course, was the unofficial president of the quorum. Here he reigned supreme—guarding with an almost fiendish jealousy and delight the interests of the Bard, and doing everything he could to prepare his entries with an expertly timed "Now Robert . . ." or: "Wait till you hear the Bard."

There was nothing that came amiss to this quintet. Even Schetky, whose knowledge of the language was rough and approximate, had an excellent grip of Scots slang; and, from Nicol's tuition, an even better grip of Scots venereal slang. They could (and did) pass from politics and solemn philosophy to a song of melting sentiment or one of rollicking bare-buttocked bawdry. And as in politics and philosophy so in bawdry: when Nicol wanted a theme capped or an exposition crowned, he called for the Bard, who, glad to have his weary hours of isolation lightened by friendship, would prove his superiority. Whereupon Nicol would slap Schetky on his broad back and roar—"Ye canna beat the bluidy Bard, Geordie —neither in my country nor in yours," to which Schetky would raise his glass, burbling: "I dispute not, my dear Villie, I dispute not."

And sometimes they would come in when he was just beginning a letter to Clarinda and he would either have to abandon it or do his best to finish it in a corner while they laughed and jested. And Nicol would say: "There's the Bard writing to some puir bitch itching for his knee to be better when he'll gie her a thumping'll put love-letters out o' her head for nine months. . ."

Sometimes he cursed his visitors when they crowded into his small room and irritated him with their crude laughter. Often he cursed them the following morning for being the cause of his drinking too much. For despite what Dalrymple of Orangefield had said to him about having his stomach tanned, he still proved an indifferent drinker. . .

But on the whole he was thankful that his friends did not neglect him.

Between times when he was not writing to Clarinda or Peggy Chalmers or correcting Johnson's sheets he read the Bible. He started at the first page of Genesis and missed nothing. And he was deeply read in the Bible. . .

So he wrote to Peggy Chalmers (who was still at Harviestoun): I have taken tooth and nail to the Bible, and am got through the five books of Moses, and half way in Joshua. It is really a glorious book. . .

But Bible or no Bible, Willie Nicol or no Willie Nicol, Bob Ainslie or no Bob Ainslie, he was far from happy. Only Clarinda, the glorious amiable fine Nancy proved a distraction for him—though that was but momentary.

Again he wrote to Peggy Chalmers (and as his knee was getting better):

I begin this letter in answer to yours of the 17th current, which is not yet cold since I read it. The atmosphere of my soul is vastly clearer than when I wrote you last. For the first time, yesterday I crossed the room on crutches. It would do your heart good to see my bardship, not on my *poetic*, but on my *oaken* stilts; throwing my best leg with an air! and with as much hilarity in my gait and countenance as a May frog leaping across the newly-harrowed ridge, enjoying the fragrance of the refreshed earth after the long-expected shower . . . !

I can't say I am altogether at my ease when I see any where in my path that meagre, squalid, famine-faced spectre Poverty; attended as he always is by iron-fisted Oppression, and leering Contempt; but I have sturdily withstood his buffetings many a hard-laboured day already, and still my motto is—I DARE! My worst enemy is Moiméme. I lie so miserably open to the inroads and incursions of a mischievous, light-armed, well-mounted banditti, under the banners of Imagination, Whim, Caprice, and Passion, and the heavy-armed veteran regulars of Wisdom, Prudence, and Forethought, move so very, very slow, that I am almost in a state of perpetual warfare, and alas! frequent defeat. There are just two creatures I would envy, a horse in his native state traversing the forests of Asia, or an oyster on some of the desert shores of Europe. The one has not a wish without enjoyment, the other has neither wish nor fear.

But his deepest trouble concerned his future. There was still no word from Creech; he was still in a dilemma concerning the Excise; he was worried, deeply worried, about Jean Armour; he was worried about Gilbert and Mossgiel. The moment his mind was not preoccupied by some distraction, worry settled her vulture claws deep in him and he could do little more than writhe in impotent agony.

Lang Sandy Wood could see how deeply worried he was and he rallied him on it.

"There's nae guid lying here, Rab, worrying your guts oot. You can do naething till that knee's better. You're coming on fine—but it'll need a week or twa yet. Are you itching to get awa' back to Ayrshire?"

"I've nae place to go to, to itch aboot, Sandy. Creech has still to settle accounts wi' me."

"He's the damndest procrastinator, is Willie Creech. He'll no' pairt wi' his money. He's aey been like that. You'll need to force it oot o' him."

"How, Sandy?"

"Juist tell him ye maun hae it!"

He laughed shortly. "You dinna ken Creech as I ken him, Sandy.'

"And what about that farm ye were thinking o' taking frae Patrick Miller?"

"I canna tak' the place without money."

"So that's what's eating ye up?"

"If I could get put on the Excise list——"

"Are you still determined on that?"

"Can you think on a better standby?"

"Weel . . . maybe no'—a' things considered. If you're determined, Rab, I'll see what can be done for you. There'll be something far wrong gin I canna get you on the Excise list for a common gauger. D'ye no' ken ony o' the Commissioners?"

"What about Graham o' Fintry—I met him at the Blair o' Atholl during my tour o' the Highlands?"

"Bob Graham? Aye . . . he wad dae. And what about your patron Glencairn?"

"I mentioned it to Glencairn a while back—when I first came to Town, as a matter of fact. He didna like the idea."

"No. . . I can understand that Glencairn wouldna like to patronise a common gauger—a different proposition a'thegither frae a heaven-taught ploughman-poet. Imphm. . . Leave it to me, Rab. You'll maybe need to write Bob Graham —and Glencairn. But no' afore I advise ye. I'll mak' sure everything's clear for ye afore ye do onything. Ye ken, of course, that ye're a wee shady on the wrang side wi' your politics?"

"What the hell, good or bad, can my politics do?"

"Quite so! But you're no' ower keen on Geordie."

"Are you?"

"The difference atween you and me, Rab, is that I keep my political sentiments to mysel'. You're inclined to advertise yours. And no' juist being a Government man doesna gae doon weel in Government circles—if ye ken what I mean."

"I ken fine what you mean, Sandy. And listen—if I've got to go doon on my knees and beg to be put on the list; if

I've got to write mortifying soliciting letters to the Great—then I'll do without."

"Aye, juist exac'ly: you'll dae without. You're a damn dour dirty cauld bitch o' a thrawn beggar when ye like, Rab. Ye haena enough i' your pouch to crack a louse under yer thoomb and ye wadna bow the knee, so ye wadna! Weel, weel . . . that's what comes o' being bred to the plough an honest rustic. Noo, had ye been properly brocht up and bred to the college ye'd hae gaed a different road to the well. Na, na: I'm no' blaming ye, Rab: I'm juist thinking—thinking how best I can bow the knee for ye. And seeing how your knee's dislocated I can ease my conscience on that score——"

"Then you needna bother, Sandy: when I canna beg for mysel' I'll no' ask my friends to do it for me."

"Aye . . . so I hear. . ."

Lang Sandy Wood was a kind-hearted man. He could not help thinking, as he sat beside the Bard in the attic, that it was a damned shame to tell a man he was a genius, that he was a credit to his country—aye, and one of the greatest credits the country had ever known—and then leave him to fend for himself as best he could. Here was the greatest poet of the age sitting in a high bare attic wondering whether to go back to his plough or turn a common gauger. Aye, and worrying his guts out how he was to become a common gauger. . .

Well, if none of the Edinburgh gentry would do anything for him, he would see what could be done—and done without inflicting any humiliating conditions on the man.

MASKS OFF

Still, there was the immediate consolation of Clarinda. A man could have all the men friends in the world; but still he needed a woman. Or *he* did. He might as well admit it. The woman wasn't born who could fill a man's life completely. Maybe the man wasn't born who could do the same for a

woman. But in different ways. A woman bore children. . .
But then fathers were often fonder of their children than were
mothers. . . Or were they? He couldn't argue things out any
longer. Clarinda had caused him to write more bluidy lies
than anybody ever had.

Were they really lies? If so, why did he write them?
Because he was in love with her. And becoming pretty desperate in his love for her—and she for him, if he was any judge
of a letter. That was the intoxicating part of it. Clarinda was
in love with him and becoming every bit as desperate as he
was.

By the third of January (a Thursday) her desperation was
at breaking point. After enclosing him some lines—Talk not
of love it gives me pain, for love has been my foe—she dropped
the mask:

Do you think you could venture this length in a coach,
without hurting yourself? I go out of Town the beginning
of the week, for a few days. I wish you could come to-morrow
or Saturday. I long for a conversation with you, and lameness
of body won't hinder that. 'Tis really curious—so much *fun*
passing between two persons who saw one another only *once*!
Say if you think you dare venture:—only let the coachman be
' adorned with sobriety.'

On Friday he wrote her a long letter in reply, saying among
other things:

To-morrow evening I intend taking a chair, and paying
a visit to Park Place to a much-valued old friend. If I could be
sure of finding you at home (and I will send one of the chair-
men to call), I would spend from five to six o'clock with you,
as I go past. I cannot do more at this time, as I have something on my hand that hurries me much. I propose giving you
the first call, my old friend the second, and Miss Nimmo as
I return home. Do not break any engagement for me, as I
will spend another evening with you at any rate before I
leave town. . .

Many happy New Years to you, charming Clarinda!

I can't dissemble, were it to shun perdition. He who sees you as I have done, and does not love you, deserves to be damned for his stupidity! He who loves you and would injure you, deserves to be doubly damned for his villainy! Adieu.

Yet it was an effort for him to get downstairs and take his seat in the sedan-chair—a much bigger effort than he had anticipated. But he was out of his prison, out into the noise of the Edinburgh streets.

He was much weaker than he thought and he was still in considerable pain. But he made a great effort and with the aid of the chairmen reached Clarinda's door in good spirits.

She had a seat ready for him by the fireplace that jutted well into the room between two windows.

They looked at each other shyly—not daring to look. Had they done so they would have immediately been in each other's arms—and the time for that was not yet.

Clarinda busied herself for a moment, offered him tea, a drink—but he would have nothing.

She took a chair on the opposite side of the narrow fire.

"Now . . . we can talk. If you only knew how dreadful the time has been waiting to hear your voice. . . But I mustn't waste any of our precious minutes. Tell me about yourself."

"What would you like to know, my dear Clarinda?"

"About your life in Ayrshire—about your Jean—about— oh, I want to know everything."

"In an hour? I'll let you have a copy of my letter to Dr. Moore in London—it contains my life story—such as it is. But pray, madam, who is this Jean of mine, as you put it?"

"Oh, I have no wish to pry into your private affairs, Robert. . . I'm so glad that within these walls I may call you Robert. I had merely thought when Miss Nimmo could discuss your Jean—as she called her—so openly that there was no secret about her."

"Apparently there are no secrets about her. My Jean, my

dear madam, was the girl—as you will no doubt have heard—was the girl I had intended to make my wife. But I wasn't good enough for her family and they persuaded her . . ."

"But surely . . . and she had twins?"

"She paid me double."

"And have you never tried to make it up?"

"There are some things, Clarinda, that cannot just be made up."

"How true. Oh, I know how true."

"I suppose you have heard all my wretched story?"

"Not wretched, my dear Robert—nothing could be wretched where you are concerned. I do feel so sorry for your Jean—what a husband she missed."

"Clarinda—I have come here to-night to talk about the present—not the past. Talk not of love, you command. But you know that I love you."

"No, Robert: I must forbid you to talk of love."

"My love for you is something I must talk about—it is that kind of love."

"Are there so many kinds of love?"

"Just as many kinds as there are kinds of human beings. Even then a human being may love in many ways——"

"To me there are only two kinds of love—sexual love and the love of the bosom guided by religion. I have had too much of the former and too little of the latter."

The Bard looked at her intently. She was more glorious than he had pictured from his first meeting. She was more than ever desirable: the voluptuous curves of her body shrieked desire.

"Please dinna think, Robert, that I dinna understand how men need sexual love. I can understand how a man needs a certain amount of intercourse."

A smoke film clouded the Bard's great smouldering eyes.

"I could even forgive infidelity on the part of a husband."

The smoke film cleared, the eyes seemed to stare, to probe deeply. Clarinda hesitated.

"Perhaps I speak too frankly to the man I consider above all things my dearest friend?"

"No, Clarinda, you do not speak too frankly: you cannot speak too frankly to me who am your friend."

"Oh, if you only knew how much I need your friendship. You are a passionate man, Robert, and I, God help me, am a passionate woman. But you have a mind and a heart that can soar above the heat of sexual passion—and so have I. Robert, when I wrote Talk Not of Love—I meant sexual love. If you and I are to be friends it must be understood that there can never be anything of that kind of love between us. . ."

The fire flickered in the grate; the candle, on the narrow ledge above, burned with a steady flame; soft shadows flitted about the room and the bed by the wall seemed to stir uneasily. The curtains on the windows moved slightly in the draught that pierced in at the ill-fitting sashes.

Eternity was in this hour. There was peace and quiet and the presence of an adorable woman in every inanimate object. But eternity ticked away on well-oiled wheels.

The strain and the excitement were beginning to tell on him. Sweat broke on his brow: he was damnably weak. . .

Yet what a peace and contentment was here in this soft woman-impregnated room: Clarinda's bedroom: her living room. The blood hammered at his heart. It was nonsense that this woman should deny herself the only love that meant anything between two passionate lovers. It was the bloodiest utter rubbish, this love of the bosom—and if he had her for five minutes on that bed he would convince her so.

And yet, and yet: the damnable thing was that she had—by her letters—half-convinced him that he was half-wrong. Here was a passionate woman whose married life had been one long series of brutal rapings by a beast who did not know the rudiments of sexual love. And yet his rasping rapings had not brought on her a sexual revulsion. But instead of bruising her teats with the whoredoms of Assyria she had succeeded in sublimating her passion and laying it before the feet of the Almighty. . . Either that or she was in terror of conceiving another child to another man when she was still tied to her husband. . .

She had brains—indeed, there was nothing she hadn't: except money and the independence it ensured.

Yet he must be careful. This woman could not be taken by storm. She would have to be wooed: her scruples would have to be undermined before they could be overcome. And if he could manage this in time it would be well worth the effort. If he could take this glorious woman to bed it would be his greatest victory in the lists of love—and (if he was any judge of the signs) by far the sweetest.

Then his eyes misted again as he watched her. He would need to hold himself in check. By all that was holy and much that wasn't he was beginning to fall in love with her—beginning to believe in the sincerity of the attitude he was building up to her. . .

Then his eye caught the clock and he remembered his appointment with John Tait of Harviestoun at Number Two Park Place. Tait had promised to see what could be done about the Excise and to advise him with regard to Creech. . .

But Clarinda wasn't anxious for him to go. She talked quickly, nervously, but with a wonderful command of language.

They came close together at the narrow doorway. She ran her fingers under the lapel of his coat: he could feel the soft yielding of her breasts. His nostrils dilated.

". . . and you'll come again soon, Robert . . .?"

He put an arm lightly on her shoulder; her chin uptilted; he kissed her gently, without a flicker of the passion that was beginning to seethe in him.

He promised to return with all speed.

John Tait concluded by saying: "Get Supervisor Nimmo to give you his Certificate of Examination—he knows the form. Enclose this to Mr. Graham of Fintry and ask for an Order for Instruction. This, Robert, you will do in your best manner. As for Creech—write him a keen letter to which he must reply: let me see his reply. . .

"And now, since Miss Chalmers is in the adjoining room with the ladies, you must say how do to them. . ."

TO GRAHAM OF FINTRY

The Bard read over his letter to Fintry:

Sir,
When I had the honour of being introduced to you at Atholl-house, I did not think of putting that acquaintance so soon to the test. When Lear, in Shakespeare, asks old Kent why he wished to be in his service, he answers, ' Because you have that in your face which I could like to call Master;' for some such similar reason, Sir, do I now solicit your Patronage. You know, I dare say, of an application I lately made to your Board, to be admitted an Officer of Excise. I have, according to form, been examined by a Supervisor, and to-day I give in his Certificate with a request for an Order for Instructions. In this affair, if I succeed, I am afraid I shall but too much need a patronising Friend. Propriety of conduct as a Man, and fidelity and attention as an Officer, I dare engage for; but with any thing like business I am totally unacquainted. The man who till within these eighteen months was never the wealthy master of ten guineas, can be but ill-acquainted with the busy routine. I had intended to have closed my late meteorous appearance on the stage of Life, in the country Farmer; but after discharging some filial and fraternal claims, I find I could only fight for existence in that miserable manner, which I have lived to see throw a venerable parent in the jaws of a Jail ; where, but for the Poor Man's last and often best friend, Death, he might have ended his days.

I know, Sir, that to need your goodness is to have a claim on it; may I therefore beg your Patronage to forward me in this affair till I be appointed to a Division; where, by the help of rigid Economy, I shall try to support that Independence so dear to my soul, but which has too often been so distant from my situation.

I have the honour to be, Sir,
your most humble servant . . .

567

But here was a worrying letter from Gilbert. He couldn't pay the wages at the end of December. The family were on their beam ends. And Jean had been thrown out into the world by her father. In her distress she had approached Gilbert and Gilbert had yoked the pony and driven her, at her request, to the Muirs of Tarbolton Mill. . .

The Bard fumed and raged and cursed and grat. If ever a man was born under an evil star he was that man. He would have to write to Willie Muir of the Mill—and he would have to write to Gilbert. If only he was well enough! If only that creeping crawling hell's evil broth of a bastard Creech would pay up. If only he could secure his Excise commission. . . If. . . If. . . If. . .

But he must get money for Gilbert: he couldn't let the family starve. . .

He cast his mind in every direction. Gilbert must have the money quickly. . . What about John Ballantine in Ayr who should have the money for his subscription copies—or some of it? He would write to him care of Gilbert and ask him to try and accommodate him until such time as he could get back to Ayrshire. John Ballantine would understand: he would tell him how he was confined to his room and so couldn't lay hands on ready cash. . .

He was ill and fevered. He had gone out too soon; and the exertion had proved too much for him. . .

And running through his fever like shooting neuralgic pains was the thought of Clarinda. Here she was coming to Saint James's Square in the hope of looking up and catching a glimpse of him at the attic window. . . What other woman had shown such an interest, affection, regard, love—for him?

Even with regard to Jean she was charitable beyond all other women. He searched her last letter for the reference: "I can't understand that bonnie lassie: her refusal after such proofs of love, proves her to be either an angel or a dolt. I beg pardon: I know not all the circumstances. . ."

By the holy, if she knew all the circumstances! Aye, but she would never know them. He could never explain even to the charitable Clarinda (let alone any other woman) what Jean meant to him. Clarinda would never understand that he was going back to Ayrshire immediately he had settled his affairs, and his knee permitted, to take her under his protection. . .

If he raved and raged, who shall blame him? If he worried himself sick and weary; if he turned in relief to Clarinda's letters; if he promised her the Kingdom of Heaven and the moon and the stars and vowed his love for her through life and beyond life, who shall blame him?

For this was just what he did. He would—he must—leave Edinburgh soon. Clarinda knew—there was little this woman did not know—that when he was back in Ayrshire their affection would die a natural death. She had said as much in her letters. . .

But he wasn't away from Edinburgh yet. And in Edinburgh, at General's Entry in the Potterrow, was a woman of his own age with ripe red lips, a full bosom and outlined in voluptuous curves. . .

BEHIND THE SCENES

Seven days after his first visit to General's Entry he was back again—so astutely had Clarinda composed her daily letter in the interval.

They were both much distracted and their nerves were taut and brittle. What both of them needed more than anything else was the utter abandonment of the bed and the relaxation that would have followed.

But Clarinda was not prepared to risk that yet—she would have to secure a firmer hold on Robert Burns before that could be risked. Her experience of life had taught her that the moment—(and it was a brief moment) that men satisfied their sexual appetite a blank and callous indifference immediately followed. She had hoped that Sylvander might be different but she had no reason to suppose that he was.

Before the visit was over she had reason to know differently; for Sylvander gave her a couple of hours of preliminary love-making that almost melted the marrow in her bones. The very delicacy of his fondling produced transports she had never before dreamed possible. And in the transport of her physical mood she allowed him liberties she had not thought to guard against. . .

Yet there was no verbal acknowledgment of this between them. Their verbal intercourse was still on the plane of friendship of the highest sensibility, suffused with the Religion of the Bosom.

The Bard was almost as transported as Nancy. He had never quite made love to any other woman as he now made it. And never had he made love to a woman who had had four children. It was a new experience and an exquisite one. There was even a deep satisfaction in postponing the final consummation. He was well content to leave this final approach to come from Nancy herself when she was ready. But he had no doubt that it would come—and before he left Edinburgh.

Yet not even in the height of his transport could he bring himself to believe he really loved Nancy. Not at least as he had loved Jean Armour or Mary Campbell. He still could not escape the comparison—despite all the differences—with Jean Glover. He had never loved Jean Glover although he had had a strange touching affection for her. He found himself developing a strange touching affection for Nancy Craig.

Maybe those men were luckiest who could satisfy their need for sex at the brothel—without being involved emotionally. But his emotions to a greater or lesser degree had always to be involved and nearly always deeply. At least there had to be an affection that went beyond the physical needs of a particular physical moment.

Yet never before had he made love to a sophisticated cultured woman like Clarinda. He had never got close enough to Peggy Chalmers to make physical love to her. But then he had longed for Peggy as a wife—there was something about his relationship with Peggy that he could not define and yet it was something almost devoid of physical passion.

But such thoughts flitted only momentarily across his mind—brightly though they were illuminated. He was lying beside Clarinda conscious that he was displaying his love-prowess to her in a way that was more successful than he had hoped. . .

And the next day brought confirmation of this. His eyes misted as he read her letter:

"I will not deny it, Sylvander, last night was one of the most exquisite I ever experienced. Few such fall to the lot of mortals! Few, extremely few, are formed to relish such refined enjoyment. That it should be so, vindicates the wisdom of Heaven. But, though our enjoyment did not lead beyond the limits of virtue, yet to-day's reflections have not been altogether unmixed with regret. The idea of the pain it would have given, were it known to a friend to whom I am bound by the sacred ties of gratitude, (no more) the opinion Sylvander may have formed from my unreservedness; and, above all, some secret misgivings that Heaven may not approve, situated as I am—these procured me a sleepless night; and, though at church, I am not at all well.

"Sylvander, you saw Clarinda last night, behind the scenes! Now, you'll be convinced she has faults. If she knows herself, her intention is always good; but she is too often the victim of sensibility, and, hence, is seldom pleased with herself. . ."

In his reply he did his best to comfort her and to allay her fears:

That you have faults, my Clarinda, I never doubted; but I knew not where they existed; and Saturday night made me more in the dark than ever. Oh Clarinda! why will you wound my soul by hinting that last night must have lessened my opinion of you? True, I was behind the scenes with you; but what did I see? A bosom glowing with honour and benevolence; a mind ennobled by genius, informed and refined by education and reflection, and exalted by native religion, genuine as in the climes of Heaven; a heart formed for all the glorious meltings of friendship, love and pity. These I saw: I saw the noblest immortal soul creation ever showed me.

I looked long, my dear Clarinda, for your letter; and am vexed that you are complaining. I have not caught you so far wrong as in your idea, that the commerce you have with one friend hurts you if you cannot tell every tittle of it to another. Why have so injurious a suspicion of a good God, Clarinda, as to think that Friendship and Love, on the sacred inviolate principles of Truth, Honour and Religion, can be anything else than an object of His divine approbation?

I have mentioned in some of my former scrawls, Saturday evening next. Do allow me to wait on you that evening. Oh, my angel! how soon must we part!—and when can we meet again? I look forward on the horrid interval with tearful eyes. What have I lost by not knowing you sooner! I fear, I fear my acquaintance with you is too short, to make that lasting impression on your heart I could wish.

HEAVEN—AND CLARINDA

With each succeeding meeting they explored each other more fully. And then immediately after, Clarinda, fearing she had gone too far and had run the risk of cheapening herself in his eyes or demeaned herself intellectually, was full of doubts and fears. She even came to the point when, having allowed him intimacies that could hardly be squared with the Religion of the Bosom, she wrote:

I am wishing, Sylvander, for the power of looking into your heart. It would be but fair—for you have the key of mine. You are possessed of acute discernment. I am not deficient either in that respect. Last night must have shown you Clarinda not ' divine '—but as she really is. I can't recollect some things I said without a degree of pain. Nature has been kind to me in several respects; but one essential she has denied me entirely: it is that instantaneous perception of fit and unfit, which is so useful in the conduct of life. No one can discriminate more accurately afterwards than Clarinda. But when her heart is expanded by the influence of kindness, she loses all command of it, and often suffers severely in the recollection of her unguardedness. You must have perceived this; but, at any rate, I wish you to know me, as ' I really am.' I would have given much for society to-day; for I can't bear my own: but no human being has come near me. Well as I like you, Sylvander, I would rather lose your love, than your esteem: the first I ought not to wish; the other I shall ever endeavour to maintain. But no more of this: you prohibit it, and I obey.

For many years have I sought for a male friend, endowed with sentiments like yours: one who could love me with tenderness, yet unmixed with selfishness: who could be my friend, companion, protector, and who would die sooner than injure me. I sought—but I sought in vain! Heaven has, I hope, sent me this blessing in my Sylvander! Whatever weaknesses may cleave to Clarinda, her heart is not to blame: whatever it may have been by nature, it is unsullied by art. If she dare dispose of it—last night can leave you at no loss to guess the man. . .

Presently he was replying:

Oh, what a fool I am in love! what an extravagant prodigal of affection! Why are your sex called the tender sex, when I never have met with one who can repay me in passion? They are either not so rich in love as I am, or they are niggards where I am lavish. . .

But the next bout of incompletely consummated love-making brought her fears to the fore again:

I am neither well nor happy to-day: my heart reproaches me for last night. If you wish Clarinda to regain her peace, determine against everything but what the strictest delicacy warrants.

I do not blame you, but myself. I must not see you on Saturday, unless I find I can depend on myself acting otherwise. Delicacy, you know, it was which won me to you at once: take care you do not loosen the dearest, most sacred tie that unites us. Remember Clarinda's present and eternal happiness depends upon her adherence to Virtue. Happy Sylvander! that can be attached to Heaven and Clarinda together. Alas! I feel I cannot serve two masters. God pity me!! . . . You and I are capable of that ardency of love, for which the wide creation cannot afford an adequate object. Let us seek to repose it in the bosom of our God. . . My servant (who is a good soul) will deliver you this. She is going down to Leith, and will return about two or three o'clock. . ."

JENNY CLOW

Jenny Clow, who had explicit instructions to deliver the letter into the hands of Robert Burns, was greatly excited at the prospect of meeting him. She knew Mrs. Mac and he were on very friendly terms. Jenny had a suspicion that the terms could not be friendlier.

She sat in the chair while the Bard scanned the letter which he did, she thought, very hurriedly. Then he turned his great eyes on her with some curiosity: Jenny at once knew that he was interested in her.

"What's your name, my dear?"

"Jenny Clow, sir."

"And you work for Mistress MacLehose?"

"Aye . . . off and on, sir."

"And you're coming back for an answer to take to your mistress?"

"Aye . . . I'll be back about half-past twa, sir—if that'll be convenient to you."

"Yes . . . quite convenient, Jenny. And where do you bide in the Town?"

"The Potterraw, sir: twa closes doon frae Mrs. Mac's— roun' the back and up a wee stair on your left, sir. You couldna miss it . . . I bide my lane, sir!"

The Bard smiled despite himself. "I didna say I was coming to see you, Jenny—though I dinna suppose ye wad mind if I did?"

"Oh, I'm no' that kind, sir: I'm nae whore. If Mrs. Mac thocht onything like that—— Oh, you wouldna say ocht to her, sir, would you?"

"No more than you'll say ocht about me."

"Aye . . . that's richt sensible, sir. You're an awfa handsome big man, sir, if ye dinna mind me remarking—I've heard an awfa lot aboot ye. Maybe I'm forgetting my place, sir— but I dinna mean ony offence. . . I've read some o' your poems, too, sir—oh, they're awfa like the thing."

The Bard stood with his hands in his breeches pockets looking down at her where she sat—for she did not seem to be over-anxious to continue her journey.

She was a good-looking lass in her early twenties. She had the delicate but attractive complexion of the consumptive; and there was the consumptive's burning love for life in her grey eyes. She was quick-witted and bright mentally.

The Bard reached for a chair and sat down in front of her.

"You wad like to tell folks how you met the Poet Burns, Jenny—is that it?"

"I needna tell onybody unless I like, sir."

"True enough, Jenny. And why were you so interested in me?"

"I've heard sae much about ye, sir—and then you being friendly wi' Mrs. Mac——"

"Just what d'you know about my friendship wi' Mrs. Mac, as you address her?"

"Oh, she's a nice woman, Mrs. Mac—and it's a gey pity for her wi' that man she had."

"Yes, I know she's a nice woman, but dinna evade my question, Jenny—what d'you know concerning my friendship with Mrs. MacLehose?"

"D'ye want the God's truth, sir—and ye'll no' tell on me . . .? Aye, weel then: she's daft about ye. . . And I dinna blame her—ony woman wad be daft aboot ye if she got the chance."

"You can lay on the butter, Jenny. So you wadna mind the chance yourself?"

"What chance have I, sir?"

"You're a woman, aren't you?"

"D'ye want proof——?"

"What time d'you get the Leith fly?"

"I've a guid half hour yet——"

The Bard rose and put the bolt in the door.

Half an hour after Jenny had gone, he got up, drank a glass of wine, took paper and pen and wrote:

Clarinda, my life, you have wounded my soul. Can I think of your being unhappy, even tho' it be not described in your pathetic elegance of language, without being miserable? Clarinda, can I bear to be told from you, that ' you will not see me to-morrow night—that you wish the hour of parting were come'! Do not let us impose on ourselves by sounds: if in the moment of fond endearment and tender dalliance, I perhaps trespassed against the *letter* of Decorum's law; I appeal, even to you, whether I ever sinned in the very least degree against the *spirit* of her strictest statute. Now, my Love, do not wound our next meeting with any averted looks or restrained caresses: I have marked the line of conduct, a line I know exactly to your taste, and which I will inviolably keep; but do not *you* show the least inclination to make boundaries: seeming distrust, where you know you may confide, is a cruel sin against Sensibility.

I had proposed bringing my bosom friend, Mr. Ainslie, to-morrow evening, at his strong request, to see you; as he has only time to stay with us about ten minutes, for an engagement; but—I shall hear from you: this afternoon, for mercy's sake! for, till I hear from you, I am wretched. O Clarinda, that tie that binds me to thee, is entwisted, incorporated with my dearest threads of life!

Later in the evening Bob Ainslie called with a bottle of prime port. Over the glass the Bard said with a deep sigh of satisfaction.

"The Deil's aey guid to his ain, Bob. My glorious Clarinda sent her servant wi' a note to me on her way to Leith and called in on her road back—and what d'you think?"

"Have you met the servant before? No! And what's she like."

"As nice a piece as you'd find in a day's travel."

"Then she got her licks."

"Aye . . . afore she went to Leith—and the same when she came back. By the Lord, Bob, if she was needing it so was I—I feel completely renewed."

"How d'you do it, Robert?"

But the Bard's reply was unprintable and Ainslie's eyes grew pained with envy.

"What if she tells Clarinda?"

"A contented lass never tells, Bob—never. And Jenny Clow's a contented lass the nicht."

"Maybe Clarinda'll no' be so easily contented?"

"Clarinda's in an entirely different category, Bob—entirely different. She'll have to be contented in an entirely different manner—but she'll be contented, never fear."

The Bard thought little or nothing of Jenny Clow. He had not deceived Jenny: Jenny had not deceived him. Both were completely satisfied with the tasty dish of life's meal. Maybe Jenny was the happier of the two. She had experienced something beyond her wildest dreams: she would have gnawed her heart out for the rest of her short life if she had refused him. Whatever slavery or drudgery life had held and might continue to hold for her, she would never forget how the Poet Burns had taken her in his arms. Her fondest hope was that he would come soon to her door.

HUMILIATION

But the hour was approaching when he must leave Edinburgh. His leg, though still stiff and sore, was vastly better. Creech had promised to pay up within a few days: this time he believed Creech was in earnest. Sandy Wood assured him that he would get his Excise commission. Once he had Creech's money in his hand he would take the first fly to Glasgow. Captain Richard Brown, his old comrade of the Irvine days, was waiting there for him; and Willie would bring Jenny Geddes to meet him there too. If only Creech would hurry and the Excise Commissioners would hurry, he would be away to-morrow. Schetky had set his Clarinda song to music and he was almost finished with Jamie Johnson's second volume. There was little in Edinburgh to keep him.

But an aristocratic old hag in Alison Square was soon to let him know differently. She was condescendingly friendly to the Nimmos—and Henry Dundas was condescendingly friendly to her.

He met her one afternoon at Miss Nimmo's, drinking tea.

"I understand, Mr. Burns," she said, haughtily, "you wish to enter upon the Excise?"

"That, madam, is my expectation."

"Then you will require to mend your manners, Mr. Burns." The Bard flushed darkly and his eyes carried a lowe from the pit of hell. But he restrained himself. This woman was apparently influential with the Commissioners.

"In what way, madam?"

"In every way, I should imagine. I've had a first-hand account o' the horrid lines you wrote on a window in a Stirling inn. Treasonable lines, sir—indescribably low and vile in their sentiment. I am shocked to think any true-born Scot wrote them—far less a man claiming to be Scotland's poet. In view of these lines, Mr. Burns, I think it's highly improper for you to apply for service in His Majesty's Excise. . ."

A diabolical rage gathered inside the Bard; but he bit his lip and said nothing.

His silence infuriated Mrs. Stewart who was not used to contempt of any kind and who found silent contempt (or so she judged the silence) the hardest to bear.

But no matter how she rated and questioned he answered briefly in deadly delayed monosyllables or not at all. . .

Back in Cruikshank's attic he wrote to Clarinda:

I have almost given up the Excise idea. I have been just now to wait on a great Person, Miss Nimmo's friend, Mrs. Stewart. Why will Great people not only deafen us with the din of their equipage, and dazzle us with their fastidious pomp, but they must also be so very dictatorially wise? I have been questioned like a child about my matters, and blamed and schooled for my Inscription on Stirling window. Come, Clarinda—' Come, curse me, Jacob; come, defy me, Israel!'

To this Clarinda replied with a masterpiece of composition, good sense, subtle coquetry and diabolical feminine cunning:

Sylvander, when I think of you as my *dearest* and most attached *friend*, I am highly pleased; but when you come across my mind as my *lover*, something within gives a *sting* resembling that of guilt! Tell me why is this? It must be from the idea that I am another's. What! another's wife! O cruel Fate! I am indeed bound in an ' iron chain '! Forgive me, if this should give you pain. You know I must (I told you I *must*) tell you my genuine feelings, or be silent. Last night we were happy! beyond what the bulk of mankind can conceive! Perhaps the ' line ' you had marked was a *little* infringed —it was really; but, though I *disapprove*, I have not been *unhappy* about it. I am convinced no less of your *discernment* than of your *wish* to make your Clarinda happy. I know you *sincere*, when you profess horror at the idea of what would render her miserable forever. But we must *guard* against going to the *verge* of danger. Ah! my friend, much need had we to 'watch and pray'! May these benevolent spirits whose office it is to ' save the fall of Virtue struggling on the brink of vice ' be ever present to protect and guide us in right paths!

I had an hour's conversation to-day with my worthy friend Mr. Kemp. You'll attribute, perhaps, to *this*, the above sentiments. 'Tis true, there's not one on earth has so much influence on me, except Sylvander; *partly* it has forced me ' to feel along the mental intelligence.'   However, I've broke the ice. I confessed I had conceived a tender impression of late—that it was mutual, and that I had wished to unbosom myself to him (as I did), particularly to ask if he thought I should, or not, mention it to my *friend*? I saw he felt for me (for I was in tears); but he bewailed that I had given my *heart*, while in my present state of bondage—wished I had made it friendship *only*—in short, talked to me in the style of a tender Parent, *anxious* for my happiness. He disapproves altogether of my saying a syllable of the matter to my friend; says it could only make him uneasy; and that I'm in no way bound to do it by any one tie. This has eased me of a *load* which has lain upon my mind ever since our intimacy. Sylvander, I wish you and Mr. Kemp were acquainted—such worth and sensibility! If you had his piety and sobriety of manners, united to the shining abilities you possess! you'd be ' a faultless monster which the world ne'er saw.' He too has great talents. His imagination is rich, his feelings delicate, his discernment acute; yet there are *shades* in his, as in all characters: but these it would ill become Clarinda to point out. Alas! I know too many blots in my own!

Pray, what does Mr. Ainslie think of her! was he not astonished to find her merely human? Three weeks ago, I suppose you would have walked into her presence *unshod*; but one must *bury* even divinities when they discover symptoms of mortality! (Let *these* be interred in Sylvander's bosom!)

My dearest friend, there are two wishes uppermost in my heart; to see you think alike with Clarinda on religion; and to see you settled in some creditable line of business. The warm interest I take in both these is perhaps the best proof of the sincerity of my friendship, as well as the earnest of its

duration. As to the first, I devolve it over into the hands of
the Omniscient! May He raise up friends who will effectuate
the other! While I breathe these fervent wishes, think not
that anything but pure *disinterested* regard prompts them.
They're fond, but chimerical ideas. They are never indulged
but in the hour of tender endearment, when

> ' Innocence
> Looks gaily smiling on; while rosy Pleasure
> Hides young Desire amid her flowery wreath,
> And pours her cup luxuriant, mantling high
> The sparkling heavenly vintage—Love and Bliss! '

'Tis past ten; and I please myself with thinking Sylvander
will be about to retire, and write to Clarinda. I fancy you'll
find this *stupid* enough; but I can't be always bright; the *sun*
will be *some times* under a cloud. Sylvander, I wish our kind
feelings were more moderate; why set one's heart upon
impossibilities? Try me merely as your friend (alas! all I ought
to be): believe me, you'll find me most rational. If you'd
caress the ' mental intelligence ' as you do the corporeal frame,
indeed, Sylvander, you'd make me a philosopher. I see you
fidgetting at this *violently* blasting rationality. I have a headache which brings home those things to the mind. To-morrow
I'll hear from you, I hope! This is Sunday, and not a word
on our favourite subject. O fy! ' divine Clarinda.' I intend
giving you *my* idea of Heaven in opposition to your heathenish
description (which, by the bye, was elegantly drawn). Mine
shall be founded on Reason and supported by Scripture; but
it's too late, my head aches, but my heart is affectionately
yours. . .

I am not sorry almost at the Excise affair misgiving.
You will be better out of Edinburgh: it is full of temptation
to one of your social turn. Providence (if you be wise in future)
will order something better for you. I'm half-glad you were
schooled about the Inscription; 'twill be a lesson, I hope, in
future. Clarinda would have lectured you on it before, ' if
she durst.' Ah, Sylvander! my peace *must* suffer; yours

cannot. *You* think, in loving Clarinda, you are doing right; all Sylvander's eloquence cannot convince me that it is so! If I were but at liberty—O how I would indulge in all the luxury of *innocent* love! It is, I fear, I fear, too late to talk in this strain after indulging you and myself so much; but would Sylvander shelter his Love in Friendship's *allowed* garb, Clarinda would be much happier!

' To-morrow,' didst thou say? The time is short *now*; is it not *too* frequent? Do not sweetest dainties cloy soonest? Take your chance—come half-past eight. If anything particular occur to render it improper *to-morrow* I'll send you word, and name another evening. Mr. Kemp is to call to-night, I believe. *He*, too, ' trembles for my peace.' Two such worthies to be interested about my foolish ladyship! The Apostle Paul, with all his rhetoric, could not reconcile me to the *great* (little souls) when I think of them and Sylvander together; but I *pity* them.

> If e'er ambition did my fancy cheat,
> With any wish so *mean*, as to be great,
> Continue, Heav'n, far from me to remove
> The humble blessings of that life I'd love.

Till me meet, my dear Sylvander, adieu!

THE BARRIERS DOWN

But neither he nor Clarinda could stay the pace of sexual dalliance and erotic endearments. All the barriers were finally swept aside. Yet at the final climax fear overcame Clarinda.

In the morning he felt relieved that their union had not been complete. To make Clarinda pregnant was the last thing he wanted to do. Indeed it would have been an overwhelming disaster for both of them.

He realised the delicacy of Clarinda's position. She had pleaded with him to take no risk that would jeopardise her future and the future of her children. And in the end he realised that she was weaker in her emotions than he was—that to betray her was to betray the trust she had in him.

But though Clarinda was exalted, elated and thrilled to her inmost marrow with Sylvander's love-making—she was devastated with anxiety and fear. There was just the possibility that she might have conceived.

She anticipated the possible future by confessing to the Reverend Kemp. It was a skilful confession and she took great care to confess that her heart only had been given to a lover. The Reverend John was almost beside himself with jealousy. Clarinda saw this and shifted her ground deftly. . .

Sylvander was a bit dubious when Clarinda wrote him about her unburdening to Kemp—of whom he had an instinctive dislike. Yet he dared not tell her his true thoughts about him. She was completely under his spiritual dominance—that at least.

On the other hand, he had succeeded in persuading her to get her silhouette done by Miers, so that he could take her image with him back to Ayrshire. . .

Clarinda held him with her physical endowments. Her entire personality was composed of sweet voluptuous curves. Her thoughts were sweetly curved and the tones of her voice were just as sweetly curved. There was nothing angular or broken-edged about any aspect of her. But above all, her letters were written in a series of connecting and convoluting curves so that they spiralled into his mind and gave a twist to all his thoughts about her.

And in his hectic last days in Edinburgh when he was almost driven to madness by the desperate nature of his situation, Clarinda was the only touchstone that kept him sane. She distracted him completely from his more important if more mundane worries.

Soon—too soon—he would have to face Ayrshire, face Jean, face Gilbert—and face them with what? With an Excise commission and his money from Creech in his pocket? Or with empty pockets and no commission?

From such worries he hurried to Clarinda . . .

And as the fever of worry mounted, so the fever mounted in his relationship with Clarinda. And as the fever mounted to its dizzy heart-aching, heart-throbbing climax, he finally was persuaded that he did in fact and deed and thought and spirit love Clarinda above and beyond all other women and that he would love her to all eternity.

And Clarinda catching something of the fever believed him.

But she was worried. The visits were becoming too frequent—folks were talking—and talking scandal.

She grappled Sylvander to her with every hook she could summon to her aid; and she played on every chord of his sympathetic nature and fevered emotions. Sometimes she acted despair. He would forget her the moment he was away from her; he would be unfaithful to her the moment he returned to Ayrshire and his Jean; the fact that she was pregnant and about to lie-in would be sure to win his sympathy. . . Was he not hurrying back to Ayrshire to be at her side? Then why was he hurrying back?

There were no lovers' embraces during these scenes. Sylvander hated the scenes and wanted the embraces. Sometimes he retreated to Jenny Clow who alone could release the terrible tensions that thwarted him.

Then he would retire to the attic and write to Clarinda and assure her that he could not possibly forget her; that he would carry her image (about to be supplied by Miers) with him into the country and it would console him for their physical separation: hadn't he got Schetky to set his song on her to fine music. . .?

Clarinda shifted her ground. How she pitied his poor Jean —what a tragedy for the "bonnie lassie." What about his son by her—the little Bobby that was being cared for at Mossgiel —all his namesake! Kindness, charity and motherly protection oozed out of every pore—and she produced the unfinished little shirts she was making for him so that he could take them back to Ayrshire with him.

Then she was pregnant; she was sure she was pregnant. Horror upon horror! If she were, what was she to do? He would have to support her. She would try to get a divorce. She would have to tell cousin Craig: she would have to tell Mr. Kemp: the whole town would know. All Scotland would know. . .

Sylvander's blood curdled at the thought. Then he would do everything he could to comfort her, to assure her that her fears were groundless; and Clarinda would throw her arms about him and become passionate and weep and groan. . .

But he was determined to get out of Edinburgh without any scene—without sending Clarinda flying to Kemp or Craig with some scarifying tale which, if made public, would ruin his chances with the Excise—Lawyer Craig might even try to arrest his money in Creech's hands. Lawyers—especially of the Craig breed—were capable of anything.

He wrote to Clarinda:

I met you, my dear Clarinda, by far the first of woman-kind, at least to me; I esteemed, I loved you at first sight, both of which attachments you have done me the honour to return. The longer I am acquainted with you, the more innate amiable-ness and worth I discover in you. You have suffered a loss, I confess, for my sake; but if the firmest, steadiest, warmest friendship; if every endeavour to be worthy of your friend-ship; if a love strong as the ties of Nature and holy as the duties of Religion; if all these can make anything like a compensation for the evil I have occasioned you; if they be worth your acceptance, or can in the least add to your enjoy-ments—so help Sylvander, ye Powers above, in his hour of need, as he freely gives these all to Clarinda!

I esteem you, I love you, as a friend; I admire you, I love you, as a woman beyond any one in all the circle of creation. I know I shall continue to esteem you, to love you, to pray for you, nay, to pray for myself for your sake.

Expect me at eight; and believe me to be ever, my dearest Madam, Yours most entirely. . .

THE FIRST PARTING

But though he was distracted, worried and deeply agitated, the Bard did not lose his head; and his immense reservoir of common sense never served him in better stead. Many of his friends thought they had never seen him calmer or more business-like.

Indeed, what business he had to do he did promptly and efficiently. Patrick Miller sent for him and asked him his intentions about Ellisland.

He promised Miller he would look over the farm some time early in March and give him his decision when he returned to Edinburgh. (He would have to come back to Edinburgh for his Excise instructions as soon as he had settled things for Jean Armour and squared up with Gilbert.)

Miller was satisfied: the Bard seemed determined, resolute, absolutely in command of himself. Miller was confident he meant business.

He overcame his intense physical dislike of Creech, bearded him in Craig's Close, came away with fifty pounds, and the definite promise of the balance on his return—certainly final settlement. And Creech now knew that he would have to keep his word.

James Johnson found him keen and exact as ever and happy beyond words at getting the second volume fully completed.

But indeed this last-lap wave of business-like activity served not only to distract the Bard—it flowed from the sharpening of events.

He had definitely committed himself to leaving Edinburgh for at least a fortnight or three weeks. Sandy Wood and Graham of Fintry had assured him that his application had been accepted and that only the formalities and the issuing of his "instruction" fell to be arranged. This might come before he left Edinburgh—if not, certainly against his return.

Only to Ainslie and to Willie Nicol did he convey anything of his real feelings. He told Nicol little or nothing about

Clarinda—Nicol would have leapt out of his skin in fury at the Bard wasting his time with such a woman. But he could and did tell Nicol all about Mrs. Stewart and his Excise ups and downs. And he confided much in his letters to Peggy Chalmers. . .

Only to Bob Ainslie did he confide anything about Clarinda. He had introduced him to her and Ainslie had been much impressed—besides, Ainslie had his eye on Clarinda's friend, Mary Peacock. If anything happened to Clarinda that would necessitate delicate ambassadorial work, Bob Ainslie would be the man to do it. Besides he had a genuine affection for Ainslie who seemed quite touched at the thought of doing him any service.

Ainslie marvelled at the Bard's way with women. He hoped to spend many an hour with Clarinda, drawing her out about the Bard's ways with her. Even if she was a bit older than he was, he wouldn't mind making love to her. . .

By Sunday, the 17th of February, after clearing up some correspondence, he was free to take leave of Clarinda.

Clarinda knew that this interval of separation would prove much—might indeed prove everything. Both Craig and Kemp were hot on her heels and were demanding to know the name of the man with whom she was philandering—both had heard that it was Robert Burns and they were anxious to have this either confirmed or denied.

This troubled the Bard and he told Clarinda that neither of them was entitled to be assured either way.

It wasn't the happiest of partings. They were both strained, worried and ill-at-ease. Neither put all their cards on the table, even while they protested that they did.

"What's worrying you, Nancy?"

"That you'll make things up with Jean Armour, Robert."

"And what makes you think that—after all that has passed between us—after all I've told you about Peggy Chalmers?"

"Aye—I ken, Robert. But I can count as well as the next one. Jean Armour refused you; her twins were born before you came to Edinburgh last year. Then you went back to

Machlin in the summer and, despite what had happened, she conceived again. The fruits of that conception are about due? And you are going back again."

"Well, Nancy, you needna worry about my conduct wi' Jean Armour: my name's Robert Burns—not James MacLehose."

But the moment he had said this he realised he had spoken entirely out of his Sylvander character and that he had hurt Nancy more cruelly than he had intended. It took him some time—and no little skill—to pacify her.

But his roughness had done her a lot of good.

"It's just that I love you, Robert—and yet have no right —am not free to love you—and I fear to lose your friendship. Have you any real idea how lonely it is for me living here? My two boys are asleep in the far room. The long winter nights I sit here alone sewing and knitting. Occasionally Mary comes to see me: occasionally Jenny watches the children while I visit Miss Nimmo or pay a duty call on cousin William . . . Life is very lonely for me. And if I had not the rock of my religion to build my faith on I were indeed lost. . . Maybe you havena independence, my love; but you have fame and many, many good friends—and you have your poetry. . ."

The Bard sighed deeply and cast a glance round the room. Aye . . . he could understand how Nancy felt. She was indeed a woman in a thousand who could endure such a life. And yet this was the only life she could endure. She would be hopelessly out of place in the country. It was quite impossible to imagine her in the narrow confines of Machlin—it was even more impossible to imagine her on an Ayrshire farm. She probably hadn't the faintest idea—despite all her reading— what the actualities of farm life were like. It was utterly beyond the limits of possibility that she could enter the kitchen of Mossgiel and be introduced as his wife. And he knew that he could not endure a lifetime of the Edinburgh environment that was her essential background.

What had started as an amorous flirtation, as a deliberate essay in seduction, had become unbelievably involved. There was a day—and that but six weeks ago—when he had thought that he would end up by taking her to bed and giving her interest for what she reciprocated.

But it had worked out differently. He had become involved with her to a degree he had not anticipated. There was now no question of enjoying her as he enjoyed Jenny Clow. She had become emotionally involved with him.

They had indeed become emotionally entangled in a way that was frightening—and it was impossible to see what the outcome might be. . .

"You'll write me every day that you're away . . .?"

"I'll write you every day. . ."

"And you'll sign yourself Sylvander——?"

"And you'll sign yourself Clarinda?"

"And every night you'll meet me at the Throne of Grace."

"Remembering all that the Throne of Grace means to us."

"Oh Robert, my beloved—were ever two beings destined to love as you and me—and not able to avow and openly acknowledge that love. . ."

He took her in his arms and comforted her—and they fused in passion and tears. . .

"At the most, dearest Nancy—three short weeks till we meet again. . ."

The candle had burned down and guttered itself out; the sea-coal had sunk to death in the iron grate and the clock on the wall had softly chimed the wee short hours before the Bard crept down the stairs and hugged his way by the wall of the Potterrow, tired and exhausted; too much drained of emotional and physical energy to notice the swath of stars that shone above the serrated roof tops of Auld Reekie. . .

THE THOUGHT FOR THE DEED

It was Saturday the 23rd of February, a cold clear but sunny day that the Bard came round by Adamhill from Kilmarnock and jogged Jenny Geddes on to Tarbolton and Willie's Mill.

He had taken five days to come from Auld Reekie but already it seemed far behind him; and he sniffed the keen West-country air, blowing over the great bare rolling uplands from the sea, with deep satisfaction. His foot was on his native heath once more and he felt much the better for it.

Tarbolton was as busy as ever this Saturday morning and the clack of looms was heard from every door. Standing at his wonted corner at the centre of the village was Saunders Tait, the Tarbolton tailor and rhymer. Saunders bore the Bard an undying grudge for his poetry. His Edinburgh success had nearly driven him demented. But Fate was delivering him into his hands. Round the corner and down the hill was Jean Armour about to deliver the second cargo laid in by the blackguard Burns. Saunders was awaiting developments with impatient interest. There was a poem in this—a fine blistering satire that would hold up the Bard of Ayrshire and of Scotland to ridicule and expose him in his true colours. . .

As the Bard trotted down past the Kirk, Saunders clawed at his yellow-white beard and screwed up his eyes. Damned, here was the notorious rake and celebrated blackguard himself trotting along as if he was one of the gentry with a fine skirted riding coat, polished high boots and wide brimmed black hat.

Saunders spat and girned and involuntarily did a few quick steps like a hen on a hot girdle. Damned, but the blackguard was larger than life and as handsome as ever—bad cess to him!

The Bard wheeled his pony to the left and without even a look in Saunders' direction turned down to Willie's Mill. Saunders performed a shuffling dance into the middle of the road and watched him as he turned the corner again beyond the town's House.

Only when he had disappeared from sight did Saunders stop clawing his beard. He spat viciously on the roadway and then decided to follow him down to Willie's Mill. . .

Willie Muir, fat and dusty, came out of the mill to greet the Bard.

"Man, Rab, are we no' glad to see you . . . and how are you? God, lad, but you're looking weel. . . Aye . . . Jean's in the hoose hinging ower the ingle. . . Damnit, Rab, ye'll need to be guid to her. The way James Armour's treated her's something dastardly—doonright diabolical. Aye, Rab, you'll need to be guid to her and dae what you can—for she's in a sair hauden-doon condition. . ."

"What d'you think I cam' home for, Willie?"

"God, you're limping, Rab: is that knee no' better yet?"

"It's better than it was. . . No, Willie, I'll do what I can for Jean—and I canna say a' my thanks to you and the guidwife for taking Jean in in her trouble. . ."

"Hoots. . . Awa' in an' see her."

He stood with his back to the fire and Jean sat in the elbow-chair. The Bard looked down at her and his heart was full. Jean didn't present too pretty a picture. She was pale and drawn and she was enormously swollen.

"God, Jean, don't tell me you're carrying twins again?" Immediately he thought of Peggy Cameron's triplets and feared the worst.

"I dinna ken, Rab. I juist dinna ken; but I wish to God it was a' ower."

"When are you due?"

"Onytime now. What are we to do, Rab?"

"Plenty, Jean. Dinna worry: I'll get John MacKenzie to attend you—you'll no' lack skill, so dinna worry on that account."

"I'm past worrying about mysel', Rab: it's you I aey seem to get into trouble. And I'm at my wits' end for I canna go back hame—and I canna bide here."

"Mrs. Muir'll be back in ony minute—d'you think you could walk oot to the stable wi' me?"

"Aye . . . . I'm no' that bad."

She rose up and he was almost frightened at her bulk. And when she was on her feet she smiled to him. It was a wan worn smile; but it was Jean Armour's smile, a smile that came back across so many happy memories.

"This is the least o' my worries, Rab."

"God, Jean, there's never been a lass like you. Come on: give me your arm and I'll help you out."

They went slowly round the house between the Fail burn and the wall and round behind the millhouse to the stable. He drew the bolt on the door and spread a bundle of hay on the dry moss-litter.

"Sit doon, Jean lass, and ease the weight you're carrying. Gie me a kiss, lass, for you've had a hell o' a time."

He kissed her tenderly yet she could feel his old passion stirring in the kiss.

The tears swam in her large dark eyes.

"I'm so glad you're back, Rab. If you only kent what it means to me. I'm surely no' to blame a'thegither for getting like this every time?"

"No: I'm mair to blame nor you, lass."

He put his arm round her to support her back.

"I'm sorry I'm like this, Rab—but I'll soon be better again."

"You still feel the same way?"

"I'll aey feel the same way about you, Rab, whatever happens. I juist canna help it. What about you?"

"Me? Juist the same. If it wasna for your condition I'd lay you doon on that horse litter and give you sic a thundering scalade as would electrify the marrow o' your bones."

"Aye . . . and I'd let you—even now, if I dared risk it."

"I know you would, Jean. But what wi' you the size you are and me wi' my broken knee, we'll juist need to tak' the thocht for the deed. . . .

" . . . now I dinna want you to worry, Jean. I'm going

down to Dumfries wi' John Tennant of Glenconner to view that farm. I havena meikle hope o' that coming off. But when I get back to Edinburgh I'll get my Excise instructions. . . I've nae idea where I'll be posted. You've got to go where you're ordered—but as soon as I get settled down I'll send for you and the bairn. Meantime, this is no' a handy place for Doctor MacKenzie. I'll see if I can get a room for you in Machlin. . . And I'm for seeing Daddy Auld. There's to be nae mair cutty stools for you and me. 'Coorse, I'll need to lie low for a bit: I canna juist rush things like a bull at the gate. But you're no' going back to the Cowgate and we're getting a place o' our ain. If we'd been able to get a place o' our ain at the beginning, this wad never hae happened——"

"No: it wad never hae happened, Rab."

"Well, what d'you think o' my plans?"

Jean wept silently; but then she spoke bravely through her tears.

"Oh Rab, Rab: this is something I dinna deserve. But just to hae a place o' my ain and a wee bit privacy so that when we shut the door we ken we hae the place to oorsel's. If we could only get that, Rab, it would be mair than worth a' we've cam' through."

"Aye, and fine I ken what it is to lack a place o' my ain. I'm twenty-nine now, Jean, and I've never kent what it was to stand independent on my ain hearthstane. I'm going in to Machlin to see about a place. I've nae desire to bide at Mossgiel after a' that's happened. . ."

And so he consoled Jean, delighted the Muirs, and rode home to Mossgiel by the old familiar road that took him past the Lochlea road end. But he had little time to occupy his mind with memories of his trudgings to and from Tarbolton.

He was worried. He had not anticipated that Jean would have had just such a devastating effect on him. But there was no escape—and he didn't know that he wanted an escape. Jean and he had been through a lot together. There was no doubting now that he loved her—and he was not sure that there had ever been any real deep-down doubt. . .

In any case, Jean and he understood each other. He could be natural with Jean in a way he could be with no other woman. And damnit, Jean was Ayrshire and had the rich Ayrshire tongue and the couthy homely Ayrshire manners. What a relief she was after the artificiality of Edinburgh. Thank God he would soon be finished with Edinburgh and for ever. . .

CLARINDA SHOWS HER CARDS

A cold enough reception awaited him at Mossgiel from his mother and sisters—the scandal of Jean Armour hung heavily about the house.

Gilbert and he retired to the stable. The Bard sat on the corn kist in order to ease his knee which was painful from his riding.

"What are you for doing about Jean Armour?"

"Taking her under my wing."

"Where?"

"In Machlin."

"In Machlin?"

"What's wrong wi' Machlin?"

"Are you mad?"

"Possibly."

"How d'you mean, take her under your wing?"

"Provide her wi' a house."

Gilbert's torn expression was lugubrious in the extreme.

"It's quite simple, Gibby. I'll take a room in Machlin so that Doctor MacKenzie can attend her. And so that I'll have a home o' my own for once in my life. I notice how welcome I am here."

"Oh, you're welcome enough. It's the shame that's worrying everybody. Holy Willie and Lamie and the others are making a stink that won't die down for a hunner years. I'm damned if I ken how you can go about the countryside wi' your head up, far less brazen things out by taking Jean to

Machlin. If you're for bairning her ever year, it would be better to marry her."

"I am married to her."

"Since when?"

"I married her once; and as far as I am concerned that's often enough to marry any one woman."

"Listen, Robin, I've nae patience to listen to ony damned sophistry. All I can say is that if you're determined to make a bigger laughing stock o' us than you have already done, then you've damned little to do."

"Aye—a'richt, Gibby. You've gotten a different outlook from me—so we'll no' argue. I'm taking a room for Jean in Machlin if I can get one. Then Monday or Tuesday I'm going down to Ellisland with Auld Glen. Then I'm going back to Edinburgh to get my Excise instructions. In six weeks' time I'll either be a working gauger or a working farmer—though I fully expect it'll be the Excise. If I get posted to the north o' Scotland I'll tak' Jean Armour with me and then you'll be able to lift your heads and walk about the parish freely. How much money do you need and how much did you get from John Ballantine?"

They discussed finances for some time and Gilbert finally agreed to all that Robin could see his way to loan him.

Once money matters had been settled between them, and Gilbert was touched to see how generous his brother proposed to be, his immediate burdens fell from him.

"Oh, by the way, Robin, here's a letter that came for you: I clean forgot all about it."

Handing Robin the letter, Gilbert walked out of the stable.

The Bard's hand shook as he broke the seal: it was Clarinda's handwriting. It was a long rambling letter. Clarinda was obviously much depressed—and both Craig and Kemp were still on his trail. It was more than obvious that Clarinda would cause trouble if she got the slightest clue as to what his real intentions were about Jean.

One line stuck in his gizzard: "My dear, I write you this to Machlin, to be waiting you. I hope, nay I am sure, 'twill be welcome."

Very welcome, my dear Clarinda. Girning your face off, are you, because you're not getting a long love-letter every day . . .?

He rode into Machlin, called in at Ronald's in the Back-causeway and, taking a table in the corner of the room, wrote to Clarinda. He was determined to throw her off the scent so that she would never have the slightest suspicions of his intentions with regard to Jean:

I have just now, My ever dearest Madam, delivered your kind present to my sweet, little Bobby; who I find a very fine fellow. Your letter was waiting me. Your interview with Mr. Kemp opens a wound, ill-closed, in my breast; not that I think his friendship of so much consequence to you, but because you set such a value on it. Now for a little news that will please you. I, this morning, as I came home, called for a certain woman. I am disgusted with her; I cannot endure her! I, while my heart smote me for the profanity, tried to compare her with my Clarinda: 'twas setting the expiring glimmer of a farthing taper beside the cloudless glory of the meridian sun. Here was tasteless insipidity, vulgarity of soul, and mercenary fawning; there, polished good sense, heaven-born genius, and the most generous, the most delicate, the most tender Passion. I have done with her, and she with me.

I set off to-morrow for Dumfriesshire. 'Tis merely out of Compliment to Mr. Miller, for I know the Excise must be my lot. I will write you from Dumfries, if these horrid postages don't frighten me.

> ' Whatever place, whatever land I see,
> My heart, untravelled, fondly turns to thee:
> Still to "Clarinda" turns with ceaseless pain;
> And drags, at each remove, a lengthened chain! '

I just stay to write a few lines before I go to call on my friend, Mr. Gavin Hamilton. I hate myself as an unworthy sinner, because these interviews of old, dear friends make me for half a moment almost forget Clarinda.

Remember to-morrow evening at eight o'clock: I shall be with the Father of mercies, at that hour, on your account. Farewell! if the post goes not to-night, I'll finish the other page to-morrow morning.

That would take care of Clarinda till he got back to Edinburgh.

PROVISION FOR JEAN

As he folded the letter he looked up and found Baldy Muckle from the Backcauseway coming in with a pint stoup in his hand.

"Hullo, Baldy, hullo! And how are you?"

"Oh, it's you, Rab. You're a stranger—and a bluidy famous one. Are ye back to settle doon . . .?"

After a pleasant crack the Bard came to business.

"I was wonderin', Baldy. . . D'ye ken where I could get a room or a couple o' rooms in the village?"

"For yoursel'?"

"Weel . . . yes. You ken how things are wi' Jean Armour?"

"Fine, Rab: the hale bluidy kintraside kens."

"Aye . . . weel, I'm looking for a place for her . . . and me. I want it kept as quiet as possible."

"Just so . . . you want a place whaur she can hae her bairn noo that James Armour has put her oot o' the hoose? I understand fine, Rab: it does you credit."

"D'you ken o' a place?"

"Weel, no, I dinna—but I'll gie you a room in my hoose."

"I'll pay you rent, Baldy."

"Ach, we'll no' talk about that the noo. Ye ken my place —up the stair abune John MacKenzie's surgery. . ."

"The very thing, Baldy. Can I come across after and see it?"

"I canna gie ye a bed, Rab—or dishes or onything. . ."

"You give me the room and I'll damn well provide the furnishings. Here's the very man."

Matthew Morison, the cabinet-maker, came in, and the Bard hailed him over.

". . . noo to a wee bit business, Mattha. Can you put me onto a decent-like bed?" He explained the position.

"As a matter o' fact, Rab, I've just finished the verra thing for you. The party I made it for's in nae hurry, so I can make anither. But . . . it's mahogany—a fine bed."

"Good, Mattha. I want nothing but the best. That's one thing I've aey promised myself—a good bed. Damnit, a body spends half his life in bed."

"Aye . . . you're born in bed and ye die there—if you're fortunate. So you're for settling in the Backcauseway, Rab?"

"No . . . but I'll settle Jean there, the noo. God knows where I'll settle ultimately—my plans are as yet uncertain. . ."

Now that he had settled the question of Jean's immediate problem he felt mightily relieved. He had still many friends in Machlin to visit. Now he would visit them with confidence and assurance. There were John MacKenzie, Gavin Hamilton, Jock Richmond and Jeannie Smith to call on. . .

Jeannie Smith was the most elated by the news.

"I micht as well be frank wi' you, Rab. If you hadna done richt wi' Jean I was finished wi' you. Noo I'm telling you. I ken Jean—or her folks, rather—didna do fair wi' you. Still Jean's suffered sair for you, Rab. And you couldna get a better wife gin you searched Scotland through. And I'm awfa glad, Rab, things are turning oot this way. I was feared you would get nabbed by ane o' thae Edinburry dames. . . But you've done the richt thing and there'll be a blessing on you for it. I'll dae everything I can for her. . . But I think you should see her mither. Oh aye . . . I think you should. Jean'll want her mither by her side at a time like this. James Armour's awa' frae hame the noo. Swallow your pride, Rab, for Jean's sake. Her mither would never hae put her frae the hoose: it was James Armour—and he was egged on by the Session. . . On you go noo and dinna waste ony mair time."

Mrs. Armour was a broken woman. The fight was gone from her.

"It's a terrible thing, my ain dochter being brocht within sicht o' my ain window very near and me no' allowed to bring her here. Oh God, what a disgrace the pair o' you hae brocht on us. . . Mind ye, Maister Burns, I'll never forgie you for what you've done. But at least I'm thankful for what you're doing now. I canna answer for Mr. Armour—but I'll dae what I can for Jean—bedding and things. I'll dae what I can. Aye, I suppose you'd best get Doctor MacKenzie—he's a guid man. Oh God, I hope and pray you'll be sensible noo and live decently, the pair o' you. I'll never be able to lift my head in Machlin again—and Mr. Armour's a broken man—heart-broken. . . And what does Mr. Auld say . . .?"

"I've no idea. . . But I'll tell you this, Mrs. Armour: if neither you nor your husband can hold up your heads in Machlin—dinna blame me—or Jean. Blame your own rotten stinkin' purse-proud respectability. Dinna think that I'll go about Machlin wi' my head among my feet. When you threw Jean out o' the house you didna care whether or not she found shelter or died in the ditch. Maybe you were glad she landed away out o' Machlin in Tarbolton. But I'm bringing her back and setting her down in the middle o' Machlin—and you and Daddy Auld and Holy Willie and who else likes can try their damndest to stop me."

THE RECANTATION OF FATHER AULD

Daddy Auld held out his thin bony claw.

"Give me that certificate o' your bachelorhood, Mr. Burns."

Auld took the document, rose and lit an end of it in the fire. He waited till it was burned to ashes.

"That's the end o' that, Mr. Burns. It should never have been written. As you say, you married Jean Armour. Though your union wasna blessed by the Kirk, nevertheless it was a marriage of sorts. It's a sair business, Mr. Burns, a sair business. There'll be trouble wi' my Session, of course. That canna be avoided. And ye canna expect me to want it avoided. The pair o' ye hae sinned greatly: ye canna weel be ocht but an abomination in the sight o' the Lord. But apparently it's God's will that the pair o' ye should come together. An inscrutable business, Mr. Burns. Aye. . . I had great hopes o' Jean Armour . . . the flower o' my parish. . . Aye, and you pu'd that flower, Mr. Burns. . . Ah well, maybe you had some queer notion o' doing richt when ye gave Jean the lines . . . The Kirk'll censure the baith o' you. . . Just how and when I havena decided. You're a man that stands high in the estimation o' your country, Mr. Burns. I wish you stood half as high in the estimation o' God's Kirk. But grievously as ye hae sinned, Mr. Burns, I hae nae ill-will to you or Jean Armour—and gin I thocht the pair o' ye had at last set your feet on the path o' righteousness I wad give you my blessing and the blessing o' the Kirk maist willingly. In the meantime I can only hope that baith o' ye will be unremitting in your prayers to God that ye may be brocht to a state o' Grace and full repentance. . ."

THE MAHOGANY BED

Holy Willie was almost beside himself. It had been fun hunting Burns when he was but an idle rhymer and a common blackguard in Mossgiel. But now he was the celebrated Robert Burns, the Scottish Bard. Willie Fisher wheezed and almost yelped with excitement. He took his stance in Nance Tinnock's so that he could look across the gap of the Backcauseway into Baldy Muckle's door and up at his windows. Here he was presently joined by Saunders Tait from Tarbolton. Willie and Saunders were well acquainted: both hated New Light heretics and both hated the very sight or sound of Robert Burns.

They got together round their pint stoups.

"Aye, aye, noo, Saunders—what's the latest frae Tarbolton? What's the word o' Jean Armour?"

"By God, Willie, the first thing he did when he cam' round by Adamhill—frae Kilmarnock as I heard after—the first thing he did was to call for her at Willie's Mill. And by God, he was no' lang in wi' her when oot he comes wi' her on his arm—and her like a coo in calf—and takes her into the stable and bars the door. . . I was cooried down on the banks o' the Fail . . . and I heard the bolt rattlin' hame. I couldna hear what they were saying—but maybe they werena saying ocht. But I ken what they were doing, Willie, by God, and so dae you." Saunders bared his rotten green-brown stumps of teeth and tee-heed like a goat.

Holy Willie bobbed up and down on his stool. "Ooooh aye, Saunders: I hae an idea! An' were they in a while?"

Saunders clawed in his yellow-white beard: "Aye, he'd be wi' her a guid half-hour, the fornicating son o' Auld Symie. I noticed he was limping a bit. . ."

"Ooooh aye: seems he dislocated his knee in Edinburry."

"Bad cess till him: it's a pity he didna dislocate his ram-tam. . . Aye, but what's this I hear about him bringing his clockin' hen till Machlin?"

"Across the way there—Baldy Muckle's front room. Aye, I hear he's bringing her in the day—wi' a cairt. Ooooh aye . . . he's gotten fully bold sin' he went to Edinburry."

"An' what are you doin' aboot a' this i' the Session, Willie?"

"Ooooh we'll be doing plenty: hae nae fear o' that. But danged, Saunders, that's the bit I canna understand aboot Mr. Auld—danged he has a saft side till the pair o' them. Ooooh but the Session canna look ower this affront. The Session garred James Armour put her frae his hoose: the Session'll no' stand for seeing her brocht back under their verra noses and set up in open sin. Na, na. . ."

There was a rattle of a barrow on the Backcauseway cobbles. Tait and Fisher nearly collided making for the window. Holy Willie yelped in unintelligible excitement and teethered on his toes.

"A bed, be-danged, a bed!" he squealed in excitement.

"A byornar bed!" hoarsed Tait, slavering into his dirty beard.

"A mahogany bed!" yelped Fisher, "a mahogany bed—be-danged! To the door, Saunders, to the door, till we get a richt keek at it!"

Even Nance Tinnock, much as she hated Holy Willie, was infected with the excitement. But then the whole of Machlin couldn't go about its business for excitement. The news buzzed into every doorway and down every chimney: "A mahogany bed! A mahogany bed! Rab Burns has bocht Jean Armour a mahogany bed!"

"By God!" roared Saunders, doing a kind of hornpipe on his heels—and in a voice that everybody gathered around could hear—"By God, he means her to lie-in in state—damned, that's a bed would hae done for the Queen o' Sheba. By God, that's a bed'll tak' twenty yairds o' bed hangings. . . He didna buy that bed a penny under forty shillings. . . Damned, that's a bed the Roman Billie could rowe about in wi' the Scarlet Whore for a month and never weary. . ."

But the progress of the bed from Matthew Morison's workshop through the Machlin streets had been followed by everybody with intense interest. It was not only that it was a mahogany bed or that it was the bed being provided for Jean Armour at the expense of Robert Burns. All this was interesting enough. What was much more interesting was the fact that Burns was setting up Jean Armour in Machlin after she had been put from her own home and after all the fuss and bother and scandal there had been about their last lapse from grace. This was the boldest moral act that had ever been done in Machlin. Certainly Robert Burns didn't do ordinary things in the ordinary way.

Lizzie Paton's Bess was at Mossgiel. There, too, was Jean Armour's Robert—extraordinary and inexplicable conduct! Never before in long records of tradition had a man assumed —and apparently been glad to assume—the responsibility for his illegitimate children. And now to set up an illegitimate

' wife' in the heart of Machlin and with only the graveyard separating her from her parents' roof-tree. . .

Machlin couldn't grasp the boldness of this stroke: its effect was stunning. . . But the folks sorted themselves out in opposing camps—and then the rival camps again divided.

There were those for the Bard and those against. There were those for Jean Armour and those against. But those against Jean Armour were not necessarily for the Bard and those for the Bard were not necessarily for Jean Armour. To complicate matters some were in favour of both and others against both.

But few could make up their minds on the true significance of the mahogany bed.

The excitement was spreading beyond Machlin. Saunders Tait was drunk with excitement. Centred in Tarbolton he had been the bard of several parishes before Burns had appeared in Lochlea. Now he had material for a poem that would re-establish his position; and when, in the afternoon, Robert Burns drove into Machlin from Willie's Mill with Jean Armour at his side, Saunders was not the only man who nearly went mad.

The mahogany bed had been no idle gesture—he was setting Jean Armour up in the Backcauseway! This was no tit-bit of scandal—this was the entire carcase. Machlin was to worry over that carcase for many a year and chew over the bones for many a decade.

ON THE BANKS OF THE NITH

Auld Glen paced over the ground that sloped sharply to the banks of the river Nith. Here and there he would take up a handful of soil and work it through his fingers.

The Bard walked behind him doing his utmost to concentrate on the agricultural aspects of Ellisland. It was a bright day for the last day of February. Certainly he could not have chosen a better time to make up his mind about it. After the long dead winter everything was at its lowest. If Auld Glen could assure him that these dead barren-looking acres constituted good arable and grazing ground, then nobody could claim that he had been misled. It was essential that he should face the bargain in its least tempting prospect.

For himself he was doubtful. The ground seemed to him to be in very poor heart. But otherwise the site on the Nith's banks was tempting enough even though there wasn't a vestige of green on the trees by the river's banks. But a fine rolling piece of Galloway countryside it was, and with a long broad stretch of the river constituting one of the marches— Dalswinton lay on the northerly bank—he was certain that it would be a grand place in the summer.

At last Auld Glen gave his verdict.

"Aye . . . a guid place, Rab. You could do weel here. The whole place needs liming—and plenty o' manure. And you could do wi' a bit draining. Is your laird for helping you to enclose? You'd be the better o' a length or twa o' dyking. But the place lies i' the sun: it's sheltered. You'll hae a guid depth o' soil for the river banks are saft. And you're for biggin a new steadin'? In about here somewhaur? You'll catch the road fine and handy——"

"You think it's a guid proposition then, Glen?"

"I do, Rab, I do. Damn the doubt: it could be made intil a grand place. You should begin to reap the benefit by your second back-end. What rent is this Mr. Miller asking?"

"Seventy pounds a year after the first three years. Fifty pounds a year for the first three years."

"You should manage that, Rab. And what about your biggins?"

"We havena decided on that yet—but the figure of two hundred was mentioned."

"Haud oot for three, Rab. You need to make a richt job o' the place to start wi'. Everything'll need to be carted here —and that costs money. You're what—six miles frae Dumfries? Aye, stick out for three hundred, Rab."

"And you think there's nae fear o' me making my way here?"

"I don't, Rab. Mind you: it'll be hard work for a year or twa. But nothing like Lochlea or Mossgiel—and a Garden o' Eden compared wi' Mount Oliphant. I wad tak' it gin I were you. You've enough money to stock the place?"

"I should have."

"Aye, weel . . . and you're taking Jean Armour doon wi' you?"

"Definitely."

"That's the plan, Rab. You couldna do better. You'll settle doon and bring up your family and live a peaceful, God-fearing life. Och aye, a guid chance, Rab—you'll go a lang road afore you get a better."

It seemed that the die was cast: that he would turn farmer and settle down on the banks of the Nith. And yet on that February day he was filled with gloomy premonitions. He had still to make his final settlement with Creech—and he had yet to undergo his Excise training. He had still to secure his commission. There was Jean still to come through her trouble. His family were up in arms at his taking Jean to the Backcauseway; his enemies were active in Machlin. Clarinda was writing suspicious letters. Unless he could throw her off the scent she would make trouble. If by any chance she was pregnant—and got the slightest wind of what he had done about Jean—she would unleash all the hell-rankling furies in her ample bosom. She might sue him. She might get her hands on Creech's money. She might, through Miss Nimmo, ruin his chances with the Excise. Bob Ainslie seemed to be missing no opportunity of her company. It was a hell's broth of a business and Nancy Craig wasn't a simple Peggy Cameron, not by a thousand miles.

He would see Jean through her ordeal and then get back to Edinburgh and force the pace what he could with Creech and the Excise. By then Daddy Auld would damn-well have to accept the fact that Jean and he were man and wife by habit and repute.

As soon as he got back to Machlin he would write Ainslie and put him off the scent about Jean so that if Clarinda quizzed him he would not be in a position to give him away.

Aye, divine Clarinda didn't trust him out of her sight. That was a devilish cunning trap she had set, asking him if he knew a Miss Nelly Hamilton in Ayr! She wished much to write to her, did she? So that Miss Hamilton could give her all the Ayrshire news—especially about Jean. Well, he hadn't sprung that trap. But he would spring one on Ainslie as soon as he got back to Machlin—and Ainslie, unwittingly if he liked, could spring it on Clarinda.

He was playing high stakes and he was playing them hard and ruthlessly. He now knew that he was playing against the most clever, the most ruthless woman he had ever encountered. Clarinda wanted to tie him to her for life. To this end she would fight with every weapon she possessed. He could do no other than fight with his weapons.

So on the morning of March the third, Monday, he left Jean in the care of her mother and some neighbour wives (she had been in sore labour all the previous night) and went across to Ronald's Ballroom and wrote to Ainslie. He would have gone into Nancy Tinnock's, but he learned that Holy Willie and Saunders Tait were ensconced there.

My dear Friend,

I am just returned from Mr. Miller's Farm. My old friend whom I took with me was highly pleased with the bargain, and advised me to accept of it. He is the most intelligent, sensible farmer in the county, and his advice has staggered me a good deal. I have two plans before me: I shall endeavour to balance them to the best of my judgment, and fix on the most eligible. On the whole, if I find Mr. Miller in the same favourable disposition as when I saw him last, I shall in all probability turn farmer.

I have been through sore tribulation, and under much buffeting of the Wicked One, since I came to this county. Jean I found banished like a martyr—forlorn, destitute and friendless; all for the good old cause: I have reconciled her to her fate: I have reconciled her to her mother: I have taken her a room: I have taken her to my arms: I have given her a mahogany bed: I have given her a guinea; and I have ****** her till she rejoiced with joy unspeakable and full of glory. But—as I always am on every occasion—I have been prudent and cautious to an astounding degree; I swore her, privately and solemnly, never to attempt any claim on me as a husband, even though anybody should persuade her she has such a claim, which she has not, neither during my life nor after my death. She did all this like a good girl, and I took the opportunity of some dry horse litter, and gave her such a thundering scalade that electrified the very marrow of her bones. O, what a peacemaker is a guid weel-willy ******. It is the mediator, the guarantee, the umpire, the bond of union, the solemn league and covenant, the plenipotentiary, the Aaron's rod, the Jacob's staff, the prophet Elisha's pot of oil, the Ahasuerus' sceptre, the sword of mercy, the philosopher's stone, the horn of plenty, and Tree of life between Man and Woman.

I shall be in Edinburgh the middle of next week. My farming ideas I shall keep quiet till I see. I got a letter from Clarinda yesterday, and she tells me she has got no letter of mine but one. Tell her that I wrote to her from Glasgow, from Kilmarnock, from Machlin, and yesterday from Cumnock, as I returned from Dumfries. Indeed, she is the only person in Edinburgh I have written to till this day. How are your soul and body putting up?—a little like man and wife, I suppose.

Your faithful Friend. . .

That would send Ainslie hopping mad—if he knew him. Hopping mad; and if he went hopping round to Clarinda, he could tell her what it contained—in his own language. Or he could show it to her. And that would send *her* hopping mad to renew her acquaintance with the Peacemaker. And by all that was holy, he would let her know what the Tree of Life meant when he got back to Edinburgh!

Then he took a good drink and sat brooding by the fire. Life was one long struggle to keep out of the jaws of death and away from the gates of hell.

But it was Jean Armour who was in the jaws of death.

She was labouring, though she didn't know it, with twins—and it was a dry labour.

The brow of the first twin, struggling into the world, was pressing on the pelvic bone; and all Jean's down-bearing pains could do nothing to release it.

Mrs. Markland twisted a towel round the post of the mahogany bed and gave the ends to Jean to clutch: she knotted a napkin and gave it to Jean to bite into in her agony. . .

. . . Mrs. Markland came out to look for the Bard.

"Get Doctor MacKenzie, Rab: we're beaten. On you go now. Tell him to come at once. Is she bad? God, Rab, if you knew what she's coming through you'd go and lib yoursel' wi' a kail-gully. Dinna halt in your step till you get John MacKenzie. . ."

It was some hours after that John MacKenzie sat in the Sun Inn and drank a glass of toddy with the Bard.

"I never hope to face the like o' that again, Robert. Oh, Jean'll pull through a' richt—but I doubt for the bairns. I had nae choice, Robert. I had to use brute force. The infants —twa bonnie girls, if they live—got sair abuse. But at least I've saved the mother and my conscience is clear."

"I'm glad o' that, John. Oh God, if onything had happened to Jean, I'd have lost what little reason I've left—and that's bluidy little, John. Bluidy little."

"Dinna worry too much, Rab. Give her another hour and then slip down and see her. She's lost a hell o' a bluid. . . But she's got the constitution o' a Galloway mare. She'll be a' richt in a day or two. But mind: she had a sair time—as sair a birth as I've ever kenned. Thank God for that mahogany bed. Two-three times I thocht Jean and me were down through it—ony other bed and we would hae been."

The Bard's mind was dumb. There was nothing he could say for the good reason that there was nothing could be said. . .

Mrs. Armour met him at the bottom of Baldy Muckle's wooden stair. She was distraught.

"No: ye canna see her. And maybe ye'll never see her

again in this world—and you'll never see her in the next, ye black-hearted damn dirty low lecherous vermin ye! On ye go back to your tinklers' midden at Mossgiel and write mair o' your dirty tinklers' poetry. . . My everlasting curse on ye, Burns, ye rotten dirty brock! Gin Mr. Armour was in Machlin the noo he could dae waur nor kick the rotten tinkler's guts oot o' ye."

Mrs. Markland came to the rescue. "Never mind puir Mrs. Armour, Rab. Jean's a' richt—but come back the morn."

The Bard turned away, his mind a dull aching blank. He hadn't heard what Mrs. Armour had said to him. He only saw her distraught grief-contorted face.

NO QUESTION OF BAPTISM

Holy Willie looked slyly at Mr. Auld: a foxy, side-long glance.

"Aye: twins. Lassies. A sair birth, I understand. A sair birth. Ooooh aye, the wicked are aey punished for their sins. . . . Ooooh aye: they had to send for Doctor MacKenzie— dragged them oot by main force, I understand—a kin' o' butcher's job; but Mr. Auld kens what Doctor MacKenzie is. . . . Of course there'll be nae question o' baptising the bastards, Mr. Auld—there'll be nae question o' that."

"Leave me to intercede on their behalf with the Almighty, Mr. Fisher. And remember, sir, that ye are no' oot o' this warld—yet."

When Fisher had gone, Father William Auld stood for a long time with his back to the fire. Jean Armour, the flower of his parish, that but yesterday he had baptised, that only this morning, it seemed, had been running to school a bare-footed lassock with all the innocence of the Holy Lamb of God stamped on her fair brow. . .

Father William Auld reckoned that he must be getting very old in the service of the Lord. Any day now the Lord might choose to call him to his long rest. He would lay down his burden gladly when He called. But he would lie happier in the Machlin graveyard if, before he was called, he could bring Robert Burns and Jean Armour to a full and contrite repentance.

Aye . . . the flesh was weak, terribly weak. The hot sweet flesh of youth was weakest of all—but then youth didna ken that till it was ower late.

Aye . . . and as Fisher had said, there could be no baptism of Jean Armour's second twins—yet. Not until things had been straightened out. . .

They would take a bit of straightening out. It was not likely that Robert Burns would give the Session any trouble. And yet. . . Well, it had been an audacious thing too, and an act that called for great courage, to set Jean Armour up in Muckle's house before the case had been dealt with by the Session. He could only hope that Burns had done it for the best, that it wasn't the act of ungovernable headstrong defiance.

At least he hoped not. His fighting days were done. But if by any chance Robert Burns, thinking he was a done man, sought to defy the Kirk, then he must be sharply made aware that the Kirk of Scotland was still the Kirk of Scotland in Machlin—whatever it might be in Edinburgh.

But there must be a way out of this sair business without creating too much hardship. . .

TAIT'S MASTERPIECE

Saunders Tait scribbled away in a high furious glee. He had never been so inspired to write; and, for Saunders, he was writing extremely well.

As soon as this effort was finished he would circulate it far and near and revel in Burns's discomfort.

And when the effort was finished he was well pleased with his handiwork. He read it aloud to himself with great gusto and elaborate gesture. He even announced the title to his imaginary audience: "Burns's Hen Clockin in Machlin"— that would arouse immediate interest.

> Ye whunstane hearted Machlin wretches!
> Wha wallop aey in deep debauches,
> Wi' me ye hae got merry catches,
>   'Tis truth I'm saying,
> I have a chicken in my hatches,
>   To me she's layin'.
>
> I catch'd her in a green kail yard,
> I neither neb nor feathers spared,
> But a' my strength on her I wared,
>   To mak' her clock,
> Now she's fa'en till't, he this out raired,
>   Come help, guid fouk!
>
> The wives they up their coats did kilt,
> And through the streets so clean did stilt,
> Some at the door fell wi' a pelt,
>   Maist broke their leg,
> To see the Hen, poor wanton jilt!
>   Lay her fourth egg.
>
> The wives they sat them down to rest,
> And viewed poor Chuckie in her nest,
> To see how Robin had her drest,
>   For sic a breeze,
> She's now a ship amang the rest,
>   On foamin' seas.
>
> The wives they let the anchors fall,
> And at the cables they did haul,
> And mounted up the sails so tall,
>   Then gave a swear,
> The anchor grip, it held so baul,
>   She wadna steer.

Then Robin he fell on his knees
And prayed to Clootie for a breeze,
That to his mind would give great ease,
    And settle strife,
That she might skip the roarin' seas,
    And save her life.

But Robin's prayers had na strength,
MacKenzie then he cam' at length,
And pulled the ship out by main strength,
    With skill o' notion,
And then she trimly swims at length
    Upon the ocean.

Now she is sailing in the Downs,
Calls at the ports of finest towns,
To buy bed hangings, and galleons,
    Away she goes;
So trimly, as she sails the rounds,
    'Mang the Chinose.

She's got some packs o' human leather,
Wi' lugs wi' een, wi' tongue to blether,
And a fine cap and peacock feather,
    And wi't she's douce,
With a grand besom, made o' heather,
    To sweep her house.

Now she returns so tight and clever,
As fast as woodcock, snipe or pliver,
MacKenzie he does her deliver
    In Machlin town;
I'm sure twa came out through the river,
    A double round.

MacKenzie gets a double dram,
Wi' a good slice o' bacon ham;

The wives sit down, drink aff ram-tam,
    The soldier's joy!
Burns is the clever vale de cham,
    Wi' his hautboy.

The Holy Fair they sit and read,
And wi' twa pipes blaw anet-seed,
And cracks o' mony a maidenhead,
    O' Tam and Sue;
Then off they come, as clean's a bead,
    Adieu, adieu!

GAVIN HAMILTON'S CLAY FEET

The Bard had no easy time of it during his Machlin interlude.
He knew he was, in himself, a subject of much gossip, some
admiration and a lot of envy. But his immediate relationship
had brought him a notoriety he did not welcome. He had
made his gesture to Machlin—but he did not look forward to
the gesture being permanent.

If he did turn farmer, then it would be best to turn farmer
on the banks of the Nith. Best to be away from Machlin and
creatures like Holy Willie and Saunders Tait. And best of all
to be away from the Armours—aye, and the long-suffering
shamed martyred faces at Mossgiel.

For the folks in Mossgiel (always with the exception of his
hero-worshipping younger brother, Willie) had taken his
affair with Jean very badly. It was not that they said much.
It was how they looked that hurt him and made him realise
how much they deprecated his conduct.

Not that he cared much what they thought. But the
Mossgiel atmosphere made domestic intercourse very difficult.

No: things weren't at all easy. Here was Gavin Hamilton
asking him to stand security for Gilbert for another seven
years' lease. He hadn't expected that from Gavin.

He spoke to John Richmond about it.

"Well, Robin, I always told you that Gavin Hamilton thinks of himself first and onybody else a long way after. I ken fine Hamilton has his good points; but I worked wi' him too long no' to ken his bad ones. A grasping, mean character, Hamilton, at bottom. Now that he thinks you've got money he wants you tied up—in his favour. Speaking for mysel', Robin, I'd see him in hell first—but please yourself."

"It's no' only mysel', Jock: I've Jean and the bairns to think about now. Much as I hate to quarrel wi' Hamilton, I'll need to refuse. And I can see quite well that when I do, the friendship will finish. But it's damnable that a few pounds can ruin a friendship."

"When money enters by the door, Robin, friendship flies out the window. How are the twins doing? Jenny Surgeoner was telling me she didn't like the look o' them."

The Bard's eyes clouded.

"I've little hope o' the poor mites, Jock. Little hope. They might have been twa bonnie lassies. But it was a hell o' a birth—bluidy diabolical."

"Aye: so I heard. But Jean's coming on fine?"

"You couldna kill Jean. Physically, of course, she's what she's always been—perfect. But she's got courage too, Jock— great courage. Between oursel's, Jock, I'm glad I didna get tied up wi' ony o' yon Edinburgh dames."

"If that's how you feel about it, Robin, then you've done the right thing. Mind you, it's no' usual—but a' the lassies were on Jean's side. I mean they were more on Jean's side than they were on yours. And you ken yoursel' that's no' usual. . . But I'm real sorry, Robin, to hear about the twins."

TO ROBERT MUIR, DYING

The Bard's sorrow was deeper than he cared to express. But though his sorrow was deep it did not render him inactive. Rather he renewed, with something akin to desperation, his applications for his future security.

He wrote to Patrick Miller and committed himself to a written offer for the farm of Ellisland and he kept in touch with the 'rotations' concerning the Excise.

And he kept in touch with his friends. Coming in by Kilmarnock he had found Robert Muir far gone in consumption. This grieved him for Robert Muir was one of his best friends—certainly his dearest friend in Kilmarnock. He had promised to spend some time with him but circumstances had prevented this. But despite his own load of troubles he did not forget Robert Muir. To him he wrote—and to him he wrote his honest mind. There had never been anything but the deep honesty of friendship in their relationship.

I have partly changed my ideas, my dear Friend, since I saw you. I took old Glenconner with me to Mr. Miller's farm, and he was so pleased with it, that I have wrote an offer to Mr. Miller, which, if he accepts, I shall sit down a plain farmer, the happiest of lives when a Man can live by it. In this case I shall not stay in Edinburgh above a week. I set out on Monday, and would have come by Kilmarnock, but there are several small sums owing me for my second Edition, about Galston and Newmilns; and I shall set off so early as to dispatch my business and reach Glasgow by night. When I return, I shall devote a forenoon or two to make some kind of acknowledgment for all the kindness I owe to your friendship. Now that I hope to settle with some credit and comfort at home, there was not any friendship or friendly correspondence that promised me more pleasure than yours—I hope I will not be disappointed. I trust the Spring will renew your shattered frame and make your friends happy. You and I have often agreed that life is no great blessing on the whole.

The close of life indeed, to a reasoning eye, is ' dark as was chaos, ere the infant sun

> Was rolled together, or had tried his beams
> Athwart the gloom profound '—

But an honest man has nothing to fear. If we lie down in the grave, the whole man a piece of broke machinery, to moulder with the clods of the valley—be it so; at least there is an end of pain, care, woes and wants: if that part of us called Mind, does survive the apparent destruction of the man— away with old-wife prejudices and tales! Every age and every nation has had a different set of stories; and as the many are always weak, of consequence they had often, perhaps always been deceived: a man, conscious of having acted an honest part among his fellow-creatures; even granting that he may have been the sport, at times, of passions and instincts; he goes to a great unknown Being who could have no other end in giving him existence but to make him happy; who gave him those passions and instincts, and well knows their force.

These, my worthy friend, are my ideas: and I know they are not far different from yours. It becomes a man of sense to think for himself; particularly in a case where all men are equally interested, and where, indeed, all men are equally in the dark. . .

Adieu, my dear Sir! God send us a cheerful meeting!

CLARINDA'S CLAWS

Yes: he had partly changed his ideas. He had partly changed his ideas about Clarinda. For one thing he was tired of her whining complaining nagging letters.

The sentences stuck like burrs in his mind. " Mr. Ainslie called . . . to tell me he had heard from you. You would see by my last, how anxious I was even then to hear from you. 'Tis the first time I ever had reason to be so: I hope 'twill be the last." "I wished you had written me from Dumfries, as you promised. . . . I hope I shall never live to reproach you with unkindness . . . two lines to have said ' How do ye, Clarinda ' would have saved me days and nights of cruel disquietude." "When you meet young Beauties, think of Clarinda's affection—of her situation—of how much her happiness depends on you."

Aye, these sentences stuck and irritated in their sticking. But there were odd sentences in her letters that puzzled him for the revelation of her character. She had asked him to kiss his son, his ' little lamb ' for her. Just what did she mean by this? "Did you execute my commission? You had a great stock in hand; and, if any agreeable customers come in the way, you would dispose of some of them, I fancy, hoping soon to be supplied with a fresh assortment. For my part, I can truly say I have had no demand. I really believe you have taught me dignity, which, partly through good nature and partly by misfortune, had been too much laid aside; which now I never will part with. Why should I not keep it up?"

He puzzled at odd moments over this paragraph. He had thought he had her measure. Now he was certain that he was not the first man she had known since James MacLehose; and he was equally certain he would not be the last. Even in his absence he was fairly sure that when Kemp wasn't on the scene Bob Ainslie would be trying his hand.

Very well: she was no sweet little dove of chastity. He knew that perfectly well. But her intimate knowledge of the way of a man with maids displayed too accurately that she was a maid who knew the ways of men from first-hand experience. He wouldn't forget that when he got back to Edinburgh —but he would never let her know that he knew. And he would be careful to part with her on good terms—on terms which her Religious Bosom would be assured were the terms of life rent and whatever lay beyond; and he would give her enough physical love-making to do her a lifetime and make any other man she might know in the future an insipid and fiddling amateur. Yes, before he left Edinburgh he would pay back Clarinda in a coin of passion nothing in her physical treasury could pay interest on. But for all that, the interest would be compound; and she would struggle with her emotional debt to him for the rest of her life. . .

WEAL OR WOE

He bade Jean good-bye in their room in the Backcauseway. Jean was sufficiently recovered to be up. But she was deeply worried about the twins.

"I'm feared we're for losing them, Rab. . . I canna tell you how feared I am. But it'll no' be my faut, Rab."

"No, Jean: it'll no' be your faut or onybody's faut. . . I am away back to Edinburgh, Jean. But I'll no' spend a day there more than I can help. I'll no' keep you waiting here. If the worst should happen, the Kirk may refuse to baptise the innocent mites; but they canna refuse them a corner in the Kirkyard. Though I've no doubt they would do that too —if they dared. It's a'richt, Jean lass: I hae my reasons for being bitter. . . Now listen, lass, I ken you'll no' waste ony money—but grudge nothing that's necessary. And keep you your courage, my love—for weal or woe you and me'll ca' through life to the end, come that early or late. We've had our troubles and they're no' a' bye yet. But the future must have some happiness for us. . ."

"I've a' the happiness I want if I hae you, Rab . . . and ye ken that. . . I hope you get this farm doon in Dumfries. I'd like to get away frae Machlin."

"If things go the way I think they will, I'll be back this day se'enight wi' the lease o' Ellisland in my pocket. But I want my Excise commission as well, Jean, so that gin the farm turned a failure on my hands I'd aey hae a brose and butter job to fa' back on. . . Noo dinna worry. . ."

AULD REEKIE AGAIN

The ten March days he spent in Edinburgh were among the most hectic he had ever spent. Twice during this period Creech promised a settlement without fail; and twice he broke his promise. But Patrick Miller was a man of his word. He had drafted out a lease for Ellisland. It was a comprehensive, water-tight agreement of three and a half folio pages, protecting the Laird of Dalswinton from every possible contingency. Rent of £50, for the first three years, was to begin from November. Thereafter the rent was to be £70. But though the lease was not to begin before November, the Bard was to build his dwelling house and steadings before November —and he was to start enclosing. For this Patrick Miller was to advance him £300. The first advance of £150 would be made as soon as he had made a start with the foundations of the buildings.

Patrick Miller watched him keenly as he read the document. When he had finished the reading Miller said:

"Any objections, Burns?"

"No. . . It seems to be a tight enough agreement. . . I must complete the building of the house and barns this summer."

"The house before Martinmas at the latest—else you stand to lose £100 in forfeiture o' the agreement."

"But accidents could happen——"

"That's the purpose o' an agreement, Burns. Accidents may happen—sae I've got to protect myself against a' possible manner o' contingency. Of coorse, Burns, I'll no drive you to the *letter* o' the agreement—I'll see, gin you put your best foot forrit, that its terms are interpreted as liberally as I can afford. Oh aye, I'll no press you ower sair. But juist in case o' ony disagreement atween us, weel, there's the document setting forth the conditions o' the bargain. If you agree, come round the morn at eleven o'clock to John Gordon's office at twenty-two Saint Andrew Square, and we'll sign the document legally in the presence o' witnesses. Aince the legal flummery's ower you can start to mak' your plans. Thomas Boyd i' Dumfries wad be your man to see aboot the biggin o' the buildings. I'll want to see the plan, of coorse. . . Well, I think ye hae made a guid move, Burns; and I dinna think ye'll ever hae cause to rue it. Aye, aye—and you're for takin' a country lass for a wife down wi' ye. That's the plan, Burns. A guid healthy country lass that kens how to milk and mak' butter and bake. . . I'm glad to see that I was richt about you frae the start, Burns. Man, Edinburgh's no' the place for you at a'. But mind: you'll need to stick in at Ellisland and make a job o' it."

"I'll have no alternative, Mr. Miller—even though I wanted one. Once I get my house built and my wife settled in and my harvest home. . ."

"There'll maybe no' be much o' a harvest, Burns—but next year wi' proper manuring. . . Ye canna draw stuff oot o' the ground barring you put plenty back into the ground. . ."

THE SECRET CHAMBER

The Bard turned out of Nicolson's Square and made for General's Entry in the Potterrow. Clarinda was desperate to receive him.

But at first the Bard was rather depressed.

"To-morrow morning when I sign that tack, I'll be committed to farm Ellisland. Between you and me, Nancy, I have my doubts and fears—he's a bluidy tight-fisted man, Patrick Miller Esquire."

"I ken nothing o' business matters, Robert—but I'm glad you've got settled for your future. If it wasna so far away."

"Two days' riding, Nancy—nothing to it. No, but it'll be hard work for a couple o' years and my jaunts to Edinburgh will be few and far between, I'm afraid."

"You're depressed, Robert. I hae some o' yon excellent wine left. I'll pour you a glass."

"And one for yoursel', Nancy. Fill up the rosy wine and let's try and banish this bluidy gut-worrying gloom."

"And when are you leaving?"

"I've still to settle wi' that low bastard Creech."

"Language, my dear! Even though you've turned farmer you mauna forget you're a poet."

"Poet! Who the hell cares whether I'm a poet——"

"I care, Robert."

"Aye, you care, Nancy. But you canna lease me a farm or give me a commission in the Excise."

"But surely you'll drop the Excise now?"

"Nae fear. Drop the Excise! This is entirely between oursel's——"

"Everything's between oursel's, my love."

"Fill up the glass—thou first o' womankind, for I could drink the wine like water the nicht."

"Dinna let's drink too much to-night, beloved. I'm weak-willed enough without wine to undermine my resistance. . . But you were for saying something about the Excise——"

"Forget about the Excise, Nancy. You mind yon first night we drank wine thegither?"

"Could I ever forget, Robert? But—about your farm. Will you no' want a wife to help you?"

"How many kye can you milk?"

"And if I said I could milk kye?"

"I would say you were the sweetest-lipped liar that ever drew the breath o' life."

"So you want a wife on your farm who can milk? Canna your Jean milk? But forgive me, my love: I promised I would never mention her name again and since you are finished with her and she with you——"

"Precisely, Nancy, precisely. . . Drink up the rosy wine and let us live for the present moment for you ken as well as me that only too soon will the present lapse into the past. Nancy—I've loved you from the first moment I clapped eyes on you—and you loved me."

"I still love you, Robert."

"And I still love you, Nancy."

"Sometimes I think you could fall in love with any woman —I mean any pretty woman, any bonnie lassie?"

"Of course I could—that's part o' my folly, Nancy—but there are degrees o' love just as there are degrees o' women——"

"And yet you'll be writing me to-morrow telling me you love me and me alone; and like the silly woman I am, I'll believe you."

"And you'll do right to believe me, dearest Nancy. You see: I've never loved any woman as I've loved you because I've never loved any woman like you. You are unique, Nancy——"

"And what will that do for me when you are on your farm and I'm sitting here alone crying out my soul for you?"

"It'll no be easy, my dear—only too well do I ken that. But there's no alternative. Fate doesna deal out alternatives. Neither you nor me have money. Hence we have no independence. I maun go and earn my daily bread in a distant parish by the sweat o' my brow; and you maun sit here and wait till your boys grow up and support you. Even if you werena tied by the legal fiddle-faddle o' marriage to MacLehose —wad you come wi' me to Ellisland and share my fate as well as share my bed? Would you?"

"Oh—we canna think o' that. We do wrong even to think about it. Robert—before my God, I canna live without you. I'll break my heart when you go and I'll pine and die. It's a terrible sin and I deserve to suffer deeply for my sin; but I hold you dearer than life itself: hold you dearer than honour, truth and virtue. For love of you, Robert, I've sinned away my immortal soul."

"No, no, my dear, you havena sinned in the Almighty's sight—sinned only in the sight of man's petty laws. Never fear on that score. Take your courage as you tak' your love, in your own soft-strong hands——"

"Oh, but had we never loved, this parting would never have been such an anguish. . . Oh, I feel my heart even now swelling up in my bosom so that I feel it will burst its walls . . . Put your arms round me, Robert. Kiss me, make love to me, before I cry out. . .

" . . . oh promise, promise, Robert, promise you'll wait

for me. Something must happen to give me my freedom. I know it—my heart tells me it will be so. Only wait for me so that when I'm free we can be thegither for ever—through life and through death and beyond death into eternity. . . Robert, my beloved . . . my eternal sweet-loving, Robert."

By this time they were in bed together. . . In the troughs of the waves, waves that were running emotional mountains high, he whispered:

"Nancy thou first of women—and bitch o' hell—you were created for this and this above all else. You were made for love, dearest Nancy; made to lie in a man's arms; made to receive the impact of a man's passion; and add interest and receive interest. You think you're an angel, Nancy—and so you are, in your soul. But if angels had lips and breasts like yours, mankind would have been thirled to religion long ago. This is the only true religion, mistress of my soul, this is the only Throne of Grace twixt man and woman."

"——that's no' what you called it in your letter to your friend Ainslie, my love—what did you mean by the pleni-potentiary?"

"So you read my letter to Bob Ainslie? You're enjoying his acquaintance now, Nancy?"

The storm abated; the waves subsided; the tide ebbed on a long low trembling wave . . . out to the black edge of the unconscious . . . of utter absorption into the mindless ecstasy of non-awareness, drifting, drifting . . . till every sentient feeling was drained away. . .

The Bard came back to consciousness quicker than Clarinda. He slipped his arm from under her neck, left her drained body still a-swoon, dressed himself and then went over and stirred the dying fire back to life.

He poured himself a glass of wine and sipped it slowly, letting the spirit soak into his parched gums and dry tongue. From dark heavy dreaming eyes he watched Clarinda come slowly, slowly back to full awareness.

God! but she was a great woman to love for an hour in bed—a glorious woman. Aye, he'd loved her to-night as she'd never been loved, as she would never be loved again. She was

—as he had told her—a bitch o' hell, jealous as only hell's bitches can be jealous and passionate, frantically passionate as only such bitches can be and invariably are.

Aye, but he loved her too, puir bitch. She wanted him tied to her for ever and ever. She could forgive infidelity in a husband! She would never forgive infidelity in him—once she was sure she had him tied. And Ainslie had showed her that letter, had he? He thought he would. . .

Before they parted that night (or early the next morning) she broached that subject:

"I hadna meant to tell you that Mr. Ainslie showed me your letter. I rated him soundly for his presuming I would understand it and he begged me frantically that I would never tell you. You won't chide him about it—he is a dear good boy really but young and inexperienced."

"You think so?"

"But tell me, Robert—you didn't do to Jean Armour what you told Ainslie, did you? You couldn't have—not in her condition. Do men generally tell each other what they do?"

"Divine Clarinda should not have read that letter—and Ainslie did very wrong to show it to you. In charity I'll forget that you ever saw it."

"In the same charity then, I shall forget that you ever wrote it. Oh, Robert, nothing must come between us . . . nothing. How many nights have we left together, my love?"

"Maybe this is our last night, my dear, I have to sup wi' some great folks in the Excise——"

"Oh no, no—I couldna bear that! However late you sup come to me afterwards—as long as you come sober so as to make no noise . . . the chain will be off the door. . . Promise me you'll come."

THE EXCISE COMMISSION

Still Creech delayed. . . He refused to pay over until he himself had been paid every penny. The Bard forced a certain amount out of him; but it was far from representing the £500 he had been promised at the beginning of their talks.

And when he demanded that he get his £100 for the copyright of his poems as per the agreement drawn up by Henry MacKenzie, Creech said flatly that he couldn't pay—not in the meantime. . . He thought he might be able to do something by May. . .

John Tait of Harviestoun, in his capacity of Writer to the Signet, advised the Bard to wait till May. . . As long as Creech paid something to account there was little could be done about him.

And then in the midst of his despair, the Excise agreed that he could take his six weeks' instructions in practical gauging from Exciseman James Findlay in Tarbolton. When his instructions had been satisfactorily completed he would be given his commission.

He explained his position to Graham of Fintry.

"You see, sir, I had to do something to secure my livelihood. . . So I had to take the lease of a small farm from Mr. Patrick Miller on the banks of the Nith at his estate of Dalswinton. Had I been put on the list earlier, it is unlikely I would have entered into an agreement with Mr. Miller. But his offer was a reasonable one; and I had already delayed long enough in settling with him. Had I lost Mr. Miller's farm *and* the Excise I would have been in desperate straits."

"Well, if you're turning farmer, Burns—and I think you are wise—why trouble with the Excise?"

"I am not too happy about farming, Mr. Graham. My recollections anent farming are gloomy in the extreme. I hope for the best. But can I be blamed for fearing the worst? I am determined on my commission, sir, so that should the worst overtake me I may have the Excise to fall back on."

"I see—oh, and I understand, Burns. I've nae doubt but you're wise. You're a wise and extremely practical man to be a poet——"

"But I hope I am a poet too."

"No doubt, my dear Burns—not an element of doubt. No: what I was thinking . . . weel, but, of course, things are difficult in this world . . . I mean that something better might have been found for you. . . If your farm prospers you'll be happy enough?"

"The farming life is the finest life that can be lived, sir— always provided a man can make his living by it."

"Then you would rather be a farmer than anything else?"

"That is so."

"Aye . . . I think you're right. But I hope you're not going to bury yourself entirely in the country. Ayr, Kilmarnock and Machlin provided you wi' mony a theme for your muse. Of course, there's Dumfries. A fine little town, too. Well, I can only wish you all success and every happiness, Burns. And should you at any time feel you would like to venture on the Excise, let me know. I'll say nothing about your farming venture until you get your commission. . . No, no, Burns, dinna thank me: I'm in your debt, as all Scotland is. I'm only sorry I canna do more for you. . ."

JAMES JOHNSON

He did not manage to say good-bye to all his Edinburgh friends. But he did manage a night to the Crochallan Club and take his leave of Willie Dunbar, Bob Cleghorn, Willie Smellie, Alexander Cunningham, Bob Ainslie. . .

He even managed to thank Henry MacKenzie and Dugald Stewart for their kindness to him, though he did not manage to meet with Lord Monboddo, Dr. James Gregory, Bishop

Geddes or William Greenfield. He missed Nasmyth; but he bade adieu to John Beugo and their French teacher, Louis Cauvin, for many a happy and instructive hour they had spent on the French language.

And there was Allan Masterton, Stephen Clarke and a few others, like Schetky, he managed to have a word with; and, of course, his best friend in this circle, his best friend in Edinburgh, Willie Nicol.

His difference with Creech made no difference between Creech's head clerk, Peter Hill, and himself. Rather otherwise, for Peter was thinking of quitting Creech and setting up a bookshop of his own. . .

And there was Jamie Johnson, the good-natured, well-intentioned but rather easy-going music engraver.

The Bard and he found it convenient to slip into John Dowie's in Libberton's Wynd to say good-bye over a drink of strong ale.

Johnson was beginning to look upon the Bard as the director of his *Musical Museum*—he was worried to know how to set about his third volume.

"But noo that you've turned farmer again, Robert, and that sae far away, I wonder how I'm to make shift for the third volume?"

"Dinna worry about your third volume, Jamie. I'll attend to that—and the three or four or five volumes to come after that."

"Oh God, Robert, I doubt nor the third volume'll exhaust us completely."

"Na, na, James, you mauna despair o' your venture sae easy. I gave you thirty-five songs for the second volume. And I'm only starting: on the lang winter nights on my farm I'll have time and plenty to go over the auld tunes and rake oot or eke oot words for them. Indeed I'm looking forward to that more than to farming gin the truth were known. I've that volume o' Highland airs you gave me to go over—there's bound to be plenty o' good tunes there. My tours in the Highlands hae given me a different appreciation o' Gaelic music. . . I heard a lass singing by the roadside on the way to Inverness; I heard a woman sing at Bannachra on the banks o' Loch Lomond. I heard a fair maid sing in the drawing-room o' Kilravock—all o' them singing Gaelic to exquisitely pathetic Gaelic airs—and those Gaelic airs are part—and maybe no' the least part—o' our national music. I wish sometimes I had studied Gaelic instead o' French for there maun be some grand words in Gaelic to fit these fine old tunes. Think o' MacPherson's Ossian. . . You maun get someone i' the Town here to translate some o' them. No, James, I'm looking forward to a lifetime's devotion to your publication. And as long as you'll engrave and publish, I'll undertake to supply the material. Only you must impress on Clarke that the lines must be set out the way I want them. There's a touch o' the irregular about our old music that canna do to be squeezed into mathematical proportions. We must keep the wildness and the wild sweet flavour o' the melodies. Tapping them oot wi' an even beat o' the toe'll no' do. Tak' a tune like Cornwallis's Lament. Ta-ra, ra, ra, tee ee ree ee—you've got to stretch out the teeee. . . Teeeee . . . ee ree ee. You see, if you hold the teeee then you slip down wi' a nice round curve on the ree ee; whereas, if you dinna hold the tee, then you come clattering down on the ree ee and you've got to rest on the ee and that takes away the sweet bend on the line and sticks in a couple o' damned sharp corners. . ."

Johnson, chin on hands, listened to him crooning and was enchanted. Damnit, but he could fairly bring out the magic o' a melody—the pure magic of it. When he lilted a tune you'd swear it was the best tune you'd heard—until you heard him lilting another.

"But whaur i' the name o' God did you get a' this, Robert?"

"What does it matter? Instinct? Or did I drink it in wi' my mother's milk? And mind ye, James—best o' a' I'm going back to yoke wi' a lass that has the finest wood-note wild in the West Country. . . No . . . I'm telling nobody her name —yet. I'll tell you a' about it in good time. But, between us, we'll fill you a dozen volumes. . . And now here—to practical matters. You ken how I stand wi' that low crawling creeping bastard Creech? Aye. . . Well, here's his note to pay me the hundred guineas for the copyright o' my poems. He promised it for May. Will you collect it for me and send it on?"

"I will that, Robert—and it'll be a real pleasure to watch Creech pay up. Send me word when you want me to collect—and I'll collect. Weel, Robert, we've had a grand session and for my part I could sit a' day and a' nicht listening to you. By God, sir, but I'll miss you——"

"And I'll miss you, my good sir. There's a few good friends i' the Town I'll miss. But I've dallied in Edinburgh too long for my own good. Mind you—it's a stinking hole is Auld Reekie—but a grand place for the long winter nichts. But man, when the spring comes, I juist canna thole it. . . Mind a puir exiled devil o' a poet wi' a letter now and again: I'll aey be interested to learn your news—and the news o' the Town. . ."

The Bard shook hands and parted with James Johnson—the poor ill-educated but enthusiastic lover of his country's songs. Folks wondered what he saw in Johnson: the Bard wondered that folks saw so little in the engraver and were so blind to his great worth and the greatness of the work he was doing—now and for posterity. The Bard had no doubt about the verdict of posterity. Johnson would never make money out of his venture; but posterity would remember James Johnson when his own name was perhaps forgotten or remembered only for the songs he had given him.

THE INSTALLATION OF AINSLIE

"Well, Bob, the measured hour has come for you and me and Auld Reekie. We've had many a happy time thegither. . . Come and see me on my farm sometime. You would enjoy the West Country. . . I'm leaving Clarinda in your care, Bob. You'll visit her and comfort her, what you can?"

"I may look her up once in a while, Robert—for your sake. I winna deny: she's a fine woman. If it wasn't that she was yours."

"I hereby install you in full rights, Bob—in my absence. I'll no' see Auld Reekie for mony a day. Clarinda canna be expected to wait a' that time. So don't let ony consideration o' me weigh on your conscience."

"You can hardly pass her on as if she were a whore——"

"Who's suggesting that? She's yours only on condition that you play your cards right. And your safest card is your devotion to truth, virtue, honour, sensibility—and the Reverend John Kemp's branch o' Calvinism."

"Personally, Robert, I'm not sure that I don't agree with Mr. Kemp's Calvinism."

"What, you? Dinna tell me you'll be running to weep on his bosom and tell him how often you've broken the sixth commandment?"

"I'm serious, Robert: I've aey been convinced of the essential truth of our Calvinistic doctrine—I—I don't mean in any narrow sense, you understand——"

"No, I dinna understand, Bob; but Clarinda will. She hopes to enjoy the best of this world *and* the hereafter. But watch that Kemp doesna light the candle on you at the critical moment. Mind you, Bob, I'm very fond o' Clarinda . . . too damned fond for my own peace of mind."

"You're fond o' her—but you don't love her?"

"Of course I love her, you blin'-eyed bat! And aey will. . . . She's one o' the few I hae really loved in my day. Had I met her the first winter I came to Town—but . . . that's a' past now, lad. Clarinda belongs to the past—and the land of might-hae-beens. At least she'll belong to the past when I have kissed her good-bye to-night—or early to-morrow morning. And when the sun sinks to-morrow evening I'll be back in the West—I like the West, Bob—I dearly like the West. . ."

Ainslie sat on the edge of the bed as the Bard busied himself packing his saddle-bags.

He was genuinely sorry he was going. It had been a wonderful experience knowing Robert Burns. But did he really know him? He was far from sure. And he didn't know how to take him about Clarinda. Maybe he was setting a trap for him—to see how far he would go with her. Little did the Bard know how far he'd already gone with her. . . Or so Ainslie thought.

JENNY'S BAWBEE

Jenny Clow said: "What's the guinea for—ye ken I dinna tak' money?"

"That's why you'll take the gowden guinea, Jenny—to buy yourself a bit ribbon for your bonnet. So that when you sally forth frae the Potterrow and see a' the lads winking at you, you'll no' forget me."

"I'll no' forget you—ever. D'ye gie every lass a guinea?"

"I'm hardly the Chancellor o' the National Exchequer, Jenny. No: you can put a hole in that, thread a ribbon through it and wear it next your skin."

Jenny held the coin to the light of the taper.

"They say a man can get his pick o' the Toon's weemin for a shilling. I wadna sell myself for a cairt load o' thae."

She dropped the bright coin down the bodice of her dress.

"I'll be gey hard ca'd when I spend that—I hope you can say as much for Mistress Mac."

"Mistress Mac worries you, Jenny?"

"I wadna say she worries me. But if she was daft about ye afore, she's clean wud on ye noo. But gin you bided wi' her ye wad ken the other side o' her."

"Meaning?"

"I'm glad you're no' taking her wi' ye."

"Ah, Jenny, you women are a' the same—it's your nature, I suppose. Well . . . good luck to you, lass; and I hope you'll get a lad that'll be able to mak' you a good husband. . ."

"I've to thank you, sir, for . . . being sae nice to me. I've enjoyed every minute wi' you and I dinna think ye've ony regrets yoursel'."

"As lang as you've nae regrets, Jenny, I'll hae nane. . ."

Clarinda was quieter than he had known her—quiet and strangely subdued. Deep down she was terribly depressed. She was losing the man, the one man whom she loved almost beyond life itself. She knew, as only a woman in love can know such things, that he didn't love her with half the depth of her love. In physical passion, yes—there he could equal her where she had never thought to be equalled. No: he didn't love her as she had hoped he would or he would never have taken a farm so far away as Dumfries. What she had feared would happen, had indeed happened. Since he came back from Machlin she had given herself utterly to him. Now he didn't really want her—not half as much as she wanted him.

Loving him had been a devastating experience. His loving of her had been but another *variety* of experience. Clarinda had not devastated him though she had given him a deep and abiding experience.

But Clarinda could not help forgetting that the letter she had received from him that morning promised nothing more tangible than his correspondence—even though it did contain the sentence: "Will you open with satisfaction and delight a letter from a man who loves you, who has loved you, and who will love you to death, through death, and for ever?"

That was this morning (though the sheet was dated: "Friday at nine o'clock, evening"). Now it was Saturday, Saturday evening of the twenty-second of March. On Monday he would be gone—and maybe for ever. Maybe she would never see him again. It was all very well for him to promise to love her—to death and through death—but she would much rather he loved her in life and through life.

As it was he came with a present of a pair of drinking glasses and a copy of the poet Young's *Night Thoughts*. The inscription on the fly-leaf gave her no thrill—but maybe he intended it for public showing. There was no Divine Clarinda here—merely a bald sentence saying: "To Mrs. MacLehose—

this poem—the sentiments of the heirs of Immortality—told in the numbers of Paradise—is respectfully presented by—Robert Burns."

He saw she was disappointed in the inscription.

"You can show that to Miss Nimmo and Mary Peacock—or Mr. Kemp or Mr. Craig. You can show it to the whole Town. It will make nobody the wiser—and allay a lot of suspicion. But here's a pair o' drinking glasses—and these shall be sacred to the Throne of Grace. We'll hansel them to-night, my dear—and then you can put them bye till we meet again."

"How weel bye am I to put them?"

"The first year'll be the worst, my dear. Maybe gin next winter I'll be able to spend a week wi' you. We'll hope for that anyway. . ."

"Hope? Robert . . . that's all that's for us. And believe your Divine Clarinda that *my* night thoughts will not be Young's."

"My dear glorious witty Clarinda! Come, fill up the glasses! For this is our parting night—the measured time hath come—Clarinda, mistress of my soul."

"Your wit and your gallantry is forced like the wine, Sylvander. You're not Robert Burns to-night—you're Sylvander—and I am *not* Clarinda—nor Nancy either: I'm Mistress MacLehose—hated name!"

"Damnit, Nancy—we agreed at the commencement of our love that we would have to dissemble in so far as the world —and our less understanding friends—was concerned. Miss Nimmo, for instance, kens how warmly I'm interested in your happiness——"

"Miss Nimmo kens that we have made carnal love to one another—that's why she's so cold to me."

"Well—damn Miss Nimmo and everybody that cuts you—or me either for that matter. . ."

There was no quivering heights of ecstasy between Robert Burns and Agnes MacLehose on the night of their parting in the cosy room in General's Entry, Potterrow. Certainly the rosy wine was sparkling enough and the chamber as secret as anyone could wish. . . But then it was their parting hour; and both of them knew the essential insincerity of it. The artificiality of their relationship immediately came to the surface the moment they were not warmed by the heat of amorous dalliance that is the forerunner of sexual fulfilment.

Their letters had been a literary exercise in the avoidance of literary amorous dalliance—the not too skilful cloaking of it in sensibility and mock-religious sentiment. Clarinda believed much less in religion than did Robert Burns—her religion was an escape from the hellish isolation, the damnable waste of her life. But this religion of escape (not forgetting John Kemp) had become the essence of her veriest prattle and the chief stock-in-trade of her verbal intercourse. She had posed so successfully as a pious mother, deserted by her worthless husband, that she had come to believe in the truth of her piety.

Had Robert Burns told her that she was nothing less than a self-deceiving sentimentalist (if not indeed a sentimental hypocrite) she would have been deeply and honestly shocked.

That is: had he told her so in cold blood. But in the drumming dithyramb of sexually-simmering blood he could tell her anything—call her bitch and whore and much that was less elegant in phraseology. All this Clarinda did not mind. Indeed, it thrilled her to be spoken to in this manner— it added (such is female perversity) to the sensation of heavenly bliss and earthly ecstasy.

It was easy for Robert Burns to write blithering bombast to Mrs. MacLehose—nothing easier.

But it was quite impossible for him to make artificial *physical* love to her. Mrs. MacLehose liked the blithering bombast (especially coming from Robert Burns). But what drove her to the verge of dementia was his physical presence and his physical love-making. She was unable to separate the bombast from the man. Always she was quiveringly aware of the man: the bombast did not register *in itself*.

But now the physical presence was to be torn from her— torn from her at the very time of its deepest root-taking. Little wonder she was depressed and her spirit grey. Little

wonder the gay butterfly-wing fluttering in her plexus gave
way to the grey gnawing worm of cancerous doubt.

She drank; but the drink did not warm her. She kissed;
but neither the kisses she gave nor received fired her blood nor
melted her marrow.

Finally she broke; and then all her weakness, her loneliness,
her despair, her lack of faith . . . finally all the hollow emptiness of her life and all life . . . (the utter bloody ruthless
inconsequentiality of all life under the sun . . . born to death
and beginning to die in the moment of birth . . .) finally
the pit of individual apartness yawned beneath her and she
glimpsed the senseless grave her father had dug for her in her
mother's womb . . . even as theirs had been dug for them
out of flesh and bone and stinking corpses from the Fall, the
why and wherefore of which could never be known since the
part could never comprehend the whole. . . . Finally Clarinda
(vehicle for a procreative purpose as blind and utterly meaningless as it was totally miraculous and completely ruthless) could
no longer support herself; and the worm-eaten, cancer-
gnawed, core-blighted pillars of human imbecility—that
fundamental human imbecility that deceives itself into
believing that which is beyond belief (and having faith in
that which is faithless since that something is for ever beyond
knowledge, intuition, belief . . . or indeed any manner of
intelligent comprehension) disintegrated.

So finally in the General's Entry, Potterrow, came sorrow
and despair and the hell of unbelief which is doubt.

But nothing of this Clarinda *knew*: else her reason would
have broken down and she would have turned her face to the
wall of life.

Nothing of this she *knew* in terms of intellectual abstraction; but her quivering senses received the full and devastating
impact of this experience.

"Oh, Robert, I canna bear the future without you. God
sent you to me to let me ken what joy was, only to take you
away from me because I'm sinful and have disobeyed His
commandments. We maun a' be punished for our transgressions and the transgressions of those that came before us.

If God had blessed our love—if He had approved of it—He would never have taken you from me nor left me to suffer alone and in silence——"

"Clarinda, Clarinda: dinna break your heart, woman. Life, as I've told you before, is nothing but a drop of sweetness in a draught of gall. To ken the sweetness you hae to swallow the gall. Sometimes the gall is no' sae bitter; and sometimes the sweetness is honey sweet. But the sting and the honey, the rose and the thorn, gang thegither. Dinna weep your heart oot, woman, dinna weep out your heart. I told you Fate was a heartless bitch and Fortune but a poxed whore. In my moods o' melancholy I think o' Fate and Fortune in terms I wadna like to repeat to you. But what a stupid silly blind-bat bitch o' a woman you can be, Nancy, wasting away your life because o' a few mouthfu's o' mumbo-jumbo frae the Lads in Black. You're sma' boned but sweetly fleshed. You've gotten brains that are sweetened by sensibility; you've a voice like the far awa' cooing o' a cushat dove. . . You're gifted wi' body, gifted wi' mind, gifted wi' soul, gifted wi' a personality o' flesh and mind and spirit far above the lave. And yet, wi' mind-forged manacles you're hauden doon into the Pit o' Denial. . . Aye: you're the Mistress o' my Soul: I've told you that. But what kind o' soul hae I got? If I hae a soul! If. . . Aye: you'll no' trade in ony ifs. You maun hae certainty. And what is certainty for you but the certainty o' Calvinism— which is nae certainty at a' but the bellowing o' Blind Man's Buff. Blind Man's Buff—bellowing like a blinkered bull against the denial o' desire. . . Hell roast you, Clarinda: you hae the brains o' a philosopher—and the ideas o' a fiddling, petty-fogging priest. What's the mouldy mouth-trappings o' every priest, despite his calling—Denial! Thou Shalt Not! Bluidy auld wives' trash to frighten bairns i' the dark. God! as if the world wasna dark enough.

"Faith, Clarinda, is but a candle lichted against the dark. But blow the candle oot (and life blaws gusts nae candle-lowe can sustain). . . Blaw out the candle and let your een grow accustomed to the darkness. After a wee while there's nae darkness at a'. You can see; but dimly maybe—but you can

see. Aye . . . in the blackest darkness. But aey *you* maun see
the taper licht as the licht o' temptation. . . There's only ae
darkness, Clarinda, Mistress o' my Soul—the darkness o' the
grave. . . Noo I've looked on this darkness long enough to
convince me o' its inevitability, to convince me that there and
there alone shall we all lay down the burden o' life—and lay
it down to all eternity. We'll lay it down for a long time
onyway—and we'll hae nae consciousness to ken how lang. . .
Love then, Nancy: what else are we to do? For me: I'll laugh
and sing and shake my leg as lang's I dow—and you ken where
I said that? I ken the blackbird's sang, Nancy, and the sang
o' the mavis and the lark . . . and the gowdspink. Watch the
gowdspink bobbing on the thorn tree—bobbing joyously on
the green spray o' life. . . I didna bob much on the green
spray o' life when I was young. God no: life was too grim
an honour for ony bobbing. Still: I've done my best to make
up for time lost. . . Nancy, my dear, I'm leaving you. I
understand how I'm leaving you—in sorrow and pain. All
parting is sorrow—but this is no' the parting o' death. We'll
meet again some other day—may that day be soon: that's a'
I ask. . .

   "Dearest Nancy . . . if there was anything I could do to
soften our parting; if there was anything I could do to make
it easier—for you and for me. . . There's so much you understand—and so much you dinna. . . But I come back full
circle. You're a woman—a glorious fine amiable woman, a
woman made for love, made for life. Dinna deny the life your
Creator gave you in such bounty—for that's a mockery and
denial o' His gift. And aey mind that when you give yourself
on the Throne o' Grace you give yourself to His glory—and
no' to John Calvin's or John Kemp's. . .

   "Had we never loved sae blindly, Nancy, we would never
hae been like this the nicht. . . And for that I canna juist
a'thegither blame mysel'. 'Deed neither o' us is to blame,
Nancy. . . Neither o' us. . . There's nobody . . . nothing
to blame. And it would be senseless to blame life for that
would be blaming God or the Divine Architect o' the Universe
or . . . or blaming the red rose for its beauty and its scent

. . . and whatever way you would look at it, that would be blasphemy. . . The deepest, darkest, bluidiest treachery. . . And treachery, my dear, treachery to man or beast in life or in death—but especially in life—Nancy, that is the vilest, perhaps the *only* unforgivable, sin here or hereafter. . ."

And so he held her in his strong arms, she who was weak in her strength; and lilted, almost with a mystical rhythm, strong words of sense to her, propping up her courage all round with the sturdy timbers of sound sense. . . And maybe he blethered a bit too as even a strong man will when holding a fine woman in his arms—a fine woman needing comfort. And such was the strength of him and the strength in the soft gold of his voice that she absorbed the most shattering of heresies in a way she had never absorbed the arid life-denying orthodoxies of John Kemp.

But maybe she was not so comforted as she was drugged and dazed. Her heart ached with a gorging of emotion. For what did any words matter and what did it matter what they conveyed? She was losing Robert Sylvander Burns—dearest of all earthly lovers, most upright and magnificent of men. And yet she who had led him—the wonder of all the gay world that was Edinburgh and the cot-houses and the mansion-houses of Scotland—she who had led him to her parlour and had revealed to him all her mysteries (and many she had never known she possessed) had been unable to hold him. And this was something she was unable to support. . .

FAREWELL TO AULD REEKIE

The Bard left Edinburgh, the gay grey sordid stinking happy Auld Reekie, without regret. But he was not without a twinge of sadness—an anticipatory twinge. His Edinburgh days had not all been unhappy. He had spent many a happy day and many a happier night here in Scotland's capital. Here, crowned as Caledonia's Bard, he had tasted the cup of fame, filled brimming to the lip. . . And he had drained that cup to the lees. . . As far as fame was concerned he had no more heights to scale. . . And of the few illusions he had retained from his Ayrshire days none remained to shatter. He had had his glorious hour of triumph—a triumph given to few men. . . But he'd had to wait a damnable time for his due reward in terms of hard cash and tangible employment. And the long months of gut-worrying waiting had taught him the value of fame and allowed him to measure the hollowness of men's praise.

Yet he had pressed the imprint of his personality on Auld Reekie and he had taught a wide variety of men and women that he could neither be seduced, flattered nor corrupted. And all this was something to give satisfaction. . .

Above all he *had* made friends in Auld Reekie—good solid hearty friends who deeply regretted his going from them. Willie Nicol had summed that up:

"Damnit, Robert, you and me hae had mony a wordy battle and mony a sair clash we hae been in; but, by God, sir, we've had our moments too. . . Glorious times, Robert. . . Aye, and we'll meet again some ither day. . . On that I hae set my heart. And if I can get a wee bit o' an estate somewhaur beside you on the Nith, then I'll be wi' you every summer; and mony a peck o' maut we'll brew thegither. And to think it was only twa winters ago you cam' fresh to Town, the ploughman-poet! Hell roast you, you black-browed beggar! I could bluidy greet if I hadna grat my een oot as a bairn in Annan lang ago. . . Guid luck to you, Robert—and wherever blessings come from—if they come frae onywhaur—let them shower on you . . . and your Bonnie Jean. . ."

And so he rode out of Edinburgh in the cold grey March daylight, whipped by a snell east wind from the Firth of Forth. He had entered Edinburgh with his bachelor's certificate: he was leaving with his tack agreement for Ellisland (and his Excise instructions up his sleeve).

But as he left the grey dragon of Auld Reekie crouching on the rock, and turned his face to the West, he was saddened in his thoughts that one of Jean's twins was dead and that her tiny sister would probably be dead by the time he reached the Backcauseway. This sad news caused his breast to overflow to Jean as it had never overflowed before. . .

But by now his back was turned on the gay world of Edinburgh. . .

Part Six

OF A' THE AIRTS

A CRACK WI' ADAMHILL

JOHN RANKINE of Adamhill welcomed the Bard in his usual boisterous fashion.

"So you're finished wi' Edinburry, Rab! Weel, you'll no' be sorry, I'll warrant. You've been a wonderfu' success there; but you're glad to be finished wi' it?"

"I am, John. . . I was little more than a nine-days' wonder there. Though I've met some honest fellows in Auld Reekie and made some good friends."

"And what about the weemin? By God, Rab, I feared for you till I heard how you'd done the richt thing wi' Jean Armour. Damned, Rab, I never feared for you till Jean was put frae the Cowgate to Tarbolton Mill——"

"Just how did you fear for me, John?"

"Weel, Rab, gin you hadna done richt wi' Armour's lass I'm afeared my opinion o' you wad hae drapped a wee! Ah, but I kent you wad dae the richt thing. It's a pity aboot the twins, though. Aye, a sair pity after a' the lass cam' through. By God, sir, did you see the verses auld Tait wrote on you and Jean?"

"I saw them."

"You'll need to blister Tait oot o' Tarbolton wi' a satire."

"No. I've *some* dignity—and Tait's beneath it."

"Ah weel, Rab, I'm beyond giving you advice noo. . ."

"Far from it. No: I'm tired o' Machlin, John. I'm finished wi' this part o' the country and it wi' me. At least for a time. Jean and me'll be far better settled in Dumfries."

"By certes, Rab, but it was a bold move settling Jean up in the Backcauseway. By God, sir, that staggered a wheen o' parishes round about. By certes, it did. But how are you for settling matters wi' Daddy Auld?"

"The twins were buried unbaptised. I'm no' likely to forget that. No' that I blame Auld; but I blame the bluidy vermin o' his Session. Oh, it makes little odds to me that they werena baptised—but Jean feels it."

"Of coorse, you no' being married——"

"Fegs, I'm married. But this, for the moment, between ourselves. The lines I gave Jean that Armour destroyed still stand. I thought at the time when they were destroyed that that was that. But no: I was wrang. Bob Aiken did it thinking he was helping me. But my lines were perfectly legal and canna be disputed. Jean and me are set up in Baldy Muckle's: that'll prove co-habitation, as it were——"

"I think you've already proved that wi' fower weans in: what . . . seventeen months?"

"Aye; but we must *live* together as man and wife—under one roof—in the same bed."

"The mahogany bed!"

"That bed gave them plenty to talk aboot. . . Well, I've put the case to Daddy Auld and Auld assures me he'll see that things are put right."

"But how can Auld dae that when he gave you a bachelor's certificate?"

"Apparently you canna destroy marriage lines even by burning them in the fire. But the like fire can destroy a bachelor's certificate."

"Oho! So that's the way o'it, is it? Damned, but Auld's a cunning beggar too. . . So he's for recognising the marriage, is he?"

"When he's talked the Session round to his views."

"By God, Rab, but that's good! Damned, you've beat them to it. Holy Willie'll hae his teeth ground doon to the gums! God, sir, but this is glorious . . . glorious. . . And when are you for Dumfries?"

"I've been down and made arrangements to hire a married man and a labourer. I've house and barns to build this summer. But first I've to complete my training for the Excise wi' Jamie Findlay in Tarbolton."

"I heard aboot that. What's this aboot you turning farmer and gauger at the same time?"

"It's a lang story, John—and a damned heart-breaking

one. . . I'm no sure o' the farm—Miller's farm. I'm dubious, after a' my experience, o' trusting to a farm for my livelihood. Actually, until a few weeks ago, I didna know whether I was to have the farm or the Excise. I plumped for both in case one should escape me. Now both have come up. And I'm for working them both. If the farm fails, I'll have the Excise. If the farm prospers, I can drop the Excise."

"You've gotten damnably lang-luggit, since you gaed to Edinburry."

"I'm wise——"

"Wise! Damnit, that's perfect. You canna lose either way. Wise! by God. . . Mind you, I'd rather see you farmer than gauger. You're a far better farmer than Gilbert. Noo, then! I've kent the pair o' you lang enough to mak' my verdict. Gilbert's a' richt; but fu' o' hare-brained schemes. You can plough, sow and reap wi' ony man. You're a farmer."

"Look at my hands, John. Lily-white and saft as a woman's bosom. My muscles are gone. I've grown saft—saft as ony gentle dame o' Auld Reekie——"

"To hell wi' that! A week's wark'll put you back in fettle."

"No: nor a year's work. Besides I've been indolent wi' haunting Edinburgh so long—bad cess to Creech, my agent. Damnit, John, I nearly got hooked by an Edinburgh widow."

"Widow!"

"Well—her husband was in Jamaica."

"Husband!"

"Well, he'd as good as deserted her."

"Ony weans?"

"Two living——"

"And dead?"

"Two dead."

"Twa dead and twa living!"

"But what a woman, John."

"What a woman! Wi' four weans!"

"Aye; and as ticht as ony virgin that ever was . . . and I should ken! But she nearly had me."

"When was this?"

"I said farewell to her as I left Edinburgh. Of course, I never had ony other real thoughts but Jean."

"By God, sir, a widow! A married woman wi' four weans!"

"You would need to hae seen her——"

"By God, I would. Mind you: I wasna wrang. I kent some o' thae Edinburry dames wad be after you. And I'll warrant she wasna the only one. By God, sir, the quicker you get down to Dumfries wi' Daddy Auld's blessing, the better."

"I never was in ony danger, John. Except wi' this woman. She was the same age as me—and wrote poetry. The Blackbird in the Museum's by her. A glorious fine woman, John. And could she ride to kirk or market . . .! But I'd a gallop in me she didna bargain on——"

"By certes, you've gone your mile in Edinburry. . . But you've settled doon, wi' Jean."

"And glad to be settled. I've never kent what it was to have a corner o' my own: it's a great comfort. . ."

"Aye, you've had a sair life o' it, too, Rab. Poverty and hard work and mony disappointments. . . But what aboot your verses?"

"Well, I've as good as taken over James Johnson's Museum. I want to write songs—hundreds o' songs. And rescue as many more from oblivion and neglect. I've years o' work afore me. . ."

"Aye, man: I'm glad to hear that. . . But I hope you'll no' miss us wi' an odd satire or twa!"

"Oh, there'll aey be something to tickle my fancy. . ."

"Och aye; and though you're awa' doon in Dumfries that's a damn sicht nearer nor Edinburry—to say nocht o' Jamaica."

"That's right: I'll be seeing you often enough once I get settled in. But I've a house to big and dykes to put up——"

"Gin you lead in your second hairst you should ken how things are gaun. But I dinna blame you for wanting quit o' Machlin . . . in the circumstances. A fresh start's the plan. And I hae nae fear o' you. Especially wi' Jean Armour to haud you to the bit and cool your ardour—unless that Edinburry widow's cooled it for you. . ."

Adamhill was still the same Adamhill: rough rude ready-witted Rankine; and the Bard found that his affection for him increased with the passing of time. . . .

CONCERNING THE EXCISE

Meanwhile he had lost no time in becoming familiarised with the duties of the Excise.

James Findlay, the officer based on Tarbolton, was a young fellow of his own age. He was an excellent officer and a man of likeable qualities.

"There's mair to the Excise than meets the eye, Robert. But you'll manage."

"It's a lot to manage in six weeks, Jamie."

"Aye; but you're about through now."

The Bard had certainly worked hard. And the work had been onerous.

They were sitting together in Johnny Dow's—enjoying a social glass.

"Let me see that Excise letter again, Jamie. The more I read it the more it impresses."

Findlay handed him the document he had got from the Excise Office in Edinburgh. It read:

"The Commissioners order, that you instruct the bearer, Mr. Robert Burns, in the art of gauging, and practical dry gauging casks and utensils; and that you fit him for surveying victuallers, rectifiers, chandlers, tanners, tawers, maltsters, etc.; and when he has kept books regularly for six weeks at least, and drawn true vouchers and abstracts therefrom (which books, vouchers, and abstracts must be signed by your supervisor and yourself, as well as the said Mr. Robert Burns) and sent to the Commissioners at his expense; and when he is furnished with proper instruments, and well instructed and qualified for an officer (then and not before, at your perils), you and your supervisor are to certify the same to the Board,

expressing particularly therein the date of this letter; and
that the above Mr. Robert Burns hath cleared his quarters
both for lodging and diet; that he has actually paid each of
you for his instructions and examination; and that he has
sufficient at the time to purchase a horse for his business. I
am, your humble servant,

A. Pearson.

Excise Office.
Edinburgh, 31st March, 1788."

"It's a marvellous document that, Jamie: it doesna leave
enough loop-hole for a bug to escape. Folk are apt to get the
notion that a common gauger is equivalent wi' a common
idiot."

"Oh, the Excise is the strictest service in the country,
Robert—it takes a good man to win to a supervisorship. But
I'll be surprised if you dinna go richt through to the Board
o' the Commissioners—in time. I'm serious, Robert—you've
picked up things amazingly weel. . . There's only one danger
in the Excise, as I see. Watch your heart doesna get the better
o' your head. Sometimes you've got to come down gey hard
on folks—especially poor folks. I'm no' saying there's no'
times when you canna side-step a minor offence. But you've
got to be damned sure o' that. Folks like to tak' advantage o'
the Excise and everybody aids and abets them—as you ken
'yoursel'. No' only that: clypes and spies and tale-bearers
abound everywhere. You let somebody off lightly; and instead
o' keeping their mouth shut they go and boast of it—that
rouses jealousy and presently your supervisor gets a complaint
—and then you're in for it. . . Another thing, Robert, is
bribery—this can take a thousand-and-one forms. I ken you
too well to insult you by mentioning the open bribe o' money
—but be on your guard for all kinds o' flattery and subtle
kindnesses: there can be nae friendship touching on the work
o' the Excise. . . Forgive me talking like this to you,
Robert——"

"On the contrary, Jamie, I'm much in your debt. I understand fully what you're driving at. . . Aye: the Excise isn't

going to be too easy—and there's a damnable amount o' clerking in the work . . . damnable. An Exciseman earns his salary and half his supervisor's. . . But I'm more than fortunate in having trained under you, Jamie—more than fortunate. If there's onything I can do for you now or in the future——"

"Well, there is one thing, Robert. . ."

"Come on then: out wi' it. I'll be happy to be of any service to you that lies in my power."

"You couldna arrange another meeting wi' Jean Markland?"

"Jean Markland! Now a word between friends, Jamie. I'm well acquaint wi' Jean and I hae a very high and special regard for her. If it's fun you're after I canna be a party to that—you maun gaun your ain gate there; but——"

"I'm serious, Robert."

"You're in love wi' the lass?"

"Well. . . Aye, I'm in love wi' her—if she'll hae me!"

"Good for you, Jamie Findlay! My heartiest congratulations! She's a fine lass: as straight as a die and as clean's a whistle. I can put in a word for you, Jamie, without Jean kenning that I'm doing so. But you'll need nae word frae me. Dinna beat about the bush. Tell the lass you love her and tell her what you mean to do about it. . . I'll tell you what! Come round to the Backcauseway about eight o'clock—ostensibly for me. Your Jean and my Jean are pack and thick thegither. Jean will be there visiting my wife. . . It looks like being a grand nicht and you can convoy her hame the lang road round—you dinna need me to tell you."

"Thanks, Robert. . . I kent you would understand. . . And dinna worry ony mair about the Excise—you'll get your commission without ony bother. . ." `

SONG WITHOUT WORDS

He had been twice to Ellisland; and he was much worried about it. Now that he had turned farmer and had to assume responsibilities and make decisions he had every cause to be worried.

He had had to engage a couple of men; and in his absence he had to trust to their integrity. And he had to spend money right and left and commit himself to bills that would pile up against him.

Jean saw he was worried.

"You're worrying, Rab—is it about Ellisland—or the Excise?"

"Them baith, lass. The Excise has been damned hard work —though Jamie Findlay has done a' he could for me. I'm mair worried aboot Ellisland. If I had my house and barns built and you down beside me——"

"And could I no' come down the noo, Rab . . .? I could sleep onywhere."

"God no, lass. . . You canna bide at Ellisland. It's bad enough for me. . . See: this is how things are doon there. The outgoing tenant, Davie Cullie, lives in a broken-doon house at a place ca'd The Isle. Why it's so-called, dinna ask me: I've that to find out yet. Cullie's done for farm-work— and been done this while back. Of course I've a wheen acres added on to my tack. But never mind that. The only place I can bide is wi' Cullie. But while *I* can thole it for a time, I wadna ask you to thole it wi' me. When we set up on the banks o' the Nith we'll set up in a proper house—the best I can get built for the money. . . Besides, I need you here until we get things fixed up wi' Daddy Auld."

"D'you think you'll get matters fixed?"

"Dinna worry about that, my love. When I tak' you doon to Ellisland it'll be wi' Daddy Auld's blessing. You ken I have my worries up the road? My mither'll no' move until Daddy Auld has recognised our marriage. And I've other bits o' annoyances to put up wi'. But dinna you worry about my Mither. She'll come round a' richt. In fact, she's coming round already. . . I tell you what: I've been thinking, Jean. I'll need to work Ellisland as a dairy farm. It'll be easier worked that way—and bring more money. So you'll need to learn how to make butter and cheese—and milking. Now you couldna learn better than from my sisters at Mossgiel. What d'you say to that?"

"I'll dae onything I can, Rab: you ken that. But . . . I'm no' sure o' your sisters. . . I ken they havena a good opinion o' me. . ."

"Aye. . . But listen, Jean: once our marriage is recognised by the Kirk that'll change. My sisters would do anything for me . . . anything at all. And once they get to know you they'll do onything for you for your own sake. They're quiet honest lassies that have had to work ower sair. . . No, lass: that's our only salvation—a dairy farm."

"Whatever you say, Rab. Only I'll be glad to get oot o' Machlin . . . for a while. When are you going back to Ellisland?"

"In about a week's time, Jean—and then I count every hour till I'm wi' you again."

"And I count every minute. If you tell me the night you're coming hame, I'll walk doon the road to meet you."

"Will you? How far?"

"You let me ken the day you leave Ellisland and I'll meet you. Then you'll see."

"That's a bargain, Jean. . . Damnit, Jean, I'm fonder o' you than I've ever been. . . If only we could have come together like this twa year ago. A wee bit hoose o' our ain——"

"And a mahogany bed!"

"God! You and me could hae managed on the floor—an' could yet."

"Could you find your road back to the green thorn tree?"

"That's an idea, lass. Damnit, we'll go back there some fine nicht. What d'you say?"

"You're daft enough as it is, Rab."

"No: no' half daft enough! Wait till we get settled down on the banks o' the Nith."

"You haena put the words to my sang yet?"

"Miss Gordon's Strathspey?"

"Aye. . ."

"No: I havena put the words thegither . . . yet. But I'll see what I can do when I'm back at Ellisland. When you come doon the road to meet me I'll see what I can do. Mony a time in Auld Reekie I thocht on your tune, Jean—I even thocht aboot it when I was at Castle Gordon. . . And mony a time it brocht tears to my e'en. . . Surely to God, lass, now that we're thegither at last there'll be some kind o' life for us in the years ahead?"

"As lang as we're thegither, Rab, I carena what comes; for I ken we'll get ower a' our difficulties."

She was still a girl; and God! but she was bonnie. Looking at her as the evening sun streamed in the window and caught her hair and suffused her warm wholesome face, he wondered that he had ever been attracted by another woman. Clarinda was but a vague taper-lit dream in comparison.

But it wasn't only her beauty and her warm wholesome looks that melted his affections. Her mental qualities captivated him. She was far and away the most natural woman he had ever known. There was no strain in her company. Above all there was not the slightest need to pose in her presence. He could be so utterly himself with her that he could completely relax in every physical, mental and spiritual sense. Her presence soothed him; she was balm to his wounds; she came between him and the wall of the world. . .

And she made no demands of him. None. She accepted him in all his moods and vagaries. Nor did she ever stop to criticise the gift of his love and the blessing of his companionship. He was the man she loved: wholly and without equivocation; and without reserve. She did not idolise him: neither was she servile to him. Their love was as natural and inevitable as sunshine or green grass or spring rain or clouds in the sky. She had won him after sore trial and much tribulation. She had won him under the green thorn tree; she had lost him momentarily under the dire pressure of domestic events. . . Now she had won him back again before the altar of their own fireside. And she had won him this second and final time from the gay world of fashion and letters where he had been the toast and the wonder. From how many women she had won him she did not know. Nor, now that she had won him, did she care. She accepted the fact of other women as she accepted life—with a quaint philosophic fatalism. There was nothing dejected and hang-dog about this fatalism. It gave her a quiet confidence and a deep acceptance that was at once soft, sturdy and assuring. . .

That there had been many other women in her husband's life she knew; that there would be many more in the future she was equally certain. But this did not unduly worry her. She was quietly confident that she could hold him against all opposition. And if in the end he did not want to be held— well, if that ever came, she would face it. She had enough love for him and enough trust in him to put that possibility at the very faintest.

Their mutual love indeed could not have been deeper or happier. It was a love of total understanding and unquestioning acceptance. After a spell of Ellisland and the miserable lodging he shared in the smoky spence of David Cullie's house, it was heavenly to return to Jean and the comfort of the mahogany bed. He wanted nothing more now than that they should remain man and wife for the rest of their days.

But if there was deep happiness in their love (and such domestic life as Baldy Muckle's room allowed them) there was plenty to worry about elsewhere. . .

"Well, Mr. Burns," said the Reverend William Auld who had just come in from strolling in his garden. "A fine night —if the midges werena so fierce. . ."

But for all Auld's pleasantries, the Bard came quickly to business.

"Is there any further word anent my marriage, Mr. Auld?"

"Your marriage? Jean and you are settling down, I understand. Uhuh! Well, Mr. Burns: my Session have given me a lot o' trouble on your account though some o' them are for letting bygones be bygones."

The Bard had a savage rejoinder on his lips; but he bit it back.

"Aye . . . but your marriage now. You have no lines. Yes, yes: I understand why. Now, if you had twa independent witnesses to certify that you had been before a justice and had contracted an irregular marriage, I think that would satisfy the Session."

"In other words, Mr. Auld, twa bits o' paper are to take the place o' one that was destroyed?"

"I'm trying to help you, Mr. Burns—and Jean. The bits o' paper may satisfy my Session—you and Jean hae yet to satisfy your Maker. You're for settling down, I understand, as farmer about Dumfries. Uhuh. . . Of course the pair o' ye will need to be compeared; and the censure will require to be noted in the minutes."

"Censure, Mr. Auld?"

"Aye, censure, Mr. Burns. The Kirk's ordinances maun be observed in the letter. But I'm mair concerned about the spirit. I wad like to have your assurance that you intend, in all your future behaviour, to act on true Christian principles, and that you will strive to be a faithful son o' the Kirk and an upright husband before God. I maun hae that assurance, Mr. Burns, from your own lips."

"You can have that assurance now, Mr. Auld. I didna

take the step I have in ony frivolous state o' mind. It's a serious step I have taken and I mean to discharge my duties as a husband and a father in all faith and sincerity. I chose my partner for life; and I chose neither rashly nor on the impulse of the moment."

"Impulse . . . aye! And—eh—you're for settling down in Dumfries quite soon?"

"Well, I've my house and barns to build, sir, afore the summer's out. But as soon as my house is ready, Mrs. Burns will take up house with me. Meantime, now that my Excise instructions are over, I'm about a week on my farm and a week up here."

"Well, I hope you prosper, Mr. Burns, as I've nae doobt you will. And do you intend to cultivate your muse in Dumfries?"

"I canna neglect her altogether. But for the moment I've got to cultivate all my energies on my farm—and on the sober science of life."

"I see. Oh, but dinna neglect your gifts, Mr. Burns. I hae hopes o' ye singing the Lord's praises yet and singing them wi' deep reverence. . . Well, bring your attestations, Mr. Burns, and I'll see that my Session gives them their speedy consideration. . . Tell me, Mr. Burns, afore you go—just how is your worthy mother taking a' this?"

"Well, Mr. Auld, I fancy that she'll no' withhold her blessing on our marriage a moment after you have given yours."

"Aye . . . a worthy woman, your mother, sir—a worthy woman. Oh, but a verra worthy family."

"Excepting me—as scapegoat?"

"Well, of course, after a manner you'll aey be excepted, Mr. Burns. Ye see, when God gave you the gifts He did, He made an exception o' ye—that's *your* cross, sir; but it's your ain responsibility how you bear your cross. . . But I think you're shaping for the right road now. . ."

Daddy Auld, in so far as the Bard was concerned, had mellowed. No longer did he thunder at him; no longer did he exhort.

Auld was ageing and he was feeling the burden of his days. And he was wearied. The heart of man was deceitful and above all things desperately wicked. The heart of man had not changed much during his forty-odd years as the shepherd of Machlin parish. Certainly it had not changed as manners and dress had changed. . .

Auld had softened towards Robert Burns. He was rather proud of him. And he was rather flattered that Robert Burns, instead of defying or mocking him, sought his advice and listened to his counsel. Immune from corruption, William Auld was sensible of the subtle flattery of this.

And the Session, with the exception of the die-hard Lamie and the embittered Fisher, basked in the reflection of this subtle flattery. In a way Mr. Burns was humbling himself before them. They were in the mood to let it go at that. And some there were (and here Holy Willie was divided in himself) who thought discretion the better part of valour. They could be contemptuous of Rab the Ranter from Mossgiel; but Mr. Burns as Caledonia's Bard was a boar with a very different and much more formidable tusk. He might write a lampoon on them; and he might *publish* it. . .

THE MOTHER

One day, not long after his interview with Daddy Auld, Mrs. Burns took advantage to speak to her first-born. They were alone in the kitchen together at Mossgiel.

"I had a word or twa wi' Mr. Auld the other day——"

"And what was Daddy saying?"

"He telt me that your marriage to Jean Armour wad get the solemn confirmation o' the Session."

"Were you ever in ony doubt aboot that, Mither?"

"I've had cause to hae mony a doubt aboot ye, Robin—mony a sair doubt."

"Aye . . . I've had mony a sair doubt mysel', Mither.

But you'll be glad to learn I'm properly married and about to receive the blessing o' the Kirk?"

"Weel . . . I'm no' sure what difference it mak's to the Almighty; but it eases us a' o' a lot o' heart-break and shame. You brocht us a' a gey lot o' shame, Robin——"

"I'm sorry about the shame, Mither."

"No' you—you never gave shame a thocht since your father died. But . . . I'm glad to see you settled at last. And since Jean Armour's had sae much shame wi' you it's only fair she should be bound wi' you."

"I'm lucky having Jean for a wife, Mither. You'd like her—gin you got to ken her."

"Aye . . . well, I've been haeing a word with Nancy and Bell; and they think it would be decent-like if you brocht her up—Mr. Auld thocht so too."

"I'm very grateful for that, Mither. You ken I'll be taking Jean wi' me to Ellisland? And if Nancy or Bell would tak' her in hand to learn her the milking and butter and cheese-making . . ."

"Ah weel, we could be doing that bravely enough—but we'll need to see her first——"

It was at this point that Nancy came bustling in. Mrs. Burns added:

"He's wanting you to learn Jean Armour the dairying."

"Who? Me? I'm far ower busy to learn onybody what they should ken already."

"You're never too busy to teach my wife, Nancy—and your good-sister."

"Oh, she's maybe your wife but she's nae good-sister o' mine."

"Not even if the Reverend Mr. Auld says she is?"

"There's nae need to bring Mr. Auld into this."

"And what if Gilbert says she is?"

"Oh, you can talk Gilbert round nicely when it comes up your humph. You micht at least bring her up so that we can see her."

"All right: I'll bring her up. But you'll be civil to her?"

"Oh, I'm aey civil to them that's civil to me."

"Except me! And I've aey been civil to you!"

"Ach, you're a pest, getting. When is she to come, Mither?"

"Jean Armour can come ony time noo. And dinna worry, Robin: we'll no' eat the lass."

"But mind you," said Nancy, still fighting a sham retreat, "we'll no' put oorselves aboot for her."

Robin rose and patted her affectionately on the shoulder. "Aye, you'll put yoursel' aboot, Nancy—and you'll learn her the dairying into the bargain—and maybe you'll come doon to Ellisland and see her started on the right lines there. . . In fact, you'll a' come doon and see how your famous brither's making out as farmer."

"Oh, I've heard stories like that afore. You may be a famous man in Edinburgh, my braw birkie; but *we* ken you. Come on noo, and no' keep me aff my work ony longer. And if you're for setting up as a farmer, it's aboot time you were getting your hand in: it must be a long time since you did ony work."

ETERNITY IN A SIGH

The initial ordeal was a bit terrifying for Jean; but Nancy and Bell and Isa soon put her at her ease and Gilbert thawed enough to be polite.

Mrs. Burns had a private word with Jean.

"I ken you'll mak' a guid wife to him, lass. . . It's to your credit that you didna yield to him till he gave you that marriage line, though you should hae kent better than trust to ony bits o' paper. . . Your bairn's doing weel here and we a' like him: so he needna gang to you till you're settled into your new farm. Mind you, lass: you'll no' hae your sorrows to seek with Robin. He's a queer man and he was aey a queer laddie though he was a guid bairn. There's something aboot him I dinna understand the way there was a something aboot his father. But he's still my laddie—and I want him to get on and do well for himsel'. So if him and you dae well for yoursel's you'll be doing well for me. . . Maybe you gave your faither and mither as sair a heart as Robin gave me . . .? Noo forget the past and come in to ane anither's backs like guid bairns. Me and the lassies'll dae a' we can for you. . . Mind ye, Jean, you'll need to hae a lot o' patience wi' him for he can be thrawn and dour and oh, awfa wayward. But when he's in his guid moods! Dear-a-dear, he wad wile the bird frae the bush. . ."

They walked down from Mossgiel together in the summer gloaming when the world was hushed and drawn. The western sky still held the broken light-suffused fragments of a glorious sunset. The distant hills were but folded shadows and the woods and shaws lay like skeins of ravelled dusk. . .

They held each other's hands as they trudged down the hill to Machlin. To-night they hadn't a care in the world. And Jean wondered at the deepness of her happiness. She didn't want to go up the narrow stair to Baldy Muckle's room in the Backcauseway. She wanted to walk on and on into the gathering gloaming. . . If only they could walk thus for the rest of their days.

"I dinna feel like going in the now, Jean. What about a walk doon by Barskimming and the green thorn tree?"

She squeezed his hand in response: "I could walk wi' you onywhere, Rab. If you asked me to walk to Ellisland it would be nae bother."

"We'll cut doon here by Netherplace, then . . . you're happy, Jean?"

"Aye . . . I'm happy, Rab. Your folks couldna hae been nicer to me."

"What did my mither say to you?"

"You tak' after your mither, Rab, mair nor you ken. I like your mither—and I was feared I wouldna."

"My mither's no' easy. . . But, by God, she's had a hard life—a hard bitter slave-driven life. Yet there was a time, Jean—at Alloway and when we first went to Mount Oliphant —when she could sing as sweet as you."

"I'm no much o' a singer, Rab."

"Aye, you can sing, lass—nane like you. And mind: when I get you to Ellisland, you'll need to do some singing for me. I've dozens o' sangs I want you to lilt ower."

"I'll need to work, Rab. . ."

"Oh aye, you'll need to work: we'll baith need to work. But there's a close to every day; and an hour by the fireside in the evening. . . Me at the table-end scribbling awa' and you trilling ower your wood-notes wild——"

"And you'll never think lang on the delights and pleasure o' Edinburry?"

"Jean, lass, I've tasted a' the joys a man can taste—but one."

"And what's that one?"

"Independence! But we'll win to that yet—wi' luck. I'm no' complaining. Apart from that I've tasted a' the joys a man can taste. . . When I was up there in Mossgiel, afore I published my Kilmarnock volume, a' I thirsted for was honest fame—recognition o' what merit I had. Well, I got fame, Jean, in a' the measure a man can want. I've nae mair fame to win. I've won to the title o' Caledonia's Bard—and a' I ever aspired to be was the Bard o' Ayrshire. . . I've been acclaimed by the highest and the lowest in the land. I've been acclaimed by peers and praised by peasants. There was a time in Edinburgh when I had to tack up a sheet o' paper listing a' the breakfasts and dinners I had invitations to from the nobility. . . I've stood in the High Street o' Edinburgh when a friend hailed me and a crowd gathered to stand and gape at the sicht o' me. And I've lived to ken what the worth o' fame is, Jean— it's like a mouthful o' stale bread. Fame's but a harlot, Jean, faithful only for the paid hour. I had to pay her wi' my verses; and she favoured me just as long as they had a novelty value. That value spent, and she was on wi' some other body. . . You dinna need to worry about me hankering after Edinburgh. But dinna think I'm bitter, lass. It's one thing being the wonder o' a gay world o' fashion and dissipation; and it's another thing being wondered at. Mind you: I'm as proud as Lucifer o' the fame I've won and merited—I'll let nobody belittle that or treat it cheaply. But life and happiness, Jean

—I've aey kent the true secret o' them—only I ken the secret better now than ever I did——"

"If happiness hae not her seat and centre in the breast . . .?"

"Jean, Jean: dinna tell me this is you quoting my ain verses!"

"I've read them a', Rab—I used to go ower them wi' Jeannie Smith."

"God bless you! Well, here's the secret o' my happiness, Jean. You and me walking thegither hand in hand i' the gloaming—wi' a bairn o' our ain and a hame in the offing. What had Edinburgh and fame to offer me compared wi' this?"

"I think I understand, Rab. . . And were there nae lassies in Edinburry?"

"Yes—there were lassies, Jean. I wouldna deceive you about that. But they were puir creatures compared wi' you, lass. You ken I'm weak where a lass is concerned."

"Fine I ken, Rab."

"Just how fine do ye ken, Jean?"

"As fine as I want to ken. And if ever you want to leave me for anither lass, I'll no' haud you."

"God Almighty, Jean—it's no' natural to say that. Hae you nae jealousy for me?"

"Aye, plenty—but what's the guid o' it? If you want to gang you'll gang, and I'll no' be able to haud you—you ken that fine."

"But, Jean lass, there's nae question o' me leaving you. I've made up my mind. And how can you be happy wi' me if you fear that some day I'll leave you for another?"

"Oh Rab, dinna ask me to explain. . . I hope and pray you'll never leave me. I ken you'll never leave me. But——"

"But what, lass?"

"I wadna have you unhappy, Rab, nae matter what happens to me."

"My dear: this is something beyond love. . . No man's worthy o' such a love: me least o' a'."

"Ah weel, Rab, that's the way I feel about you—and that's the way I want to feel about you. . . You'll never ken what

it meant to me when you cam' in that morning to the Muirs o'
the Mill: I was gey near finished. . ."

The earth stopped in its spinning. The river Ayr ceased
to gurgle itself to sleep. Not a leaf turned on its twig. The
far hills prostrated themselves beyond the shadows and all
living things were transfixed in silence. For a century and
more all movement, all animation was suspended.

Suspended, held in wonder, till he withdrew his lips from
hers. Then, with a gentle sigh, the world revolved again on
its axis and the Ayr gurgled to the sea. Rabbits nibbled again
at the short grass; moths stirred; and the goatsucker gyrated
round the topmost branches of an old whispering elm. . .
And the sap flowed again in the green thorn tree.

THE WORDS AND THE SONG

It was a long and hard day's riding from Machlin to Ellisland.
By the time he had called in on Annie Rankine and her
husband John Merry, to ease himself from the saddle and give
Jenny Geddes a drink, he was fit for no more than a drink
and a bite when he reached Brownhill Inn, four miles from
Ellisland. . . And it was gey dreich country between New
Cumnock and Thornhill. But from Thornhill to Ellisland
the countryside was more rugged and broken and pleasing
to the eye. . .

Jenny Geddes did not like coming down into Nithdale and
she did not like Ellisland. But she was a faithful mare and if
she trudged dowie enough yet she trudged.

Now that he was committed to Ellisland, the Bard wasn't
so sure that he liked it. Yet he realised it was not Ellisland
that he disliked so much as his separation from Jean.

The days that he spent away from her were unbearably
lonely. The old couple at the Isle at Ellisland were no company
for him; and if Brownhill Inn was four miles away it was
four miles back again. . .

Sometimes it rained; and then it could be bitterly cold

even for summer. Old Nance Cullie would light a fire in the hovel of a spence. . . God knows, the Isle needed the comfort of a fire. The roof leaked; there were cracks in the gable that let in piercing draughts; the earthen floor got soggy and damp. The smoke sought a vent everywhere but in the roof-hole; and every other gust of wind sent it spewing through the room.

Alone in this wretched hovel (and the few buildings there were about Ellisland were equally wretched) he was beset with worries. Boyd, the Dumfries builder, kept putting him off about the planning and contracting for his house and barns. Old David Cullie who had farmed the place for years (and who had refused a lease from Patrick Miller on account of his age) was as poor a farmer as the Bard had ever encountered. It was obvious that long before he had quitted the farm he had lost heart in it. Being an indifferent farmer he had no sympathy for modern methods and even considered enclosing to be the height of needless extravagance. The Bard got little sympathy or change from him.

Willie Stewart, the Closeburn factor, alone was helpful; but he was busy with the supervising of the Closeburn estate and the rebuilding of the Hall that had been destroyed by fire. . .

Stewart was occupying the only habitable portion of the ruined Closeburn Castle with his daughter and wife and step-daughter. It was pleasant to visit there and enjoy their hospitality. And occasionally he met Stewart in Bacon's Inn at Brownhill; but John Bacon was not a Stewart; and though his wife was a sister of Willie she resembled him in no way. But these visits only served to bring home to him the isolation and discomfort of Cullie's biggin—and sharpen his desire for Jean.

Indeed, despite all his worries, he could not drive her from his mind. . .

And as he worked on his hundred and seventy acres, sometimes weeding, sometimes ditching and sometimes helping with the dry-stone dyke enclosures, he would be humming her favourite tune—*Miss Gordon's Strathspey*. . .

And then one wet morning while he was pacing out some ground and planning, for the twentieth time, where exactly he would have his farm-house, a man came to him.

"Wad you be Mr. Burns the poet?"

The Bard, eyeing him rather abstractedly, nodded.

"I'm the fiddler you wanted—Mr. Stewart o' Closeburn sent me ower."

"God, but you're welcome, fiddler—have you your fiddle wi' you?"

"I wadna be much guid withoot it?"

"And what's your name, fiddler?"

"D'ye need to ken that?"

"No . . . no' unless you're ashamed o' it?"

"Ah weel: I'm kent as Fiddlin' Sandy."

"Fiddlin' Sandy—aye, a good name. And you can play from the music?"

"Aye; and write it too."

"I've some Highland tunes I want gone over—what's your fee, Sandy?"

"You'll feed me?"

"You'll get what I get: I'm in lodgings."

"Would you grudge a shilling?"

"Your playing would need to be damned rank and bad afore I grudged you that, fiddler. But come wi' me to Davie Cullie's yonder and I'll hear what you can do."

Fiddling Sandy was indeed an able fiddler and it was at once obvious to the Bard that he had not acquired his art by the roadside.

He was a queer fellow. He had a thin expressionless face, very sallow of colouring; and, when he doffed his bonnet, his long black hair was dank and lustreless. He had long thin fingers, strong as steel: his bowing, as he tuned, was confident in its movements.

His tuning completed in a business-like fashion he said: "Have you a favourite I could warm myself up on?"

"D'you ken Miss Admiral Gordon's Strathspey?"

"William Marshall's! A grand composer."

It was glorious to sit in Cullie's spence and listen to this fine strathspey played by a fiddler who was as able as he was sensitive. But apart from an occasional wrinkling of the forehead he betrayed no sign of interest or emotion.

And then the Bard propped up on the rickety table Patrick MacDonald's *Collection of Highland Vocal Airs*. The fiddler gave the opening page a casual glance and tucked the fiddle under his chin. . . .

For two days they went at it, stopping only for meals and sleep. The rain lashed in torrents: the fire smoked: they let it go out and played on. The fiddler remained stoical to the end. And he never complained of exhaustion. The Bard made fantastic demands of him. He would ask him to play a tune again and again. Sometimes he would study the music for a while and then make suggestions regarding interpretation. To these suggestions Sandy complied to the letter. Sometimes the Bard stopped him while he took notes.

The Cullies were convinced that both the Bard and the fiddler were mad—or worse: maybe they were devil worshippers!

It was at the end of the second day that the fiddler allowed himself an observation.

"I've been told you're a poet, Mr. Burns. For mysel' I never read onything now-a-days—so I mak' no apology for my ignorance. But I ken music—and I ken something about playing a fiddle. And I've played before a wheen knowledgeable folk in my day. But you've a bluidy uncanny ear for a tune, Mr. Burns. Aye . . . I've played more for you than I wad play for King Geordie even if he gave me a wing o' his palace. But you've played me done. Still, if you want the same ower again, I'll do it."

"That's generous o' you, fiddler—you've been a grand help to me. Though I've only got one tune worth a damn so far. When are you leaving the district?"

"I should have been left. Will I come back in a couple o' days?"

"Aye, come back as soon as you can manage. I'll need a day or two to mull over what I've learned. Now: one thing afore you go, fiddler, and I'll no grudge you twenty times the fee you asked. Play me over Miss Admiral Gordon's Strathspey again."

The rain had cleared away and the evening was mild and clear. He walked slowly along the river bank. The Nith was swollen and red with the rains. Full-throated it rushed to the Solway. And full-throated the birds sang—especially the blackbird and the mavis. Apart from these the air vibrated with minor bursts of bird melody: hedge-sparrows, linnets, pipits, wrens and shelfies. Along the Nith were martins and sand-pipers. . . Above the fields lapwings tossed and cried. Through everything came the immemorial call of the curlew.

The grass, though sodden to the feet, was incredibly green; the trees and shrubs were coming into fullness with virginal intensity.

But though conscious of all this, the melody still dominated his mind.

He raised his eyes to the west. There, not here, was home. Beyond those hills and woods and rivers was Ayrshire; and in Ayrshire, not here, was Jean, his wife. God knows but he had loved a wheen lassies in his day. Many he had loved deeply: all of them he had loved kindly. All of them had given him something—something rich in experience and happiness. . . And some had brought him sorrow.

But all the women he had loved could not make up the sum of Jean Armour. She was queen of all the women he had known.

He had thought he had nothing new to experience in love —not even with Jean. But now, strolling in the calm of a summer's evening by the banks of the Nith (and a river's bank was the most glorious place in the world to stroll), he realised that Jean as a wife, in their own tiny corner of Machlin, had brought a depth and satisfaction to his experience of love that was wonderfully revealing. . . Indeed it was the greatest revelation that had yet come to him regarding life between man and woman.

Still warm with this knowledge he looked to the west in

great longing—almost as if his eyes could penetrate into the Backcauseway of Machlin itself. But the mood of creation was on him and the creative eye could annihilate time and space.

And yet the creative and the visual eye were in complete harmony. If anything the visual eye was a shade sharper than normal. There was nothing it missed.

He had reached the spot in the middle of his farm where he had decided to build his home. It was a flat stretch of ground that lay adjacent to the farm road that ran from the Isle at the south end of his ground. From the edge of the flatness the ground sloped quickly to the water's edge, and he intended that from most windows of his future home he would be able to see the Nith, see across the rich holm lands of Dalswinton to the rising hills beyond. But no matter how his windows were placed there would be glorious views and vistas leading into a background of hills. . .

Here he paced up and down, every faculty of creation at work. From what direction was the wind blowing? But then the wind could blow from any direction—from a' the airts. . .

From a' the airts? Of a' the airts. He had it! He turned the lines over in his mind; he lilted them to the tune. He was still pacing the river bank when the gloaming came down so that it was quite dusk before he realised how time had passed.

He went back to Cullie's: lit a candle: took a fresh sheet of paper and placed stumpie in the ink.

Occasionally the old pair could hear him lilting and tapping his foot. This went on far into the night. But by this time they were quite convinced he was mad. But when at last he snuffed the candle and drew the blankets over him, he did so with a grand feeling of satisfaction. He had put the words to the song in the green thorn tree. Jean's song—the song to which he had written honeymoon words, the song that would be their honeymoon song. . .

When he rode back to Machlin the song was still in his throat. . .

Jean had set off that afternoon to meet him, walking on

her bare feet and but lightly clad for the day was a perfect June day. She was as anxious to meet her husband as he was to meet her. Life had taken a wonderful turn: so wonderful that, despite the death of her twins, she was dazed with her happiness.

And there was pride in Jean too, great and glowing pride in her husband who had loved her before he was famous and who, now that he was famous, loved her more than ever.

There was nothing to mar their happiness. Even her father now approved of what had happened and accepted her marriage. And her particular friends, Jean Smith, Jean Markland, Jenny Surgeoner, Helen and Lizzie Miller were all delighted that Robin had done the right thing by her.

No: there was nothing to mar their happiness. And at Mossgiel where she went every day (and where she delighted in the company of her first-born, the young sturdy Robert), Mrs. Burns and her daughters could not be more friendly or more helpful. . .

There was nothing to mar this happiness but this periodic separation from him. But this could be borne for it made their meetings so much more intense.

And so Jean went lilting down the warm dusty road on her bare feet in the hot June sun. . .

She thought of the first time she had seen him (apart from the kirk services): at the race-dance in Ronald's ballroom. How she had longed to meet him just from hearing Jeannie Smith and Jean Markland speaking about him. And Wee Jamie Smith! Jamie had been a good friend to both of them —and still was.

And then that day she had met him on the road to Mossgiel. Him leading the horse; and stopping; and looking at her so intensely with his great eyes. . . And then his voice: a voice that struck deep vibrating echoing chords in her. . .

And then those summer nights in the gloaming under the green thorn tree! Oh, there would never be nights like them ever again. She had given everything to Rab on those nights —her inmost soul not excepted. She had loved him and he had loved her.

Aye: she knew there were other lassies. It couldna be otherwise wi' a lad like Rab. Since lassies couldna resist him how was he to resist them?

She had suffered for loving him; but she would forget all the suffering. Indeed she had already forgotten it. What was suffering, in retrospect, compared to the happiness that was now hers?

And maybe it was better that she had suffered. She had had many long weary days and nights to suffer. So much had she suffered that she could have been forgiven if her love had turned to hate. But no, no: never as long as she had breath in her body could she bring herself to hate Rab Burns.

But the suffering had deepened her love—deepened it a thousandfold. If she had loved him so deeply in her agony, how much deeper did she love him now?

When everybody had lost faith in him—even Jeannie Smith —she never had. So there could be no mistake in loving him now.

And since they had both suffered so deeply for their sins maybe their suffering was at an end.

It must be at an end. Everything was settled now—on the road to settlement. He had gotten a farm and he had passed his Excise training.

What was there that could go wrong—now? She could think of nothing.

And so she trudged forward along the dusty road singing under her breath, her heart filled to bursting with deep inward ecstasy. She flicked the hazel wand about her bare legs and sometimes waved it in the air from sheer happiness. She didn't feel her feet on the dusty road; she didn't feel the miles passing behind her; she was unconscious of the riders that passed her or overtook her. The farther she walked the nearer she was coming to Rab—the nearer he was coming to her. And had the road been a hundred miles long her spirit would not have been daunted.

As it wore on towards evening she kept a look out for a vantage spot by the roadside where she might rest against his coming—a spot that would provide, in the immediate offing, a sheltered place where they could exchange their mutually desperate embraces. . .

He dismounted from the saddle. His feet were hardly on the ground before Jean was in his arms. . .

It was a calm evening, perfect as only an evening in the Scottish June can be perfect. They were sheltered by a bank of broom; and a burn purled gently at their side. Jean had bathed her dusty feet in the burn and her small evenly-spaced toes glowed pink though her feet and legs were berry-brown. . .

The almost physical agony of their reunion was spent. They lay relaxed on the soft turf. . .

He sat up and said very quietly:

"I've put the words on your sang, my love—the sweetest words I ever put to any tune."

"Sing them to me, Rab."

"You ken I canna sing, Jean, but I can croon them to you. I've been doing that a' the road up."

And so he crooned:

> "Of a' the airts the wind can blaw
> I dearly like the west,
> For there the bonnie lassie lives,
> The lassie I lo'e best.
> There wild woods grow, and rivers row,
> And monie a hill between,
> But day and night my fancy's flight
> Is ever wi' my Jean.
>
> I see her in the dewy flowers—
> I see her sweet and fair.
> I hear her in the tunefu' birds—
> I hear her charm the air.
> There's not a bonnie flower that springs
> By fountain, shaw, or green,
> There's not a bonnie bird that sings,
> But minds me o' my Jean."

She was completely melted by them and the tears welled unrestrainedly from her black eyes and ran down her brown cheeks. But there was no sobbing in her throat for they were tears of deepest happiness.

The Bard, affected by these silent tears, could not keep the tears from his own eyes. . .

The gloaming came down from the slow-rounded Ayrshire hills. It came slowly and softly and the burn seemed to pitch its song in a lower key.

He kissed her very gently and his voice was dreamy in the dusk.

"Come hame, my love, come hame. The dew's on the grass and I canna have you risking a chill. . ."

"Rab, Rab!" she murmured, putting her arm round his neck. "I could lie wi' you here to a' eternity. Surely we hae God's blessing on us noo . . .?"

"Surely, Jean, surely. I've never doubted but that He blessed you when He made you. . ."

He swung her up behind him on Jenny Geddes. She put her arm round him and rested her cheek on his shoulder.

Jenny tossed her head and gave a low whinny. Her head was turned towards Machlin and home. She trotted eagerly into the soft quiet night.

And quietly and softly he crooned their honeymoon song that she had baptised with the happiness of her tears.

Never, since man had loved woman, had there been a love so deep, so perfect, so natural and inevitable as this love between Jean Armour and Robert Burns. It had been purified in the fires of life and tempered in suffering. It had emerged as strong and durable as the stuff of life itself. . .

Or so at least did Jean Armour and Robert Burns, maid and man, wife and husband, comprehend their love as they journeyed home in the June gloaming . . . with the dew-laid dust on the ground and the pale sky aquiver with a dusting of stars—and an urgent mare hungry for a stimpart of oats.

THE END

She was completely misled by them and the tears welled
unrestrainedly from her black eyes and ran down her brown
cheeks. But there was no sobbing in her throat for they were
tears of deeper happiness.

The bard, affected by those silent tears, could not keep the
tears from his own eyes.

The plaintive air died down from the slow-rounded Ayrshire
hills. It came slowly and softly and the tune seemed to
merge into a lower key.

He raised his voice gently and his voice was dreamy in
the dusk.

'—come hame, my love, come hame. The dews on the
grass, and I maun have you biding a chill.'

'Weel, Rab,' she murmured, putting her arm round his
neck. 'I could lie wi' you here to a' eternity. Surely we hae
God's blessing on us noo.'

'Surely, lass, surely. I've never doubted but that He
blessed you when He made you.'

He swung her up behind him on Jenny Geddes. She put
her arm round him and rested her cheek on his shoulder.
Jenny tossed her head and gave a low whinny. Her head
was turned towards Mochlin and home. She trotted eagerly
into the soft after-night.

And slowly and softly he crooned and hummed a song
that she had fashioned with the happiness of her tears.

Never since man had loved woman, had there been a love
so deep, so pure, so natural and inevitable as this love
between Jean Armour and Robert Burns. It had been purified
in the fires of bliss and tempered in suffering. It had emerged
as among the durablest things, the stuff of life itself.

Or so at least did Jean Armour and Robert Burns, maid
and man, wife and husband, comprehend their love as they
journeyed home in the June gloaming, with the dew-laid
dust on the ground and the pale sky aquiver with a quaring
of stars—and an urgent mare hungry for a sappart of oats.

THE END

Map indicating the Main Routes traversed by Burns in Scotland and England.

Places where he slept overnight shown thus ●

SCALE OF MILES

0   10   20   40